David Farland began writing at the age of seventeen, and in the years since has published over forty fantasy and science fiction novels for both adults and young adults.

Over the years, he has worked the typical writerly jobs – as a missionary, a prison guard, a meat cutter, an editor, a contest judge, a writing professor, a video game designer, and as a movie producer.

He currently lives in Saint George, Utah, with his wife and five children, where his hobbies include hiking, fishing, and working-out.

Find out more about David Farland and other Orbit authors by registering for the free monthly newsletter at www.orbitbooks.net

By David Farland

THE RUNELORDS
The Sum of All Men
Brotherhood of the Wolf
Wizardborn
The Lair of Bones
Sons of the Oak

BROTHERHOOD OF THE WOLF

The Runelords: Book Two

David Farland

www.orbitbooks.net

ORBIT

First published in the United States in 1999 by Tor,
Tom Doherty Associates, LLC
First published in Great Britain in 2000 by Earthlight,
an imprint of Simon & Schuster UK Ltd
This paperback edition published in Great Britain in 2007 by Orbit
Reprinted 2007 (twice)

A CIP catalogue record for this book
is available from the British Library.

ISBN 978-1-84149-561-3

Papers used by Orbit are natural, recyclable products made from
wood grown in sustainable forests and certified in accordance with
the rules of the Forest Stewardship Council.

Typeset in Berkeley Book by Palimpsest Book Production Ltd,
Grangemouth, Stirlingshire

Printed in Great Britain by
Clays Ltd, St Ives plc
Paper supplied by Hellefoss AS, Norway

Orbit
An imprint of
Little, Brown Book Group
100 Victoria Embankment
London EC4Y 0DY

An Hachette Livre UK Company

www.orbitbooks.net

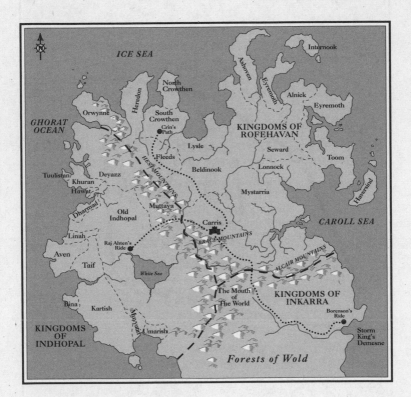

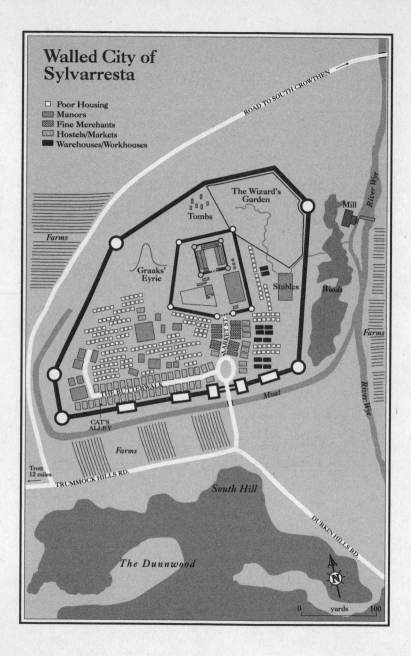

Walled City of Sylvarresta

□ Poor Housing
▨ Manors
▧ Fine Merchants
▨ Hostels/Markets
■ Warehouses/Workhouses

ROAD TO SOUTH CROWTHEN

River Wye

Mill

The Wizard's Garden

Tombs

Farms

Graaks' Eyrie

Stables

Woods

Farms

MARKET ST.

THE BUTTERWALK

Moat

River Wye

CAT'S ALLEY

Farms

Trott 12 miles

TRUMMOCK HILLS RD.

South Hill

DURKIN HILLS RD.

The Dunnwood

N

0   yards   100

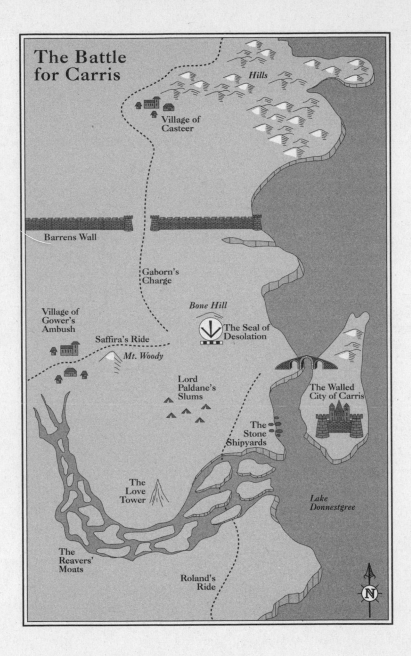

The Battle for Carris

Hills

Village of
Casteer

Barrens Wall

Gaborn's
Charge

Bone Hill

The Seal of
Desolation

Village of
Gower's
Ambush

Saffira's Ride

Mt. Woody

Lord
Paldane's
Slums

The
Stone
Shipyards

The Walled
City of Carris

The
Love
Tower

*Lake
Donnestgree*

The
Reavers'
Moats

Roland's
Ride

N

PROLOGUE

The week of Hostenfest began with its usual festive air at the Castle at Tal Rimmon in northern Mystarria.

On the first morning of Hostenfest, the spirit of the Earth King came as usual. Fathers and mothers took delight in heaping gifts of food for their children onto kitchen tables – honeycomb dripping in sweet piles, the small brown-spotted tangerines common to Mystarria, almonds roasted in butter, sweet grapes fresh from the vine and still wet from the morning dew. All of these represented the bounteous gifts that the Earth King would bestow upon those who loved the land, 'the fruits of the forest and of the field.'

And on that same first dawn of Hostenfest, the children rose and anxiously ran to the hearth. There mothers had left their daughters dolls woven of straw and dry wild flowers, or perhaps a box with a yellow kitten in it; and there young boys might find bows carved of ash, or finely embroidered woolen cloaks to help warm them through the coming winter.

So the children's joy was full, and the week of Hostenfest came to Tal Rimmon under skies so warm and blue that they belied the coming of autumn.

Summer is forever, those skies promised. No wind shook the forested hills around the castle.

And if during the second day of Hostenfest, parents spoke in hushed tones of a fortress that had fallen, few children took note. Tal Dur was far to the west, after all, and Duke Paldane, the Huntsman, who served as regent while the King was away, would be swift to repel the armies of Indhopal.

Besides, it was still a season of joy, and reminders were everywhere. New herbs were strewn on the floors: meadowsweet, pennyroyal, lavender, or rose. The icons of the Earth King were still in place beside every doorway and window, inviting the Earth King into the people's homes. It had been nearly two thousand years since an Earth King had risen to lead mankind. The old images carved of wood showed him in his green traveling robes with his staff in his hand, a crown of oak leaves woven into his hair while rabbits and foxes played at his feet.

The icons were meant to serve only as a reminder that an Earth King had once come. Yet on that day, some old women approached their icons and whispered, as if to the Earth itself, 'May the Earth protect us.'

Few children noticed.

And later that evening, when a rider said that far to the north in Heredon a new Earth King had indeed arisen, and that the name of that Earth King was Gaborn Val Orden of Mystarria, the people of Tal Rimmon erupted in jubilant celebration.

What did it matter if the same messenger bore dire news of lords slaughtered in far places, of the troops of the Wolf Lord Raj Ahten striking all through the kingdoms of Rofehavan? What did it matter that Gaborn's own father, old King Mendellas Val Orden, had fallen in battle?

A new Earth King had arisen, after all, and of all the wonders, he was Mystarria's own sovereign.

Such news filled the young ones with unaccountable pride, while the elders looked at one another knowingly and whispered, 'It will be a long winter.'

Immediately the smiths around Tal Rimmon went to work forging swords and warhammers, shields and armor for man and horse. The Marquis Broonhurst and the other local lords all rode back to the castle early from the autumn hunt. In the Marquis's Great Hall they argued for long hours about the portent of the dispatches – the dark tidings of sorcerous attacks, of the movements of enemy troops, of Duke Paldane's call to prepare for battle.

Few children noticed. As yet their joy was undiminished.

But on that day it seemed a shift in the air brought an indefinable sense of urgency and excitement.

All week long, the young men of Tal Rimmon had been preparing for the tournaments that accompanied the end of

Hostenfest. But now the boys who prepared to fight suddenly had a feral gleam in their eyes. And at mid-week, when the first rounds began, those who jousted or took part in mock combat attacked their opponents with abnormal ferocity. For now they did not seek to win honor only among themselves, but fought for the right to someday ride into battle with the Earth King himself.

The Marquis noted the change, and when he told his lords, time and again, 'It is a good crop this year, the best I've ever seen,' he was not speaking of apples.

At mid-week the skies darkened, and an afternoon thunderstorm flashed above Tal Rimmon and shook the city. Many of the local children huddled abed with their mothers and fathers, safe beneath their quilts. That night, five hundred powerful Runelords rode from the east, answering Duke Paldane's summons to defend Carris, the largest castle in western Mystarria. For the latest reports said that the Wolf Lord, who had been retreating toward his homeland in Indhopal, had suddenly struck south toward the heart of Mystarria.

The Marquis Broonhurst could not sleep so many lords with his troops, so he had many of them wait out the storm in his Great Hall or in the hostels just outside the castle proper. There the lords and knights argued long and forcefully about how to repel the impending invasion.

Raj Ahten's troops had taken three border fortresses already. Worse, he had taken endowments from perhaps twenty thousand people. He had taken to himself their strength, wit, stamina, and grace, turning himself into such a fierce warrior that none could best him in battle. He sought to become the Sum of All Men, a being that old stories said would be immortal. Some feared even now that he could not be killed.

Worse, he had taken so many endowments of glamour that his beauty outshone the sun. Hundreds of miles north in Heredon, when his troops besieged Castle Sylvarresta, King Sylvarresta's people had taken one look at Raj Ahten's face and thrown their weapons over the castle walls, welcoming him as their new lord. And at Longmot, it was said that Raj Ahten

had used the tremendous power of his Voice to shatter the
stone of the castle walls, as a songmaster might shatter crystal.

It was nearly dawn when Raj Ahten struck Tal Rimmon.

He came pulling a handcart filled with onions, a battered
cloak pulled low over his forehead to keep out the night's rain.
The guards at the castle gates paid him little notice, for other
peasants had also brought their carts to the gates. They stood
sheltered from the rain beneath the eaves of a weaver's shop.

Raj Ahten began to sing a song that was not words, but
instead a low throaty moan of incredible volume, a sound that
made the stone walls of Tal Rimmon hum at first, and that made
the bones of a man's inner ear vibrate as if a hornet were
trapped within his skull.

The gatekeepers swore and drew weapons. The few farmers
near Raj Ahten grasped their heads in pain as his song began
to slowly shatter their skulls. They dropped unconscious
before they died.

Within seconds the stone of Tal Rimmon's towers began to
shiver violently. Bits of stone flaked away as if artillery battered
the walls.

In moments the castle's battlements trembled, heaved, and
then toppled, as if struck by a mighty fist.

Raj Ahten stood in his ragged cloak and lifted his voice
high, until the Marquis's towers collapsed in on themselves
and his Great Hall fell in a protest of screaming timbers.

The Runelords within those edifices were crushed under
stones. Broken oil lamps spilled their contents into the timbers
and tapestries, setting much of the castle aflame.

No common man could approach Raj Ahten without being
slain. Two Runelords had enough endowments of stamina to
withstand his Voice. But when they charged from the ruins
of a hostel and tried to draw steel upon him, Raj Ahten drew
his own dagger in a blur and spilled their guts.

Once the castle and most of the buildings in the market
were down, Raj Ahten turned and fled down dark city streets,
into the shadows.

*   *   *

Moments later, he reached his own Imperial warhorse, tied behind a farmer's barn at the foot of a low hill. Two dozen of his Invincibles had gathered there in the darkness, waiting for his return.

A flameweaver named Rahjim sat upon a black horse and gazed hungrily toward the ruins of Tal Rimmon, toward the sheets of flame twisting up into the sky. This was the third castle his master had destroyed in a single night. He breathed rapidly in excitement, vapors of smoke issuing from his mouth, an unnatural light gleaming in his eyes. He had no hair, even on his eyebrows. 'Where to now, O Great Light?' the flameweaver asked.

As Raj Ahten drew near, he felt the dry heat of the creature's skin. 'Now we ride to Carris,' Raj Ahten answered.

'Not to the Courts of Tide?' the flameweaver pleaded. 'We could destroy their capitol before their lords ever learn of the danger!'

'Carris,' Raj Ahten said more firmly, determined to resist the flameweaver's arguments. He did not wish to raze all of Mystarria yet.

Mystarria's king was still safely secluded far to the the north in Heredon, holed up deep within the Dunnwood, protected by the spirits of his ancestors.

'To strike down the capitol at the Courts of Tide would be a fell stroke,' Rahjim urged.

'I shall not attack it,' Raj Ahten whispered in a deadly tone. 'The boy will not come if I leave him nothing to save.'

Raj Ahten leapt to the back of his warhorse, but for a long moment he did not ride for Carris. Tal Rimmon could be seen bright as day beneath columns of firelit smoke. Distantly, people screamed and tried to throw water upon their burning homes or to pull the fallen from beneath collapsed buildings. He could hear the children crying.

Raj Athen watched the city burn while reflected flames danced in his dark eyes.

BOOK 6

DAY 30 IN THE MONTH OF HARVEST

A DAY OF CHOICES

1

THE VOICES OF MICE

As King Gaborn Val Orden rode toward Castle Sylvarresta on the last day of Hostenfest, the day of the great feast, he reined in his horse and peered up the Durkin Hills Road.

Here the trees of the Dunnwood had been cleared back from the road, three miles from town. The sun was just rising, casting a sliver of silver light over the hills to the east, and the shadows of leafless oaks blotted the road ahead.

Yet in a patch of morning sun around the bend, Gaborn spotted three large hares. One hare seemed to be on guard, for it peered up the road, ears perked, while another nibbled at sweet golden melilot that grew at the margin of the road. The third just hopped about stupidly, sniffing at freshly fallen leaves of brown and gold.

Though the hares were over a hundred yards distant, the scene seemed preternaturally clear to Gaborn. After having been underground in the darkness for the past three days, his senses seemed invigorated. The light appeared brighter than ever before, the early morning birdsong came clearer to his ears. Even the way the cool dawn winds swept down from the hills and played across his face seemed new and different.

'Wait,' Gaborn whispered to the wizard Binnesman. He reached behind his back, untied his bow and quiver from his saddle. He gave a warning glance to his Days, the skeletal scholar who had followed him since his childhood, bidding the Days to stay behind.

The three were alone on the road. Sir Borenson was

following some distance behind them, bearing his trophy from the Hostenfest hunt, but Gaborn had been in a hurry to get home to his new wife.

Binnesman frowned. 'A rabbit, sire? You're the Earth King. What will people say?'

'Shhh,' Gaborn whispered. He reached into his quiver, pulled his last arrow, but then paused. Binnesman was right. Gaborn was the Earth King, and it seemed fitting that he should bring down a fine boar. Sir Borenson had slain a reaver mage, and was dragging its head into town.

For two thousand years, the people of Rofehavan had looked forward to the coming of an Earth King. Each year during the seventh day of Hostenfest, this last day of the celebration, the day of the great feast, served as a reminder of the promise of the Earth King who would bless his people with all the 'fruits of the forest and of the field.'

Last week the Earth Spirit had crowned Gaborn, and charged him to save a seed of humanity through the dark times to come.

He'd fought long and hard these past three days, and the reaver's head belonged as much to Gaborn and Binnesman as it did to Sir Borenson.

Still, if Gaborn brought in nothing more than a single hare for the great feast, he could imagine how the mummers and puppetmasters would ridicule him.

He braced himself for the mummers' scorn and leapt lightly from his charger, whispering 'Stand' to the beast. It was a force horse, his fine hunter, that had runes of wit branded along its neck. It stared at him knowingly, perfectly silent, while Gaborn put the lower wing of his bow on the ground, stuck a leg between the bow and the string, then bent the bow and pulled the upper end of the string tight into its nock.

With the bow strung, he took his last arrow, inspected the gray goose quills, and then nocked the arrow.

He crept forward, staying low along the brushy side of the road. Wizard's violet grew tall here by the roadside, its flowers a dark purple.

When he rounded the corner, the hares would be in full sunlight. So long as he stayed in the shadows, they'd not be likely to see him; if he remained silent, they'd not hear him; and while the wind blew in his face, they'd not smell him.

Glancing back, Gaborn saw that his Days and Binnesman remained on their mounts.

He began stalking down the muddy road.

Yet he felt nervous, more nervous than mere hunting jitters could account for. He sensed a vague apprehension dawning. Among the newfound powers that the Earth had granted him, Gaborn could sense danger around those people he'd Chosen.

Only a week ago, he'd felt death stalk his father, but he'd been unable to stop it. Last night, however, that same over-powering sense had enabled him to avoid disaster when the reavers staged an ambush in the Underworld.

He felt danger now, but vaguely, distantly. Death was stalking him, as surely as he stalked these rabbits.

The only weakness of this newfound power was that he could not know the source of the danger. It could be anything: a crazed vassal, a boar lurking in the underbrush.

Yet Gaborn suspected Raj Ahten, the Wolf Lord of Indhopal, the man who had slain Gaborn's father.

Riders on force horses had brought word from Mystarria that in Gaborn's homeland, Raj Ahten's troops had taken three castles by subterfuge just before Hostenfest.

Gaborn's great-uncle, Duke Paldane, had marshaled troops to contain the problem. Paldane was an old lord, a master strategist with several endowments of wit. Gaborn's father had trusted him implicitly, and had often sent him out on campaigns to track down criminals or to humble haughty lords. Because of his success, he was called the 'Huntsman' by some, the 'Hound' by others. He was feared throughout Rofehavan; if any man could match wits with Raj Ahten, it was Paldane. Surely Raj Ahten could not march his troops north, risk the wights of the Dunnwood.

Yet danger approached, Gaborn felt certain. He placed his

feet carefully on the dry mud of the road, moved as silently as a wraith.

But when he reached the bend in the road, the hares had left. He heard a rustling in the grass by the roadside, but it was only mice stirring, scampering about under dry leaves.

He stood a moment wondering what had happened. *Ah, Earth*, he said in his thoughts, addressing the Power he served. *Could you not at least send a stag from the forest?*

But no voice answered. None ever did.

Moments later, Binnesman and the Days came trotting up the road. The Days bore the reins of Gaborn's dun-colored mare.

'The hares are skittish today, it seems,' Binnesman said. He smiled slyly, as if pleased. The morning light accentuated the creases in the wizard's face and brought out the russet hues of his robes. A week ago, Binnesman had given part of his life to summon a wylde, a creature strong in the earth powers. Before that, Binnesman's hair had been brown, and his robes the green of a leaf in summer. Now his robes had changed color, and the fellow seemed to Gaborn to have aged decades in the past few days. Worse yet, the wylde he'd sought to summon had vanished.

'Aye, the hares are skittish,' Gaborn answered suspiciously. As an Earth Warden, Binnesman sought to serve the earth, and claimed that he cared as much about mice and snakes as he did mankind. Gaborn wondered if the wizard had warned the hares off with some spell, or perhaps something as simple as a wave of the hand. 'More than a little skittish, I'd say.' Gaborn swung up into his saddle but kept his bow strung and his arrow nocked. They were close to the city, but he imagined that he still might see a stag by the roadside, some enormous old grandfather with a rack as big as his arm span, come down out of the mountains to eat one sweet apple from a farmer's orchard before it died.

Gaborn glanced over at Binnesman. He still wore that secretive grin, yet Gaborn could not tell if it was a sly grin or a worried smile.

'You're happy that I missed the hares?' Gaborn ventured.

'You'd not have been pleased with them, milord,' Binnesman said. 'My father was an innkeeper. He used to say, "A man with fickle innards is never pleased."'

'Meaning?' Gaborn said.

'Choose your quarry, milord,' Binnesman answered. 'If you are hunting reavers, it's silly to go chasing after hares. You wouldn't allow your hounds to do it. Neither should you.'

'Ah,' Gaborn said, wondering if the wizard meant more than he said.

'Besides, the reavers proved a harder match than any of us had bargained for.'

Bitterly, Gaborn realized that Binnesman was right. Despite the powers of Gaborn and Binnesman combined, forty-one strong knights had died fighting the reavers. Besides Gaborn, Binnesman, and Sir Borenson, only nine others had made it from the ruins alive. It had been a bitter struggle. The nine were back with Borenson now, dragging the reaver mage's head to town, opting to stay with their trophy.

Gaborn changed the subject. 'I didn't know that wizards had fathers,' he teased. 'Tell me more about yours.'

'It was long ago,' Binnesman said. 'I don't remember him much. In fact, I think I just told you everything I recall about him.'

'Certainly you recall more than that,' Gaborn chided. 'The more I know you, the more I know not to believe anything you say.' He didn't know how many hundred years the wizard had lived, but he suspected that Binnesman must have a story or two.

'You are right, milord,' Binnesman said. 'I don't have a father. Like all Earth Wardens, I was born of the Earth. I was but a creature that someone sculpted of mud, till I formed this flesh for myself of my own will.' Binnesman arched an eyebrow mysteriously.

Gaborn glanced at the wizard, and for just a moment, he had the nagging suspicion that Binnesman spoke more truly than he pretended.

Then the moment passed and Gaborn laughed. 'You are such a liar! I swear, you invented the art!'

Binnesman laughed in turn. 'No, 'tis a fine skill, but I did not invent it. I merely seek to perfect it.'

At that moment, a force horse came thundering along the road from the south. It was a fast horse, with three or four endowments of metabolism, a white charger that flashed in the sunlight as it moved between shadows and trees. Its rider wore the livery of Mystarria, the image of the green man upon a blue field.

Gaborn reined in his horse and waited. He'd felt danger. Now he feared the courier's news.

The messenger rode up swiftly, never slowing his mount, until Gaborn raised a hand and called out. Only then did the messenger recognize Gaborn, for the King wore nothing now but a simple gray traveling robe, stained from the road.

'Your Highness!' the messenger cried.

He reached for a leather pouch at his waist, then proffered a small scroll, its red wax seal bearing the mark of Paldane's signet ring.

Gaborn opened the scroll. As he read, his heart sank and his breathing quickened.

'Raj Ahten has moved south into Mystarria,' he told Binnesman. 'He's toppled castles at Gorlane, Aravelle, and Tal Rimmon. This was near dawn two days ago.

'Paldane says that his men and some Knights Equitable made Raj Ahten pay. Their archers ambushed Raj Ahten's troops. You can walk from the village of Boarshead to Gower's Ridge on the backs of the dead.'

Gaborn dared not relate more of the horrific news. Paldane's notes were extremely detailed and precise, noting the exact type and number of enemy casualties – 36,909 men, the vast majority of whom were common troops out of Fleeds. He also noted the number of arrows spent (702,000), defenders slain (1,274), wounded (4,951), and horses slain (3,207) versus the amount of armor, gold, and horses captured. He then gave precise notes on the movements of enemy troops along with the current dispositions of his own men. Raj Ahten's reinforcements were converging on Carris from Castles Crayden, Fells, and Tal Dur. Paldane was reinforcing Carris, convinced that Raj Ahten would seek to capture the mighty fortress rather than casually destroy it.

Gaborn read the news and shook his head in dismay. Raj Ahten had engaged in savagery. Paldane had paid him in kind. The news revolted Gaborn.

Paldane's last words were: 'Obviously, the Wolf Lord of Indhopal hopes to draw you into this conflict. He has decimated your northern border, so that you cannot come south with the hope of bringing in fresh troops of any consequence. I beg you to remain in Heredon. Let the Huntsman bring this dog to bay.'

Gaborn rolled the scroll back up, tucked it into the pocket of his robe.

This is maddening, Gaborn thought. To sit here nearly a thousand miles away and learn when my people died days after it happened.

He could do little to stop Raj Ahten. But he could get news faster . . .

He glanced at the messenger, a young lad with curly brown hair and clear blue eyes. Gaborn had seen him at court on many occasions. He looked the young man in the eyes and used the Earth Sight to stare beyond his eyes, into his heart. The courier was proud, proud of his position and his riding skill. He was daring, almost eager to risk his life in his lord's service. A dozen wenches at inns across Mystarria thought they loved him, for he tipped well and kissed even better, but the fellow was torn between his love of two women who had vastly different personalities.

Gaborn did not think particularly well of the young man, but saw no reason not to Choose him. Gaborn needed servants like this, needed messengers he could count on. Gaborn raised his left hand, stared the lad in the eyes, and whispered, 'I Choose you for the Earth. Rest now, but head back for Carris today. I currently have one Chosen messenger there. If I sense danger to you both, I'll know that Raj Ahten plans to attack the city. If ever you hear my voice warning you in your mind, obey me.'

'I dare not rest, Your Highness,' the messenger said, 'while Carris is in danger.'

To Gaborn's satisfaction, the lad wheeled his mount to the south. In moments he was gone, only the dust hovering above the road to show that he'd come to Heredon at all.

With a heavy heart, Gaborn considered what he should do. He would have to notify his lords in Heredon of this disturbing news.

As they rode through the dawn, Gaborn suddenly had the urge to get away. He put his heels to horseflesh, and his roan hunter raced under the shadowed trees along the road, with Binnesman's mount easily keeping pace beside and the Days on his white mule struggling along behind. At last they reached a wide bend on a hilltop that afforded them an unobstructed view of Castle Sylvarresta.

Gaborn drew in his reins; he and the wizard halted, staring in surprise.

Castle Sylvarresta was set on a small hill at a bend in the river Wye, its high walls and towers rising like pinnacles. All around that hill squatted a walled city. Beyond the city walls, there was normally just the countryside – empty fields with a few haycocks, orchards, and farmer's cottages and barns.

But over the past week, as news of the rise of an Earth King spread, lords and peasants from all across Heredon – and even from kingdoms beyond Heredon – had begun to gather. Gaborn had a premonition of what was to come. The fields before Castle Sylvarresta had been burned black by Raj Ahten, yet already so many peasants had amassed that the grounds around the great walled city of Sylvarresta were covered by pavilions. Not all of the pavilions belonged to peasants; many tents belonged to lords and knights from around Heredon – armies that had marched when they'd heard of the invasion but had arrived too late to offer any aid. Banners of Orwynne and North Crowthen and Fleeds and various merchant princes from Lysle mingled among the hosts, and off on one hill camped thousands of merchants out of Indhopal who – after having been driven off by King Sylvarresta – had hurried back to see this new wonder, this Earth King.

The fields around Castle Sylvarresta were dark, but they were no longer dark from the blackened grass. They were dark with the massed bodies of hundreds of thousands of men and animals.

'By the Powers,' Gaborn swore. 'Their numbers must have quadrupled in the past three days. It will take me the better part of a week to Choose them all.'

Distantly, Gaborn could hear music drifting above the smoke of cooking fires. The sound of a jousting lance cracked across the countryside, followed immediately by cheers. Binnesman sat ahorse, gazing down, just as the Days rode up. All three mounts breathed heavily after their short run.

But something caught Gaborn's eye. In the sky above the valley, a flock of starlings flew, thousands strong, like a living cloud. They weaved one way, then another, swooped and then soared upward. It was as if they were lost, searching for a place to land but unable to find safety. Starlings often flew thus in the autumn, but these birds seemed peculiarly spooked.

Gaborn heard the honking of geese. He looked along the Wye River, which wound through the green fields like a silver thread. A hundred yards above the river, miles away, the geese flew in a V along the river course. But their voices sounded strained, crass.

Beside him, Binnesman sat upright and turned to Gaborn. 'You hear it, too, don't you? You feel it in your bones.'

'What?' Gaborn asked.

Gaborn's Days cleared his throat as if to ask a question, but said nothing. The historian seldom spoke. Interference in the affairs of mankind was forbidden by the Time Lords that the Days served. Still, he was obviously curious.

'The Earth. The Earth is speaking to us,' Binnesman said. 'It is speaking to you and to me.'

'What does it say?'

'I don't know, yet,' Binnesman answered honestly. The wizard scratched at his beard, then frowned. 'But this is the way it usually speaks to me: in the worried stirrings of rabbits and mice, in the shifting flight of a cloud of birds, in the cries of geese. Now it whispers to the Earth King, too. You are growing, Gaborn. Growing in power.'

Gaborn studied Binnesman. The wizard's skin was oddly tinged a bit of ruddy red that almost matched his baggy robe. He smelled of the herbs that he kept in his oversized pockets, linden blossom and mint and borage and wizard's violet and basil and a hundred other spices. He looked like little more than a jolly old man, except for the lines of wisdom in his face.

'I will look into this. We shall know more tonight,' Binnesman assured Gaborn.

But Gaborn was unable to lay aside his worries. He suspected that he would need to convene a war council, but dared not do so until he knew the nature of the threat that his Earth senses warned him against.

The three riders headed down the road into a deep fold between two hills that had been burned black last week.

There, at the base of the hill, Gaborn saw what he took to be an old woman sitting by the roadside with a blanket draped over her head.

As the horses came stamping down the road, the old woman looked up, and Gaborn saw that she was not old at all. Instead, it was a young maiden, a girl he recognized.

Gaborn had led an 'army' from Castle Groverman to Longmot a week ago. The army had consisted of two hundred thousand cattle, driven by peasant men and women and children and a few aging soldiers. The dust of their passage as the herd crossed the plains had ben ruse enough to dislodge the Wolf Lord Raj Ahten from his attack on Longmot.

If Raj Ahten had discovered Gaborn's ruse, Gaborn felt sure the Wolf Lord would have cut down every woman and child in his retinue out of sheer spite. The girl at the foot of the hill had ridden in Gaborn's army. He remembered her well. She'd carried a heavy banner in one hand and a nursing babe in the other.

She had acted bravely and selflessly. He'd been glad for the aid of people like her. Yet Gaborn was astonished to see her – a mere peasant who probably didn't have access to a horse – here at Castle Sylvarresta, more than two hundred miles north of Longmot, only a week after the battle.

'Oh, Your Highness,' the girl said, ducking her head as if to curtsy.

Gaborn realized she'd been waiting by the roadside for him to return from his hunt. He'd been gone from Castle Sylvarresta for three days. He wondered how long she'd been here.

She climbed to her feet, and Gaborn saw that the dirt of the road stained her feet. Obviously, she had walked all the way from Longmot. In her right hand she cradled her babe. As she stood, she put her hand beneath her shawl to ease her nipple from the babe's mouth and cover herself properly.

After giving aid in a victorious battle, many a lord might have come to seek a favor. Gaborn had seldom seen a peasant do so. Yet this girl wanted something of him, wanted it badly.

Binnesman smiled and said, 'Molly? Molly Drinkham? Is that you?'

The girl smiled shyly as the wizard dismounted and approached her. 'Aye, it's me.'

'Well, let me see your child.' Binnesman took the infant from her arms and held it up. The child, a dark-haired thing who could not have been more than two months old, had put its fist in its mouth and was now sucking vigorously, eyes closed. The wizard smiled beatifically. 'A boy?' he asked. Molly nodded. 'Oh, he's the very image of his father,' Binnesman clucked. 'Such a precious thing. Verrin would have been proud. But what are you doing here?'

'I come to see the Earth King,' Molly said.

'Well, here he is,' Binnesman said. He turned to Gaborn and introduced Molly. 'Your Highness, Molly Drinkham, who was once a resident of Castle Sylvarresta.'

Molly suddenly froze, her face pale with terror, as if she could not bear the thought of speaking to a king. Or perhaps she fears only to speak to me, the Earth King, Gaborn thought.

'I beg your pardon, sire,' Molly said too shrilly. 'I hope I'm not disturbing you – I know it's early. You probably don't remember me . . .'

Gaborn alighted from his horse, so that he would not be sitting high above her, and sought to put her at ease. 'You're not disturbing me,' he said softly. 'You've walked a long way from Longmot. I remember the aid you gave me. Some great need must have driven you, and I'm eager to hear your request.'

She nodded shyly. 'You see, I was thinking . . .'

'Go on,' Gaborn said, glancing up at his Days.

'I wasn't always just a scullery maid for Duke Groverman, you see,' she said. 'My father used to muck stables for King Sylvarresta's men, and I lived in the castle. But I did something that shamed me, and my father sent me south.' She glanced down at her child. A bastard.

'I rode with you last week,' she continued, 'and I know this: if you're the Earth King, then you should have all of Erden Geboren's powers. That's what makes you an Earth King.'

'Where did you hear this?' Gaborn asked, his tone betraying his concern. He suddenly feared that she would ask some impossible task of him. Erden Geboren's deeds were the stuff of legend.

'Binnesman himself,' Molly said. 'I used to help him dry his herbs, and he would tell me stories. And if you're the Earth King, then bad times are coming, and the Earth has given you the power to Choose – to Choose the knights who will fight beside you, and to Choose who will live under your protection and who won't. Erden Geboren knew when his people were in danger, and he warned them in their hearts and in their minds. Surely you should be able to do the same.'

Gaborn knew what she wanted now. She wanted to live, wanted him to Choose her. Gaborn looked at her a long moment, saw more than her round face and the pleasing figure hidden beneath her dirty robes. He saw more than her long dark hair and the creases of worry lines around her blue eyes. He used his Earth Sight to stare into the depths of her soul.

He saw her love for Castle Sylvarresta and her lost innocence there, and her love for a man named Verrin, a stablemaster who had died after being kicked by a horse. He saw her dismay to find herself at Castle Groverman doing menial work. She wanted little from life. She wanted to come home, to show her babe to her mother, to return to the place where she'd felt warm and loved. He could see no deception in her, no cruelty. More than anything, she was proud of her bastard son, and she loved him fiercely.

The Earth Sight could not show Gaborn everything. He suspected that if he peered into her heart for long hours, he might get to know her better than she knew herself. But time was short, and in a few seconds he saw enough.

After a moment, Gaborn relaxed. He raised his left hand. 'Molly Drinkham,' he intoned softly as he cast his spell. 'I Choose you. I Choose to protect you through the dark times to come. If ever you hear my voice in your mind or in your heart, take heed. I will come to you or lead you to safety as best I can.'

It was done. Immediately Gaborn felt the efficacy of the spell, felt the binding, the now-familiar tug in his gut that let him feel her presence, that would warn him when she was in danger.

Molly's eyes widened as if she felt it, too, and then her face went red with embarrassment. She dropped to one knee.

'No, Your Highness, you misunderstand,' she said. She held up the infant in her arms. The boy's fist flopped from his mouth, but the child seemed to be half-asleep, and did not mind. 'I want you to Choose him, to make him one of your knights someday!'

Gaborn stared at the child and began to shiver, unnerved by the request. The woman had obviously been raised on tales of Erden Geboren's great deeds, and so she expected much of an Earth King. But she had no comprehension of Gaborn's limits. 'You don't understand,' he tried to explain softly. 'It's not that easy. When I Choose you, my enemies take notice. My war is not with men or with reavers, it is with the unseen Powers that move them. My Choosing you puts you in greater danger, and though I might be able to send knights to your aid, more often than not you must help yourself. My resources are far too thin, our enemies too numerous. You have to be able to help yourself, to help me get you out of danger. I – I couldn't do that to a child. I couldn't put him in danger. He can't defend himself!'

'But he needs someone to protect him,' Molly said. 'He doesn't have a da.' She waited for him to speak for a moment, then begged, 'Please! Please Choose him for me!'

Gaborn studied her face, and his cheeks burned with shame. He looked from side to side, from Binnesman to his Days, like a ferrin caught in a dark corner of the kitchen, hoping to escape.

'Molly, you ask that the child be allowed to grow up to become a warrior in my service,' Gaborn stammered. 'But I don't think we have that long! Dark times are coming, the darkest this world has ever seen. In months perhaps, or maybe a year, they'll be on us in deadly earnest. Your child won't be able to fight in battle.'

'Then Choose him anyway,' Molly said. 'At least you'll know when he's in danger.'

Gaborn stared at her in utter horror. A week ago, he'd lost several people that he'd Chosen in the battle for Longmot: his father, Chemoise's father, King Sylvarresta. When they'd died, he'd felt stricken to the core of his soul. He hadn't sought to explain the sensation to himself or anyone else, but he felt as if . . . they each had roots, and were pulled from his body, leaving dark holes that gaped and could never be filled. Losing them was like losing limbs that could never be replaced, and he was mortified by the thought that their deaths were a sign of his own personal failure. He carried the guilt as if he were a father who, through neglect, had let his own children drown in a well.

Gaborn wetted his lips with his tongue. 'I'm not that strong. You don't know what you ask of me.'

'There's no one to protect him,' Molly said. 'No father, no friends. Only me. See, he's just a babe!'

She unwrapped the sleeping boy, held him up, and stepped in close. The child was thin, though he slept soundly and did not appear to be hungry. He had the sweet scent of a newborn on his breath.

'Come now,' Binnesman urged her. 'If His Majesty says he can't Choose the child, then he can't Choose him.' Binnesman gently took Molly by the elbow, as if to steer her toward town.

Molly turned on Binnesman and shouted viciously, 'So what would you have me do, then? Dash the little bastard's head against a stone by the road and be done with him? Is that what you want?'

Gaborn felt dismayed, cast adrift. He glanced at his Days, and feared what might be written of his choice. He looked to Binnesman for help. 'What can I do?'

The Earth Warden studied the babe, frowned. With the barest movement he shook his head. 'I fear that you are correct. Choosing the child would not be wise, nor would it be kind.'

Molly's mouth dropped in shock, and she stepped back as if she'd just recognized that Binnesman, an old friend, had become an enemy.

Binnesman tried to explain, 'Molly, Gaborn has been charged by the Earth to gather the seeds of mankind, to protect those he can during the dark times to come. Yet even all that he does might not be enough. Other races have passed from the face of the earth – the Toth, the duskins. Mankind could be next.'

Binnesman did not exaggerate. When the Earth had manifested itself in Binnesman's garden, it had said much the same thing. If anything, Binnesman was being far too gentle with Molly, holding back the truth from her.

'The Earth has promised to protect Gaborn, and he has sworn in turn to protect you as best he can. But I think it best you protect your own child.'

This was how Gaborn planned to save his people – by Choosing lords and warriors to care for their charges. Before the hunt, he'd Chosen over a hundred thousand people around Heredon, had selected as many as he could – old and young, lords and peasants. At any moment, if he considered one of those people, he could reach out in his mind, know their direction and distance. He could find them if he had to, and he knew if they were in danger. But there were so many of them! So he'd begun Choosing knights and lords to protect certain enclaves. He struggled to Choose wisely, and he dared not reject the frail, the deaf, the blind, the young, or the weak-minded. He dared not value these less than any other man, for he would not make of them human sacrifices to his own conceit. By placing a lord, or even a father and mother, in charge of the safety of his or her own charges, he relieved some of the pressure he felt. And to a great degree, he'd done exactly that. He'd been using his powers to instruct his lords, requiring them to prepare their defenses and weapons, prepare for war.

Molly paled at the thought that she would be placed in charge of her infant, looked so stricken that Gaborn feared she would faint. She wisely suspected that she could not protect it adequately.

'And I too will help protect your child,' Binnesman offered in consolation. He muttered some words under his breath, wet his finger with his tongue, and knelt by the roadside to swirl the finger in the dirt. He stood, and with muddy fingers he painstakingly began to draw a rune of protection on the child's forehead.

Yet clearly Molly believed the wizard's aid would not be enough. Tears coursed down her cheeks, and she stood in shock, trembling.

'If it was yours,' Molly begged Gaborn, 'would you Choose it? Would you Choose it then?'

Gaborn knew that he would. Molly must have read the answer on his face.

'I'll give him to you then,' Moly offered. 'A wedding

present, if you'll have him. I'll give him to you, to raise as your son.'

Gaborn closed his eyes. The despair in her tone struck him like an axe.

He could hardly Choose this child. It seemed a cruel thing to do. This is madness, he thought. If I Choose it, how many thousands of other mothers might justly ask the same? Ten thousand, a hundred thousand? Yet what if I don't Choose it and Molly is right? What if by my inaction I condemn it to die? 'Does the child have a name?' Gaborn asked, for in some lands, bastards were never named.

'I call him Verrin,' Molly said, 'like his father.'

Gaborn gazed at the child, looked beyond his sweet face and smooth skin, deep into his small mind. There was little to see – a life unlived, a few vague longings. The child felt relieved and grateful for his mother's nipple and for the warmth of her body and the way she sang sweetly to get him to sleep. But Verrin did not comprehend his mother as a person, did not love her in the way that she loved him.

Gaborn stifled a sob. 'Verrin Drinkham,' he said softly, raising his left hand. 'I Choose you. I Choose you for the Earth. May the Earth heal you. May the Earth hide you. May the Earth make you its own.'

Gaborn felt the binding take force.

'Thank you, Your Highness,' Molly said. The girl's eyes glistened with tears. She turned and headed toward Castle Groverman, ready to walk the two hundred miles home.

But as she did, Gaborn felt a powerful sense of dread; the Earth was warning him that she was in danger. If she went south again, she'd die. Whether she'd be waylaid by a bandit or take ill from her journey or face some more dire fate, he did not know. But although he could not guess what form the danger would take, his premonition was as strong as on the day that his father had died.

Molly, Gaborn thought, that way lies death. Turn and go to Castle Sylvarresta.

She stopped in mid-stride, turned her big blue eyes on him

questioningly. For half a second she hesitated, then spun and raced north up the road toward Castle Sylvarresta as if a reaver were chasing her.

Gaborn's eyes filled with tears of gratitude at the sight.

'Good girl,' he whispered. He'd been afraid she would not hear his warning, or would be slow to heed it.

On his white mule, Gaborn's Days glanced from Gaborn to the girl. 'Did you just *turn* her?'

'Yes.'

'You felt danger in the south?'

'Yes,' Gaborn answered again, not wanting to express the vague fear that was creeping over him. 'Danger for her, at least.'

Turning to Binnesman, Gaborn said, 'I don't know if I can keep this up. I didn't expect it to be this way.'

'An Earth King is not asked to carry easy loads,' Binnesman said. 'After the battle at Caer Fael, it is said that no wounds were found on the body of Erden Geboren. Some thought he'd died of a broken heart.'

'Your words comfort me,' Gaborn said sardonically. 'I want to save that child, but by Choosing it, I don't know if I did well or ill.'

'Or perhaps nothing that any of us does matters,' Binnesman said, as if he might resign himself to the knowledge that even their best efforts might not save mankind.

'No, I have to believe that it matters,' Gaborn countered. 'I must believe that it is worth the struggle. But how can I save them all?'

'Save all of mankind?' Binnesman said. 'It can't be done.'

'Then I must figure out how to save *most* of them.' Gaborn looked back at his Days, the historian who had followed him since childhood.

The man wore a plain brown scholar's robe, and his skeletal face peered at him with unblinking eyes. But when Gaborn stared at the man, the Days looked away guiltily.

The sense of foreboding Gaborn felt was discomforting, and he believed the Days could warn him of the source of that danger, if he would.

But the Days had long ago given up his name, given up his own identity in service to the Time Lords. He would not speak.

Still, though the Days' devotion to the Time Lords was supposed to leave little room for meddling in the affairs of man, Gaborn had heard tales of Days who had forsaken their vows.

Gaborn knew that far away in the north, in a monastic settlement in the islands beyond Orwynne, lived another Days – one who had given Gaborn's Days an endowment of wit and who had received from him the same endowment in return. Thus the two Days now shared a single mind – a feat that had seldom been duplicated outside the monastery, for it led to madness.

Gaborn's Days was called a 'witness,' and he had been charged by the Time Lords to watch Gaborn and to listen to his words. His companion, the 'scribe,' acted as recorder, noting Gaborn's deeds until his death, when the book of Gaborn's life would be published.

And because the scribes all lived in a common settlement, they shared information. Indeed, they knew all that transpired among the Runelords.

Thus Gaborn felt that the Days knew too much and imparted their wisdom too seldom.

Binnesman caught the accusatory stare that Gaborn shot toward the Days, and he wondered aloud: 'If I were choosing seeds for next year's garden, I do not know if I would seek to save most of them, or only the best.'

2

STRANGE BEDFELLOWS

The village of Hay in the midlands of Mystarria was a blight on an otherwise unremarkable landscape, but it had an inn, and an inn was all that Roland wanted.

He rode into Hay past midnight, without waking even one of the town's dogs. The sky to the distant southwest was the color of fire. Hours past, Roland had met one of the king's far-seers, a man with half a dozen endowments of sight who had said that a volcano had erupted, though Roland was too far from it to hear the blast. Yet the light of its fires reflected from a column of smoke and ash. Its distant pyre added to the starlight, making everything preternaturally clear.

The village consisted of five stone cottages with thatch roofs. The innkeeper kept pigs that liked to root at his doorstep. As Roland dismounted, a couple of hogs grunted awake and staggered to their feet, sniffing the air and blinking wisely. Roland pounded at the oaken door and stared at the Hostenfest icon nailed there – a tattered wooden image of the Earth King, dressed in a new green traveling robe and wearing a crown of oak leaves. Someone had replaced the Earth King's staff with a sprig of purple-flowered thyme.

The fat innkeeper who greeted him wore an apron so dirty that he was almost indistinguishable from his swine. Roland silently swore to ride far before he breakfasted. But he wanted sleep now, so paid for a room.

Since the rooms were full up with travelers fleeing from

the north, he was forced to bed with a huge fellow who smelled of grease and too much ale.

Still, the room was dry while the ground outside was not, so Roland climbed into bed with the fellow, shoved him onto his side so that he stopped snoring, and tried to sleep.

The plan went afoul. Within two minutes the big fellow rolled back over and snored loudly in Roland's ear. While still asleep, he wrapped a leg over Roland, then groped Roland's breast. The man had a grip so firm it could only have come from taking endowments of brawn.

Roland whispered menacingly, 'Stop that, or I'll be leaving a severed hand in this bed in the morning.'

The big man, who had a beard so bushy that squirrels could have hidden in it, squinted at Roland through the dim firelight shining through a parchment window.

'Oh, sorry!' the big fellow apologized. 'Thought you were my wife.' He rolled over and immediately began to snore.

That was some comfort. Roland had heard tales of men getting buggered under such circumstances.

Roland turned aside, letting the fellow's backside warm his buttocks, then tried to sleep. But an hour later, the big fellow was at him again, clutching Roland's breasts. Roland gave him a sharp elbow to the chest.

'Damn you, woman!' the fellow groaned in his sleep, rolling back over with a huff. 'You're all bones.'

Roland promised himself that tomorrow night he'd sleep with the rocks in the field.

The thought had hardly crossed his mind than he woke from a deep slumber.

He was entangled in the fellow's arms again, arms as big as logs. His bedfellow had kissed him on the forehead.

A dim morning light shone through the window. His eyes closed, the man seemed fast asleep, breathing deeply.

'Excuse me,' Roland said, catching the man by the beard and yanking this way and that. He shoved the fellow's head back. 'I admire a man who can show affection, but please refrain from showing it to me.'

The fellow opened his bloodshot eyes and gazed at Roland for half a second. Roland expected the brute to offer an embarrassed apology.

Instead, he paled in dismay. 'Borenson?' he shouted, coming fully awake. He scuttled his three hundred pounds of bulk back against the wall and huddled there quivering, as if terrified that Roland might strike. 'What are you doing here?'

He was an enormous man with black hair, and a good deal of gray in his beard. Roland didn't recognize him. But I have been asleep for twenty-one years, he thought. 'Do I know you?' Roland asked, begging a name.

'Know me? You nearly killed me, though I must admit that I deserved it. I was an ass back then. But I've repented my ways, and I'm only half an ass now. Don't you know me? Baron Poll!'

Roland had never met the fellow. He's confusing me with my son, Ivarian Borenson, Roland realized, a son he'd only learned about after waking from his long sleep.

'Ah, Baron Poll!' Roland said enthusiastically, waiting for the fellow to recognize his own mistake. It didn't seem likely that Roland's son would look so much like him, with his flaming red hair and pale complexion. The boy's mother was fairly dark of skin. 'It's good to see you.'

'Likewise, and I'm glad you feel that way. So, our past is forgotten? You forgive me . . . the theft of your purse? Everything?'

'As far as I am concerned, it's as if we've never met,' Roland said.

Baron Poll suddenly seemed mystified. 'You're in a generous mood . . . after all those beatings I gave you. I suppose it turned you into a soldier, though. One could even say that you're in my debt. Right?'

'Ah, the beatings,' Roland echoed, still astonished that the fellow didn't realize his mistake. Roland knew only one thing about his son: he was a captain in the King's Guard. 'That was nothing. Of course I gave as good as I got, right?'

Baron Poll stared at Roland as if he'd gone utterly mad.

Roland realized that his son really hadn't given as good as he'd gotten. 'Well . . .' Poll ventured suspiciously, 'then I'm glad we're reconciled. But . . . what are you doing down here? I thought you'd gone north to Heredon?'

'Alas, King Orden is dead,' Roland said solemnly. 'Raj Ahten met him at Longmot. Thousands of our men fell in battle.'

'And the Prince?' Poll asked, his face pale.

'He is well, as far as I know,' Roland answered.

'As far as you know? But you're his bodyguard!'

'That is why I'm in a hurry to get back to his side,' Roland said, climbing off the bed. He threw his new bearskin traveling robe over his shoulders, pulled on his heavy boots.

Baron Poll heaved his bulk up on the side of the bed, stared about dumbly. 'Where's your axe? Your bow? You aren't traveling weaponless!'

'I am.' Roland was in a hurry to reach Heredon. He hadn't taken the time yet to purchase weapons, had only learned last night that he might need them, as he began to meet refugees fleeing the north.

Baron Poll studied him as if he were daft. 'You know that Castle Crayden fell six days ago, along with Castle Fells and the fortress at Tal Dur? And two days ago Raj Ahten destroyed Tal Rimmon, Gorlane, and Aravelle. Two hundred thousand of Raj Ahten's men are marching on Carris and should reach it by dawn tomorrow. You're heading weaponless into that kind of danger?'

Roland knew little about the lay of the land. Being illiterate, he could not read a map, and until now he had never been ten miles from his childhood home at the Courts of Tide, but he knew that castles Crayden and Fells defended the passes on Mystarria's western border. He'd never heard of Tal Dur, but he knew of the castles that had been destroyed to the north.

'Can I reach Carris before they do?' Roland asked.

'Is your horse fast?'

Roland nodded. 'It has an endowment of stamina and one of strength and metabolism.' It was a lordly animal, such as the king's messengers rode. After being on the road for a week, Roland had met a horse trader and purchased the beast with money he'd inherited while he slept.

'You should easily make a hundred miles today, then,' Baron Poll said. 'But the roads are like to be treacherous. Raj Ahten's assassins are out in force.'

'Fine,' Roland said. He hoped that his mount would be up to the challenge. He turned to leave.

'Here now, you can't go out like that,' Baron Poll said. 'Take my arms and armor – whatever you want.' He nodded to a corner of the room. Baron Poll's breastplate was propped against the wall, along with a huge axe, a sword as tall as a man, and a half-sword.

The breastplate was too wide for Roland by half, and he doubted he could even heft the tall sword well enough to use it in battle. Roland was a butcher by trade. The axe was no larger than the forty-pound cleavers that Roland had used for splitting beeves, but he doubted that he'd ever want such a clumsy weapon in a brawl. But there was the half-sword. It was not much larger than a good long knife. Still, Roland could not take such a gift by deception.

'Baron Poll,' Roland apologized, 'I fear that you are mistaken. My name is Roland Borenson. I am not a member of the King's Guard. You mistake me for my son.'

'What?' Baron Poll spat. 'The Borenson I knew was a father-less bastard. Everyone said so. We teased him mercilessly for it!'

'No man is fatherless,' Roland said. 'I served as a Dedicate in the Blue Tower these past twenty-one years, giving metab-olism in service of the King.'

'But everyone said you were dead! No. Wait . . . I remember the story better now: they said you were a common criminal, a killer, executed before your son was born!'

'Not executed,' Roland objected, 'though perhaps my son's mother might have wished it.'

'Ah, I remember the harpy well,' Baron Poll said. 'As I recall, she often wished *all* men to death. Certainly she damned me enough.' Baron Poll suddenly blushed, as if embarrassed to pry any further. 'I should have known,' he said. 'You look too young. The Borenson I knew has endowments of metabolism himself, and has aged accordingly. In the past eight years, he would have aged more than twenty. If the two of you stood together, I think you would look like father and son now – though he would seem the father, and you the son.'

Roland nodded. 'Now you have the way of it.'

Baron Poll's brows drew together in thought. 'You're riding to see your son?'

'And to put myself into service to my king,' Roland answered.

'You've no endowments,' Poll pointed out. 'You're not a soldier. You'll never make it to Heredon.'

'Probably not,' Roland agreed.

He headed for the door.

'Wait!' Baron Poll bellowed. 'Kill yourself if you want, but don't make it easy for them. At least take a weapon.'

'Thank you,' Roland said, as he took the half-sword. He had no belt to hold the scabbard, so he tucked it under his shirt.

Baron Poll snorted, displeased by his choice of weapons. 'You're welcome. Luck to you.'

Baron Poll got out of bed, shook Roland's hand at the wrist. The man had a grip like a vise. Roland shook hard, as if he had endowments of brawn of his own. Years of knife work had left him with strong wrists and a fierce grip. Even after decades asleep his muscles were firm, his calluses still thick.

Roland hurried downstairs. The common room was full. Peasants fleeing south clustered at some tables, while squires who were heading north with their lords sat at others. These young men were sharpening blades or rubbing oil into leather or chain mail. A few of the lords, dressed oddly in tunics and hose and quilted undermail, were seated on stools along the bar.

The smells of fresh bread and meat were inviting enough to make Roland repent of his vow to leave here hungry. He took a vacant stool. Two knights were arguing vigorously about how much to feed a warhorse before charging into battle, and one of the men nodded at Roland, as if encouraging him to enter the fray. He wondered if the fellow knew him, or if he believed Roland was a lord because of the fine new bearskin cloak he wore, and his new tunic and pants and boots. Roland knew he was dressed like a noble. But soon he heard a squire whisper the name Borenson.

The innkeeper brought him some honeyed tea in a mustache mug, and he began to eat a loaf of rye bread, dipping it in a trencher of rich gravy thick with floating chunks of pork.

As Roland ate, he began to muse about the events of the past week. This was the second time in a week that he'd wakened to a kiss . . .

Seven days earlier, he'd felt a touch on his cheek – a gentle, tentative touch, as if a spider crawled over him – and bolted awake, heart pounding.

He'd been startled to find himself in a dim room, lying abed at midday. The walls were of heavy stone, his mat of feathers and straw. He knew the place at once by the tang of sea air. Outside, terns and gulls cried as if in solitary lament, while huge ocean swells surged against battlements hewn from ancient rock at the base of the tower. As a Dedicate who gave metabolism, he'd slept fast for twenty years. Somehow, over the many years that he'd slept, Roland had felt those waves lashing during storms, making the whole keep shudder under their impact, endlessly wearing away the rock.

He was in the Blue Tower, a few miles east of the Courts of Tide in the Caroll Sea.

The small chamber he inhabited was surprisingly sparse in its decor, almost like a tomb: no table or chairs, no tapestry or rugs to cover the bare walls or floor. No wardrobe for clothes, or even a peg on the wall where one might hang a robe. It was not a room for a man to live in, only to sleep in for endless ages. Aside from the mattress and Roland, the small chamber held only a young woman who leapt back to

the foot of the bed, beside a wash bucket. He saw her by a
dim light cast from a salt-encrusted window. She was a sweet
thing with an oval-shaped face, eyes a pale blue, and hair the
color of straw. She wore a wreath of tiny dried violets in her
hair. The touch of her long hair on his face was what had
awakened him.

Her face reddened with embarrassment and she crouched
back a bit on her haunches. 'Pardon me,' she stammered.
'Mistress Hetta bade me cleanse you.' She held up a wash rag
defensively, as if to prove her good intentions.

Yet the moisture on his lips tasted not of some stale rag
but of a girl's kiss. Perhaps she had meant to cleanse him, but
decided to seek more enticing diversion.

'I'll get you some help,' she said, dropping her rag into the
bucket. She half turned from where she huddled.

Roland grabbed her wrist, quick as a mongoose taking a
cobra. Because of his speed, he had been forced to give his
metabolism into the King's service.

'How long have I slept?' he begged. His mouth felt terribly
dry, and the words made his throat itch. 'What year is it?'

'Year?' the young woman asked, barely fighting his grasp.
He held her lightly. She could have broken away, but chose
instead to stay. He caught the scent of her: clean, a hint of
lilac water in her hair – or perhaps it was the dried violets.
'It is the twenty-second year of the reign of Mendellas Draken
Orden.'

The news did not surprise him, yet her words were like a
blow. Twenty-one years. It has been twenty-one years since I
gave my endowment of metabolism into the service of the
King. Twenty-one years of sleeping on this cot while young
women occasionally clean me or spoon broth down my throat
and make sure that I still breathe.

He'd given his metabolism to a young warrior, a sergeant
named Drayden. In those twenty-one years, Drayden would
have aged more than forty, while Roland slept and aged not
a day.

It seemed but moments ago that Roland knelt before

Drayden and young King Orden. The facilitators sang in bird-like voices, pressing their forcibles into his chest, calling the endowment from him. He'd felt the unspeakable pain of the forcibles, smelled flesh and the hairs of his chest begin to burn, felt the overwhelming fatigue as the facilitators drew forth his metabolism. He'd cried in pain and terror at the last, and seemingly had fallen forever.

Because Roland was now awake, he knew that Drayden was dead. If a man gave use of an attribute to a lord, then once that lord died, the attribute returned to the Dedicate. Whether Drayden had died in battle or abed, Roland could not know. But now that Roland was one of the Restored, it meant Drayden was certainly dead.

'I'll go now,' the girl said, struggling just a bit.

Roland felt the soft hairs on her forearm. She had a pair of pimples on her face, but in time he imagined that she would become a beauty.

'My mouth is dry,' Roland said, still holding her.

'I'll get water,' she promised. She quit struggling – as if by relinquishing she hoped he might let her go.

Roland released her wrist, but stared hard into her face. He was a handsome young man – with his long red hair tied back, a strong chin, piercing blue eyes, and a svelte, muscular body.

He asked, 'Just now, when you were kissing me in my sleep, was it me you wanted, or did you fantasize about some other man?'

The girl shook with fright, looked to the small wooden door of Roland's chamber, as if to make sure it was closed. She ducked her head shyly, and whispered, 'You.'

Roland studied her face. A few freckles, a straight mouth, a delicate nose. He wanted to kiss her, just behind her small left ear.

To fill the silence, the girl began to chatter. 'I've been washing you since I was ten. I . . . in that time, I've come to know your body well. There is kindness in your face, and cruelty, and beauty. I sometimes wonder what kind of man you are, and I hoped that you would awaken before I married. My name is Sera, Sera Crier. My father and mother and sisters all died in a mud slide when I was small, so now I serve here in the keep.'

'Do you even know my name?' Roland asked.

'Borenson. Roland Borenson. Everyone in the keep knows you. You are the father of a captain of the King's Guard. Your son serves as bodyguard to Prince Gaborn.'

Roland wondered. He'd had no son that he'd ever heard of. But he'd had a young wife when he gave his endowment, though she would be getting old by now. He had not known when he'd given his metabolism that she carried a child.

He wondered if this girl spoke aright. He wondered why she was attracted to him. He asked, 'You know my name. Do you also know that I am a murderer?'

The girl drew back in astonishment.

'I killed a man,' Roland admitted. He wondered why he told her that. But although the man had died twenty years ago, for him it had happened only hours ago, and the feel of the man's guts in his hand was still fresh on his mind.

'I'm sure you had good reason.'

'I found him in bed with my wife. I slit him open like a fish, yet even as I did, I had to wonder why. Ours was an arranged marriage and a poor match by any measure. I did not care for the girl, and she hated me. Killing the man was a waste. I think I did it to hurt *her*. I don't know.

'For years you have wondered what kind of man I am, Sera. Do you think you know?'

Sera Crier licked her lips. Now she began to tremble. 'Any other man would have lost his head for such a deed. The King must have liked you well. Perhaps he too saw some kindness masked by your cruelty.'

'I see only waste and stupidity,' Roland answered.

'And beauty.' Sera leaned forward to kiss Roland's lips. He turned his head a bit.

'I've given myself,' he said.

'To a woman who disavowed you and married someone

else long, long ago . . .' Sera answered. Roland felt certain that she knew what she spoke of when she mentioned his wife. The news saddened him. The girl had been another butcher's daughter – and she'd had a wit sharper than her father's knives. She'd thought him stupid, he'd thought her cruel.

'No,' he answered, feeling that she did not see the deeper truth. 'I'm not given to my wife, but to my king.'

Roland sat up in his cot, gazed down at his feet. He was dressed in nothing but a tunic – a fine red cotton garment that would breathe in the moist air. Not the old work clothes he'd worn twenty-one years ago when he gave his endowment. They'd rotted away.

Sera fetched him some trousers and a pair of lambskin boots, then offered to help dress him, though he needed no help. He had never felt so completely rested.

Though today was the second time in a week that Roland had wakened to a kiss, Sera Crier's lips had been far more desirable than Baron Poll's.

As Roland ate, a young knight in splint mail came in through the front door. 'Borenson!' he shouted in greeting. At the same instant, Baron Poll had just come down the stairs and stood at the landing. 'And Baron Poll!' the fellow said in dismay.

Suddenly the room swirled in commotion. The two lords beside Roland dove to the floor. The knight at the door pulled his sword, ringing from its scabbard. The squires in the corner shouted variations of 'Fight!' 'Blood feud!' One of the lads flipped a table over and hid behind it as a barricade. A girl who was serving the peasants threw a basket filled with bread loaves into the air and ran for the buttery shrieking, 'Baron Poll and Sir Borenson are in the same room!' The innkeeper ran out from the kitchens, face pale, as if hoping to rescue his furniture.

Everywhere Roland glanced, he saw frightened faces.

Baron Poll just stood on the landing, studying the scene, an amused smile playing on his lips.

Roland enjoyed the joke. He furrowed his brow, drew the half-sword, and eyed Baron Poll menacingly. Then he chopped a loaf of bread in half and plunged the sword tip into the counter, so that it stood there quivering.

'It appears the stool beside me has been vacated, Baron Poll,' Roland said. 'Perhaps you will join me for breakfast.'

'Why, thank you,' Baron Poll said courteously. He waddled over to the stool, sat down, took half the loaf, dipped it in Roland's trencher.

The whole crowd gaped in wonder. Roland thought, They'd not look more astonished if Baron Poll and I were a pair of toads flying about the room like hummingbirds, chasing flies with long tongues.

Horrified, the young knight exclaimed, 'But you're not to be within fifty leagues of each other – by the King's own command!'

'True, but last night, by mere happenstance, Borenson and I were thrust into the same cot,' Baron Poll replied contentedly. 'And I must say, I've never had a more cordial bedfellow.'

'Nor I,' Roland offered. 'Not many a man could warm your backside as well as Baron Poll. The man is as big as a horse and as hot as a smithy's forge. Why, I suspect he could warm a whole village at night. You could fry fish on his feet or bake bricks on his back.'

Everyone stared at them as if they were daft, so Roland and Baron Poll loudly discussed such mundane topics as the weather, how the recent rains had aggravated the gout that Poll's mother-in-law suffered from, the best way to cook venison, and so on.

Everyone watched them warily, as if at any moment the truce might break, and the two men would go at it with knives.

Finally, Borenson slapped Baron Poll on the back, went outside into the early morning light. The village of Hay was aptly named. Haycocks stood everywhere in the fields, and black-eyed Susans grew huge so late in the summer. The margin of the road out of town was a riot of yellows and deep browns. The countryside was flat, and the grass had grown tall in the summer, but now was sun-bleached white and dying.

At the front of the inn, the pigs had wisely fled. A couple of red hens pecked in the dirt by Roland's feet. Roland waited while a stableboy went to fetch his horse.

He stood looking up into the hazy sky. The air was moist with wisps of morning fog. Volcanic ash drifted in the mist like flakes of warm snow.

Baron Poll came out, stood with him a moment, staring up and stroking his beard. 'There's mischief in this volcano blowing, and powerful magic,' he predicted. 'Raj Ahten has flameweavers in his retinue, I hear. I wonder if they're mixed up in this?'

Roland thought it unlikely that the flameweavers had anything to do with the volcano. It had blown far to the south, and Raj Ahten's soldiers were converging on Carris a hundred miles north. Still, it seemed ominous.

'What is this about the King's command?' Roland asked. 'Why are you not to get within fifty leagues of my son?'

'Ah, it's nothing.' Baron Poll grinned with embarrassment. 'Old news. I'd tell you the story, but you'll hear some minstrel sing of it soon enough, I imagine. They get most of it right.' Baron Poll sheepishly glanced at the ground and wiped some fallen ash from his cloak. 'I've lived in mortal terror of your boy these past ten years.' Roland wondered what his son would have done if he'd wakened in this man's arms. 'But dark times can make even the worst of enemies into friends, eh?' Baron Poll said. 'And men can change, can't they? Wish your son well for me, if you find him.'

His expression begged Roland for forgiveness, and Roland would have been happy to give it to him, but he could not speak for his son. 'I'll do so,' Roland promised.

Far down the dirt road to the south, fifty knights were racing north, the hooves of their chargers thundering over the earth.

'Perhaps your road north won't be so dangerous after all,'

Baron Poll said. 'But mark my word. Beware of Carris.'

'Aren't you coming north? I thought you'd ride with me.'

'Pah,' Baron Poll spat. 'I'm going the wrong way. I have a summer estate outside Carris, so my wife wanted me to remove a few valuables before Raj Ahten's men looted the place. I'm helping the servants guard the wagon.'

That seemed cowardly, but Roland said nothing.

'Aye,' Baron Poll said. 'I know what you're thinking. But they'll have to fight without me. I had two endowments of metabolism until last fall when some of my Dedicates got slain. I'm feeling too old and fat for a real battle. My armor fits me no better than would my wife's undergarments.'

Those words had come hard. The Baron did want to come. Still, Baron Poll looked no more than forty-odd years. If he'd had the Dedicates for ten years, he'd now be twenty years old chronologically. Roland's age.

'We could skirt this battle at Carris,' Roland suggested, 'and find one more to your liking. Why don't you come with me?'

'Hah!' Baron Poll guffawed. 'Eight hundred miles to Heredon? If you're not worried for your own health, or mine, at least you could show pity to my poor horse!'

'Let your servants haul off your treasures. They don't need you guarding them.'

'Ah, my wife would give me such a tongue-lashing – the shrew! Better to anger Raj Ahten than her.'

A maid came out of the inn and expertly grabbed one of the hens that had been pecking in the dust, snatching it by the neck. 'You'll be coming with me. Lord Collinsward wants your company for breakfast.' She wrung the chicken's neck and was already pulling off feathers as she carried the hen round the back.

In moments, the knights from the south reached the village, wheeled their horses toward the stable. Apparently they hoped to rest, get some news, and care for their mounts.

When the stableboy brought the horse around, Roland mounted, gave him a small coin. The filly was well rested, frolicky. She was a huge red beast with a blaze of white on her hooves and forehead. She acted ready for a brisk run in the cool morning air. Roland took off along the road, through a field shrouded with mist that soon turned into a low fog.

Roland sniffed at the ashes. On the road north ahead was Raj Ahten's army – an army said to contain sorcerers and Invincibles and frowth giants and fierce dogs of war.

He could not help think how unfair life could be. That poor chicken back at the inn hadn't had a second's warning before it died.

Moments later, while Roland was preoccupied with such grim thoughts, the sound of a horse riding hard startled him.

He glanced behind, worried that it might be a robber or assassin. He was riding through a thick fog, and could not see a hundred feet ahead.

Spurring his mount off the road, he reached for his half-sword just as a huge shape came thundering from the mist behind him.

Baron Poll bounced up on his horse. 'Well met!' the fat knight cried, sitting precariously on his charger. The beast looked about with a terrified demeanor, eyes wide and ears back, as if afraid its master would give it a good cuffing.

'Aren't you going south with your treasures?' Roland asked.

'Damn the treasures. The servants can abscond with them for all I care! Let them take that harpy of a wife, too!' Baron Poll bellowed. 'You were right. It's better to die young with the blood hot in your veins, than to die old and slowly of being too fat!'

'I never said that,' Roland objected.

'Pah! Your eyes said it all, lad.'

Roland sheathed his sword. 'Well, now that my eyes are so eloquent, perhaps I'll give my unruly tongue a rest.' With that, he wheeled his horse into the mist.

3

HOSTENFEST

Myrrima woke at dawn with tears in her eyes. She wiped them away and lay wondering at the strange sense of melancholy that had overwhelmed her each dawn for the past three days. She did not know for certain why she woke crying.

She should not have felt this way. It was the last day of Hostenfest – the day of the great feast – and it should have been the happiest day of the year.

Moreover, in the past few weeks, she had won several small victories. Instead of sleeping in her shack outside Bannisferre, she had wakened in her room in the King's Tower at Castle Sylvarresta. Over the past three days, she'd become a close friend to young Queen Iome Orden, and she'd married a knight with some wealth. Her sisters and her mother were here in the castle, living in the Dedicate's Keep, where they would be taken care of for life.

She should have been happy. Yet she felt as if the hand of doom weighed on her.

Outside her window, she could hear the King's facilitators chanting out in the Dedicates' Keep. Over the past week, thousands of people had offered to dedicate their attributes into the service of the Earth King. Though Gaborn was an Oath-Bound Lord and had sworn not to take a man's brawn or wit or stamina unless it was freely given, and those had been freely offered, he still had not taken a single endowment. Some feared that he had forsaken the practice altogether, yet he did not forbid his knights to take endowments.

King Gaborn Val Orden seemed to have an endless supply
of forcibles, and for the past week, the chief facilitator had
worked with his apprentices night and day, doling out endowments to Heredon's knights, trying to rebuild the kingdom's
decimated troops. Still, the Dedicate's Keep was only half full.

A soft knocking came from Myrrima's door, and she rolled
over on the satin sheets of her bed, glanced out through a
window of the oriel. The morning light barely glowed through
the stained-glass image on the window – mourning doves
winging through a blue sky, as seen through a screen of ivy.
She realized that the low knocking had wakened her.

'Who's there?'

''Tis I,' Borenson said.

Throwing back the sheets, she leapt up, rushed to the door,
and yanked it open. He stood in the doorway, a lamp in his
hands, its small flame wavering in the drafty castle. He looked
huge there in the darkness, grinning like a boy with a joke
to tell. His blue eyes twinkled, and his red beard fanned out
from his face.

'You don't need to knock,' she laughed. They'd been married
now for four days, though he'd run off and spent the last
three on a hunt. Worse, they had never consummated their
marriage, and Myrrima had to wonder at him.

Sir Borenson seemed smitten enough by her, but when
she'd thought to bed him on her honeymoon night, he'd
merely said, 'How can a man take such pleasures, while tonight
he will hunt in the Dunnwood?'

Myrrima was inexperienced with men. She did not know
if it was right to feel so hurt by his rejection. She'd wondered
if he really was overexcited by the hunt, if that was natural,
or if he had a war wound that kept him from showing affection. Perhaps Borenson had married her only because Gaborn
had suggested it.

For days she had felt hurt and bewildered, and had longed
for Borenson's return. Now he was home.

'I was afraid you'd be deeply asleep,' he said.

He stepped forward, ventured a small kiss, holding the

lamp far out to his side. She took the lamp from him and set it on a trunk. 'Not like that,' she said. 'We're married.' She grabbed him by the beard and pulled him down, kissed him roughly, leading him toward the bed. She hoped that by now he might have settled down.

Almost immediately she regretted it. He was covered in dirt, and his ring mail was caked with mud. It would take someone hours to get her bedclothes clean.

'Ah, that will have to wait.' Borenson grinned. 'But not too long, of course. Just until I get cleaned up.'

She stared up into his face. The melancholy she'd felt only moments before had dissipated completely. 'Go wash, then.'

'Not quite yet,' Borenson chortled. 'I've got something to show you.'

'You killed me a boar for Hostenfest?' she laughed.

'No boars this Hostenfest,' he answered. 'The hunt didn't go as anticipated.'

'Well, I suppose the lords at the table could make do with a rabbit,' she teased. 'Though I shan't want anything smaller. I never have developed a taste for field mice.'

Borenson smiled mysteriously. 'Come on. Hurry.' He went to her wardrobe and pulled down a simple blue dress. Myrrima threw off her night-clothes, pulled on the dress, and began to tie the laces of the bodice. Borenson watched, delighted to be entertained by his new bride. She pulled on some shoes and in moments he had her rushing down the steps of the keep, trying to catch up.

'The hunt didn't go well,' Borenson said, taking her hand. 'We had some casualties.'

She wondered at that. There were still black-furred nomen prowling in the woods, and frowth giants. Raj Ahten had fled south from here more than a week ago, abandoning those troops that were too tired to flee. She wondered how the lords had been killed. 'Casualties?'

He nodded, unwilling to say more.

In moments they reached the cobblestone street. The morning air carried a keen cold bite, and Myrrima's breath fogged. Borenson hurried her through the portcullis of the King's Gate, rushing down Market Street to the city gate. There, just beyond the drawbridge, beside the moat, a huge crowd was gathering.

The fields before Castle Sylvarresta were full of bright pavilions that sprawled like a city of canvas. In the past week, another four hundred thousand peasants and nobles from Heredon and kingdoms beyond had gathered here, come to see the Earth King, Gaborn Val Orden. The fields were becoming an endless maze of tents and animals, enough so that now the tents covered nearby hills, and whole towns were springing up on the plains to the south and west.

Everywhere, merchants and vendors were setting up booths, creating impromptu markets among the host. The scent of cooking sausages hung over the throng, and because this was a feast day, hundreds of minstrels were already warming up their lutes and harps under every tree.

Four peasant boys ahead were singing so badly to pipes and lutes that Myrrima didn't know if they were serious or if they simply mocked others' poor efforts.

Borenson nudged aside some peasants and chased away a couple of mastiffs so that Myrrima could see what was at the crowd's center.

What she saw revolted her: a lump of gray flesh as huge as a wagon lay on the grass, the eyeless head of a reaver. Its feelers hung like dead worms around the back of its skull, and the rows of crystalline teeth looked terrifying as they caught the morning sun. The thing was dirty, having been dragged for many miles. Yet beneath that grime, along the forehead, she could see runes tattooed into the monster's horrible flesh – runes of power that glowed even now like dim flames. Every child in Rofehavan knew the meaning of those facial runes.

This was no common reaver. It was a mage.

Myrrima's heart pounded as if it were trying to batter its way out of her chest. She found herself breathing hard, feeling faint. She went suddenly cold, and stood letting the heat of strangers' bodies warm her while the mastiffs sniffed at the reaver's head and wagged the stumps of their tails nervously.

'A reaver mage?' she asked dully. No one had killed a reaver mage in Heredon in over sixteen hundred years. She studied the thing's head. The monster could have bitten a warhorse in half. Or a man.

Peasants tittered; children reached out to touch the horrible thing.

'We caught her in the Dunnwood, down in some old duskin ruins, far underground. She had her mates and offspring there, so we killed them all and crushed her eggs.'

'How many died?' Myrrima asked, dazed.

Borenson did not immediately answer. 'Forty-one good knights,' he said at last. 'They fought well. It was a fierce battle.' He added as modestly as he could, 'I killed the mage myself.'

She wheeled on him, full of rage. 'How could you do this?'

Surprised by her reaction, he sputtered, 'It wasn't easy, I confess. The mage gave me a hard time of it. She seemed loath to lose her head.'

Suddenly she saw it all clearly: why she had wakened every morning full of melancholy, why she could hardly sleep nights. She was terrified. She'd sought to wed a man for his wealth, and instead had fallen in love. Meanwhile, her husband seemed more interested in getting himself killed than in making love to her.

She turned and stalked off through the crowd, shoving away bystanders, pushing toward the castle gate, blinded by tears.

Borenson hurried after her, caught her at the foot of the drawbridge and turned her with one big hand. 'What are you so mad about?'

The sound of his voice was so loud that it startled a fish down in the reeds of the moat. The water swirled as something large swam away. A throng of people heading into the castle made way for Borenson and Myrrima, skirting them as if they were islands in a stream.

She turned up to face him. 'I'm mad because you're leaving me.'

'Of course I'm leaving you – in a few days,' he said. 'But not by choice.'

Borenson had killed King Sylvarresta, and Myrrima knew that it shamed him, despite the fact that Sylvarresta had given an endowment to Raj Ahten, lending wit to the Wolf Lord. Though Sylvarresta had been a good man, one who had only given his endowment under duress, the truth was that in such a horrible war as this, friend could not spare friend. Brother could not spare brother.

By granting an endowment of wit to Raj Ahten, King Sylvarresta had made himself an enemy to every just man, and Borenson had felt bound by duty to take the life of his old friend.

Once the deed was done, the King's daughter, Iome, was loath to punish Borenson, but neither could she forgive him. So in the name of justice she'd lain a quest upon Borenson, commanded him to perform an Act Penitent – to go to the lands beyond Inkarra and find the legendary Daylan Hammer, the Sum of All Men, and bring him back here to Heredon to help fight Raj Ahten.

It seemed a fool's quest. Though rumor said he lived, Daylan Hammer could not still be alive after sixteen centuries. Sir Borenson seemed loath to go, when he saw better ways to protect his people. Still, he was bound by honor to depart – and he'd do so soon.

'I don't *want* to go,' Borenson said. 'I have to.'

'It's a long way to Inkarra. A long way for a man to travel alone. I could come with you.'

'No!' Borenson insisted. 'You can't. You'd never make it alive.'

'What makes you think you will?' Myrrima asked, though she knew the answer. He was a captain in the King's Guard, with endowments of brawn and stamina and metabolism. If any man alive could make it through the enemy territories, Borenson could. Inkarra was a dangerous place: a strange land where northerners weren't tolerated. Neither he nor Myrrima could travel easily in Inkarra: the Inkarrans all had skin as pale as ivory, with straight hair the color of silver. Borenson and Myrrima couldn't disguise themselves enough to hide their foreign birth.

For the most part, the Inkarrans were a nocturnal people who worked and moved by night. By day, they spent much of their time at home or in the shadowed woods. Evading them would be nearly impossible.

And if Borenson were captured, he'd be forced to fight in their dark arena.

In order to stay alive, he'd have to travel secretly at night, as best he could, never risking contact with the Inkarrans.

He said, 'I can't take you. You would slow me down, get us both killed.'

'I don't like this,' Myrrima said. 'I don't like the idea of your going off alone.' A vendor pulling a handcart moved close, and Myrrima stepped from his path, dragging Borenson with her.

'Neither do I, but you can't believe for a moment that you could help me.'

Myrrima shook her head, and a tear splashed down her cheek. 'I told you about my father,' she said. He'd been a fairly wealthy merchant who had apparently been robbed and killed and then had his shop burned down around him to cover the crime. 'I sometimes wonder if I could have saved him. On the night he was killed, he was not the wealthiest merchant in Bannisferre, or the most feeble. But he was alone. Perhaps if I had been with him . . .'

'If you had been with him, you too might be dead,' Borenson said.

'Perhaps,' she whispered. 'But sometimes I think I'd rather be dead than live without knowing if I could have been of help.'

Borenson stared hard at her. 'I admire your loyalty, I cherish it. But the worst day of my life came last week when I learned that you had ridden to Longmot, hoping to join me in battle.

I want you to sleep by my side, not fight by my side – even though you have a warrior's heart.' He kissed her tenderly.

For just a moment their eyes met. She held his outstretched hand. A plea. 'If I cannot come with you,' she said, 'I will not be happy until you return.'

Borenson smiled and leaned his forehead against hers, kissed her nose. 'Let us agree, then. Neither of us will be happy until I return.'

He held her for a long moment, letting the crowd of peasants heading for the castle stroll past.

Behind her, she heard a couple of men talking. 'Chose that whore Bonny Cleads, he did, not half an hour ago! Why would the Earth King Choose someone like her?'

'He says he Chooses those what love their fellow men,' a fellow said, 'and I don't know of no one that's loved more of 'em than she.'

Myrrima felt Borenson stiffen in her arms as his attention focused on the peasants. Though he bridled to hear such criticism of the King, he did not challenge the men.

Myrrima heard a shout and a splash, as if someone had thrown something into the moat, but paid it no mind until Borenson pulled his head back from her and turned away.

She looked to see what had caught his eye. Four young men stood on the levee, looking down into the moat, about a hundred yards upstream. They were perched on a small rise, beneath an enormous willow.

The sun was bright and the skies clear. An early morning mist rose off the dark waters. As Myrrima watched, a huge fish came up to the surface of the moat and swam about lazily. One boy hurled a spear at it, but the fish darted nimbly forward and dove again.

'Hey,' Borenson shouted as if angry. 'What are you boys doing?'

One lad, a thin boy with straw for hair and a triangle for a face, said, 'Catching a sturgeon for Hostenfest. Some big ones swam into the moat this morning.'

Even as he spoke, an enormous fish some six or eight feet

long rose to the surface and began finning, whirling about in strange patterns. It ignored a duckling that nosed about in some nearby reeds. The huge fish did not seem to be hunting for flies. One lad readied a spear.

'Stop – in the name of the King!' Borenson commanded. Myrrima had to smile to hear him appropriate the name of the King.

The spear-bearing lad looked at Borenson as if he were mad. 'But never has such a huge fish swum into the moat,' he said.

'Go get the King – now!' Borenson commanded. 'And the wizard Binnesman, too! Tell them it's an emergency, that there are some exceeding strange fish in the moat.' The boy looked longingly at the sturgeon, spear poised at his shoulder. 'Do it now!' Borenson roared. 'Or I swear I'll gut you where you stand.'

The boy glanced back and forth between Borenson and the fish, then threw down his spear and ran for the castle.

By the time Gaborn reached the moat, holding hands with his wife Iome while the wizard Binnesman walked behind, a great crowd of peasants had gathered at its banks. They seemed both perplexed and angry to have a knight standing there protecting the enormous sturgeons that swam not twenty feet from shore. There was much grumbling about how the fish were 'good enough for the King's belly, but not for ours.'

Borenson had been gathering information about the fish for several minutes. Nine sturgeons had been spotted at dawn, swimming into the moat from the Wye River. Now all nine fish finned at the surface, just outside the castle wall, performing a strange and sinuous dance.

Iome came and stood with Myrrima, smiling radiantly to have her husband home. Gaborn's and Iome's Days followed at their backs.

'You look well,' Myrrima said. 'In fact, you are glowing.' It was true.

Iome only smiled at the remark. In the past few days, Iome

had invited Myrrima to dine with her at every meal, as if Myrrima were some woman born to the court. Myrrima felt odd and apprehensive about such behavior, as if she were merely pretending to be a gentleman's wife, though Iome seemed in every respect to be genuinely pleased by Myrrima's company.

Iome's Maid of Honor, Chemoise, had departed this week to an uncle's holding in the north. For six years, Iome and Chemoise had been constant companions. But now that Iome was married, she no longer required a Maid of Honor to constantly remain in her presence. Still, Myrrima wondered if Iome craved a woman's company. Certainly Iome had sought to befriend her easily enough.

Iome kissed Myrrima's cheek and smiled in greeting. 'You look well, too. What is the excitement all about?'

'Big fish, I guess,' Myrrima said. 'I think our lords and knights are all still boys at heart.'

'Indeed, our husbands are acting oddly today,' Iome said, and Myrrima merely laughed, for both of them had been married only four days past, and neither she nor Iome were used to speaking of 'our husbands.'

In moments young King Orden knelt beside the moat, a dark-haired, blue-eyed young man squinting into the depths beside the pink water lilies. The Earth Warden Binnesman followed, wearing his wizard's robes in shades of scarlet and russet.

When Gaborn saw the fish, he stared in frank amazement. He came and stood at the riverbank with Borenson, then sat down on his haunches, watching the fish as they wheeled and dove.

'Water wizards?' Gaborn asked. 'Here in the moat?'

'That's what it looks like,' Borenson said.

'What do you mean, "water wizards"?' Iome asked Gaborn. 'They're fish.'

The Earth Warden Binnesman gave Iome a patient look as he stroked his grizzled beard. 'Don't assume that one must be human to be a wizard. The Powers often favor beasts. Harts and foxes and bears often learn a few magical spells to help them hide in the woods or walk quietly. And these fish look as if they are quite powerful.'

Gaborn beamed at Iome. 'You asked me just the other day if my father had brought any water wizards for our betrothal, and now Heredon surprises me with a few of its own.'

Iome grinned like a child and squeezed Myrrima's hand.

Myrrima stared at the fish, marveling. There were rumors of ancient fish up at the headwaters of the Wye, magical fish that no man could catch. She wondered what they were doing here.

Iome asked, 'But even if the Powers do favor them, what good can they do us? We can't speak to them.'

'Perhaps we cannot communicate well,' Binnesman said. 'But Gaborn *can* listen to them.' Gaborn glanced up at the wizard, as if surprised that the Earth Warden thought him capable of the feat. 'Use the Earth Sight,' Binnesman told him. 'That's what it's for.'

Behind them a crowd of children and onlookers gathered. Several large boys had now brought fishing nets from the banks of the river, and others had gathered spears and bows, hoping to make a meal of the sturgeons, if the King would allow it. They seemed a bit forlorn at the prospect of missing a meal.

Now that the sun had risen a bit more, slanting in, Myrrima could see the huge sturgeons easily enough, their dark blue backs. They were circling near the surface, their fins slicing through the water as they swam about in curious patterns. To a casual observer, it might have appeared that they were finning the surface like salmon, preparing to spawn.

'What has happened to the water here in the moat since this began?' Gaborn wondered aloud.

'The level of the moat is rising,' Binnesman said. 'I'd say that it has come up at least a foot this morning.' He climbed down to the edge of the moat and dipped his fingers in. 'And the water here has become much clearer. The sediment is settling out of it.'

One fish swam a lazy **S**, then dipped below the surface and rose again, just so, to put a single dot at the end, then slashed through it. Gaborn traced the pattern with his finger.

'See there,' Binnesman said, pointing at the sturgeon. 'That fish is making runes of protection.'

Gaborn said, 'I see it. It's a simple water rune that my father taught me as a child. What do you think they want protection from?'

'I don't know,' Binnesman said, staring deeply, as if to read the answer in a sturgeon's eye. 'Why don't you ask them?'

'In a moment,' Gaborn promised. 'I've never tried to use my Earth Sight on an animal before. Let me gather my thoughts first.'

Some deep-green dragonflies buzzed past, and Myrrima and Iome stood hand in hand for several long moments, studying the runes that the fish drew. They noticed that each of the sturgeons had taken an area free of reeds and lily pads.

Gaborn and Binnesman, meanwhile, discussed the meaning of the runes. One sturgeon kept tracing runes of protection next to some cattails. Gaborn said that another drew runes of purity near the center of the pond – a rune to cleanse the water. A third was sketching runes that Binnesman recognized as runes of healing. Over and over again.

Farther away, a fish was moving in the depths of the moat, tracing runes that neither Gaborn nor Binnesman had ever seen before. Even Gaborn, a king raised in the Courts of Tide where water wizards were common, could not divine the purpose for all the runes. But Binnesman ventured a guess that the rune would make the water colder.

'Do you think the water really is much colder?' Iome whispered to Myrrima.

'I'll see,' Myrrima said. She climbed down and touched the water, too, though no one else on the shore dared. Binnesman was right. It was bitterly cold, as cold and fresh as the deepest of mountain pools. And the shoreline in the moat was indeed higher than it had been this past week.

Myrrima nodded to Iome. 'It's freezing!'

Gaborn climbed down to a huge flat rock by Myrrima, leaned out over the glassy surface of the moat and began to trace runes on the water, simple runes of protection. He was mirroring the sturgeon.

A great sturgeon swam up, just under his hand, its dark-blue back close to Gaborn. Its gills expanded and contracted rhythmically as it studied him, watching his fingers as if they were something edible. The fish was tantalizingly close to Myrrima.

'That's right. I'll protect you if I can,' Gaborn whispered to the fish in an easy tone. 'Tell me, what do you fear?'

He continued drawing the runes, stared into the fish's eyes, and into its mind, for long minutes. He frowned as if what he saw confused him. 'I see darkness in the water,' he murmured. 'I see darkness, and I taste metal. I can feel . . . strangulation. I can taste . . . metal. Redness coming.'

The young King stopped speaking, almost seemed to stop breathing. His eyes lost their focus and rolled back in his head.

'King Orden,' Binnesman called, but Gaborn did not move.

Myrrima wondered if she should grab Gaborn to keep him from falling in, but Binnesman climbed down to the water's edge and touched his shoulder.

'What?' Gaborn asked, rousing from his stupor. He leaned on the flat rock.

'What is it they fear?' Binnesman asked.

'They fear blood, I think,' Gaborn said. 'They fear that the river will fill with blood.'

Binnesman drew his staff up tight against his chest and frowned, shaking his head in dismay.

'I can't believe that. There is no sign of an army approaching, and it would take a great battle to fill the river with blood. Raj Ahten is far away. But something odd is happening,' he said. 'I've felt it all night. The Earth is in pain. I feel the pain like pinpricks on my flesh – north of here, in North Crowthen, and again far to the south. It trembles in far places, and there are slow movements even here, beneath our very feet.'

Gaborn tried to make light of it. 'Still, it comforts me to
have these wizards here in our moat.' He turned and addressed
the crowd of boys with their spears and bows and nets. 'Let
no man fish in this moat or foul its waters in any way. Let
no one swim in it. These wizards will stay as our guests.'

Gaborn asked Binnesman, 'Can we seal the moat off from
the river?'

Myrrima knew it should not be hard. A small diversion
dam upriver let water spill into the canal that fed the moat.

'Of course,' Binnesman said. He glanced about. 'You, Daffyd
and Hugh, go close the raceway. And hurry.'

Two stalwart boys ran upstream, elbows and shirttails flying.

Myrrima watched the wizard draw himself to his full height,
look up at the early morning sun.

She held her breath, strained to listen as Binnesman spoke.
'Milord,' he said so softly that most of those nearby could not
have heard. 'The earth is speaking to us. It speaks sometimes
in the movements of birds and animals, sometimes in the
crash of stone. But it is speaking nonetheless. I do not know
what it is saying, but I don't like this business of rivers filled
with blood.'

Gaborn nodded. 'What would you have me do?'

'Raj Ahten had a powerful pyromancer in his retinue, before
you killed her,' Binnesman said thoughtfully. 'Yet I'm sure that
whole forests are still being sacrificed to the powers that the
flameweavers serve.'

'Yes,' Gaborn said.

'I would not speak of plans that I want held secret now in
open daylight. Nor would I do so before a fire, not even so
much as a candle flame. Hold your councils by starlight if
you must. Or better yet, in a darkened hall of stone, where
the earth can shield your words.'

Myrrima knew that powerful flameweavers sometimes
claimed that if they listened to the whispering tongues of
flames, they could clearly hear words spoken by others of
their ilk hundreds of miles away. Yet Myrrima had never seen
a flameweaver who could really perform such feats.

'All right,' Gaborn agreed. 'We will hold our councils in the Great Hall, and I will have no fires lit therein throughout the winter. And I shall pass orders that no man is to discuss military strategies or secrets with another by daylight or firelight.'

'That should do,' Binnesman said.

With that, the King and Iome and their Days and Binnesman went over to see the reaver's head, then walked back up to the castle. Borenson stayed behind for a few moments and posted some lads beside the moat, charging them to care for the fish.

Myrrima stood by and wondered. During the past week, much in her life had changed. But Binnesman's warning to Gaborn hinted of dire portents. Rivers of blood. With the hundreds of thousands of people camped around the city of Sylvarresta, it seemed as if the whole earth were flocking to Heredon, to the courts of the Earth King. Whatever change was coming, she stood near the center of it all.

She climbed up the levee and stood looking out over the vast throng, over the pavilions that had risen up here in the past week. Dust was rising to the south and west, from the numerous travelers moving on the road. Last night, Myrrima had heard that merchant princes had come from as far away as Lysle.

The whole earth shall gather here, Myrrima realized. An Earth King's powers are legendary, and are given only in the darkest of times. Every person in every land who wants to live will come here. There are reavers in the Dunnwood and wizards in the moat. Soon there will be enough people to bleed rivers of blood.

That knowledge made her feel small and helpless, worried for the future. And now that Borenson was leaving, she knew she wouldn't be able to rely on him.

I must prepare for whatever is to come, Myrrima thought.

Myrrima walked with Borenson back up to the castle. She stopped on the drawbridge for a few moments and watched the great fish finning in the moat. She felt relieved by their presence. Water wizards were strong in the arts of healing and protection.

That morning, Myrrima finished breakfast in the King's Tower, with only King Gaborn and Queen Iome and their Days in the room. Though Myrrima was becoming friends with Iome, she still felt uncomfortable to be dining in the presence of the King.

Indeed, the meal was filled with uncomfortable silences: Gaborn and Borenson refused to discuss their hunt over the past three days, saying very little at all. Gaborn also had received disturbing news out of Mystarria, and all morning long he looked haunted, somber, withdrawn.

They were nearly finished with breakfast when the elderly Chancellor Rodderman came to the door of the dining hall, looking resplendent with his white beard combed and wearing his black coat of office. 'Milord, milady,' he said. 'The Duke of Groverman is waiting in the alcove and has requested an audience.'

Iome looked at Rodderman wearily. 'Is it important? I haven't seen my husband in three days.'

'I don't know, but he's been skulking out here for half an hour,' Rodderman said.

'Skulking?' Iome laughed. 'Well, we mustn't have him skulking.' Though Iome smiled at Rodderman's choice of words, Myrrima sensed that she did not much care for the Duke.

Presently, the Duke entered the room. He was a short man with gangling limbs, a hatchet face, and dark eyes that were set so close he looked nothing short of ugly. In a family of warriors and nobles, he seemed out of place. Myrrima had heard it rumored that a stable mucker had sired the Duke.

In honor of Hostenfest, Groverman was wearing a gorgeous robe of black embroidered with dark-green leaves. His hair was freshly combed, his graying beard expertly trimmed so that it forked from his chin. For an ugly man, he groomed and dressed well.

'Your Highnesses' – the Duke smiled graciously and bowed low –'I hope I did not disturb your meal?'

Myrrima realized that Groverman had asked Rodderman to wait until the King and Queen finished eating before notifying them of his presence.

'Not at all,' Gaborn said. 'It was kind of you to wait so patiently.'

'Truly, I have a matter that I think is somewhat urgent,' the Duke said, 'though others might not agree.' He looked pointedly at Iome. Myrrima wondered what he might mean by such a warning. Even Iome seemed baffled. 'I've brought you a wedding gift, Your Highness – if I may be so bold.'

Over the past few days, every lord in the kingdom had been plying the new King and Queen with wedding gifts; some were expensive gifts that would hopefully curry favor. Most of the lords had brought sons or trusted retainers to help rebuild the lists of the King's Guard. Such sons served quadruple duty: they not only rebuilt the King's army, but they also served as a constant reminder to the King of a lord's loyalty. A trusted son at court could seek favors for his father, or serve as his spy. Last of all, it allowed the boy himself to form new alliances with other nobles who might live in far corners of the kingdom, or even in other nations.

Over the past three days the ranks of new soldiers had filled so quickly that it looked as if Gaborn would not even have to levy his subjects for more troops, despite the fact that Raj Ahten had decimated the King's Guard. Instead, it seemed to Myrrima that Gaborn would have problems finding posts for all of his new soldiers to fill.

'So,' Iome asked, 'what gift have you brought that is so urgent?'

Groverman got to the point. 'This is a somewhat delicate matter,' he said. 'As you know, I've not been blessed with sons or daughters, else I'd offer one of them into your service. But I have brought you a gift that is just as dear to my heart.'

He clapped his hands and looked expectantly toward the dining hall's door.

A boy came through, walking with arms outstretched. In each hand he held a yellow pup by the scruff of the neck. The pups looked about dolefully with huge brown eyes. Myrrima was not familiar with the breed. They were not mastiffs or any form of war dog. Nor were they hounds or the type of hunters she was familiar with, or the lap dogs popular with ladies in colder climes.

They could have even been mongrels, except that both pups had a uniform color – tawny short hair on the back, and a bit of white at the throat.

The boy, a ten-year-old in heavy leather trousers and a new coat, was as clean and well groomed as Duke Groverman. He handed a pup each to Gaborn and Iome.

One little bundle of fur smelled the grease from the morning's sausages on Gaborn's hand. The pup's wet tongue began to slide over Gaborn's fingers, and the dog nibbled at him playfully. Gaborn ruffled the pup's ears, turned it over to see if it was male or female. It was a male. It wagged its tail fiercely and scrambled upright, as if intent on doing damage to Gaborn's fingers. A real fighter.

He studied the creature. 'Thank you,' Gaborn said, taken aback. 'But I'm not familiar with this breed. What do you do with them?'

Myrrima glanced at Iome, to see the Queen's reaction to her pup, and was astonished. There was such a glare of rage in her eyes that she could barely contain herself.

The Duke had not missed her look. 'Hear me out,' he said to Gaborn. 'I do not offer these pups lightly, Your Highness. You have taken endowments from men, and I know that as an Oath-Bound Lord you feel some reluctance in doing so. Indeed, though many have offered to serve as your Dedicates this past week, neither you nor the Queen has taken endowments. Yet we must prepare for whatever is to come.'

Myrrima was startled to hear Groverman repeat aloud the thought that had been preying upon her but an hour before.

'It's a grave decision,' Gaborn agreed. His eyes were haunted, full of pain. Myrrima had agreed to take endowments of glamour and wit from her sisters and mother. She understood the price of guilt that came from committing such an atrocity.

'I will not take another man's strength or stamina or wit lightly,' the King said. 'But I have been considering whether to do it, for the welfare of the kingdom.'

'I understand,' Groverman said honestly. 'But I ask milord, milady, to consider the propriety of taking endowments from a dog.'

Iome stiffened. 'Duke Groverman,' she hissed, 'this is an outrage!'

The Duke looked about nervously. Now Myrrima recognized the breed. Although she had never seen such pups, she had heard of them. These were pups raised for endowments – dogs strong of stamina, strong of nose.

'Is it any less of an outrage to take endowments from a man?' Groverman countered defensively. 'It takes the endowments of scent from fifty men to equal one from a dog, they say. I believe that my pups' noses are a hundred times better than a common man's nose. So I ask you, which is better, to take endowments of scent from a hundred men, or from one dog?

'As for stamina, these pups are bred for toughness. For a thousand generations, the Wolf Lords have fought them in the pits, so that only the strongest survive. Ounce for ounce, no man alive can provide you a better source of stamina.

'Metabolism and hearing too can be gained from such dogs, though I fear my pups are too small to give brawn. And whereas a man must give an endowment willingly and therefore can often fail to transfer an attribute completely, if you feed these pups and play with them for a day or two, they will develop such an undying devotion to you that their attributes can be transferred without loss. No other animal loves man as completely, will give themselves to you as wholly as these pups.'

Iome looked so furious, she could not speak. To take endowments from a dog was considered an abomination. Some high-minded kings would have thrown the Duke into

the nearest moat for suggesting that pups be used for endowments.

Gaborn himself was an Oath-Bound Lord, and Iome was
the daughter of an Oath-Bound Lord. An Oath-Bound Lord
swore only to take endowments from those vassals who gave
them freely. Such vassals would be men or women who had
some great attribute, such as a quick wit or tremendous
stamina, but often lacked the other necessary attributes to be
good warriors. Knowing that they couldn't serve their lord as
warriors, they might opt to give their wit or stamina into their
lord's use, subjecting themselves to the indignity of the forcible
for the greater good of those around them.

But not all of the lords in Rofehavan were Oath-Bound.
Gaborn's own father had once considered himself a 'pragma-
tist.' Pragmatists would often purchase endowments. Many a
man was willing to sell the use of his eyes or ears to his lord
in return for gold, for many a man loves gold more than he
loves himself. But Iome had told Myrrima that even Gaborn's
father had eventually given up his pragmatic ways, for King
Orden could not always be sure of a man's motives when
selling an attribute. Often a peasant or even a minor lord who
suffered from heavy debts would see no way out, and would
therefore try to sell an endowment to the highest bidder.

Gaborn's father had been confronted by the realization that
his own pragmatic ways were unscrupulous – for he could
never be completely certain what drove a man to sell his
endowments. Was it greed? Or was it hopelessness or plain
stupidity that led a man to trade his greatest asset for a few
pieces of gold?

Indeed, Myrrima knew that some rapacious lords hid their
lust for other's attributes beneath a cloak of pragmatism. Such
lords would gladly accept endowments in lieu of payment for
taxes, and time and again, in such kingdoms, whenever a king
raised the taxes, the peasants were forced to wonder what he
really sought.

Worst of any lord, of course, were the Wolf Lords. Since a
vassal had to be 'willing' to give an endowment before an

attribute could be transferred, the Wolf Lords constantly sought ways to make men more willing. Blackmail and tortures both physical and psychological were the Wolf Lords' coin. Raj Ahten had blackmailed King Sylvarresta into giving away his wit by threatening to kill his only daughter, Iome. After King Sylvarresta complied, Raj Ahten then had forced Iome to give her own endowment of glamour, rather than to watch her witless father be tortured, her friend Chemoise be murdered, her kingdom taken from her. Raj Ahten was thus the most despicable kind of man – a Wolf Lord.

The euphemism 'Wolf Lord' had been coined to name those men of such relentless rapacity that they stole attributes even from dogs. In dark times past, men had done more than take endowments of scent, stamina, or metabolism from dogs; some had taken even endowments of wit. It was said that doing so increased a man's cunning in battle, his thirst for blood.

The very notion of taking endowments from dogs had therefore become anathema in Rofehavan. Though Raj Ahten, Gaborn's great enemy, had never stooped to take an endowment from a dog, he was called a 'Wolf Lord' still. Now, Groverman dared affront Iome by begging her to become a Wolf Lord.

'So long as a man does not take a dog's endowment of wit, it is not a bad practice,' Groverman said as if encouraged by the fact that no one argued with him. 'A dog that has no sense of smell makes a fine pet. So long as one has a good dog handler to care for the animal, it can be well maintained. Even loved. It will give you its sense of smell, even as your children wrestle with it on the floor.

'Indeed, I have calculated the number of farmers and tanners and craftsmen and builders and clothiers that it takes to sustain a Dedicate. I figure that it takes the combined labor of twenty-four peasants to care for a single human Dedicate, and another eight for a Dedicate horse. But it only takes a single man to care for each seven Dedicate dogs. It makes for a frugal trade.

'For a king at war, fine dogs are as necessary as arms or

armor. Raj Ahten has war dogs in his arsenals – mastiffs with endowments. If you will not let these pups serve as Dedicates to your warriors, consider at least that they could give endowments to your own war dogs.'

'This is an outrage!' Iome said. 'An outrage and an insult!' She looked at Gaborn pleadingly.

'It is meant as neither,' Groverman said. 'I mention the possibility only to be practical. While you were dining, I stood for half an hour outside your door, and you never knew it! Had I been an assassin, I might well have set an ambush for you. But if you had an endowment of scent from a single dog, you'd have no need to see me or hear me to know that I hid outside your door.'

'I will not be called a "Wolf Lord,"' Iome objected. She set her pup on the floor. It wandered over to Myrrima, sniffed her leg.

She scratched its ear.

Gaborn seemed not to be perturbed by the proposal. Myrrima wondered if it was because of his father's influence. His father had always been recognized as a prudent man. Could a man of principle be both an Oath-Bound Lord *and* a Wolf Lord, she asked herself.

'Your Highness,' Duke Groverman urged Gaborn, 'I must beg you to consider this. It is only a matter of time before Raj Ahten sends his assassins. Neither you nor your wife is prepared to meet an Invincible, and it is already noised about that Your Highness has sworn to be an Oath-Bound Lord. I don't know how you plan to stand against Raj Ahten. Indeed, the lords of Heredon worry about little else. But it may be that you will stand in sore need of Dedicates, if you refuse to pay men for their endowments.'

Gaborn thoughtfully stroked the fat ball of fur under its nose. The pup growled and bit hard on Gaborn's thumb.

'Take your mongrels and get out of here,' Iome told Groverman. 'I want no part of it.'

Gaborn smiled fiercely, looking from Iome to the Duke, then merely shook his head. 'Personally, I have no need of endowments from dogs,' Gaborn said. Turning to Iome, he said, 'And if you will not be a Wolf Lord, then so be it. We can still train the pup to bark at strangers, and keep him in your room. The pup will be your guard, and perhaps in its own way, it can save your life.'

'I'll not have it in my sight,' Iome said. Myrrima picked up the Queen's pup protectively. It nuzzled its head between her breasts, then just stared in her eyes.

'So our choice is made,' Gaborn said to Iome. 'But as for the troops, Groverman is right. I'll need scouts and guardsmen with strong noses to sniff out ambushes. I'll let my men choose whether it be a compliment or curse to be called a Wolf Lord.'

Gaborn nodded acceptance of the gift to Groverman. 'My thanks to you, Your Lordship.'

He turned his attention to the boy who'd brought in the pups, and Myrrima realized that the gift did not consist merely of dogs, but of the boy. He was a dark-haired lad, rangy. Like a wolf himself.

'Tell me, what is your name?' Gaborn asked.

'Kaylin,' the boy answered, dropping to one knee.

'These are fine dogs. You are their keeper, I take it?'

'I been helping.' The boy's language was uncouth, but his sharp eyes marked his intelligence.

'You like these puppies?' Gaborn asked. The boy sniffed and blinked back a tear. He nodded.

'Why are you so sad?'

'I been watchin' 'em since they was born. I don't want nothin' to happen to 'em, Yer Highness.'

Gaborn met Groverman's eyes. The Duke smiled and nodded toward the boy.

'Then, Kaylin,' Gaborn asked, 'would you be willing to stay in the castle, and help care for them for me?'

The boy's mouth dropped in astonishment. As Myrrima had guessed, Groverman had not forewarned the child of the possibility.

Gaborn merely smiled pleasantly at the Duke. 'How many of these pups can you provide me with?'

The Duke smiled. 'I've been letting them breed at will now for four years. I smelled trouble brewing. Would a thousand suit Your Highness?'

Gaborn grinned. It was a princely wedding gift, in spite of the fact that Iome looked as if she were about to fly into a rage and tear out the Duke's hair.

'You think we could have that many by spring?' Gaborn asked. 'It seems a large number.'

'Far sooner than that,' Groverman said. 'Seven hundred pups are waiting outside – in wagons. The others will be ready within a few weeks.'

Autumn was not normally the best time of year to get pups, Myrrima knew. More births occurred in early spring and summer. These seven hundred had to have been born within the last sixteen weeks or so.

'My thanks,' Gaborn said. He put his pup on the floor and returned to the breakfast table as Groverman left with Kaylin in tow.

The King's pup came and worried at Myrrima's shoe for a moment, trying to drag her foot from her leg, until she gave it a sausage from her plate.

Iome seemed so upset by the presence of the pups that Myrrima offered to put them out with the others. When Iome agreed, Myrrima grabbed the pups and a plate of sausages. She went outside the keep, and found Kaylin on the green, looking somewhat forlornly at a wagon of pups.

Gaborn's new counselor, Jureem, who had served Raj Ahten until only recently, was standing next to the boy with his back turned to Myrrima, giving instructions to Kaylin. To be heard over the yapping of the creatures, Jureem spoke loudly.

'You will of course be tireless in your service,' Jureem said. 'The dogs will depend on you for food and water and shelter and bathing. You must keep them strong.'

The boy Kaylin nodded vigorously. Myrrima stopped behind Jureem. She had seen Jureem instructing the house-hold staff over the past few days, badgering a chambermaid here, a horse groom there. Now, she was curious to hear what this former slave from a far country had to say.

'A good servant gives his all to his lord,' Jureem intoned with mock exaggeration in a thick Taifan accent. 'He never lets himself tire, never shirks his duty. He must never become weary of performing his tasks well. He serves his lord in every thought and every deed, administering to his lord's needs before they are ever voiced. He gives up his own life – his dreams and pleasures – to serve his lord. Can you do that?'

'But,' the boy said, 'I just want to take care of the pups.'

'When you serve them, you *are* serving your lord. That is the task he has chosen for you. But if he should choose a different task for you, then you must be prepared to fulfill his every command. Do you understand?'

'You mean he might take me away from the pups?' the boy whined.

'Someday, yes. If you do this job well, he will expand your duties. In addition to the kennels, he might place you in charge of his stables or ask you to train dogs for war. You might even be called upon to become a guard and bear arms – for even the Dedicate dogs of the kennels might be a target for Raj Ahten's assassins.

'Watch the King. He works for his people tirelessly. Learn from his devotion. We all live in service to one another. A man is nothing without his lord. A lord is nothing without his servants.' Jureem walked away, hurrying to fulfill some other obligation.

The boy seemed to consider the counselor's words, then looked up at Myrrima and caught his breath. He smiled at her in that hopeful way that men did ever since she'd been endowed with glamour.

She put both pups down by her feet, and stroked them as they wolfed their sausages. Until that moment, even Myrrima had not known what she would do.

But she knew that she must prepare, and Jureem's words convinced her that she had to begin doing so tirelessly, to anticipate the threat before it arrived.

'The pups like you,' Kaylin mused.

'You know the pups well?' Myrrima asked. 'Do you know which dogs were born of which bitches?'

Kaylin nodded soberly. Of course he did. That was the only reason that Groverman had sent the boy to serve young King Orden.

'I'll want four of them,' Myrrima said softly, lest someone overhear. She was terribly conscious of the fact that she planned to take these pups from her own king without asking. But Kaylin would never know that she was stealing. Hadn't he just seen her dining with the King and Queen? The boy would assume that she was some lord who had a right to the pups. Myrrima hoped that if she worked hard, perhaps she *could* truly earn that right. 'Two for stamina, one for scent, and one for metabolism. Can you pick out the best ones for me?'

Kaylin nodded vigorously.

After breakfast, Iome and Gaborn retired to their bedchamber for a moment, and closed the doors behind them, leaving their Days out in the alcove.

Iome could not feel perfectly at ease in this room. The huge bed, with its images of fools and lords carved into its posterns and the pineapples at its top, had been her mother and father's bed a week ago. Her mother's perfumes and cosmetics were in their case beside the oriel, where the morning light was best. Her father's clothes were still in the wardrobes; Gaborn had brought few of his own clothes from Mystarria, but her father's garments fit Gaborn well enough.

But more than the objects in this room, the scent of it reminded Iome of her parents. She could smell her mother's hair on her pillow, her body oils, her perfume.

Should I tell him? she wondered. Iome was carrying Gaborn's child, she felt certain. They'd been married for only four days, and Iome felt no nausea. She would not know for a few days yet whether she had even missed her time of month. But she did feel a strangeness to her body, and Myrrima had seen it today. She'd said that Iome was 'glowing.'

But was that proof enough? Iome doubted it. She dared not speak of her hopes to Gaborn.

Iome sat on the edge of the bed, wondering if Gaborn would want her, but he merely went to the oriel and stared south for a long time, deep in thought.

'Have you decided what to do yet?' she asked. Before the wedding, he'd been in constant turmoil, wondering how he could best fight Raj Ahten, wondering where Raj Ahten would strike next. As Earth King, he was the protector of mankind, and now Gaborn shuddered at the very thought of taking a human life, even the life of an enemy. This morning's news of Raj Ahten's attacks had left him deeply worried.

She'd encouraged him to go on the hunt, hoping that by having a few days away, slipping into some sort of routine, he might be able to clear his mind, while at the same time it would ease concerns among his people.

'Will you take endowments? Thousands have offered themselves as your Dedicates.'

Gaborn bowed his head in thought. 'I can't,' he said. 'Of that I am becoming more and more certain.'

A week ago, both of their fathers had been slain. Afterward, Gaborn had wanted to take endowments, to take the strength of a thousand men and the grace of another thousand and to take the stamina of ten thousand and the metabolism of a hundred men – and use it all to slay Raj Ahten.

Yet now that deed seemed beyond him. Taking a man's endowments was risky. A man might give them willingly enough, but there was always a danger. A man who gave brawn would find that his heart was suddenly too weak to beat, and might pass away within moments. A man who gave grace could not properly digest his food, or relax his lungs enough to let out a breath, so might fall prey to starvation or suffocation. A man who gave stamina to his lord could die from infection the next time an illness swept through the castle.

So a man who took another's endowments could soon find himself poisoned by guilt. Worse than that, since a powerful

Runelord was so nearly Invincible, only a fool would attack him directly. Instead, the Runelord's Dedicates became the targets of his enemy's wrath. If one were to slay a lord's Dedicates, he would sever the magical link that raised the lord's attributes, and in doing so, he would make the lord himself more human, more vulnerable to attack.

Borenson had slain Iome's own Dedicates a week ago. The pain of it was astonishing. Good men and women had died. She'd wept bitterly about it night after night, for the Dedicates were often friends, people who had loved the kingdom and therefore sought to strengthen it so that they could better maintain her realm.

As Earth King, Gaborn sought to defend his people. He could lock his Dedicates in towers, guard them with his most powerful knights, provide the best physicians to care for them. Still it might not be enough.

Gaborn's arguments against taking endowments were morally sound. Yet Iome had to wonder. He was the Earth King, the hope of the world. But how great a king could he be, if he left himself open to attack?

'Last week,' Iome said, 'you swore to me that you would be an Oath-Bound Lord. Are you forsaking endowments completely? I can't imagine why. You are a good man. If you take endowments only from your Chosen, I know that you will use them wisely, and prudently. You will be a better king because of it. And because you are the Earth King, you will know when your Dedicates are in danger, and be better able to preserve them.'

'Knowing that a man is in danger and rescuing him are entirely different matters,' Gaborn said heavily. 'Even with all of my powers, I may not be able to protect them.'

'But what of Raj Ahten? What will happen when he does send his assassins? Surely he will!'

'If he sends assassins, then I will sense the danger, and we will flee.' Gaborn says. 'But I will not fight another man ever again, unless I have no choice.'

Iome felt confused by such talk. She valued life, valued the lives of her people above all. But she couldn't just turn her back on Raj Ahten. She'd never be able to forgive him for what he'd done. Iome's mother and father were dead at his hands. Gaborn's mother and father, too.

Gaborn should have been shouting for vengeance. Even now, Raj Ahten was marching on his homeland in Mystarria. All of Gaborn's counselors had agreed that Heredon's forces were too weak to pursue the Wolf Lord south. They lacked the warriors and force horses to do so. Raj Ahten's troops had stolen all of the good horses in Sylvarresta's stables when they fled. One of the first things that Gaborn did when he reached Castle Sylvarresta was to learn from the stablemasters the names of every horse that had been taken, and the names of their Dedicates. Then he'd sent the list to Duke Groverman, where the Dedicate horses were kept, and had the Dedicates slain.

It was a desperate effort to slow Raj Ahten in his flight toward Mystarria. Raj Ahten's knights would have been forced to ride common mounts. Perhaps because of this slaughter of Dedicate horses, hordes of Knights Equitable had been able to mount ambushes that took a toll against Raj Ahten's Invincibles.

Gaborn had bought Duke Paldane the time he'd need to set his defenses against the Wolf Lord, and might well have made it possible to run some of Raj Ahten's forces into the ground. Gaborn's home country of Mystarria was the largest and richest realm in all the kingdoms of Rofehavan. A full third of all the force soldiers in the north were under the command of Paldane the Huntsman.

But Iome doubted that Paldane could stop Raj Ahten's armies. She only hoped that Paldane could somehow hold the Wolf Lord at bay until the kings of the north could combine their armies. Gaborn had sent messengers all across Rofehavan, begging for aid.

Still, Gaborn had not sent men from Heredon to help Paldane.

'Why?' Iome asked. 'Why won't you stop Raj Ahten? You

don't have to do it yourself. Many are gathering here, lords from all over Heredon. You have men who could fight, the lords of Heredon are eager for revenge! *I* would fight! I hesitate to ask you this, but are you afraid of him?'

Gaborn shook his head, looked at her as if hoping she would understand. 'I am not afraid of him,' Gaborn said. 'Yet something holds me back.

'There is something . . . I feel so profoundly . . . and I cannot express it well. Perhaps I cannot express it at all. But . . . I am the Earth King, and am charged with saving a seed of mankind through the dark season to come. I don't feel that the people of Indhopal are my enemies. I cannot harm them. I will not willingly destroy men and women. Not when I fear that the reavers are my true enemies.'

'Raj Ahten is our enemy,' Iome said. 'He is as bad as any reaver.'

'He is,' Gaborn admitted, 'but think of this: for each four hundred men and women alive, we have but one force soldier, one protector capable of stopping a reaver. And if that one protector dies, then it is probable that four hundred people will die because of that loss.'

It was a terrifying thought, and Iome herself had worried about little else but logistics for the past seven days as she began to consider the enormity of the problem. How many warriors could Gaborn spend fighting Raj Ahten? Was even one warrior one too many?

Time and again Gaborn hinted that he thought so. With the forty thousand forcibles that Gaborn's father had captured at Longmot, Gaborn might equip four thousand force soldiers. It was a number ten times what Iome's father had had. Yet it would be a small force compared to what Raj Ahten could marshal.

And there was the Wolf Lord himself to contend with. Raj Ahten had thousands of endowments of his own. Gaborn had talked about using the forcibles to make himself Raj Ahten's equal, so that he could fight the Wolf Lord man to man.

But if Gaborn did so, if he drained endowments from even several hundred men, he worried that he would be wasting resources. He did not know if he'd ever get another forcible again. Jureem had warned him that the blood-metal mines of Kartish were played out. These forty thousand forcibles were Gaborn's best weapons against the reavers.

But suddenly Iome understood something that had eluded her. 'Wait, are you saying that you don't want to kill Raj Ahten?' Until this moment, she had thought that Gaborn would merely stay here in Heredon, hide behind the protective borders of the Dunnwood, and let the shades of his ancestors protect him from Raj Ahten. But Gaborn seemed nervous, and there was an intensity to him, a pleading demeanor, that made her realize that he needed to tell her something she would not want to hear.

Gaborn turned aside and looked at her from the corner of his eye, as if he could not bear to face her fully. 'You have to understand, my love: the *people* of Indhopal are not my enemies. The Earth has made me its king, and Indhopal is my realm also. I must save those I can. The people of Indhopal also need a defender.'

'You can't go to Indhopal,' Iome said. 'You can't even be *thinking* such a thing. Raj Ahten's men will kill you. Besides, you'll be needed *here*.'

'I agree,' Gaborn said. 'Yet Raj Ahten has the most powerful army in the world, and he is the most powerful Runelord of us all. If I fight him, we may all be destroyed. If I ignore him, I surely do so at my own peril. If I try to flee him, he will catch me. I can see only one alternative . . .'

'Are you saying that you would use your power to Choose him? After what he has done?' Iome could not hold back the shock and anger in her voice.

'I hope to arrange a truce,' Gaborn admitted, and she knew from his tone that his decision was final. 'I have discussed the possibility with Jureem.'

'Raj Ahten will not grant you a truce,' Iome said with certainty. 'Not unless you return the forcibles your father won

with his own life. And *that* would not be a truce; *that* would
be surrender!'

Gaborn nodded, stared at her evenly.

'Don't you see it?' Iome said. 'It wouldn't even be surrender
with honor, for once you give the forcibles back, Raj Ahten
would use them against you. I know my cousin. I know him.
He will not leave you alone. The fact that Earth has given you
dominion over mankind does not mean Raj Ahten will concede
the honor.'

Gaborn gritted his teeth, looked as if he would turn away.
She could see the anguish in his features. She knew that he
loved his people, that he sought to protect them as best he
knew how, and that right now he could see no way to bring
Raj Ahten down.

'Still, I must ask for a truce,' Gaborn answered. 'And if a
truce cannot be won, then . . . I must ask for honorable conditions of surrender. Only if such conditions cannot be met,
will I be forced to fight.'

'There can be no surrender,' Iome said. 'My father surrendered, and once he did, Raj Ahten changed the terms to fit
his whim. You cannot be Raj Ahten's Dedicate *and* the Earth
King!'

'I fear you are right,' Gaborn said with a heavy sigh, and
he came and sat on the bed next to Iome, took her hand. But
it was cold comfort.

'Why can't you just kill him and be done with it?' Iome
asked.

'Raj Ahten has perhaps ten thousand force warriors in his
service,' Gaborn said. 'Even if I defeated him roundly, and lost
half as many men, would it be worth the price? Think of it,
four and a half million children, women! Could I knowingly
throw away the life of even one? And who is to say that it
would stop there? With so many warriors lost, would it even
be possible anymore to stop the reavers?'

Gaborn paused. After a moment, he held a finger up to his
lips, motioning for Iome to keep quiet, and went over to King
Sylvarresta's old writing table. He drew out a small book from

the top drawer, and began pulling out papers hidden in its bindings.

He brought them to Iome and whispered, 'In the House of Understanding, in the Room of Dreams, the Days are taught thus about the nature of good and evil,' Gaborn said. This surprised Iome. The teachings of the Days were hidden from Runelords. Now she knew why he whispered. The Days were right outside their doorway.

Gaborn showed her the following diagram:

The Three Domains of Man

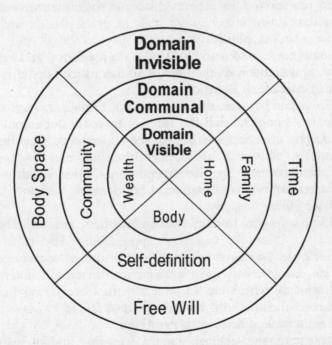

'Every man sees himself as a lord,' Gaborn said, 'and he rules over three domains: the Domain Invisible, the Domain Communal, and the Domain Visible.

'Each domain can have many parts. A man's time, his body space, his free will, are all part of his Domain Invisible, while all of the things he owns, all of the things he can easily see, are part of his Domain Visible.

'Now, whenever someone violates our domain, we call him evil. If he seeks to take our land or our spouse, if he seeks to destroy our community or our good name, if he abuses our time or tries to deny us our free will, we will hate him for it.

'But if another enlarges your domain, you call him good. If he praises you to others, enlarging your stature in the community, you love him for it. If he gives you money or honor, you love him for it.

'Iome, there is something I feel so deeply about, and I can only express this way: the lives of all men, their fates, are all here, a part of my domain!'

He pointed to the drawing, waving vaguely toward the Domain Communal and the Domain Invisible. Iome looked up into his eyes, and she thought she understood. She'd been a Runelord all her life, had been entrusted in small ways with the affairs of state. She had accepted the hopes and dreams and fates of her people as part of her domain.

'I see,' Iome whispered.

'I know you do, in part,' Gaborn breathed, 'but not in full. I feel . . . I feel the cataclysm approaching. The Earth is warning me. Danger is coming. Not just danger for you and for me, but for every man, woman, and child I've Chosen.

'I must do what I can to protect them – everything I can to protect them, even if I am doomed to failure.

'I must seek alliance with Raj Ahten.'

Iome noted the vehemence in his demeanor, and knew that he was not just stating his resolution. He was soliciting her approval.

'And where do I fit in your circles?' Iome asked, waving to the drawing in Gaborn's lap.

'You are all of it,' Gaborn said. 'Don't you understand? This is not my bed or your bed. This is *our* bed.' He waved at himself. 'This is not my body or your body, it is *our* body. Your fate is my fate, and my fate is yours. Your hopes are my hopes, and my hopes need to be yours. I don't want walls or divisions between us. If there are any, then we are not truly married. We are not truly one.'

Iome nodded. She understood. She'd seen couples before, seen how over time they'd shared so much, become so close, that they'd picked up even one another's oddest habits and notions.

Iome craved such union.

'You think you're so wise,' she said, 'quoting forbidden teachings. But I've heard something from the Room of Dreams, too.

'In the House of Understanding, in the Room of Dreams, it is said that a man is born crying. He cries to his mother for her breast. He cries to his mother when he falls. He cries for warmth and love. As he grows older, he learns to differentiate his wants. "I want food!" he cries. "I want warmth. I want daylight to come." And when a mother soothes her child, her own words are but a lament: "I want joy for you."

'As we learn to speak, nearly all of our utterances are merely cries better defined. Listen to every word a man speaks to you and you can learn to hear the pleas embedded beneath every notion he expresses. "I want love." "I want comfort." "I want freedom."'

Iome paused for a moment, for effect, and in that profound and sudden silence, she knew that she had his full attention.

Then she voiced her plea. 'Gaborn, never surrender to Raj Ahten. As you love me – as you love your life and your people – never surrender to evil.'

'So long as I have the choice,' Gaborn said, at last listening to reason.

She pushed his book to the floor and took Gaborn's chin in her hand, kissed him firmly, and drew him down to the bed.

*   *   *

Two hours later, guards atop the castle wall called out in dismay and pointed to the Wye River, where it snaked among the verdant fields. The river upstream had turned red, red as blood.

But the flood of red washing downstream bore the strong mineral smells of copper and sulfur. It was only mud and silt thick enough to foul the waters, to clog the gills of fish and slowly suffocate them.

Gaborn took his wizard to investigate. Binnesman stood knee-deep in the water, experimentally dipped his hand in and tasted it, then made a sour face. 'Mud from the deep earth.'

'How did it get in the river?' Gaborn wondered. He stayed on the riverbank, not liking the smell of the fouled water.

'The headwaters of the Wye,' Binnesman said, 'spring up from deep underground. The mud is coming from there.'

'Could an earthquake cause this?' Gaborn asked.

'A shift in the earth *could* cause it,' Binnesman mused. 'But I fear it didn't. The ruins where we slew the reaver mage are near the source of the water. My guess is that reavers are tunneling there. Perhaps we didn't kill them all.'

Because so many lords had gathered outside Castle Sylvarresta for the celebration of Hostenfest, it was not hard to gather some worthy men quickly and ride the thirty miles into the mountains. Six hours later in the early afternoon, a full five hundred warriors reached the ancient duskin ruins, with Gaborn and Binnesman leading the way.

The ruins looked exactly as they had the night before, when Binnesman, Gaborn, and Borenson had emerged. The gnarled roots of a great oak on a hill half hid the entrance. The men lit their torches and made their way down an ancient broken stairway, where the earth held a thick mineral smell. Gaborn could tell that the scent had changed since yesterday.

The entrance to the ancient duskin city was a perfect half-circle some twenty feet in diameter. The stones along the walls were enormous, and each was perfectly carved and fitted, so that even after thousands of years, they still held solid.

For the first quarter mile, there was a myriad of side tunnels and chambers, houses and shops where duskins had once lived, now overgrown with the strange subterranean fauna of the Underworld – dark rubbery leaves of man's ear and spongy mats of foliage that clung to the wall. The place had been picked clean of any duskin artifacts ages ago, and now was the abode of glowing newts and blindcrabs and other denizens of the Underworld.

The troops had not gone half a mile down the winding stairs when it ended abruptly.

The path ahead had recently been shorn away. Where the stair should have been leading down – miles and miles to the Idymean Sea – instead a vast tunnel crossed the path.

Binnesman edged close to the bottom stair, but the rock cracked and shifted under his feet and he leapt back. He held a lantern high, peering down.

The tunnel opening was a huge circle, at least two hundred yards across, and had been hewn through thick dirt and debris. The bottom was a mess of sludge and stone. No human could have dug this passage. No reaver, either, for that matter.

Binnesman stared down, stroking his beard. Then he picked up a stone and dropped it. 'So, I did feel something stirring beneath my feet,' he mused aloud. 'The Earth is in pain.'

Just then, a flock of small dark creatures flew through the black tunnel below, creatures of the Underworld that could not easily abide the light of day. They made shrieking sounds of pain, then wheeled away from the lanterns.

Nervously, Borenson broke the silence. 'What could have burrowed such a tunnel?'

'Only one thing,' Binnesman answered, 'though my bestiary of the Underworld describes it as a creature only witnessed once before by a single man, and therefore describes it as a thing of legend. Such a passage could only have been dug by a *hujmoth*, a world worm.'

4

THE REAVERS

'Skyrider Averan,' the beast master Brand said, 'you are needed.'

Averan turned to look at him in the predawn light, but not too quickly. In the huge shadowy loft of the graak's aerie, she located Brand more by the sound of his footsteps than by sight. She was feeding some fledgling graaks and dared not look away from the reptiles. The graaks stood fourteen feet at the shoulder and could easily swallow a child like Averan whole. Though the graaks adored her and she'd been feeding them since they first clawed their way out of their leathery eggs, the graaks were likely to snap when hungry. Sometimes they would try to hook meat from her hand with a long wing claw. Averan did not want to lose an arm, as Brand had done so long ago.

Skyrider, she thought. He called me 'skyrider.' Not 'beast handler.' At nine years of age, Averan was too big, too old, to be a skyrider. She hadn't been allowed to fly in two years.

Brand stood in the doorway to the aerie, the dim morning light casting a halo around him. The haunch of a young lamb was tied to his belt with a coil of rope, a lure for the graaks. He squinted and stroked his gray beard with his left hand.

She wondered if he'd had too much new wine last night, had forgotten how old she was. 'Are you—'

'Sure? Yes.' Brand grunted, and his words were clipped, strained. She suddenly realized that he was shaking. 'And we must hurry.' He turned then, and headed for the lofts.

In the dim light, Averan and Brand climbed stairs chiseled in stone, into the upper aerie. The nests up here smelled fetid. The older graaks carried a scent not unlike that of a snake, and after centuries of habitation, that odor permeated the very rock of the aerie. Averan had learned to like the smell long ago, just as some people were said to enjoy the stench of horse sweat or the odor of dogs.

The stairs opened into a wide chamber with a single narrow entrance chiseled in the east side of the hill. In the dim light, Averan could see that the chamber was empty. The graaks were out for their morning hunt. The cool autumn weather tended to make them restless and hungry.

Averan followed Brand onto the landing. He stood for a moment, took the haunch of lamb from his belt and made sure that the rope was tied snugly between a ligament and the bone at the joint. Then he stood swinging the huge clumsy lure. It took a full-grown man to swing the graak bait like that.

'Leatherneck!' he called. 'Leatherneck.'

The graak was trained to respond to his name. The lamb would serve as a reward for the monster's obedience, when he came.

Averan searched the morning sky. The reptile was nowhere in sight. Leatherneck was old and large, a beast of great stamina, but not much speed. He was seldom used as a mount anymore. Over the past summer, he'd taken to hunting farther and farther afield.

To the west, the Hest Mountains rose, their sheer peaks white from last night's dusting of snow. On the mountainside below the aerie, Keep Haberd rose – five stone towers – its walls spanning both sides of the narrow pass that led into the mountains. People were running about within the castle walls, shouting. Some still bore torches. Their voices sounded dim and distant. Women and children were climbing onto wagons down on the green, seeking to escape.

Only then did Averan realize that something was terribly wrong. 'What's happening?'

Brand set down the haunch of lamb as if weary, measured her with a gaze. 'A squire just rode in with news out of the hills of Morenshire. A volcano erupted in the Alcair Mountains last night, spewing ash. Reavers are approaching in its wake. The rider estimates that among the reavers are some eighty thousand blade-beaters, and another thousand lesser mages with at least one fell mage. A cloud of gree flies above them, blackening the skies. You must get the news to Duke Paldane at Carris.'

Averan struggled to understand the implications of what Brand had just said. Morenshire was a region in the farthest west of Mystarria, bordering the juncture of the Hest and Alcair mountains. The citadel here, Keep Haberd, the nearest fortress, was old and stalwart. It served as a refuge for travelers in the mountains, and the soldiers here mostly kept the trails safe against robbers and reavers and other vermin. But the fortress would never hold out against a force like the one that Brand described. The reavers would overrun the walls in an hour, and they wouldn't take prisoners.

Duke Paldane was the King's strategist. If anyone could defeat the reavers, Paldane could. But Paldane had his hands full. Raj Ahten's men had taken or destroyed several castles on the borders, and lords and peasants alike were fleeing from the north.

'Our lord thinks that the volcanic eruption has flushed the reavers from their lairs,' Brand went on. 'It happened once that way, in my grandfather's time. The volcano filled their burrows with lava and all the monsters fled in its wake. But this eruption will bring greater misery than that one did. The reavers have been breeding unchecked in those hills for far too long.' He rubbed his whiskers.

'What about you?' Averan asked. 'What will you do?'

'Don't worry about me,' Brand said. 'I'll take them on with one hand, if I must.' He wiggled the stump of his right arm and laughed painfully at his own joke.

But she could see the terror in his eyes.

'Don't worry about me. You just take old Leatherneck,'

Brand said. 'You'll fly without benefit of saddle or food or water – to keep your weight down.'

'What of Derwin?' Averan asked. 'Shouldn't *he* take the message to Duke Paldane?' Derwin was younger. At the age of five, he was the official skyrider for Keep Haberd.

'I sent him off late last night on another errand,' Brand answered, gazing off to the south, searching for his beast. Then he muttered bitterly, 'Our fool of a lord – sending skyriders to fetch letters to his mistress.'

Averan already knew that. Years ago, she'd often carried letters and roses from her Lord Haberd to Lady Chetham in Arrowshire. In return, the lady would send notes of her own with lockets of her hair or a perfumed handkerchief. Lord Haberd apparently believed that he could hide his adulterous affair more easily if he used children for messengers rather than one of his older soldiers.

The fertile plains to the east were shrouded in morning fog that turned a a dim gold as the sun's first rays touched upon it. Here and there, a green hill rose like an emerald island from the mist. Averan watched among the valleys for sign of the graak. Leatherneck would be there, searching for something slow and fat to eat.

'How soon will the reavers be here?' Averan asked.

'Two hours,' Brand answered. 'At the most.'

Hardly time to mount a defense. If Lord Haberd called for aid from the nearest fortress, it would take a day, even for knights riding forces horses. She wondered if the men here could hold out so long.

Brand put his hand to his mouth, called again. In the far distance. Averan saw a winged speck rise from the mist, tan-colored flesh aglow with the morning light – Leatherneck answering the summons.

'Leatherneck is old,' Brand said. 'You'll have to stop and rest him frequently.'

Averan nodded.

'Fly above the woods to the north, then cut across the ridges to the Brace Mountains. It's only two hundred and forty miles

– not far. You can reach Carris by nightfall.'

'Won't resting slow me?' Averan asked. 'Maybe I should just fly on through.'

'This is safer,' Brand said. 'No need to kill the beast in your hurry.'

What could he mean? she wondered. Of course she had to hurry – and the death of her mount was nothing compared with the deaths of the men.

She realized the truth then. Keep Haberd was isolated. Nothing that she did would make any difference. No help could arrive in time. Lord Haberd had probably already sent out messengers riding force horses. And the horses would make better time than she could. Her top speed was forty miles per hour, and flying north at this time of the year, she might have to battle headwinds. A fast horse, one with enough endowments of metabolism and strength and stamina, could easily run eighty.

'You're not sending me out to carry a message,' Averan said. Her voice felt tight in her throat, and her heart was pounding.

Brand glanced down at her, smiled fondly. 'Of course not. I'm saving your life, child,' he admitted. 'Take the message to Duke Paldane if you want. There's always a chance that the horsemen won't get through.'

He leaned over and whispered conspiratorially. 'But if you take my advice, I wouln't stop there. The palace at Carris is a death trap. If the reavers head that way, they could take it in a fortnight, and there's no guarantee that Paldane will let you ride out on the beast you flew in on. Tell Paldane that you've been instructed to carry a message of warning farther north, to our lord's second cousin at Montalfer. Paldane wouldn't dare hold you back then.'

Leatherneck was laboriously winging his way up from the foggy downs, carrying some shepherd's ewe in his great maw. He flew eagerly, his small golden eyes gazing all around.

The beast dropped to the landing, flapping his great wings so that the air whipped Averan's hair. Leatherneck took a clumsy bounce, then gently laid the sheep's carcass at Brand's feet, as if he were some giant cat making a present to his master of a dead mouse. The graak stood panting, the folds of skin at his throat juggling, as he sought to catch his breath.

He leaned forward, nuzzled Brand's chest.

Brand smiled wistfully, reached out with his one good hand and patted the brute's nose, pried a chunk of meat out from between Leatherneck's saberlike teeth.

'I'm going to miss you, old lizard,' Brand said. He tossed the haunch of lamb up into the air as high as he could. Leatherneck snagged it before it could touch ground.

To Averan, Brand said, 'I used to ride him as a lad, you know, forty years back – as did King Orden. This is a kingly mount you'll ride.'

Leatherneck was one of the oldest graaks in the aerie, not the one she'd have chosen to take. But he was well trained, and Brand had always held a special affection for the monster. 'I'll take good care of him,' Averan said.

Brand made a fist, palm down, and the great reptile leaned forward, crouching so that Averan could mount. She ran a step and leapt onto its back. Like all skyriders, she had an endowment of stamina and of brawn. She had more strength and endurance than any commoner, and with her small size she was easily able to leap up and scramble over the monster's back. Beyond those endowments, she had one of wit, and could therefore recount verbatim almost any message her lord ever wanted her to deliver. Such endowmenets set her apart from other children. She was only nine, but had learned much in that time.

Averan settled in before the first horny plate on the beast's neck. She scratched the graak's leathery hide.

'Never fall,' Brand said. It was the first rule a skyrider was taught as a child. It was also a farewell among the skyriders, an invocation to begin every journey.

'I never shall,' Averan answered. He tossed her a small bag that clanked when she grabbed it, the sound of coins. His life's savings, she imagined.

She clasped her legs around the graaks's neck, felt his muscles tense and ripple as he awaited her command.

She wished that she had more time to say goodbye to Brand. A part of her could not quite imagine that the reavers were really coming. The keep this morning looked the same as on any other autumn day. Here on the landing, high above the castle, maidenhair ferns and a few morning glories trailed up the rock, their purple flowers opening wide. The air was still and peaceful. The smell of cooking fires wafted up from the strongholds down below.

Her mind rebelled at the thought of leaving. Normally she would feed her graak better before such a long flight. She wished now she could allow Leatherneck to eat more, but the beast would hardly be able to bear her weight and that of a full belly.

Averan's throat felt dry. Bitter tears stung her eyes. She sniffed, and asked, one last time, 'And what of you, Brand? What will you do? Will you leave the castle? Will you promise to hide – if not for yourself, for me?'

'It would be death to run before the reavers,' Brand said. 'They'd cut me in half like a sausage. And I fear that in my current condition, I'd make a poor bowman to man the walls.'

'Hide for me, then,' Averan begged. Brand was everything to her – father, brother, friend. She had no family. Her father had died in a skirmish with reavers before she was born, and her mother perished from a fall when Averan was a toddler – a fall from a chair while lighting a lantern in the lord's keep. Averan had seen her mother fall but had never quite accepted that someone could die so easily from a fall. She herself had dropped fifteen feet on more than one occasion when her reptile jarred her free on landing, but Averan had taken no harm from it.

'I promise that I'll hide, if hiding will do any good,' Brand said.

She studied his eyes to try to see if he was lying. But Averan had always been terrible at seeing behind other people's eyes. What other people really thought, what they meant, often seemed an unfathomable mystery.

So she had to satisfy herself with the hope that Brand would hide, or run, or somehow escape the reavers.

Brand had been staring at her, but suddenly his eyes focused on something behind her, and he caught his breath.

She turned. On a far hill up the canyon, she suddenly saw them, the reavers scurrying forward on their six legs. Their leathery hides were pale gray in the morning, and at this distance, one could not make out how many runes were tattooed into their skins. One could see only their blades flashing in the sunlight, and the gleam of fiery staves. From a distance, the six-legged creatures looked only like some strange insects, scurrying from beneath a rock. But Averan knew that every one of those fell beasts was three times the height of a man.

A dark cloud flew up behind, the gree swarming out in alarming numbers. The gree were smaller than bats, larger than June bugs. They flew out of caves sometimes. Averan had never seen so many that they darkened the sky.

'Go, now!' Brand said. The reavers would not be here in two hours. At the speed they ran, they would be swarming the walls in five minutes.

'Up,' Averan shouted.

The graak turned and leapt off the cliff. Averan felt nauseous for a moment when the lizard fell. She looked down over his neck to the jumbled rocks hundreds of feet below.

For a moment, she forgot about the reavers. Many a young skyrider had fallen to those rocks over the centuries. Averan had watched little Kylis fall last year, had heard the girl's death scream. Now for one eternal moment Averan feared that Leatherneck would not be able to bear her weight, that she would carry them both to their deaths.

Then the graak's wings caught on the air, and she soared.

She glanced back. Brand waved at her from the rocky perch of the graak's aerie, as the morning sun glanced off his face, then he walked manfully back inside the upper lofts.

It looked to Averan as if the mountain swallowed him. She felt half-tempted to circle the city for a few moments, to see what the coming of the reavers might bring, but knew that she did not want such memories to haunt her in years to come.

So with little nudges of her feet and spoken commands, Averan steered Leatherneck north, above the roiling fog that glistened like the waves of the sea. She wiped bitter tears from her eyes as Leatherneck bore her away.

5

BEAR STORIES

'So then your son throws his javelin at the old tusker,' Baron Poll chortled at Roland, 'and he thinks himself a marksman, aims right between the eyes. But that old boar must have had a skull as thick as the King's fool's head, for the javelin hits the skull and merely grazes the beast!'

Baron Poll smiled at the memory, and Roland looked up the road. They were still half a day from Carris, riding slowly in the mid-afternoon, letting the mounts catch their breath.

'So the old tusker is mad, and he lowers his snout and paws the ground, blood flowing down over his tusks. Now you know that the boars of the Dunnwood are as tall as a horse and all as shaggy-haired as a yak. And your son, being only thirteen at the time, sees that this tusker is about to charge and hasn't the wit to do what any man should.'

'Which is?' Roland asked. He'd never hunted boars in the Dunnwood.

'Why, turn his mount and run!' Baron Poll shouted. 'No, your son sits there looking at the beast, making a fine target of his horse, and no doubt he's peed his breeches about now.

'Well, that old boar charges and catches his mount right under the belly with a good upper thrust that disembowels the horse and throws your son about four feet in the air.

'Now, as I said, it was about an hour past that we'd lost the hounds, and we'd been riding to find them. We could hear them yapping off in the hills, you see.

'So your son comes down off his horse, and it's sort of

limping away, and the boar sees your lad standing there, and your son takes off running so fast, I swear by the Powers I thought he'd taken flight!'

Baron Poll's eyes were wide with delight at telling the story. It sounded as if he'd told this one many a time before, and he'd honed it well.

'So then young Squire Borenson, upon hearing the hounds yapping, thinks to himself – as we later found out – *I'll run to the dogs! They'll protect me!*

'And so he takes off running through the bracken, with that boar right behind him.

'Now, at the time, your son had just taken two endowments of metabolism – so you can imagine how fast he's running. He's sprinting along at thirty miles an hour, shouting "Murder! Bloody murder!" – as if he's raising the hue and cry – and every time he slows, that boar puts the fear of death into him.

'Now, he's run about half a mile, all uphill, and I start to thinking it's about time to save his life, so I go charging up on my own mount, right behind him and the boar. But they're running so fast through the underbrush that I keep having to weave around them, looking for a clearer course, and so I never can quite get within throwing distance of that boar.

'And then your son reaches the dogs. They're all sitting down at the base of this big rowan tree, their tongues hanging out, and every once in a while one of the hounds would howl as if to have something to do to pass the time, and your son thinks, *Ah, I'll climb that tree, and the dogs will promptly save me.*

'Your son leaps into the tree, and all the hounds jump up expectantly, looking at him and wagging the stumps of their tails, and young Borenson shinnies up about twenty feet.

'And then the boar leaps in amid the thick of the dogs. Now this old tusker had been around, it seemed, and it loved the dogs no better than it did your son, and seeing that the dogs were all fagged out and a bit astonished to find a fifteen-hundred-pound monster in their midst, the tusker lowers its snout and throws the first dog it sees about forty feet in the air and slices another two open before they can even get to their feet.

'So the rest of the hounds – there were only about five or six of them in this little pack – decide that it's time to tuck what's left of their tails between their legs and head for the nearest pub. Then Squire Borenson starts screaming for me: "Help – you son of a whore! Help!"

'Well, I think to myself, that's no way to address someone you're asking to save your miserable life, such as it is. So since I can see that he's safely up a tree, I proceed to slow my horse, as if giving it a breather.

'And just then, I hear this most peculiar sound – this deafening roar! And I look up, and see why your son is screaming. It turns out that the tree he'd climbed had bears in it! Three big bears! The hounds had treed them!'

Baron Poll laughed so hard at the memory that he roared himself, and by now he was nearly weeping.

'Now your son is stuck in this tree, and the bears are none too happy to have him there, and the boar is down underneath it all, and I start laughing so hard I can hardly sit in my saddle.

'He curses me soundly – we were never friends, you know – and orders me to come rescue him. Well, I'm two years his elder, and at fifteen I figured I'd rather be damned than ordered about by a boy who'd been twelve two weeks before. Keeping a goodly distance from the tree, I shout, "Did you call me a son of a whore?"

'And your son cries, "I did!"

'Well, it didn't matter that he spoke the truth,' Baron Poll continued. 'I was not about to be so cursed by a thirteen-year-old. So I shouted up at him, "Call me 'sirrah,' or you can save yourself!"'

Baron Poll fell silent, became thoughtful.

'What happened then?' Roland asked.

'Your son's face became dark with rage. We'd never been friends, as I said, but I never had guessed how much he hated me. You see, I'd always ridden him mercilessly when he was a child, damning him for a bastard, and I think he saw through me. He knew I was of low parentage, so he thought I should treat him better than the other boys did – not worse. So I deserved his hatred, I guess, but I never knew a boy could hate so much. He said, "When you're dead, if you die with honor, then I'll call you 'sirrah'! But not a moment before!"

'Then he drew his knife,' Baron Poll added more soberly, 'and climbed up that tree and started laughing and going at the bears himself.'

'With nothing but a knife?'

'Aye,' Baron Poll said. 'He had endowments of brawn and stamina in his favor, but he was still not much more than a boy in stature. The bears had climbed out onto some big limbs, and I don't know a man in his right mind who would have fought them thus. But your boy went after them, maybe just to prove to me that he could do it.

'I think he would have killed them, too. But the bears saw him coming and jumped first. So when the boar saw bears dropping like plums from the tree, he decided to give up on your son and go hunt acorns, instead . . .' Baron Poll chuckled at the memory.

'That was when I first realized that young Squire Borenson would someday become captain of the King's Guard,' Baron Poll continued. 'Either that or he'd get himself killed. Maybe both.'

'Both?' Roland studied Baron Poll's face now. The man was enormous – three hundred pounds of fat, all covered with hair as dark as night. But his expression was thoughtful.

'Men who become captain of the King's Guard seldom keep the post long. You know that King Orden's family was attacked by assassins three times in the past eight years?'

Three attacks in eight years seemed like a lot. In recent history, Roland had never heard of anything like it. When he'd given his endowment of metabolism into the King's service, he'd never quite imagined that he would waken to such dark times. His own king dead, the whole kingdom of Mystarria under attack from invaders.

'I hadn't known,' Roland said. Having been asleep for twenty years, he hadn't really had a chance to catch up on recent history. He wondered if Orden had had any local troubles – neighbors who might have wanted him dead. 'Who sent the assassins?'

'Raj Ahten, of course,' Baron Poll said. 'We could never prove it, but we've always suspected him.'

'You should have sent an assassin down to waylay *him*,' Roland replied, seething with righteous indignation.

'We did – dozens of them. Among all the kingdoms of Rofehaven, we've sent hundreds, maybe even thousands. We've tried to kill him and his heirs, wipe out his Dedicates and his allies. And the Knights Equitable spent their own forces, as well. Damn it, this is no little border skirmish we're engaged in.'

It was astonishing that one Wolf Lord could repel so many attacks and still be as powerful as Raj Ahten was rumored to be.

Yet evidence of it was everywhere. All this afternoon, as Roland and Poll had been riding, they'd met peasants fleeing from the north. Men and women pulling carts loaded with bundles of clothes, some scraps of food, and the few valuable possessions they had to their name. They also saw signs of recent movements of armies – Mystarria's warriors heading north into battle.

Roland fell silent.

'Uh-oh,' Baron Poll muttered. 'What do we have here?'

They rounded a bend and looked down a rise. On the road ahead, a horse was down. Broken leg by the looks of it. The beast had its head up, looking around weakly, and its rider was trapped half underneath it. The man was dressed in the garb of a king's messenger – a leather helm and green cloak, a midnight-blue vest with the image of the green knight on its chest.

The messenger had passed them not an hour before, shouting for them to get out of his way. Now the fellow wasn't moving.

Roland and Baron Poll raced forward. The low spot in the road was muddy from rains two days past, not so muddy that you'd notice it right off, but Roland could see where the horse had slid as it rounded the bend, skidding a hundred yards. After skidding, the horse had apparently twisted its leg and gone over. Riding a force horse at full speed – one with three endowments of metabolism – could be dangerous. A horse that tried rounding a bend at sixty miles an hour could misplace a foot, charge full speed into a tree.

The messenger obviously was dead. The man's head rested at an unsightly angle, his eyes were glazed. Flies danced in the air around his tongue.

Roland hopped down, grabbed the fellow's message case from within his tunic, a long round scroll pouch made of green lacquered leather. The injured horse looked up at Roland, uttered a cry of pain. Roland had seldom heard that sound from a horse.

'Show the beast some mercy,' Baron Poll said.

Roland took out his short sword, and when the horse looked away, he gave it a killing stroke.

Roland opened the message case, pulled out the scroll, and studied it for half a second. He did not know how to read or write more than a few words, but he thought he might recognize the wax seal. He didn't.

'Well, open it up,' Baron Poll said. 'At the very least, we must find out where it should go.'

Roland broke the wax seal, opened the scroll, found a hastily penned missive. He recognized some of the words: 'the,' 'a,' 'and.' But Roland couldn't figure out the larger words no matter how hard he squinted.

'Well, out with it, damn you!' Poll cried.

Roland gritted his teeth. He wasn't a stupid man, but he wasn't educated, either. He hurled the message at Baron Poll. 'I can't read.'

'Oh.' Baron Poll apologized, taking the scroll. He appeared to read it all in a glance.

'By the Powers!' he shouted. 'Keep Haberd was overwhelmed at dawn by reavers – thousands of them. They sent news to Carris!'

'I doubt that Duke Paldane will rejoice to hear more bad news,' Roland said.

Baron Poll bit his lower lip, thinking. He looked south, then north, obviously worried about which way to go. 'Paldane is the King's great-uncle,' he said, as if Roland might have forgotten over the past twenty years. 'He rules now as regent in the King's stead. But if he's put under siege at Carris, as seems likely, there will be damned little that he can do about the reavers. Someone should take this news back south to the Courts of Tide, to the counselors there, and to the King.'

'Surely more than one rider was sent,' Roland said.

'We can hope,' Baron Poll said.

Roland made to mount his horse, but Baron Poll cleared his throat loudly, nodded toward the dead messenger. 'Best grab that man's purse. No need to let it go to the scavengers.'

Roland felt queasy robbing a dead man, but he knew that Baron Poll was right. If they didn't get the fellow's purse, the next man on the road would. Besides, he told himself, if he was going to deliver the King's message, he ought to get a messenger's pay.

He cut the purse loose, found it to be heavier than expected. The man was probably carrying his life savings.

Roland shook his head. This was twice in one week that he'd found himself in possession of a small fortune. He wondered if it were some sort of sign that this war would go well for him.

He leapt onto his horse and shouted to Baron Poll, 'I'll race you!'

Then he put his heels to horseflesh and they rode like a storm in its fury. Baron Poll had the faster mount, but Roland knew that the fat man's beast would tire sooner.

On a hillside a dozen miles north from where Roland and Baron Poll had found the dead messenger, Akhoular the far-seer stood in the crook of the branches of a tall white oak. He leaned his head against one limb and watched two men race north along a muddy road in the early afternoon.

These were not peasants, he knew, fleeing the battle to come at Carris. Nor were they mounted soldiers riding to war.

They did not appear to be king's messengers, for they were not wearing the proper livery. Yet Akhoular had to wonder . . .

His men had killed several messengers in the past week, disposed of the bodies along the roadsides. Perhaps the king's messengers were becoming wiser, traveling in disguise.

Akhoular had five endowments of sight. Even from a mile away, he could make out the men's determined faces. The younger fellow, a big man on a fleet-footed horse, bore a dark-green leather message case on his wrist. The fat fellow was well armed.

Yes, the king's messengers were getting wiser. They were riding now without the king's colors, and this one had a knight to guard him.

Akhoular whistled to the camp at the base of the tree. He was growing short on men. He'd lost three assassins this week. Yet he called a young man, a Master in the Brotherhood of Silent Ones.

'Bessahan, two riders! They carry a message,' he said. He pointed toward the road, though the assassin below him would not be able to see through the forest.

Akhoular said, 'They ride fast toward Carris. You must kill them.'

'They shall not reach Carris,' Bessahan assured the far-seer. The Silent One leapt onto his force horse and drew his dirty brown hood low over his face. With one hand, he reached back behind the saddle, checked to make sure that his hornbow was still tied to his saddlebags.

He spurred his horse and raced down the mountainside.

6

AMONG THE PETTY LORDS

'Here now, that's much better,' Sir Hoswell said. Myrrima watched her arrow arc into the air and hit its target eighty yards distant. Her shot fell a foot low of where she wanted, but it was the third time in a row that she'd hit within the red circle of cloth pinned to the haycock, and she felt proud.

'Good, milady,' Sir Hoswell said. 'Now if you do that ten thousand more times, you will internalize it. Learn to shoot that distance, and then learn to shoot farther and farther. Soon you'll shoot with your gut, not your head or hands.'

'I'll have to raise my aim,' she corrected. The thought of shooting ten thousand more times worried her. Already her fingers and arms were sore from the labor. 'That shot wouldn't have stopped an Invincible.'

'Pah,' Sir Hoswell said. 'Maybe you wouldn't have killed him, but you would have made an eunuch of him. And if stopping him from rape was your aim, he'd definitely walk with a limp in more appendages than one.'

Myrrima glanced sideways at him. Sir Hoswell smiled broadly. He was a wiry man with a bushy moustache, a thin beard, and the heavily lidded eyes of a lizard as it lies half-asleep on a warm stone. His smile would have been pleasant if his teeth hadn't been so crooked.

Sir Hoswell stood close, too close. Myrrima could not help but feel uncomfortable. They were in a glade in a narrow valley not far from the tents put up by petty lords of Heredon. Yesterday hundreds of boys had been practicing archery here, but today was the day of the great feast. Trees hunched close within fifty yards on either side of her, and Myrrima could not help but feel alone and vulnerable.

She'd known Sir Hoswell nearly all her life – he was from Bannisferre, after all – yet somehow today she did not trust him. It was growing late in the afternoon, and she wondered if she should head back to the castle.

The oak trees on the hills here formed a natural barrier that shielded them from view. Myrrima had no other witness present. She knew that being alone with a man other than her husband might seem scandalous, but now that she'd decided to prepare herself for war, she did not want to attract Borenson's attention. If her husband guessed her intent, she feared he'd forbid her. She needed someone to teach her martial skills.

Lord Hoswell had been a friend to her father, and he was a fine bowman. When she'd found him here practicing his skills, she'd asked him to give her lessons for the afternoon, and he'd agreed. With the endowment of wit her mother had granted her two weeks past, Myrrima found that she was learning the basic skills of archery much faster than she'd thought possible.

'Try again,' Lord Hoswell urged her. 'And this time, pull that bow back harder. You need to hit him firm, to get deep penetration.'

Myrrima drew an arrow from her quiver, glanced at it quickly. The fletcher had done a hasty job. One of the white goose feathers wasn't glued and tied properly. She wetted her finger with her tongue and smoothed the feather into place, then took the arrow firmly between her fingers, placed its notch on the bowstring, and drew the arrow back to her ear.

'Wait,' Sir Hoswell said. 'You need to work on a firmer stance.'

He stepped up behind her, and she felt the warmth of his body, the warmth of his breath on neck. 'Straighten your back, and turn your body a little more to the side – like this.'

He reached up and took hold of her left breast, adjusted her stance by half an inch, and stood there holding her, quivering. The man's legs shook.

She felt her face redden with embarrassment. But in her

mind, she heard the voice of Gaborn, the Earth King, warn her, 'Run. You are in danger. Run.'

Myrrima was suddenly so frightened that she loosed the arrow by accident. But Sir Hoswell did not release her breast.

As swiftly as she could, so that even with his endowments of metabolism he could not avoid it, she twisted around and brought her knee up into his groin.

Sir Hoswell half collapsed, but he had her blouse in his hand, and he tried to pull her down with him.

Gaborn's voice came a second time. 'Run!'

She punched at his Adam's apple. He tried to draw back, and in doing so let go of her blouse enough so that after she landed the blow, she broke free.

She turned to run.

He grabbed her ankle, tripping her. Myrrima shouted 'Rape!,' turned and kicked at him as she fell.

Then he was on her.

'Damn you, you bitch!' he hissed, slapping a hand over her face. 'Shut your yap, or I'll shut it good.'

He twisted his hand, putting his palm against her chin and pushing with incredible force so that her neck arced backward painfully. Then he adjusted his fingers, pinching her nostrils closed. With his palm over her mouth, she could not breathe. With the weight of his body on her, she could not escape. She tried to fight him off – rammed her thumbnail into his right eye so hard that blood gushed from the socket.

'Damn you!' he cursed. 'Must I kill you!'

He punched hard in her guts, knocking the air from her, making the gorge rise in her throat. For a long moment she struggled silently, fighting only to get a breath as he worked to untie his belt with his free hand. Her lungs burned with the need for air, and her vision went red. Her head began to spin, as if she were falling.

Then she heard a snapping sound, and all the air went out of Sir Hoswell. He rolled from atop her.

Someone had kicked him – kicked him hard enough to break ribs.

Myrrima gasped for fresh air, felt her lungs fill and fill again, yet still she could not get enough air.

'Here now, what's going on?' a voice asked. It was a woman's voice, and the accent was so thick that at first Myrrima did not recognize that the woman spoke Rofehavanish.

Myrrima looked up. The woman standing over her had blue eyes and wavy black hair that fell in ringlets about her shoulders. She looked to be twenty years old. Her broad shoulders hinted of more strength than even a working drudge might have. She wore a plain brown robe over a shirt of stout ring mail, and she had a heavy axe in her hand.

Behind her stood a mousy woman in scholar's robes, a Days.

Myrrima glanced over at Sir Hoswell, and she half wondered if the woman had dealt him a deathblow with the axe. This was no commoner. She was a Horsewoman of Fleeds, a warrior with enough endowments of brawn and grace that she'd likely be a match even for Hoswell.

But Sir Hoswell was still alive, holding his ribs, hunched over like a whipped cur. Blood flowed down his face. Yet he snarled, 'Stay out of this, you Fleeds bitch.'

'Och, I would not be addressing a girl so harsh like, especially when she's wielding an axe and you've had no proper introduction.' The woman smiled in mockery of a lady's courtly manners. Yet her smile was full of malice.

She studied him for half a moment, then frowned.

'Och, if Heredon doesn't breed better warriors than this,' she mused, 'I'll never get bedded.'

Myrrima was gasping, terrified by all that had happened. The woman's words barely registered, but Myrrima understood it as a joke.

The Horselords of Fleeds had bred horses for a thousand generations, bred them for strength and beauty and intelligence.

In the same way, noblewomen of Fleeds bred themselves to get children. A highborn woman might ask a dozen worthy men to sire children on her during her lifetime, she might even marry a man, but a husband would never rule her.

Women alone carried the right to title, since in Fleeds it was believed that 'No child can know its father.' The women of Fleeds laughed at the queer notion that men should rule. Thus, in Fleeds a 'king' was only a man who had married a queen. And if she chose to dispose of him and choose another mate, then he would lose his title.

'I – ah,' Myrrima stammered. Hoswell held his bleeding forehead, then half dropped, as if weary.

'You, ah, what?' the woman asked.

'I'm sorry,' Myrrima said. 'I only asked him to teach me to use a bow.'

The woman spat at Hoswell. 'You'd think your northern lords would *want* to teach women to fight, what with Raj Ahten knocking your castles down.'

Myrrima couldn't argue. She knelt over him. Hoswell coughed and began feebly trying to crawl to his knees.

She tried to help him up, but Hoswell gaped at her and slapped her hands away. 'Leave me, you Mystarrian whore! I should have know you'd be trouble.'

He made it to his knees, then got up and lurched away, swaying from side to side.

Myrrima didn't know quite how to feel. She was stung by his words: 'Mystarrian whore.' She'd been born and raised here in Heredon. Hoswell knew her. Did he dare call her a whore for marrying a man from Mystarria?

The woman of Fleeds said, 'Don't make any sad faces for that one: I know his kind. At dinner, he'll be telling them all that he had his way with you, then tripped and hit his face on a rock.'

'We should go get a physic,' Myrrima said. 'I'm not sure he can make it back to camp.'

'It will just lead to a fight,' the horsewoman said. 'If you want to avenge your honor, just put an arrow into the fellow's back now.'

'No,' Myrrima said.

'Then leave him.'

Myrrima frowned. She didn't think herself a paragon of

virtue, but she'd never thought she'd leave a wounded man to fend for himself.

I should be mad as hell at that blackguard, not feeling sympathy for him, she thought.

Myrrima hardened her jaw. If she were going to go to war, she'd see worse than some man staggering around with a knot above his nose.

'Thank you,' Myrrima said to the horsewoman. 'I'm lucky that you happened by.'

'Oh, I didn't happen by,' the Fleeds woman said. 'I was around the spur of that hill, and the Earth King said someone here needed help.'

'Oh,' Myrrima said, surprised.

The horsewoman studied Myrrima frankly. 'You're a pretty thing. What endowments do you have?'

'Two of glamour, one of wit,' Myrrima said.

'What are you? Highborn, or a wealthy whore? Though I don't see much difference between the two.'

'Highborn . . .' Myrrima said, then hesitated, for it was a lie. 'Sort of. My name is Myrrima. My husband is in the King's Guard.'

'Have *him* teach you the bow,' the woman said, not hiding her disgust at northerners and their dullards' ways. She turned as if to march up into the trees.

'Wait!' Myrrima begged.

The woman turned.

'Whom do I have the pleasure of addressing?' Myrrima thought her manners sounded far too dainty, too refined for such a rough woman.

'Erin, Erin of Clan Connal.'

She was a princess, daughter of the High Queen Herin the Red.

'I'm sorry for your father,' Myrrima said, for she could think of nothing else to say. Word had reached Heredon several days past that Raj Ahten had captured the High King Connal, and fed him alive to frowth giants.

Lady Connal merely nodded, her green eyes flashing. She

could have said something deprecatory about her father, demeaned his prowers in war. Such deprecations passed for humility in her land. She could have given some sign that she loved him. A child's love for her father was also a worthy emotion. She did neither. 'Many warriors died,' was all she said. 'Men *and* women. The dead ones are the lucky ones. Some things are worse than death.'

Erin reached down and picked up Myrrima's bow and quiver. She nocked an arrow and drew the shaft full, then let it fly. The arrow struck the center of the target on the haycock.

She's showing off, Myrrima realized. She wants me to respect her.

Thirty thousand warriors of Fleeds had been impelled to join Raj Ahten's army. The Wolf Lord had so many endowments of glamour and of Voice that few could withstand his persuasive powers.

Myrrima suddenly understood Erin Connal. She was proud of her father, proud to have him dead rather than converted.

Half a moment before, Myrrima would have been afraid to beg a boon from this lady. But on seeing Erin's own embarrassment, Myrrima could also see the woman's humanity. We are no different, she realized.

'Princess Connal, can you teach me?' Myrrima asked.

'If you can learn,' Connal said. 'But the first thing you'll have to learn is not to call me "Princess," or "Lady," or any of your courtly titles. I'll not be spoken to as if I was some man's pet. And in my own land, a woman becomes High Lord of the Clans by working for it, not being born to it, so I've little right to your titles. You'll call me Connal, or if you want a title, call me "horsesister," or just "sister," for short.'

Myrrima nodded numbly.

Sir Hoswell had just rounded the bend, passing through a screen of trees. Sister Connal said, 'Let's get out of here, before that weasel finds some friends and comes back.'

Myrrima took her bow and arrows, and Sister Connal led her up through the woods, with Connal's Days walking discreetly behind. The grass in the fields felt dry to the touch, but once they got under the trees, the rains from two nights past had softened the grass stalks and the fallen leaves, so that it felt as if they walked upon a soggy carpet.

They climbed through the oak forest, and Sister Connal watched Myrrima disapprovingly from the corner of her eye. 'You'll have to work on your stance. The problem with being a woman archer is that your breasts get in the way. And you've got more than most. You could use a rag, to help tie them down. Better yet, I've seen some women just wear a leather vest.'

Myrrima grimaced. She'd always been proud of her breasts, and didn't fancy the notion of tying them down or covering them in leather.

They reached the top of the knoll and stood a moment. Here, beside the old Durkin Hills Road, the petty lords had set their camp, and from the top of the knoll, Myrrima could see down over the pavilions to the lands all around the castle.

The fields before Castle Sylvarresta were a sea of canvas and silk. Here by the roadside camped the petty lords, men and women who could claim to be gentlemen only from a single line or two, people whose fathers or grandfathers had been knighted and thus raised in stature above the common peasants. A high lord would normally be knighted on all four lines, and his ancestors had won the honor generation after generation, confirming his noble blood. But as far as Myrrima was concerned, knighthood was no great honor. Any brute could win it on a good day. Most men among the petty lords had ancestors who were knighted only because their skill with a weapon matched a rude temperament and nasty disposition. For instance, 'Sir' Gylmichal in the tent below her was from Myrrima's home in Bannisferre. The man had been spawned by a foul-mouthed drunkard who somehow discovered that he could find both righteous anger and courage in a mug of whiskey. His father, upon hearing that some bandit had attacked a traveler, would drink himself into a blind rage, usually late after midnight, and then take his hunting dogs and go murder the bandit in his sleep. For that, the peasants would have to bow and scrape the floor with their hats to his descendants for generations to come.

Gylmichal was thus a petty lord, a man with a title but without the breeding or status to rub shoulders with the major lords, whose larger and more ornate pavilions were pitched off to the east side of Castle Sylvarresta.

To the west of the castle, and at its front, peasants had pitched a few shabby tents – or slept with nothing better than the sky as a roof for their heads.

Even farther to the west stood a few bright silk pavilions pitched by the merchants out of Indhopal.

Sister Connal stood atop the knoll for a moment, gazing out over the multitude of tents. 'That's my pavilion,' she said, pointing down to a dirtstained canvas tent. Whereas the pavilions of Heredon were always pegged at four corners, and numerous poles held up the roof, Connal's tent was round, with a single pole at its center, in the inelegant style used by the Horselords.

Directly below Myrrima, at the center of the pavilions pitched by the petty lords, was a muddy tournament field, surrounded by posterns with rails atop them, so that spectators could watch the proceedings. Some of the rails were hung with colorful tapestries, to protect the spectators' fine clothing from spattering mud. Vendors of pastries and roasted hazelnuts milled through the crowd, calling out their wares.

The sides of the knoll where Erin and Myrrima stood were so steep and filled with brush and rock that no one bothered to stand here to watch the performance below. Still, Myrrima found that it was almost a perfect spot to see over the crowds into the arena, and the sound carried remarkably well. She gazed down over the crowd some eighty feet below, clinging to the rough bark of an oak, and watched the game with Erin Connal and her Days.

Jousting was considered a game for boys in Rofehavan – young men still in training for war. Among Runelords, who were made powerful with endowments of brawn, even a casual blow from a lance could be devastating. So a time came in a warrior's life when he quit jousting.

In the tournament field, two young men in full armor were mounted on chargers. The boy on the west side of the field looked to be of fairly common stock. He wore tournament armor, which consisted of an extremely heavy helm and a breastplate that was customarily thicker on the right side – where a lance was more likely to strike with any degree of force – than on the left. It looked to be old armor cobbled together from mismatching outfits borrowed from other knights. His only decorations were a horse's tail, dyed a vivid purple, stuck into the helm, along with his lady's favor, a yellow silk scarf, tied to the shaft of his lance. Myrimma's heart went out to the lad.

The boy on the other side of the field was wealthier. His tournament armor was new, and had obviously been a year in the making. The matching breastplate, helm, pauldrons, and gauntlets were made of burnished silver covered in red enamel, showing an image of three fighting mastiffs. He wore a cape of cloth-of-gold, with bleached peacock feathers in his cap.

The Lord of the Games, Baron Wellensby, sat in a special pavilion off to one side with his three fat daughters and enormous wife. The Baron was ridiculously accoutred in a bright purple houppelande with arms so baggy that children could have hidden in them. Over this he wore a white hat with a wide brim that fell low enough over his face so that he obviously thought no one would notice if he slept through the tournament. His wife, who was no paragon of fashion, wore an emerald-colored cotehardie with gorgeously embroidered floating sleeves. She kept her hands tucked into the slit pockets in front of her, petting a small dog that was peeking out of her pockets just enough to bark when the knights came charging by. During a moment of silence from the crowd, her few shouts of encouragement to the warriors sounded curiously like the dog's bark.

This was obviously but one pass of many that these boys had taken. Their names had been heralded already, and if they fought for any particular honor, then the terms of the fight had been named and the conditions set.

Now, Baron Wellensby dropped his lance. At this signal, the young men on chargers dropped their own lances into a couched position and shouted, digging their heels into their mounts' ribs.

The warhorses responded by shaking their heads and charging forward, their armor clanging, hooves thundering in the mud. The young man who wore the cape of cloth-of-gold had tied dozens of silver bells to the mane and tail of his mount, so that the horse made music as it ran.

Behind the Baron's pavilion, a gaggle of minstrels sat playing a quick riff on the horns and pipes and drums, providing climactic music for a charge that likely would end with nothing more than a couple of shattered lances. The lances, after all, had been hollowed so that the warriors wouldn't actually skewer one another, but only knock their opponent from his horse. Upon impact against a warrior, the lances would shatter with a cracking sound that could be heard for miles. The audience was sure to applaud.

Yet Myrrima could not resist the thrill of the battle. Men did get hurt in these affairs. Even a poor blow with a lance could leave a man badly bruised, and a knight who faltered in the way he handled his lance could rip a tendon. A lance could take a man through the visor and thus lodge in his brain, or a fall from a horse could snap a person's neck.

Mounts sometimes fell in the combat, too, rolling over and crushing their riders. It was a rare festival that didn't end with at least a couple of deaths, and the spectacle was all the more visceral because the contenders were known to the spectators. One of the knights was bound to be someone that you knew and admired or envied or hated or loved.

The horns pealed and the drums rolled and the chargers raced together with the sound of bells and jangling armor and through it all Myrrima held her breath.

These were force horses, each with one endowment of metabolism, so that they raced toward one another with blinding speed, hooves moving so swiftly that they blurred. Goose bumps thrilled up her spine.

'The poor boy on the left will win,' Connal said, disinterested. 'He's got the stance.'

Myrrima doubted it would happen soon. A jousting match might require the combatants to make twenty or thirty passes before a victory could be won. These young men looked weary and muddied. They'd already made several passes.

The warriors met, and the air filled with the sound of splitting lances and the screams of horses. The rich lad went down, bowled over backward by a lance that took him full in the gorget and snapped his head backward. He tried to hold on to the heavy reins, but they snapped under his weight.

The audience cheered and thundered its approval, while those who'd bet against the fallen knight hurled insults.

'Ah, the lad dirtied those nice white peacock feathers,' Myrrima whined in mock sympathy.

Sister Connal chuckled. 'They'll need a hammer and tongs to get that helm off him.'

But the lad got up from his fall quickly and bowed to assure the crowd that he was all right. He hobbled from the field and squires rushed forward and began stripping off his armor, casting it into a pile to become the prize for the victor. Myrrima felt glad for the poor knight.

The smell of freshly roasted hazelnuts cooked in butter and cinnamon rose from vendors among the crowd, making her hungry. She wanted to go join the celebration.

'Could you beat that knight?' Myrrima asked as the victor circled the field with his broken lance held high.

'Aw, sure,' Sister Connal said. 'But where's the sport in it?'

Myrrima wondered. The Horselords of Fleeds were fearsome warriors who honored a leader's strength more than her bloodline. Sister Connal was likely among the toughest of the lot, and she'd have the endowments of brawn and stamina and grace to take on any warrior.

As the wounded knight left the field, heralds came forward to shout the names of the next contestants. As the first herald approached, there was a sudden dull roar, a tittering of excitement. From up here, over the myriad cries, Myrrima missed hearing the name of the warrior that the herald announced, yet immediately she realized that this was not a common fight. The herald who spoke from the far side of the field was no boy, but a grizzled old veteran warrior with a horribly scarred face. He wore no king's tunic emblazoned with the device of the lord he served, so Myrrima took him to be a Knight Equitable, sworn only to fight against evil.

At the far end of the field a knight rode out on a huge black mount, a monster of a horse with so many runes of power branded into it that it no longer seemed to be a creature of flesh and bone. It moved with surety and power, like some creature of iron come to life.

The man mounted on that beast seemed no less a monster. This fellow had to stand head and shoulders taller than any man Myrrima had ever seen, as if he had giant's blood flowing through his veins.

He was a huge man, dark and brooding. He bore the blank shield of a Knight Equitable, but he wore armor in a strange foreign style. The shield itself was shaped like a winged eagle, with a single spike issuing from the eagle's eye. His helm had horns on it, in the style of warriors out of Internook, and his chain mail was unusually long. It would have hung down to his ankles when he stood, and covered his feet in the stirrups. The sleeves of the coat came down to the wrist.

But he was not wearing tournament plate for mail. His chain mail, no matter how well made, would be punctured by a lance as easily as a needle pierces cloth.

This would be no ordinary match. Among powerful Runelords who rode force horses, *any* blow with a lance could shatter bones or turn a man's innards to jelly. Plate mail could not be made thick enough to protect a man and still let him ride a horse. So among powerful lords the art of the joust had evolved into a new kind of contest. Such lords could not trade blows, nor could armor do much to protect them.

Instead, Runelords had to use grace and wit and speed to avoid or deflect blows. A man's defensive prowess became his surest armor – in effect, his only real armor. Hence, few

Runelords ever wore plate that would inhibit their full range
of motion, and instead wore ring mail or scale mail over thick
layers of leather and cloth that would help deflect blows.
When Runelords fought in tournaments, the spectacle was
thrilling, with lords charging on fast force horses and clashing
at a hundred miles per hour. Men would leap from their horses
to avoid blows, or cling to their horses from the belly, or
perform other phenomenal stunts. It was high entertainment,
fit for the king's tournament.

It was also a deadly contest, not to be undertaken lightly.

The lord in the arena was not wearing tournament plate.
This monster had not come to fight for wealth or glory; he
had come to take a life – or lose his own.

'Here now, what is this?' Sister Connal said. 'This looks
interesting.'

'Who is it?' Myrrima asked. 'Who's fighting?'

'The High Marshal, Skalbairn.'

'The High Marshal is here, in Heredon?' she asked numbly.
She'd never seen the man before, had never heard that he'd
even crossed the border. He normally wintered in Beldinook,
three kingdoms to the east.

But of course he'd come, she realized, as soon as he heard
that an Earth King had arisen. The whole world is coming to
Heredon. And he rode so swiftly that no messenger could ride
ahead to announce him.

Now he was here, the leader of the Knights Equitable.
Myrrima felt astonished. Among the Knights Equitable, there
were no lords. A common boy who joined their ranks might
climb in station as quickly as a prince might. They were sworn
to one thing only: destroying Wolf Lords and bandits, fighting
for justice.

No man held the title of 'lord' among the Knights
Equitable, but there were ranks – squires, knights, and
marshals. High Marshal Skalbairn was the leader of them
all. In his own way, he held nearly as much power as did
any king in Rofehavan.

And one did not gain the rank of High Marshal without

shedding blood. Myrrima had never seen the man. Skalbairn was said to be a madman, a berserker who fought like one who wished himself dead.

But she recognized the herald who came out on the near side of the field. The stout Duke Mardon strode round from the back of the main pavilion, dressed in his best finery. He held his hands high, to silence the crowd.

'Duke Mardon,' Myrrima whispered in awe. If a duke was acting as herald for the warriors, then this was no petty bout. It meant that some great nobleman was about to fight, perhaps even a king, and Myrrima had a flight of fancy in which she imagined briefly that young Gaborn would do battle.

Yet if a nobleman were to fight, Myrrima wondered, why would he fight here? The high lords had another arena up on the castle green, and this bout should have been fought there. Unless the high lords wanted to keep this match a secret from someone at court until it was over.

'Ladies and gentlemen,' Duke Mardon bellowed in a voice that carried across the fields. Then his voice was lost to the surge of cheers and premature applause, and Myrrima could not hear anything until he bellowed louder. '. . . slew a reaver mage in the Dunnwood only yesterday . . . Sir Borenson the Kingslayer!'

Myrrima's heart beat so loudly, she was sure Sister Connal could hear it.

The cheers and screams that arose from the crowd below were deafening. Some cheered for her husband, others called for his death. Angry peasants shouted, 'Fool!' 'Bastard!' 'Whoreson!' 'Kingslayer!'

In the pandemonium that broke out, people came rushing from nearby tents, swelling the audience alarmingly.

Now Myrrima thought she understood why this battle would be fought here. Her husband had slain King Sylvarresta, slain him upon the orders of King Orden after the battle of Longmot. And though King Sylvarresta had given an endowment of wit to Raj Ahten, and was therefore nothing more than a pawn in the hands of an enemy, he had been a good king in his time, and was beloved by his people. As a punishment for his crimes, Iome Sylvarresta had sentenced Myrrima's husband to commit an Act Penitent. But apparently that wasn't enough for the High Marshal. He would want blood to atone for blood, and so he had challenged Sir Borenson. Young King Gaborn Val Orden would never have sanctioned such a combat. He'd not have allowed it to be fought in the high arena. So they battled here among the petty lords and the cockfighters and bear baiters.

'By the Powers,' Sister Connal swore lightly. 'The only man in this kingdom I'd want between my legs, and here he's fighting a death match!'

Myrrima glanced up into the horsewoman's face, astonished by the insult, until she realized that Sister Connal could not know that Sir Borenson was her husband.

Then Borenson rode out onto the west end of the field. He sat upon a gray charger, wearing his own splint-mail armor, carrying a simple round shield that had been blanked. His long red hair flowed down his back, his blue eyes smiled. He studied his opponent, gauging the thickness of the man's arms, his size.

A knight wearing the colors of King Sylvarresta rushed forward with a heavy war helm, and Borenson donned it.

Myrrima was appalled. She was astonished that her husband was in the arena preparing to fight without having spoken a word about it to her.

Knights came rushing out, bearing lances. These were no brightly painted parti-colored pieces of hollow wood. They were sturdy war lances of polished ash, bound with iron rings and tipped with steel. The steel tips were blackened with pitch, so that they would not slide across a man's shield or armor on impact but instead bore straight through. Each lance had to weigh in excess of a hundred and fifty pounds, and was tapered at the base to a diameter of eight inches. Once a man was skewered, the lance would wedge apart his flesh and bones, creating a huge gaping wound from which no man, even with endowments of stamina, could ever recover.

These lances were weapons of murder. The High Marshal bore a black lance, a color that symbolized vengeance. Boreson bore a red one, the color of innocent blood. Tied to its haft was Myrrima's red silk scarf.

The minstrels began playing a clamorous melody before the charge.

'I must go,' Myrrima said, feeling ill to her stomach. She looked around desperately, searching for a way down from the knoll. The steep ground was covered with big rocks, and small oaks thrust up between them.

'Where?' Sister Connal asked.

Myrrima groaned and pointed. 'Down there. That's my husband!'

The look of astonishment on Sister Connal's face was a relief to behold. Myrrima had begun to think the woman a stoic, and Myrrima's own emotions – the shock and horror of all that she'd been through today – made her feel weak and volatile in comparison.

Myrrima turned away and began racing down the steep hill as fast as she was able. By the time she made it to the bottom and crossed the Durkin Hills Road, the mob was thick around the tournament field.

She tried to force her way through the throng, and couldn't, until she suddenly found Sister Connal at her side, shouting, 'Out of our way!' and shoving people aside.

Myrrima looked up to thank her. Sister Connal apologized for her earlier remark, saying simply, 'I didn't know he was your husband.'

By the time they fought their way through the crowds close enough to see well, the horses were already charging.

This would not be a boys' tournament battle, twenty-five passes with the lance, with the loser suffering nothing more than bruised ribs.

The wild shouting of the crowd was deafening. Myrrima glanced at the taut, giddy faces of those nearby. They were hoping for blood.

Both warriors had chosen odd stances. Sir Borenson rose

in his stirrups and leaned far to his right, as only a warrior with many endowments of brawn could do. Furthermore, he did not hold his lance in the couched position, but instead held it overhead as lightly as if it were a javelin.

The High Marshal on the other hand leaned far forward on his black charger, trying to make his enormous bulk into a smaller target. On seeing Borenson's stance, he muscled his lance out and held it side-armed, in a position that Myrrima had never seen a warrior use. Furthermore, he chose not to carry a shield in his other hand. Instead, he bore a short sword.

It appeared that Borenson meant to jab down into the High Marshal's visor from above, while perhaps the High Marshal hoped to pierce Borenson's armpit, where the lack of armor left the flesh exposed.

Yet as they met in mid-field, both men swirled into furious motion.

The two horses streaked toward one another. The men atop them blurred as each sought the advantage, taking various defensive stances. Myrrima watched Borenson rise up, then crouch, then sweep his shield down in an effort to drive Skalbairn's lance tip aside.

As for Skalbairn, she could not really watch him and her husband at the same time, but she saw him roll to the left, perhaps even dropping to the ground for half a second in an effort to avoid Borenson's lance and then leaping back on his horse.

The men met, a vicious, seething blur.

Myrrima heard the clash of arms and armor. Someone cried out in pain, while the audience cheered and horns blared. Borenson's shield swiped up brutally while Skalbairn hacked with his short sword.

Metal flashed, and a helm went flying. Sir Borenson tumbled backward on his horse.

For one eternal moment, Myrrima thought that her husband had been decapitated. A scream of terror escaped her lips as the silver helm arced up, then tumbled to the earth. The musicians blared their trumpets at the sign of a kill, and the crowd cheered wildly.

Myrrima felt faint, grabbed for Horsesister Connal's shoulder.

In the next instant she realized that both men had fallen – and both still lived!

They struggled with supernatural swiftness in the muddy field, roaring and beating at one another with mailed fists as they sought to disentangle.

Borenson leapt up first, jumping back a pace. Even with his armor on, he moved lightly, for he had seven endowments of brawn, and thus had the strength of eight men. Blood flowed down the side of his face. The audience jeered.

Borenson reached to his belt, pulled a morningstar, and whipped the thing about expertly, the heavy balls becoming a blur at the ends of their chains. He crabbed sideways to regain his shield.

The air smelled of mud and blood.

But the giant Skalbairn gained his feet just as easily, raced across the field to his horse. He pulled a huge axe from a horseman's scabbard.

He whirled it and advanced on Sir Borenson, easily standing a foot and a half taller.

Only then did the crowd fall silent long enough for Myrrima to hear if the warriors spoke. Her husband was laughing, uttering the mad battle chuckle for which he was noted.

Borenson swung his morningstar, aiming for the High Marshal's head, a warning blow meant to drive the monster back.

The High Marshal pivoted to his right and dodged. A moment later they exchanged a flurry of blows so fast that Myrrima could not see, with no man the clear victor. Yet when Borenson stepped back a pace to catch his breath, she glimpsed the blood still streaming from his brow.

Again they lunged at one another. The High Marshal aimed a vicious swing with the axe. Borenson tried to parry, but the axe cleaved through his shield's steel exterior and shattered the wooden braces underneath. The shield came apart on Borenson's arm while he swung his morningstar, aiming a blow at the High Marshal's face. The spikes on the steel balls grazed the High Marshal's chin, but the main force of the blow was deflected by his sturdy helm.

With his defenses crumbling, Borenson leapt in the air and swung down full force, seeking a quick strike.

Once again the men's actions became a blur. Myrrima sensed more than saw the High Marshal duck away from the attack and bring his axe up, entangling the weighted balls of the morningstar.

Then fists flew, men groaned. A kick from Skalbairn swept Borenson's legs from beneath him.

Borenson went down, tried to climb back up, and Skalbairn drove a mailed fist into Borenson's face.

Stunned, Borenson slumped to his back, momentarily unconscious.

Skalbairn drew his long dagger and leapt to the ground, pressing its blade under Borenson's chin. Myrrima tried to climb over the railing, for she feared that the High Marshal would shove the dagger into her husband's throat, but Sister Connal caught her by the shoulder and shouted in Myrrima's ear, 'Stay out of it!'

'Do you yield? Do you yield?' the big man Skalbairn began roaring.

From the crowd came scattered applause for the High Marshal, along with curses. 'Kill him!' 'Kill the whoreson blackguard!' 'Kingslayer!'

Such curses were normally only reserved for the worst cowards or oafs. Myrrima was dismayed by the vehemence of the insults. Her husband had killed a reaver mage and brought its head to the gates of the city. He should have been hailed as a hero.

But the people here would not forget that her husband had slain King Sylvarresta. Myrrima began to realize that they would never forget her husband's deed, nor forgive it.

'Mystarrian whore,' Sir Hoswell had called her. 'Kingslayer,' the crowd shouted at her husband. She glanced at those nearby, saw their faces flushed with excitement. Nothing would give them more joy than to see her husband killed.

She had hardly noticed the minstrels playing all during the charge, but now the drum rolled and a single horn blared the high, curdling call for the death stroke.

It sickened Myrrima, sickened her to the core. He's better than any one of you, she wanted to shout. He's better than the whole lot of you put together!

The crowd hushed to hear Borenson's response above the drum roll.

And there, lying in the muddy field while an angry giant held a dagger to his jugular vein, Borenson responded by laughing uproariously, laughing so heartily that Myrrima wondered if the fight had been staged for the benefit of the petty lords.

Perhaps this was not a death match after all, Myrrima hoped. Two skilled warriors, feigning a deadly grudge just to thrill a crowd. It had been done before.

'Do you yield?' High Marshal Skalbairn roared again, and the tone of his voice that made it clear this was no jest.

'I yield,' Sir Borenson laughed, and he made as if to get up. 'By the Powers, I've never met a man who could handle me like that.'

But the High Marshal snarled viciously and shoved Sir Borenson's head down, poking the long knife harder against his throat.

Under the rules of formal combat, Sir Borenson put his life into the High Marshal's hands by yielding. His life belonged to Skalbairn now, and he could be slain or allowed to live, according to Skalbairn's whim.

But the formal code of chivalry observed on the battlefield was seldom taken seriously here in the arena. A defeated knight might be asked to pay a ransom of arms or armor, sometimes even money or land. But he was never slain outright.

'You'll not get off so handily!' the High Marshal bellowed

like a bull. 'Your life is mine, you scurvy bastard, and I intend to take it!'

Sir Borenson lay back, astonished by the High Marshal's battle fury.

Another man might have fought on, hoping to save himself. But true to his word, Borenson lay back and taunted his opponent. 'I said "I yield." If it's my life you want, take it!'

The High Marshal smiled savagely, and the giant hunched over him, as if eager to dig the knife blade into Borenson's throat.

'First, a question,' the High Marshal demanded, 'and you must answer honestly, or it's your life.'

Sir Borenson nodded, his pale blue eyes going hard as stone.

'Tell me,' the High Marshal bellowed, 'is Gaborn Val Orden truly the Earth King?'

Now Myrrima understood that the High Marshal did not want her husband's life, only information. And he'd wanted that information so badly, he'd been willing to risk his own life for it.

A knight who yielded on the battlefield was bound by honor to speak truly. Borenson would answer truly now, so long as his answer did not betray his lord.

The High Marshal had shouted so that the entire field hushed to hear the answer. Speaking in a voice that brooked no argument, Borenson said, 'He is truly the Earth King.'

'I wonder . . .' the High Marshal said. 'In South Crowthen I heard strange rumors. It's said that in the House of Understanding, your king studied in the Room of Faces and in the Room of the Heart – he studied mimicry and motives in a place where a dishonest man might better learn to deceive. And then when he announced himself to be Earth King, on that very day, his first act was to perform an elaborate ruse to drive Raj Ahten from his lands! Some think it an odd coincidence that Young Orden "happens" to become the Earth King just when Heredon needs him most. It seems a too convenient tale, one to rouse a peasant's hopes. So I ask you once again, is he truly the Earth King – or is he a fakir?'

'On my honor and my life, he is the Earth King.'

'Some call him a cur, without natural affection,' the High Marshal growled. 'Some wonder why he fled Longmot, leaving his men and his father to die at the hand of Raj Ahten. Surely if he is the Earth King, he could have withstood even Raj Ahten. But you've known the boy for ages – raised him from a pup. *What say you?*'

Borenson's voice shook with rage. 'Kill me now, you lousy knave, for I'll not listen to poisonous lies spread by that fool King Anders!'

There was a whispered hush, and many in the crowd glanced to the far end of the field from whence Sir Skalbairn had ridden. There at the gate stood a tall man in a fine robe. He had wispy blond hair, a hatchet face, and a grim demeanor. He looked to be thirty, but if he had endowments of metabolism, he might have been far younger than that. Myrrima had not seen him before, would not have noticed him in a crowd, but now people whispered, 'Prince Celinor.' 'Anders's son.'

The giant smiled grimly and looked up at Prince Celinor as if seeking his approval. The Prince nodded; he appeared satisfied.

So, Myrrima realized. King Anders's boy was behind all of this. But did he demand to know whether Gaborn was the Earth King because he sought confirmation, or did he do so because he wanted to plant doubts in the minds of the peasants? If it was for the latter reason, he could not have chosen a better venue for this spectacle than here among the petty lords.

High Marshal Skalbairn sheathed his knife, then offered Sir Borenson his hand. He said, 'Arise, then, Sir Borenson. I would see this boy king myself.'

In moments, the arena filled with young boys and minor nobles who rushed up to see the High Marshal, the man who had bested Sir Borenson. Some went to retrieve his lance, others to bring him his horse.

Borenson got up shakily, and no one came to offer him

comfort or congratulate him on a good fight. Instead, he went to his cracked lance and knelt to untie Myrrima's red scarf from it, the sign of her favor.

Myrrima climbed over a rail of the arena, found herself in the thick mud, looking for an easy path to her husband. She struggled through the deep mud, and when she reached Borenson, she found herself shaking, unsure of what she should say to him.

He'd gotten the scarf untied, and stood with his back to her, wrapping it around his own neck. He tried to tie it while wearing his gauntlets, but the thick leather and ring mail left him fumbling.

Myrrima went around to the front of him, tied the damned thing for him, and found that her own hands were trembling so badly that she was as clumsy as he was. She looked at his face. His hair was smeared with mud, and blood was thickening from a deep gouge above his right eye.

'You saw?' he asked.

Myrrima nodded wordlessly, finished tying the scarf. She could not see it anymore. Tears were filling her eyes.

'Damn you, I could be tying this around your corpse right now.'

Borenson laughed, a short nervous bark.

'Do you think so little of me that you didn't even tell me?' She thought now that he must have fought here so that she wouldn't see.

'I *tried* to find you,' Borenson explained. 'But you weren't at the King's feast, you weren't at the royal games. No one had seen you since this morning. And Sir Skalbairn had called me to task, demanding battle before sundown. It was a matter of honor!'

Myrrima realized that of course no one had seen her. She'd been careful not to let anyone know where she was going. 'You could have waited. Do you love me less than your own honor?'

She had not spoken to him before of love. Gaborn had arranged their marriage, and she had agreed. In all, she'd not known Borenson for a week. Yet she'd married him, and in spite of their short time together, she knew that she was in love. She wanted to hear Borenson admit the same.

'Of course not,' Borenson said. 'But what is a life without honor? You could never grow fond of me if I were any less of a man.'

Just at that moment, Borenson looked up over Myrrima's shoulder, and Myrrima glanced back to see the object of his attention. It was Horsesister Connal, bringing Myrrima her bow and quiver. Myrrima had dropped them on the knoll outside the arena. Borenson smiled at the horsewoman.

'Milady,' Horsesister Connal said, 'you dropped these.'

Myrrima took them in one hand.

'Erin Connal, well met!' Borenson said in greeting. 'I hadn't heard that you were in camp.'

'I've been here since yesterday,' Horseister Connal said, 'with nothing better to do than stare at that rotting reaver head you dragged in at dawn.'

'You two have met?' Myrrima asked.

'A couple of times,' Borenson said hesitantly. 'Old King Orden was a friend of her mother's, so he usually stopped at her palace when he rode through Fleeds.'

'Good to see you,' Erin said, ducking her head like a shy lady.

Myrrima didn't like this. Didn't like the idea that they knew each other, that Connal was attracted to her husband. She asked her husband bluntly. 'Did you know that she wants to have your babies?'

Borenson snorted in surprise and his face turned red. 'Well, of course she wants to have my children, what Horsewoman wouldn't?' He spoke as if to a crowd of drinking companions. Then he faltered as if he realized that he'd spoken too soon, and added jokingly, 'But, of course, we won't sell her any of our precious offspring, will we, my pet?'

Myrrima smiled with tight lips, hardly placated.

7

THE HIGH MARSHAL

Borenson turned aside, wishing he could run from his wife. He dared not ask her what she was doing with a bow, or why she was in the company of Erin Connal.

Fortunately, he had to clear his gear from the field for the next challengers, so he went to his horse, led his mount and the women toward the High Marshal.

The High Marshal was deep in whispered conversation with the Prince. But of course Borenson had two endowments of hearing and caught the tail of it. 'Tell your father he can keep his damned money,' the High Marshal whispered. 'I'll not winter my armies in Crowthen if this boy is the Earth King. I'll send them where they are needed.'

'Of course, of course,' Celinor said in almost a pleading tone. Then he looked up and saw Borenson coming.

Borenson smiled and called across the short distance, 'Prince Celinor, Sir Skalbairn, may I present my wife.'

The High Marshal nodded in greeting, and Prince Celinor merely let his gaze sweep appreciatively from Myrrima's head to her feet.

'I'll get my horse,' Celinor said, turning aside. As he passed, Borenson smelled the stench of alcohol strong on him. Celinor headed through the throng at the north end of the field.

'What was that all about?' Borenson asked the High Marshal, looking up into the big man's face. Skalbairn lumbered above him like a bear. 'What is this about wintering in Crowthen?'

The High Marshal studied Borenson, as if gauging just how

much to tell him. Obviously, what he had to say was not anything King Anders of South Crowthen would want spoken in public. But the High Marshal was a tough man, and he seemed not to care what effect his words might have. 'Word reached me in Beldinook of Raj Ahten's attack here about four days ago. But King Anders's messengers, who begged that I bring the Righteous Horde of the Knight Equitable to South Crowthen, carried the word. And they brought money to pay for our travel. There's too much money by half. It smelled of a bribe to me.'

'He wants to bribe the Knights Equitable?'

'I could understand Anders's distress,' the High Marshal continued. 'What king wouldn't want the Knights Equitable camped in their realm with Raj Ahten's armies moving about. Indeed, it seemed a logical move. Instead, we drove Raj Ahten into the mountains and I ordered my men to hound him.

'But when I reached Crowthen last night, I found that Anders still wants my armies to stay in Crowthen, ignoring the greater threat to Mystarria. His son just pressed me to hold to their bargain, at least for now.'

'What will you do?'

'Anders will be furious. I'm sending back his gold – at least most of it.'

'Anders sounds craven,' Borenson said.

At that, the High Marshal's black eyes glittered dangerously. 'Don't underestimate him. I fear he's worse than a coward.'

'What do you mean?'

'He wants my troops, and he wants them badly. A coward would want them for protection. But as I rode to Crowthen, I was thinking, what if he is not afraid of Raj Ahten? What if he really fears the Earth King?'

'Gaborn?' Borenson said in astonishment, for he could not imagine that Anders would fear the lad.

'I got proof of it at the border. King Anders had troops stationed at the road, and he's forbade any peasants and even merchants from entering Heredon. His troops proclaim Gaborn a fraud and say that it is a waste of men's time to come see him, and harmful to Anders's interests.'

'If Anders had no interest in learning the truth himself,' Borenson said, 'that would be one thing. But to forbid his people from coming? That's evil.'

'Look at it from his point of view,' Skalbairn said. 'There has not been an Earth King in over two thousand years. In Erden Geboren's day, he was honored as the one and only true king of all Rofehavan. But since then, lesser men have been called kings, and the lands have been divided and squabbled over.

'What will happen to Anders if the people rise up and offer to serve House Orden? Will he be relegated to the status of a petty lord? Or will he be asked to bow and scrape the knee like some common peasant?

'You and the commoners may think it is a fine thing to have an Earth King, but mark my words: if Anders could kill the boy now, he'd do so. And he's not the only lord in Rofehavan who will feel that way.'

'Damn,' Borenson whispered. He glanced back. Myrrima and the horsewoman were close enough to have heard everything the High Marshal had said.

'My mother says that if ever an Earth King were to rise in our day, he would come out of House Orden,' Horsewoman Connal said. 'She's asked me to verify whether he is the Earth King, and if he is, to offer the clans to back him up.'

'As will I,' the High Marshal said, 'if he is the Earth King.'

'He is,' Myrrima said forcefully. 'Ten thousand men at Longmot saw the ghost of Erden Geboren crown him. And I myself have heard Gaborn shout his commands into my mind.'

'I met him this morning,' Erin told Skalbairn, 'and learned the truth of it. I'll be backing him.'

'Yet King Anders ridicules the tale of his coronation as the babbling of a spooked army,' High Marshal Skalbairn objected. 'He points out that the Earth Warden Binnesman was present, and that the old wizard may have had a hand in some fakery.'

'That's a vile thing to say,' Myrrima objected.

'Yet Anders may believe it is true,' Skalbairn said. 'He points out that his own line is every bit as true as Orden's, and that the Earth King could as easily come from his own loins.'

'He would name Prince Celinor the Earth King?' Horsesister Connal said. 'Celinor the sot? I've heard too many sad tales about him.'

'Of course not,' the High Marshal whispered. 'Why should Anders bother to put his son forward, when he so loves himself?'

Borenson laughed scornfully.

'I think,' the High Marshal said, 'that his son is no more than a pawn. The boy has come ostensibly to pledge his sword into the King's Guard, like some petty lord's son. But he talks more like a spy, on his father's errand. Just listen to him when he returns!'

'So, tell me,' Borenson asked the High Marshal. 'If the Earth King summoned your men to battle, how many could you bring?'

The High Marshal grunted, and his flinty eyes flickered. 'If we brought everyone? Our numbers are down. The Righteous Horde numbers some thousand mounted cavalry, and another eight thousand archers, six thousand lancers, five hundred artillery men, and of course another fifty thousand squires and camp followers.'

In giving these numbers, the High Marshal did not bother to mention the quality of his troops. His thousand cavalry were worth more than any ten thousand mounted by any other lord, while many of his 'archers' were seasoned assassins who often went into dangerous territory to ambush whole armies.

'Shhh . . .' Myrrima whispered.

Prince Celinor led his mount near, while his Days followed a few paces behind. Though his was a force horse, the beast had drooping ears and looked as if it would need a good meal in the king's stables after riding a hundred and fifty miles since daybreak.

Prince Celinor smiled innocently. 'Shall we go?' he asked. Borenson began to lead them all through the throng. The streets were crowded this evening, with peasants from the camps all going from one table or tournament to another. Celinor weaved through the crowd deftly, but with rubbery legs. He seemed pretty far into his cups.

No one spoke, leaving Prince Celinor to fill the clumsy silence, which he accomplished quite handily by babbling, 'I find all of this incredible. I mean, I *knew* Gaborn. I went with him to the House of Understanding, but I did not speak to him much. I seldom saw him. He did not spend much time in the alehouses—'

Horsewoman Connal said, 'And of course we couldn't expect you to truly befriend someone who doesn't spend all his spare time in alehouses.'

Celinor ignored the jibe. 'I meant that he was an odd lad. Since he studied in the Room of Faces and in the Room of the Heart, he did not study arms or tactics. So of course I did not know him well.'

'Perhaps you speak poorly of him because you are jealous,' Connal said.

'Jealous?' Celinor asked. 'I could never be the Earth King. And I mean no disrespect toward Orden. But when I was a child, I sometimes dreamed that an Earth King would be born in my lifetime. And I always imagined someone bigger than me, and older – someone with a look of profound wisdom dripping from his brow, with the strength of a whole army bulging in his chest, someone of legendary stature. But what do I get? Gaborn Val Orden!'

Myrrima had to wonder at Prince Celinor's words. The young man sounded innocent enough, like a carefree lad just babbling. But was it innocent babble? Everything he said seemed calculated to engender doubt in others.

'Gaborn serves his people,' Borenson told Celinor. 'He serves them more truly than anyone I've ever met. Perhaps that is why the Earth has chosen Gaborn, made him our supreme defender.'

'Perhaps,' Celinor said. He smiled in a cold, superior way, and inclined his head to the side as if in thought.

*   *   *

When Borenson reached the Great Hall with Prince Celinor, High Marshal Skalbairn, and Horsewoman Connal in tow, dozens of lords and barons were busily feasting around tables that circled the room. At the center of the tables, minstrels sat on cushions and played softly, while serving children scurried back and forth between the kitchen and buttery, bringing food and drink as it was wanted, then clearing the tables.

At the far end of the Great Hall, Gaborn smiled and stood in greeting as Borenson entered the doorway, with the others crowding behind him.

Gaborn called, 'Sir Borenson, Lady Borenson, Prince Celinor, and Lady Connal, welcome. Let the servants bring you chairs and plates.' Then he looked up at the High Marshal and asked, 'And who do we have here?'

The minstrels left off at playing their lutes, tambours, and drums. Gaborn stared hard at Skalbairn.

'Your Highness, may I present High Marshal Skalbairn, Master of the Knights Equitable.'

Borenson expected Skalbairn to nod curtly and study Gaborn from afar. Instead, the High Marshal acted without hesitation. He said gruffly, 'Milord, some claim that you are the Earth King. Is it true?'

The question astonished Borenson, for he'd thought the man convinced. But he realized belatedly that the High Marshal had only been convinced that Borenson believed Gaborn to be the Earth King.

'I am,' Gaborn said.

The High Marshall said, 'It is said that Erden Geboren looked into the hearts of men and named some to be his protectors. If you have that power, then I beg you, look into my heart and choose me, for I would serve the Earth King with my life. I bring with me the Righteous Horde of the Knights Equitable, thousands of warriors who fight beside me.'

He drew his sword and stepped forward to the King's table, then knelt and drove the blade into the floor, resting his hands upon the hilt.

Borenson immediately felt embarrassed. This was not an honor that one demanded of the Earth King in public. But Gaborn did not seem taken aback by the High Marshal's blunt manners.

Around the King's tables, lords began to murmur in astonishment. Some questioned the man's upbringing, but the High Marshal was a renowned warrior, one of the greatest in all Rofehavan, and they knew he could bring tens of thousands of warriors to swell the Earth King's armies. This would be a great boon. So no one dared to criticize openly.

Moreover, no High Marshal had ever offered to swear fealty to a king.

Until now.

Gaborn leaned forward across the table, placing his hands on either side of his silver platter, and looked down steadily into the High Marshal's eyes for a long moment.

High Marshal Skalbairn stared back with eyes as black as obsidian.

Gaborn's face went slack, as it did when he performed the Choosing. He gazed deeply into the High Marshal's eyes and raised his left arm to the square, as if to perform the ceremony.

Then he dropped his hand and stared in shock, trembling.

'Get out!' Gaborn said, his face going pale. 'Get out, you foul . . . thing! Get out of my castle. Get away from my lands!'

Shocked, Borenson recalled the people Gaborn had Chosen this past week: paupers and fools and old women who couldn't bear a dagger in their own defense, much less a sword.

Now one of the greatest warriors of the age knelt before him, and Gaborn wanted to cast the man away!

The High Marshal smiled in secret triumph. 'Why, my lord?' he asked casually. 'Why would you send me away?'

'Must I speak it?' Gaborn asked. 'I see your guilt written in your heart. Must I speak it, to your eternal shame?'

'Please do,' the High Marshal answered. 'Name my sin, and I will know that you are the Earth King.'

'No, I will not speak it,' Gaborn raged, as if the very notion sickened him. 'There are women present, and we are feasting. I'll not speak of it now – or ever. But I refuse your service. Begone.'

'Only the *true* Earth King would know that I am unworthy to live,' the High Marshal said, 'and only a true gentleman would refuse to name my sin. My offer still stands. I give myself into your service.'

'And I reject you still,' Gaborn answered.

'If I cannot live in your service,' Skalbairn said, 'then still I will die in your service.'

'Perhaps that is best,' Gaborn said.

High Marshal Skalbairn stood and sheathed his sword. 'You know of course that Raj Ahten is driving south, into the heart of your own Mystarria. You will have to engage him – and soon. Your enemies would like to see him defeat you.'

'I know,' Gaborn said.

'The Righteous Horde is moving south. I will fight beside them, though you hate me.'

There was utter silence in the crowded room as the High Marshal turned and strode from Heredon.

Borenson marked the look upon Prince Celinor's face. The Prince only cocked his head to the side, watching the whole spectacle with a calculating gaze.

Borenson noted that the young Prince did not dare to offer his own sword in public.

8

THE GREEN WOMAN

As Averan flew, she kept watching behind her, gazing in the distance toward the fortress and the beast master Brand for any sign that things might have changed. She expected to see the smoke of burning buildings or to hear the peal of doom.

But the fortress merely gleamed in the morning sun, the white stone of its towers sparkling as always, until it receded from her view, its few towers becoming a distant speck on the horizon. Then it was swallowed completely as the clouds began to rise from lowlands. Even if Averan had had the eyes of a far-seer, she'd have lost the castle in the mist.

She remained aloft for hours. The world flowed beneath the wings of her mount. Cool air beat upon her face, and the sun warmed her side and back. As the clouds continued to rise from the lowlands, some of them extended up into the air, became crystalline pillars, weird sculptures. Flying into them was always a mistake, Averan knew. They were filled with fragments of windblown ice, and the air currents around them could be dangerous.

Even to get close to them was to feel their cold bite. Averan wished that she still had her leather riding gloves to keep her hands warm.

She hunched low to the neck of her mount, to feel the heat of Leatherneck's body and to listen to the subtle rhythms of his breathing so that she could learn when he began to tire.

Twice during the day, she let Leatherneck drop below the mists and rest for short times on the ground. He was an old graak, old and easily tired. She feared that if she rode him too hard, his heart would give out.

As they traveled, the mountains of Alcair receded from sight until they were lost in a haze, and the mountains of Brace rose up from the clouds off to her left and spurred to a point ahead. Averan knew every peak by name, and knew that she was rapidly approaching Carris just beyond a saddleback ridge seventy miles ahead. She doubted that she'd reach Carris by dark, and hoped only that the cloud cover was thin enough so that she could see the city's lights from above.

So it was that in the near dusk, Averan rode with stomach tight from hunger, her mouth dry from thirst, not wanting to make her mount bear any more than he was able. She was lying against his neck, listening to the steady thump-ump, thump-ump, thump-ump, of his heart, wondering if she should let him rest again.

Thus she was distracted at the single most important moment of her life. For just at dusk, the green woman plummeted like a comet from a cloudless sky.

Averan heard a wordless shout – a piercing wail – and looked up.

The sky above was the perfect blue of a robin's egg.

And a green woman fell from the sky.

Averan spotted her two hundred yards off. The woman tumbled head over heels, naked as a newborn babe. She was tall, thin of build, her ribs showing plainly beneath her small breasts. The hair of her head and the dark V between her legs was the color of pine needles, while her skin was a more muted shade, almost flesh in tone.

Averan could make out few other details.

She glanced skyward, to see if the woman could have fallen from some vehicle. Flameweavers sometimes rode in hot-air balloons, and it was said that the Sky Lords traveled in ships of cloud, though Averan had never seen one.

Neither cloud nor balloon was above her, or anywhere near.

In that moment, Averan felt the cold wind numbing her hands, blowing through cracks in her robe and on her face.

She could see clearly. Could hear the woman's cry.

Something in Averan broke.

She'd seen her mother fall from a chair and dash her head on the paving stones at the foot of a fireplace. She'd seen her five-year-old playmate Kylis tumble from the landing of the aerie, drop to the cliff base far below.

She could not idly watch another person fall to her death.

Without a thought of her mission to carry a message to Duke Paldane at Carris, she leaned back, clasped Leatherneck tightly with her legs, and cried, 'Down! Fast!'

The graak folded his wings in close, shot after the green woman like a hawk diving for a mouse.

For a moment, the woman stared up at Averan, hands outstretched, pleading for aid. Her mouth was a round O of horror, fangs bared, her long green fingernails extended like claws.

Not human, Averan realized. This woman was not human. It did not matter. She seemed close to human, though it was hard to tell. In seconds she plummeted into the clouds, and was lost from sight.

Averan followed her into the mist. Drops of moisture beaded on her skin.

Leatherneck flapped his wings and slowed, refused to dive blindly into the fog. From below came the snapping sound of cracking wood, and the green woman's shriek was stilled.

When the great reptile emerged beneath a low ceiling of cloud, Averan saw the green woman at once.

She'd dropped into an orchard, among a trio of crabapple trees. One tree had snapped under the impact, a slash of white where its uppermost branches had ripped away.

The graak glided over the orchard. Averan's mind seemed to go numb as she urged Leatherneck to the ground. The great reptile flapped his wings, and Averan leapt to the ground almost before the beast touched down.

In seconds she was at the green woman's side.

The woman lay slightly askew, her right hand over her head, her legs spread. She'd impacted so hard onto the moist ground that her body now rested in a mild depression.

Averan could see no overt sign of broken bones. Nothing poked through the green woman's flesh. Yet she saw blood, so dark green and oily it was almost black, smeared across the woman's left breast.

Averan had seldom seen a naked woman – had never seen one like this. The green woman was not merely handsome; she was beautiful, unearthly, like some fine Runelord's lady, gifted with so many endowments of glamour that a common woman could only look at such a creature and despair.

Yet even with the perfect features of her face, her flawless skin, the green woman was obviously not human. Her long fingers ended in claws that looked as sharp as fishhooks. Her mouth, faintly open, dribbled green blood and showed canines longer than those on a bear. Her ears were ... somehow wrong. They were dainty and graceful, yet tilted forward a bit, like the ears of a doe.

The green woman was not breathing.

Averan put her head to the woman's chest, listened for a heartbeat. She heard it, beating softly, deeply, as if the green woman rested in slumber.

Averan felt the green woman's arms and legs, searching for wounds. She wiped away some green blood near the woman's neck, found what looked like a puncture wound from the woman's own nails. Wiping away the blood from the woman's lips, she checked in her mouth.

She'd bitten her tongue in the fall, and it was bleeding badly. Averan twisted the woman's head to the side, afraid that the blood flowing freely into her throat might choke her.

The green woman growled, low in her throat, like a dog disturbed by dreams of the hunt.

Averan suddenly leapt back, afraid for the first time that this woman might be some animal. Feral. Deadly.

A dog began baying.

Averan looked up.

She was at the edge of a farm. A cottage stood not far off, a hut made of fieldstones and covered with a roof of thatch.

A fierce wolfhound barked by the edge of the rail fence, but dared not approach the graak. For its part, the graak merely studied the dog hungrily, as if it hoped the hound would lunge.

The green woman opened her eyes to slits, and grasped Averan's throat.

Averan fought to scream.

9

THE RESCUE

Roland and Baron Poll had been riding hard all day, having traveled at a pace that would kill a normal horse, when they heard the snarling and yelping of a hound, accompanied by a child's scream.

They had just rounded past a village near the base of the Brace Mountains and Roland's horse had slowed, winded. The sky was overcast, and with the hills so close, the night's shadows were already beginning to thicken.

When Roland heard the shriek, he was nearing a small farm with an orchard of woodpear and crabapple trees behind it.

A quick glance showed him a graak in the orchard, lunging and snapping at a huge wolfhound, while under the shade of a tree, a girl was shrieking in terror.

'By the Powers, it's a wild graak!' Baron Poll shouted, spurring his charger. Wild graaks often attacked peasants' animals out here, so close to the mountains. Yet it was rarer for them to eat humans.

Roland's heart raced.

Baron Poll reached behind him, drew his horseman's axe, and spurred his mount past the cottage, frightening some nervous ducklings that milled about by the cottage door. Then his horse jumped the rail fence. The hound, emboldened by Baron Poll's presence, leapt after him and charged toward the graak.

Roland's horse suddenly leapt over the fence, and Roland realized that he too had charged the graak without thought.

He reached into his tunic for his half-sword, though it would do little good against such a large lizard.

The whole world seemed to narrow to that moment. Roland could hear the child shrieking farther back in the orchard, could see the great beast rise up and spread its wings. Baron Poll's charger reared back and pawed the air.

It was an old lizard, by the look of it, huge. Teeth like daggers, its golden eyes blazing.

The hound leapt in at it, and the graak snapped down, catching the hound in its long jaws. It gave the dog a vicious shake, snapping its bones.

At that moment, while the lizard was distracted, Baron Poll raised the axe in both hands and hurled with all his might, catching the reptile cleanly between the eyes.

'Hah, take that, foul creature!' the Baron shouted as if in parody of some great hero.

The graak jerked back its head, as if stricken by surprise. Blood welled from the horrible blow that Baron Poll had dealt. The graak batted its wings once, then pitched to the side and collapsed.

Roland sat in his saddle for half a second, feeling exuberantly victorious, stupidly clutching his own sword.

Still, the child screamed.

As the body of the graak settled to the ground, Roland saw the child better, for she'd been momentarily hidden behind its wings – a girl of seven or eight years kneeling beside the trees. The girl had half turned toward him. Piercing green eyes and wavy hair, the same red as Roland's.

She wore a hooded cloak of midnight-blue with the king's coat of arms on it – the image of the green man, a face circled by oak leaves. Above it a graak was sewn in red.

A skyrider. The blood drained from Roland's face. We've killed a mount for the king's messenger, he realized. All the gold he had would never repay the new King.

The child screamed again, and Roland realized something else. The crabapple tree that the child sat beneath was broken, as if struck by a bolt of lightning. And in the tall brown grass beneath the tree was something green.

One of its claws was hooked in the skyrider's cloak.

The child had not been attacked by a graak at all. Something else had her in its grip.

'Helllp!' the child wailed.

Roland rushed forward a few paces for a better look, suddenly cautious, until he had a full view of the green woman lying there in a pool of blood of the deepest green.

He had never seen anything like this monster. The green woman was beautiful and strange beyond anything that Roland had imagined. She held the child's robe firmly in her claws, merely held it, staring at the sigil emblazoned on the girl's chest. Mesmerized, she moved the girl this way and that, gazing at the colored threads that made up the image of the green man.

Roland felt confused. 'Get away from that thing, child,' he whispered. 'Stop screaming, and let the beast have your robe.'

The girl turned to him, her face an ashen white. She quit screaming but began to whimper as she shrugged out of the robe, tried to disentangle herself.

Meanwhile, Baron Poll had dismounted, and came huffing toward them, having recovered his axe.

Roland leapt from his own horse, sword at the ready.

The green woman almost did not notice the two men, until the girl tried to move back. Then it lashed out and grasped her forearm, studied her from eyes as dark green as her own blood.

'Let her go!' Roland shouted, stepping forward, brandishing the half-sword. Baron Poll stepped up beside him.

The green woman turned on them, stared at Roland and through him. She tossed the child aside like a rag doll, then rose to a crouch, sniffing the air like some animal, her small breasts swaying as she shifted from side to side. She caught a scent, stared fixedly at Baron Poll.

Roland's heart was pounding in fear.

'That's right,' Baron Poll said. 'I'm the one you're after. I'm the one you want. You smell blood? You want some? Come and get it.'

The green woman leapt at Poll, covered sixty feet in three
bounds. Roland prepared for her charge. He set his feet, raised
his sword, and timed his swing so that it would lop off the
green woman's head.

With a mighty shout he whirled the blade, just as the green
woman reached Baron Poll.

Roland threw his full weight into the blow, brought the
sword down on the green woman's neck, and felt as if he'd
struck the blade against stone. The blade clanged into her,
bounced off her neck and slapped Roland's left wrist.

The pain of it stung him, left his sword arm throbbing.

Then the green woman had Baron Poll. He'd fallen backward, too astonished to swing, and she crouched over him,
grasping the handle of his axe.

Baron Poll struggled to move the blade from side to side, but
even with his endowments of brawn, he could hardly budge it.

She held the axe, studying it. She sniffed the graak's blood,
then with a long sensual tongue, experimentally licked the
gore from the blade.

Roland fell back a pace as the monster closed her eyes,
relishing the taste of blood.

The girl child was still whimpering. Blood pounded in
Roland's ears and sweat poured down the front of his tunic.

It seemed obvious that the green woman craved blood as
a drowning man craves his next breath.

'By the Powers, get her away from me!' Baron Poll said,
grunting in terror. He held the axe, tried to tear it away, as
the green woman began to lick the blade clean.

Roland had never seen anything like this, had never heard
of anything like this green woman. She had to be a summoned
being, perhaps some fell monster drawn from the netherworld.
Dark-green blood flowed from a couple of small wounds.
Green, like green flames, he thought.

Nearby, the king's skyrider still whimpered. Roland called
to her softly, 'Get out of here, child. Walk slowly. Do not run.'
He backed away himself, knowing that he could be of no use
to Baron Poll.

The green woman stopped licking the axe blade, turned and watched Roland, then repeated in a soft voice, matching his every tone and inflection, 'Get out of here, child. Walk slowly. Do not run.'

Roland did not know if the beast sought to command him or was merely repeating his words. He backed away a step, his feet crunching in the dry brown grass. A twig snapped beneath his heel.

The green woman licked the axe blade and shouted at Baron Poll, 'I'm the one you're after. I'm the one you want. You smell blood? You want some? Come and get it.'

Baron Poll nodded as she licked the blade clean, let the axe go in her hand. 'Blood,' he whispered. 'Blood.'

The green woman stopped licking, stared at him. 'Blood,' she said, running her tongue over the blade. 'Blood.'

Roland had backed up a dozen paces by now, wondered if he should turn and run. You never run from a dog, he knew, or a bear. The movement of your legs only enticed the animals. He decided that he should not run from the green woman, either.

He backed away and turned. In half a heartbeat, the green woman pounced, caught him from behind.

'Blood!' she said, hefting him in the air. She sniffed his wrist, where he had scraped himself only moments before, inhaled deeply the scent of his blood.

'No!' he cried as she set him down, shoved him onto his side. Dirt entered his mouth, and he smelled the bitter scent of wild carrots, the fragrant mold upon the wild barley that grew about.

Then there was a burning pain as the green woman shoved one long claw into his wrist. He struggled to escape, tried to kick at her face. She held him, ran her tongue over his left wrist, savoring his life's blood.

He kicked her ankles. Though she looked delicate as a dancer, every muscle in those legs seemed to be a cord of steel. His struggling availed him nothing. She held him tighter, crushing his arm.

He gasped in pain.

The green woman sucked at his wound, pulling out his vital juices with a soft slurping sound. He cried out, fought for his very life, fearing that at any moment she would bite into his throat.

'Help!' Roland shouted, looking for Baron Poll. But the fat knight had gotten up shakily, and stared at Roland in helpless horror.

By the Powers, he thought. Asleep for twenty years, and I wake up only to die after the first week.

Suddenly, the child raced to Baron Poll, grabbed his axe, and leapt toward them. 'No! No!' Roland cried.

The girl swung the axe blade down on the green woman, and there was a dull thud.

The green woman stopped, loosed her grip a little.

The woman stared at the child. She shouted, 'No! No!'

Then the green woman let him go completely, and Roland was free. He tried to scramble through the grass, but tripped and fell three paces off.

The green woman eyed him hungrily.

'No,' the child repeated. 'Not him.' She swung the axe down a second time, hitting the green woman in the skull.

The green woman crouched on the ground. She looked up at the child, parroted, 'No.'

The girl dropped the axe. She'd put a notch in the green woman's skin, just the barest of cuts. Dark blood oozed from it.

The child reached down and stroked the woman's hair at the front of her scalp. The green woman arched her back, as if pleased by the attention.

'When training a dangerous animal,' the girl said softly to Roland and Baron Poll, 'you must reward it for good behavior, and punish it for bad.'

Roland nodded. Of course the girl would know about the training of beasts. She was a skyrider, after all, and would have to tend the graaks.

Roland had been the king's butcher. As a child, one of his

first duties had been to carry bones and scraps of offal to the kennels, so that beast master Hamrickson could train the king's war dogs. He thought he knew what she was asking of him.

He backed off carefully, to avoid drawing the green woman's attention, then painfully limped toward the dead graak.

'No, I'll do it,' the girl said. 'She should think of me as her master.'

She hurried past him, circled the lizard. Her eyes seemed blank with pain as she looked at the reptile. Then she leaned over and pulled the hound's carcass from its jaws. It was not a small feat. The wolfhound was a huge dog that easily weighed a hundred pounds, yet the child hefted its carcass easily.

I am a fool, Roland thought. The girl is a skyrider, with at least one endowment of brawn. Despite her small size, she is stronger than I am. I had thought to save her, and instead the child saved *me*.

She brought the hound back, laid it at the feet of the green woman. 'Blood,' she whispered. 'For you.'

The green woman sniffed the hound, began licking blood from its pelt. When she seemed assured that no one would take the thing from her, she tore into the carcass and ripped into its back and haunches.

'Good girl,' the child said. 'Very good.'

The green woman looked up at the child. Blood foamed at her mouth as she parroted, 'Good girl.'

'You're a smart one, too,' the child said. She pointed to herself and whispered, 'Averan, Averan.' The green woman repeated her name. She pointed to Roland, and he gave his own name. Baron Poll finally came close, gave his own name. Then Averan pointed to the green woman.

The green woman stopped eating and stared blankly.

10

THE GEM

Tears of rage and pain threatened to blind Averan as she worked – rage and pain that came from seeing her graak dead. She didn't want to seem a child, didn't want to act like a child. But she found it nearly impossible to keep up a façade of indifference.

So after Roland and Baron Poll introduced themselves, she busied herself tending Roland's wound, moving about numbly as if in a dream. The green woman's fall from the sky, the shock of seeing Leatherneck dead, the horrors that she knew had occurred at Keep Haberd, all left her feeling dazed and wrung out. She wanted to scream.

Instead, she bit her lip and worked.

Averan knew that the wound in Roland's wrist stung like a hornet when she washed it. The wound was deep, ragged, and it bled badly. She went to a well beside the cottage for a bucket of water, then poured it over him and blotted the wound. He stifled a cry, and the green woman drew near eagerly, like a dog begging for scraps.

'No,' Averan warned the green woman. 'This one's not for you.' Baron Poll grabbed the axe. The fat knight shook it threateningly. The green woman backed off.

Roland laughed miserably. 'Thank you, child, for not feeding me to your pet.' Averan finished wiping the water away. Her lightest scrubbing had opened the wound again, and she used part of Roland's tunic as a compress, holding the wound closed.

'She's not my pet,' Averan objected, trying to hold in her own pain.

'Try telling *her* that,' Baron Poll said. 'In half an hour she'll be rolling over for you and trying to nose her way into your bed.'

Averan knew that they were right. The green woman had accepted her, had accepted her from the moment that she woke to find Averan kneeling over her. She was like a baby graak that way, new from its egg. But just because the Baron was right didn't mean she had to like him. He was the oaf who had killed Leatherneck, after all.

The green woman thinks I'm her mother, Averan realized. Averan shook her head. She didn't know what to do with the beast.

'Did you summon the creature?' Baron Poll asked.

'Summon her?' Averan asked.

'Well, it's not a natural creature, is it?' Baron Poll said, eyeing the green woman warily. 'I've never heard of its like. So it must have been summoned.'

Averan shrugged. Baron Poll's question was beyond her, beyond any of them. She knew nothing of magic, aside from what one might hear from an occasional hedge wizard. Keep Haberd had seldom entertained anyone with power.

'It's the green of fire,' Roland said. 'Flames can be green. Do you have any power over fire?'

The green woman got off her haunches, went to the dead body of Leatherneck, and began to feed. Averan winced and looked away.

'No,' Averan said mechanically. 'I sometimes light the fire in the hearth at our aerie; it's all I can do to keep one going. I'm no flameweaver.'

Averan wiped the last of the blood from Roland's wound with a corner of Roland's tunic. 'The earth can be green, too,' she said. 'As is water.' She blinked a tear from her eye.

Roland didn't answer, but Baron Poll did. 'You're right, girl, but the summoner's art is practiced by *flameweavers*, not by earth magicians or water wizards.'

'She fell from the sky,' Averan said. 'That's all I know. I saw her drop out of the air in front of me. I was above the clouds. Maybe she's a creature of the air.'

Baron Poll half turned to look down at her. 'Summoned,' he said thoughtfully, sure of himself.

Averan frowned. She had an endowment of wit, and so was a quick learner. But she was only nine years old, and she'd never studied the magical arts. 'You think I am the summoner? You're daft.'

Baron Poll was the oldest, and even Roland looked to him for counsel. He said, 'Maybe so, but I've heard it said that the Powers have their own reasons for doing what they do. Perhaps you didn't summon it; it may have been sent.'

That seemed just as unlikely. Roland's bleeding had finally stopped, and the wound looked clean enough.

Averan noticed that some of the green woman's blood was on her fingers. She dipped them in the bucket and tried to scrub the blood off, but the green stuff had already soaked into her skin, staining her hands as if she'd spilled ink, leaving irregular blotches. She supposed it would wear off.

'I'm sorry about your graak,' Baron Poll said for the third time since he'd introduced himself. 'Can you forgive me?'

Averan fought back bitter tears, Leatherneck was not *my* graak, she told herself. It was the King's, or Brand's, more than it belonged to anyone else.

Still she had fed the beast for years, had groomed it and scraped its teeth and filed its claws. She'd loved the old lizard.

She'd known he was old, that he'd only had another summer or two left, at most.

She knew that she should not blame Baron Poll for killing it. Brand had always said, 'Never punish a beast for having a good heart. Even the kindest brutes will sometimes nip you by mistake.'

The same was true with men, she supposed. Even fat old knights who should have known better. Tears flooded her eyes.

'It is forgotten, Sir Paunch,' Averan said, trying to make light of it, trying to keep the pain from her voice.

'Go ahead, child, hurl insults if it will make you feel better,' the old knight said. 'You can do better than that!'

Averan wanted to hold her tongue, but it hurt too much to keep the pain in. Still, she dared not be too rude to a lord. 'If it pleases you, Sir Breadbasket, Sir Greasebarrel, Sir Broadbutt.'

'That's better, child,' Poll said with a sullen expression.

'Though he is a baron,' Roland corrected the girl, 'and should more properly be called *Baron* Broadbutt.'

Averan smiled weakly, sniffed and wiped her tears away, satisfied with the name-calling, at least for now.

Baron Poll asked, 'Where were you going? Are you carrying an important message?'

Averan considered. It was the most important message that she'd ever carried: news of an impending invasion. 'Paldane has heard by now,' Averan said truthfully. 'Reavers were coming down to Keep Haberd from the mountains. By now, Haberd has fallen. I was to bear a message to Duke Paldane, but riders on force horses were also sent. Master Brand had me fly out only to save my life.'

'We found your messenger,' Baron Poll said, 'earlier today. He'd had a bad fall, so I suppose that Paldane has yet to learn your news. 'Tis bitter tidings these days. The King dead, Raj Ahten advancing on Carris – all of it! Now the reavers.'

'We're going north to Heredon,' Roland said as he sat up. 'We'll bear your news to Paldane in Carris – and then to the King, too.'

Baron Poll added, 'We can drop you off in Carris.'

She remembered Brand's warning that she should head north for safety. 'I don't want to go to Carris,' she said. 'I'm going to Heredon, with you!'

'Heredon?' Baron Poll said. 'I don't think so. It's bound to be a dangerous trip, what with Raj Ahten on the move. There's no need for you to go. We'll carry the message.'

'I know the way to Heredon,' Averan offered. 'I know the roads, and the mountains, and I know faster ways for a man on a good horse to travel. I could guide you.'

'Have you flown there?' Baron Poll asked.

'Yes, twice,' Averan lied. She'd seen the maps, memorized the lay of the land. But she'd never even flown as far as Fleeds.

The men looked at one another meaningfully. They could use a guide.

'No, we've only got two horses,' Roland said. 'We'll drop you off somewhere safe.'

'I could ride with you,' Averan said to Roland. Given Baron Poll's stomach, she could not sit double with him on a horse. 'I'm small, and I've an endowment of strength and stamina. If your horse tires, I can get down and run.'

This was important, she knew. She wanted to get to Heredon now; she had an unreasoned and unreasonable craving to do so. Her message to Paldane was important, but her need was even more compelling. Her whole body shook with the desire. In fact, she knew almost exactly where she wanted to go. She closed her eyes, and recalled the maps: In the middle of Heredon, almost nine hundred miles north of here, beyond the Durkin Hills. Castle Sylvarresta. In her mind's eye, she saw something that resembled a green glowing gem.

'Do you have family in Heredon?' Baron Poll asked.

'No,' she admitted. 'Not really.' Yet it was important that she get there.

'Then why are you so determined to go?' Roland asked.

Averan knew that because she was small, because she was a child, others expected her to act like a child, prone to tantrums and unreasonable fits. But Averan was not like other children; she never had been. Brand had said that he chose her from among all of the orphans in Mystarria because when he looked in her eyes, he saw an old woman there. During her short life, she had lived more than others had.

'That is where I was heading,' she lied, 'after I gave Duke Paldane the message. My master Brand has a sister there at Castle Sylvarresta. He hoped she would take me in. He gave me a letter for her, and money for my keep.' She jingled the purse tied to her belt.

Roland did not ask to see the letter. Words on paper were

obviously above him. And Baron Poll was a lazy man. He didn't want to bother reading letters. Averan hoped that the lure of money might hook them.

'And what of your pet?' Baron Poll asked, nodding toward the green woman. 'Will she follow us, do you think?'

'We'll leave her,' Averan answered, though something inside warned against it. What if Baron Poll was right? What if one of the Powers had summoned the creature for her? It would be wasteful to abandon it, perhaps even dangerous. Still, Averan did not see how they could bring the creature with them.

Baron Poll considered thoughtfully. In a tone that brooked no argument, he said, 'We dare not take you far. I'll drop you off somewhere safe, north of Carris if you like. I've got a cousin in a small town north of there. She could help arrange for your care.'

Averan was used to dealing with lords. They were often inconsiderate and never liked being told that they were wrong. Baron Poll's tone warned her that she could expect nothing better from him.

But in her heart she vowed, If you leave me, I'll run behind you if I must, and follow you every step of the way.

Averan ran and fetched Roland's piebald filly, along with Baron Poll's dun stallion, and they prepared to depart. The sun had nearly set, yet the owner of the cottage had still not come home.

Baron Poll picked a few woodpears and crabapples from the small orchard, then grabbed some turnips and onions from a garden behind the cottage. A few scrawny ducks, hatched in the past eight weeks, waddled around the front of the house. Baron Poll left them.

Averan wondered who might live here. An old woodcutter she imagined, for the orchard was too small to provide a living for even one person and the hills were wooded to the south. She wondered what he would think when he discovered his dog dead, and a graak lying beside it in his backyard. She opened the purse that Brand had given her, found that it contained not only some northern coins, but also a couple of golden trade rings like those used by merchants from Indhopal. The rings were as precisely weighted as any coin, and were struck with the symbols of Muyyatin, but could be worn on the fingers or toes, or on a string about the neck, and therefore were not as easily lost as a northern coin.

After selecting a single piece of silver, Averan laid it atop the body of the dog.

Then she sat before Roland on his mount, and she and Baron Poll and Roland raced away from the cottage, up a winding road toward the forests of the Brace Mountains.

When they left the cottage, the green woman was still feeding on Leatherneck's corpse. She did not even look up, except to cast an unconcerned glance in Averan's direction.

A mile farther on, the road began to climb the hills in earnest. The highway was lined with alders, their leaves going golden in the early autumn. Higher up, a few pines also marched along the hill.

The road here became a lonely place, the hillside windswept. In some places, boulders had rolled down the mountain and blocked parts of the road, so that Roland maneuvered the horse around them. This highway had been well tended a dozen years ago, but the bandits in these hills were so thick that the king's men didn't bother to maintain the trail any longer.

It was an hour after sunset, and Bessahan had been riding hard all afternoon, trying to catch the king's messengers. But his horse had thrown a shoe in the woods, and he'd had to stop and fix it, wasting nearly an hour.

Bessahan found the graak by the roadside almost by chance. Near a cottage beside the road, a hefty woman stood with a battered lantern, staring at the dead reptile in her orchard. The lantern was hooded with a cloudy ceramic that did not let out much light. In the darkness, the woman mistook Bessahan for someone else.

'Eh, Koby, is that you?'

Bessahan had a limited command of the Rofehavanish tongue. He dared not let her hear his accent, so he merely grunted in return.

'Did you see this? Someone killed this graak right here by the house, split its head clean open. There's tracks here from a pair of horses. Was it you who did it?'

Bessahan shook his head no.

'And the damned monster killed my dog, too.' The fat woman shook her head in disgust. She was an old thing with stringy hair and a greasy apron. Bessahan had taken endowments of scent from two dogs. He could smell lye soap on her, even at fifty paces. A dirty woman who washed clothes for others.

'Whoever killed it did me no favors,' the old woman groaned. 'If they'd have said to me, "Kitty, you want us to kill that monster in your backyard?" I'd have answered, "No. You leave it alone. Killing it won't bring Dog back to life – and you can let it have my worthless ducks, too." But would anyone ever listen to me? Nooo!'

Bessahan's opinion of the woman lowered even more. She was not only fat and greasy, she talked much while thinking little.

'Well,' she asked, 'will you help me get rid of it? The carcass will only draw wolves. In fact, it looks as if one has already been after it. It's all ripped apart.'

Bessahan looked up the road. The messengers had probably gone that way, into the mountains, into the dark. But night was falling, and he wondered if they would risk the mountain trails by night. No, it would be wiser to stay nearby. They could be camped anywhere – in the orchard, up the hill.

And rain was coming. He could smell it on the wind. It might be hard to track them by scent.

He rode his horse up to the old woman in the dim lamplight. She looked up at him through hooded eyes, suddenly wary.

'Hey, you're not Koby!' she accused.

'No, I am sorry,' Bessahan answered in his thick accent. 'I am not your Koby. My name is Bessahan.'

'What are you doing here?' she asked, backing up a step, suddenly defensive.

'I am searching for the men who killed the graak,' Bessahan answered.

'What for?' the old woman demanded. Bessahan let his horse step closer.

'Bessahan?' she asked, suddenly frightened. 'What kind of name is that!'

She had obviously not seen the men, had no further information of any value. So he told her the truth.

'It is not a name, so much as a title. In my country, my name means "Hunter of Men."'

The old woman put her hand on her mouth, as if to keep from crying out.

Bessahan leaned over quickly, grabbed the old woman by the hair with his right hand, and drew his khivar, a long-bladed assassin's knife, with his left.

He slashed hard with his knife, so that the blade snicked through bone, and the old woman's body tumbled into the dry grass at his horse's feet. He cut off a single ear, then tossed her head beside the body.

She had died without a cry.

Bessahan put the ear in a coin pouch, then leapt from his horse and picked up the lantern. He cleaned his blade and circled the carcass of the graak. He caught the scent of a young man in a cotton tunic, and an old man whose sweat was more like a boar's scent. All of these northerners ate too much cheese and drank too much ale. Their very skin smelled bad to Bessahan, like curdled milk. And they were dirty besides.

But he smelled something else – a girl's scent on the beast's neck. This was no wild graak, he suddenly realized. He held the lantern near, saw where the scales of the graak's neck had been polished smooth by young legs there near the base of the beast's shoulders. A skyrider had been on that beast!

So, she had joined with the king's messengers.

The prints of hooves near the graak's carcass showed that two mounts had indeed headed north on horseback.

Bessahan removed the hood from the lantern, then blew out the wick and left it on the grass. He preferred that the old woman's body not be found until morning.

In the darkness, he stretched his back and looked up. A ragged hole in the clouds showed stars gleaming like a thousand diamonds in a perfect sky.

A beautiful night, with just a touch of cold. On such a night back home, he would have taken a pair of girls to his room to keep him warm. He had been without a woman for too long.

He let the hood fall back from over his head, shook his long dark hair out in the starlight, and sniffed the air in consternation.

He smelled something odd, something . . . unlike anything he had ever encountered. Rich, earthy. Like freshly turned soil or like moss − yet sweeter.

I am in a northern forest, he reminded himself, far from home. Of course there are plants here that I have never smelled before.

Yet something bothered him. He could sniff the air, taste the scent, but he could not locate the source of the smell itself. It was as if some strange animal had passed this way.

Bessahan got on his mount and rode into the night.

11

POLISHED STONES

Iome and Gaborn stood atop the King's Keep, gazing down on the fields below Castle Sylvarresta. It was the last evening of Hostenfest, and the great feast was over, though Gaborn had not eaten a handful of food all day. Now, by tradition, was a time of song.

For a thousand years or more, the end of Hostenfest had been celebrated in song as families gathered round the hearth and cast handfuls of fragrant dried leaves and flower petals upon the fire – rose and jasmine, lavender or mint.

Then they had sung together, in hope of the new King.

Two hundred thousand tents and pavilions covered the fields before Castle Sylvarresta, and each one shone from the lanterns within it, so that the light shining through made the edifices glow in colors of gold and silver, iridescent blues and vivid greens. Moreover, the people of Heredon stood before their tents and held aloft small oil lamps. The essence of flower petals filled the air, and the light of the lamps reflected from their faces.

Every kind of man stood upon that field: lords and ladies in their finery, peasant farmers by the drab hundreds of thousands, scholars and fools, minstrels and laborers, whores and healers, merchants and huntsmen. The sick, the healthy, the lame, the dying. The astonished, the joyous, the skeptical, the true believers, the terrified.

The people were giddy and wild-eyed. It was the last day of Hostenfest, the celebration of the Earth King. The people celebrated, but even in their celebration there was an undertone of terror.

Together the people sang an ancient hymn.

'Lord of the Forest, Master of the Field,
To whom each knee must bow and heart must yield,
Great shall be my joy when thy reign has come.
Gather me when you bring the harvest home.

'We'll stand together when the darkness falls
Shoulder to shoulder on the castle walls.
I'll lend thee my sword, if you'll be my shield,
Lord of the Forest, Master of the Field.'

As the people sang, Iome looked down in wonder, for beside the opalescent lights shining from the pavilions and lamps around the castle, a strange sapphire light glowed in the moat.

The great sturgeons swam wildly, drawing runes of protection about the castle, as if they too offered support to the Earth King.

When the song ended, horns began to trumpet upon the walls of Castle Sylvarresta and throughout the vast horde. Hundreds of thousands of voices united in shouting, 'All hail the new Earth King! All hail the Earth King.'

Their voices echoed among the hills and reverberated from the castle walls. Men, women, and children raised their fists as they cried out in wonder. Many an animal bucked wildly at the shouting and began to run through the camps. A throng of at least five hundred thousand people began racing forward to kneel with their weapons proffered in support of Gaborn. Men shouted and women cried, the horns kept blaring. Upon the castle walls boys wildly waved the banners of Sylvarresta.

Iome had never imagined such a noise or tumult. A chill coursed down her spine.

This is only the beginning, Iome realized. People remember the legends. Every man, woman, and child who desires to live knows that he must serve the Earth King, gain his protection.

Millions upon millions of people are coming. The whole world will gather here.

Thus Gaborn Val Orden stood on the walls of Castle Sylvarresta in triumph.

Iome looked to his face to see his reaction. Gaborn stood rigid, and peered to the south as if listening to a distant trumpet.

Iome looked off at the edge of the forest, could see nothing beyond the dark trees. Yet Gaborn trembled as he gazed beyond the southern hills with a faraway look in his eye.

'What's wrong?' Iome asked.

He breathed heavily. 'Iome, I feel a warning like never before! The Earth's warning. The fields here are black. My death is coming! The death of us all is coming!'

'What do you mean?' Iome asked.

'We must prepare to flee,' he said. He offered no further explanation. Instead he gripped her hand as he turned and raced from the top of the King's Tower, through the open hatch, down the stairs, descending six stories until he reached the old cellars where no man had lived in Iome's lifetime.

Gaborn's and Iome's Days raced to keep up.

Iome was vaguely aware that the Earth Warden Binnesman had converted this dirty hole into his den, since Raj Ahten's flameweavers had burned his cottage in the garden, but when Gaborn threw open the door, she was not at all prepared for what she saw.

The wizard Binnesman stood in the cellar, whose scent of mildew, sulfur, and ash was made tolerable only by the bundles of herbs tied to the rafters. Binnesman had no candles or lamps of any kind lit in that room. Yet half-buried in the dirt on the floor lay a Seer's Stone. It was an enormous round stone, a polished agate of purest white. Other, smaller crystals were laid around it, pointing inward toward this vast stone, and the wizard had drawn magic runes in the dirt around the entire assembly. The crystals and the great polished agate were all glowing with their own light.

Binnesman stood leaning on his staff and staring down at

the glowing stone, watching an image. As Iome looked at the stone, she could see four mountains spouting smoke and ash and fire. Distantly thunder rumbled, seeming to shake the floor beneath her. The stone reavealed an image of volcanoes erupting.

Or at least that is what she thought at first. For these were not common volcanoes. Instead, they were but small domes, where lava gushed like water, and reavers by the tens of thousands boiled out of the ground.

Nor did the Seer's Stone convey the image alone. Iome realized that the odor of sulfur and ash in the air issued from the stone, and the heat radiated by the Seer's Stone warmed the room like a baker's oven. Indeed, she could smell and feel and hear and see everything, just as if she were watching the volcanoes from afar.

Yet Iome had never heard that Binnesman dabbled with Seer's Stones. In fact, he'd denied ever having done so when confronted by Raj Ahten.

Iome stared at the image in the stone, astonished.

'Reavers have surfaced in North Crowthen,' the wizard said matter-of-factly. 'Others are coming to ground farther south, along the Alcair Mountains. Your keep at Haberd is toppled. Raj Ahten's defenses in Kartish are faring no better.'

Even as he said it, the whole of Castle Sylvarresta suddenly trembled as the earth shook. At first Iome thought it was a residual effect from the Seer's Stones arranged on the floor, but the wizard stared up at the walls of the castle, concerned. 'It is but a minor tremor,' the wizard said. 'The Earth is in pain.'

Iome glanced at the pair of Days who had taken sanctuary in the dark corner behind her. With their minds paired to those of their fellows, they knew more about the affairs of the earth than anyone in this room, including the wizard Binnesman. What she saw worried her. Gaborn's Days stared at the scene in horror, mouth gaping.

'What is Raj Ahten doing, attacking me at a time like this?' Gaborn demanded. 'Does he even know the danger?'

'I doubt that he sees the calamity yet,' the wizard answered. 'Last I saw, his troops were marching toward Carris, it seemed. At least, they were a few hours ago.'

'Where are they now?' Gaborn asked.

Binnesman bowed his head and closed his eyes, as if too weary to continue. Ever since he'd raised his wylde and lost it, he'd suffered from fatigue. 'It has been a long day. But I'll try.'

The wizard reached down to the dirt floor and rubbed fresh soil upon his palms and on his face. Then he picked up a few crystals, moved them about the edge of the Seer's Stone, pulling some back, moving others left or right, his face a study in concentration.

The process took several minutes, for the wizard had first to locate Raj Ahten's troops, as if seen from a distant mountain, then progressively move to better vantage points.

Yet what Iome eventually saw made the hair stand up on her arms: Raj Ahten's troops were massed about a village, a hundred stone houses with thatch roofs. A low wall of stone surrounded the village, one that a knight mounted on a good force horse could easily overlap.

There were no watchmen on the walls, no distant sound of barking dogs. It appeared that the settlement was unaware of the approaching threat.

'I know that place,' Gaborn said. 'That is the village of Twynhaven.'

The frowth giants in Raj Ahten's army raised their muzzles and sniffed the air hungrily, as if trying to catch the scent of fresh blood. The knights in the retinue held their lances and war axes ready.

But it was Raj Ahten's sorcerers who took the lead.

Three flameweavers spread out in a line, just outside the village wall, and began to chant, soft and reedy. Iome could hear them plainly, yet she could not make out their words, for their chant was a song of fire and consumption, the flickering sounds of flames, the crackle of a log.

Around each of them, grass and bushes suddenly erupted.

Green flames shot skyward, and the flameweavers were engulfed. Iome smelled ash, felt the heat of their flame. They began stalking toward the village, climbed the low stone wall.

Suddenly, the dogs in the town caught sight of them and several began to bay. A horse whinnied nervously.

Still, no voice was raised in alarm.

The flameweavers leapt over the wall, and by now the fires behind them had grown substantial, so that Iome watched the sorcerers from beyond a screen of flame.

Around the village wall, the late summer sun had bleached the grass, sucked all the moisture from it. The flameweaver to the far left pointed to his left, and a tendril of flame shot from his hand and raced around the wall faster than a good horse could run. The flameweaver to the right did the same. In seconds, the two bolts of flame met at the far end of the hamlet, and it was circled in fire.

Then the fire leapt skyward and began to rush toward the center of the circle.

A woman screamed and ran from her house at the edge of the village, gaping in dismay. Others began to follow her from their homes – children and mothers. Some horses knocked down a corral, raced round the settlement, bucking wildly.

The flameweavers advanced on the village now. The rising inferno was feeding them, giving them energy. One flameweaver pointed at a large barn, and the thatch of its roof caught fire, seemed almost to explode.

Seconds later, one of his fellows approached a house, sent a rope of flame twisting toward it, so that its roof and all its timbers inside were consumed at once. The heat of it fairly smote Iome.

People screamed within the house, and a burly townsman raced from it, his hair and clothes afire. A woman and her son raced out, the boy bearing a shield. His armor and his eyes reflected the flames. Firelit smoke made the scene bright.

The smell of smoke came strong to Iome's nostrils.

The whole town suddenly erupted into an inferno, and the flames whirled high into the air, a hundred, two hundred yards. The flameweavers began chanting louder as they walked into that inferno, and they themselves became glowing worms of light, writhing beside the townspeople who died.

'They're sacrificing those people to the Power they serve,' Binnesman said in horror, and the wizard turned away from his Seer's Stone. 'This is a black summoning.'

'This is the source of my terror,' Gaborn said.

The flames encompassing the village slowly turned green, the several fires within it coalescing into some strange wonderland of otherworldly shadows. Within moments, the rock walls of the cottages and the stone fences all began to dissolve into molten puddles.

It happened quickly, Iome thought. The settlement was soon leveled; the bones of every carcass, both of man and animal, were licked clean by flames.

It did not take the normal hours of teasing and coaxing that Iome thought would be required to perform a summoning. Perhaps the sacrifice strengthened the flameweavers' spell. The flameweavers sang and danced like living flames.

Within an hour, a green glowing portal appeared on the ground, and the flameweavers stood before it, calling in the tongues of flames and ashes.

Nothing came forth, until one flameweaver walked to the portal and disappeared into the netherworld.

Almost instantly, the flames around the hamlet diminished, puffed out into utter blackness. Only an occasional coal in the blackness still burned.

For a long moment, Iome held her breath, believing that a flameweaver had died, that he'd disappeared into the netherworld, never to return.

Then, among the ashes, she saw two forms take shape, writhing like wrestlers, she thought at first. But no, she decided, they were writhing like men who have struggled to crawl the last few yards of a long and difficult journey.

One was the dark shape of the flameweaver, half covered with ashes.

Beside him was a larger form, like that of a dark man with

a shaggy mane of long curly hair. But he glowed with a pure blue light, as if he were made of crystal. Flames rippled and played on his flesh.

The lumbering fellow staggered to his feet, and fanned wide his resplendent wings. Lightning seemed to flicker across his brow, and it glowed fiercely in his eyes.

Everywhere, among the ranks of Raj Ahten's troops, hardened soldiers cried out in astonishment, while war dogs backed away and snarled in terror.

'By the Powers,' Gaborn said, 'he's summoned a Glory!'

But what kind of Glory? Iome wondered. For in the ages past, it was said that at the battle of Vaderlee's Gorge, the Earth King Erden Geboren once fought with one Glory on his right hand and another on his left. They were said to be irrepressible opponents. She'd thought them to be the beneficiaries of mankind.

Yet this youth had a fell look in his eye as he wrapped his wings about his shoulders, and the light streaming from him became the blackest abyss.

'Do not be misled,' Binnesman said. 'He is not like the Glories revered in ancient tales. He is a Darkling Glory. This creature comes to slay an Earth King, not to save one.'

'How soon?' Gaborn asked. 'When will it come?' Binnesman went to a small table and retrieved a large tome, an illuminated manuscript that depicted various creatures of the earth. He flipped through his bestiary, to the pages that dealt with creatures of the netherworld. The notations for a Darkling Glory were scant, and lacked even a crude drawing. Obviously, even among the wise, this beast was the stuff of mere legend. 'It is a creature of air and darkness,' Binnesman said. 'It will fly to you, and most likely it will wait to attack until night. I think it is too far away to reach us today. But tomorrow night, or the night after, it will surely come.'

'What should I do?' Gaborn asked.

Binnesman didn't answer, merely frowned as he read the entry on Darkling Glories. Iome realized that he had no answer.

'That fool, Raj Ahten,' the wizard muttered, 'to loose such a monster now.'

Binnesman knelt by his crystals, nudged one a hairsbreadth, and shifted his view so that he could better see Raj Ahten's army.

For a long moment he stared, then he spoke to Gaborn. 'I don't see Raj Ahten himself. Where could he be?'

Gaborn studied the image, too. 'It's dark there. Maybe he's in the shadows, near the rear.'

'No,' Binnesman said. 'He would be at the forefront, to greet his new ambassador. He's gone. He's split off from his main army for some reason.'

'But why?' Gaborn asked. 'Can you find him?'

Binnesman shook his head and frowned. 'I doubt it. An army, a volcano – these are easy to spot. But one man, riding in the night? It could take me days, and I'm at the end of my strength.'

Binnesman turned away from the Seer's Stone, and the image faded altogether, though the glowing crystals still provided some small light for the room. In that light, he looked ill-used. Only a week before, his robes had been green, the color of leaves in high summer. But then he'd tried to summon a wylde, a creature of the Earth that would strengthen his powers. Unfortunately, the wylde had been lost, and Binnesman was now weary and weakened.

'I have been studying the volcanoes,' he said glumly, 'trying to figure out the reavers' plan of attack.

'I must admit that it makes little sense to me. The reavers are surfacing in places that are far apart from one another, and most of them are far from any human habitation.

'But one thing I have noticed. They arise in places where there is already an old volcano nearby, or regions filled with hot springs or geysers.'

'Which means?' Gaborn asked.

'There is a realm of fire at the heart of the earth,' Binnesman said, 'as I saw when I travelled to the Idymean Sea.

'I think,' Binnesman continued, 'that in some places, this realm of fire comes closer to the earth's surface than in others. That is where hot springs form, and volcanoes arise. Now I wonder if perhaps the heat is driving the reavers to the surface.'

Gaborn changed the subject. 'It is of more immediate concern that Raj Ahten is preparing to attack Mystarria in earnest. I'll need to convene a council with my war leaders.'

'War with Raj Ahten?' Binnesman asked. 'Are you *sure* that is wise, with so many reavers surfacing?'

Gaborn sighed heavily. 'No. But if I do not at least give some sign that I will fight him, Raj Ahten may do more damage. I can only hope that once he learns of the damage in his own lands he will retreat to Indhopal and look after his own defense. I may even be able to negotiate a truce.'

The wizard studied Gaborn thoughtfully. 'You may try to reclaim Raj Ahten if you want,' Binnesman said. 'But I don't know if even *you* can save him. Remember that I cursed him a week ago. Such curses take time to reach their full effect, but I suspect that now you cannot help him.'

'For the sake of my people, I must try,' Gaborn said.

Binnesman peered up at him from beneath a bushy brow. 'And for the sake of your people, I must warn you: Raj Ahten is not likely to take counsel from an enemy. You will be placing yourself in grave danger when you go before him. It may be that he is even trying to draw you into battle, for he knows that he cannot attack you here, so close to the Dunnwood, where the wights protect you.'

'I know,' Gaborn said uneasily. 'Will you come with me, then?'

'You know that I have no strength in war,' Binnesman said, 'but I may follow in a day or two and offer what help I can. As for now, I must prepare to face the Darkling Glory, and I must meet it alone.'

'You?' Gaborn asked. 'Alone, without a wylde? I can marshal fifty thousand knights to fight at your side.'

'And they would avail you nothing – merely get themselves killed,' Binnesman said.

'What weapons can you muster?' Gaborn asked.

'I . . . don't know yet,' Binnesman said. 'I'll have to think of something. As for you, convene your war council. Your men know how to fight better than I do. At dawn, warn the people to flee Castle Sylvarresta. Certainly you feel the approaching danger. And now, I must rest.'

With no more preamble than that, he staggered toward a corner and lay down in some thick loam. The loam could not have been here long, Iome realized. The floors here in the cellar were paved with a few flagstones thrown over hardened dirt. The wizard must have obtained that soil himself; Earth Wardens often administered healing soils to the sick. Iome wondered if the soil he slept in now had any special properties. He pulled handfuls of dirt close to him, and sprinkled some over him, and soon was sleeping peacefully.

Iome looked around. Now the room smelled only faintly of mildew and the clean scents of the wizard's herbs. She could feel earth power here, that strange tingling sensation she got whenever Gaborn or the wizard drew near. Only here it was stronger. Unbidden, the blessing that she'd heard so often lately from Gaborn came to mind. 'May the Earth hide you. May the Earth heal you. May the Earth make you its own.' This was a place surrounded by Earth.

'Let's go,' Gaborn said.

12

IN THE KING'S COUNCIL

Sir Borenson woke Myrrima with only a little shaking, and told her his news: Gaborn had requested her attendance at a council meeting.

'Are you certain that he wants *me*?' Myrrima asked, bewildered. She'd come after dinner to lie on the bed and had fallen asleep in her clothes. She sat up stiffly.

'I'm sure,' Borenson said.

'If he wants to know which autumn flowers will look best in the Great Hall,' Myrrima said, 'I could counsel him till dawn. But I know nothing of war.'

'Gaborn likes you,' Borenson said, somewhat at a loss himself. She had no skill at war, and Borenson suspected that Gaborn had invited Myrrima as a mere courtesy to him, so that he could spend more time with his new bride before leaving for Inkarra. But he dared not hurt his wife's feelings by telling her so. 'Did he not say when he first met you that he wanted you in his court? He respects your opinion.'

'But . . . I feel as if I'm an imposter.'

'I'm sure the King feels the same way himself,' Borenson ventured. 'A week ago, his greatest worry was whether or not to wear a feather in his cap when he came before Iome to ask for her hand. Now his father is dead, and he must plan a war. A week ago, I am sure that Iome worried most about what color thread to use in her embroidery, but she'll be at the council, too.'

'It sounds as if he has invited everyone in the kingdom to his council!' Myrrima said in surprise.

'Not everyone. Chancellor Rodderman and Jureem will attend, as will Erin Connal, King Orwynne, High Marshal Skalbairn, and Lord Ingris of Lysle.'

Frowning thoughtfully, Myrrima rose from the bed, glanced in a mirror, and began combing out her long dark hair.

Borenson felt unsure of his own place at this council. He was now, after all, a blank shield by avowal.

A few days ago, he had promised to give himself two weeks to prepare for his journey to Inkarra. He'd wanted time to say goodbye to his homeland and to his wife. He'd thought he'd have that time. But then Borenson had also believed that Raj Ahten would flee home to Indhopal for the winter. Instead, the Wolf Lord was driving south, straight into the heart of Mystarria, giving Gaborn no respite. Now Gaborn was stuck up here in Heredon, all but severed from his own realm and from his counselors.

So Borenson had not been able to bring himself to head south on his quest to Inkarra. Not while his friend still needed counsel. Though as a Knight Equitable, Borenson was free to leave, until tonight, he'd chosen to stay.

But he knew that if Gaborn rode south to Mystarria, Borenson would ride, too. And once he set his back to Heredon, and to his wife, he would not return until his quest ended.

'What of the herbalist Binnesman? Won't he be at the council?' Myrrima asked.

'He's asleep,' Borenson said, 'and cannot be disturbed.' Of all those missing from the council, Borenson wondered most about Binnesman. He'd offered to put a boot to the wizard's ribs and roust him from bed, but Gaborn had forbidden it.

'Then what of Prince Celinor,' she inquired, 'or the other merchant princes of Lysle?'

Borenson frowned. Everyone present at court these last few hours had heard how the merchant princes had come to town and set up camp, then bade Gaborn come to their pavilions and Choose them, as if he were their servant rather than the Earth King.

Borenson would have damned the lot of them, but to everyone's surprise, Gaborn had complied, Choosing several of the uppity lords.

'I suspect that the King does not fully trust Celinor,' Borenson answered. 'And though Gaborn has invited Lord Ingris, he apparently thinks that the other merchant princes would be of as much help as a gaggle of geese.'

'It seems to me that other lords could be in camp by now,' Myrrima said. 'What of North Crowthen, or Beldinook?'

'We've had no word out of North Crowthen,' Borenson said. 'The Iron King never liked Sylvarresta, and it may be that like his cousin King Anders, he has no interest in the Earth King. Or it may be that he faces problems of his own. Reavers are surfacing in North Crowthen tonight. Gaborn has already sent messengers to the Iron King, offering aid.

'As for Beldinook, King Lowicker is frail . . .' Borenson did not know what more to say. Lowicker had always been a friend to House Orden, but Borenson did not trust the man. It seemed to him that Lowicker used his frailty as an excuse for inaction whenever it came in handy. Still, Borenson parroted Gaborn's assessment of the situation. 'Lowicker had to contend with Raj Ahten marching through his lands on his way to Mystarria, after all. It is no wonder that he has not yet sent emissaries.'

When Myrrima had combed her hair, she stood for a moment studying her reflection by candlelight. She looked beautiful and desirable.

Borenson offered his hand, and escorted his wife downstairs to the Great Hall. They found Gaborn sitting in darkness at a table with his back to the wall. No candles or lamps lit the room, no fire warmed the hearth. The room had but one open window, to let in a little starlight. The rest of the windows remained shuttered.

In the darkness, King Orwynne had taken a place to Gaborn's left. Iome sat away from the table, at Gaborn's back. To Gaborn's immediate right was the popinjay Lord Ingris – a gracefully aging fellow in a tritipped maroon felt hat adorned with an enormous dyed ostrich feather. His silk blouse glowed pearl-white in the darkness, and rings and necklaces and buckles sparkled even in the wan light. Jureem sat next to him, his southern attire for once outmatched in gaudiness. Gaborn motioned for Borenson to sit next to Jureem.

Myrrima went to the back wall and seated herself beside Iome, taking the Queen's hand. Borenson watched his wife. Iome clutched Myrrima as if seeking support. The Queen's face was limned by starlight. Borenson could see from the set of her jaw that Iome was terrified.

Borenson glanced at Gaborn. In the starlight he could see the sheen of sweat on the King's brow. They're both frightened, Borenson realized. This would indeed be no ordinary council.

A few moments later, Erin Connal entered the room and took a seat at the far end of the table from Gaborn, next to Chancellor Rodderman. The Days all lined up against a wall behind the lords.

'We searched the camp for the High Marshal,' Rodderman said, 'but there's no sign of him. He's already gone.'

'I feared as much,' Gaborn said.

'You gave him little choice,' Borenson said, not bothering to hide the challenge in his tone. He thought Gaborn had been wrong to reject the High Marshal's offer of service, and by the Powers, though no one else would ever dare chastise the Earth King for his error, Borenson would not hide his feelings.

'Are we to speak here in the dark?' Lord Ingris asked in an effeminate tone, trying to head off an argument.

'Yes,' Gaborn said. 'No flames. I've had a servant extinguish even the coals of the hearth. No one must repeat what is spoken here – in daylight, or before an open flame.'

Gaborn took a deep breath. 'We are going to battle. The Earth has warned me that we are in grave danger, and tonight the Wizard Binnesman used Seer's Stones to show me our enemies. Right now, reavers are surfacing in North Crowthen.'

'What?' Lord Ingris said. 'When do we march?'

'We don't – at least not against the reavers,' Gaborn said.

'The Iron King has refused to answer any correspondence in the past week, and I do not know if he would welcome our troops in North Crowthen even now.

'Nor do I believe that King Anders will allow us to march through his realm.

'So, half an hour past, I sent Duke Mardon north to Donyeis with reinforcements, should the reavers strike in our direction, and I have sent both King Anders and the Iron King offers of aid. I shall do nothing more.'

'Then,' Lord Ingris asked, 'you think the reavers contained?'

'Not at all,' Gaborn said. 'Reavers have destroyed Keep Haberd in Mystarria. Others are in Kartish. And there may be more outbreaks still.'

In the darkness, the lords looked at one another. One swarm of reavers to the north was disquieting. But Gaborn's mention of multiple outbreaks to the south aroused solemn terror. This bespoke no isolated incident.

It bespoke the beginning of a wholesale invasion.

Borenson had heard about the outbreaks only moments before the meeting, but could hardly imagine any worse news. All his life, reavers had rarely trod the earth's surface. Yet ancient tales warned that it had not always been so, and everyone feared that someday reavers would surface by the tens of thousands.

'So we are facing a serious threat,' Gaborn continued, 'one that for the moment we can do nothing about. But there is a second threat just as dire, for while the reavers nibble at our borders, Raj Ahten strikes at our heart.

'For the past week, Raj Ahten's troops have fled south. Weariness and the Knights Equitable have taken a terrible toll on the Wolf Lord's forces. He left Fleeds with over forty thousand men. Duke Paldane's scouts estimate that Raj Ahten now has but four thousand troops marching with him – only half of which are Invincibles – along with some few archers, frowth giants, war dogs, and sorcerers.'

'It sounds as if his forces are foundering,' Lord Ingris said hopefully. 'They can't run forever.'

'It's true that Raj Ahten's men are exhausted,' Gaborn said, 'and the mounts he picked up in Fleeds are outworn. He has left behind a ghastly trail of fallen giants, war dogs, and common soldiers, all too weary to match his pace.

'Yet at the moment, Raj Ahten himself eludes us. He has left those four thousand men behind, eighty miles north of Carris. Chancellor Rodderman and I have consulted the maps, and it may be that he himself has gone to rendezvous with his troops at the fortress at Tal Dur, though he may be heading to Castle Crayden or Castle Fells.'

'He won't run to Fells,' Erin Connal said. 'I got news an hour ago. One of our scouts says that Raj Ahten's troops have all but abandoned Castle Fells. The majority of them seem to be moving toward Carris – over a hundred thousand men out of Fells alone, most of them common soldiers. Raj Ahten will join up with them. Your "Huntsman" Paldane is about to become the hunted!'

Borenson himself had warned Gaborn of this probability. He could not imagine the Wolf Lord retreating to some hill fort like Tal Dur when the mighty Castle Carris beckoned.

Horsesister Connal said, 'My mother has ordered the Bayburn Clan to take Fells back for Mystarria.'

Connal's news obviously surprised Gaborn, for Borenson heard him catch his breath.

'That is well done!' King Orwynne said, while Lord Ingris clapped his hands.

In his mind's eye, Borenson imagined how Raj Ahten's troops must be converging. Carris was the strongest fortress in western Mystarria, and of great value, but Raj Ahten had used his Voice to destroy Longmot. Perhaps now he would do the same at Carris. Borenson could only hope he did not.

'If Raj Ahten succeeds in taking Carris,' Borenson warned, 'half of Mystarria will fall this winter. We must stop him.'

Jureem folded his hands, elbows on the table, and put his fists under his pudgy chin. Speaking in his thick Taifan accent, he said to Gaborn, 'Borenson is right, but I would be cautious, O Great One. Like a wolf, Raj Ahten hopes to strike at your soft underbelly, and that underbelly is Mystarria. He hopes to draw the Earth King into battle, force him to leave the Dunnwood. He *will* attack Carris.'

Gaborn said softly, 'I know, and that fear has preyed much upon my mind. But there is one more threat that Binnesman showed me. Tonight, Raj Ahten's flameweavers summoned a Darkling Glory from the netherworld.'

Lord Ingris gasped in surprise, while the others took the news quietly. Borenson felt uncertain how to react to such news. He had heard of Glories, of course, creatures of light and goodness that inhabited the netherworld. And he knew vaguely that they had enemies, creatures of darkness with arcane powers. But he knew nothing more about them.

'We have feared assassins,' Chancellor Rodderman said. 'It seems inevitable that Raj Ahten will strike at the Earth King. Will the Darkling Glory come here?'

'No,' Jureem ventured. 'I think Raj Ahten will use it against Mystarria, against Paldane at Carris.'

'You're wrong,' Gaborn said. 'The Darkling Glory is coming. The Earth has warned me.'

'So be it.' Jureem nodded in acquiescence. 'A week ago, I knew Raj Ahten's strategies, but now the game has changed.'

'We'll need to plan our strategies, fight this creature,' King Orwynne said.

Gaborn shook his head. 'No. I'll have the people flee.'

'Then we'll notify them at once,' King Orwynne said.

Gaborn shook his head. 'If word of this leaks out tonight, there will be blind panic. The plains are dark and full of horses and oxen – and children who would be crushed under their hooves. Half the men camped out there are drunk after Hostenfest. No, as hard as it is to bear, I will wait until first light to issue the warning. The danger is profound, but still distant.'

Erin Connal abruptly asked Gaborn, 'Your Highness, can you be sure that the Darkling Glory comes for you, and not against someone else – even Fleeds?' Borenson thought her prudent to be considering her own lands first.

'After I Chose my father,' Gaborn said, 'I felt danger around him, a suffocating aura, like a black cloud. He died within hours. Ever since this morning, I have felt that aura growing around each person in this room – indeed, around everyone here at Castle Sylvarresta. For the past week, we have feared that Raj Ahten would send an accomplished assassin to our camp. Now I believe an assassin is coming, although it is something far more fell than any Invincible. And all of us here at Castle Sylvarresta are its targets. Vassals that I Chose at Longmot – and those on the road north – are in little danger. But every one among us here must be on our guard.'

'If you feel *our* danger,' Lord Ingris said, 'then can you not sense Mystarria's danger, or Lysle's? Perhaps *you* could tell us where Raj Ahten plans to strike next?'

Gaborn shook his head sadly. 'Until I see a man, I cannot Choose him. And this power is new to me. Aside from a few of my messengers who have been sent to Carris and the Courts of Tide, I haven't yet Chosen anyone in Mystarria or Lysle, so that I might gauge what is to come. We must therefore consider a plan of action, find a way to defend ourselves against Raj Ahten.'

'You should know,' Lord Ingris said, 'that other lords have already moved against Raj Ahten. Upon first hearing of the invasion of Mystarria, we merchant princes struck against him – and we are not alone.'

'How so?' King Orwynne asked.

'While you defend yourselves with arms and men,' Lord Ingris said, 'in Lysle our best defense has always been our wealth. We hire mercenaries to fortify our own borders and we pay tribute to our neighbors. Upon hearing of the attack, we sent messages to certain lords in Inkarra, offering bribes if they would send their assassins to slay Raj Ahten's Dedicates in the Southern Provinces, where he will least expect it.'

'Well done!' King Orwynne said. 'I've a thousand good force soldiers in Orwynne who can attack from the north!'

Ingris smiled broadly. 'The warlords of Toom may beat you to it, from all that I hear . . .'

Sir Borenson sat and listened in dismay. He himself had slaughtered Raj Ahten's Dedicates here in Castle Sylvarresta, in the Dedicates' Keep not two hundred yards up the road. It had been a grisly deed, one that broke his heart. Though he told himself that he had acted under orders, and it was needful, he could hardly bear to sit here and listen to more talk of such blatant butchery.

He was about to speak when Gaborn himself cried 'No!' and looked hard at Ingris and Orwynne. 'I reject such a plan!'

'Why?' Ingris asked. He pulled out a silk handkerchief from his pocket, dabbed at his nose, and tossed the soiled kerchief to the floor.

'The price is too high,' Gaborn said. 'I battle not against Raj Ahten, but *for* mankind. To send our warriors against one another is folly!'

Lord Ingris said matter-of-factly, 'The arrows have already flown. It may be that you cannot save Raj Ahten from his doom.'

Surely, Borenson thought, the man is overconfident. After all, we have been sending assassins for years. But to Borenson's surprise, Gaborn looked very distraught.

Gaborn asked, 'Tell me, when did you reach this decision, to hire assassins from Inkarra?'

Lord Ingris considered. 'It was in the afternoon, about a week ago. The day your father died.'

Gaborn stared hard at Lord Ingris. 'On that very afternoon, the wizard Binnesman cursed Raj Ahten to death. Like you, he fears that the curse cannot be recalled. I cannot help but wonder at the timing. You may have been an instrument in the Earth's hands.'

Lord Ingris chuckled as if rejecting an unearned compliment. 'I doubt it. If Raj Ahten dies, it will be *my* gold and the Inkarrans' greed that killed him, not the curse of some Earth Warden.'

From behind Gaborn's chair, Iome spoke up. 'And where did your gold come from,' she asked, 'if not from the Earth?'

In the silence that followed, Borenson had to wonder if it

was really possible for a few assassins to strike so great a blow?

He doubted it. Raj Ahten had far too many Dedicates strewn across far too vast a kingdom, and they were well guarded. Though Raj Ahten might be wounded, Borenson knew that he could not easily be killed.

Raj Ahten would have to lose certain key endowments first. If he lost stamina, for example, he might retain his strength yet still fall to a particularly nasty blow. Or if he lost metabolism, he might slow enough so that even the most mundane warrior could slice off his head.

Under the right circumstances, a few assassins *could* have a devastating impact on the Wolf Lord.

Gaborn shook his head and said, 'In good conscience, I cannot wish any man's demise. I certainly cannot condone the killing of innocent men, women, and children whose only crime is that they allowed themselves to grant an endowment to Raj Ahten. I will stand up to him if I must, but for now, I wish only to stop him – or, better yet, turn him if I can.'

'Damn your fool pardon,' King Orwynne grumbled, half rising from his chair, 'but I knew you would say that!'

'You object to our lord's wisdom?' Jureem asked.

King Orwynne's face hardened. 'Forgive me, Your Lordship,' he said, struggling to control his wrath. 'You cannot risk allowing Raj Ahten to live. It would be more than imprudent, it would be foolish.'

'I do not make this choice because it is cunning,' Gaborn said. 'I make it because I feel that it is the right thing to do.'

'You are a young man, full of noble-sounding ideals, and you have the Earth Powers to aid you,' Lord Ingris said to Gaborn. 'You may hope to turn Raj Ahten but how, may I ask, do you propose to do it?'

'I captured forty thousand forcibles at Longmot,' Gaborn said evenly.

King Orwynne, Lord Ingris, and Erin Connal all started in surprise.

'I've already used five thousand to renew Heredon's army and rebuild its cavalry,' Gaborn continued. 'The remaining

forcibles are enough to grant endowments for a small army –
or enough to create a single lord as great as Raj Ahten.

'Last week, after the battle of Longmot, I'd thought I would
do just that – become a lord equal to Raj Ahten, and then try
to best him. Like you, I want to fight.

'But I am loath to call even Raj Ahten my enemy, though
he has attacked my people. I am going to propose a truce.'

King Orwynne was flabbergasted. 'He has carried his battle
to us,' he said, speaking too loudly. 'We can't just walk away
from him.'

'He's right,' Jureem said. 'My old master will not grant you
a truce – unless you yourself were to give him an endowment. He will want your wit or your brawn, something to
cripple you so that you can never rise against him.'

'Perhaps,' Gaborn said. 'But I will propose one just the
same. I will send a messenger bearing these words: "Though
I hate my own cousin, the enemy of my cousin is *my* enemy."
By the time that message reaches him, he will have heard of
the fall of Keep Haberd, and perhaps even of his own troubles in Kartish. I will remind him of the threat of reavers, and
inform him that I am now his cousin through marriage. To
seal the peace, instead of my endowment, I will offer him
twenty thousand forcibles. He knows that without them, I
will be crippled enough. But I'll give the forcibles to him only
on the condition that he agree to leave Rofehavan.'

Borenson licked his lips. Raj Ahten was not likely to listen
to reason, but at the same time, he could hardly turn away
from twenty thousand forcibles.

'Other men have borne such appeals,' Jureem warned. 'He
will not buy what he believes he can take by force. I suspect
that he will not listen. He might even kill your messenger.'

'Perhaps,' Gaborn said. 'But what if the petition were borne
by one of his own people, one whom he loved and could not
easily dismiss?' Gaborn leaned to his right, gazing hard at
Jureem. 'Jureem, you told me a few days ago that Raj Ahten
has hundreds of wives secreted at the Palace of Concubines
in Obran. You say that no man is allowed to see them, upon

penalty of death. Which is his favorite wife? Would *she* hear my plea? Would *she* bear my petition?'

'Saffira is her name, milord,' Jureem said, stroking his goatee. 'The daughter of Emir Owatt, of Tuulistan. She is the prize of his harem.'

'I know her father by reputation. The Emir is a good man,' Gaborn said. 'Surely his daughter shares some of his goodness and strength.'

'Perhaps,' Jureem said. 'But I have never seen her. Once a wife enters the palace, she does not come out.'

'Raj Ahten is a vain man,' Iome said. 'I can think of only one reason why he would hide the women of his harem away from his own people. How many endowments of glamour has he lavished upon his favorite wife?'

Jureem considered. 'You guess wisely, milady. It is his custom to grant an endowment of glamour to his wife each time he lies with her, so that on his next visit she will be even more beautiful than he remembers. Saffira has been his favorite for five years. She must have more than three hundred endowments by now.'

Borenson sat back in astonishment. A woman with a dozen endowments of glamour left men dizzy with desire. He could not imagine how a woman with hundreds of such endowments might affect him. Perhaps the notion *could* work.

But Borenson still felt uneasy. 'I can't believe that no one has considered using her as a weapon.'

'I was my lord's most trusted servant,' Jureem said. 'It was my duty to provide baubles and endowments for the concubines. Aside from two or three others, no man has been allowed to know the extent of the harem.'

Gaborn's gaze shifted to each of the others. 'What do you say? I propose to send a message to Saffira, and let her carry it to Raj Ahten.'

'It could work,' Jureem said doubtfully. 'But I hesitate to believe that Raj Ahten would take her counsel. She is, after all, only his wife.'

Borenson wondered. In many parts of Indhopal, it was

considered unmanly to listen to the counsel of a woman.

'It *could* work,' Iome said more hopefully. 'Binnesman suggested that Raj Ahten has gone mad simply because he has been listening to his own Voice. She might persuade him.'

'And what if I were to give her another thousand endowments of glamour and Voice,' Gaborn asked, 'as a token of my goodwill, so that even Raj Ahten could not resist her?'

'There *are* facilitators at Obran who are skilled at giving such endowments,' Jureem admitted.

'And we have the forcibles to do it with,' Chancellor Rodderman cut in. 'But it might take a day or two to find women who would serve as Dedicates.'

'I'd offer my glamour,' Myrrima said.

She glanced nervously toward Borenson, as if afraid of his reaction. She'd used that beauty to try to lure him into marriage. She had to know that it was unfair to offer to give it away now. Yet Borenson admired her all the more for making the offer.

'There are already women at Obran,' Jureem said. 'Raj Ahten has many concubines, all of whom have been endowed with glamour or Voice. Some of them have suffered greatly because of this long war. They too hope for peace, and I suspect that some of them, perhaps many of them, would act as vectors . . .'

'You would be taking a great risk,' King Orwynne said. 'We don't know this woman – nor do we know how such power might affect her. What if she too turns against you?'

'We must try,' Gaborn said. 'Raj Ahten is not our greatest enemy. I need his strength. I want him to fight the reavers.'

It seemed a slim chance, one that Borenson would not have considered himself.

'Perhaps,' Erin Connal said. 'But we should move forward with a doe's caution. You say that you feel an aura of great danger around us. Even if you send riders tonight, it will take days to reach Indhopal—'

'Not with the right horse,' Jureem countered. 'The fortress at Obran is in the northern provinces, just south of Deyazz, barely seven hundred miles from here.'

Borenson said, 'I've never heard of Obran. But if it's that close, then with a king's mount and a little luck, I could take the Raven's Pass out of Fleeds and be there by early afternoon tomorrow. If she consents, Saffira could deliver the message to Raj Ahten the following night.'

He spoke the words without considering the matter. It sounded like a fool's quest. He wondered at his own reasons for wanting to go. In part, he wanted to do it because he knew that he was a good man for the job. He'd performed dozens of dangerous missions in the past.

He could also see that this would give him the opportunity to spy on Indhopal's defenses and study the movements of enemy troops along the border. And as he did so, he would be heading far south, toward Inkarra.

Thus he would begin the quest Iome had set for him.

But a small part of him knew that he wanted something far more: he wanted redemption.

Both Lord Ingress and King Orwynne spoke casually of killing Dedicates, of holding to the endless tradition of butchery that had defined the battle strategies of Runelords in the past. Their strategies were so horrific in part because they were reliable.

But Borenson had little stomach for it now. Gaborn's plan, no matter how poorly conceived, offered some slim hope that Indhopal and Rofehavan could reach an accord, put an end to the madness.

And it was the only such plan on the table.

Borenson had the blood of over two thousand men, women, and children on his hands. Perhaps if he could bring this off, he reasoned, he might someday feel clean again.

'I would not put all of my hopes on this one throw of the bones, Your Highness,' King Orwynne said. 'You must look to your own defenses.

'Saffira may not be able or willing to do as you ask, and you would not have called this council if you did not plan to bestir yourself, and ride to the defense of Mystarria. You need to prepare to battle Raj Ahten in person, if need be . . .

'Or you could select a champion. I have a nephew – a lion of a man – Sir Langley. He's here in the camps.'

'It's all very well to send a champion,' Horsesister Connal urged Gaborn, 'but you should not let Orwynne or Heredon fight alone. Raj Ahten may fear Duke Paldane, but if you ride from the north, he'll fear *you* more. And it would rally every man in the north to fight beside you. The horse clans would ride with you.'

Gaborn sat pondering the proposals of his supporters.

The idealistic lad actually hopes to get out of this without fighting Raj Ahten, Borenson realized. But he suspected that Gaborn would never pull it off. A war with Raj Ahten was coming whether Gaborn or any of them willed it or not.

'What will you do?' Borenson pressed him.

Gaborn reflected for another half a second, nodded. 'The fate of the world rests upon our decision. I would not make such a decision hastily, and in truth I have thought about little else for the past week.

'My people cannot hide from Raj Ahten, and I cannot drive him away. I would fight him, if I believed that in fighting we could prevail. But I don't believe that. So I must hope to turn him, however slim that hope might be.'

Gaborn looked at Borenson. 'You'll take *my* horse and leave within the hour.'

Borenson slapped the table with a fist and rose from his chair, eager to be away, but found himself lingering momentarily as a courtesy.

Gaborn turned to King Orwynne. 'I've met Sir Langley. He has a good heart. I'll give you two thousand forcibles, to equip him as he wishes.'

'You are most generous,' King Orwynne said, seemingly astonished that the Earth King would grant such a boon. Even ten years ago, when blood metal was amply available, the whole kingdom of Orwynne had probably not seen two thousand forcibles in a single year.

Last of all Gaborn turned to Connal. 'You're right. If I march at the head of our armies, Raj Ahten cannot ignore me. I'll ride south, and Fleeds will have two thousand forcibles, too.'

Connal grunted in wonder. Her poor realm had probably never seen two thousand forcibles in any five years.

With that, the meeting ended. The lords pushed their chairs back from the table, began to rise. Gaborn reached into the pocket of his vest, drew out the keys for the king's treasury, and tossed them to Borenson.

'Milord,' Jureem said, 'May I suggest that you have him take seven hundred of glamour, three hundred of voice?'

Gaborn nodded. 'As he says.'

Borenson left the room, headed for the treasury in the Dedicates' Keep. Myrrima followed behind, and once they were outside, she accompanied him along the stone wall a couple of steps.

She grabbed his hand. 'Wait!'

He turned to look at her in the starlight. The night was a bit chill, but had no teeth that bit. Myrrima stared up at him with worry in her eyes. Even in the starlight, she was gorgeous. The sinuous curve of her waist and the gleaming sheen of her hair tempted him.

'You won't be back, will you?' she said.

Borenson shook his head. 'No. Carris is nine hundred miles south of here. I can reach the northern border of Inkarra only three hundred miles farther on. I'll head south.'

She studied him. 'Do you even plan to say goodbye?'

Borenson could see that she wasn't going to make this easy. He wanted to hold her, to kiss her. He wanted to stay. But duty called him elsewhere, and he had ever been loyal to his duty. 'There's not much time.'

'There's time,' she said. 'You've had all week. Why did you even remain in Heredon, if not to say goodbye?'

She was right, of course. He'd chosen to stay in order to say goodbye to her, to all of Rofehavan, perhaps to his own life. Yet he'd not had the strength to speak of it.

He kissed her lips, tenderly, and whispered, 'Goodbye.'

He began to turn away, but she grabbed his arm again. 'Do you really love me?' she asked.

'As best I know how.'

'Then why have you not bedded me? You've wanted me. I've seen it in your eyes.'

Borenson had not wanted to broach the subject, but he answered her now as honestly as he could. 'Because to do so would risk siring a child –'

'And you don't want me to carry your child?'

'– and bringing a child into the world requires one to accept certain responsibilities—'

'You think I'm not ready for such responsibilities!' Myrrima said too loudly.

'If I should die, I would not want my child called a bastard!' Borenson raged. 'Or the son of a kingslayer! Or worse!'

The blood came hot to his face, and Borenson found himself trembling with rage.

But despite his rage he was able to detach himself – as if he were viewing himself from somewhere outside his own body – while he mused about past and present. Ah, it's funny how the old pains can still hurt, he thought. Here he was, kingslayer, reaver slayer, guardian to the Earth King, one of the most feared warriors in all of Rofehavan – and rightfully so. Yet deep inside he was still just a child running through the stucco-walled alleys on the Isle of Thwynn while other boys hurled insults and mud and sharp stones.

Borenson had always felt the need to prove himself. It had driven him to become one of the mightiest warriors of his time. Now he did not really fear any other man on earth.

Yet the notion that a child of his might be hurt as he himself had been hurt seemed unbearable.

He still feared the tauntings of little boys.

'Love me!' Myrrima demanded, trying to pull him close.

But Borenson pointed a finger in her face and said more firmly, 'Responsibility.'

'Love me,' she pleaded.

He shook her hand from his sleeve and said, 'Can't you see? This is how it's done. And should I die – as seems likely – you'll have my name, my wealth . . .'

'I've heard it said that you're a lusty man,' Myrrima accused. 'Have you never bedded a woman?'

Angry now, Borenson sought to control himself. He could not express in words his own self-loathing, his desire to unmake his own past. 'If I have, it was a mistake,' he said, 'for I never imagined that I would meet someone like you.'

'It's not responsibility that drives you from my bed,' Myrrima accused. 'You're punishing yourself. You think you're punishing yourself, but when you do, you're also punishing me – and I don't deserve this!'

She sounded so certain of herself, so sure. Borenson had no reply to her accusation, only the solid belief that ultimately she would come to see that he acted in her best interest.

He squeezed her hand, then left.

Myrrima felt cheated as she watched him turn to go. The *ching, ching* of his mail echoed between the stone towers. In a moment he reached the portcullis to the Dedicates' Keep, and was swallowed beneath its shadows. She stood for a moment, watching how the starlight washed the paving stones here in the bailey.

She knew that he thought he was right. Loving someone meant taking responsibility for that person.

But as he went of to fetch his forcibles, Myrrima began to fume. Borenson would not allow this to work both ways.

A few minutes later he came back out of the keep, bearing a leather bag filled with forcibles. He saw her but turned and headed for the stables, as if to avoid her.

She said, 'I have one word for you: "responsibility."' Borenson stopped and gazed at her half a second. 'Why do you insist on being responsible for me, but I cannot be responsible for you?'

'You're not coming with me,' Borenson said.

'Do you think I'm less capable of love than you are?'

'You're less capable of staying alive,' he answered.

'But—'

'And even if you weren't, there's not a horse in Heredon

that can keep pace with the mount I'll be riding tonight.' He looked toward the stable.

She thought he'd leave then, but to Myrrima's astonishment, Borenson returned to her, put one huge hand behind her neck, and kissed her passionately. He stood for a long time afterward with his forehead against hers, just staring into her eyes. No gleam of starlight reflected from his pale-blue eyes. They seemed just empty wells in the night.

But still he had a fierceness to him. She could see it in his will to live, to fight, to return. She could feel it in the way that his powerful hands cupped the back of her head. At last he said evenly, 'When I come back, I *will* love you as you wish – as you deserve.'

Then he turned and hurried off. With his endowments of metabolism, his pace surprised her. She stood for a long moment, still smelling him, still tasting his lips on hers. She thought to follow him into the king's stable across the green, but as she gathered her wits and took a few paces, he hurriedly saddled Gaborn's horse and then came riding out like a gale, shouting for the guards to open the gates.

She folded her arms, to fight the night's chill, and watched him go.

As soon as her husband left, Myrrima fetched a lantern and went to the kennels where the boy Kaylin had caged her pups. She'd only been able to sneak away twice to see them today, yet as soon as they caught her scent, the pups began to yap and wag their tails, and soon dozens of pups were yelping for attention.

The boy Kaylin was at the back of the kennel, lying asleep on a bed of straw with at least twenty pups around him, and nothing else to keep him warm.

Myrrima laid her cloak over the boy, then went to the cage that held her pups. She lifted the latch.

She'd brought a few scraps from the table, and she gave these to the pups, spoke to them and made cooing noises, until at last they settled down enough so that she could get them in her arms. 'Yes, little ones,' she whispered. 'You'll sleep with me tonight.'

She managed to get two pups in each arm, and went to the kennel door. As she was juggling the door latch, it opened wide.

Iome Sylvarresta stood there with a servant at her back, and her Days behind. Only the stars winging through the heavens lit them.

Myrrima felt sure that Iome had followed her in an effort to catch her stealing the pups. 'Why, Your Highness,' she said, 'what a surprise!'

Iome glanced down at the pups, looked back toward the keep, as if just as dismayed at having been found out herself.

Then she suddenly set her jaw and looked stern.

'Is the boy Kaylin sleeping here?'

Pups ran out and circled the Queen, leaping up at the hem of her dress, whining and yapping for attention.

'Yes, he's here,' Myrrima said.

Iome did not apologize for what she planned to do. Even as a princess, she had refused to take endowments from another person, to risk a human life.

'I'll need some of those, too,' Iome said stiffly. 'If I'm to be of any help to you.'

Late that night, after the lords had left, Gaborn stood awake in Sylvarresta's old study on the fourth floor of the King's Keep, gazing southwest across the hills. The floor had recently been strewn with dry meadowsweet, and so his passage across the planking as he crushed the golden flowers had infused the room with a delightful, pleasant scent.

Borenson had left the keep nearly three hours past. Iome had gone to her room hours ago, though Gaborn did not imagine that she would sleep. They were newlyweds, after all, and he imagined that she would be awake, worrying, as he worried.

But perhaps not. He hoped that she slept. A week past, when Borenson had slain her Dedicates, Iome had lost all of her endowments of stamina. She needed sleep now, as much as any commoner did. But Gaborn still had his endowments of stamina and brawn. He did not sleep much at all in times of stress, but instead preferred to rest on his feet, sometimes letting his mind retreat to a waking dream.

He hoped that Iome would not wait up for him. He wanted solitude this night.

Part of the Queen's garden was back there beneath the study. A pair of frogs sang in the water of a reflecting pool. A ratlike ferrin wearing scraps of cloth came and drank at the pool. The frogs went quiet as the creature gazed about with bright eyes. Gaborn tasted the scent of fresh air flowing from the open window, looked out in the starlight.

The camps below town were dark now, and the people huddled in a mass. Gaborn could still feel danger about them, could feel it closing in, like a noose around his own neck. The Darkling Glory was coming. Gaborn could feel the danger rising as it flew steadily north.

Half a million people, all under his protection – along with their horses and cattle – asleep and unaware.

'May the Earth hide you. May the Earth heal you. May the Earth make you its own,' Gaborn whispered, reciting the ancient blessing.

He dreaded what he had to do. At dawn he would leave his people, head south to war. He could only hope that they would escape the wrath of the Darkling Glory.

So many people depended upon him, and he wanted to save them all, to do everything in his power. Yet though he was the Earth King, his powers were still new to him, and they were growing. He felt clumsy. Incompetent.

If any of us survive these dark times, he thought, I will have to live with the memories of those I let down. For the sake of my own conscience, I dare let no one down.

For a long time he pondered some words from the small book written by the Emir Owatt of Tuulistan – not the forbidden words from the House of Understanding, but a silly poem about self-definition. He had not committed it to memory, could only recall two lines.

Love and lovers may not always sustain,
But I choose to love still.

Thought heart might fail me and the battle be lost,
I choose to strive still.

As did the Emir, Gaborn saw wisdom in the struggle. The universe was a powerful foe. In time death overtakes all men. But while he breathed, Gaborn was free to choose the kind of man he would become. It was essential that he remain the kind of man he could live with.

He thought of Emir Owatt of Tuulistan. The little book he'd sent to King Sylvarresta intrigued Gaborn. The Emir was obviously a jewel among men. And now Gaborn was placing great hopes on his daughter Saffira.

A flicker of ghost fire caught his eyes up on the hill at the edge of the Dunnwood just at the tree line, a shimmering gray light.

A wight sat there, on its ghostly mount in the darkness, staring toward the castle at the huddled masses.

He's watching over my people, Gaborn realized, just as I commanded him to do. Like a shepherd on a hill, watching his flocks by night.

Gaborn could not see from so far away who it might be. He imagined that it was the spirit of Erden Geboren himself, or perhaps his own father.

Gaborn missed his father's counsel now.

He wondered idly if the wights would be able to fight the Darkling Glory. He doubted it. A wight's cold touch could kill a mortal man, but wights dissipated when in light. A campfire would drive them off. Sunlight banished them. And if the Darkling Glory came from the Realms of Fire in the netherworld, it would surely have some control over that element.

At the back of the room, Gaborn's Days coughed.

Gaborn turned and looked at the man in the shadows, wondered what he knew.

'Tell me,' Gaborn said in an easy tone. 'What think you of our plans? Did I do well or ill today?'

'That, I cannot say,' the Days answered in a tone that told Gaborn precisely nothing.

Gaborn asked rhetorically, for he knew the answer, 'If I were drowning in deep water, a foot from shore, would you save me?'

'I would note in my records the moment that you went under for the last time,' his Days said, amused by the game.

'And if mankind sank with me?' Gaborn asked.

'It would be a sad day for the books,' the Days said soberly.

'Where is Raj Ahten? What does he plan?'

'Everything in its own time,' the Days said. 'You will know all too soon.'

Gaborn wondered. Had Raj Ahten sped north, too? Could he be coming with the Darkling Glory? Or did he have more dire plans in mind?

'Your Highness, may I ask *you* a question?' the Days said.

'Of course.'

'Have you considered the fate of the Days? Have you considered whether you will Choose me – or any other Days?'

Seizing the moment, Gaborn stared the man in the eyes, gazed beyond them, into the Days' hopes and dreams.

Gaborn had looked into his father's heart, and it had been clear. He'd looked into the heart of Molly Drinkham's child and seen that it loved nothing, was only grateful for its mother's nipple and for the warmth of her body and the way she sang sweetly to get him to sleep.

Yet even that child, with its vague longings, seemed clearer, more comprehensible, to Gaborn than did the Days.

Through the Earth Sight, he saw not a man, but a man and a woman – a woman with a quill and parchment, a woman with wheat-colored hair and emerald-green eyes.

Gaborn had never guessed that the scribe to his witness would be a woman. Now he saw that the two loved one another, that for them sharing a mind was a joy and an intimacy that Gaborn had never quite imagined.

He looked deeper still, and saw that they shared something more than that: a love of old tales and deeds and songs, a childlike joy that came from merely watching events unfold, the way that an old gardener loves to watch the first crocuses of spring spread wide their white petals, or seeds sprout green from a newly planted field. For them, the study of history was a constant delight, an ever-present joy.

And neither of them wanted anything more than to simply watch. They did not want to better the world or lessen another's pain. They sought no gain.

They were content to watch.

Gaborn could not fathom it, he was amazed. He had never quite imagined that any man's heart could be as odd as what he saw beating within the historian.

Gaborn considered. He'd told Iome that he wanted much the same kind of unity earlier in the day, that his domain and hers were one, and that he wanted to grow together with her. Yet so long as they remained two creatures apart, perhaps that could never be achieved. But the Days had seen a possibility, a way to unite two people so that they became of one mind and one heart, and they had followed that path.

Gaborn almost envied them. He would have spoken to Iome of the possibility, but it was too late for them. She'd already granted an endowment of glamour to Raj Ahten's vector, and though the vector was dead and Iome's beauty had returned to her, the fact that she had given an endowment now made it impossible for her to ever give another.

She and Gaborn could never share such intimacy.

'I will consider the possibility,' Gaborn answered.

'Thank you, Your Highness,' the Days said.

Gaborn resumed looking out the window, letting the fresh night air blow into his face as he listened to the frogs. For long hours, he sat taking his rest as Runelords do, eyes awake, wandering through a realm of dream.

In his dream, he was a young man, riding a stallion through a dark chasm along a narrow mountain road he'd once ridden with his father.

He knew this place, knew this bleak landscape. Last week he had asked his Days why the Days were once called the 'Guardians of Dreams.' His Days had said that someday soon, in his sleep, he would visit this place: this land in his dreamscape where all of his terrors lay hidden. He'd told Gaborn to seek out that place.

Only in this dream, he was alone and spiderwebs as strong as bands of steel barred his way. In crevasses among the dark rock, he could see spiders larger than crabs scuttling in the shadows, eyes glittering like bright crystals.

Now, Gaborn looked up the dark ravine, thick with cobwebs. His heart pounded with terror, and his chest was tight. Sweat beaded on his brow. He drew his saber and cut through the strong strands, so that they snapped like lute strings. He urged his mount forward.

He missed a strand, and it hit his forehead, slashed his face before it broke. Gaborn rode on with blood running down the bridge of his nose, into his clenched lips.

This is the land of fears, he realized. This is where my terrors reside. He raced now to face them.

He ducked low and rode hard up the narrow ravine, fearing death, hoping instead to find his father there, or his mother, or some other proper reward.

But ahead the crevasse turned and twisted. It splayed into a wide passage where a dim light shone.

There, above him, tall upon a dark horse, sat his Days. His narrow skull was a dark V, his close-cropped hair unkempt. He looked almost skeletal, merely bones wrapped in a bundle of cloth. He held a wavering green light in his palm, like the flame of a wind-blown lantern, though the light did not issue from any device.

'I've been waiting for you,' the Days said, holding up the thin light, as if to pass it into Gaborn's hand.

'I know,' Gaborn answered. 'I'll try not to disappoint you.' Gaborn reached to take the light. 'What is this?' he asked as it touched his palm.

'The hope of the world and all its dreams,' the Days said, thin lips pulling into a ghastly smile.

Gaborn trembled to see how small the light was; his hand shook so that the flame dropped and fell toward the stony ground.

BOOK 7

DAY 31 IN THE MONTH OF HARVEST
A DAY WITHOUT CHOICE

13

THE FOURTH EAR

Even in the shifting winds, Bessahan smelled the smoke of the messenger's fire from three miles down the trail. He was high in the Brace Mountains, in the deep pines. The clouds had scudded in just at sunset, smelling heavy with rain, and in half an hour the rain was pelting down while lightning flashed. The winds shook the great pines, knocking branches down in the roadside. Falling leaves swirled about. His quarry dared not ride in such brooding darkness, and so they had been forced to stop beneath the trees. After an hour, the lightning had abated, and now only brief flashes sometimes lit the northern horizon. But the rain still fell.

He approached the smoke quietly, walking along the road, so that he made no noise, keeping low, until the smell of the wood smoke came strongest.

He had expected to find them camped by the highway, but after passing the source of the scent, he realized that they were being wary. They'd taken a side trail, climbed up the mountain to a hidden glade. From the road, he could not even see their fire.

So Bessahan got off his horse, tied it to a tree, and strung his bow. Then he pulled out his khivar and inspected it. He'd cleaned the blade after beheading the old woman. Now he took a moment with an oilstone to hone it sharp, in the darkness, working by feel alone.

When at last he felt prepared, he took off his hard shoes, letting his bare feet grip the cold muddy road as he prepared to ascend the hill.

For a Master in the Brotherhood of the Silent Ones, it was not a great challenge. To climb through brush in the darkness was not difficult, only cold and miserable and sometimes painful. He had to feel his way through the underbrush, letting his fingers and toes search for twigs that his eyes could not see.

So it was that he began his slow ascent. The trail was not hard, he soon discovered. The moss here was thick, and he found himself crawling through a bed of deep ferns higher than a man's chest. The trees here were old, had stood like this for a hundred years, and twigs were scarce on the forest floor. The few he encountered were small, and because they were wet and old and rotten, they snapped softly. The ferns and the pelting rain muted any sounds of breakage.

Only once in his journey did he encounter any difficulty. As he crawled along his palm sank into the moss and hit something sharp, possibly a ragged piece of bone left by a wolf. The wound it caused was small, a tiny puncture that hardly bled. He ignored the pain.

In half an hour, he reached the summit of the hill, topped a small rise, and glimpsed the fire. A great pine had fallen, a tree perhaps twelve feet in diameter, and it rested against the hillside at an angle.

The party was camped beneath the windfall, using it for a roof. They'd peeled off some of the drier bark to build a fire, but it was wet and smoky.

Now they lay in blankets beside the fire, talking to one another. The huge knight, the big red-haired messenger, and a girl child.

'Stop fretting,' the big red-haired messenger said. 'You'll get no sleep worrying.'

'But it's been an hour since we heard her. What if she's lost?' the child asked.

'Good riddance, I say,' the fat knight replied.

'It was your fire that scared her,' the child accused the knight. 'She's sore afraid of it.'

Bessahan halted, heart thumping. He'd thought he was hunting three people, but there appeared to be a fourth. His lord paid him for his killings by the ear. He'd want that fourth woman's ear.

If she was looking for them, it would not be long before she stumbled into camp. Even a person without the benefit of a wolf's nose would smell that fire.

Bessahan backed away, decided to wait.

Yet as he eeled backward on his belly, down over the lip of the hill, he bumped against something solid.

He glanced back, looked up. A naked woman with dark skin smiled down at him stupidly. The fourth ear.

'Hello?' he whispered, hoping to keep her from shouting in alarm.

'Hello?' she whispered in return.

Was she a fool? he wondered briefly. Then she knelt on her haunches and studied him. In the dim light that reflected from the branches overhead, he could barely discern her. She was long-haired and shapely.

He'd been too long without a woman, and decided to enjoy her before he killed her. He reached up quickly, slapped a hand over her mouth, and tried to pull her down.

But she was stronger than she appeared. Instead of toppling down on him, she merely grabbed his hand and sniffed, an expression of pure ecstasy on her face, as if she were smelling a bouquet of flowers.

'Blood,' she said longingly, tasting the scent of his wound. She bit into his wrist, and pain blossomed. Her bite snapped clear through the tendons and ligaments, and blood gushed from an artery, spraying up like a fountain.

He tried to pull away, but the woman held him firmly. With three endowments of brawn to his credit, he pulled hard, trying to break free. The bones of his wrist snapped as he twisted, yet she continued to hold him tight. Catching a glimpse of her hand, he realized that what he'd imagined were long fingernails were not nails at all but claws or talons. She was not human!

The woman opened her mouth in astonished delight, watched the blood fountain out of him.

Bessahan brought his khivar up in a dreadful slash, attempting to rip out her throat. The thin steel blade caught in her skin, but despite his endowments of brawn, the point hardly pierced her. Instead, the blade snapped off clean.

Blood had spurted all over his face and hands. Now the woman knelt down as if to lick it up.

He struggled silently as the woman forced him down and licked the blood from his face with a raspy tongue. As she began chewing at his chin, gnawing like a kitten that has not yet learned to kill the mouse it eats, he fought fiercely. Until the green woman's teeth found his throat. Then he finally went still, although his feet continued to kick and jerk until long after he knew no more.

It was well near dawn when the green woman entered camp. Roland had been asleep when suddenly he felt her touch as she lay down next to him.

Averan spooned against his belly, and the green woman came and tried to lie down at Roland's back.

She trembled from cold; the fire was but a smoking ruin, having gone out. For the last hour, the rain had been mixed with snow.

Roland slept beneath a blanket, and his new bearskin cloak lay over the top of that. He half woke, took the cloak and pulled it protectively over the green woman's naked skin, then he urged her with a few whispered words and motions to get under the blanket with him and Averan.

The green woman complied slowly, as if not sure what he desired. Once he had her lying between him and the child, where the body heat of them both would warm her, Roland merely wrapped a big arm and leg over her, to speed the process.

In minutes she had quit trembling so violently, and lay next to him, luxuriating.

In the creeping dawn, Roland could make out the green woman's features. She was one of the most beautiful women he had ever seen, even with her odd skin tone, her dark-green lips.

She lay next to him, but he became aware that she was watching the smoking embers of the fire, still terrified.

'Don't worry,' he whispered. 'It won't hurt you.'

She grasped his wounded hand, sniffed at the bandage. 'Blood – no!' she said softly.

'That's right,' Roland answered. 'Blood, no! You're a smart one. And obedient. Two qualities I admire in a woman – or whatever you are.'

'You're a smart one,' she parroted. 'And obedient. Two qualities I admire in a woman – or whatever you are.'

Roland smelled her hair. It was odd, like . . . moss and sweet basil combined, he decided. He could smell the coppery tang of blood on her, too. She was a large thing, as tall as him, and more muscular.

He grasped her thumb, and whispered, 'Thumb. Thumb.'

She repeated his words, and in minutes he taught her all about hands and arms and noses and moved on to trees, the autumn leaves, and the sky.

When he grew tired, he drifted back toward sleep, and hugged the green woman tightly. He wondered where she had come from, wondered if she felt lonely. Like Roland and Averan, she had no connections to anyone that he could see. All three of them were terribly alone in the world, cast adrift.

I should heal that wound, Roland thought. I could petition Paldane to become Averan's guardian. The world is too full of orphans, and she has my color of hair. People will think I'm her father. He promised himself he would talk to Averan about it tomorrow.

Perhaps because he held a woman in his arms, because he craved a woman's company, and because he still remembered a wife who had rejected him twenty years ago, he thought about Sera Crier, and the sense of duty that had sent him north.

He recalled his waking seven days earlier . . .

As he pulled on the loose-fitting trousers, Roland had said to Sera Crier, 'I gave my endowments years ago, to a man named Drayden. He was a sergeant in the King's Guard. Do you know the name?'

'Lord Drayden?' she corrected. 'The King let him retire to his estates several years ago. He is quite old – yours was not the only endowment of metabolism he took, I think. But he still travels each year to Heredon, for the King's hunt.'

Roland nodded. Most likely Lord Drayden had been thrown from a horse, he thought, or had met with one of the old tuskers of the Dunnwood. The great boars were as tall as a horse, and skewered many a huntsman.

The thought had hardly passed through his mind when a cry rang through the narrow stone halls of the Dedicate's Keep. 'The King is dead! Mendellas Draken Orden has fallen!' And from elsewhere in the keep, someone cried, 'Sir Beaufort has died!' Some woman shouted, 'Marris is fallen!'

Roland wondered why so many lords and knights were dying at once. It bespoke more than coincidence, more than an accident.

He'd finished pulling on his boot and shouted, 'Lord Drayden has found his rest!' Then cries from the Dedicates of the Blue Tower came fast and furious as deaths were reported, too many names, too many knights and lords and common soldiers, for any man to keep track of.

Boars did not slay so many men at once. There had to have been a great battle. And as dozens of voices began to meld together as the fallen were named, he thought, Nay, not even a battle. This speaks of slaughter.

Roland rushed from his chamber into the narrow hall of the Dedicate's Keep, found that his tiny berth stood at the top of a stairwell. A woman staggered out from a chamber nearby, massaging her hands, recently restored from having given grace. Across a hall, another man blinked in amazement, gawking about. He'd given the use of his eyes to a lord.

Sera Crier followed at Roland's heels.

Shouts of grief rang through the Blue Tower, and, people raced down the stairs, toward the Great Hall.

The Blue Tower was ancient. Legend said it had not been built by men, for no man could have shaped and hefted rocks so massive as those that formed its barrier walls. Many thought the tower had been formed by a forgotten race of giants. The keep loomed thirty stories above the Caroll Sea. With its tens of thousands of rooms, the Blue Tower was a great sprawling city in itself. For at least three millennia it had housed the Dedicates of Mystarria, those who had given their wit or stamina or brawn, their metabolism or glamour or voice.

Roland darted around a group of people in the hall who stood in his way, pushed past a fat woman. Sera hurried to keep up. He took her hand, shoved his way through the clotted halls, nuzzling past others until at last he and Sera gazed over the edge of a balcony into the Great Hall, a fine chamber where thousands of Dedicates and servants were gathering.

There was much shouting and crying. Some people shouted for news, others wept openly for their love of a lost king. One old woman screamed as if her child had been torn from her breast and dashed against the flagstones.

'That's old Laras. She's a cook. Her boys are in the King's retinue. They must be dead, too!' Sara said, confirming Roland's thoughts.

Down in the great room the Dedicates who were now Restored gathered in a crushing crowd, along with the cooks and servants who normally attended them. A fight erupted as one burly fellow began pummeling another, and a general melee ensued. Those who wanted news shouted for everyone else in the crowd to hold silent. The resulting tumult filled the room, echoed from the walls.

The Great Hall had an enormous domed ceiling some seventy feet high, and balconies encircled the hall on five levels. At least three thousand former Dedicates were gathered in the hall. They spilled out of every doorway and stairwell, and leaned precariously over the oaken rails of the balconies.

Roland was hardly able to comprehend the scope of what was happening. Thousands of Dedicates Restored at once? How many valiant knights had died in battle? And so quickly!

Seven men of varying ages took seats around an enormous

oak table. One man began to beat a huge brass candelabrum against the table, yelling, 'Quiet! Quiet! Let us all hear the tale! The King's Wits can give it best!'

These seven men were the King's Wits, men who had endowed King Mendellas Draken Orden himself with the use of their minds, letting their skulls become vessels for another man's memories. Though the King had died, fragments of his thoughts and recollections lived on in each of these restored men. In days to come these men would probably become valued counselors to the new King.

After a moment, the screaming woman was pulled from the Great Hall, and the others stifled their sobs and their shouts. Sera Crier pressed against Roland's back, half climbed his shoulders to get a better view of the turmoil below.

It felt to Roland as if the crowd breathed in unison, every man and woman among them waiting expantly to hear news of the battle.

The King's Wits began to speak. The oldest among them was a graybeard named Jerimas. Roland had known him at court as a child but barely recognized him now.

Jerimas spoke first. 'The King surely died in battle,' he said. 'I recall seeing a foe. A man of dark countenance, dressed in armor of the south. His shield bore the image of a red wolf with three heads.'

It was a scrap of memory, an image. Nothing more.

'Raj Ahten,' two of the other wits said. 'He was battling Raj Ahten, the Wolf Lord.'

'No. Our king did not die in that battle,' a fourth Wit argued. 'He fell from a tower. I remember falling.

'He was joined in a serpent ring,' old Jerimas added. 'He felt the pain of a forcible before he died.'

'He gave his metabolism,' another fellow croaked as if he were ill and could hardly speak. 'They all gave metabolism. I saw twenty lords in a room. The light of the forcibles hung in the air like glowing worms, and men cried out in pain at their touch.'

'Yes, they had formed a ring. A serpent ring, so that they could battle Raj Ahten,' another Wit agreed.

'He was saving his son,' Jerimas said. 'Now I recall. Prince Orden had gone for reinforcements . . . and was bringing an army to Longmot. King Orden was wounded, and could battle no more, so he threw his life away, hoping to break the serpent ring, and thus save his son.'

Many of the King's Wits nodded. Once, as a child, Roland and some friends had gone into an old ruin, a lord's manor house. In ages past there had been a mosaic of colored tiles on the floor. Roland and his friends had sat one morning piecing together the tiles, trying to guess what picture they might make. It had been an image of a water wizard and dolphins as they battled a leviathan in the deep ocean.

Now, he watched as the King's Wits picked up the tiles of Orden's memory, similarly trying to piece them into a cohesive picture.

Another man shook his head in confusion and then added, 'There is a great treasure at Longmot. All the kings of the north will want it.'

'Shhh . . .' several others hissed in unison. 'Do not speak of that in public!'

'Orden battled to free Heredon!' one of the King's Wits shouted at the fellow who mentioned the treasure. 'He wanted no treasure. He fought for the land, and the people he loved!'

After that, there was only silence for a long moment as the Wits considered. None of them could recall all of what Orden had known. A snippet here, a scrap there. An image, a thought, a single word. The pieces were there, but the King's Wits, even doing their best, could hardly fit them together. Many crucial pieces would be missing – the memories that Orden had taken with him to his grave.

A king was dead.

Roland considered his duty, saw where it lay. In the land of Heredon, his king had died. In the land of Heredon, his own son served the new king.

'What of Prince Orden?' Roland shouted. 'Was anyone here a Dedicate to the Prince?' Roland had never seen this prince, only knew of his existence because Sera Crier had mentioned him. King Orden had married only a week before Roland became a Dedicate.

For several heartbeats Roland waited. No one answered. None of the Prince's Dedicates had been Restored.

Roland turned and thrust Sera Crier away. He began pushing through the crowd, intending to leave the keep and go in search of a boat. He needed to leave the Blue Tower as quickly as possible. The King's Wits might be hours telling their tale of woe. But within moments, he knew, others among the Restored would begin hurrying back to the mainland, to visit loved ones. He wanted to beat the others to the boats.

Sera grabbed his sleeve, held him. 'Where are you going?' she asked. 'Will you return?'

He glanced back into the crowd, saw Sera's stricken face, blood leaching from it. He knew that his answer would not sound gentle to her ears, no matter how softly it was spoken, so he said bluntly, 'I don't know where I am going. I – I just need to get away from here. But I am never coming back.'

'But—'

He touched his forefinger to her lips. 'You served me well, for many years.' Roland knew that men learn to love best those whom they serve most wholeheartedly. Sera Crier had cared for him for years, had lavished affection on him in his sleep, had perhaps dreamed of what he might do when he awakened.

Those who served in the Dedicate's Keep were often stray children who performed menial chores in return for the barest necessities. If Sera remained, she'd likely wed some lad in the same predicament, and the two of them would raise their family here in the shadows of the Blue Tower. She might never walk on the green mainland under the full sun again; she would be forced to listen to the pounding of the surf and the calls of the gulls for the rest of her days. Clearly, Sera Crier hoped for something better. Yet Roland had nothing to offer her. 'I thank you for your service, both for myself, and for my king,' he told her. 'But I'm no longer a Dedicate, and have no place here.'

'I . . . I could come with you,' she suggested. 'With so many men Restored, freed from their servitude today, no one would really miss me if I left.'

I am a good servant, he thought. I give my all to my lord. You should do the same.

He squinted toward the nearest door, a dark passage crowded with bodies. He prepared mentally to shove past them all. He had few connections to the living. After twenty-one years of sleep, his king was dead. His mother and his uncle Jemin had been old even back then. In all likelihood, they were gone. Roland would never again see them. Though men would now call him 'Restored,' in fact he felt he had been restored to nothing. He had only one thing left: a son to find.

'Sera,' he whispered, 'take care of yourself. Perhaps someday we will meet again.'

He turned and left. Roland was the first to reach the little harbor at the Blue Tower . . .

Now Roland smiled as he nuzzled the green woman's hair and wondered if he'd ever see Sera again.

Baron Poll wakened him. 'Good morning to you all!'

Roland looked up. The sun was well over the hill, and Baron Poll stared down at him with a playful grin. He had a day-old loaf of bread in his hands, and he tore a piece off and munched contentedly.

Averan came awake, wrapped in the green woman's arms. She turned over, gazed at the green woman. 'What's she been eating?'

Roland rose up half an inch. Earlier, in the predawn light, he'd not noticed the dried blood smeared liberally all over the green woman's chin.

'It looks like she caught something,' Roland said.

'Not our horses,' Averan intoned with relief. The mounts were lying beneath the windfall.

'She didn't catch a something,' Baron Poll said with evident gusto. 'She caught a *who*. I'd say she waylaid him quite well. Come and see the evidence.'

'Some traveler?' Averan cried in dismay.

Baron Poll did not answer, merely turned and led them downhill. Roland leapt up, as did Averan, and they followed Baron Poll over the top of the hill. The green woman followed them, apparently curious about the excitement.

'How did you find him?' Averan asked.

'I was searching for some fortunate sapling upon which to empty my bladder,' Baron Poll offered, 'when I stumbled upon the remains.'

At just that moment, they reached a slight depression. The grisly sight that awaited them would be forever indelibly impressed upon Roland's mind.

Averan did not cry out in horror as other children might have done. Instead, she went up to the remains and studied them with morbid fascination.

'He was creeping up on us, I'd say,' Baron Poll conjectured, 'when she pounced on him from behind. See here, he had an arrow nocked, and a long knife. But it's broken now.'

Roland had been the king's butcher. He knew knives, and had bought one like this in the market once. 'A khivar,' he corrected. The man had worn a black cotton burnoose under his robe. A broken necklace near his ragged throat was decorated with gold trade rings. 'One of Raj Ahten's assassins?'

'He had a little purse full of human ears,' Baron Poll confirmed. 'I doubt he was a surgeon.'

Roland bent over and pulled the necklace of trade rings free, slipped them into his pocket. He glanced up at Baron Poll. The Baron grinned. 'Now you're learning, man. No use leaving them for the scavengers.'

'Blood,' the green woman said. Then she said more softly, 'Blood – no.'

At that, Averan grinned wickedly and said in a loud voice, 'Blood – yes!' She walked over to the corpse, pretended to wipe her finger in the mess, and said, 'Good blood! Mmm . . . blood – yes!'

The green woman stared, the dawn of comprehension glowing in her eyes. She went over to the body, sniffed it.

'Blood – yes.' But apparently she wanted none of it.

'She likes them fresh,' Roland suggested.

'Are you sure that's a good idea?' Baron Poll asked Averan. 'Teaching her to kill people?'

'I'm not teaching her to kill,' Averan said. 'I just don't want her to feel guilty about what she did. She saved us. She didn't do anything wrong!'

'Right, and because she's got the blood lust out of her system, I'm sure she'll be of cheery temperament all day,' Baron Poll said. 'But of course, next time she's hungry, she'll just grab someone by the roadside.'

'No she won't,' Averan said. 'She's very smart. I'm sure she knows more than you think.' She reached out and scratched the green woman's head, as if she were a dog.

'Oh, she's smart all right,' Baron Poll said. 'And the next time the High King levies taxes, I'll have her right over to figure my dues.'

Averan glared at the Baron. 'Baron Globbet, have you ever thought that maybe she could be of use to us? What if she killed this man because she knew he was trouble? What if there are more assassins on the road? She could kill them for us. She seems to have a strong nose, and they all smell like ginger and curry. She might smell them out. Don't you think so, Roland?'

Roland merely shrugged.

'I like a bit of curry myself,' Baron Poll argued. 'And I don't fancy the notion of having my innards ripped out because some inn chooses to serve it for dinner.

'Besides, she's not smart,' Baron Poll continued. 'I've seen crows that mimic your words as well as she does!'

Averan's belief in the green woman seemed far-fetched, Roland thought, but the green woman *had* learned a lot of words this morning. Given a day or two, they might teach her to hunt.

More to the point, he wasn't quite sure what they could do about her. He hadn't had any luck at killing her yesterday.

They'd tried to outrun her, leave her behind last night, and the green woman had merely loped behind their mounts, shouting for blood.

No, the green woman was a problem, maybe one that only the King and his counselors could fathom. She was Averan's charge for the moment, and Roland didn't have any fancy notions about how to handle her.

14

DEYAZZ

Dawn found Sir Borenson far from Heredon. He'd spent most of the night riding south to Fleeds, and then to the Raven's Pass.

Now he was racing Gaborn's dun-colored mare through the red foothills above Deyazz, heading down roads that Jureem had named, but still unsure of his destination. The name Obran was a contraction of two Indhopalese words: *obir*, to age, and *ran*, city of the king. It was best translated as 'City of the Ancient King.' It sounded like the name for the capital of a province. But Borenson had never heard of the damned place, and Jureem's directions would lead him only to the northern borders of the Great Salt Desert, a home to Muttayin nomads. It seemed an unlikely place to find a palace.

Jureem assured him that he would need a guide to show him the palace's location; the guide would have to be a minor lord himself. Borenson carried a standard in his left hand – the green pennant of truce above the Sylvarresta boar.

The morning air was bracing, invigorating. His steed ran long and far between each stop for rest. The breath came cold from Borenson's mouth, and his armor rang with each hoof-beat of his mount. The horse worked its lungs like a bellows. The roads hereabout were narrow and treacherous, though not from mud, as was common in Mystarria; rocks sometimes rolled down the hills from above, and the little tan-colored ground squirrels prevalent in this region seemed not to recognize the danger when they heard the thud of hooves on the hardpan.

Despite the danger, Borenson raced his mount down the hills at speeds of up to fifty miles per hour.

The landscape below him was a vast savanna dotted with drab olive-green trees. The grasses were the color of sand where the red clay did not show through. A single broad river silvered the landscape on the edge of the horizon, and cities of tents and adobe glittered at its border, with fields of wheat and orchards of oranges and almonds all along the water-course. He had not yet passed a village. The citizens of Deyazz lived only along its great rivers.

He'd passed through the mountains during the night with surprisingly little resistance. Often he'd met small caravans filled with merchants heading north. Yet it was too late of the season for them to be coming for trade. He could think of only one reason they would trek north: they were refugees fleeing Indhopal, eager to see the Earth King.

Once he'd circled a large army bivouacked in a mountain pass. Though he'd borne a torch on the pole of his standard, so that all might see that he flew the colors of truce, three times assassins had chased him.

But Borenson rode a kingly mount, one that this week had been given two more endowments of metabolism and two of sight, so that it would run swiftly and with clear vision, even by starlight. He'd outraced his pursuers with nothing more than an arrow that snapped off in his mail to show for the trouble.

Yet even Borenson could not outrace the doubts that nagged him.

He worried that he had been too harsh when he'd said goodbye to Myrrima. She may have been right when she said that he punished both himself and her for his murders.

The road ahead to Inkarra and his mission in Obran were also cause for apprehension.

He worried most of all for Gaborn. The lad was naïve to think that he could sue for peace or seek to bribe Raj Ahten. King Orwynne had been right. Gaborn could have better spent his time using his forcibles to prepare for war.

Borenson had always imagined that when an Earth King

appeared, he would be a stately fellow with the wisdom of the ages on his brow. He'd be as strong as the hills, with muscles as gnarled and as powerful as tree roots. He'd have the respect of all, and a certain implacable demeanor.

The Earth King he'd always imagined bore absolutely no resemblance to Gaborn.

Gaborn had no great skill in battle, no vast stores of wisdom. He was but an unskilled lad who loved his people.

But he had an asset that Borenson had seldom considered. He recalled the words of Gaborn's father in discussing what would happen if he ever went to battle with a certain duke in Beldinook who was giving him trouble. He'd said, 'Duke Trevorsworthy I can handle. It's his wife and that damned Sergeant Arrants who terrify me.'

Borenson had laughed at the idea of a king being terrified of a woman and a mere sergeant, but the King had cut him short. 'The wife is a brilliant tactician, and Sergeant Arrants is perhaps the most inspired artilleryman I've ever seen. He could build a catapult out of a butter churn that would knock down a castle wall or put an iron ball between your eyes at four hundred yards.'

The he'd taught Borenson this lesson: 'Remember, a lord is never a single man. He is the sum of all the men in his retinue. When you fight a lord, you must consider the strengths of each man that he commands before you can get a true measure of his stature.'

Borenson therefore had to consider Gaborn's human assets. There were thousands of gentlemen of various rank and title in Mystarria, everything from petty lords to Gaborn's wise great-uncle Paldane. Some were sailors or builders, men who commanded great hordes of peasants in the field, men who trained horses or hammered shields. A nation's strength had to be measured by more than its warriors.

And if one measured a lord by the strengths of the men that he commanded, the Earth could have done no better than to choose Gaborn. Mystarria was the largest, wealthiest nation in Rofehavan.

Perhaps the Earth had chosen Gaborn, in part, because of the strength of his people.

If that was true, then the Earth had not merely chosen Gaborn to be Earth King on his own merits, it had chosen Gaborn because it knew that Borenson could be counted on to be the Earth King's protector.

That notion startled Borenson, and humbled him. For it meant that he might be more tightly entangled in this whole affair than he'd imagined.

It meant also that perhaps the Earth required his best efforts. It might even mean that Borenson needed to protect Gaborn from himself.

He'd need a man who would stand up to the reavers when they issued from their caves. He'd need a man who knew Gaborn's weaknesses, and who would not despise him for being only a young man, instead of a proper Earth King.

Such thoughts drove Borenson as he rode into Deyazz, racing along the narrow mountain trails. He rounded a bend as a flock of crows flew up from the road. Suddenly, on the hairpin turn before him, a troop of soldiers a hundred strong came riding.

The road to the right was too steep to climb. To the left it was nearly a vertical fall. His horse was wise enough to skid to a halt before Borenson thought to draw in the reins.

Yet the animal had been trained to hate the colors of Raj Ahten's troops. It pawed a hoof in the air and stamped and snorted and fought at the bit upon seeing so many golden surcoats sporting the crimson trio of wolf heads.

The captain of the troop was an Invincible, a big man with a crooked nose, pocked skin, and glowering dark eyes. He carried a long-handled horseman's mace. At his back, several men drew bows.

Behind him, Borenson suddenly heard the beat of horses' hooves. He glanced back up the road. Another troop of lancers rode in behind him. They must have come down off the hill above. He'd never even seen their scout.

Trapped. He was trapped.

'Where do you go, red hair?' the Invincible asked.

'I carry a message from the Earth King, and come under the banner of truce.'

'Raj Ahten is not here in Indhopal, as you well know,' the big fellow said. 'He is in Mystarria. You would trouble yourself less to ride back to your own lands.'

Borenson nodded in acquiescence, eyes half-closed in sign of respect.

'My message is not for Raj Ahten,' Borenson said. 'I carry a message to the Palace of Concubines in Obran, to a woman named Saffira, the daughter of the Emir of Tuulistan.'

The Invincible tilted his head in thought. He clearly was not prepared for such news. Behind him, an old man in a fine gray silk burnoose, beneath a yellow traveling robe, whispered to the captain's ear, '*Sabbis etolo! Verissa oan.*' Kill him! He seeks forbidden fruit.

Borenson fastened his eyes on the old man. He was obviously not a soldier, merchant, or traveler, but a sort of counselor to Raj Ahten. Most probably he held the rank of *kaif* – which would be translated as 'old man' or 'elder.' More importantly, he seemed to be Borenson's adversary.

'It is forbidden fruit to look upon the concubines,' Borenson said. 'I had not heard that it is forbidden fruit to deliver a message.'

The old fellow glared at Borenson and looked askance, as if to argue with one of his rank were an affront.

'You speak truly,' the Invincible said. 'Though I am surprised that you have heard of the palace at Obran. Among the hundred here, only the *kaifba* and I have ever heard it.'

Kaifba. Great elder. 'Then may I deliver my message?'

'What need has a messenger for armor and weapons?' the Invincible asked.

'The mountain passes are dangerous. Your assassins did not respect the banner of truce.'

'Are you sure they were *my* assassins?' the Invincible asked, as if Borenson had affronted him. 'The mountains are full of robbers, and men who are worse.' The Invincible knew damned well that they were his assassins. He looked pointedly at Borenson's war axe and armor.

Borenson dropped his shield. He unsheathed his axe, threw it to the roadside. Then he pulled off his helm and ring mail, dropped them also.

'There, are you satisfied?' Borenson asked.

'A messenger has no need of endowments,' the Invincible said. 'Take off your tunic, so that I may see whose strengths you wear.'

Borenson stripped off his tunic, showed the jagged white scars where the forcibles had kissed him thirty-two times. Stamina, brawn, grace, metabolism, wit. All were here.

The Invincible grunted. 'You say you are a messenger for a king, yet you bear a blank shield like a Knight Equitable. Often they come to kill my lord's Dedicates. Yet I must ask myself, what Knight Equitable would be so stupid as to ride in plain sight like this? And now I must ask myself, what Knight Equitable has so many endowments?'

'My name is Borenson, and I was once guard to the Earth King. Now I am a blank shield, free to do as I wish, and right now I wish to bring the Earth King's message and sue for peace.' He stood, breathing hard, defiant. Without arms or armor, he would be no match for even this one Invincible, much less the others. They had him at their mercy.

'Assassin,' the men in the ranks muttered, and they eyed him darkly. One man said, 'Take him to the precipice – teach him how to fly!'

But the kaifba muttered, 'You tell an interesting story, hard to prove, hard to disprove. You know of the Palace of the Concubines, when no man of your country has ever heard of it. And I have not heard of this Saffira, though I know that the Emir has many daughters.' He seemed secure in the knowledge that if she were a person of import, he would have known her name.

'It is forbidden fruit to speak her name in your land,' Borenson said. 'I learned it from a man who once served as a counselor to the Great Light himself – Jureem. He now sits at

BROTHERHOOD OF THE WOLF

the elbow of the Earth King and counsels him.' A kaifba would surely know Jureem, who had been Raj Ahten's high counselor.

'What is your message?' the kaifba asked. 'Tell it to me, and perhaps I will give it to her.'

Among the Deyazz, a message might easily be delivered by a second without giving affront to either the sender or receiver of the message. But Borenson knew that gifts had to be given in person. 'I bear a gift, a favor, for Saffira,' Borenson said, 'along with the message.'

'Show me the gift,' the kaifba said. Among royalty, a gift of gold or perfume might have been an acceptable favor to offer before asking a boon. Borenson wondered if such items might not tempt these soldiers. The men shifted uneasily on their mounts.

He reached into his saddlebags, picked up as many forcibles in one hand as he could. He held perhaps seventy. 'It is the gift of beauty. Seven hundred forcibles of glamour. Three hundred of Voice.'

The soldiers began to talk excitedly. Forcibles were worth far more than their weight in gold.

'Silence!' the Invincible shouted sternly at his men. Then he turned a deadly glare upon Borenson and demanded, 'Tell me the message.'

'I am to say to her, "Though I hate my cousin, the enemy of my cousin is *my* enemy." And then I am to ask her to bear this message for us to Raj Ahten, in the name of the Earth King.'

'Kill him,' the kaifba whispered. Some of the soldiers urged the same. Their horses stamped their feet, feeling the tension in the air, the electric thrill.

Borenson steeled himself for a deathblow. He did not doubt that if the kaifba ordered his death, the others would fulfill that order.

But the captain of the Invincibles tilted his head to the side and considered, ignoring the command, as only a military officer might.

After a long moment, he ventured, 'And you think the Great Light of Indhopal will listen?'

'It is only a hope,' Borenson said. 'The Earth King is Raj Ahten's cousin by marriage now. And we have word that reavers are attacking Kartish and the south of Mystarria. The Earth King hopes to put aside this conflict, now that greater enemies confront us.'

The Invincible nodded, said, 'These sound like the words of an Earth King. He sues for peace. My grandfather always said that if an Earth King were to arise, "He will be great in war, but greater in peace."'

He glanced at the kaifba, and the old man glared at him, angry that the captain did not kill Borenson outright.

'You will deliver your message,' the Invincible said. 'But only if you consent to wear manacles while in our land. You must vow not to break our laws. You may not enter into the palace, and you may not look upon a concubine. Also, I will ride at your side at all times. Do you agree?'

Borenson nodded.

In moments, a fellow brought the manacles – huge iron affairs, made especially to bind men who had endowments of brawn – and he locked them onto Borenson's wrists. Then he chained the manacles around Borenson's back, so that he could not lift his hands.

When the fellow was done, Borenson expected him to offer the Invincible a key. But he did not.

Instead, the Invincible took the reins to Borenson's mount and began walking it down the mountain.

'Do you have the key to the manacles?' Borenson asked.

The Invincible shook his head. 'I do not need one. A smith will remove the manacles – if it ever proves necessary.'

Borenson got an uneasy feeling. A new fear took him. Raj Ahten seldom killed men. He did not steal their lives. He stole their endowments.

A man like Borenson would be a prize.

The Invincible smiled coldly when he saw that Borenson had understood.

Borenson had surrendered without a fight.

15

THE SCATTERING

At dawn, after a night of fitful sleep, Iome wakened to a voice ringing in her mind. 'Arise, all you Chosen who reside at Castle Sylvarresta. A Darkling Glory comes, and time is not great. You must prepare to flee into the Dunnwood. Arise.'

The effect was astonishing. Iome had never felt so completely . . . dominated by the will of another. The voice rang inside her skull like a bell, and every fiber in her sought to obey. Every muscle seemed to react.

Her heart pounded wildly, and she gasped for breath. She leapt from the bed, grabbing only a quilt to throw around her shoulders, scattering the pups that had slept beside her.

All right, I've risen! she thought distractedly. Now what?

Run! she decided in a blind panic. The Darkling Glory is coming.

She would have raced away from the castle in that quilt alone before she realized that it was too immodest. She leapt to her wardrobe and threw on a chemise and skirt, along with a traveling robe and her riding boots, while her five yellow pups circled her and yelped and leapt and wagged their tails, wondering what new game this might be.

She thought only of the stables, tried to determine the quickest route to her stables and her mount. She was about to flee the castle with nothing else in hand when she stopped cold.

Wait, she thought, panting. Binnesman had said that the Darkling Glory would not arrive until tonight. Which meant that she had all day to make good her escape.

Yet the Earth King had warned her through his powers, had warned everyone in and around the city to arise and flee. No, not to flee, to 'prepare' to flee.

As she considered, she realized what a feat it would be. There were tents to move, and animals, baggage, and stores by the wagonload. Worse than that, people had been traveling to Castle Sylvarresta from all across Heredon and environs beyond. Never had the city hosted more than a hundred thousand people, yet now the fields around the castle were cluttered with seven times that number. If everyone fled at once, every road out of town would be jammed.

Gaborn had decided to warn them all now so that he could give them a head start. Instead of running for the forest, as every instinct warned her to do, Iome stooped and stroked each of her pups for a moment. Outside, she heard a few thousand people crying out in dismay, and the sounds of the people camped outside the castle rose to a dull roar. Gaborn had warned them only to prepare, yet it sounded as if the mob were panicking. Iome closed the pups inside her room, and raced to the top of the King's Keep.

There she found Gaborn staring out over the city. The place was bedlam.

Thousands of people were running for the Dunnwood, screaming and crying, many carrying nothing but the clothes on their backs. Others tore down their pavilions as quickly as possible. Horses bucked and grew frightened, racing from their desperate owners. Yet not everyone did as Gaborn had commanded. Many among the camp had not yet been Chosen, and therefore had not heard Gaborn's command. Thousands of these raced for the castle, as if to seek verbal orders or possibly defend the keep. Others had decided that running north, away from the Dunnwood, was more sensible. They blindly surged toward the town of Eels, some two and a half miles north of Sylvarresta.

At the far edge of the camp, King Orwynne had mounted some five hundred knights, and another thousand lords of Heredon stood with him, prepared to head south. They included every lord or knight among Gaborn's retinue who could command a force horse.

It was not a large force to send against Raj Ahten, but a powerful one, comprised only of those force horses capable of traveling two hundred miles a day. The warriors looked eager to ride as they awaited Gaborn, many of them glancing back over the camps.

Yet the Earth King stood on his tower, awestruck, dismayed at the madness he had caused by issuing his warning through the earth powers. Gaborn wore a simple shirt of horseman's mail beneath his cape, and had put on his riding boots. But he had not yet donned his helm, so that his dark hair hung down to his shoulders.

'What are you doing?' Iome demanded. 'You nearly frightened me to death! You nearly frightened all of us to death.' She put one hand over her chest, vainly trying to still her heart, to calm her breathing.

'I'm sorry,' Gaborn said. 'I'd hoped it would go better. I've been fighting the urge to issue the warning all night. I had to give them as much time as possible to flee, but I dared not have them running blindly in the darkness. I don't want to panic them.'

His tone was so apologetic that Iome knew he meant it. He was concerned only with the welfare of his people.

Suddenly his voice rang through her mind again. 'Calm yourselves. You have the whole day. Work together. Save the old and the young and the infirm. Get as far from the castle as you can by nightfall.'

People were still running, though many of them stopped and tried to obey his newest command.

He pointed down to the roiling mass of falling tents and fleeing citizenry. 'You see what happened? Many of those people camped by the river came out of West Heredon, and they would have trampled everyone in camp as they dashed for their homes.

'And down there, see that red pavilion where the children are crying? Their mother and father fled without them! I applaud the parents' obedience, but I had hoped for a more measured response.

'Yet I chose the man and woman in the tent next to them, and neither of them have bestirred themselves to get out of their beds at all, as far as I can tell! They must be packing, I think, but what if the danger were more immediate? Should I applaud them for their measured response, or will they someday die because of it?

'And see up there, many people have reached the edge of the Dunnwood already, and now they mill about in confusion, unsure what to do next. And others may not stop running – no matter what I say – until they faint from exhaustion. Who among them is right? Those who follow the very letter of my command, or those who strive too hard?

'And over there, you see that old woman struggling to escape? She must be ninety. She cannot possibly walk more than two miles in a day. Do you think anyone will help her?'

As Gaborn studied the swirling miasma of humanity, his mouth gaped open in astonishment and horror.

Iome understood now. He was so new to his power, so unused to it, that he wielded it clumsily. He could not afford to wield it so. His power was like a sword, a weapon that was only useful if the arm that wielded it could parry and thrust with accuracy. He was trying to learn his strokes now.

And so much depended on those strokes – the lives of every man, woman, and child in this vast throng.

But even as she watched, she realized that he witnessed an even greater horror. As Earth King, he had power to warn his people, but he could not force them to obey. He could not compel them to act in their own best interests.

With the issuing of his second command, the confusion began to ease. Gaborn sent them a third warning, asking them to calm themselves and care for one another. People all took a moment to stop and stare up at Gaborn. Tents and pavilions still fell with marvelous rapidity, but now parents raced back to their children, while strangers went to help the elderly. Iome no longer worried that people in the lead might be crushed under the feet of those behind.

Gaborn nodded in approval, turned to Iome and hugged her.

'Are you leaving now?' she asked, not wanting him to go.

'Yes,' he said. 'King Orwynne and the others are already mounted, and we have far to travel today. Few of the horses will be able to handle such a pace. I've sent messengers to Queen Herin the Red and on into Beldinook, asking them each to host us for a day. We'll travel without cooks or any other camp followers.'

Iome nodded. It would be a hard march without any camp followers, without cooks or washwomen or tents or squires to care for the armor and animals. Yet if they were to travel quickly, they'd have to make do. In troubled times like these, no lord would dare refuse to feed his company. They'd be glad for the reinforcements, and a night's food and lodging would be small recompense.

Then Gaborn asked something unexpected. 'Will you ride with me?' It was not common for a lord to take his wife to war, but it was not common for a lord to desert his wife within six months of the wedding, either. She suspected that it was a hard thing for him to ask.

'You ask me to come now?' she said. 'You could have asked me hours ago. I'd have been ready.'

'I looked in on you hours ago. You slept fitfully, and you don't have the stamina to go without sleep and then ride all day. So I had the idea of asking Jureem to stay a few hours this morning and take notes, watch the camp and learn what he can, so that next time I must warn a city to flee, I'll know how to do it. I thought that you could stay with him, then ride later this morning. Your horses are fast enough so that you should catch up quickly.'

'May I bring Myrrima?' Iome asked. 'She'll want to come, too. I'll need a lady to keep me company.'

Gaborn frowned in thought. He did not want to take another lord's wife on what might prove to be a dangerous journey, but saw his wife's need to follow the rules of propriety.

'Of course,' he said, but sounded uncertain.

He stared hard at her, his dark-blue eyes gauging her. 'I saw the pups in bed with you.'

'You weren't there,' she said in her own defense. 'I needed something to keep me warm.'

'Are the nights so cold?'

'"The Knights are Hot in Heredon,"' she said, quoting the title of a bawdy ballad that she'd never heard openly sung in her presence.

Gaborn laughed uproariously and his face reddened. 'So, my wife wants to be a wolf lord and slouch about alehouses now, singing bawdies and showing her legs!' Gaborn said. 'Queen of the byways! People will say I'm a bad influence.'

'Do you disapprove?'

Gaborn smiled. 'No. If I did not have my endowments already, I might have slept with some pups last night. I'm . . . relieved that you accepted Duke Groverman's gift. He will be delighted that he has served you so well.' Gaborn considered for a moment. 'I'll have the treasurer set aside forcibles for your personal use. A hundred should do.'

'I will have Jureem bring some extra puppies for you, too, then,' Iome said. 'You are going into battle soon.'

Iome grabbed him and kissed him on impulse, then suddenly realized she was kissing him here on the tower, while probably not less than ten thousand eyes were watching. She pushed back in embarrassment. 'Sorry,' she said. 'The people are staring.'

'They saw us kiss at the wedding,' Gaborn said, 'and as I recall, some cheered.' He kissed her again. 'Until this afternoon, then?'

'Thank you,' she replied.

Gaborn bit his lip, smiled worriedly, and said, 'Never thank a man for taking you into battle until after the war is over.'

Then he turned and raced down the hatch at the top of the tower. In moments she saw him striding out of the keep, along the cobbled streets to the King's Gate, then he was lost as he moved down to the blackened corner of Market Street, where he'd killed the flameweaver last week. Masons had been hard at work repairing the damage to the buildings there, but cleaning and replacing the stone faces of the market would take months or years, and already the place was being referred to by the locals as the 'Black Corner.' Iome imagined that four hundred years from now, strangers getting directions to some establishment would be told, 'Aye, the silversmith's shop is up on the Black Corner, toward the portcullis,' and everyone would understand what it meant.

If we are lucky enough to live so long, she thought.

Then she got to work. She packed her own things, then had some servants and a new guardsman – a powerful young lad named Sir Donnor out of Castle Donyeis – go with her to the king's treasury to remove all the gold and precious spices and armor and forcibles.

Gaborn had taken twenty thousand forcibles south to return to Raj Ahten, in hopes that the Wolf Lord would agree to his terms for a truce. Yet he still had ten thousand forcibles in the treasury, along with other gifts that had been given recently by lords of Heredon. The gifts included plate mail for Gaborn and barding for Gaborn's horse given by Duke Mardon upon their wedding, but which Gaborn would not take into this battle, because of its onerous weight. In addition, there was a good deal of gold and spices given in revenue, for the harvest taxes were normally paid during the week of Hostenfest. The sum total amounted to several thousand pounds of treasure. So she had the servants quietly haul it all up to the tombs, where she locked it in the vault among the bones of her grandparents.

This feat in itself took her two hours, and when she had finished, the thought struck her that she ought to check on Binnesman, for she had not yet seen him, and she worried that he might need the help of some servants before they all left the city.

When she went to his room down in the basement of the keep, he was not there, though a fire burned in an old hearth, and the air smelled heavily of simmering verbena – an herb with a lemony scent, often decocted to make perfumes. Indeed the fresh fragrance filled the whole basement, and smelled like liquid sunshine. In the buttery Iome found Chancellor Rodderman's daughter, a sharp-eyed girl of eight, who had stayed in the keep while her father made certain that it was properly evacuated. Binnesman had left at dawn, saying that he would search the manor gardens down in the city for goldenbay, succory, and faith raven.

Iome abandoned that concern for a moment. Instead she made her way to the Dedicate's Keep, to make sure that the Dedicates had been evacuated.

In the past week the keep had become a different place. Sir Borenson, acting upon the orders of Gaborn's father, had slain all of the Dedicates here, for Raj Ahten had forced her father's troops to grant him endowments, thus seizing attributes from thousands of Sylvarresta's people. Borenson's had been a bloody and horrific deed, and though part of Iome was grateful that someone had had the courage to do it, another part of her was still shocked and saddened. Many of the Dedicates had been servants who'd offered the use of their minds or brawn, stamina or metabolism into the service of King Sylvarresta. Their only crime had been to love their lord and seek to serve him as best they were able. Yet when the knights to whom they had granted endowments were captured, forced to grant endowments of their own, the Dedicates had become converted to the use of a monster like Raj Ahten. Since no one could hope to slay Raj Ahten, his enemies' best hope was to weaken him – which meant slaughtering the enfeebled and innocent Dedicates. Borenson's feat had been a grisly task, killing fools who did not know that their own deaths were upon them, butchering those who had given metabolism in their endless slumber, murdering those so weak from having given brawn so that they could not even raise their hands to ward off a blow.

Borenson had been cold and distant to her and Gaborn since that night. He did not handle the guilt well.

And as Iome walked through the bailey that served as the

courtyard to the Dedicate's Keep, she did not handle her own memories of this place well, either. The high narrow walls around the keep made it feel suffocating. The Dedicate's Keep carried too many dark memories.

Only a couple of small trees, stunted by lack of light, grew within the bailey. A week past, Iome's mother had lain here, her body hidden from sight after Raj Ahten murdered her. And after her father had given his endowment of wit to the Wolf Lord, Iome had stayed here a day serving him, though he did not know his own daughter to look at her. For not only was he witless, but she had given her own endowment of glamour to Raj Ahten's vector, and so had become ugly.

Iome crossed the bailey but dared not enter the keep itself, for fear that it would arouse too many memories of lost friends, for fear that she would find herself looking for bloodstains on the mats and on the floors. Although the steward assured her the beds had all been burned and the floors, walls, and – by the Powers – ceilings had been scrubbed spotless. She could not willfully try to imagine what it had looked like.

At last she sent Sir Donnor into the keep proper to find Myrrima, while she waited in the courtyard with her Days.

Several wains were parked in the courtyard, and Iome watched a few guards leading the blind to one wain, carrying those who had given grace or brawn to another. They were a sad-looking lot, these people who had offered to become cripples in service to their king.

A moment later Sir Donnor exited the keep and assured Iome that Myrrima had attended to her mother and sisters, and even now was packing in her own room.

Iome bade Sir Donnor go to the stables and prepare their mounts, then went to inform Myrrima that they would leave together, heading south with her husband. Iome wasn't surprised to find Myrrima with her pups yapping at her feet, and a longbow with a quiver full of deadly looking arrows and a wrist guard on her bed. But she was surprised to find Myrrima trying on a rather shabby, heavily quilted old vest that looked fit to be worn only while scrubbing floors.

'Do you think it smashes my breasts down enough?' Myrrima asked.

Iome stared at Myrrima in frank surprise and said, 'If you want smashed breasts, rocks might work better.'

Myrrima made a sour face. 'I'm serious.'

'All right, smashed enough for what?'

'So that they don't get in the way when I shoot!'

Iome had never fired a bow, though she knew ladies who had, and she recognized Myrrima's predicament.

'I've got a leather riding vest in my wardrobe that might work better. I'll get it for you,' Iome offered.

Then she told Myrrima that they would both be riding south. Myrrima seemed both astonished and genuinely gladdened by the prospect of following the men to war.

An hour later, Myrrima and Iome had a good breakfast with Iome's Days and Sir Donnor, but by ten in the morning Binnesman had still not come back to his room, so they sent to the stables for their horses and prepared to ride out, leaving little undone. Iome's puppies were left in the king's kitchen, until she felt sure that she would depart.

In all the confusion, Iome still had not talked to Jureem. When she reached the city gate, she found him shouting at people who loafed outside the castle.

Iome had imagined that by now everyone would have fled the grounds outside Castle Sylvarresta, but it was not so. As she looked through the city gates, she realized that the roads to the south and to the west, the roads heading into the Dunnwood, were jammed with carts and oxen and peasants, many of whom had given up on the notion of travel and were just milling about. Of the pavilions near the castle, a full quarter of them still stood, and many of their occupants seemed not to be interested in going anywhere at all.

Jureem had his hands full. Though he was a fine servant – perhaps the most capable servant she'd ever met – he could not do the impossible.

And the situation before him was clearly impossible. A full five thousand petty lords and knights and even some peasants with nothing more than longbows to use as weapons had besieged the gates of the castle and demanded entrance. The city guard – about forty men – barred their way.

'What's going on?' Iome demanded.

'Your Highness,' Jureem explained, 'these men have decided that they want to guard the castle walls.'

'But . . .' Iome could think of nothing to say for a moment. 'But Gaborn told everyone to flee.'

'I know!' Jureem said. 'But they choose not to listen.'

It astonished her that a vassal would disobey the command of his king. She looked to Sir Donnor, as if for an answer. But the blond lad merely glared at the troublemakers. She gazed out over the throng. 'Is this true?' she asked. 'Are none of you Chosen? Did you not hear the commands?'

At that, hundreds of men looked away in shame. Though they might stand up to Jureem, a mere servant, they would not do so to Iome.

Baffled, she said. 'Do you even know what a Darkling Glory is? Can you guess its powers?'

One man, a petty lord she recognized as Sir Barrows, stepped up. 'We've heard of Glories and Bright Ones – we all have,' he said. 'And if the old tales be true, they can die in battle, same as a man. So we was thinking we could stand fast on the battlements with the siege engines – the ballistas and catapults and steel bows, and kill it before it even lands.'

'Are you daft?' Iome shouted, astonished by the man. 'I know you are all courageous, but are you also daft? Did you not hear your lord's command? He told you to flee!'

'Of course we heard, Your Highness,' Sir Barrows replied, 'but surely that command was meant mainly for women and the little ones. We're all strong men here!'

At that, the men all shook their spears and axes and raised their shields and shouted in a great cry that echoed from the hills.

Iome stared in utter amazement. They had heard the word of the Earth King and had decided to keep their own counsel. She turned to the captain of the King's Guard and commanded,

'Place two hundred archers on the wall. Shoot any of these men who comes within bow range.'

'Milady!' Sir Barrows said in a hurt tone.

'I'm not *your* lady,' Iome turned on him and shouted viciously. 'If you will not follow my lord's word, then you are not *his* servant, and you are doomed to die, all of you! I may applaud your valor, but I will curse your foolishness, and I will punish it, if I must!'

'Your Highness!' Sir Barrows said, dropping to his knees, as if awaiting her order. After a moment, the others fell in line and followed his example, though some were slower to bend the knee than others.

She turned on Jureem. 'Why are people milling about on the roads?' she asked. 'Can't they get away from the city?'

'The slower travelers get in their way,' Jureem said. 'Many of the carts are heavily laden, and some have broken axles or lost wheels, so everyone must move around them.'

Iome turned to the troops that knelt before the castle gate. 'Sir Barrows, send a thousand men up each road and have them clear the carts of those who are stranded. Put them to work fixing wheels and axles. As for those folk who have chosen to remain afield, go find out why they are here. If they have valid reasons to stay, I want to know. If they don't have good reasons to stay, tell them that you have orders to kill anyone found within five miles of the castle within the hour.'

'Your Highness,' Sir Barrows cried in astonishment. 'Do you really want us to kill them?'

Iome felt bewildered by his stupidity. But then she remembered that Gaborn had said earlier in the week that he thought it wrong to ever curse a man for being a fool, for fools could not help themselves and were forever at the mercy of the cunning. 'You shan't need to kill them,' she warned. 'The Darkling Glory will do it for you.'

Sir Barrows opened his mouth in sudden comprehension. 'It will be done, Your Highness.' He turned and began shouting orders.

Jureem bowed his pudgy figure to her, the decorative hem

of his golden silk robes sweeping the dust. 'Thank you, Your Highness. I was not able to reason with them, and I dared not disturb you.'

'Next time, dare,' she said.

'There are other matters,' Jureem said.

'Such as?'

'Hundreds of people are too ill to run. Some are too old, too infirm; some are mothers who have given birth in the past few hours, or warriors who were injured in yesterday's games. They have asked permission to take cover in the castle. I've had them carried to the inns until we can decide what to do.'

'Can we load them on wagons?' Iome asked.

'I've had physics talk to those who can speak at all. Anyone who could be loaded on a wagon has already gone. Some physics have offered to stay and tend the ill.'

Iome licked her lips, grimaced in despair. Of course they could not be moved. Such people could not move five miles – or a more appropriate fifty – in a day. 'Let them stay,' she said. 'Some will have to stay hidden.'

She wondered if she should order the physics away, for she feared to lose such highly skilled men and women, but she also dared not deny the sick and the dying whatever succor she could give.

As she considered what to do, Binnesman came strolling through the crowd of warriors from someplace outside of the city. A sack on his back was overstuffed with goldenbay leaves.

Though it was still morning, already Binnesman looked spent. 'Let them stay, Your Highness,' he shouted, 'but not in the uppermost rooms of the inns. Go instead to the deepest cellars, well belowground. I shall come put runes on the doors to help conceal them, and I'll leave some herbs that might offer protection.'

Iome felt more relieved to see Binnesman than reasoning could account for. As Binnesman approached, she understood why. Often in the past, she'd felt the earth power that pooled within him, a slightly disturbing power that spoke of birth and growth and that filled her with creative longings. But this morning he must have been casting strong protective spells, for she felt as a harried rider might when fleeing enemies and suddenly has found himself safely within a castle's walls.

That is it, she realized. This morning she felt safe in his presence. 'You look over-worn. Can I do anything to help you?'

'Yes,' Binnesman said, 'I would be less worried for you, Your Highness, if you would flee the city like everyone else.'

But Iome glanced out over the fields. 'Not everyone has left, and I can't go until I've done everything possible to ensure that my people are safe.'

Binnesman harrumphed. 'That sounds like something your husband would say.' But his tone carried no hint of disapproval. He studied her and Myrrima a moment. 'There is something you *could* do, though I hesitate to ask.'

'Anything,' Iome said.

'Do you have a fine opal you would be willing to give me?' Binnesman asked. His tone suggested that she would never see it again.

'My mother had a necklace and some earrings.'

'With the proper enchantment, they can be powerful wards against creatures of darkness,' Binnesman said.

'Then you shall have them, if I can pry them loose from their mounts.'

'Leave them,' Binnesman said. 'The larger and brighter the stone, the better the protection, and opal easily breaks.'

'I'll get them,' she said. She had forgotten to move them to the treasury, she now realized. Her mother's jewelry chest was still hidden behind her desk in her room.

'You'll find me at the inns,' Binnesman said. 'Time is short.'

Iome and Myrrima rode back up to the King's Keep, and ascended to the topmost room. Sir Donnor and Iome's Days did not dare enter Iome's bedroom, and remained in the alcove outside.

The jewelry chest held Iome's mother's formal crown, a simple but elegant affair of silver with diamonds. Besides the crown, there were dozens and dozens of pairs of earrings, brooches, bracelets, anklets, and necklaces.

Iome found the necklace she recalled. It was made of silver inlaid with twenty matched white opals. A large, brilliant stone mounted on a silver pendant made up its centerpiece.

Iome's mother had said that Iome's father had purchased the stones when he'd traveled to Indhopal to ask for her hand in marriage.

Iome wondered at that. Her father had ridden halfway across the world to find his mother. It seemed a romantic journey, to travel so far, though Gaborn had done no less for her.

Yet somehow the romantic ardor of Iome's marriage to Gaborn felt diluted by the fact that their fathers had been best friends, and had both long desired the union. Marrying Gaborn felt a little like marrying the boy next door, even though she hadn't met him until ten days ago.

As she looked through her mother's chest of jewels, Iome found other opals. The large chest had served the queens of House Sylvarresta for generations, and it held items that her mother had never worn. She discovered a brooch of fire opals set like eyes in a trio of fish made of tarnished copper. Also an old teardrop pendant had an opal that shone in hues of vivid green.

She took these, since they had the largest stones, then handed them to Myrrima, since she was the one with the vest pockets. 'Let us hope these will do.'

She put her mother's jewels back into the chest, then scooted it under her bed.

When she finished, she looked out the oriel window, across the castle.

The streets of the city lay empty, silent. For the first time in her life, she did not see the smoke of even one single cooking fire rising from a chimney in town. In the distance, she saw tents folding out on the fields. Now that the knights were threatening to kill her people, they were fleeeing, racing away.

Suddenly the scene below seemed familiar.

'I dreamt this,' Iome said.

'You dreamt what?' Myrrima asked.

'I dreamt of this, last week when Gaborn and I were riding south to Longmot, or I dreamt something very near. I dreamt that Raj Ahten was coming to destroy us, and everyone in the castle turned to thistledown and floated up and away on the wind, up beyond his grasp.'

The people scattering in all directions reminded her of thistle-down blown before a fierce wind. 'Only in my dream, Gaborn and I were the last to leave. We all floated away. But . . . in my dream, I knew that we were never coming back. Never coming here again.' That thought frightened her. The thought that she might never return to the castle she'd grown up in.

Legend said that the Earth spoke to men in signs and dreams, and those who listened best rightly became lords and kings. The blood of such kings flowed through Iome's veins.

'It was only a dream,' Myrrima said. 'If it were a true sending, then Gaborn would be with you now.'

'He is with me, I think,' Iome said. 'I believe I'm carrying his child.' Iome glanced at Myrrima. She was of common stock, and Iome knew that she would not take omens lightly.

'Oh, milady,' Myrrima whispered. 'Congratulations!' Shyly, she embraced Iome.

'It will be your turn, soon,' Iome assured Myrrima. 'You cannot be near the Earth King without responding to his creative powers.'

'I hope so,' Myrrima said.

Now Iome retrieved the jewely chest from under the bed and withdrew her mother's crown and the most valuable pieces she could see. Just in case, she told herself. These pieces she wrapped in a pillowcase, thinking it would fit nicely in her saddlebags.

As she finished, someone – a girl – shouted desperately out in the courtyard before the castle. 'Hello? Hello? Is anyone here?'

Myrrima opened the oriel window. Iome leaned over the sill to look down.

A girl of twelve, a serving girl by the look of her, wearing a brown frock, saw Iome and cried, 'Help! Your Highness, I was hoping to find one of the King's Guard. Milady Opinsher has locked herself in her apartments and won't come out!'

Lady Opinsher was an elderly dame who lived in the city's oldest and finest neighborhood. Iome knew her well. She knew for a fact that Gaborn had Chosen her when she presented herself at their wedding. Certainly Lady Opinsher had heard the Earth King's warning.

'I'll be there in a moment,' Iome said, wondering at what trouble this portended.

She and Myrrima hurried down to the bailey, with Sir Donnor and the Days falling in step behind. The girl climbed fearfully onto Myrrima's steed, and they raced the mounts down through the King's Gate, into the city, and along the narrow streets toward Dame Opinsher's manor.

As they raced, Iome glanced up, caught sight of a child in an open window. It was late in the morning, she realized, and still not everyone had obeyed her husband's call.

At Dame Opinsher's manor, they stopped at the porte cochere, where white columns held up a roof above an enclosed courtyard. At the front door of the manor, two guardsmen in fine enameled plate stood at arms.

'What is the meaning of this?' Iome asked them. 'Shouldn't you have left by now?'

'We beg your indulgence,' one guard said, an old fellow with clear blue eyes and a silver moustache that dropped over his mouth. 'But we are sworn into the service of Lady Opinsher, and she bade us remain at our posts. That's why we sent the girl.'

'May we pass?' Sir Donnor asked threateningly, as if unsure what the guardsmen's orders were. If the woman had gone far into insanity, she might have ordered the guards to kill all comers.

'Of course,' the elder guard said. He stepped aside.

Iome dismounted, hurried into the house with the serving girl to lead the way.

Lady Opinsher's manor was far newer than the King's Keep. While the keep had been built two thousand years ago to serve a lord and his knights, the manor here was less than eight hundred years old, and had been built at leisure during a time of prosperity. It was also far more opulent and stately than was the King's Keep. Iome imagined that it was more like a soaring palace at the Courts of Tide. The entrance had clear windows above it, so that sunlight shone into a great room, making its way down past a silver chandelier to fall onto intricate tile mosaic on the floor. The walls were all paneled with polished wood. Fine lamps rested on tall stands.

The servant led Iome's retinue up a great staircase. Iome felt terribly self-conscious. She was wearing boots and riding clothes, and in such a fine manor, she should have been able to hear the rustle of her own skirts as she climbed the stairs.

When they reached the second floor, the servant led Iome to a huge oaken door, intricately carved with Dame Opinsher's heraldic emblem.

Iome tried to open the door, but found it locked, so she pounded with her bare fists and shouted, 'Open in the name of the Queen.'

When that brought no response, Sir Donnor pounded harder.

Iome heard the whisper of feet against stone, but still the dame did not open her door.

'Get an axe and we'll chop down the door,' Iome said loudly to Sir Donnor.

'Please, Your Highness, don't,' Dame Opinsher begged.

Sir Donnor halted as the dame unlocked her door, opened it a crack. The woman was elderly, her face covered in wrinkles, but she still had a slim figure. With her endowment of glamour still intact, the dame was a fine-looking woman, though she seldom had set foot from her house in the past three years.

'What may I do for you, Your Highness?' the dame asked with a stiff curtsy.

'You heard the Earth King's warning?' Iome asked.

'I did,' the dame answered.

'And?'

'I beg to be left behind,' Dame Opinsher said.

Iome shook her head in wonder. 'Why?'

'I am old,' the dame said. 'My husband is dead; my sons all died in your grandfather's service. I have nothing left to live for. I do not want to leave my house.'

'It is a fine house,' Iome said. 'And it should be here when you return.'

'For eight hundred years my family has lived here,' the dame said. 'I don't want to go. I won't go. Not for you or anyone else.'

'Not for yourself?' Iome asked. 'Not for your king?'

'My mind is made up,' the dame said.

I could command Sir Donnor to drag her out, fight her guards, Iome realized. She doubted that the old gentlemen would give Sir Donnor much trouble, for he was said to be a fine warrior. Borenson had fought him, and promoted him to captain in the King's Guard.

'There is a purpose to life,' Iome said. 'We do not live for ourselves alone. You may be old, but you still may serve others. If there is any wisdom or kindness or compassion left in you, you could still serve others.'

'No,' Dame Opinsher answered 'I'm afraid not.'

'Gaborn looked into your heart. He saw what's in you.' Dame Opinsher was known for her charity, and Iome believed that she understood why Gaborn had Chosen the old woman. 'He saw your courage and compassion.'

With a dry chuckle, Dame Opinsher said, 'I ran fresh out of such traits this morning. If my serving girl could buy them in the market, I'd have her fetch them and leave them by the bedroom door. 'No,' she said forcefully, 'I'll not leave!'

She closed her door.

Iome felt dismayed. Perhaps the old woman did feel compassion, but did not believe that tomorrow could be better than today, or that her own life was worth struggling for, or that she had anything of import to give. Iome could only guess at the woman's motives.

'You may stay, then,' Iome said to the door. She would not drag a woman kicking from her own home. 'But you will release your servants. You'll not let them die, too. They must flee.'

'As you will, Your Highness,' the dame answered.

Iome turned to give the command, but the serving girl was already running, glad to escape. Iome stared at Myrrima for a moment. The dark-eyed beauty was thoughtful.

'Even your husband can't save someone who doesn't want to be saved,' Myrrima offered. 'It's not his fault. It's not ours.'

'Sir Donnor,' Iome said, 'go to the city guard and have them search every building in the city. Find out how many more like her there are. Warn them in my name that they must depart.'

'Immediately,' Sir Donnor answered, and he turned and hustled off.

'That will take hours,' Myrrima said after he was gone.

Iome understood the hint of a question in Myrrima's voice. She was asking, 'And if we do this, when do *we* leave?'

Iome bit her lip, glanced at her Days as if searching for an answer. The matronly old woman held silent, as usual. 'We have fast horses,' Iome said. 'We can run farther in an hour than a peasant can in a day.'

Iome found the wizard Binnesman down at an inn, as he had promised. The inn, a reputable old establishment called the Boar's Hoard, was the largest in the city, and the cellars beneath it were a veritable maze. Huge oaken vats exuded a yeasty scent, and dried alecost hung in bundles from the rafters. The place smelled also of mice, though feral cats darted everywhere as Iome, Myrrima, Sir Donnor, and Iome's Days wandered among piles of empty wineskins and bins filled with turnips and onions and leeks, past winepresses and barrels of salted herring and eels, between moist sacks of cheese and bags of flour.

In the farthest reaches of the cellars, back where enormous vats of ale fermented, dozens and dozens of sick people had been laid out for the physics to tend.

Here in the dim light of a single candle, the wizard Binnesman worked. He'd set out leaves of goldenbay and sprigs of faith raven in front of some huge oaken doors, and he'd painted the door with runes.

When Myrrima approached and pulled the queen's jewels from her pocket, Binnesman closed the door to the sickrooms.

He took the opals with greedy hands and laid them out on the dark wooden floor, stained with countless years of grime. Between casks of oil that rose to the ceiling, it was almost as dark as a star-filled night.

Binnesman set the opals on the floor and drew runes in the dust around them. Then he knelt and made slow circular motions with his fingers, chanting:

'Once there was sunlight, that warmed the Earth.
It drenched you like a child who basks
beside the winter's hearth.

'Once the stars shone, so fiercely they streamed,
that the stones still remember
and cherish their beams.'

Binnesman stopped speaking, whispered softly, 'Awaken, and release your light.' He ceased making the circular motions and stood waiting expectantly. The stones until now had lain darkly on the ground.

But suddenly Iome saw them begin to glow as the fire caught deep within them blazed. She had often played with her mother's necklace as a child, had watched the dazzling display of color as she held an opal and shifted it in the light. She'd seen flecks of green, red, and gold all swirled within them.

But nothing prepared her for the dazzling light that blazed from these stones now. Beams of crimson and emerald and deepest sapphire and glorious white played across the room more fiercely than any fire. Staring at them was like staring into the sun, and Iome turned away, fearing that she'd go blind.

Behind her, Myrrima stood back, afraid. She gasped and looked all about the room in wonder as the quavering lights shifted and bounced, as if reflected from water.

Binnesman stared at the fiery opals. Some glowed more fiercely than others did. After long moments they began to dim, like coals going cold. He moved the fire opals off to the left with one finger, for though they shone, their ruddy light quickly faded.

He picked up the pendant that held the green opal with one hand. Though the other stones were darkening, this one still blazed so brightly that the heat of it became intense – its verdure a weapon that smote Iome.

To Iome, Binnesman had always seemed a kindly old man – until now, when the light that flared around him filled her with terror. He stuffed the pendant into a pocket of his robe, and the light still glowed like a fire through the cloth.

'My thanks to you, Your Highness,' Binnesman said. 'This is as fine a stone as I could hope to find. I have no use for the others. You will find that they are somewhat dull now, but put them in the sunlight for a few days, and their fire will return more fiercely than ever.'

He carefully laid a single earring on the floor before the closed door of the sickroom, then handed the rest of the opals back to Myrrima.

Iome stood in the gloom, bedazzled. 'Will it work?' she asked. 'Can you kill it with that stone?'

'Kill a Darkling Glory?' Binnesman asked. 'The thought hadn't occurred to me. I only hope to capture it.'

16

PATCHES OF FOG

The ride down from the Brace Mountains into Carris seemed too easy to Roland. It felt wrong all the way. He, Baron Poll, Averan, and the green woman made good time on the mountain road that morning, for the most part because the roads were empty.

That in itself seemed wrong. King Orden's chief counselor and strategist, Paldane the Huntsman, was said to be at Carris. One would have expected to see his troops racing on the highway, getting into position for the coming battle.

As they rode down from the mountains through bands of pine and aspen, Roland took a few moments to sit on an outcropping to watch the rocky plains below for sign of troops. Morning fog lay thick in patches down among some streams, fog so thick an army could have hidden beneath it. Beyond, the region was rife with other places where an army might be secreted – forested hills rose above the plain at a number of points, and a deep valley lay between two arms of a mountain off to the west. Cities and towns were everywhere.

The Barren's Wall to the north was eight miles wide and stretched between two tall hills. In ages past, Muttaya and Mystarria had fought over this realm numerous times. The fact that Mystarria had not always won was profoundly evident in the varying architecture: domed manors with enclosed porches and reflecting ponds were everywhere in the towns. The streets were much broader than in the Courts of Tide where Roland had been raised.

The names of the villages also reflected the fact that this land had much been battled over. Villages like Ambush, Gillen's Fall, and Retreat squatted beside towns with names like Aswander, Pastek, and Kishku.

All in all, Roland studied the landscape below and thought it a fine site for a strategist like Paldane the Huntsman to choose for his battles. Several fortresses could serve as rallying points. He imagined how bowmen might be secreted behind stone fences, or cavalry might hide within the gates of a larger keep.

Yet he saw no sign of troops on the plains anywhere below – no glint of morning sunlight on armor, no smoke rising from campfires, no lords' pavilions pitched in any distant valley.

Indeed, from the hills above Carris, the landscape looked dead. Roland, Baron Poll, Averan, and the green woman stood on a knoll for fifteen minutes, squinting into the valley below. Roland could see farmhouses by the hundreds, and haycocks by the scores. Fields of crops checkered the land – vineyards striping one field while hops darkened the next. Rock walls circled the farmsteads. From up here, one could see that there was an abundance of stone in Carris, enough to build homes and fences, and still so much surplus that the farmers had, in some places, just piled them into mounds. Atop many of the hills were ancient Muttayin sun domes – circular crematoriums built of stone so that they looked like the setting sun. These marked ancient battle sites.

Carris was an old land. It was said that the fortress here was older than memory even when Erden Geboren rode with his hundred thousand knights to defend it. Many of those sun domes below served as incinerators where conquering armies had tossed the losers. Wights would haunt such places.

But if there were wights about, they did not seem to bother the locals. Carris itself was hard to make out from this distance, still twenty miles away. The ancient fortress was built on a peninsula in a deep lake on the horizon. Fog lay thick on the lake, but the fortress pierced the fog, its granite walls and high watchtowers shining like gold in the dawn. Morning cooking fires left a trail of smoke hanging above the castle.

A graak flew up out of the castle, bearing a skyrider. Averan sighed, as if she yearned to be on the beast.

Yet close by, no smoke drifted up from any chimney in any home. No wind blew. No animals walked the fields.

Dead. The whole plain of Carris looked utterly dead, aside from a few flocks of geese that winged about. Even here on the mountainside, it was too quiet: no jays squawked, no squirrels scurried about.

'I don't like it,' Roland said as he stared below. 'It's too quiet.'

'Aye,' Baron Poll said. 'I was born to this land. I used to run wild here when I was a boy. I've never seen anything like it.'

He pointed to some green fields off to the left, just two miles below, where an orchard intersected a line of oaks. 'At this time of year, always a flock of crows comes winging its way from the north. If you trace a path in the sky, following that line of oaks, you should get a good idea where they fly.

'But I see nothing here today. Not a single crow. Crows are smart birds. They see danger better than a man. They know there's a battle brewing, and so they'll follow the soldiers in hope of good pickings after.

'Look down there, where that patch of fog lies thick on the downs.' He pointed now almost straight ahead, five miles north of the base of the mountain. 'See the geese flying over it? There's good oats in those fields, and ponds to swim about in. Any goose worth a gander should be down there. But the geese aren't circling the fields to make sure it's safe before they land. They're flying from one patch of fog to the next, knowing it's not safe, never daring to land.'

'Why?' Averan asked.

'They're scared. Too many men about, skulking in the fog.'

Averan looked askance, as if she believed that Baron Poll was merely trying to frighten her. The girl seemed tired or ill to Roland. Her eyes were bleary, and she hid in a cloak, as if suffering from chills.

'I'm serious. See that patch of fog, off to our left across the hills over there? It must be two hundred feet higher up than any other patch of fog, and the color is a bit too dark blue. It's traveling downhill when it should be rising, warmed by the morning sunlight. Raj Ahten's men, I'll wager, with a flameweaver hiding them. Our scouts say he used such a fog to hide in while marching through Heredon. If you were to walk into that patch of fog, you'd find war dogs and frowth giants and Invincibles by the score.

'And there, farther across the downs, is another patch of that oily blue fog.

'Then look up here to our left. A third column marching toward them.'

Roland gaped, leaned back on his mount. Baron Poll seemed to be right. The three patches of fog were converging, and no currents of wind would ever have blown them together.

'Then, down there, across from Carris, by the river. Water wizards are at work, I'll wager. See the huge fog there?'

'By its color, I'd say that is just a natural fog,' Roland said.

Baron Poll raised a brow. 'Perhaps, but it's coming off the river there and nowhere else. Water wizard's work. The fog will be of a better quality, more natural-looking than a flameweaver's smoke. *That* fog hides the number of Paldane's reinforcements coming south from Cherlance, I'd say.' The Baron hitched up his pants, the way a peasant will before going to work. 'We must take care. The roads look empty ahead, but looks can be deceiving.'

The green woman pointed at the fog on the downs, and asked, 'Fog?'

'Aye, fog,' Roland said, adding a word to her vocabulary.

She pointed to a cloud in the sky. 'Fog?'

'Cloud,' he said, wondering how he might make a better distinction. He squinted at the sun and pointed. 'And up there is the *sun*. Sun.'

'Sun, no,' the green woman said, glancing fearfully at the bright orb. She pulled the bearskin robe tight against her shoulders.

'I told you she's no creature of fire,' Averan said. She went to the green woman and put the hood of the cloak up for her, so that she could hide beneath it. 'She doesn't like the sunlight any better than she liked our campfire.'

'I suspect you're right,' Baron Poll said. 'My apologies to the gut-eating wench with the avocado complexion.'

Roland laughed.

Averan merely glared at Baron Poll. 'And I'll tell you something else –' she said, drawing her breath as if to make a great statement.

But Averan's face paled and she trembled and grew quiet. She pulled her own cloak tight about her as if she too hid from the sun.

She had a faraway look in her eyes. Roland realized that she trembled not because she feared that Sir Poll might disbelieve what she was about to say, but because she wanted to say something that frightened her.

'Well, tell me . . .' Baron Poll demanded.

'Baron Poll,' she asked distantly, 'what will we do with the green woman?'

'I don't know,' the Baron said. 'But if she would quit following us, I'd be a happier man.'

'If she follows us to Carris, what will Duke Paldane do with her?'

Baron Poll glanced at the green woman distractedly. 'I don't know, child. I suspect he will want to imprison her. She's very strong, and dangerous, and we have no idea where she came from or what she wants.'

'What if she fights him? What if she tries to protect herself?'

'If she harms one of His Majesty's subjects, he'll imprison her.'

'What if she kills someone?'

'You know the punishment,' Baron Poll said.

'He'll execute her, won't he?' Averan asked.

'I suspect so,' Baron Poll said, trying to infuse the statement with a tone of pity that he obviously didn't quite feel.

'We can't let him kill her,' Averan said. 'We can't take her to Carris.'

'We have a message to deliver,' Baron Poll said. 'By all rights, we should have pressed on through the storm last night, but I didn't fancy the notion of running into any of Raj Ahten's troops in the dark. Still, we have a message to deliver, and you, *Skyrider* Averan, are sworn to deliver it.'

'What are you afraid of?' Roland asked, for the girl was obviously terrified out of her wits.

'No one in my family has ever received a Sending,' Averan said.

'And you think you have?' Roland asked.

The girl clutched her hands, wringing them while she held them against her stomach. She trembled in agitation. 'I saw something just now. I saw the green woman dead, on the end of a pole, outside the castle walls.'

Roland was not educated, but every child in Mystarria knew lore about Sendings. 'If it was a true Sending, then it was only a warning, and you might be able to stop it from happening.'

Baron Poll squinted, knelt down to be closer to the child. 'You want to avoid Carris? We could skirt around it, I suppose, but at least one of us must go in.' He considered the possibility only that long, then added more forcefully, 'No, the roads won't be safe! We'll be better off if we stay together. I'm pretty sure I can get us through to Carris, but I won't promise anything more.'

Roland knew that Baron Poll really believed his own warning: armies were hiding down on that plain, and Raj Ahten's men had been waylaying messengers all along the roads.

'Leave me somewhere while you carry the message,' Averan begged. 'The green woman is following *me*, not you. She'll stay wherever you put me. Then you could come back for me.'

Baron Poll scratched his chin. Riding so close to Carris would be dangerous enough, but the child was asking him to risk his life going both directions.

Still, the girl was right to be worried for the fate of the green woman. Baron Poll's eyes flickered over Roland, as he considered what to do. 'It's too dangerous. I won't allow it.'

He spoke in a tone of authority, as if to end all discussion.

'First you say you won't take me north to Heredon, now you say you won't leave me here! Can't I have any say in the matter!' Averan asked.

'No,' Baron Poll said reasonably. 'I may be a fat old knight, but I am a lord and you're not. We're at war. I'm only doing what's best for you.'

'You're only doing what's best for *you*,' Averan cried. 'I don't matter.'

'I'm only thinking about what's best for *people*, not' – he waved his hand at the green woman in dismissal – 'some green monster.'

'I know what's best for me!' Averan said.

'Do you?' Baron Poll asked. 'Last night you pouted because you wanted to go to Heredon. Now you're in a fit because you want to stay here. So what's best?'

'I can change my mind,' Averan said too loudly.

'True,' Baron Poll said, 'but you won't change mine.'

He grabbed Averan roughly by the arm and dragged her to his charger. Averan yelped, and Baron Poll slapped her across the backside.

'Damn you, girl, if you call Raj Ahten's troops with all of your noise, I swear I'll cut your throat before they get me, even if it's the last thing I do.'

Baron Poll leapt up onto his charger, his great strength belying his size, and tried to pull Averan on with him.

'Wait!' Roland said. 'Let her ride with me. And I'll not have you slapping the child, or threatening to slit her throat.'

'What do you care?' Baron Poll asked. Both the Baron and the child stared at him in surprise. Roland was no knight, no warrior who could hope to best Baron Poll in a fight, yet he had spoken harshly.

'I care,' Roland said, gazing at the child. 'I was thinking last night, I could petition Paldane to become her guardian, her . . . father.'

There was a clumsy silence as the child recognized that he

spoke not just a statement, but a question. Then she lurched toward him. 'Yes!' she cried.

Roland mounted up, taking Averan in the saddle before him. In moments they were thundering down the mountainside, the green woman loping behind, and as they neared the plain, Baron Poll suddenly veered his charger sideways and raced it through the trees, cutting across a spur of the mountain on a game trail. The green woman ran at their back, struggling to keep up. Roland felt amazed that she could do so at all. No human could run with such grace and ease.

The Baron no longer seemed to trust the road, and perhaps his own fear finally touched the girl, for Averan fell silent. He raced the horses down the mountainside, and Roland leaned back in his saddle, gripping Averan before him, afraid that the girth strap on his saddle might slip or break so that he'd go rolling downhill. But Baron Poll never slowed.

After several heart-stopping minutes, they found an old woodcutter's road and raced along it for a while, then they rode the horses hard across a creek and let them leap a farmer's fence and gallop across a pasture.

For several miles they rode this way, never trusting a road, often peering off to either side. The green woman ran just behind.

They reached a large village and raced through it, let the horses stop for rest just outside. A number of walnut trees lined the lane, the nuts just beginning to split open from their green pouches, and Averan, still huddled in her robes, looked up at them longingly. 'Are we going to eat today?'

'When we reach the castle, you might get some dinner,' Baron Poll said.

'You gave me nothing more than hope for dinner last night, and now I shan't even have that to chew on for breakfast. They've done with breakfast at the castle and won't eat again until tonight. I didn't get any food yesterday at all.'

'Well,' Baron Poll said, 'all the better to help you maintain a dainty figure.'

'You should try it yourself sometime,' Averan groused. 'Your horse would like you better if you did.'

The Baron shot Averan a warning glare. The child had an endowment of brawn, but Baron Poll had more than one, and he knew he could beat her soundly.

Roland thought him a hard man, to starve a child that way. 'I'll get you some walnuts,' Roland offered, and he leapt from his horse.

The green woman had been lagging behind for several moments, and now she stood, sweat pouring off her, as she gasped for air.

Baron Poll seemed to fear that the child would ride off, so he nudged his horse toward Averan, grabbed her and hefted her onto his own saddle.

Sweat drenched Roland's horse and it breathed like a bellows. Several cottages clustered together here at the north end of the village, and there was little forage for the mounts. Sheep had eaten down the grass near the road. Roland could see no sign of the sheep now. They had probably been driven off to the castle. With little else to eat, the mount went over to a window box outside a cottage and began to chew voraciously on some white geraniums, eating as quickly as only a horse with endowments of metabolism can.

Meanwhile, Roland looked in vain for walnuts on the ground, but pigs rooted there, and they'd taken the nuts. He ended up climbing the tree to pick a few.

'I have to relieve myself,' Averan said, squirming in the saddle where Baron Poll held her firm.

'Hold it for another hour,' Baron Poll commanded her. 'A girl with an endowment of brawn can hold her bladder all day.'

'I've been holding it since last night,' Averan apologized.

Baron Poll rolled his eyes. 'Go then. There should be a privy behind the cottage.'

Averan dropped from the horse and scurried away. The green woman followed at her heels like a faithful dog.

Roland climbed into the crook of a walnut tree and began

filling his pockets. He'd been at it only a minute when he glanced back down the road to the south.

Dust rose from the road in the direction they'd just come. The dust clouds were back a couple of miles, so trees and houses obscured it. Still, at the speed a force horse could race, those riders would be on them quickly.

'Riders, coming fast,' Roland warned Baron Poll. His heart hammered. If he'd not been standing in the tree, he'd not have seen them.

'What colors?'

He saw a flash of yellow. 'Raj Ahten's, they're close on our tails.'

He leapt from the tree, landed hard enough to jar his ankles.

'Averan,' Baron Poll shouted. 'Stop peeing and get over here now!'

He spun his charger and raced around the corner of the cottage, shouting and cursing. Roland leapt onto his own mount, circled the cottage, just in time to see Baron Poll kick over a weathered privy in the backyard. No one was inside.

'The damned girl ran off!' the Baron shouted.

Roland bit his lip, struggled against panic. He did not want to lose the child or see her harmed. He wanted to help her, yet he understood her fears, and applauded her desire to do what she knew was right.

Stone fences divided the land behind this cottage from the yards and gardens behind. Roland searched nervously. He saw no sign of Averan or the green woman.

'They couldn't have gotten far,' Roland said. But he knew that it didn't matter. Even if the girl hid nearby, he couldn't take the time to search for her.

'Leave her!' Baron Poll said. 'The girl wanted to stay, let her stay!'

The Baron wheeled his mount, but Roland was slow to follow. He feared to leave the green woman and Averan there alone. He cared about them more than he'd dare admit.

He rose up in his saddle, searching for the child, vainly hoping to spot the green woman, as Baron Poll raced away.

Moments later, he began to hear the thunder of hooves on the far side of town.

'Luck to you!' Roland called to Averan. 'I'll come back for you, daughter!' he promised. He turned and sped for Carris.

Four cottages away from Baron Poll, Averan huddled behind a lilac bush by a stone fence and watched Roland and the Baron gallop north. She had taken off the green woman's bearskin cloak, so that now her skin blended in with the lilac bush, concealing her.

Averan clutched the green woman tight and cooed softly, to keep her from moving.

She could not explain to Roland and Baron Poll why she needed to leave. The men would never understand. But Averan had had a strange feeling growing in her since yesterday.

It had made her nervous to look at the campfire last night, and the morning sun hurt her eyes, made them burn. And this morning, when she'd knelt over the corpse of Raj Ahten's assassin, pretending to eat, Averan had craved the taste of the man's blood.

Now, she thought she knew what the green woman needed, probably understood it better than the green woman did herself.

She needed the Earth. She needed to be renewed by its power.

So Averan huddled with the green woman while Baron Poll cursed and Roland promised to return. Averan fought to keep tears from her eyes.

She'd been surprised that he asked to be her father, surprised and delighted. She wanted someone to take care of her, to be a friend. But right now, she had to put her own wants aside.

She dared whisper, 'Come back for me then, Father, when you can.'

Moments later, twenty of Raj Ahten's knights went racing past along the tree-lined lane, armor rattling, the hooves of their warhorses thundering on the hard road.

The green woman did not move, leaned into Averan's embrace until the Invincibles had passed. Then she lifted her nose in the air like a hound trying to catch a scent, and asked, 'Blood, yes?'

'Blood, yes,' Averan promised, glad that the green woman had recognized the scent of Raj Ahten's soldiers. 'But not now. You must rest now. I know what you need.'

Averan had seen it in a vision, she felt sure. She didn't understand what she saw, but she felt a need driving her, a craving that went to the bone. The green woman was a creature of the Earth, and right now, she needed its embrace.

Still, Averan felt afraid to move. A morning breeze sighed through town, stirred the lilac bush. The green woman stared up at the leaves, as if in terror of this ominous force.

'It's nothing,' Averan said. 'Only the wind. Wind.'

She held up the green woman's hand, let her feel the wind flow between her fingers. But the green woman jerked her hand back in terror.

'Wind, no!' she said. She looked about desperately, as if searching for a place to hide.

The Invincibles had been gone long enough, Averan decided. She led the green woman to a walled garden behind a cottage. The soil was deep and well tended, but the owners had fled. Before doing so, they'd dug up all of their carrots and turnips.

Averan tasted the rich soil, and approved. She found a mattock in a shed, and in a few minutes was able to dig a shallow trench.

Without any coaxing, the green woman stepped into the trench and lay down, spreading herself out – naked, luxuriating, delighted to feel the soil on her bare skin.

Averan stood over her, prepared to heap the dirt on the green woman, bury her there. But right now she felt a craving of her own, an itching. The sun shone fiercely on her neck, and when she glanced up, it hurt her eyes.

Her robe seemed too thin to protect her from its rays. She looked down at her fist where the green woman's blood had touched her yesterday while Averan had tried to clean her after the fall.

Dark green blotches still stained her hand. The green spots had not gone away – not even when she washed them or tried to rub the skin away. Instead, the dark green blood had merely seeped down lower, into her skin. Now it looked as if she had been tattooed with ink. The blotches would likely never go away, she realized. Or maybe someday the green woman's blood would just seep down farther into her, until it fused with her bones.

'The same blood flows through us now,' Averan said to the green woman. 'I don't even know what you are, but you and I are one.'

Having said that, Averan stripped off her own clothes and climbed into the shallow trench beside the green woman. She used her hands to pull mounds of dirt over her feet and body, to hide her skin from the sun, but she could not bury herself properly.

On a sudden inspiration, she hugged the green woman tightly and commanded the soil, 'Cover me.'

The soil responded, flowing over her like water.

Averan wondered if Roland or any Invincibles would return, see the signs of their shallow grave. Even if they did, what would they do? Dig her up?

No, she realized. We're safe. Safe from sun and fire. Safe for a little while, until nightfall.

17

BENEATH A DUSTY GARMENT

The Durkin Hills Road was a trail of dust. Erin Connal had ridden down it a couple of days ago, when last week's rains had made the road slick at its low points. But at least then the dirt had clung to the ground, and she'd been riding alone.

Now, after only a couple of days of heat, the road south was as dry as if it were midsummer. Beyond that, it had been much traveled during the past week, and the hooves of countless animals and the wheels of thousands of wagons had churned the soil and ground it into a fine powder that rose dirty and brown all about, marking their passage. Time and again, Erin wished that she could ride off into the trees of the Dunnwood, ride parallel to the army, to get clear of the dust. But the brush beside the road was thick, the trails uneven, and she could not afford to slow her trek. Right now the army had need of haste.

She rode now to war in the vanguard of the army, near the very front, beside King Gaborn Val Orden and fat King Orwynne, a gaggle of lords, and of course all of their attendant Days.

A few dozen scouts and guards were strung out on the road ahead, yet the dust of their passage rose high in the air. Grit caught in Erin's teeth and burned her eyes and sinuses. Grime clung to the oiled links of her armor and heavy powder settled in the folds of her clothes. Though they had ridden but half the day, she figured it would take a week's worth of baths to ever feel clean again.

There was nothing she could do about it for now. She was only grateful that she was not riding farther behind in the ranks, for near the rear, the dust would have been unbearable.

Many warriors in Gaborn's retinue wore helms that covered their faces, and so they merely put the visors down, affording the face and eyes some small protection from the dust. Erin envied them. She imagined that even the infernal heat inside the blasted helm would have been more bearable than the dust.

But her own helm was merely a horsewoman's helm, a round thing with guards for ears, without even a bridge for the nose. A horse's tail, dyed royal blue, adorned the top.

So she rode holding a cloth to her face. From behind, the sound of hoofbeats reverberated as a rider raced along the edge of the road.

He glanced at Erin and made to pass her, when suddenly he spotted Gaborn and reined his horse in. The man's face was a study in surprise. Erin realized that he'd been looking for the Earth King, but King Gaborn Val Orden and King Orwynne were both so dirty that one could not distinguish them from common soldiers.

'Your Highness,' the fellow implored Gaborn, 'the troops in the rear beg permission to fall back. The dust is fouling the horse's lungs.'

Erin nearly laughed. Apparently these warriors of Heredon could breathe the dust just fine. It was only their horses that suffered.

'Have them fall back,' Gaborn said. 'I see no reason to keep close ranks, so long as we all reach Castle Groverman by nightfall.'

'Thank you, milord,' the fellow said with a nod. Yet he did not fall back to spread the word. Instead, he rode beside Gaborn as if he would beg another boon.

'Yes?' Gaborn asked.

'Beg your pardon, milord, but since you are the Earth King, could you not do something more?'

'Would you like me to get rid of the dust altogether?' Gaborn asked, bemused.

'That would be greatly appreciated, milord,' the knight said, gratitude thick in his voice.

Gaborn laughed, but whether he laughed from mirth or laughed the fellow to scorn, Erin could not tell. 'I may be the Earth King,' Gaborn said, 'and I like the taste of trail dust no better than you do. But believe me, there is a limit to my powers. If I could make the dust settle, I would. Open ranks. Have every man pace his horse. Those with the quickest horses will reach Groverman first.'

The fellow studied Gaborn from head to foot. The Earth King was covered in grime. 'Yes, milord,' the fellow said, and he wheeled back, calling the orders for the formation to disband.

At that point, the kings gave the horses their heads, and raced away from the more common mounts. In moments, Erin was racing along and even Gaborn's scouts, at the very front of the line, had to hurry to keep ahead of the army.

Erin stood in her stirrups, riding to the flank of the king, and let the wind clean some dust from her clothing and from her hair.

Beside her, Prince Celinor did the same. She glanced over, caught the Prince staring at her. He turned away when she noticed his scrutiny.

Erin did not have an endowment of glamour to mar her face. Fleeds was a poor land, and so by the High Queen's decree, endowments of glamour were never given. One could not waste precious blood metal on forcibles that would enhance a woman's beauty, not when the same ore could be put to some better use.

Still, even without an endowment of glamour, men sometimes found her attractive. Yet she thought it odd that Prince Celinor would gaze at her so. He had at least two endowments of glamour, and so was a fine-looking man. His hair was platinum in color, almost white, his face narrow but strong. His eyes shone like dark sapphires. He was a big man who stood roughly twenty hands tall. A handsome man, indeed, she thought, though she had no desire to bed him. For as they said in Fleeds, 'His reputation follows him as flies follow filth.'

Celinor's Days, who rode behind him, was remarkable only in that he was nearly of the same height as his lord.

No, Erin was not interested in a sot. Last year at Tolfest it was said that Prince Celinor had gone out to distribute alms to the poor of Castle Crowthen and had ridden through the streets in a wagon, tossing out food and clothing and coins. In a drunken stupor, he had soon found himself out of alms, and so had stripped off his own cloth-of-gold breeches and tossed them to the crowd, much to the dismay of those mothers who had children. Rumor also had it that he was well endowed in more ways than one.

It was said that he drank so much that no one was quite sure whether he had ever learned to sit a horse, for he could be seen falling from one more often than riding it.

His vassals nicknamed him 'Mad Dog,' for often the froth of ale could be seen foaming at his mouth.

In an hour they reached the river Dwindell, at the village of Hayworth.

There, the lords and their Days came to a halt, riding their horses down to the riverbank east of the bridge, so that they could quench their thirst. As the animals drank, Erin climbed off her horse, gauged the water. The river Dwindell here was wide and deep, its clear waters swirling in eddies. Clouds had been moving in all day, but even behind their screen, the sun was so high that Erin could see huge trout and even a few salmon swimming in the river's depths.

Erin took the cloth that she'd had over her nose, knelt at the riverbank and dipped it in the cold water, then began to wash some of the grime off her face. She longed to strip off her armor, swim out into the river's depths. But there was no time for it.

Prince Celinor knelt by the water, too, and took off his helm, a thing of burnished silver. He filled it with water twice, swirled the water in it to get the dust off the helm, then filled it a third time and drank deeply, using it as a mug.

When he finished, he offered his helm to Erin while he washed his own face clean of grime. She drank deeply, felt the dust clear from her throat. She'd never tasted water so refreshing.

King Gaborn had halted and was letting his own horse drink, as if too weary to dismount. Gaborn was covered in grime, thick with dust.

Celinor gazed up at the King, the sunlight striking him full on the face.

'Now there is a proper Earth King,' Celinor whispered of Gaborn. 'See how well he wears his realm.' He chuckled, amused at his own jest.

'I'm thinking that none wear it better,' Erin said, for she dared not utter anything so irreverent.

'I meant no disrespect,' Celinor apologized, sounding sincerely regretful.

Erin gave him back his helm, shoved it hard into his hands. Celinor refilled it, then leapt up and carried it to Gaborn, let him drink from it. As Gaborn drank, Celinor wet a cloth in the stream, then carried it to Gaborn.

He offered the cloth for Gaborn to wash his face. Gaborn sponged himself, and thanked Celinor cordially. Yet Erin wondered if Celinor served Gaborn for her sake, or if he really had meant no disrespect.

When Gaborn's mount had watered, he and King Orwynne were quick to cross the bridge and head for the Dwindell Inn there in Hayworth, for it was well-known that strong drink clears trail dust from one's throat better than water. With so many hundreds of knights riding through, Erin imagined that it would be a boon day for the innkeeper.

Erin washed herself, preparing to join Gaborn and King Orwynne. She got on her mount and spurred it over the bridge, and could not fail to notice that Celinor rode at her side.

Yet when she reached the inn and dismounted, Celinor

only sat ahorse, watching her. She stood in the shade of the porch, glancing back. The yeasty smell of ale was strong here, having soaked into the floorboards over the ages.

'Are you coming in?' she asked.

His face looked set, determined. He merely shook his head, then apologized. 'I'll go on up ahead, let my horse rest a few moments.'

Erin went into the inn, her Days following, and sat down at a table alone, just the two of them. In moments a young serving girl hurried over, asking, 'What would please the lady?'

The owner of the hostel, a big-bellied man, sat with King Orden, talking cordially. She heard the fellow congratulating Gaborn on his recent marriage.

'I'll have ale,' she said. The waif hurried off.

In moments the hostler himself ran downstairs to help fetch up some ale kegs. Fat King Orwynne said in his high voice, 'So, Your Highness, it seems that Prince Celinor fears to join us.'

'Good,' Gaborn said. 'I'd hoped that he might have the strength to forbear this place.'

'But do you think it will take?' Orwynne said. 'I for one believe that even the railings of the Earth King will not keep him sober through the week. I'll bet you ten golden eagles, milord, he'll be falling off his horse by sundown tomorrow.'

'I hope not,' Gaborn said, though he did not accept the wager.

'Your Highness,' Erin wondered aloud, 'have you spoken to Prince Celinor?'

King Orwynne glanced at her with the dismissive look that some warlords gave the women of Fleeds. He did not respect her, but he answered her question before Gaborn could speak. 'The sot had the audacity to present himself to the Earth King this morning, before we rode out, and offer his sword in service. The Earth King rejected him, of course.'

Gaborn sat wearily, gazing down at his hands folded on the table. 'Don't be so harsh,' Gaborn said. 'The man has a good heart, but I could not in conscience Choose a man who loves strong drink more than he loves himself or his fellows.'

'So you rejected him?' Erin asked.

'Not rejected,' Gaborn said. 'I asked him for a show of contrition. I asked him to give up his greatest pleasure. In return, if he can remain sober, I will Choose him.'

Erin had not heard that the Earth King made such bargains with men. He had Chosen her outright. Yet she was glad of it, glad to know that a man might better himself to some reward.

When her ale came, she took only a small sip, then went out front where her mount was tied to the hitching rail. She poured ale into her palm for her horse, let it drink, the hairs of its muzzle tickling her palm. A good strong drink would serve her mount well, give it the energy it needed to keep up with the other lords' horses. Her own mount was a good force horse, with a single endowment each of strength and metabolism and grace, but it was not so lavishly endowed as Gaborn's charger, or those of some of the other mounts in the retinue.

She wondered at Gaborn's words. He'd said that Celinor had a 'good heart.' What exactly did that mean? Celinor had done nothing but voice his doubts about Gaborn's sovereignty yesterday. The High Marshal had hinted that he thought Celinor might even be a spy, out to destroy Gaborn. Yet Gaborn had looked into the man and seen a good heart?

It made no sense.

Perhaps, she thought, Gaborn did not mind if Celinor had reservations.

After she'd finished giving her horse some drink, she took her glass mug inside, dropped a copper dove on the table. Her Days followed. Together they rode out of town.

Erin found Celinor and his Days in a meadow dotted with yellow dandelions and white clover. Celinor brushed down his mount as it grazed.

She stopped and did the same, taking a moment to check the beast's legs and ankles. One of its shoes had lost two nails, but otherwise the horse was fine. Celinor could not keep his eyes off her.

'I am surprised that you're not with the others,' Celinor said at last. 'There will be few comforts through these hills, until we reach Bannisferre.'

She dared not admit why she'd come. Her code of honor was such that she stood by a man in battle, even if he was only a man who battled his own vices. 'Since we're allowed to open ranks, I thought it might be more of a comfort to get a head start,' she said. 'Let the others chew on *my* trail dust for a while.'

'I'm certain they'll make a fine meal of it,' Celinor laughed.

Erin smiled. So he truly had not meant to be disrespectful toward Gaborn, she thought. He merely jests by nature.

'So,' Erin asked, 'you think Gaborn is the Earth King after all? I've heard that you bent the knee to him.'

'After he rejected the High Marshal,' Celinor said, 'I reasoned that he is either the Earth King or a madman. I don't think he's mad. He rejected me, too, of course. But I'd hoped for nothing better.'

'Not rejected,' Erin said. 'I hear that he is holding his judgment in reserve.'

'Indeed.' Celinor smiled, cocked his head to the side. 'And I hope someday to be worthy of his blessing. Already I've gone twenty hours without a drink.'

Erin tried to think of a compliment appropriate for such a negligible feat, and had to wonder. Twenty hours? He'd offered his sword into Gaborn's service only this morning. Yet the alehouses around Castle Sylvarresta had been full last night as people celebrated the end of Hostenfest.

What's more, tradition required a toast to end Hostenfest before going to bed. She couldn't imagine him having gone the night without a drink.

'Twenty hours?' she asked. 'But you only offered service this morning.'

'I swore off drink yesterday,' Celinor said.

She looked at him inquisitively.

'You scorned me,' Celinor said, 'and you were right to do so. For I realized that you were correct: all of my best friends did live in alehouses. I would not have it so. I could not bear to look into your eyes and incur your displeasure.'

Erin smiled, pleased that her one remark might have inspired a change in the man. Yet she did not trust it completely.

'Will you ride with me today?' Erin asked.

'I would be happy for the opportunity,' Celinor said. They mounted up, and raced off side by side.

18

ONE FOR THE BOOKS

Gaborn sat in his chair in the Dwindell Inn. King Orwynne kept up a rambling monologue on a number of topics, but Gaborn felt too preoccupied to listen. All morning long, he'd felt a constricting sensation in his chest, the rising recognition of danger.

As his people fled Castle Sylvarresta, his fears for them eased. Yet not everyone had left Castle Sylvarresta. He felt Iome there with Myrrima, and dozens of guards and towns-people still braving the danger.

What powers might this Darkling Glory possess that it so dismayed him? A sense of doom was growing on him, and he promised himself that he would not wait too long before warning the others. So Gaborn nodded at King Orwynne's blathering, hardly speaking, hardly daring to move. He felt distracted, worried in particular for King Orwynne.

It would be foul indeed to lose him, Gaborn thought. I must take special care of him.

King Orwynne was a staunch ally, a rarity these days. And his force warriors would be badly needed on the trip south.

Gaborn prepared to leave the Dwindell Inn at well past one in the afternoon.

Hundreds of knights still poured into Hayworth, eager for a brief rest. The streets were lined with horses, and the innkeeper had brought barrels of ale to the porch. A maid filled mugs as fast as the men could drink. She had no time to clean the mugs. A man would simply pass a mug forward through the press, along with a copper dove, and she'd take the coin and fill the mug.

Thus the kings had to shoulder their way through the throng as they headed toward their horses. Gaborn went to the hitching post, untied his own mount. Time was short.

At that moment, Gaborn's Days tapped him on the shoulder. Gaborn turned and looked the scholar in the eye. The brown-robed fellow looked shaken. 'Your Highness . . .' the Days said, and he held his hands wide, as if to say *Words cannot express my sorrow.*

'What?' Gaborn asked.

'I am sorry, Your Highness,' the Days said. 'It will be a bad day for the books. I am sorry.' The aura of death surrounding Gaborn was overwhelming.

'A bad day for the books?' Gaborn said, a sense of horror rising in him.

He faced the abyss. I'm under attack, he thought. Yet he could see no attacker.

'What? What's happening?' he wondered aloud.

Fat King Orwynne had heard the words, and now he looked from Gaborn's Days to Gaborn, worry on his brow. 'Your Highness?'

Gaborn looked up at the steel-gray clouds that gathered above, and sent a warning to Iome and the others still at Castle Sylvarresta. 'Flee!'

He put a foot into a stirrup, began to leap onto his horse, and suddenly felt the earth twist.

A wrenching nausea assailed his stomach as his strength suddenly left him. Gaborn slipped from the saddle, stood for a moment leaning against his horse.

I'm under attack, he thought, by some invisible agent.

'Your Highness?' King Orwynne asked. 'Are you well?' The wrenching nausea came again, and for a second, Gaborn was stunned, dazed and unsure of where he was.

Gaborn shook his head as he shakily sat down on the porch of the inn. The porch was dirty, but warm. People moved aside to give him air.

'I think he's been poisoned!' King Orwynne shouted.

'No – no! Dedicates are dying,' Gaborn said feebly. 'Raj Ahten is in the Blue Tower.'

19

AT THE BLUE TOWER

The fog had been thick over the sea all morning as Raj Ahten rowed to the Blue Tower, lured by the call of seabirds, the sound of waves crashing over rocks.

In the thick fog, he'd bypassed the warships set to guard the tower, until he stood at its base.

His shoulder ached as he rowed. King Mendellas Orden had kicked him hard in the battle at Longmot, had crushed the bones of his right shoulder. With thousands of endowments of stamina, he would live, but over the past week he'd had surgeons cut into his flesh a dozen times and break the bones, try to straighten them. His wounds healed within minutes, but the pain had been excruciating, and still his shoulder was little better.

Damn the Mystarrians – old King Orden and his son.

In the past week, Raj Ahten had been able to retrieve enough forcibles to boost his metabolism again, enabling him to prepare for war.

Now he reached the Blue Tower, saw it rising from the fog. It was enormous, this ancient fortress that housed the vast majority of Mystarria's Dedicates.

Raj Ahten stood in the prow of a fine little coracle and made a deep sound from far back in his lungs. It was not a shout. It was more of a rumbling, a chant, a single deep tone that rattled the bones and chilled the air and sent the stone of the Blue Tower thrumming in harmony.

It was not an exceptionally loud sound. Great volume, he'd

found, did not serve him. It was the precise tone that he wanted, a note – which varied between different kinds of rock – that made stone sing in return.

For long moments he held this tone, letting his Voice mingle with the song of the stone, until he heard the explosive sound of stone splitting; until the servants in the Blue Tower began screaming in terror, their voices as distant and insignificant as the cries of gulls; until great swaths of stone crashed from the battlements and plunged into the sea, spewing foam.

Still he sang, until roofs crashed into floors and people threw themselves from windows to escape the doom.

Still he sang, until turret collapsed against turret and gargoyles fell from the walls like ghastly parodies of men, until the whole of the Blue Tower tilted to the left and dashed into the sea.

The smoke and dust of ruin rose gray in the fog. The deadly warships that guarded the Blue Tower hoisted sail and came gliding toward him.

The Blue Tower tumbled down, and surely as it fell, Mystarria would fall with it. The Dedicates inside had died, along with all of their guards.

Raj Ahten turned and put his back to the oars one more time. He slipped through the fog faster than the warships could maneuver.

His back ached, but he felt comforted to know that Gaborn Val Orden would ache even more.

20

AN EARTH KING STILL

Gaborn had never felt a Dedicate die. The sensation had been described to him, the wrenching nausea, the sense of loss as brawn or stamina were ripped away.

Now he felt it keenly. Wave after wave of nausea assailed him as his endowments were stripped away. His mail suddenly seemed to hang heavy on his frame, a suffocating weight that bore him down.

He'd not slept for three nights. With his endowments of stamina he'd taken it lightly, but now fatigue overcame him.

He felt bewildered, weary to death. King Orwynne stared in horror.

Gaborn hunched over and covered his stomach with his hand, as if reeling from a physical blow. Yet his greatest concern was not for himself.

The Blue Tower housed the vast majority of the Dedicates who served Mystarria. More importantly, the warriors of Mystarria made up nearly a third of all the force soldiers in all the kingdoms of Rofehavan.

Duke Paldane's warriors, the finest in Mystarria, would become worthless commoners in moments, or with the loss of key attributes, they might at best become 'warriors of unfortunate proportion,' perhaps strong but slow, or wise but weak.

Even now Duke Paldane was driving his men into formation before Raj Ahten's troops, while Raj Ahten's Invincibles sharpened their blades for the slaughter.

Gaborn had wondered last night what had become of Raj Ahten. Now he knew.

Mystarria would be destroyed, and most likely all of the north would collapse with it. Gaborn wondered how it had happened.

Certainly, Duke Paldane had strengthened the Blue Tower's defenses – had doubled or quadrupled its guard.

In his mind's eye, Gaborn imagined the tower walls splintering, great shards of stone cascading into the sea.

Similarly, Gaborn felt himself crumble. Strength left him as his three endowments of brawn were stripped away. His eyes dulled as the blind Dedicates in the Blue Tower fell.

He'd prided himself on all that he'd learned in the House of Understanding, yet in moments, as his twin endowments of wit fled, he forgot more than half of all he had learned; he could not even conjure Iome's image. The distant calls of warblers over the town suddenly muted as his ears went dull.

In a blind rage, as the impact of what was happening was borne home, Gaborn shouted at his Days, 'You bastard! You craven bastard! How could you not have warned me?' But his own voice sounded weak, distant, as the mutes in his service were silenced forever. 'A bad day for the books, indeed!'

'I am sorry,' the Days vainly apologized again.

King Orwynne sat down on the porch beside Gaborn, held his shoulders. 'Rest yourself,' the old man said. 'Rest yourself. Did he kill all of your Dedicates?'

Gaborn fought the urge to surrender to exhaustion, to surrender to cruelty, to surrender all hope. 'They're dead!' Gaborn said. 'The Blue Tower is gone.'

'You look, Your Highness, like a corpse,' King Orwynne said. 'What shall we do now? Where shall we go? Do you want to find a facilitator and take new endowments before heading south?'

Gaborn had twenty thousand forcibles with him, and the temptation was great. But he dared not turn back for Castle Sylvarresta now.

'No, we must ride on,' he said. He would reach Castle

Groverman by nightfall, and Groverman had a facilitator he could use if he had to. 'I have the strength of any other man. I am still the Earth King.'

He struggled up from the porch, climbed into his saddle.

Gaborn could ignore the threat to his men no longer. The Darkling Glory drew close. 'Be warned,' he sent to his Chosen warriors. 'Death is coming.'

21

THE PRICE OF A MEAL

In the early afternoon, Borenson lost his endowments. He sat in the saddle feeling his metabolism leave, feeling himself slow to the speed that other men lived.

At first he wondered at the nausea that overwhelmed him, thought that it was his stomach cramping. Then the loss of endowments came so precipitously he could not quite feel what was lost next – strength or stamina, smell, hearing or sight. All of it drained away in moments, leaving him an empty husk.

As his endowments were depleted, a sense of desolate grief assailed Borenson. He'd looked into the eyes of the young farm boys who'd given him brawn years ago. They'd been promising lads who'd bequeathed their lives to him.

They should be frolicking with some milkmaids right now, Borenson thought. Not dying in the Blue Tower. And he remembered old Tamara Thane who had given him warm scones when he was a child and an endowment of metabolism when he stood in need. All those who'd known her would miss her.

But as much as he grieved for his Dedicates, he grieved more for himself. The deaths of his own Dedicates brought fresh to mind the nightmarish images he'd seen in Castle Sylvarresta a week past, when he'd been forced to butcher the Dedicates there.

Most of the morning, Borenson's guard had been silent. They'd ridden like a gale through Deyazz, a land where the

sun shone brighter than anywhere else in Borenson's memory.
It was a beautiful land, and though he was only five hundred
miles south of Heredon, the weather had warmed dramatically west of the Hest Mountains.

Deyazz lay north of the great Salt Desert, the hottest heart
of Indhopal, and the prevailing winds swept the desert heat
in this direction. Deyazz was not a tropical land, yet the water
seldom froze even in the dead of winter.

The farmers' fields along the Anshwavi River were a lush
green. Herons hunted for insects in the oft-flooded fields.
Young boys in white linen loincloths worked with their
mothers and sisters to harvest rice in wicker baskets.

Borenson had ridden through cities of whitewashed adobe,
where the lords of the land had built majestic palaces with
domed roofs plated in gold. Beautiful dark-skinned women
in silk dresses, adorned with rings of gold and rubies in their
ears or noses, lounged among the stately columns of the
palaces or sat beside reflecting pools.

The cities had broad avenues, awash with sunlight – not
narrow streets like those in the walled cities of Heredon.
Deyazz's cities therefore smelled clean – less of man and beast
than in the north.

Yet signs of war were everywhere. Borenson had passed
column after column of troops, and the castles along the
border had been filled to overflowing. As he and the Invincible
had passed through, the common folk in the towns along
their route had watched Borenson distrustfully. Small boys
hurled figs at him, while their mothers hurled curses.

Only once or twice did he hear a hopeful call from an old
man or woman: 'Have you seen the Earth King?'

But as Borenson's endowments left him, he slumped over,
and wrapped the chains of his manacles around the pommel
of his saddle to keep himself from falling. Tears came to his
eyes.

'Help!' he called. He had not slept in days, and had not
eaten since late last night. With his endowments of stamina,
he had not felt the hunger or fatigue. But now fatigue nearly

blinded him, making it hard to focus his eyes, and hunger cramped his stomach.

His captor glanced back at him darkly, as if afraid Borenson was engaged in some ruse. They were riding through a city now, along its main market street within the gates. The vendors' stalls in the market smelled strongly of curry and ginger, cumin and anise, paprika and hot pepper. Toothless old brown men in turbans sat beneath umbrellas in the midday sun, smiling at Borenson's captor and calling to him to try their food. They offered steamed rice cooked in bamboo baskets over boiling water in brass pots. Beside the rice sat pots with various curry sauces and condiments. Some men sold doves barbecued in plum sauce and still attached to long skewers. Others had pickled starling eggs, or artichokes in huge barrels. Elsewhere were fruits: tangerines, oranges, melons, figs, candied dates, and piles of dried coconut.

'Stop!' Borenson begged again. 'Your master is at the Blue Tower in Mystarria.'

He leaned forward, straining with the effort to stay awake, for he had not slept in days. His senses reeled, and he glimpsed visions of nightmares. A deep-seated weariness overtook him, like a pain in the bones.

The Invincible glanced at him from the corner of his eye. 'The Blue Tower would be a good place to strike. I would recommend such a plan to my lord.' He studied Borenson suspiciously, but if Borenson had concocted some scheme to overpower his captor, this market was the worst possible place to try it. Finally he asked, 'Can I do anything for you?'

'Nothing,' Borenson said. There would be no balm that could assuage his horror and grief at the loss of his Dedicates. The Invincible would not be able to replace any memories that Borenson had lost, or grant him surcease from the mind-numbing weariness that assailed him now. Instead, he begged only for whatever succor his captor would grant him. 'But I'm suddenly exhausted, and starving. I don't know if I can stay awake much longer. I had not slept for days.'

'It is true, what they say,' the Invincible said. '"Warriors without endowments are not warriors at all."'

A vendor, upon seeing that they had stopped, rushed forward and presented the Invincible with a sample taste of his sweet peppered crocodile. In moments, other vendors proffered samples of their wares. But they ignored Borenson, the red-haired warrior of Mystarria.

The aroma of good warm food made Borenson's stomach rumble, and he was overwhelmed with hunger. 'Can we stop to eat?' he begged.

'I thought you were in a hurry?' the Invincible said gruffly, his mouth full of food, as the merchants circled his horse.

'I'm in a hurry, but I'm also hungry,' Borenson answered.

'Which is greater?' the Invincible said. 'Your hurry, or your hunger? I sensed your haste and therefore did not stop. Besides, a man should not be made a slave to his stomach. The stomach should serve the man. You northerners, with your fat bellies, should heed my advice.'

Borenson was a stout man, a big man; he'd never thought himself fat. On the other hand, in the course of his ride through Deyazz, he'd not seen a man as heavy as himself.

'I only want a bit of food. We do not have to stop long,' he implored.

'What will you pay me if I feed you?' the Invincible asked.

Borenson looked at the merchants' stalls. He was a captive, and had little choice in the matter. Here in the south, lords seldom fed their prisoners. Instead, family members or friends were expected to provide food, clothing, and medical treatment for captives.

As a prisoner, he would not be allowed to buy food from vendors.

'I've got gold in my purse,' Borenson said, wondering how long such gold might last if he had to pay his captor for food. The Invincible would charge heavily, to make sure that Borenson's future jailers got nothing.

The Invincible laughed, glanced back at Borenson with an expression of pure amusement. 'You are in chains, my friend.

I shall have your purse whenever I want it. No, you must come up with a better coin.'

'Name your price,' Borenson said, too weary to argue.

The Invincible nodded. 'I will consider it . . .'

The Invincible bought some roasted duckling and rice, and a pair of lemons from an old vendor who also provided cheap clay bowls to eat from.

Then the Invincible rode through the city swiftly and stopped at a bend in the Anshwavi River. An old palace had fallen into ruins here perhaps a thousand years before.

They let the horses drink and graze. The Invincible led Borenson to the water by the manacles so that he could wash in the river before eating. Then the men sat on an ancient marble pillar to dine. The green-veined stone was worn smooth, as if travelers often sat here to eat.

The Invincible cut his lemons with a curved dagger and squirted their juice over the delicately spiced duck and rice. Borenson's stomach cramped at the sight. He reached out for the bowl, but the Invincible only smiled and taunted him. 'First, your payment.'

Borenson stared expectantly, waiting for the man to name a price. Perhaps his fine bow, or a piece of armor.

'Tell me about your Earth King,' the Invincible said. 'Tell me what he is like, and speak honestly.'

Borenson considered wearily. 'What would you like to know?'

'It is said that My Lord Raj Ahten fled before him in battle. Is this true?'

'It is,' Borenson said.

'He must be a fearsome warrior,' the Invincible said. 'My Lord Raj Ahten seldom retreats.'

'Not really,' Borenson said. He did not want to speak the full truth. He was unwilling to admit that Gaborn hated to take endowments from other men, and thus was no match at all for Raj Ahten.

'He is a tall men, though?' the Invincible said. 'Strong?'

Borenson laughed outright. He saw what game the man

played. He too had sometimes dreamt that someday an Earth King would arise.

'No, he is not tall,' Borenson said, though great height was considered a virtue in some parts of Indhopal. Leaders were expected to be tall. 'He is shorter than you by a hand.'

'Yet he is handsome in spite of this, surely?' the Invincible asked. 'As handsome as My Lord Raj Ahten.'

'He does not take endowments of glamour,' Borenson admitted. 'Raj Ahten's beauty is a bonfire. My lord's beauty is . . . a cinder, shooting up into the night.'

'Ah!' the Invincible said, as if having made a discovery. 'Then it is true what I have heard, that the Earth King is short and ugly!'

'Yes,' Borenson admitted. 'He is shorter and uglier than Raj Ahten.'

'But he is very wise,' the Invincible said. 'Very cunning and crafty.'

'He is a young man,' Borenson admitted. 'He is not wise. And he would be insulted if you said he was cunning and crafty.'

'Yet he outwitted My Lord Raj Ahten in battle,' the Invincible said. 'He drove women and cattle across the plains, and frightened my lord.'

'It was luck, I suspect,' Borenson said. 'In fact, it wasn't even Gaborn's idea. His wife suggested it.'

'Ah, so he takes the counsel of women?' the Invincible asked. In parts of Indhopal, to suggest that a man took the counsel of women was to suggest that he was either unmanly or a fool.

'He listens to the counsel of men *and* women,' Borenson corrected.

The Invincible smiled at Borenson in a superior way, the pockmarks on his dark skin showing better as he angled his face against the sunlight.

'You have seen my Lord Raj Ahten?' the Invincible asked.

'I have seen your lord,' Borenson agreed.

'There is none better. There is none more handsome, or so

fierce in battle,' the Invincible said. 'His enemies rightly fear him, and his people obey him implicitly.'

Yet Borenson caught something in his tone. It was as if the Invincible were testing him somehow. 'On this we agree. None is stronger, or more cunning, or more handsome, or more feared.'

'So why do you serve the Earth King?' the Invincible demanded.

'There is none so handsome as your lord,' Borenson said, 'or so corrupt in his heart. Do I not say well that his own people fear him as much as his enemies do? And rightly so?'

'To say such things in Indhopal,' the Invincible warned, 'is death!' His eyes flared, and his hand strayed toward the curved dagger at his side. He half drew it from its scabbard.

'To *speak truly* is death in Indhopal?' Borenson said. 'Yet you are the one who bade me speak the truth. Is the price of my lunch going to be my life?'

The Invincible said nothing, so Borenson continued. 'Yet I have not answered your question in full: I serve the Earth King because he has a good heart,' he declared loudly. 'He loves his people. He loves even his enemies, and he seeks to save them all. I serve the Earth King because the Earth chose him and gave him his power, and that is something that Raj Ahten with all of his armies and his fine face will never have!'

The Invincible burst into amiable laughter. 'You have earned your lunch, my friend! You spoke honestly, and for that I thank you.' He clasped hands with Borenson. 'My name is Pashtuk.'

Pashtuk handed Borenson the bowl of rice and duckling. Borenson could not help but notice that he had called him 'my friend.' In Indhopal, such words were not spoken lightly.

That encouraged him to ask, 'When you were a boy, Pashtuk, did you also dream that someday the Earth King would come? Did you dream of being a knight in his retinue? Do you, too, intend to serve the Earth King now?'

The Invincible took a spoonful of rice and stared at it thoughtfully. 'I did not think he would be short and ugly and take counsel from women. Nor did I think he would hail from enemy lands . . .'

Borenson ate thoughtfully. The bowl of rice was not big, and barely assuaged his hunger. It filled him without making him overfull, renewed his energy a bit.

Borenson considered the implications of the deaths at the Blue Tower. If he'd lost his endowments, thousands of other warriors would have done the same. Many lords had preferred to keep their Dedicates under their own personal guard. Yet the Blue Tower had stood for thousands of years, had not been successfully attacked since the naval blockade of King Tison the Bold, four hundred years ago.

The lords of Mystarria would be in a panic.

Worse than that, Borenson had to wonder about Gaborn. Gaborn would also have lost his endowments.

Raj Ahten had not been able to flush Gaborn from his lair in Heredon, could not risk bringing his armies north so long as the wights of the Dunnwood served the Earth King. So he was seeking to force Gaborn's hand, bring him within striking range. Gaborn had counted on Duke Paldane to repel any attacks against Mystarria. Paldane was old and wise, a grizzled veteran who had led dozens of campaigns against petty tyrants and criminals in Orden's behalf. No one was more trustworthy than Paldane.

But Paldane couldn't fight with his hands tied behind his back, and Raj Ahten had succeeded in tying his hands.

Even in his weak and weary state, Borenson saw it all clearly. Raj Ahten knew that Gaborn could no longer resist the temptation to come into battle.

There could have been no more perfect a lure than the life of a nation, the lives of everyone that Gaborn knew and loved.

Borenson wished that he could speak to Gaborn now, urge his lord to flee, to return to the north. Yet he was not sure it would be the right thing to do. For if Gaborn did not go south, Raj Ahten would destroy Mystarria.

22

THE DARKLING GLORY

Erin and Celinor raced far ahead of the others. They were riding through the hills twenty miles south of Hayworth when Gaborn's warning came. 'Hide!'

It coursed through Erin, and she found her heart pounding. Immediately she glanced around, searching for the source of danger, and reined in her mount.

Celinor did the same, asking, 'What's wrong?'

Erin looked up at the steel-gray clouds. On the horizon a darker cloud rushed toward them.

Her breath came fast, and she could barely speak. 'String your bow,' she whispered, for she thought she had time.

She leapt from her horse and grabbed her bow, tried to string it, fumbling. Celinor did the same, as he gaped up at the band of approaching night. It was like a great fish swimming behind the clouds, Erin thought. A great fish that lurks in the depths, half hidden, half revealed, waiting to strike.

I'm not afraid, she told herself. I'm a horsesister. The horsewomen of Fleeds do not give in to fear.

But though Erin was a horsewoman and had often engaged in mock combat and tournaments and even the occasional brawl, she'd never faced danger like this. She'd never felt helpless.

She had her bow strung when Gaborn spoke to her again. 'Flee, Erin. Hide!'

She dropped her bow and leapt back into the saddle. She was mounted before she realized that Celinor had not been

Chosen, and had not heard Gaborn's command. He was still on the ground trying to string his bow. 'There's no time!' she shouted. 'Into the woods! Come on!'

Celinor looked up at her in surprise. He finished stringing his bow. Up ahead was a hill covered in alders, many of whose leaves had not yet fallen. Erin hoped they might hide her.

The darkness descended from the clouds, a roiling mass of night that the eye could not pierce. Above that mass only darkness stretched across the sky. A great maelstrom of fire, like a tornado, appeared to be fastened like an umbilicus to the ball of darkness, feeding all light into the center of that storm.

The fiery maelstrom writhed and twisted above the ball of darkness as it dipped toward them.

'Run,' Erin cried. Celinor grabbed his bow, leapt on his horse, and they raced away from the road.

The central mass of darkness had been sweeping directly over the Durkin Hills Road. Now it veered and dropped lower.

Behind them, Erin's and Celinor's Days cried out in horror and raced after them, trying hard to catch up to the swifter horses.

Erin's steed leapt down an embankment, raced into the forest. Her mount thundered through the sparse trees, jumping bushes and low rocks, the wind rushing in her face, all of night falling upon her.

She gazed back as the mass of darkness, half a mile in diameter, touched ground level. A great wall of wind roared through the trees on the hill, bowling them over like a ball. Great old patriarchs of the forest snapped like twigs. The trees screamed in protest, and the roar of the wind was the snarl of an animal. Branches and autumn leaves swirled into the roiling wind. Erin could see only the edges of the storm, only the wind swirling debris, but at its heart flew a cloud of blackest night.

The wind had picked up speed. The front of the wall blasted along the highway, struck Erin's Day's horse with so much power that the steed staggered sideways, rolling over its rider.

Then the wind took them both, horse and rider. It lifted the Days like a hand and tossed her into the air.

Erin recalled a line from an ancient tome, a description of a Glory in battle. 'And with it came the sunlight and the wind, a wind that swept from its wings like a gale, and smote the ships at Waysend, and lifted the ships from the water and hurled them into the deep.'

She'd always thought it a fanciful description. She'd seen large graaks in flight, and the wash of their wings had never created anything similar. But the creature that struck now controlled the wind with more than natural force. The wind and air moved like an extension of its body.

Now her Days shrieked, a cry of wild terror hardly heard above the storm, and as Erin watched, a huge spar – a pine tree stripped of all its branches – caught the woman in the midsection and impaled her, shot clean through like an arrow. Blood and entrails streamed out after it. Then the wind carried the Days' carcass and horse and the tree up a hundred feet in the sky, and all were lost as they tumbled end over end, into that impenetrable ball of darkness.

Erin had never liked her Days, had never been close to the woman. The only kindness Erin had ever extended her Days was to make her tea on the few occasions when she took sick from a cold. Yet the image of that woman, pierced and utterly destroyed, horrified Erin.

Celinor's Days reached the roadside, and his horse floundered, its rear legs suddenly pulled backward by the wind. The horse screamed as the Darkling Glory pulled it into the roiling mass. Erin did not watch.

The wall of wind raced toward her. Erin turned just as her horse landed hard in a sandy little ravine. A dry streambed wound its way through here. Celinor had turned his mount, was racing down the dry streambed for safety, fleeing the ball of darkness that chased behind, heading toward a tall stand of pines that opened before them like a dark tunnel. He fled from the wind, from the blackness.

Leaves and dry grasses suddenly swirled up around her.

Erin put her heels to horseflesh, felt the wind tearing at her cloak. She looked behind.

Not a dozen yards back, the wind howled like an animal, and she stared into the blackness as if it were a pit. Trees crashed down to each side of her. The blackness gaping behind it all was like a huge mouth, trying to swallow her. A long pole thrust out of the darkness, hitting her in the back like a lance. It exploded against her mail, shattering on impact, shoving her forward.

She reached the stand of pines. Just within their shelter, Celinor had brought his mount to a halt. Ahead, a huge logjam blocked the channel where once the stream had flooded.

'Hide!' Gaborn's voice shouted in her mind.

Erin leapt toward Celinor, and the wind half carried her to him.

She knocked him from his mount and rolled forward, ducking beneath a fallen tree, beneath the logjam.

Behind her, she heard horses whinny in terror, but dared not spare a glance backward.

Instead, she crawled under the pile of logs as the wind howled and thundered. Trees snapped and branches crackled. A tree toppled and crashed into the woodpile above her as if the Darkling Glory meant to crush them all. Its branches shielded her as darkness descended, enveloping her with the smell of pitch and evergreen.

All around their little shelter, the storm raged. Even here, even beneath the fallen trees, the wind ripped bark from ancient logs and sent stones rolling ponderously along the riverbed.

Celinor put his arms around Erin, clutched her, trying to protect her with his body. In the utter darkness, she felt he was smothering her. Yet she feared to let him go.

'Stay down!' he cried.

Now she understood why Gaborn had warned them. The power of the Darkling Glory seemed immense. No arrow could have pierced that roiling storm. No rider, no matter how courageous or proficient, could have borne down upon the beast with lance.

She could not fight it, did not know if she could even hide from it.

Lightning cracked overhead, and the dry logs above exploded like dry tinder.

In the blinding flash, she glimpsed something. Beyond the trunk of the fallen pine, between its intact branches, she saw a shimmering form. The shape of a winged man hunched low. He moved along the streambed, stalking toward them. Dark flames flickered around him, as if he simultaneously both created and devoured fire.

Erin felt the air thrill. Her hair stood on end as static electricity wreathed them. She feared that another lightning bolt would pierce her now.

In that moment, as the Darkling Glory overtook them, the wind suddenly died. In the utter blackness, Erin dared not move. She felt she was at the heart of a storm.

Above her, the dried trees and brush that shielded her roared into flame, ignited by the lightning. The Darkling Glory leapt into the air, fanned the flames with its wings.

The beast let out an unearthly howl of delight, a sound that was at once both more pain-wracked and more beautiful than any sound she'd ever heard, an aria of the damned.

Smoke billowed around her, choking her. Bits of twigs and broken bark scattered blazing through the log jam, dropping all around. A log dropped from above, thwacking Celinor on the back. A hot ember landed on Erin's hand.

She swatted it away, and the fire touched dry grasses nearby. From their wan light, Erin saw an embankment to her left. The stream had cut away some dirt, creating an overhang, and she imagined that if she could make it to the undercut, the ground above might help shield her from the inferno.

She grabbed Celinor and motioned for him to go the left, but realized with a start that he was unconscious. He'd tried to protect her with his body, but the falling log had hit him harder than she'd known. He was unconscious, if not dead.

She rolled from beneath him, grabbed the collar of his ring

mail, and began laboriously dragging him out from underneath the burning wood, inching toward safety.

A hot branch fell from above, hit Celinor full on the back with a thud. He screamed in agony and looked up, his face streaming sweat and blood, then passed out again.

She kept fighting, made it halfway through the logjam, climbing over one log and under another, when suddenly she realized that the wind had stopped. Full daylight shone through the inferno.

She looked up, daring to hope, unsure if even she alone could now escape from beneath the tangle of burning logs before they collapsed under their own weight.

But the Darkling Glory had left.

Dully, she realized that Celinor's cry might have saved them. The Darkling Glory must have thought him dead. She flipped Celinor onto his back, wondering if the Darkling Glory was right.

23

BRAVE LORDS

Gaborn could only look up in dull wonder as the Darkling Glory drew the light from the sky, focused it into a funnel of fire that swirled down into a ball of blackest night.

Gaborn felt wearier than he'd ever been, could hardly focus his eyes, much less his thoughts. Without having slept for days, and with the sudden loss of his endowments, he could barely hold up his head.

As the beast approached, the wind of its passage whipped and howled. It flew low over the dirt highway, just as an owl will sweep along a winter's road in the moonlight, hunting mice.

The wind of its passage uprooted trees, hurled great stones. Half a mile ahead, men and horses scattered from its path, but not fast enough, seldom fast enough.

Lightning crackled from the cloud, firing like ballista bolts, blasting men in half, gutting horses.

Thunder snarled through the afternoon air, mingling with death cries and the sounds of snapping trees.

As the tempest thrashed the road, dust swirled into the mix, obscuring everything.

'To me,' cried fat King Orwynne at Gaborn's side. 'For Orwynne and Mystarria!'

The old fool thinks to protect me! Gaborn realized. I've lost my endowments, and Orwynne thinks me a commoner.

I've underestimated the speed of the Darkling Glory, Gaborn thought. I have to get my people to move faster.

He was riding at the van of his army, with his knights scattered miles behind. He sent a warning to his Chosen warriors: 'Hide! Don't dare fight!'

But his warning did not deter King Theovald Orwynne. The fat king dropped his lance into a couched position, the haft of the lance resting in the crook of his arm, and spurred his mount forward, charging that swirling orb of blackness and storm.

His eldest son, Barnell, was only sixteen years old, but he was a fighter. He bravely drew his warhammer, and charged on his father's right, while King Orwynne's most trusted guardsman, Sir Draecon, hurtled forward at his left.

A hundred knights surged to cover Orwynne's attack. Some began hurling lances into the maelstrom, while archers shot wildly into the black orb, sending up shaft after shaft, creating a steady hail of arrows.

The archers availed nothing. Spears and arrows veered in the whirling magical winds controlled by the Darkling Glory, thrown wildly from their course. In moments, arrows hurtled back toward the attackers.

So men fought to protect their king, but only King Orwynne, his son Barnell, and Sir Draecon proved brave enough to charge that darkness.

Behind Gaborn, someone shouted, 'Milord – this way!' Someone raced up and grabbed the reins of Gaborn's horse.

Gaborn was so bone weary – so weak from his loss of endowments and lack of sleep – that he could not think what to do. He let himself be blindly led. Without his endowments of stamina, he felt more enervated than he'd ever been. Without his brawn, he could hardly hold himself upright in the saddle. Without his endowment of wit, he could no longer think straight, could not recall the names of most of those he'd Chosen in the past week, men whose faces flashed before his eyes as he sensed their danger.

So he felt debilitated both in mind and body.

Gaborn's Days raced at his side. Through a seeming haze, Gaborn now recognized the young knight who led his horse –

Sir Langley, Orwynne's champion. He was grateful to see that the best of Orwynne's men were bright enough not to follow him to their deaths.

The mounts raced from the storm toward a stand of alder, gray-white trunks rising splendidly among golden autumn leaves.

Gaborn glanced back. King Orwynne and his men bore down, their swift force horses gaining speed, the mounts' braided manes whipping in the wind.

A sudden hope arose in Gaborn, a hope that they might succeed in their charge, even as the earth powers in him warned that they could not.

Lightning forked from that dark orb.

One tong slammed into Sir Draecon on Orwynne's left, while the other blew a ragged hole through young Barnell on the right.

Only King Orwynne was left, roaring a battle cry as he urged his armored mount to charge into that churning orb of obscurity.

Just when it looked as if Theovald Orwynne's mount might penetrate that darkness, an irresistible wind struck the horse, lifting it and fat King Orwynne into the air.

Suddenly Orwynne twisted horribly, like a rag being wrung by a washwoman.

King Orwynne had several endowments of voice, and the agony in his death shriek was astonishing in volume. It promised to be the thing of nightmares for weeks to come.

The King's armor crumpled with his bones. Blood poured from the twisted wreckage. The stomach cavity of his charger burst like a melon, spilling innards, and then the whole grisly spectacle – king and mount – went hurling high into the air, as if tossed up in celebration.

'The Bright Ones protect us!' Sir Langley exclaimed at Gaborn's side.

Gaborn's and Sir Langley's chargers finished climbing up a small knoll into the alders. The horses snorted and huffed in terror. Gaborn stared back wearily as King Orwynne and his charger dropped a quarter of a mile from the top of their arc. Gaborn felt fatigued in heart and mind.

He could go no farther. I'm not tired just from lack of endowments, he realized. I'm mentally exhausted.

Being tied by his earth powers to hundreds of thousands of people, being cognizant of their danger, sending warnings to each of his Chosen when he recognized a threat – it was more than he could bear.

But despite his inordinate fatigue, he felt terrified to sleep. He feared that if he slept, he would not be able to use his powers, could not warn his Chosen.

Weakly he sent a warning to all of his Chosen. 'Hide!'

From this vantage he could see the road behind for nearly two miles back. He gazed down the road, watched his men scatter, split off the road and race into the woods.

The Darkling Glory roared in frustration, veered across the valley to the nearest visible target, a knight who had fallen from his horse. The orb of darkness swooped, and this time no lightning bolts flashed out, no claws of air ripped him to shreds.

Instead, the dark orb settled over the poor fellow, and Gaborn was left to imagine from the fellow's prolonged death shrieks what kind of horrible fate he'd met.

Then the swirling wind and debris and blackness began to rise, veered ever so slightly toward him.

'Come,' Sir Langley said. He took Gaborn's reins, and urged his mount forward; they raced under the trees, leaping a windfall, galloping down a long slope.

'If you have the power to save us,' Langley said lightly, 'now would be a good time to use it.'

Gaborn felt inside himself, wondering. Yes, the danger was still strong.

'Go left!' Gaborn warned, ordering Langley to head into sparse cover. To the left, most of the golden leaves of the alders had fallen. They lay in deep piles on the forest floor. Logically, riding into the open seemed wrong.

The Darkling Glory came, a roaring wind that whipped low

through the woods, racing after them just above the treetops.

It dove toward them, and the golden leaves on the forest floor began swirling, swirling everywhere in a maelstrom. The wind shrieked.

Lightning flashed, blasted a tree beside Gaborn.

'Left,' Gaborn shouted.

Sir Langley and Gaborn's Days veered, racing to beat the wind.

Suddenly Gaborn realized what the Earth wanted. The Darkling Glory could not see through the swirling leaves any better than he could. Gaborn had been circling the monster, stirring up the leaves, and they had blinded the beast.

'Now drive hard right!' Gaborn shouted. Langley complied. Gaborn's Days raced at his tail.

In a moment they were galloping south over a trail through the trees, running parallel to the path of the Durkin Hills Road, while the Darkling Glory roared in confusion behind.

They drew into a copse beneath the shelter of a few dark pines and hid there while the horses wheezed and trembled in terror.

In moments the Darkling Glory rose from the forest floor and winged north, attacking any man foolish enough to remain on the road.

'It has lost us,' Sir Langley whispered. 'We were fortunate.'

Gaborn shook his head. Mere luck had not saved him. Gaborn recalled his meeting with the Earth spirit in Binnesman's garden more than a week past. The Earth had drawn a rune of protection on Gaborn's forehead, a rune that hid him from all but the most powerful servants of fire.

Gaborn smiled grimly. Binnesman said that the Darkling Glory was a creature of air and darkness, a creature that consumed light rather than served it. Gaborn suspected that the beast had not known he was here, would not have been able to find him in any circumstance, and had only chased after Langley and Gaborn's Days.

'Hide!' Gaborn sent the message to his troops once more. Almost as if in response to his command, the Darkling

Glory flew high into the air, momentarily breaking off the attack. The swirling coil of flame above it grew thicker, broader.

The beast let its own powers expand, drew light from the farthest reaches of the skies, as if all its hunting had made it hungry.

It's like a cat, Gaborn thought. It only attacked because we were easy prey. So long as it has to work for its pleasure, it wants none of us.

Then the Darkling Glory did something unexpected. In an instant it shot across the horizon at a speed that not even a force horse could hope to match.

It sped toward Castle Sylvarresta, seventy miles back. But at the speed it suddenly attained, it would reach the castle in moments.

Gaborn let tendrils of his power creep out. Distantly, he felt the death aura wrapped around Iome like a cloak, and he wondered why she had not yet left the castle.

'Flee!' he sent one last time. 'Flee for your life!'

The effort of making so many sendings cost him. He was so dizzy, so weary and fatigued from the loss of endowments that he still felt as if leaves swirled around him, swirled and swirled with him at the center.

Too thoroughly drained to remain astride his horse, he clutched for the pommel of his saddle as fatigue took him, and then dropped to the forest floor.

24

WAITING FOR DARKNESS

Myrrima had been right when she told Iome that it would take hours for her garrison to search the city.

Iome had them search it anyway. Iome took her pups and let them run in the bailey just inside the city walls, while she held court, having the city guard drag in every townsman found haunting the place.

A large city surrounded Castle Sylvarresta, an old city with thousands of homes. Some were fine manors, like Dame Opinsher's, while others were hovels perched above the crowded market streets along the Butterwalk.

Everywhere the soldiers looked, they found people. They caught thieves ransacking the empty homes of the wealthy and poor alike.

Iome didn't want to execute the thieves, but feared that to leave them or imprison them with the Darkling Glory coming was the same as killing them. Most of the thieves were not evil so much as stupid – witless old men and women, relentlessly poor beggars who failed to rise above temptation when they saw so many empty homes.

These people she relieved of their goods and sent away, warning them to do better.

Yet other looters were shifty-eyed creatures of foul disposition whom Iome would never want to meet in a dark alley. Such cunning and cruel people troubled her. She'd wanted to save her people, not take their lives.

These were not fools tempted into wrongdoing, but clever

men and women who made a profession of bringing misfor-
tune to others. So she had the guards place them in the
dungeon.

Not all those found within the walls were thieves. Some
were crude or ignorant. One old codger complained that the
King was making a 'big to-do' about nothing.

On and on it went. Iome seemed determined to bring her
dream to pass, to make sure that she was the last bit of human
fluff to ride the wind away from Castle Sylvarresta.

A gale blew in, a strong steady wind from the south, driving
steel-gray clouds that lay low against the hills, promising rain.
The clouds brought a chill that raised goose pimples on
Myrrima's arms. She worried for her mother and sisters, traveling south in such weather.

Iome dared not flee herself, though she ordered those city
guards who did not have force horses to race for the Dunnwood.

All day, Binnesman the wizard hurried about the King's
Keep, strewing herbs, drawing runes above the gates.

At two in the afternoon, Gaborn's command came stronger
than ever before. 'Flee now, I beg you! Death is upon you!'

Binnesman raced down from his tower. 'Milady,' he called
to Myrrima, for Iome was engaged in a discussion with a
clothier who would not leave his shop. He was dying wool
in scarlet, and if he pulled the wool from the vats early, it
would be a muddy pink. If the cloth was not turned, the dye
might take unevenly. If he left it too long, the wool would
expand and loosen the weave, ruining the cloth.

'Milady!' Binnesman urged Myrrima again. 'You must get
Her Highness away from here *now*! The Earth King has spoken.
There can be no more delays!'

'I am her servant,' Myrrima said. 'Not her master.'

Binnesman reached into the pockets of his robe, drew out
a lace kerchief filled with leaves. 'See that you give some of
these to Iome and Sir Donnor and Jureem. There's potent
goldenbay, and root of mallow and leaf of chrysanthemum
and faith raven. It should offer some protection from the
Darkling Glory.'

'Thank you,' Myrrima said. Binnesman's power as an Earth Warden let him magnify the potency of any herb. Even a small bundle of his herbs would prove a great boon.

Binnesman turned and hurried up the Butterwalk, toward the Boar's Hoard.

Myrrima went to Iome. 'Milady, I beg of you, let's go. Most of the town has been searched, and it's growing late.'

'Nightfall is not for hours yet,' Iome argued. 'There will be others left here in town.'

Jureem stood a few yards away, hands folded under his chin, looking apprehensive.

'Leave the city guard to care for them,' Myrrima begged. 'You can appoint a commander to issue judgment in your stead.'

Iome seemed flushed and anxious. Beads of perspiration stood on her brow. 'I can't,' she whispered, so that none of the city guard would hear. 'You see how they are. They're rough men. I have my people to care for.'

Iome was right. The captain of the guard seemed overjoyed to have found so many thieves. After years of hunting criminals, he was ready to dispatch just about anyone he found. Iome could not trust the guards to exercise her degree of constraint and compassion.

Myrrima pleaded with her. 'Remember, you have a child to care for, too.'

The expression of anguish that crossed Iome's face was such that Myrrima knew she had said the wrong thing. Iome *was* thinking about her child. She probably worried about little else.

But Iome said coolly, 'I can't let concern for one child growing in my womb cause me to neglect my duties.'

'I'm sorry,' Myrrima said. 'I misspoke, Your Highness.'

At that moment, the captain of the guard brought a club-footed boy up out of the Butterwalk. He did not drag him as if he were a thief, but instead steadied the boy's arm, helping him. The boy was in pain and seemed hardly able to drag his monstrously swollen leg.

Caught between manhood and childhood, he probably felt too afraid to ask others for help, yet could not flee alone.

'What have we here?' Iome asked.

'Orphan,' the captain of the guard answered.

Myrrima checked on the horses, tied to a hitching post not far off. But Jureem had already cinched the girth straps tight, had tied water bottles and packs onto each beast. He'd also gathered the puppies, tied them into two wicker picnic baskets. The pups barked and wagged their tails as Myrrima neared.

Sir Donnor stood by the mounts. 'Milady,' he said. 'We must go. I'd feel better if you'd leave the castle at least.'

'Leave Iome?' Myrrima asked.

'She'll have me to guard her,' Sir Donnor said. 'Her horse is faster than yours. Even if you accompanied Jureem a few miles down the road, you could have a good head start. You would be able to hide under the trees, if necessary.'

Jureem, who already sat ahorse, said frantically, 'He is right, let us reach the edge of the woods at least.'

Before she had time to reconsider, she'd mounted up and was thundering over the drawbridge, out of the castle.

Myrrima glanced into the moat, saw the huge sturgeons wheeling in desperation, still drawing their runes, though they had been here for a night and a day. Out in the field, larks wheeled about in a cloud, nervously shifting this way and that, as if fearing the approach of winter and unsure which way to flee.

The sky above them had been darkening steadily the past few hours, so that now it was a dirty lead-gray. But beyond it, Myrrima thought she saw a great black thunderhead rushing from the south.

They raced uphill, and Jureem veered toward the shelter of the autumn woods. The pups in his basket snarled and yapped like hounds who have scented a boar.

As they galloped under the shelter of trees with limbs nearly barren of leaves, Myrrima touched the pouch of herbs in her vest pocket, suddenly realized that she had not dispensed them as Binnesman had asked.

The black cloud rushing from the south disturbed her deeply. She looked up, realized the source of her apprehension: the cloud was not blowing with the wind, but moved at an angle to it. Lightning flashed in the heavens, and thunder pealed.

The Darkling Glory would not wait for nightfall to strike, for it brought the darkness with it.

And I have left milady defenseless, Myrrima thought.

She grasped the reins from Jureem's hand, turned her mount, and raced back toward the castle.

25

AT THE KING'S KEEP

Iome interviewed the clubfooted boy in the lower bailey. He stood on the cobblestones with his head down, clearly embarrassed to have been dragged before the Queen. His embarrassment did not concern Iome so much as his infirmity.

His right leg was a swollen monstrosity, so large that he could not have worn pants. He wore nothing but a tunic of old sackcloth that looked as if the poorest inhabitant of the castle might have discarded it.

'How old are you?' Iome asked gently.

'Ten,' the boy said. Then after a long moment he added, 'Yer High . . . uh . . . Ladyship.'

Iome smiled. He might have addressed her as 'Your Highness' or 'milady,' but had instead invented his own uncouth concoction.

'Ten years?' she asked. 'Have you lived in Castle Sylvarresta so long?' She'd never seen him before.

'No,' the boy said slowly, never daring to look up. 'I come from Balliwick.' It was a village on Heredon's western border.

'That is a long way, nearly a hundred miles,' Iome said. 'Are you an apprentice to a carter? Who brought you?'

'I come to see the Earth King,' the boy said. 'I walked. I got here Wednesday, but he was at the hunt . . .'

The boy's leg was as swollen as a melon and his foot twisted inward at a horrible angle. No boot would have fit it, so he'd merely wrapped the thing and walked about on the bandage. She imagined that he must have had his leg broken as a babe, and that it had healed poorly. Yet she could not imagine that anyone with such a leg could walk all the way from Balliwick. He'd have dragged it, painfully, step by aching step.

'The Earth King is gone,' Iome said, 'headed south into war.'

The boy stared hard at the ground, fighting tears. She wondered what to do with the lad.

I could put him in the inn with the others who are sick, she thought. But to leave him here in the castle would be dangerous.

This boy had walked a hundred miles to see her husband, but Gaborn was riding south, and Iome realized that this child was so slow he might never catch the Earth King, might never be able to obtain his lord's blessing. While the merchant princes of Lysle hadn't bothered to walk from their camps to see her husband, this boy had crawled halfway across Heredon for an audience.

She couldn't abandon him. She couldn't easily take him, either. 'I'm going south,' Iome decided at last. 'You could ride with me. But first you must get into some proper clothes.'

The boy looked up in wonder, for no pauper would have hoped for such a boon. But as he looked up, Iome fretted. Myrrima had already left the castle with Jureem. But by the sun, it could not be much later than two o'clock. Nightfall was hours away. She had almost managed to bring her dream to life. The city guard had searched the whole east end of the city, gathered every last one of her vassals and sent them south.

'Go to the King's Keep,' Iome told the boy. 'On the top floor, take the hallway to the left. There you will find my apartments. Look in the guest wardrobe to the left and get yourself a decent tunic and a traveling cloak, then take a moment to wash in the horse trough there in the bailey. When you finish, come back and wait until we can leave.'

'Yes, Yer Lordship,' the boy said. Iome winced at his use of a masculine title for her. He leapt up and half limped, half ran on his twisted, clumsy foot, lumbering up Market Street.

Iome closed her eyes, savored the moment. The guards had

only to search the north end of the city. Two more hours. That is all it would take to clear the city.

But now Gaborn's warning rang through her. 'Hide! You are too late to flee. Hide – all of you!'

Iome started. From here in the bailey, she could not see over the castle walls. A watchman on the gate tower cried, 'Your Highness, it's coming from the south – a great shadow above the clouds.'

Even as he spoke, thunder cracked over the Dunnwood. Lightning strobed. Nearby, Iome's horse jumped, pulling at its tethers.

Sir Donnor grabbed the reins to Iome's mare, and mounted his horse, as did Iome's Days. 'Your Highness,' Sir Donnor shouted, 'we must away!'

'Hide!' she ordered him, astonished that he wanted to flee – for the Earth King had told them to hide.

'But we've fast mounts,' Sir Donnor urged, 'faster than anything that flies.'

Perhaps Sir Donnor is right, she thought. A swift force horse *might* outrun such a creature – Ah, who am I fooling? I would never risk it.

'Hide!' Gaborn's warning struck her again.

Iome ran and leapt on her mare. Sir Donnor turned his mount and sped out the city gates, over the drawbridge and away from Castle Sylvarresta, never looking back. He'd been certain that she would follow. Iome's Days raced hot on his heel, but after years of keeping her eyes on royalty, the matronly woman spared a glance backward, realized that Iome was not following.

The Days' face was stricken, pale with fear.

But Iome could not leave the clubfooted boy. 'I'll get the boy!' she shouted.

Iome wheeled her mare and raced up Market Street, the beast's hooves clattering over the cobblestones, its breath coming hot from its mouth. Her Days followed a hundred yards behind.

As Iome's charger hit the Black Corner, turned and sped

under the portcullis of the King's Gate, she glanced back down over the valley. She could see the fields before Castle Sylvarresta from up here: the river Wye twisted like a silver thread among the green fields on the east of the castle, the autumn golds and reds of the Dunnwood rose above the fire-blackened fields to the south.

And there on the blackened fields, Sir Donnor spun his mount, galloping back toward the castle, having realized that Iome was not following.

To Iome's dismay, Myrrima was racing down from the hills, too. She passed Sir Donnor.

Even as Iome watched, a great sphere hurtled from the clouds. Blackness suddenly filled the sky above, darker than any night. A tornado swirled above the sphere, a tornado of light and heat and fire all whirling down into the heart of blackness.

The Darkling Glory drew the light and heat from the sky like some consummate flameweaver, channeling the power to himself. Within the heart of the sphere, swirling air and veils of night concealed the Darkling Glory.

Yet it plunged toward those who raced for the castle, swept toward Sir Donnor like a hawk for the dovecote.

Myrrima galloped across the downs, gouging her heels into the flanks of her charger, hoping for greater speed. She clutched the bag of herbs Binnesman had given her. Myrrima had never owned a horse, had learned to ride only because the boys in Bannisferre had sometimes insisted that she ride with them.

Yet now she galloped for the castle, drove mercilessly as the Darkling Glory came on, the wind screaming at her back. Sir Donnor had been racing toward her, fleeing the castle. Now he wheeled his mount and shouted wordlessly, trying to pace her.

With the Darkling Glory came a night darker than any winter's eve.

Myrrima's horse plunged through thickening gloom. She

glanced up at the city, saw a flash of movement. Iome's horse was racing across the barren green at the crown of the hill, toward the King's Keep. Iome's traveling cloak flapped like a banner in the wind.

It seemed to Myrrima that the Darkling Glory slowed abruptly, that it hovered just at her heel, silently.

She hoped that she'd be able to outpace the beast, for with each second, the castle drew nearer, with its tall battlements and stone towers and the promise of safety.

Her charger rounded a bend. Myrrima clung tight, tried to keep from falling. She glanced back. Sir Donnor galloped behind, struggling to catch up. The knight half turned to the side, drew his great horseman's axe. He looked as if he would wheel and do battle.

A ball of wind hurtled from the darkness. Myrrima saw it skim across the blackened field, picking up ash from last week's fire, blurring like a hand to cut the legs from beneath Sir Donnor's charger.

Sir Donnor shrieked as his mount went down, and he pitched forward to meet the ground.

Myrrima screamed for her horse to run. She grabbed her bow and quiver from off her pack.

Sir Donnor shouted, but his cry was drowned out in the rising roar of the wind that whipped all about. Myrrima glanced back. Sir Donnor was lost to the darkness.

Myrrima peered forward. She had almost reached the draw-bridge. She saw it through the darkening gloom. 'Jump!' she shouted to her charger, vainly hoping that somehow the beast would leap faster than it ran.

She heard a lightning bolt snap, felt her horse jerk and quiver. Its impetus suddenly redoubled as a lightning bolt hurled it forward. The horse flipped in the air, head over hooves, and then she too was tumbling.

Iome never spotted the clubfooted boy. She timed her leap for the moment that her mount slowed, and ran into the keep.

'Boy?' Iome shouted. 'Are you here?'

'Milord?' he called from the top of the stairs.

Outside, thunder pealed and rattled the windows. Wind screamed over the stones of the keep like something in pain.

'Down here!' she shouted. 'The Darkling Glory!'

He came running at once, tripped and rolled down the carpeted stairs above. In seconds he stood before her, looking ridiculous in the King's finest brocaded jacket, a gorgeous thing made of cloth-of-gold with cardinal stripes. The boy had not been able to resist trying it on.

Thunder pealed, and all light seemed to flee as night descended on the castle. Wind howled through the King's Keep and hail battered the windows. Iome wheeled toward the door of the keep, just as lightning split the sky outside. Her horse screamed in pain and she heard a wet thud as its carcass dropped. The wind lifted the beast, rotated it slowly in the air about ten feet off the ground, like a cat holding a mouse in fascination.

The clubfooted boy screamed in terror. Iome glanced about in dismay. Her Days had not followed her into the keep, and Iome wondered where the woman might have gone. Never before had a Days deserted her, no matter how great the danger.

She raced for the door outside, but the wind grabbed the huge oaken door, slammed it closed in her face.

'Hide!' Gaborn's voice rang through her. 'For the sake of our love, hide.'

'This way!' Iome called to the boy, grabbed his hand. A suffocating darkness enveloped the castle. It was not the darkness one sees on a star-filled night, or even on a night of storms when clouds blanket heaven. It was a complete absence of light, the darkness of the deepest cavern.

Yet Iome knew the keep, knew all its twists and turns. She felt her way along the hall, heading for the buttery, thinking to hide in a deep corner of some vegetable bin.

But she recalled Binnesman's chamber in the cellars. She recalled the sense of power she'd felt in that room. Down in the depths of the castle, surrounded by earth.

She turned abruptly, raced for the lower passage that had seldom been used, threw open the door. The flagstones leading down were rough and uneven. The fourth one from the landing twisted loosely underfoot. She'd have to be careful on her way down. The cellar had never been meant for habitation. She led the boy as swiftly as she could.

She saw light ahead.

Iome reached the door at the top of the stairs, closed it behind her, bolted it. Outside, wind screamed. Thunder pealed and hail battered the stone walls.

Upstairs, the windows of the keep all shattered as if from a great blow. Iome winced. The stained glass of the oriels in the King's Chamber had been in place for a thousand years. The glass was a treasure that could not be replaced.

With the door sealed, Iome could see the faintest glow from a fire down below. The air smelled sickly sweet from lemon verbena that simmered on Binnesman's hearth. Iome had not seen the wizard in half an hour. The last she'd been aware, he'd taken off toward the inns in town, gone to help the sick, but he might have come back here. He might have taken one of the side roads back up to the keep.

Binnesman had planned to fight this monster. She dared hope to find him in his room.

She raced down to the cellar, found the pot of verbena still brewing, a few coals glowing in the hearth. The boy raced over to the fire.

Iome threw the door closed, looked for a way to bolt it. Binnesman's door did not even have a latch.

She searched Binnesman's room for something to hold the door closed. There were various large stones among the Seer's Stones, too large for her to roll by herself.

'Hide!' Gaborn shouted in her mind. 'It comes for you!'

Binnesman did not even have a bed to hide under – only the pile of dirt in the corner.

Myrrima woke, floating facedown in the moat. She tasted water, cold water mixed with algae.

Pain throbbed in every muscle. Vaguely she remembered falling from her horse, and she believed that she must have shattered bones on impact, then rolled into the water. Darkness hovered over her.

Her horse was screaming and thrashing in the moat nearby. The waves of its struggle made her bob on the surface like a piece of cork bark.

I'm dying, she thought muzzily.

She floated in deep water as cold as winter ice, and just as numbing. She felt so weak.

She could not move. She struggled vainly, tried to lift a hand and swim – to the shore, to the castle wall, anywhere. But she could not see a thing in such total darkness.

Above her, she felt a wind, the wash of giant wings as something hovered overhead.

It did not matter where she went, so long as she swam.

But she struggled, and as she struggled, she found herself sinking.

It does not matter, she thought. It does not matter if I die today, if I join the ghosts of the Dunnwood.

By dying, Myrrima would lose her endowments. Her sisters would be glad to get back their glamour. Her mother would regain her wit. They would work and scrape in their little house outside Bannisferre, and they might be happy. It did not matter if Myrrima died.

She struggled, and found herself falling from regions of darkness, into the perfect obscurity of the moat.

A great sturgeon swam beside her, skimmed her hand and whipped away through the water. She felt the wash of its wake as it departed, but it returned again a moment later. The big fish swam around her lazily, creating an intricate pattern, like a dance.

'Hello,' Myrrima mouthed. 'I'm dying.'

Myrrima closed her eyes and lay for a long time, letting the water numb her. The frigid water soothed her muscles, drew the pain even from her bones.

It's lovely here, she thought. Ah, if I could only stay for tea.

She found herself dozing for a moment, and woke with a start.

Some light had returned, enough to see by. She lay in the muck at the bottom of the moat.

A sturgeon floated through the water, drew near, and then held steady, one huge eye the color of beaten silver staring at her. The great sturgeon, longer than she, merely parted its bony lips, its feelers drooping like a moustache, opening and closing its mouth minutely with each opening and closing of its gills.

She felt amazed to find herself alive. Her mind was clearing, and now her lungs ached for air. Two more great sturgeons whipped past her in a frenzy, swirling in dance.

She remembered the runes they'd drawn.

Protection, healing. Over and over for days. Protection, healing. The water wizards were powerful.

With the recognition that she would live, Myrrima suddenly felt concern for others. She looked up from the bottom of the moat. The surface was thirty feet up. Darkness still covered half the sky.

She pushed her toes into the muck, feeling freshwater mussels beneath her feet, and swam upward, bursting from the surface.

She began to cough, clearing water from her lungs.

Lying weightless in the water had seemed easy. Now she found that swimming in her clothes was hard. She churned through icy water, slogged toward shore so that she could climb up through the cattails along the moat's bank.

The water weighted down her riding clothes so that she felt as if she were swimming in chain mail. She saw her bow and quiver floating nearby. Half of her arrows had spilled from the quiver.

Grabbing the weapons, she swam to the cattails and climbed up, sank wearily to the grass. The frigid water left her numb, trembling from cold. Hail began to pelt her.

There on the green grass, she looked up into the gloom. Darkness reigned all around, but mostly it centered uphill, over the King's Keep.

Myrrima crawled to her knees. Her horse was sloshing up out of the moat. She felt astonished to see it alive, for she was sure that a lightning bolt had pierced it. Yet she'd known a man in Bannisferre who had been struck by lighting on three different occasions and only had a couple of burn scars and a numb face to show for it. Either the horse had been lucky or the water wizard's spells had healed it.

Farther afield, Sir Donnor and his mount lay dead. Myrrima did not need to check them to know. Sir Donnor was hewn in more than one piece, and his mount lay so twisted and broken that it might never have been a horse.

Myrrima struggled to stand, strung her bow and nocked an arrow.

Her mount neighed in fear, managed to churn a path up the bank, then it raced away from the castle, heading back across the valley toward the hills where Jureem hid. In the gloom, Myrrima turned and ran over the drawbridge, uphill, into Castle Sylvarresta.

The clubfooted boy gazed at the wizard's room, at the bundles of herbs tied in the rafters, at the baskets made of coiled rope that held dry herbs above the mantel. Iome recalled how Binnesman had gone in search of herbs this morning, glanced about desperately for something the wizard might have used to fight with. She hoped that Binnesman might have left his staff, but it was nowhere to be seen.

She saw a bag sitting on a low stool, ran to it. It was the bag Binnesman had been hauling herbs in this morning. She turned it inside out. Dozens of goldenbay leaves, bits of root and bark, and flower petals fell out – the odds-and-ends of his craft.

Iome scooped them up, held them protectively. She cringed, listening. Her heart thudded in her ears. The clubfooted boy moaned in terror, gasping for breath. Wind whirled about the castle, making the fire sputter in the hearth.

Upstairs in my room are opals, Iome thought, recalling the light that had blazed from them under Binnesman's hand.

They were of low quality compared to the ones that she'd given the wizard, but at the moment, Iome wanted anything to protect her.

Above her she heard footsteps, a heavy foot landing on the floorboards. Her heart hammered.

Binnesman? she wondered. Could Binnesman be in the keep? Or is it the Darkling Glory?

Whoever it was, he was on the first floor.

It couldn't be the Glory, Iome told herself. Such a creature would fly up to the roof. It would land there like a graak and sit shifting its wings. It wouldn't land by the front door, enter like a common cleaning wench.

'It comes for you,' Gaborn's warning echoed in her mind.

The beast stalked across the floor. She heard claws scratching the wooden planks as it reached the door above. She heard it sniff, testing for a scent.

Then the sound of splintering wood filled the air as the door at the top of the stairs exploded inward.

Iron hinges and bolts clanked as they rolled down the rough flagstone steps. Wooden planks clattered.

The Darkling Glory drew near, kicking the remains of the door aside, sniffing as it came.

Outside, the wind had been shrieking, storming.

The winds suddenly died. Everything went quiet. Yet Iome could still feel the storm; there was a suffocating heaviness to the air.

On the far side of the door, a deep, inhuman voice whispered, 'I smell you, woman.'

Iome fought back the urge to cry out. She desperately searched for a weapon. Binnesman did not have much in the room – no sword or mace, no bow or javelin. He was not a warrior.

He had only his magic.

She heard snuffling at the door. 'Can you understand me?' the creature asked.

'I smell you, too,' she answered. The beast smelled heavily of putrefaction and hair and wind and lightning.

She glanced about. Earth Wardens used magic soils for many spells. She recalled how Binnesman had curled up in the corner, pulling topsoil over himself like a blanket.

She grabbed a handful of the dry soil, cast it into the air.

'Come to me,' the Darkling Glory said.

'You can't come in here!' Iome shouted, hoping it was true. She'd sensed the earth power in this room. Suddenly she recalled Binnesman's words: the Darkling Glory was a creature of Air and Darkness. The wizard had drawn runes of warding and earth power on the floor of this room.

And earth was ever the bane of air. Outside, the Darkling Glory had used wind to lift her horse the way a cat might use a paw. But now the winds had gone silent. The beast was crippled down here, weakened. She said again, with more certainty: 'You can't come in.'

The Darkling Glory snarled like some fell beast. 'I *can* come for you. And I will, if I must.'

Iome threw another handful of dust toward the door, hoping to drive the beast away.

'Come to me,' the Darkling Glory whispered. 'Come out to me, and I will let you live.'

'No,' Iome said.

'Give me the King's son,' the Darkling Glory said. 'I smell a son.'

Iome's heart pounded. She backed into the corner. The clubfooted boy whimpered. 'The King has no son,' Iome answered, voice quavering. 'There is only a young boy.'

'I smell a son,' the Darkling Glory assured her. 'In your womb.'

Myrrima ran with her bow, panting hard from the effort, racing up the streets of Sylvarresta toward the King's Keep. She could not see the keep. The Darkling Glory had wrapped it in veils of night.

Hail pelted the cobblestones all around, bounced noisily from the leaded roofs of the merchants' quarter.

A tornado of flames seemed to hover above the keep, and

the fire whirled and was lost in a haze of darkness. Myrrima knew that Iome must be in the keep. She'd glimpsed Iome racing toward it only moments before.

The sky above remained black as the Darkling Glory drew light from the heavens. Yet everywhere, at the limit of vision on the horizon, beams of light shone down, as if silver fires burned in the distance. By this dim reflected light she found her footing over the uneven cobblestones.

As she ran, heart racing, she considered how she might shoot this beast, this Darkling Glory.

She had been practicing the bow for only a couple of hours over the past two days. All her arrows were shot from a range of eighty yards. She didn't trust herself to try for a longer shot.

By the Powers, she thought, I don't trust myself to try for any shot at all!

She'd do best if she got close, if she got within a comfortable shooting range. Her heart hammered, her breathing came ragged.

If I miss, I'm dead, she realized. One shot is all I'll ever get.

The Darkling Glory threw bolts of lightning. She'd not get a second shot.

She reached the Black Corner. Ahead, the portcullis that led to the King's Gate rose, a darker monolith against an almost perfect black.

Hidden beneath the portcullis stood the wizard Binnesman.

He held his staff overhead, swirling it in wide motions as he chanted softly, fearfully, words that she could not hear. A dim green light issued from his staff, as if it were a flaming ember, and Myrrima could see him clearly, limned by the light. His steadfast gaze was fixed upon the orb of darkness that surrounded the King's Keep.

Something strange had happened. No winds screamed about the keep, no lightning flashed.

The Darkling Glory seemed to have fallen silent.

It's in there with Iome, Myrrima realized. The thought made her faint, and she staggered on the cobblestones.

Myrrima ran softly, afraid that the Darkling Glory might hear her footsteps.

Suddenly an inhuman cry rang from the heart of the darkness around the King's Keep. It split the night and echoed from the stone walls of the castle.

Binnesman whirled his staff and chanted in triumph.

'Eagle of the netherworld, now I curse you.
By the Power of the Earth I seal your doom.
Let the lair of stone become your tomb!'

The Darkling Glory touched the door to the room where Iome hid, so that it swung open on squeaky hinges.

The hallway behind the beast was darker than any night. A finger of blackness stole over the room. The coals in the fire began to die.

'Milady!' the clubfooted boy cried, lurching toward the fire.

In the shadows, the Darkling Glory snarled. A lightning bolt sizzled through the air, past Iome's head, and exploded against the ancient wooden walls.

Iome held up her little pouch of leaves and roots, hoping it would ward the beast away.

The Darkling Glory roared as if in pain.

Suddenly the Keep shuddered as if an earthquake had struck. Everywhere the walls rocked. The sound of splintering wood and of stone grinding upon stone filled the air. Baskets dropped from shelves. Overhead the heavy oaken beams of the rafters shrieked in protest as they shattered.

In total darkness, six stories of stone collapsed in on itself.

Gaborn lay asleep in a faint while his troops regrouped. Though men tried, none could rouse him. After listening to his heartbeat for a moment, Sir Langley merely said, 'Prop him on his horse and let him sleep, if that's what he has a mind to do. I'll whip any man among you who dares disturb his slumber.'

In his dreams, Gaborn hovered above some great and spacious building.

It might have been the Blue Tower, near the Courts of Tide, he thought, though Gaborn had never been inside.

But no, this building seemed more begrimed and sinister than any proper building should have. No tapestries adorned the walls, no lanterns hung from wall hooks. The stonework was old, the interior plaster all worn away.

The building was as cold as a dungeon. Many of its gray stones were worn or broken loose from the wall. But it was not exactly a dungeon; it was a ruin, a maze of walls without a roof.

In this dank old building, Myrrima and Iome ran from Raj Ahten with blindfolds over their eyes. Gaborn was imprisoned in a metal cage that hung from a huge tree. He gazed down over the maze, through gaping holes in the roof.

He heard the Wolf Lord's wet feet slap against stones, could hear what sounded like claws scraping the floor. He could sometimes glimpse Raj Ahten's hulking black shape. Yet Iome and Myrrima were at a disadvantage and seemed not to recognize the danger. He had to warn them.

'Hide! Hide!' Gaborn pleaded. Yet each time they tried to conceal themselves in a corner, the dark creature of dream plodded unerringly toward them.

'Hide!' he warned.

Binnesman finished chanting his spell, twirled his staff. A green bolt of light, like a touch of summer bursting through leaves, shot from his staff and raced toward the keep.

The light penetrated the darkness, and was lost.

Stones cracked and splintered in the keep as rocks toppled by the ton.

The fiery tornado above the King's Keep swirled and shattered.

Brilliant sunlight suddenly filled the sky. Dust swirled in the air, and Myrrima raced through the portcullis to stand beside Binnesman.

The wizard gazed in triumph.

Myrrima stared in horror.

The King's Keep had collapsed in utter ruin. A pile of stones fifteen feet tall littered the ground, dust rising around them. Bits of furniture and tapestries added color to the wreckage, and a stone gargoyle that had decorated the upper reaches of the keep sat tilted on the pile of broken stones, grinning as if in mockery.

Myrrima stared in shock, her mind numb.

Binnesman glanced at her. 'I've imprisoned the beast,' Binnesman said, his voice weary, 'sealed him in the Earth.' With finality he leaned on his staff and said, 'Let us only hope that I can hold him!'

Myrrima looked about the bailey. She'd seen Iome riding toward the keep only minutes before. But Iome's mare had vanished.

Suddenly she spotted it, impaled on the merlons of the Dedicate's Tower, eighty feet in the air. She pointed at the charger and shouted, 'But Iome was in the keep! You sealed them in together!'

She staggered back in rising horror.

'No!' Binnesman cried.

And with that, the hill of stone and rubble that had been the keep surged upward. Rocks were pitched aside.

A whirlwind of fire swirled above the gaping hole, and once again darkness saturated the sky, more complete and blacker than ever before.

Binnesman shouted in terror. Myrrima could think of nothing to do but follow the counsel of the Earth King. She raced under the portcullis and put her back to the wall, quivering.

Winds rose and screamed through the portcullis, battered the castle. The stone wall at Myrrima's back shuddered under an icy blast, but Binnesman stood in that storm, and drew runes on the ground with the tip of his staff, shouting words that the gale tore from his lips and carried away.

Yet Myrrima saw something amazing: though the wind blasted around him, it did not touch him. It did not so much as lift the hem of his robe.

Lightning streaked from the darkness and blasted at his feet, but Binnesman's spells of protection were powerful enough that no bolt could pierce him. Green light glowed steadily from his staff, and Binnesman gazed on in determination.

He reached into his pocket, pulled out the opal. It suddenly blazed in his hand.

Myrrima thought at first that it was sending out light, as it had done in the darkened storage room of the Boar's Hoard. But she realized that something else was happening instead. The stone now drew light. The tornado of fire that the Darkling Glory pulled from the skies suddenly twisted, and now that light funneled into the stone. Light began to fill it as water fills a sponge.

The gloom softened, and the raging storm that ripped through the castle suddenly weakened, becoming only a stiff gale. The shadows lifted, so that the sky above seemed only to be as dark as evening.

From the deeper shadows surrounding the ruins of the King's Keep, Myrrima heard laughter – a deep, inhuman voice.

'You think to steal my power, little wizard? Your stone is too small to hold it all!'

Myrrima trembled. She clutched her bow tightly. Her arrow had come loose, and she nocked it.

She drew the arrow now to her ear, felt the sting on her fingers where practice over the past two days had rubbed the skin off.

She took a deep breath and ran to the mouth of the portcullis, wheeled.

Ahead in the deep shadows stood the Darkling Glory. He was eight or nine feet tall, looked like a tall man covered with dark hair. Vast wings rose at his back. Cold white flames licked his naked flesh, and he regarded her with contempt.

She did not try for a fancy shot. The brute stood roughly sixty yards away, and she could not hope to hit anything other than his midsection, if even that.

She took quick aim and loosed an arrow. The wind around her suddenly howled as the Darkling Glory swept his wings.

A bolt of lightning surged from the monster's palm and crashed into the stone archway above her head. Splinters of rock rained down upon her neck.

Her arrow flew high of its mark, and looked as if it would race above the monster's head.

But the Darkling Glory's wings had lifted him a foot in the air, and the arrow struck home, piercing the creature's shoulder.

The Darkling Glory's head snapped back, and he convulsed. He fell to the cobblestone pavement of the bailey and writhed, wounded, trying to cover himself with his wings, trying to shelter himself. He screamed in pain and terror.

Myrrima grabbed another arrow and raced toward him, the blood lust pounding in her veins. Light still funneled from the skies into Binnesman's opal.

Now Gaborn's shout roared in her mind, and his command came with such force that she could not fight it. 'Strike! Strike now!'

Myrrima raced to the Darkling Glory. The creature hissed at her like a snake. He peered up at her in horror and contempt from behind the folds of a wing.

She drew her shaft full and let it fly, taking the beast in the eye.

Full daylight came streaming from the skies, and Myrrima stood over the Darkling Glory, panting.

She suddenly realized that she was screaming at the thing, had been shouting all along: 'Damn you, foul thing! Damn you, I'll kill you!'

She raced up and began to kick his still-convulsing form. The monster seemed to reach for her with a hairy three-fingered claw. She danced back a step and found herself still yelling, crying out in terror and relief and pain.

'Get back!' Binnesman shouted. He raced up behind her.

At that moment, the Darkling Glory arched his back, spread his wings wide, and raised a claw to the air. A sound came from his mouth, a dry hissing rattle, nothing at all like the death rattle of an animal.

A black wind tore from his throat, raising an inhuman cry. The force of that magnificent wind drove the beast hard into the ground, and Myrrima struggled to backpedal, to lift her legs and flee.

Numb, she realized that she had killed the Darkling Glory's body, but had not reckoned with the elemental trapped within.

A great roiling fist of wind slammed into her, driving her back several paces and knocking the breath out of her. Her ribs ached as if she'd been hammered with a truncheon. She lost her footing, and the wind took her, sent her skittering back along the paving stones. It screamed about her with a thousand voices, like the wails of disembodied spirits.

The blast howled through the bailey, transformed itself into a tornado, carrying the body of the Darkling Glory up and up. The base of the tornado tore the cobblestones from the pavement, swirled them up into the mix with a sound like an earthquake. Lightning flashed at the tornado's crown, arcing into the heavens. The roiling mass of air whirled violently once and then slammed to the north. The walls of the Dedicates' Keep rumbled and shattered. Huge boulders heaved into the air.

Three bolts of lightning struck beside Myrrima in rapid succession. The tornado veered toward her. She felt fingers of air tug at her, inviting her into the heart of the maelstrom. Binnesman was shouting, and Myrrima twisted and scrabbled to grab some paving stones.

The wind lifted her off the ground, held her for a heart-beat as if pondering what best to do with her.

And then Myrrima saw Binnesman. The old wizard struggled through the wind, as it ripped at his hair and pummeled his robes. He thrust the end of his staff toward her, and frantically Myrrima grabbed it, felt its gnarled and polished wood in her grasp. A great boulder came bouncing down from the Dedicates' Keep, two tons of stone rolling toward them as if hurled with unerring precision.

Binnesman raised his hand, warding it away, and the boulder's course suddenly shifted left, narrowly missing them.

'I claim you for the Earth! Live now, live for the Earth.' Binnesman shouted.

The wind ripped at Myrrima with powerful fingers, tried to pull her away, and Myrrima clung to the staff with all her might.

Binnesman hurled a handful of leaves from his pocket, sent them scattering. The wind took them, sent them whirling. 'Begone, fiend!' Binnesman shouted. 'She is mine!'

Suddenly the wind stilled nearby, and the great tornado roared. It ripped stones from the ruined Dedicate's Keep, sent them roaring into the air, then let them rain down uselessly all around Binnesman and Myrrima.

A dozen bolts of lightning slashed the air nearby, leaving Myrrima blinded by the light.

Then the elemental was gone, screaming north through the king's tombs, uprooting cherry trees that had stood for a hundred years. It leapt down cliffs to the north, and raced then among the fields, meandering almost aimlessly as it knocked down cottages, smashed carts, ripped apart haycocks, tore through fences, and gouged a black scar in the earth.

For long minutes, bits of hay and dust still hung heavy in the air. But what was left of the Darkling Glory had departed.

Myrrima sat on the ground, quivering, mortified. Her ribs ached. Dozens of small abrasions covered her legs and hands where bits of stone had pummeled her.

She felt astonished to even be alive.

Binnesman held her, drawing her close, seeking to comfort her.

She began trembling uncontrollably as the terror and blood lust left her. Her heart pounded in her ears so hard, she could hardly hear, couldn't quite make sense of Binnesman's words.

'That, milady, should not have been possible!' he said in astonishment. 'No common mortal could slay a Glory! And then to live – to live through it?'

'What? What do you mean?' she asked.

But he merely held her for a moment longer and said in a tone of infinite wonder, 'You're wet. You're wet, every bit of you!'

She leaned against him for support. Tears filled her eyes. She stared over his shoulder at the pile of stones where the King's Keep had fallen. There was a huge rent there now, a crevasse from which the Darkling Glory had escaped.

Iome will be down there, Myrrima realized. I should look for her body, give it a proper burial.

But even as the thought lodged in her mind, she saw movement at the edge of the pit.

Iome, covered in dust, stuck her head up from the wreckage, gazing about curiously. The clubfooted boy poked his head out after her.

'We hid in your room,' Iome said as she related her tale to Binnesman. 'The earth power was greatest there, and the Darkling Glory didn't want to draw near. When the keep collapsed, the boy and I got trapped in the corner, beneath some beams.'

'We was lucky,' the clubfooted boy shouted. He looked as if he'd play the fool in his cloth-of-gold coat. 'The Queen has got luck!'

'No, it wasn't luck,' Iome said, shaking her head in warning. 'I felt Gaborn warn me, telling me to hide. I pushed us toward that corner because it felt safe, and when the roof collapsed, the beams were strong enough to shelter us.'

'You can thank the King for your life, when next you see him,' Binnesman said.

Iome glanced off toward the valley, where the tornado wandered to the east. She shuddered before continuing. 'Afterward, when the Darkling Glory broke out, we simply crawled through the rubble until we got free. The wind was howling so! I didn't dare climb up until I heard you and Myrrima talking, and knew it was safe.'

Myrrima looked at the pile of rubble where the Darkling Glory had been sealed beneath the earth. It seemed impossible for any human inside that building to have survived when it collapsed.

Binnesman let Myrrima go. She still trembled, but not so badly as before.

'I still don't understand.' Binnesman shook his head in wonder. 'No common arrow should have been able to pierce that beast.'

He retrieved one of Myrrima's arrows from the ground, and examined it closely. He studied the narrow blade of cold iron at the bodkin's tip. He felt the white goose feathers on the arrow's fletching.

He cocked a brow at Myrrima. His voice was thick with suspicion. 'It's wet.'

'I fell in the moat,' Myrrima explained.

Binnesman smiled as if perceiving something important. 'Of course. Air is an element of instability. But water counters its unstable nature. Like earth, water can also be a counter to air. A shaft made of earth alone could not pierce the Darkling Glory, but one of earth *and* water maybe . . . And, of course, I was draining the Glory's power at the time.'

It sounded suspiciously to Myrrima as if the wizard were trying to take credit for her kill, when she felt quite certain that she was the one who had saved *his* life. Binnesman did not sound persuaded by his own conjecture as to the cause of the monster's death.

Moments later, Jureem came galloping up to the keep, leading Myrrima's mare. The horses' hooves clattered against the stone.

Her mount had a white burn on its rump where the lightning bolt had struck it. Myrrima was amazed the horse could even walk. But it was a force horse, she reminded herself, with endowments of stamina, and therefore could endure much more than a common mount.

Jureem leapt from his charger and set down the baskets of puppies. The dogs yelped with excitement, and one pup pushed its nose through the lid of the basket and leapt out, raced to Myrrima's side.

She reached down and petted it absently.

Jureem glanced from person to person, as if making sure everyone had survived.

Iome laughed nervously and said to Myrrima, 'Your

husband slew a reaver mage and brought home its head yesterday, and today you must best him. What trophy will you gather next?'

'I can think of only one better,' Myrrima said. 'Raj Ahten's head.'

In point of fact, Myrrima could not feel easy about her kill. The air around them hung heavy and smelled of a storm. There was no corpse to the Darkling Glory, nothing that could prove she'd killed him.

She felt almost as if he were still here, hovering close, hanging on her every word.

Binnesman himself was glancing about furtively, gauging the air. It smelled thick with dust and lightning.

'He is dead, isn't he?' Myrrima asked. 'It is over?'

Binnesman gazed at her, held his tongue as he considered his answer. 'A Glory is not killed so easily,' he warned. 'He is disembodied now, diminished. But he is not dead, and he is still capable of much evil.'

Myrrima looked out over the valley, to where the tornado now whirled and seethed two miles off. 'But . . . he can't touch us now, can he?'

Binnesman answered warily. 'I've driven him away.'

Iome stared off into the distance, breathing hard. 'So he will lose form, the way that a flameweaver's elemental does?'

Binnesman gripped his staff, stared thoughtfully at the heaving maelstrom. The tornado moved erratically, striking in one direction, turning in another. Like a child in the throes of a tantrum.

'Not exactly,' Binnesman said heavily. 'He will lose form, but I think he will not dissipate quickly, not like an elemental of flame. Nor do I think he will leave us alone.'

Down below, in the city, the city guards all began to come out of hiding, gazing nervously uphill to the ruined keep. She saw four of them standing down at the gate.

In all of the commotion, Myrrima had dropped her bow, and now she saw it lying across the bailey. She picked her way toward it among fallen stones and rubble. The Darkling

Glory had so devastated this part of the castle that she was astounded to be alive.

Suddenly on the ground before her, she saw a part of the Darkling Glory, a severed hand with three clawlike fingers, their dusky nails as sharp as talons. Blood leaked from the stump at its end.

To Myrrima's horror, the hand was moving, grasping the air rhythmically.

She stomped on it and kicked the horrid thing away. It lay on the ground and groped at the paving stones, lumbered about like an enormous spider. Her pup ran after it, barking and snarling even louder.

Myrrima picked up her bow, returned to where the others stood. Jureem eyed the moving hand nervously, while Iome kept staring at the pup.

It snarled savagely, took a nip at the vile hand.

'That pup wants to protect you,' Iome said. 'It's ready to give you an endowment.'

It surprised Myrrima that the pup would be ready to give an endowment so soon although Duke Groverman had said pups of this breed were quick to bond to their masters.

Myrrima dared hope for a boon. She had slain the Darkling Glory, slain him while good men like Sir Donnor and the city guards had failed.

She knelt to face Iome, presented her bow at the Queen's feet. She had hoped to be considered worthy of becoming a warrior, had hoped to earn the right to use the King's forcibles. The cost of taking endowments was tremendous. And with blood metal so scarce these days, she knew it would be impossible to gain the use of forcibles any other way.

'Your Highness,' Myrrima said. 'I come before you to swear my troth. I offer my blade and my life to you, and beg for the honor to bear weapons in your service.'

Iome stood a moment, as if unsure what to do.

'She has a warrior's heart,' Binnesman said, 'and more. She fought on while stouter men hid.'

Iome nodded her head; the decision was made. She glanced about for a sword of her own. Jureem drew a curved dagger from its sheath, and handed the ruby-encrusted blade to Iome.

Iome touched Myrrima's head and each shoulder with the blade, and said solemnly, 'Arise, Lady Borenson. We accept you into our service gladly, and for your deeds this day, I shall award you ten forcibles from my personal stores, along with the maintenance of your Dedicates.'

Ten forcibles. The very thought brought tears to Myrrima's eyes, and she thought vainly that if she were to become a warrior, she ought not cry. But with ten forcibles, she could take enough endowments to become a warrior. It was a great gift, far more than she dared hope. Yet when she considered what she'd done for the kingdom, she knew that Iome felt so many forcibles were merely payment well earned.

Myrrima took her bow in hand and stood. By right, she was now a warrior of Heredon, equal in stature to any knight. She felt . . . relieved.

Iome went off to the tombs. While she was gone, Iome's Days came out of hiding, her face still pale with fear, and Binnesman and Jureem recounted for her the manner in which the Darkling Glory had been slain.

But Myrrima did not speak. Instead, she sat on the ground with her yellow pups and played with them, felt the prick of their sharp teeth, let them kiss her face with their tongues.

Her dogs. The key to her power. By tonight they would reach Castle Groverman, and there a facilitator would sing his chants and take an endowment from a pup. The pup that had sought to protect her was bred for stamina. Myrrima would sorely need the attribute if she were to continue her training.

A wolf lord. By morning she would be a wolf lord. Rumor said that those who took endowments from dogs became more feral. She wondered if it would really change her, if in time she would become no better than Raj Ahten.

When Iome returned from the tombs, she had more than three dozen forcibles. She knelt beside Myrrima and said, 'I brought extra, for me. I wouldn't want you to be the only wolf lord in Heredon.'

'Of course not,' Myrrima said. They mounted up. Jureem gave Iome his own horse, and went to the stable to fetch a spare mount left by the King's Guard. Myrrima and Iome each held their baskets of pups, while the wizard Binnesman rode with the clubfooted boy.

As they ambled down the cobbled streets, Myrrima kept gazing back at the skyline of the city. It looked wrong without the King's Keep standing, without the towers of the Dedicate's Keep.

When they reached the drawbridge, Myrrima spotted the reaver's head still lying at the far side. She stopped her horse on the bridge, and gazed down into the water. She could see no fish; none finned the surface, none drew their runes of protection as they had over the past two days.

At last she spotted a sturgeon resting in the shadows beneath the bridge, among a bed of golden water lilies.

Resting. No longer seeking to protect the castle. The water wizards knew what they'd done, she suspected. Perhaps more than anything else, their spells had helped bring down the Darkling Glory.

'Binnesman,' Myrrima said. 'We should do something for the wizards. We must thank them in some way.' She felt guilty for her remark, for yesterday morning she'd hoped to eat one. Now she realized just how great a debt she owed these fish.

'Of course,' Binnesman said. 'The river is clearing of silt today. We could go unblock the spillway now, let the wizards go where they will. That's not something they can do for themselves.'

Myrrima tried to imagine being a fish, imprisoned in the moat. The river had to be better, with its frogs and eels and ducklings and other delicacies.

With the help of Binnesman and Jureem, Myrrima pried loose the boards that dammed the spillway, opening the channel from the moat to the river.

As she climbed up out of the millrace, she saw the dark

shapes of the wizards, their blue backs shadowy in the depths. The huge fish wriggled their tails and shot off into the river, heading upstream toward the Dunnwood and the headwaters of the river Wye.

26

OBRAN

Borenson rested his eyes as he rode toward the Palace of the Concubines, still weak and reeling from fatigue and grief. He was never quite sure if he'd fallen asleep for only a moment or for an hour. The horses thundred on relentlessly; it seemed only moments before Pashtuk began prodding Borenson's ribs.

'We are here,' Pashtuk said, indicating the valley down below. 'The Palace of the Concubines.'

Borenson lifted his head. He did not feel refreshed by his respite, did not feel as if he'd slept at all. And the 'palace' did not live up to his expectations. He'd imagined an opulent edifice of stone, like the golden-domed palaces to the north, with soaring arches above the porticoes and vast open courtyards.

But there, on the valley's far side, a smattering of ancient stone buildings leaned against the rock face of a cliff.

It seemed an old place from afar, a deserted ruin. The valley around it was strewn with jagged stones and ancient boulders and spinebush and greasewood. He could not smell water nearby. He saw no sign of flocks or herds, no camels or horses or goats. No fires seemed to burn in the city. He could see no guards on any walls.

'Are you sure?' Borenson asked.

The Invincible merely nodded.

'Of course,' Borenson realized. 'He would not hide his greatest treasure in the open.' The palace was concealed, an anonymous ruin in the wastes. Obran. Borenson had thought the word meant 'City of the Ancient King.' But now another possible translation came to mind: 'Ruins of the King.'

Pashtuk led him down the trail.

Even as his horse ambled within the gates of the ancient city, Borenson saw no sign of guards. Indeed the gatehouse was an indefensible pile of stones that had collapsed hundreds of years before. The piled-up stones of what he'd thought was the palace looked upon closer inspection to be a fine abode for scorpions and adders.

Everywhere he went, large gray lizards sunned on stones. They dashed off at his approach. Birds were plentiful, desert sparrows among the greasewood, yellow-crested flycatchers dipping along the trail.

There is water here, he realized. Animals would not be so plentiful otherwise. Yet he could see no sign of water – no wells, no lush trees growing in profusion.

He rode through the streets of the city, up to a large ancient ruin, a state house or manor of some kind, and the Invincible led him, still ahorse, right into the building, as if they'd not bother to dismount upon entering a lord's throne room.

Inside the manor, the roof had collapsed. The walls had once been brightly painted with murals of ancient lords in long white silk coats, all of whom seemed to have curiously curly hair. But now the sun had bleached the murals to the point that in most places only a few faded earth-toned pigments still showed.

Finally, Borenson saw evidence of life. At the far wall to the throne room, someone had recently dug through, revealing a small, narrow chasm.

At this end, the chasm was dark, but ahead he could see that it opened wider, for sunlight filtered down to light the path ahead.

Now he saw the guards.

Two Invincibles stepped from the shadows and began speaking loudly to Pashtuk in a dialect of Indhopalese that Borenson could not follow. Pashtuk showed them the forcibles and described Borenson's message. In broken Rofehavanish, the Invincibles offered the normal death threats that Borenson was beginning to realize constituted the majority of any guard's conversation in this country.

Borenson was so weary after having lost endowments that he frankly did not care if they killed him or not.

One Invincible ran through the chasm to bear the message that Borenson sought an audience. When he returned twenty minutes later, Borenson left his horse behind as the guards ushered him ahead.

The first thing he noted as he entered the narrow ravine was the smell of wet earth and lush vegetation. An oasis had to be ahead.

He walked through the chasm, looking up at the golden shafts of sunlight that played on the yellow sandstone. The walls of the cliff were over one hundred feet high, and all the light that reached the chasm floor now, so late in the day, reflected from the walls above.

The chasm walls were smooth, creamy in color. Borenson imagined that this place had been hidden for thousands of years, and was only newly discovered.

Odd, he thought. Terribly odd, that water, such a precious commodity here in the desert, would be lost for so long a time. He wondered at the story. What lord had hidden this oasis, walled up the entrance behind his throne? And how had the presence of the water ever been forgotten?

The chasm wound like a serpent through the hills, and spilled into a small triangular valley. To the east and west, high cliffs reared up, meeting in a V three miles farther to the south. To the north hunkered a ridge of broken rock that no beast could have traversed.

.And here in the hidden valley, beside a small lake where palm trees grew in abundance, squatted the palace that Borenson had dreamed of.

Its cream-colored exterior walls rose forty feet, while the square guard towers at odd intervals each rose forty more. Over the palace spanned an enormous central dome, open to the air around the sides, so that it would serve as a veranda under the stars. The dome was all plated in gold, while copper plating served to highlight the tower walls. With the blue of the lake, the vibrant emerald of the grass, the lush palms, and the strands of wild honeysuckle and jasmine that trailed up the palace walls, in some ways it was perhaps the most exquisite palace Borenson had ever seen. It was simple, yet elegant.

Borenson approached the palace in manacles, lugging his bundle of forcibles. A thousand forcibles weighed about ninety pounds, and without his endowments of brawn, Borenson found himself grunting and panting from exertion long before he reached the palace.

Pashtuk stopped him at the palace gate, a huge portal of blackened wrought iron backed by gold-plated wood.

He could not see past the gate, so Borenson stared about in wonder at the dozens of hummingbirds that flitted about, drinking from the deep-throated flowers that dripped saffron and pink from the palace wall.

Borenson could not see beyond the gate, but he could hear the splash of a fountain behind it.

A guard standing above the gate spoke in a loud, high voice to Borenson in Tuulistanese.

Pashtuk translated. 'The eunuch says that Saffira will entertain you here in the courtyard. He will open the gate so that you may speak. By royal decree, you must not to look upon her. If you choose to do so, by king's command you may be slain.' In a softer voice, he added, 'However, I should warn you that if Saffira decides to intervene in your behalf, that sentence can be commuted, and instead she may elect to have you castrated, so that you can remain in the palace as her servant.'

Borenson snickered. He had never seen a woman with more than ten endowments of glamour, had never even considered the possibility, but he understood the danger. A man who took glamour might be terribly handsome, but Borenson had never felt any sexual attraction to such a man – even Raj Ahten's astonishing beauty left him cold – though he knew others who could not say the same. So he'd never struggled with his feelings when looking upon a lord.

Sometimes, when he saw a queen or high lady with several endowments of glamour, he'd found himself striving against certain unsavory temptations. A woman's glamour affected him far more powerfully than a man's. But though Borenson admired women, he'd always felt that high ladies with several endowments of glamour were above him – untouchable, so gorgeous that they seemed more than human. Saffira, with her hundreds of endowments, presented an exquisite temptation.

'I'll forgo the pleasure,' Borenson said. 'I've always been somewhat attached to my walnuts.'

'I also am loath to sever such attachments,' Pashtuk said.

Borenson grinned. Pashtuk nodded a signal. The guards cranked the winch, raising the gate.

'Close your eyes tight,' Pashtuk warned, dropping down to his hands and knees in a formal gesture of obeisance. 'Squint, so that the guards know that you do not see. Since you are a northerner, they may seek excuse to kill you. Indeed, they could offer you a blindfold, but they may prefer to have a reason to kill you.'

Borenson squinted tightly and felt a bit unsure of himself. Courtly manners differed from land to land. Saffira's stature was hard to define. As a member of a royal harem, she was not quite as elevated in status as a queen. She would not have a Days at her side. Yet she was also Raj Ahten's favorite, a diamond that he secreted away.

Borenson decided to treat her as a queen. He wearily climbed down to his hands and knees on the hot, sun-washed paving stones, so that his nose was even with the ants.

It was a difficult feat, wearing manacles.

To his astonishment, when Saffira spoke, her clear voice came to him in Rofehavanish, with only the faintest trace of an accent.

'Welcome, Sir Borenson,' she said. 'Never have we had a visitor from Rofehavan. It is a singular pleasure. I am delighted to see that the tales are true, that there are men in the world with pale skin and fire for hair.' He listened hard to her voice.

It was soft and sensual, melodic and surprisingly deep. He imagined that Saffira must be an elegant woman, with dozens of endowments of Voice. Furthermore, since she spoke Rofehavanish so perfectly without ever having seen a man from his realm, he suspected that she also had garnered one or more endowments of wit.

Saffira drew close, the rustle of a woman's silks announcing her. In moments her shadow fell upon him, blocking the sun's rays, and he smelled a mild, exotic perfume. Borenson did not answer, for she had not yet given him permission to speak.

'What is this?' Saffira asked. 'You have brown spots upon your head! Are these tattoos?'

Borenson nearly laughed. Apparently her study of language was not all-encompassing. Now that she had asked a question, he was free to speak. 'The spots are natural, Your Highness,' Borenson said. 'They are called "freckles."'

'Freckles?' she said. 'But are not the spots on trout called "freckles"?'

'In northern realms of Rofehavan, they are called that, Your Highness, though in Mystarria and the southern realms we call such spots "speckles."'

'I see,' Saffira said, amused. 'So even in your own lands, you cannot agree what to call them.'

Borenson heard the patter of small feet. Children were coming out of the courtyard, drawing close.

'Sir Borenson,' Saffira said, 'my children are curious. They have never seen a man of Rofehavan, and are naturally afraid. My eldest living son wishes permission to touch you. Do you object?'

Borenson had dragged the head of a reaver to the gates of Castle Sylvarresta only yesterday. Children and even many old people had gathered around to study it. Women had touched its rubbery gray flesh and screamed in mock terror. Now, he realized, the children here would do the same to him.

Have we sent so many assassins to this realm, he wondered, that they fear me so?

But of course the answer was yes. These children had been

born here, hidden all their lives. And many a Knight Equitable, if he'd known of this 'eldest living son,' would have considered the boy a proper target. Indeed, Borenson wondered what had happened to the eldest *nonliving* son.

'Your children are welcome to touch me,' Borenson said. 'Though I am a Knight Equitable, I will not hurt them.'

Saffira spoke quickly and softly to the boy, and the child groaned to hear that Borenson was a Knight Equitable. With hesitant steps he drew near and tentatively touched the bald spot on Borenson's head, then raced away. Immediately after, Borenson heard the steps of a smaller child come rushing forward, and again he was touched. Last of all came a toddler, a child who could not have been more than a year or two, who grabbed Borenson's hair and patted him as if he were a kitten.

Three children, Borenson realized. Jureem had said that Saffira had been Raj Ahten's favorite for five years. He had not allowed himself to wonder if she'd borne him one child, much less three.

At his mother's command, the youngest child withdrew.

'You have a message for me, and a gift?' Saffira said.

'I do, Your Highness,' Borenson answered, aware that he was being treated with some hostility. Custom dictated that she offer him food and drink before asking his quest, even if such offers were only an informal gesture. But Saffira made no such offer. 'I have come from Heredon, with a gift and a message from Gaborn Val Orden, the Earth King.'

There was a long pause, and Saffira drew a sharp breath. Borenson realized that she had not heard, here in this remote place, that an Earth King had risen in Heredon.

'But Heredon is ruled by King Sylvarresta, is it not?' Saffira asked.

'We are at war,' Borenson said. 'Your husband attacked—'

'He would not have killed King Sylvarresta!' Saffira said. 'I forbade him to. He promised leniency. Sylvarresta was a friend to my father!'

All the air came hard out of Borenson's lungs, causing him to cough in surprise. It was true that Raj Ahten had shown

Sylvarresta uncommon courtesy, had taken his endowment of wit instead of his life. But never in Borenson's wildest imaginings had he considered the possibility that a woman's influence had won Sylvarresta such a reprieve.

Now he began to wonder. He'd thought he'd come on a fool's quest, seeking to speak to Saffira at Gaborn's insistence. Had not Pashtuk said it best when he suggested that Gaborn was a weakling for listening to the counsel of women?

Yet it appeared that Saffira *could* sway Raj Ahten.

'Your Highness,' Borenson admitted, 'your husband was true to his word. Raj Ahten did not kill King Sylvarresta.'

'Can you name the warrior who killed him?' Saffira said. 'I will see that he is punished.'

Borenson dared not speak the truth. He dared not say, 'I, who kneel before you, slew King Sylvarresta.' He only hoped that the red of embarrassment did not show in his face.

Instead he averred, 'I cannot say, Your Highness. I know only this, Gaborn Val Orden is in Heredon, and he has been chosen by the Earth to become its king.'

Saffira paused. 'Gaborn Val Orden – the Prince of Mystarria – claims to be an Earth King?'

'It is true, Your Highness,' Borenson said. 'The spirit of Erden Geboren himself appeared to a company of more than ten thousand men, and the spirit crowned Gaborn with leaves.'

She whirled and began shouting at the gatekeepers in Taifan. Borenson could easily guess the nature of her question: 'Why was I not told?'

The enuchs made apologetic noises.

Saffira turned her attention back to Borenson. 'This is grave news. And you say that the Earth King has sent me gifts and a message?'

'He has, Your Highness,' Borenson said. He opened the bag of forcibles, and spread them on the ground gently so that the soft blood metal would not dent. 'He offers you gifts of glamour and of Voice.'

Saffira drew an astonished breath at the sight of so many forcibles. It was an impressive gift.

'And he bears this message. Gaborn has recently wed Iome Sylvarresta, so that he is now your husband's cousin by marriage. There is news of reavers attacking in the south of Mystarria, and in Kartish. The Earth King wishes to put aside this conflict with your lord Raj Ahten, and he begs you to carry this message: "Though I hate my cousin, the enemy of my cousin is *my* enemy."'

When Saffira drew a breath of astonishment, the sound was pure ecstasy. Sir Borenson waited for her answer. She knew what he asked. She knew that she would have to put the forcibles to use, travel to the battlefront in Rofehavan.

'The men who killed my son wish a truce?' Saffira asked. Borenson silently cursed. Jureem had not mentioned a murdered son.

'We do,' Borenson answered, as if he himself bore some responsibility for her son's death.

'If my husband agrees to this,' Saffira asked, 'does that mean that you will quit sending the Knights Equitable against us? Will you quit slaughtering our Dedicates, and the members of the royal family? Does the Earth King have that much power?'

Borenson hesitated. It was common here in Indhopal to insist on conditions when making a bargain, in hopes of getting stronger assurances. The woman wanted confirmation that she and her children would no longer have to face the fear of murder at the hands of the Knights Equitable. It was a fair request.

But Gaborn had refused to Choose the High Marshal of the Knights Equitable, though High Marshal Skalbairn had offered to turn over command of his troops. Could Gaborn truly claim to command the Knights Equitable?

The answer was both no and yes. Gaborn did not currently command that force, but he could do so if he chose.

Still, Saffira would not want to hear a no. Could he promise her safety? Would Gaborn offer to Choose the High Marshal, if doing so would guarantee a truce?

What had Gaborn seen in the High Marshal's heart that made him wish the man dead?

Borenson felt certain that no matter what foul deeds Skalbairn had committed, Gaborn would surely Choose him if he understood how much was at stake. The answer was yes.

'The command of the Knights Equitable has been offered to the Earth King,' Borenson said, skirting the truth. 'Gaborn Val Orden would ensure peace.'

'Where is my husband now?' Saffira asked. Borenson noted that it was not the first time she had called him 'my husband.' So the woman *was* married to him. She was indeed more than a mere concubine, she was the Queen of Indhopal.

'Raj Ahten slew the Dedicates at the Blue Tower in Mystarria more than two hours ago,' Borenson said. 'I believe he will ride hard now to slaughter Duke Paldane's troops, which are amassed at Carris.'

Again Saffira drew in a sharp breath. She had to see how much depended on her. An entire nation now lay at her husband's mercy, like a convict with his head on the chopping block. At this very moment, Raj Ahten would be racing for Carris. The axe was falling; perhaps she alone could stop it.

'Carris is far,' Saffira said. 'If I am to take endowments and ride there, we must hurry.'

'Please, do,' Borenson said.

She sighed deeply, as if she'd made up her mind. With a hint of desperation, she said, 'My lord has drawn most of the palace guard off into his service. I have no one to escort me to Carris, no one but my personal guards to guide the way, and I fear that I will need the guidance of a soldier of Mystarria.'

Borenson dreaded what was coming. Of course she'd need him. A cohort of riders coming out of Indhopal would face the risk of ambush by Mystarrian troops. And Borenson knew full well that even if Saffira carried a standard of truce, the soldiers at his borders were no more likely to honor such a truce as Indhopal's guards had been.

She needed him. He'd imagined that she'd ride with a thousand troops at her side, that once he delivered his message, he'd be free to leave.

Saffira said heavily, regretfully, 'Pashtuk, Sir Borenson, would you escort me to Carris? Knowing the cost, would you enter my service?'

Borenson felt dizzy. Of course he was her best choice for a guide, her only choice if she wanted to reach Carris alive. But the price?

He was newly married. He loved his wife.

To give up his manhood! The very thought left him reeling, made him feel weak as a babe. Worse, it filled him with a sense of profound loss. What if I should never be able to consummate my love for my wife?

Could I do it? Dare I do it, even for Mystarria?

Pashtuk answered first. His answer was restrained, but spoken with a certain heaviness. 'I will do so, if it pleases Your Highness.'

Borenson hedged, seeking escape. 'Your Highness,' he apologized, 'I fear that I cannot. Unlike Pashtuk, I have no endowments of brawn or stamina. If I were to give up my manhood, I could not ride a horse for six yards, much less six hundred miles!'

Pashtuk was an Invincible, with endowments of stamina and brawn. He might give up his manhood, and though the ride a few hours later would be painful, he could probably accomplish it. But Borenson could never manage such a feat.

'Of course,' Saffira said, 'I would be lenient on you, Sir Borenson. I would forbear the requirements until after I have reached my lord.'

On fast horses, he realized, they would reach Carris sometime tomorrow, near dawn.

At dawn he would pay the price, if he agreed.

The thought unnerved him. Yet he was a warrior of Mystarria, bred to battle, and his people needed him. He had no choice.

'You Highness, I will,' he offered, proud of the fact that his voice did not quaver.

'Then, Pashtuk, Sir Borenson, look upon me,' Saffira said.

Sir Borenson raised his eyes hesitantly, looking up from the sandstone pavement into the resplendent courtyard. His gaze lingered on the children. Before him stood a handsome little boy of four or five, with finely chiseled features and eyes as dark as Iome Sylvarresta's, but with skin that was even a shade darker than hers. He wore a princely costume of embroidered red cotton sewn with pearls and looked fierce as he stood protectively by his three-year-old sister and eighteen-month-old brother.

The children huddled next to their mother, as frightened children will. Borenson hardly noticed the ornate fountain behind her in the empty courtyard, or the tall Invincibles that made up her personal guard, standing at her back.

For all he could see was Saffira, a slight figure of a woman with skin as dark as karob, the elegant bones and grace of a doe. All that existed was Saffira. He did not hear his own racing heart, or his own in-drawn breath.

To say that her beauty was exquisite would be meaningless. No flower petal had ever seemed so lovely and delicate. No single star in the night sky had ever filled a man with such hopeless longing. No sun had ever blazed so fiercely as she did. Borenson focused on her fully, completely, and was lost.

Every muscle in his body tightened until his legs ached and he found himself gasping, having forgotten how to breathe. He could not close his eyes, did not dare to blink.

When next Saffira spoke he was not even conscious of what she asked. When she gathered her children and led them into the palace to take her endowments, Borenson found himself scrabbling up off his aching knees, eager to follow, until Pashtuk stopped him.

'You can't go in there,' Pashtuk yelled into his ear. 'There are other concubines.'

Borenson struggled to escape Pashtuk's grasp, but he had no endowments of brawn anymore. He had not a tenth of the Invincible's strength.

So he scrabbled to the edge of the fountain in a daze, and satisfied himself with the thought that he could sit here, he could sit here and wait until Saffira returned.

Borenson did not regret his bargain. Cared not at all that within a day, he too would have to pay the price for having looked upon Saffira. It was worth it, he thought. It was well worth the trade.

So he sat like a wretch beside the cool fountain, and waited for a long hour before he fell asleep. As he did, three things became clear to him.

The first was that his captors no longer needed to keep him in manacles. He was a captive now, as much a slave to Saffira's beauty as any man could be.

And the second thing he realized was that Saffira was not at all what he'd expected.

Raj Ahten was a man in his mid-thirties, who had aged far beyond that by reason of his many endowments of metabolism. Thus, he was rapidly becoming quite elderly.

So Borenson had naturally assumed that Saffira would have been a mature woman. But this beauty, this mother of a five-year-old son, still seemed a mere child herself.

Saffira looked as if she could not have been more than sixteen.

The thought pained him. He'd known that in Indhopal, women often married young, much younger than in Mystarria. But Saffira could not have been more than eleven years old when Raj Ahten first bedded her.

Even here, the notion bordered on the obscene.

So the third thing that Borenson realized followed from the first two. In a rage so fierce that it colored the whole palace red to Borenson's eyes, he vowed silently that – truce or no – he would find a way to make a eunuch of Raj Ahten before he killed the man.

27

LOST IN THE MIST

I paid all of that money for a good horse, and now I'm just going to kill it, Roland thought as he raced for Carris with Raj Ahten's knights chasing close behind.

His charger thundered across a wooden bridge, dashed across the countryside. His mount wheezed as if each breath would be its last. Its ears lay flat, and foam lathered its mouth, dripped from the bit and bridle. The force horse easily ran at sixty miles per hour, but the Invincibles were gaining.

Baron Poll's mount had surged ahead half a mile from Roland. It galloped over a hill. Poll was far enough in the lead that the big knight had little to worry about.

Roland had been born to a family of shipbuilders on his mother's side. He began to wonder if he might gain more speed by jettisoning cargo. But he wasn't a man with arms or armor; he really had nothing heavy in his saddlebags. He'd given the green lady his heavy bearskin cloak. His purse was laden with gold. Though he'd never had a sentimental attachment to wealth, he decided he'd rather die with it than without.

The only item that really weighed him down was the half-sword that Baron Poll had given him, and he reasoned that it might be worth more in his hand than not.

So he galloped his horse, kicked its flanks, hunkered low, and clung tight.

Carris was but eight miles away, cloaked in a dense fog, yet from any hilltop he could see its white towers rising from the mist.

He looked back. The Invincibles had closed to within two hundred yards. Two bowmen at the van had strung their horse bows, preparing to shoot. Roland raced for the hilltop; his mount went airborne for a moment before its hooves thudded to the dirt road.

The force horse stepped left to avoid a rut. That alone saved Roland's life, for just then two arrows whipped past Roland's shoulder, missing his back by less than a foot. His mount burst ahead as it raced toward a stand of heavy oaks, their browning autumn leaves blowing in a light breeze, their trunks and branches twined with dark-green ivy.

Roland hoped the road ahead was winding, for the trees might give him some extra cover. He raced for the grove, glanced back over his shoulder.

The Invincibles drew to a halt at the crest of the hill, the morning sun glistening from their brass-colored helms and saffron surcoats.

They gazed down at the wood, then turned their steeds and raced away.

Roland wondered if they feared an ambush. Perhaps friendly troops hid in these oaks.

Or perhaps another of Raj Ahten's patrols guarded them. Roland never slowed, and not once did he spot anyone in the small wood – either friend or foe.

When he came out on the other side, the road wound on before him. Baron Poll was nowhere to be seen. The dirt highway led up over the downs, past a small village. Hedgerows marched along the left of the road, stone fences to the right. And still no sign of Baron Poll.

I've lost him, Roland realized.

He'd seen a couple of paths in the wood, trails that led to uncertain destinations. Baron Poll must have taken one. But Roland had no idea which, and he wasn't about to turn back.

So he kept racing over the downs, past the village, until the trail dropped precipitously into a patch of fog. He was close to Carris now, only five miles. And if Poll was right, this fog hid friendly troops, Duke Paldane's troops.

He slowed his horse, not wanting to charge blindly into the mist where he could well encounter pikemen or bowmen.

A dozen yards into the thick of the mist, he knew that Poll had been right: this was no common fog.

He'd never seen such a dense fog, not even in the Courts of Tide. The mist was thick as butter, and though it had been a bright and warm morning not a hundred yards back, now it turned dark and sultry as night. Sitting on his horse, he soon found that he could not even see the road at his feet.

He feared that his horse might stumble over an embankment, so Roland climbed from the charger's back. When he knelt so that he was at a height of no more than four feet, he could barely discern the road at his feet and the grass nearby.

So it was that he led his charger, droop-eared and wheezing, through the mist.

He'd seen the tops of the white towers at Carris rising from the fog, and he'd guessed the distance to be five miles.

Yet when he got off his horse and led it for many hours through the mist, sometimes stumbling from the road, sometimes slipping in puddles, always unsure what direction he was going, he seemed to make no headway.

The difficulty of finding a trail at all greatly increased when he reached a city or village, for then the road met many byways, and he twice found himself wandering around city blocks.

The road twisted and turned like a damned serpent, and though he followed the margin where grass met mud, after three hours he knew that he must have forked off somewhere, for he'd certainly gone more than five miles.

In all that time, he'd spotted not a single soldier of Mystarria, not a single defender. The water wizard's mist might have hidden a hundred thousand men within easy bowshot of the road, but he'd never have seen one.

As he walked, he worried for Averan, a little girl hiding in some town south of here. He knew that she must be terrified, and he cursed himself for a fool for not staying with her.

And if truth be told, he realized that he was just as worried for the green woman. She'd never done him any harm, aside from having tried to suck blood out of his hand. But his feelings for her ran deeper than mere compassion.

He didn't quite know how to express it. She was as beautiful as a Runelord's fine lady. Though Roland fancied that he was no starry-eyed lad, he knew quite frankly that her beauty attracted him.

But he doubted he'd really ever fall in love with a woman who had fangs and green skin.

Nor could he say that he was attracted by her strength of character. So far as he could tell, she didn't have any character. He didn't know whether she had faith or charity or confidence or any other human virtue.

But there was one thing that he could say for the green woman: in the past day, he'd discovered that he felt . . . safe, when she was near.

Beyond that, he felt that she needed him, needed his wisdom and his counsel, needed him to teach her the name for the color blue, and how to wear shoes, and how to ride a horse.

No other woman had at once seemed so formidable and yet so vulnerable.

She was as impenetrable to him as the fog. The very mystery of her attracted him.

He swore to himself that as soon as he delivered the message to Paldane, he'd return south under cover of night and search for Averan and the green lady.

Roland had no illusions about himself. He did not believe that the green woman could ever love him.

He was after all a worthless man — everyone told him so. His wife had let him know it time and again. His king had thought him good for nothing but providing an endowment of metabolism. He couldn't read words or do numbers, couldn't fight.

Roland was reminded of Gaborn, and realized he'd never given much thought to how he would react to the rise of an Earth King.

Now, he realized it did not matter. No Earth King would Choose a man like Roland Borenson, a man who had nothing left to offer. It meant that Roland's short, bitter life would probably remain just that – short and bitter.

When at last he did trudge out of the mist, he found that he'd gotten thoroughly lost. The sun was up well past noon, and he could still see the towers of Carris off in the distance, some five miles. Yet he'd somehow managed to bypass the castle completely, for Carris was now south of him.

He stood for a moment, feeling weak. His tunic was wet from the mist, so drenched that he took it off and wrung it out, letting the water spill into the dirt at his feet. Then he put his tunic on and trundled back into that damned fog, wondering if perhaps he'd see better if he carried a torch.

Hours later, he found himself again outside the fog, and outside Carris, to the west this time. Now it was late afternoon.

He gritted his teeth and went back under that infernal oppressive cloud, into the gloom, vowing to watch his feet more carefully.

He had not gone far, perhaps two miles, when he heard a bell chime six times, off to his left. It was getting late, and Roland realized that a message he should have delivered shortly after dawn had been delayed now till evening. He'd spent the day wandering through this fog.

He soon found a road heading left, and after a mile was greeted by the happy sounds of castle life: the ring of hammers on mail, the curses of some lord who demanded that the vassals secure the hoardings to the castle walls, roosters crowing at the last rays of daylight.

More than all of that, he heard the sounds of crows cawing, and pigeons cooing, and gulls shrieking in the air above him.

Allowing his ears to guide him toward the city, he found a narrow road that led out to a causeway. He knew he was on a causeway because he could hear water lapping at both sides of the road, and the fog had suddenly begun to smell of algae.

At last he reached a barbican, an enormous stone gate set in front of the road.

The fog was so thick that when he approached the gate, no guards hailed him, for they could see him no better than he could see the castle.

'Is anyone there?' Roland called.

A booming voice laughed from overhead, atop the barbican. 'There's about a million of us here, good fellow. Searching for anyone in particular?'

'I've a message for Duke Paldane,' Roland said, feeling foolish. 'A message from Baron Haberd of Keep Haberd.'

'Well, come to the side gate, man, so we can have a look at you!'

Roland followed the huge iron gate to the right, found only a narrow tower with archer's slots above and some holes for pikemen to attack through. He peered into one of the holes, and could see into the tower. Torches burned there, and at least twenty men in armor sat inside. An ignorant-looking fellow playfully thrust his pike at Roland and shouted, 'Woo!'

Roland followed the iron gate back to the left, found a small portcullis with several guardsmen waiting for him. In the fog, Roland could not see much of them, only shadowy shapes.

'Sorry,' Roland said. 'I can't see my own damned feet in this fog.'

'I'll give the wizards your compliments,' the captain of the guard said. He took Roland's message pouch, inspected the seal. 'This seal has been broken.'

'I'm not a messenger myself,' Roland admitted. 'I found the messenger dead on the road, and brought the pouch. I had to open it to know where to deliver it.'

'Smart fellow,' the captain of the guard said.

He opened the portcullis gate and urged Roland onto the drawbridge, to a second barbican, then a third. Each barbican was successively more heavily guarded. Men with warhammers and pikes were stationed below, while archers and artillery threatened from above.

The fog was so dense, Roland could not see the water on either side of the bridges, though he smelled it and heard it lapping against the piles.

Walking through the fog for mile after mile, Roland had begun to worry that the castle was totally undefended. He'd not seen so much as a single guard posted on the roads.

Once he got inside, it became obvious that men were everywhere. Knights by the thousand bivouacked down in the bailey, and the walls crawled with troops.

But it was not until he got past the bailey, into the walled city of Carris proper, that he began to realize how many people had fled here. When the guard on the wall had said, 'there's about a million of us,' Roland had known he was jesting.

Still, Carris was a large island, as he'd seen from afar. Numerous towers jutted up from the walls, and the defenses inside Carris included dozens of walled manors and fortresses. The streets were full of urchins getting underfoot, serious-looking women rushing hither and thither, and men-at-arms swarming everywhere.

Crows and gulls and pigeons perched at every rooftop. Smelly goats nibbled at low-hanging laundry; nervous chickens ran underfoot; geese waddled about honking; horses whinnied in the stables, while yellow cows merely squatted in the road.

So many people and beasts in such close quarters caused a fetid smell. Even after only a few minutes of walking through the stench, Roland longed to escape to a tower or castle wall – or better yet, return to the road far from here and join Averan and the green lady.

The guards escorted him up through the city, into the main bailey of Castle Carris itself, and from there to the Duke's Keep – an enormous tower that rose above all others.

The furnishings in the keep were as rich as any king's. The wood on every doorpost and chair and table was oiled to a shine. The decorative brass lamp holders on each wall were covered with costly glass hoods out of Ashoven. The carpets were rich underfoot, and the plaster walls had been nicely painted with fields of red poppies.

The Duke, a crafty-looking fellow with a triangular face, was cloistered in the uppermost tower, surrounded by counselors whom Roland recognized. They were men who had granted endowments of wit to King Orden and had been Restored at the Blue Tower a week before.

With a nod toward the king's messenger standing nearby, one of the counselors said, 'If the Earth King has ordered us to flee, then we must flee.'

But Duke Paldane slammed his fist on an oak table. 'It's too late,' he said. 'I have four hundred thousand civilians in my care, and Raj Ahten's troops surround us. I can't ask them to *flee* out onto the plains, where his Invincibles will cut them down for sport.'

The old counselor Jerimas shook his hoary head. 'I don't like it. If the Earth King has warned us, we should listen, my Duke.'

'Listen to what?' Paldane asked. 'He has given us no direction. Flee? Flee where? How? When? From what?'

'You act as if you think the walls of Carris can protect us,' old Jerimas said. 'You put great faith in stone, even after all that has happened. Perhaps you should put faith in your King.'

'I have faith in my King,' Paldane argued. 'But why does he burden me with contradictory commands?'

The counselors looked worried. Roland could see that they had too many questions and not enough answers. They looked as if they were already beaten.

The Duke glanced up, saw Roland, and his mouth dropped in surprise. 'Sir Borenson? What are you doing here? Do you bring further direction from the King?'

'No,' Roland said. 'I'm not Sir Borenson, though we are kin.'

Roland handed the message case to the Duke, who unrolled the parchment, glanced at it distractedly, and then handed it back to Roland with a curt 'Thank you.'

Reavers had overrun Keep Haberd, and Duke Paldane did not bat an eye.

'Milord?' Roland asked.

'I know,' the Duke said. 'Baron Poll brought the same message hours ago. There's nothing for it. We're under siege here, and the king's messengers simply ask me to flee!'

'Siege, milord?' Roland asked in surprise. Raj Ahten had not moved siege engines near the walls. Indeed, he seemed to have no troops within miles.

'Siege,' the Duke said, as if Roland were simpleminded.

'Milord,' Roland asked. 'I was hoping to leave the castle. I have some friends hidden to the south, a young girl who needs me.' He wanted to plead for license to become Averan's guardian, but knew that this was not the time.

The Duke considered for half a second. 'No one leaves. It's too dangerous, and with the Blue Tower destroyed, our walls are hopelessly undermanned.'

'Destroyed?' Roland asked, unsure he'd heard right.

The Duke nodded solemnly. 'Every stone is down.'

Roland choked back a cry of astonishment. He'd served as a Dedicate in the Blue Tower for twenty years. He might have been killed in his sleep there. He had escaped just in time.

But without force soldiers to man the walls of Carris, he realized, those who died in the Blue Tower might be the lucky ones. 'How did it fall?' Roland dared to ask.

Paldane shrugged. 'I don't know, but as far as we can tell, four hours ago, everyone in the tower was killed.' He studied Roland with a critical eye. 'You look like a Borenson. Tell me, have you any training in war?'

'I am a butcher by trade, milord.'

Duke Paldane grunted, noted the half-sword tucked into his belt. 'Now you're a guardsman. You'll take the south wall – between towers fifty-one and fifty-two. Gut any man or beast that comes over the wall. Understand? We'll be down to knife-work here before daybreak, and a butcher will be of use to me on the wall.'

Roland stood, dumbfounded, until a squire led him to his post.

28

A PLOT UNMASKED

By the time Erin Connal reached Castle Groverman on the banks of the Wind River, she felt no desire to celebrate. True, Gaborn had wakened from his faint an hour before and given the good news: the Darkling Glory was dead – or at least disembodied, made much less dangerous.

But Erin had been left horseless, and Prince Celinor had been injured by a falling brand. The skin on the back of his neck had burned and bubbled. With his endowments of stamina, the Prince would live, but he'd not have an easy recovery. By the time Erin had dragged him from under the burning logs, the pain of his wounds had Celinor gibbering and weeping like a child. He'd fallen unconscious shortly afterward, and so had been carried behind the saddle of one of Duke Groverman's men, and had gotten lost from Erin's sight during the ride.

Erin rode behind a knight from Jonnick into the bailey outside Duke Groverman's keep. Upon entering, she learned that she was not the first to arrive at the keep – far from it.

Hundreds of knights had already arrived and were feasting. Groverman's servants had brought baskets with loaves of bread into the bailey and dispensed the food freely while a serving woman opened flasks of ale. A great bank of fires lined the east wall, where cooking boys turned whole calves on spits. Minstrels played from a balcony of the Duke's keep, and a crier beside the city gate welcomed them by shouting, 'Eat your fill, gentleman. Eat your fill!'

The Duke spared nothing for the Earth King's army. But Erin was not yet ready to eat.

She went to find Celinor. Duke Groverman's men had laid him on a saddle blanket near a dark wall of the keep. Moonflowers grew along the wall, and now their pale white blossoms opened wide to the night air and the moths that fed on their nectar. A well-intentioned soldier was hunched over Celinor, trying to force whiskey down his throat.

'Drink, good sirrah,' the knight said. 'It will ease your pain.'

But Celinor clenched his teeth, and, with tears of pain in his eyes, turned his head away. The knight tried to wrestle Celinor's head around, to force him to drink, obviously believing that the Prince was delirious.

'I'll have at him,' Erin said, urging the knight to leave. 'He'll take the poppy better.'

'Perhaps,' the knight said, 'though I don't know why he'd prefer a bitter poppy to sweet whiskey.'

'Find a physic and ask for the poppy,' Erin said wearily, and she knelt by Celinor, brushed his brow. He was sweating, and looked up at her with pain-filled eyes.

'Thank you,' he managed to whisper.

The Earth King had bidden him to put aside strong drink. Now Erin saw that he really would avoid it at any cost. 'It's nothing,' she told Celinor, then she held him a moment. He seemed to sleep.

At times he spoke deliriously, as if in evil dreams. Once he shouted and tried to push her away.

But after several long minutes, he woke. His eyes were glazed with pain, and sweat soaked his brow. 'The Earth King has lost his endowments,' he said. 'I heard someone say it. Is it true?'

'Sure,' Erin answered. 'He's a common one now – if an Earth King can be called "common."'

'Then you can look upon him without his glamour. Have you seen him?'

She'd seen him on the ride toward Castle Groverman this evening, dead asleep. Even with his endowment of glamour, the young man had not been handsome. Now he looked downright plain.

'I saw him with my own eyes,' she said, thinking Celinor's comment was merely a subject chosen by delirium.

She patted his cheek, noticed that he wore a silver chain around his neck with a silver oval locket.

As he fell back, wincing in pain, the silver locket fell out from his tunic, up by his throat. She knew immediately what it was – a promise locket. Many lords, when they had sons or daughters whom they sought to wed, would commission an artist to paint a miniature portrait of the young lord or lady who sought a match, and would then insert the portrait into a locket. Such a locket would then be sent to distant lands, to be shown to the parents of a prospective spouse, so that lords and ladies might choose a match for their son or daughter without ever having seen the person in question.

Such lockets were never trustworthy. The artists who painted them tended to ignore a child's flaws and accentuate his or her beauty to the point that sometimes the image on a locket bore only a slight resemblance to the young lord or lady pictured therein.

Still, such lockets often inspired romance. Erin recalled that when she was twelve, her mother had shown her the image of a young lord from Internook. Erin had carried the locket about for months, dreaming of the fierce-looking blond-haired lad, until it became clear that boy had seen Erin's own image on her promise locket and not been impressed.

Celinor seemed too old to be swooning after some child on a locket. He had to be twenty-five, and should have married years ago. But then Erin realized that no right-thinking lady would have had him.

'What, Father?' she imagined some twelve-year-old girl asking. 'You want me to wed the "Sot of South Crowthen."'

'Not the boy,' the father would say, 'just the kingdom. And while he drinks himself into an early grave, he'll run about begetting bastards on every tavern slattern within

three kingdoms. And after you've slaughtered all his wee
bastards, Crowthen will be yours.'

She couldn't imagine any girl welcoming the match.

Yet Celinor wore a promise locket, like some lovesick boy.

Erin wondered what twelve-year-old girl had caught his
fancy. She glanced at Celinor, who lay breathing heavily, apparently asleep.

She surreptitiously flipped the tiny latch on the locket
and caught her breath. The image of the twelve-year-old
girl on it had blue eyes and long dark hair. She knew the
painting instantly, even in the wan firelight reflecting from
the far wall, for it was Erin's portrait, painted ten years ago,
back when she'd dreamt that such protraits meant something.

Erin snapped the locket closed. No suitor had ever come
begging for the hand of a girl from the horse clans of Fleeds.
She wasn't sure what she'd have done if a suitor had come.
She was a warrior, after all, not some fine lady raised with no
more purpose than to bear a man sons. And it was only in
kingdoms like Internook that a warlord sometimes wanted a
wife who was strong enough to fight beside him.

Yet now Celinor wore her promise locket. Had he carried
it for the past ten years?

Her mother might have sent it to South Crowthen, but
Erin's mother had never mentioned a possible match with
Celinor. No, Erin knew her mother well enough to be sure
that even if King Anders had proposed such a match, her
mother would have turned him down.

Yet Celinor had her locket, had kept it for ten years.

Had Celinor dreamt of such a match? It made sense, in a
small way. South Crowthen shared a border with Fleeds.
Celinor and Erin could have married, enlarged their kingdoms, despite the differences in their cultures.

But King Anders would have seen it as a bad match. Fleeds
was a poor country, after all, with nothing to offer. If their
parents exchanged lockets, it was only as a matter of courtesy. Neither lord would have wanted the match.

Yet Celinor had kept the locket for ten years, had perhaps even worn it for ten years.

Celinor the sot.

She looked into his face. He'd come awake. He stared at her with narrow, pain-filled eyes.

Erin's heart hammered.

'Tell me,' Celinor asked with surprising ferocity. 'Young King Orden, does he look like you?'

'What?' she begged in surprise. 'I'd be a sorry sight if he did.'

'Does he look like you?' Celinor asked. 'Like brother to sister, as my father says? No flame-headed man of Fleeds gave you that dark hair.'

Erin felt her face flush with embarrassment. She'd been imagining that he loved her. Now she saw the truth of it: Gaborn's father, King Orden, had made an annual pilgrimage to Heredon for the autumn hunt with King Sylvarresta. On those pilgrimages, he'd passed through Fleeds, and had become a friend to Erin's mother.

If her mother had thought Orden to be a suitable match, it was only reasonable that she'd have wanted to breed with him. It could have happened. But it hadn't.

Still, both Erin and Gaborn had black hair and blue eyes, though Erin had her mother's build, not King Orden's broad shoulders.

So King Anders imagined that King Mendellas Draken Orden was her father, making Gaborn her half brother – her younger brother.

Erin dared not name her true father.

On the day that Erin had first begun her monthly bleed, her mother had taken Erin to the study, shown her a book that named her sires, told of each man's and woman's times and deeds. They were great men and women, heroes of old, and her mother had made Erin swear to keep the tradition, to breed with only the finest of men.

Erin knew the name of her father, but under the circumstances, she thought it better not to reveal her patronage.

'Is that the only reason you wear my promise locket?' Erin asked. 'You wanted to measure my face to his?'

Celinor licked his lips, nodded barely. 'My father . . . seeks to expose Gaborn's deceit, label him a criminal.'

Erin wondered. If she were Gaborn's brother, what would be the repercussions?

By the laws of Fleeds, having a royal father from another realm meant nothing. Erin's title as a royal was handed down from her mother, but even that title would not allow Erin to become the High Queen. That post would have to be earned, bestowed by the wise women of the clans.

But if Erin were Orden's daughter, it might have tremendous repercussions in Mystarria. Some might claim that she, as the eldest, was the rightful heir to Mystarria's throne.

King Anders wanted to use her as a pawn.

'I – I'm not following you,' she said. 'What could your father hope to gain? I'd never want the throne of Mystarria!'

'Then he would thrust it upon you,' Celinor whispered.

'Fagh! That would be a lot of trouble for nothing. I'd have no part of it.'

'You know the laws of succession: no man can be crowned a king who has won the throne by murder,' Celinor answered.

She wondered. Yesterday, before he'd met Gaborn, the High Marshal Skalbairn had warned that King Anders was spreading rumors that Gaborn had fled Longmot, leaving his father to die. Such a deed might not technically be counted as murder, but it was akin to murder.

And after the death of King Orden, was it not Gaborn's own bodyguard who had slaughtered the witless King Sylvarresta? Borenson swore that in doing so, he only fulfilled the last command spoken to him by old King Orden, to slaughter those who had given themselves as Dedicates to Raj Ahten.

But one could easily argue that Borenson told such a tale to cover the truth – that he'd murdered Sylvarresta in order for his master to gain Heredon's throne.

Gaborn now wore a double crown of kingship – that of Heredon and that of Mystarria. But Anders would argue that both crowns had been won through murder.

Thus Gaborn was not a king at all. And if he was not rightfully the king of any nation, then how could he be the Earth King?

And if Gaborn was not a king, he could justifiably be dispatched, dealt with as a murderer.

She saw it all in a flash, realized that Anders would start his war. He was probably already sending out minor lords to gather support. He had blocked his borders and forbade his people to come to Heredon to see the Earth King.

After all, if they saw Gaborn, they might be persuaded that he was indeed the Earth King. And King Anders did not want them to learn the truth.

Yet Erin knew the truth. She'd heard Gaborn's voice in her head, leading her to safety. She knew him to be the Earth King.

'What foul notions your father has, to make up such things!'

Celinor laughed painfully, as much from his burns as from the sentiment that followed. 'Some think me to be much like him.'

'You didn't need to whip your horse to a froth to check out your father's story,' Erin said. 'So why are you here?'

'My father sent me to gain any information that might help expose Gaborn. But I came to learn the truth.'

Just then, a healer woman brought the poppy resin, along with a small ivory pipe that she would use to blow the opium into Celinor's face. She set the pipe down, rolled the opium into a dark ball, then set it in the bowl of the pipe and added a hot coal from an ornate clay brazier.

Erin began to back away, to give the healer room to work, but Celinor clutched at her cloak.

'Please,' Celinor said. 'I don't know if I can go on with you to Fleeds tomorrow. You must stop my father. Have your mother issue a statement about your patronage – even if she must lie to do so.'

Erin patted Celinor's chest reassuringly. 'I'll be back in a wee bit, to check on you.'

Erin covered him with a blanket while the healer blew

opium smoke into Celinor's face. Then Erin walked down through the portcullis and stared up at the night sky. The sun had set an hour past, and all of the day's clouds had drifted off. Only a few high cirrus clouds still hung in the night sky, a veil for the stars. It would be a warm night, and it was too late in the year for mosquitoes. Celinor would be comfortable if she left him alone for a bit.

Knights were still surging into the castle by the hundreds. Erin stepped aside to let some men pass, and the crier at the gate behind her shouted again, 'Eat your fill, gentlemen!'

She looked down over the castle walls to the city below, Groverman's domain.

Damn King Anders, Erin thought. But she had to wonder. Why does he need me?

After all, if Anders wanted to argue that Gaborn was no king at all, had earned his crown only by murder and deceit, he only needed to allege murder. He didn't need to provide Erin as an alternate heir to Mystarria's throne.

Perhaps, she thought, Anders is afraid that if he kills Gaborn, the people of Mystarria will rise in war against him. By providing an alternate heir, King Anders might well hope to assuage such a war.

But that didn't seem right. If Gaborn died, and if indeed he had won his crown through murder, then the kingship would rightly fall to Duke Paldane.

Paldane the Huntsman. Paldane the schemer and tactician. Paldane, her true father.

Of course, Anders would fear him. Paldane would easily pierce any subterfuge that Anders might devise. And he would demand satisfaction. Paldane's reputation was such that no king in all of Rofehavan would want to match wits with him.

No, Anders wouldn't want the kingship to fall to Paldane after Gaborn's death, so perhaps he hoped to offer Erin as a suitable heir to old King Orden. But what would happen then?

Anders might hope that Erin Connal and Duke Paldane would squabble over the kingship of Mystarria, possibly starting a civil war.

Or perhaps Anders hoped that Paldane would strike at Fleeds itself, crushing her poor nation.

That seemed possible. In fact, after Gaborn was dead and Fleeds lay in ruins, Anders might even imagine that he could wash his hands of the mess by claiming that Erin had deceived him.

Whatever his plot, Anders was bound to be surprised when the truth came out.

Or maybe not. What if King Anders had guessed whom her father really was? What if he planned to kill Paldane so that she really would inherit Mystarria's throne?

Would Erin dare take it?

Damn my mother for choosing Paldane, Erin thought. She should have known better. At the time, it had seemed improbable that Paldane would himself ever be in line for the throne, and her mother had thought Paldane the best man in Mystarria – the best lord in all of Rofehavan. But a dozen assassinations later, now Erin stood in direct line for Mystarria's crown.

Of course, the political situation in Rofehavan had been thrown into upheaval today, now that the Blue Tower was destroyed. Mystarria's strength had easily been halved.

But *that* was something Anders couldn't have foreseen. He couldn't have known that Raj Ahten would destroy the Blue Tower.

Unless Anders was in Raj Ahten's hire.

No, Erin decided, now I'm thinking nonsense.

Erin knew she was missing something. Perhaps Anders didn't have a fully developed scheme for disposing of Gaborn – or perhaps she could not see all of it.

When Erin was a child, her mother sometimes made her perform an odd exercise. Mother and daughter played chess together with a curtain placed across the board, so that each one saw only her own half of the board. Thus she always had to be protected from players that might strike out of the darkness, and Erin had to learn to pin down opponents she couldn't see. It was an exercise in futility.

She suddenly wished that she'd played chess with King Anders.

How many moves ahead could he plot? Four, eight, twelve?

She was only looking ahead four moves, at best.

And Anders had thrown up a screen of secrecy that could not easily be pierced.

Damn, she thought. Erin needed to consult with her mother. Once Queen Herin learned of Anders's plot, she could help unravel it. King Anders had better beware!

Erin had to see her mother immediately. She needed to find a fast horse.

Castle Groverman smelled deliciously of horses and grass out on the heather. Here on the plains beside the Wind River, Groverman raised most of the horses and much of the beef cattle that supplied Heredon. Tolfest, the time when cattle were slaughtered for the winter, was just a few weeks away. Already the cattle were penned outside the city and soon they would be driven to various castles and villages in the north.

Now that Hostenfest was past, much of the real work for the horsemen was ending: hundreds of wild horses had been gathered over the past weeks and penned in stalls with the finest domesticated mounts available. These domestic mounts were warhorses, trained for combat, or horses for the use of messengers, quick beasts that could outrace the wind.

The domestic mounts all had an endowment or two of strength or stamina or wit, and now were in the process of establishing their dominance by fighting with the wild herd leaders. It was a brutal thing to do to a common horse, to pen it in together with a force horse, but vital nonetheless. Once the wild horses accepted the domestic animals as their leaders, Groverman's facilitators could take the forcibles among the wild herds and siphon off attributes for the domestics, creating force horses of tremendous worth.

With so many lords going to battle and with so many mounts now ready to take endowments, Erin knew that she would find it hard to get a decent mount. Even in a good year, force horses were hard to come by.

She headed toward the stables north of the castle, began her search for something suitable.

In the stables she found at least a hundred lords stalking about, demanding that the stableboys show them the horse's teeth by torchlight and engaging in other forms of silliness.

Erin simply went directly to the stablemaster. A stableboy had recognized her accent and told her that his master was a fine old horseman of Fleeds, a man by the name of Bullings.

She found him in the Dedicate stables, where the horses that granted endowments to others were housed. These were weak horses that had given their brawn to others, mounts that were sickly after having given an endowment of stamina. The Dedicate stables consisted of an enormous building in a walled part of the city. Here some three thousand horses were cared for, blind horses and deaf, horses kept in slings because they could not stand. Some horses that had given an endowment of grace had to be fed on oat mash because the guts of their intestines could not stretch properly to push food into their stomachs for digestion. These mounts were difficult to tend, for they suffered from bloat and therefore required frequent massage.

'Sirrah Bullings? I'll be wanting a horse to take to war,' she said. 'You know your mounts. Which is your best?'

'For a horsewoman of Fleeds?' he asked, as if unsure. She'd never met him before. By the way he spoke, regardless of the fact that they both hailed from Fleeds, Erin knew that he would hold back, sell her a lesser horse.

The stable door opened behind her, and Erin heard heavy footsteps, the *ching* of ring mail. Other knights in search of good mounts were obviously coming to speak to the stablemaster. She knew she'd not hold his attention long.

'Aye, a horse for a woman of Fleeds,' she answered. 'Any mount will be appreciated, so long as it can get me home tomorrow.'

Behind her, the Earth King himself spoke. 'Not just any mount will do,' he said. 'This horsewoman is the daughter of Queen Herin the Red, and today she saved the life of a prince of South Crowthen.'

Erin turned. She'd not told Gaborn that she'd saved Celinor, had not reported it to anyone, but apparently already tongues were wagging. Both she and Celinor had been forced to ride double with other lords.

'Your Highness,' Bullings said, dropping to one knee. The stablemaster kept his floors so clean that he need not worry about soiling his leather trousers.

Gaborn looked pale, weak. Erin wanted to tell him what she'd discovered about King Anders's schemes, but one glance warned her that she shouldn't. He looked as if he needed nothing more than to fall into bed, and her news might keep him awake for hours.

Besides, Erin thought, I can handle it.

'What is the *best* mount you've got? The very best,' Gaborn asked the stablemaster.

Bullings stammered, 'I – I've a fine warhorse, Your Highness. It's well trained, has a good heart, with fifteen endowments to its credit.'

'A fine mount,' Gaborn said. 'It should do for a horse-woman of Fleeds, don't you think.'

'But Your Highness –' Bullings objected. 'I can't be doing that. The Duke will skin my hide and sell it cheap to the tanners! That mount was to be a gift from our Duke Groverman to you!'

'If it is freely given,' Gaborn said, 'then I shall give it to whomever I want.'

'Your Highness,' Erin begged in embarrassment, 'I could never be accepting such a horse!' She spoke honestly, for such a horse was a kingly mount. She dared not to take a beast that rightfully belonged to the Earth King. 'I'll not have it!'

Gaborn smiled playfully. 'Well, if you decline, then I'm sure that the stablemaster here will find something suitable.'

'Aye, Your Highness,' Bullings said in a bluster, leaping at the opportunity. 'I've a fine mare, with a personality so sociable I'd marry her if I could! I'll bring her at once.' As if forget-ting all other duties, he raced to the back of the stables and hurried out of a door.

Erin stared at Gaborn in surprise. 'You knew he wouldn't sell me a decent horse!'

'I'm sorry he wasn't more accommodating,' Gaborn answered. 'Good horses are going to be hard to come by here in Heredon. My father killed most of Raj Ahten's warhorses, so Raj Ahten stole what he could from Sylvarresta.

'Now we've plenty of forcibles to create some good mounts and replenish our supply, but King Sylvarresta only had a few hundred warhorses in training. Duke Groverman and I have been doing our best to address the shortage. But even by granting endowments to some half-trained warhorses that shouldn't be getting endowments until next year, we'll only add four or five hundred good new mounts to take into battle. So of course Groverman will be loath to sell a decent horse at any price. In fact, he wouldn't have sold you one.'

Those were grim tidings, but Erin was relieved to see that Gaborn had been considering such matters. Erin herself was unused to thinking about the economics of war.

Without a decent cavalry, Heredon would be forced to rely on infantry and archers to defend themselves. Over the past couple of days, she'd been watching his troops practice. The fields south of Castle Sylvarresta had been filled with thousands of boys with bows, while west of the castle, thousands more had been learning to use pole-arms. Even with Heredon's vast resources in the way of smithies, however, it would take months for Gaborn to properly outfit an infantry with helms and armor. But while riding through the villages today, she'd been reassured by the ring of hammers upon anvils.

It occurred to her that the weight upon Gaborn must be tremendous. No, she would not burden him now with tales of possible treachery. As she considered, she even began to wonder if she might have been overreacting. Could Anders really be plotting Gaborn's demise? She had little evidence of it, beyond Celinor's suspicions.

She wanted more proof, and besides, Gaborn would be better equipped to contend with such matters when he was rested.

She'd never really considered what duties an Earth King might have to perform in organizing a war effort. Many a lord with a good understanding of battle tactics found that he floundered once he was faced with issues of logistics.

Gaborn would have to deal with all of the complexities of war, with the problems of supplying and training his armies, while maintaining his defenses. Add to that the concerns over strategies and tactics, and the normal duties of maintaining justice along with fulfilling his other obligations seemed overwhelming.

Yet Gaborn's responsibilities went further than that. She'd heard his voice in her mind today, heard him warn her of danger personally, and she knew for a fact that he'd done the same for thousands of other people. He did not merely rule in the manner of a common monarch. He was intimately connected to and concerned with each of his vassals.

The powers of an Earth King seemed awesome, and the burden even greater. 'Milord?' she asked, hoping to test him. 'Have you been thinking about how you will get the feathers to fletch your arrows?'

'I've commanded every lord in Heredon to have every child who plucks a goose or duck or grouse or pigeon to give the wing and tail feathers into the king's service.'

'But you've barely had time for such niggling details,' she said. 'When did you make such a command?'

'Most of the lords of Heredon presented themselves to me on the day that I reached Castle Sylvarresta, after the battle of Longmot,' he answered wearily. 'I spoke into the minds of my Chosen, just as I spoke to you today, and told them to tend to the matters of their own defense.'

'And you asked them to save feathers?'

'And nails for horses, and I warned them to make good winter cloaks that a man might sleep under as well as wear, and to store food and healing herbs, and of course to tend to a thousand other matters.'

Now as she thought about it, she'd seen it. She'd seen the people of Heredon working as she'd ridden north, had noted the intensity with which the millers ground their flour and the weavers spun their cloth. She'd seen masons working on every fortress wall.

'What would you be having me do?' Erin asked, for when others were making such heroic efforts, her own small part in this war suddenly seemed insignificant.

'Follow me,' Gaborn said. 'You listened to my voice today, and because of it, you lived. Keep listening.'

At that moment, the stablemaster threw open a door, brought in a fine-looking black warhorse, a tall mare with a spirited air, a mount with nine endowments: one each of brawn, grace, stamina, wit, sight, and smell, and three of metabolism. It was among the most noble-looking beasts she'd ever seen, almost a king's mount.

'I'll listen to you, Your Highness,' Erin promised. 'Can you be riding with me tomorrow? I have a matter we need to discuss.'

'I look forward to it,' Gaborn said. 'But as I will warn the others shortly, we must ride before dawn. We must reach Carris ahead of schedule. You'll have a couple of hours' rest, but come moonrise, we will ride as best we can.'

'How soon are you hoping to reach Carris?' Erin asked.

'For those mounts that can make it, I hope to be there by nightfall tomorrow.'

Over six hundred miles. It was a long journey for any horse, even a fine force horse like the one he'd just given her. And riding by moonlight would be dangerous. Erin nodded, but she could only wonder.

Some of the knights in this company might be able to reach Carris tomorrow at nightfall, but in doing so, they would run their horses into the ground. Even the finest knight could not fight from the back of a dead horse.

Perhaps Gaborn might excel in matters of logistics, but she had to worry at his skill as a strategist.

29

DOVE'S PASS

The facilitators had been singing in the Palace of the Concubines when Saffira left, but Sir Borenson did not hear them.

Exhausted by days of work, and deprived of the great endowments of stamina that had let him withstand the natural frailties of man, he fell asleep in the sunlight, waiting by the fountain for Saffira to return. Someone unlocked his manacles as he slept.

When at last Pashtuk and Saffira's bodyguards helped the big man into his saddle, Borenson clung to it by nature and needed no one to lash him down.

Thus he slept in the saddle for hours as Pashtuk led the group back north into Deyazz, then west past the sacred ruins of the Mountains of the Doves.

Borenson woke for a bit on that mountainous trail, looked up to the sheer white cliffs. There, four thousand feet up the mountain slopes, altars and ancient domed temples leaned precariously over the precipices. Thousands of years ago, devotees were said to have leapt to the plain, thus giving their lives to the Air.

If the devotee's act was sanctified, then the devotee might be given the power of flight. But if the Air powers rejected him, he'd fall to his death.

In this manner, it was said that even children had gained the power to fly. Yet at the base of the cliff, in the Vale of Skulls, lay ample evidence that the Air had seldom accepted the ancients' sacrifices.

Few people were crazed enough to try such things nowadays, and Borenson had never heard of anyone besides the Sky Lords who had gained powers over Air. Still, every once in a while someone would walk out the door of his home and simply follow the wind, letting it blow him toward whatever destination it would. Invariably the 'drifting ones,' or 'wind followers' as they were sometimes called, would turn to thievery and other mischief in an effort to support themselves.

Saffira's guards rode beside her, two mountainous men named Ha'Pim and Mahket. She covered her face as she traveled, wearing veils of silk so that no one would see her face. Yet no veil could cover the luster of her eyes or mask the translucence of her skin.

Though she said not a word, her very posture in the saddle attracted the gaze of everyone she passed.

From moment to moment, she grew more beautiful, for the Palace of the Concubines at Obran was home to hundreds of women, each of whom had many endowments of glamour.

Now, one by one, the facilitators gathered the glamour from Raj Ahten's concubines and funneled it into Saffira through Dedicates who acted as vectors.

She of course did not need to be present in Obran to receive endowments, for when a person gave an endowment, it opened a magical link between him and his lord, a link that could be broken only when either the lord or the Dedicate died.

Thus if a woman gave an endowment of glamour, all of her glamour was funneled to her lord. If that same Dedicate later took an endowment of glamour from another, the Dedicate did not gain any glamour. Instead it immediately transferred to her lord.

A Dedicate who acted as a link to a lord in this manner was called a vector. So the women who already served as Saffira's Dedicates were now taking endowments from others. Those who had given Saffira an endowment of glamour were taking glamour in Saffira's behalf; those who had given Voice received Voice, and so on.

In this manner Saffira made good use of the Earth King's gift of forcibles. When she pleaded with Raj Ahten for a truce between nations that had been too long at war, she hoped to have not merely hundreds of endowments of glamour, but thousands.

Pashtuk led them along the mountain trails for hours, diverting from the road when they passed Raj Ahten's armies traveling near the fortress at Mutabayim. Borenson fell asleep again as he rode.

The five had already reached the heavily guarded borders of the Hest Mountains when Pashtuk finally stopped to wake Borenson for dinner.

Night was falling, and Pashtuk pulled Borenson from the saddle saying only, 'Sleep here for an hour, while I fix dinner for Her Highness.'

Borenson landed unceremoniously in some pine needles and would have slept soundly if not for Saffira's perfume.

He woke as she passed near him. Sitting up, he watched her graceful movements, earning a warning scowl from Ha'Pim.

Pigeons cooed in nearby pines, and the dry mountain air carried the smell of a nearby stream. Borenson glanced off into the west.

He'd never seen the sun setting over the Salt Desert of Indhopal, and once having seen it, he would never forget the magnificent sight. To the west, the desert was a soft violet, seeming almost flat for hundreds of miles, and the evening wind stirred the dust over the flats just enough so that a bit of red sand dust floated in a distant haze. The sun seemed enormous as it intersected the horizon, a great swollen pearl the color of rose.

Yet even the glories of nature could not compare with the lovely Saffira. Borenson gazed raptly as she strolled downhill to the shelter of a glen, and there knelt by a rocky pool where honeybees flew about the evening primrose that grew beside the boulders. When she removed her veil and the wrap that covered her head and shoulders, Borenson felt her loveliness like pure torture. It wracked his body and eroded his mind.

She sat for half a second, poised above the pool, and studied her own reflection. Over the past few hours, the concubines had vectored hundreds, perhaps thousands, of endowments of glamour to her, while others had endowed her with Voice.

She glanced over her shoulder, found Borenson awake and staring at her.

'Sir Borenson,' she said, her voice mellifluous. 'Come sit by me.'

Borenson got up, felt his legs go weak with the effort. He manipulated the things like clumsy logs until at last he fell at her knees. She smiled pleasantly and touched his hand.

Ha'Pim moved close, and rested a beefy fist on his dagger. He was a huge man, with a dark and surly expression.

'Will I be a worthy vessel to bear your supplication for peace?' Saffira asked.

'Worthy,' was all that Borenson managed to croak. 'Completely worthy.' Her voice was like music to his ears, while his own seemed the raucous caw of a crow.

'Tell me,' Saffira begged. 'Do you have a wife?'

Borenson had to think a moment. He blinked nervously. 'I . . . do, milady.'

'Is she lovely?'

What could be answer? He had thought Myrrima lovely, but compared to Saffira, she seemed . . . overlarge, almost cowish. 'No, milady.'

'How long have you been married?'

He tried to recall, but could not quite count the days. 'A few days, more than two. Maybe three.' I must sound a fool, he thought.

'But you are quite old. Have you never had a wife before?'

'What?' he asked. 'Four, I think.'

'Four wives?' Saffira asked, arching a brow. 'That is many wives for a man of Rofehavan. I thought your people took only one.'

'No, four days since I married,' Borenson managed. 'I'm fairly sure of it. Four days.' He tried to sound as if he spoke with authority.

'But no other wives?'

'None, milady,' Borenson answered. 'I . . . was my prince's guard. I had no time for a wife.'

'That is a shame,' Saffira said. 'How old is your wife?'

'Twenty . . . years,' Borenson managed. Saffira placed her hand on the rock, leaned back. In doing so, her finger touched the knuckle of Borenson's right hand, and he stared at the spot, unable to take his eyes from his own hand.

He wanted to reach out and touch her again, to stroke her hand, but realized that it was impossible. A *thing* like him was not meant to touch a wonder like her. It had only been by purest chance that their flesh had met, an astonishing chance. The air smelled heavy with her perfume.

'Twenty. That seems quite old,' Saffira said. 'I have heard that women often wait until they are old to marry in your country.'

He did not know what to say. She looked to be no more than sixteen herself, yet Saffira had been married for years, had borne Raj Ahten four children. She must be older than she looks, he imagined. Perhaps seventeen, but no more than that – unless she has taken endowments of glamour from children.

'My lord took me to bed on my twelfth birthday,' Saffira said proudly. 'I was the youngest of his wives, and he was the most handsome man who ever lived. He loved me from the start. Some concubines he keeps to look at, others he keeps to sing. But he loves me most. He has been very good to me. He always brings me presents. Last year he brought two white elephants for us to ride, and their headdresses and the pavilions on their backs were all covered in diamonds and pearls.'

Borenson had seen Raj Ahten. The Wolf Lord had thousands of endowments of glamour to his own credit. Now as Borenson looked upon Saffira, he understood how a woman's heart might ache for him.

'I bore him his first child before I turned thirteen,' Saffira said proudly. 'I bore him four children.' He detected a hint of sadness in her voice. He feared that he had led her to a topic that was painful for her, the death of her son.

Borenson's mouth felt dry. 'Uh . . . um, will you give him more?' he asked, praying that she would not.

'No,' Saffira said, ducking her head. 'I can have no more.'

Borenson thought to ask her why, but she looked at him askance and changed the subject.

'I do not think that men were meant to have red hair. It is not appealing.'

'I . . . will shave it off for you, milady.'

'No. Then I would be forced to see all of your white skin and your speckles.'

'Then I will dye my hair, milady. I have heard that one can use indigo leaves and henna to make it black.' He did not tell her that this was how northern spies and assassins colored their hair before striking south into Indhopal.

Saffira smiled captivatingly, the most beautiful smile ever to have graced a woman's face. 'Yes, in some places in Indhopal, old people dye their hair when it starts to turn gray,' she said. 'I will send for such dye.'

She fell silent for a moment. 'My husband,' she bragged, 'is the greatest man in the world.'

Borenson flinched. He had never heard that before, and had not really thought it possible. But now that Saffira said it, he realized it was true. 'Yes, O Star of the Desert,' he said, for he suddenly thought that 'milady' was too common a word, a title that should be reserved only for dried-up old matrons with leathery faces.

'He is the hope of the world,' Saffira instructed him with perfect conviction. 'He will unite mankind, and destroy the reavers.'

Of course, now that he saw it, Borenson realized that it was a great plan. Who was more powerful than Raj Ahten?

'I look forward to the day,' Borenson agreed.

'And I shall help him,' Saffira said. 'I shall bring peace to Rofehavan, begging all men to lay aside their weapons, and thus stop the depredations of the Knights Equitable. Long has my love fought for peace, and now the Great Light of Indhopal shall shine over the whole world. The barbarians of Rofehavan will humble themselves and kneel before him, or be destroyed.'

Saffira had been speaking half to herself, as if listening in wonder to the pure tones of her own voice. From minute to minute the facilitators in her palace were adding endowments to her. 'Wahoni had forty endowments of Voice. They must be mine now,' Saffira said. 'She sang so beautifully; I will miss it, though I can sing more beautifully now.' She raised her voice, sang a few lines in such a haunting tone that the music seemed to hang in the air about her like the down of a cottonwood tree. The song sent chills down Borenson's spine.

She suddenly glanced at him distractedly. 'You should not stare at me with your mouth open,' Saffira said. 'You look as if you want to eat me. In fact, perhaps you should not look at me at all. I am going to take a bath now, and you must not look at me naked, do you understand?'

'I will close my eyes,' Borenson promised. Ha'Pim kicked at Borenson's legs, and Borenson walked away a few yards. Then he sat with his back to a warm rock.

He listened to the delicious sound as she removed her silks, smelled the sweet scent of her body as she removed her dress, and her jasmine perfume suddenly became stronger.

He listened as she stepped timidly into the pond and made a small noise of surprise to find out how cold the mountain water could be. He listened to her splash and burble, but he did not look at her.

He closed his eyes tightly, obeying her every command, willing himself to obey no matter what the cost to himself.

Yet as he closed his eyes and tried to focus on anything but the sounds Saffira made as she splashed, he began to wonder.

She had said that Raj Ahten was the greatest man in the world, and at that moment, he'd thought the words sounded wise, reasonable, and well considered.

But now doubt began to creep in.

Saffira loved Raj Ahten?

She thought him kind? The man who had destroyed every

neighboring king and now sought to subdue the world?

No, Borenson had seen Raj Ahten's cunning and his cruelty. He'd seen the dead bodies of Gaborn's brother and sisters and mother. When Borenson slew Raj Ahten's Dedicates at Castle Sylvarresta, he'd been forced to take the lives of the children that Raj Ahten drew endowments from. The Wolf Lord was a man wholly given to evil.

Raj Ahten had taken Saffira to wife as a child, and though she gloried in Raj Ahten's affection, Borenson wanted to see him die for that.

But he wondered. Saffira had gone to him willingly as a child, overpowered by his glamour and Voice. She loved him. She loved him so much that she now promised to support him against the nations of Rofehavan.

She had never seen the world that her husband ruthlessly sought to usurp, Borenson realized. She was hopelessly naïve. She'd spent all her time locked in her palace, awaiting the gifts Raj Ahten would bring, fearful of the Knights Equitable. She'd been stripped from her family at the age of twelve, and though Borenson had not been allowed to see the other concubines, he imagined that they'd be girls like Saffira – just as naïve and foolish.

Already he realized how hopelessly Gaborn's plan might go astray: Saffira offered to forge a peace between Indhopal and Rofehavan, but she would do it for her own reasons, not because the Earth King sought it.

And if Raj Ahten could not be persuaded to call a halt to his war, then Saffira would join him and use her own glamour to subvert the armies of Rofehavan.

Faintly, a voice in the back of Borenson's mind whispered that he had helped to create a monster, and that now he should destroy it, if possible.

Yet he could not bear the thought. Even if he'd still had his endowments, even if he thought himself capable of fighting Pashtuk, Ha'Pim, and Mahket, he did not think himself capable of killing Saffira.

No man *could* manage it.

And she did not deserve such rough treatment. Saffira was innocent, not evil.

Even if he had thought her evil, he knew that he would never have been able to lift a finger against her.

30

THE BOON COMPANION

It was well after sunset when Iome reached Castle Groverman. Both Binnesman and Jureem rode the fine mounts that Raj Ahten had graciously provided them a week before, and Myrrima rode Sir Borenson's mount, as swift a beast as Mystarria could offer. But the force horse Iome had been constrained to take from the king's stables had been a simple guardsman's mount with only three endowments.

It gave out after a hundred miles of hard running, so Iome was forced to slow until they could get to Bannisferre and buy a fresh mount.

Still, the stars shone brightly and the air up here high in the Dunnwood was cold and fresh, so that the evening ride was pleasant.

Once they arrived at the castle, Iome went off in search of the King. She took a retinue consisting of Jureem, Binnesman, and Myrrima, as well as her Days and the clubfooted boy.

With a few words to a captain, she caught up to Gaborn in Duke Groverman's Keep, where he had retired for dinner with a number of other lords.

Iome proceeded from the hall to to the Duke's audience chamber. She was about to open the red curtains at the entrance to the Great Hall when she heard someone addressing her husband in a harsh voice. 'This is a travesty, Your Highness!' a knight said too loudly. 'You can't let them turn back *now*, not before the chase has even begun! This speaks of cowardice!'

She knew the whiny voice. It was Sir Gillis of Tor Insell.

A deep-voiced fellow roared, 'Your Highness, I will not be called a coward by this man, nor will I have my king named one! I demand an apology!'

Iome motioned for those behind her to stop. She parted the curtain a bit. Duke Groverman had set a fine banquet, and Gaborn and three dozen lords crowded around a table that should not have held two dozen.

In the center of the room stood a young man with a pimpled face, Theovald Orwynne's son, fourteen-year-old Agunter.

Word had spread along the road of the day's events. Iome knew that King Orwynne and his son Barnell had been slain by the Darkling Glory. Agunter would be next in line for the throne. She'd also heard that Gaborn had lost his endowments.

At Agunter's side stood a big bear of a man, Sir Langley, and at his back counselors waited.

'I demand an apology from this lout . . .' Sir Langley roared at Sir Gillis, 'or satisfaction!'

With a tone of wry amusement, Gaborn turned to his left, where Sir Gillis sat at the table, several places down. 'What say you, Sir Gillis? Will you apologize for your insult, or will we all get to watch Orwynne's champion yank your tongue from your mouth?'

Red of face, Sir Gillis threw down a swan's leg he'd been gnawing at and glared over his dinner plate. 'I say it again! Orwynne swore fealty to the Earth King, and if Agunter and his knights choose to depart now before the battle, then I say they are cowards all! Rip out my tongue if you can, Sir Langley. Though it wriggle on the floor, my tongue will still declare the truth!'

Sir Langley glared at Sir Gillis, and his hand strayed toward the dagger in his belt, but he dared not draw steel in the Earth King's presence.

'If you please, Your Highness!' one of Orwynne's counselors shouted. 'It was not milord Agunter's wish to return to his lands. I have sought all day to persuade him that this is the most prudent course!'

'Speak on,' Gaborn told the counselor.

'I . . . I merely point out that Agunter is but fourteen, and though he has the size of a man about him – and a courage to equal that of any man in this room – today his kingdom suffered a tremendous loss. With King Orwynne dead, along with his oldest son, the royal family of Orwynne is now in a tenuous position. Agunter's nearest brother is but six years old, and if by some fell chance Agunter continued south and died in battle, his brother would be incapable of ruling in his stead. With our kingdom at war, we need a proper lord to lead us. For this reason alone, we petition you for leave to return to our homes.'

Gaborn sat back in the shadows, with Duke Groverman to his left and Chancellor Rodderman to his right. Now he leaned forward in his chair.

'For young Agunter here to leave is one thing,' Sir Gillis said. 'But must he take his entire retinue? Five hundred knights?'

Iome was torn at the thought. Agunter's father had indeed mounted five hundred of his best knights for this campaign, and with Heredon's forces so decimated, such knights would be sorely needed. While it was only prudent for young Agunter to turn back, it seemed excessive for him to take all of his men.

Sir Gillis was right, she decided. More than common sense lay behind Agunter's request. Agunter was sorely afraid – and with good reason.

Gaborn's father had stood up to Raj Ahten and been murdered for his trouble, as had her own father. Agunter's father was slain most terribly, crushed by the Darkling Glory right before Agunter's own eyes.

Agunter spoke now, voice shaky. 'I think that to take all of my men *would* be excessive, but for the news my father bore last night: reavers have surfaced in North Crowthen and again to the south in Mystarria. World worms shake the earth as they burrow beneath the Dunnwood. My kingdom borders the Hest, and we've spotted many signs of reavers this past summer in the mountains. How long will it be before they come at us en masse?'

'Hah! I call it robbery!' Sir Gillis said. 'The Earth King saves your whole nation and gives two thousand forcibles to make Sir Langley our champion, and then you think to ride off on your merry way with the booty. Shall Orwynne be named a boon companion?'

Young King Agunter glared menacingly at Gillis. If his champion was afraid to draw steel before the Earth King, Iome saw that Agunter was not. Though Agunter might fear Raj Ahten, that fear didn't extend to such men as Sir Gillis.

A boon companion, indeed.

Iome bit her lip. If young Agunter does not like hearing such jibes to his face, she thought, then in a year or two he'll positively loathe what is said at his back. It would be churlish for the boy to withdraw his support completely.

Gaborn had sent two thousand forcibles to Orwynne so that Langley could receive endowments. It was a tremendous investment, and Iome could see from his stance alone that Langley was receiving endowments through his vectors. He stood tall even with his mail shirt on, and he moved with incredible fluidity and swiftness, as only a man with great endowments of grace and metabolism could do.

Langley was becoming a potent warrior, minute by minute, as Orwynne's facilitators drew attributes in his behalf.

It would be churlish of Agunter to withdraw Langley from the coming battle, churlish and foolish. Iome would not have allowed it, would have pounded the table and demanded Orwynne's assistance. Instead, she watched to see how Gaborn played the lad.

Gaborn leaned forward and cleared his throat. As he bent into the wan light of a candle, Iome felt astonished by the transformation she saw in his features since only this morning. His eyes were dark and hollow, his face pale. He looked ill or weary nigh unto death. Such was the havoc that losing his endowments wrought upon him.

'Sir Gillis, you owe young King Orwynne an apology,'

Gaborn said. 'I have looked into his heart. It is full of wrath at Raj Ahten, and it is as difficult for him to turn aside from this conflict as it will be for you to watch him go.'

Addressing the young king, Gaborn said, 'Agunter Orwynne, by all means, take your men home with my blessing. Rofehavan needs Orwynne to hold the west, and to be strong against all enemies – whether they be Raj Ahten's troops or reavers. Take your father and brother home for burial. Take your knights, and may the Powers ride with you.'

Iome couldn't believe it. Gaborn was riding to battle with far too few men as it was. He shouldn't be acquiescing to a coward's demands.

'But—' Sir Gillis let out a strangled exclamation.

'I ask only one boon of you,' Gaborn told Agunter. 'Let Sir Langley come to fight as your champion. It is my hope that he will still avenge both my father and yours. If he does, I will be forever grateful for your aid.'

Iome suddenly realized what Gaborn was doing. Agunter could not bear the thought of facing Raj Ahten. He was so terrified that he dared not even ride home alone.

But perhaps by declaring that the boy had courage, Gaborn lent Agunter some. At the same time, Gaborn appealed to whatever dignity the young lad had left. No child could fail to try to avenge a murdered father. If Agunter did not let Langley fight, he would never be able to live with the scorn that his people would heap upon him. Surely Agunter saw this.

Yet Agunter trembled as he said, 'Take *him* then . . . along with a hundred knights.'

Gaborn nodded, as if surprised and impressed at the young king's graciousness.

Agunter turned and stalked from the Great Hall, his counselors and his Days flapping at his tail, eager to flee Castle Groverman, eager to return to Orwynne.

Iome stepped back from the audience chamber to let Agunter pass with his retinue.

Of all Agunter Orwynne's men, only Sir Langley stayed in the audience chamber.

He eyed Agunter's back thoughtfully for a moment, and no one in the room spoke. When Agunter was good and gone from the keep, Sir Langley bowed to Gaborn. 'I thank you, Your Highness, for letting the lad go.' Then he bowed to Sir Gillis. 'And you, good sirrah, for reminding him of his duty.'

Gaborn smiled in amusement. Sir Langley obviously wanted to fight Raj Ahten far more than his king did, and though Langley might defend his king's honor to the death, he saw the lad for what he was and felt relieved to have his lord's permission to ride south.

Langley too turned to leave the room.

'Stay if you will,' Gaborn said. 'There is more than enough room at the table.' It was an amusing statement, for lords were crammed elbow to rib at Groverman's table.

'Thank you, Your Highness,' Langley said. 'But I fear that when my king rides off, it will weaken the morale of your troops. If you would allow me, I'd like to take my dinner there, so that I can reassure them somewhat.'

'That would be appreciated,' Gaborn said.

Langley began to march for the exit, but Gaborn stopped him. 'Sir Langley, you should know that your king is a decent lad. He has a man's body, but not a man's heart – yet. In a year or two, I suspect that he will find his courage.'

Langley glanced back over his shoulder. 'I pray he does not find it too late.'

Iome let Langley pass, then proceeded into the Great Hall with Myrrima, Binnesman, Jureem, and her Days at her back. The clubfooted boy remained in the audience chamber to play with the pups.

Upon seeing her, Gaborn rose and invited Iome to sit next to him. Iome kissed him, studied him as she did. He looked ill, she decided.

She took a seat beside him when Duke Groverman offered his own chair. Iome squeezed Gaborn's right hand with her left.

She had not even settled in her chair when a page announced a messenger from Beldinook; it was the first messenger to come from Beldinook since Gaborn had been crowned as the Earth King.

Beldinook was an important nation, the second largest and wealthiest in all of Rofehavan. It bordered Mystarria on the north, and thus was a strategic ally. More than that, old King Lowicker, a frail man given to fits of indecision, had long been a friend to Gaborn's father. Gaborn needed Lowicker now, in part because Gaborn's small army would have to pass through Beldinook to reach Carris. But since Gaborn had to travel quickly, he was not able to carry all of the supplies he would need for battle.

At the very least, by the time his mounts reached Beldinook, they'd need good grain to eat, and Gaborn's warriors would need food themselves.

Queen Herin the Red had sent Erin Connal to offer such support, but Gaborn had been waiting for a pledge from Beldinook, and had been forced to proceed despite a pledge.

Gaborn needed Lowicker's assistance merely to ride through Beldinook, but he hoped for more. Gaborn faced serious supply shortages in Northern Mystarria with so many castles having fallen.

Paldane would have moved most of his remaining supplies to Carris itself, in preparation for a siege, and Raj Ahten would likely set such a siege – if he did not destroy the castle outright. Personally, Gaborn believed that Raj Ahten wanted Carris whole, so that his own troops could winter there.

Given that, Gaborn would have to break the siege by attacking Raj Ahten. If Gaborn's warriors were to fight a pitched battle, they'd need extra weapons for the fray: arrows for archers, lances for cavalry, shields, and whatnot.

Few of the knights who rode south had burdened their mounts with any barding at all. Some had chaffrons to cover the charger's heads, with only blankets quilted like gambesons to protect their necks and flanks. But full armor was too heavy for the mounts to carry so far. With force horses at such a premium these days, Gaborn was hesitant to send poorly armored mounts into battle. He would prefer full bard for the horses, along with some breastplates and great helms for his knights.

Gaborn hoped to get such goods from Beldinook.

If Gaborn could manage to drive Raj Ahten to ground – in Castle Crayden, Castle Fells, or at Tal Dur – Gaborn might have to lay siege to a fortress, in which case he might need tools for siege engines. In addition to this he might well need smiths, cooks, squires, washwomen, sappers, carters – a whole host of support personnel. Gaborn could call for aid from his own vassals in the south and east of Mystarria, but it would take weeks to get them all north, and time was of the essence.

Of necessity, Gaborn would have to rely upon his old ally King Lowicker of Beldinook, a man who some whispered might be too cautious in war, a man who some suspected would not have the spine to stand up to Raj Ahten.

Though Gaborn had sent letters to Beldinook nearly a week ago, seeking to purchase supplies should he need to ride south, Beldinook had not responded – probably because at the time, Raj Ahten was racing through the wilderness on the border of Beldinook with his own men, and King Lowicker was much occupied caring for his own defense. Iome herself had dispatched a second courier only two days past.

Now at last the messenger entered the room, still wearing the dust of the trail over his dun-colored tunic. The white swan of Beldinook was emblazoned on it. He was a small fellow, thin, with a long moustache that hung below his chin, and no beard.

Gaborn got up to speak with him privately, but the messenger bowed with a grand gesture and said, 'If it please Your Highness, Lords of Heredon and Orwynne, the good King Lowicker bade me speak openly to you all.'

Gaborn nodded. 'Please continue, then.'

The messenger bowed and said, 'My lord Beldinook bade me say this, "Long live the Earth King Gaborn Val Orden!"'

He raised his hand, and everywhere the lords at the table shouted, 'Long live the King!'

'My King apologizes for the delay in bringing you word. He dispatched documents to you nearly a week past, offering his assistance in whatever manner he may. Unfortunately, it appears that our courier did not make it alive to carry my lord's message. The roads were thick with Raj Ahten's assassins. For this lapse, my lord apologizes.

'But he wished to convey that, just as he loved your father, he has always thought of you, Gaborn, as one like unto a son to him.'

Iome did not like the sound of this. She knew that Lowicker had often courted favor with King Orden, perhaps hoping that Gaborn would be man enough to relieve Lowicker of a notoriously unattractive daughter, his only heir.

'Milord King Lowicker bids you to be easy of mind,' the messenger continued. 'He is aware of the danger brewing at Carris, and has amassed troops and supplies to aid in freeing the city. To this end, he has marshaled five thousand knights, a hundred thousand footmen, fifty thousand archers – along with engineers and an unnumbered host of support personnel – in the hopes that together we might crush Raj Ahten now, before the threat grows stronger!

'Your Highness, Lords of Heredon and Orwynne, my King Lowicker bids you be of good cheer, and to make all due haste to join him, for he himself will lead his troops to war!'

Suddenly Iome understood what Lowicker proposed. Certainly troops would be coming from the south and east of Mystarria, riding to Carris to defend against Raj Ahten. With Fleeds guarding the west, and Lowicker coming strong out of the north, Raj Ahten would find himself beleaguered on every side, like a bear caught between the hounds, and Beldinook hoped to take Raj Ahten down.

Iome grinned fiercely. Not in her wildest imaginings had she thought that frail old King Lowicker would ride to war.

The lords at the table cheered and raised their mugs in toast, and Iome felt a wave of relief wash through her such as she'd never felt in her life.

The lords saluted Beldinook's health and toasted the Powers, each man spilling ale to the floor as an offering to the Earth.

Iome studied Gaborn's reaction most of all. The lines of worry had gone somewhat from his face, and he thanked the messenger graciously, offered the man food and drink from his own table.

So, Iome thought, we lose a few knights of Orwynne, and find that we have gained a hundred times more! Her heart soared at this hope.

But Iome watched Gaborn carefully, studying his face for a reaction. He sensed their danger, after all, and she dared not celebrate until he was satisfied.

Gaborn had had but two endowments of glamour, and even with that, he had seemed only a plain and unpretentious lord. Now, stripped of glamour, she saw him truly for the first time in her life. Gaborn was not homely, she decided, but he was close to it.

She began to wonder. Gaborn's external transformation, as obvious as it might be to her, was perhaps the least important. Without his endowments of stamina, he would be prone to illness, and would be easily slain in battle. Without his brawn, he would be no match for even the lowliest force warrior. Without his endowments of tongue, he would not speak with any degree of eloquence.

Perhaps most horribly, Gaborn had lost his endowments of wit. Much of what he knew, so many of his memories, would have been stripped away.

It was discouraging for a Runelord to lose so many endowments at once, especially when he needed them more than ever.

She whispered into Gaborn's ear. 'Your Highness, you look positively . . . decrepit. I'm worried for you. At the very least, you need rest. I hope you don't plan to sit up all night feasting with your lords.'

He squeezed her hand reassuringly, and raised a finger, as if in signal. Jureem strode forward with one of the baskets that he had used to carry the pups south.

'Your Highness, Duke Groverman, lords of Heredon,' Jureem said with great fanfare. 'We all have reason to celebrate our good fortune with this news from Beldinook tonight. But I bring you something that should further lighten your hearts and lift your spirits!'

Jureem reached under the lid of the large basket, the jeweled rings on his fingers flashing in the thin lamplight, and Iome wondered if he would pull out a pup.

Instead, he drew out the hand of the Darkling Glory. Its long talons were clutched into a claw. The lords shouted and cheered and began banging their fists on the tables. Some cried out, 'Well done, Binnesman! May the Powers preserve you!' Men raised their mugs in salute, while others poured further libations upon the floor.

Dismayed at the injustice of it, Iome grabbed Gaborn's arm and whispered fiercely, 'But Binnesman didn't kill it!'

Gaborn grinned at her and raised his own mug, as if to offer another toast, and the men all quieted.

'As you know, the Darkling Glory today slew many men,' Gaborn told the lords. 'Among those dead is our good friend King Orwynne, whose support will be greatly missed.

'But of those men who died, all had one thing in common: they rejected my warnings.

'The Earth instructed us to flee, and the men did not flee. All this week, I have been wondering if the Earth will ever let us fight in our own defense. Time and again it has told us to flee.

'Finally, today, the Earth whispered that one among us should strike, should strike the Darkling Glory down!'

The lords began to pound the tables again and cheer, but Gaborn shouted over them.

'It whispered the command to a woman, a woman without an endowment of brawn or stamina, a woman without skill in war.'

He waved toward the horried trophy in Jureem's hands. 'Here is the hand of the Darkling Glory, slain by the arrow of Sir Borenson's wife, the Lady Myrrima Borenson!'

Iome was delighted to see jaws drop on nearly every lord in the room.

One fellow blurted, 'But . . . but I've seen how badly the woman shoots! That can't be right!'

Myrrima stood at the far back of the room, in the shadows

near the curtained entrance. She was so embarrassed that she looked ready to flee clear back into the audience chamber.

'It is true,' Iome said. 'She shot her bow well enough to slay the Darkling Glory. She has the heart of a warrior, and soon will have the endowments to match!'

'Well, let us see this champion then,' a lord shouted, and Binnesman urged Myrrima out of the shadows.

The cheers and whistles that erupted from the lords were deafening. The noise rang from the stone walls, and Gaborn himself led the applause for several long minutes, letting Myrrima savor the moment.

At last Gaborn raised his hands, begging the lords for silence. 'Let Myrrima's deed ever remind you of what one may accomplish with the aid of the earth powers,' he said. 'It is our protector and our strength.

'In ages past, the Earth safeguarded our forefathers. By its power, Erden Geboren withstood the dark wizards of Toth.

'Now we must strive to match his feat.

'Yesterday at dawn I heard the Earth whispering, urging me south. We rode from Castle Sylvarresta, knowing that we were few. Yet we also knew that it takes but one man to strike a grievous blow.

'Now we find that we will fight with a great army, and we fight not alone. The Earth fights with us!

'As you know,' he continued, 'I have sent dozens of Chosen messengers abroad. Three of them are even now at Carris, where Raj Ahten's troops ring them about. I feel their danger, and the Earth gives me this warning: "Hurry. Hurry to strike!"'

He pounded the table for effect.

'As you also know, I planned to ride for Fleeds tomorrow at dawn. But now I fear I must travel sooner. I leave for Fleeds at moonrise, and I will camp there tomorrow only briefly. I call upon every man who can keep pace with my mount to ride with me, and for those who cannot, to follow as best you can. I hope to join King Beldinook at Carris no later than tomorrow at dusk. There, our numbers will swell with Knights Equitable and lords from Mystarria and Fleeds. We are going to war!'

The lords continued to cheer until Gaborn himself went to Myrrima and took her elbow, led her and Jureem down to the bailey to make the same speech to the knights camped there.

31

THE SMELL OF THE NIGHT WIND

That night, after receiving her applause, Myrrima took her forcibles and went to the Dedicate's Keep, begging Groverman's facilitator to perform an act that she'd always thought an abomination.

The facilitator was weary, but understood her sense of urgency. So he bade her enter the room with her basket of pups and sit in a cold chair.

The windows of the tower were open to the starlight, and the breeze entering the room smelled crisp and fresh.

The yellow pup squirmed in Myrrima's hand. Even as she held it, she fought back tears.

Myrrima had taken endowments from her mother and sisters. At her mother's bidding, she had taken her mother's wit. At her sisters' bidding, she had taken their glamour, all so that she could make a good marriage and provide for them well.

Yet the fruit of her deeds tasted bitter.

Myrrima knew that what she'd done was evil, and now she sat prepared to repeat her deed. But while some evil acts became easier with repetition, some became more impossible.

The pup was innocent, staring up at her with big, brown, loving eyes. She knew the pain that the pup was about to endure, knew that she would hurt it grievously, withdraw its stamina for no better reason than that it loved her, that it had been born with a disposition that would allow it to love her and serve her. She stroked the pup, tried to comfort it. The pup licked her and softly nibbled her sleeve.

Myrrima had come alone to the facilitator's room in Duke Groverman's Dedicate's Keep. She'd come alone because Iome was tired and had sought a bed. She'd come alone because even though all the knights in Heredon cheered her, she felt ashamed of what she had to do.

Duke Groverman's chief facilitator was a small fellow, an old man with wizened eyes and a white beard that nearly fell to his belly.

He studied the forcible she provided carefully before he put it to use. The forcible looked like a small branding iron in shape. One long end served as a handle, while the shape of the rune at the other end determined which attribute would be magically transferred from a Dedicate to his or her lord.

The facilitator's art was an ancient practice, one that required only a small level of magical skill, but great study. Now the facilitator took the forcible for stamina, studied the rune made of blood metal at its end. Using a tiny rat-tail file, he carefully began to shave off bits of blood metal, resting the forcible over a pan so that he could capture every precious flake of metal for reuse.

'Blood metal is soft and easily damaged,' the facilitator said. 'This should have been transported with greater care.'

Myrrima only nodded. The damned thing had been carried thousands of miles since its forging. She did not wonder that it was a little dented. Yet she knew that if the facilitator had to, he could melt the forcible down and cast it again.

'Still, it is a good design,' the facilitator muttered reassuringly. 'Pimis Sucharet of Dharmad forged this forcible, and his work shows his genius.'

Rarely had Myrrima heard anyone compliment a man of Indhopal. The nations had been too long at war.

'Hold the pup tight, now,' the facilitator said. 'Don't let it move.'

Myrrima held the pup as the facilitator pressed the forcible to its flesh, began his chants, his voice piping high and bird-like.

In moments the forcible began to glow white-hot, and the

smell of burning hair and flesh filled the air. The pup yelped desperately in pain, and Myrrima pinched its legs together and held them so that it could not run or squirm. The pup nipped her as it sought to escape, and Myrrima whispered, 'I'm sorry. I'm so sorry.'

In that second, the forcible blazed white-hot, and the pup howled in torment.

Myrrima's other three pups were wandering about the floor of the keep, sniffing at carpets and mopping the floor with their tongues in search of tidbits. But as this pup howled, one of the others rushed to Myrrima's side and began barking, staring up at the facilitator, as if unsure whether to attack.

The facilitator withdrew the forcible, inspected the glowing thing. He weaved the forcible through the air, and ribbons of light hung there, as if painted in the smoky air. He stared at the bands of light for a long moment, as if juding their thickness and width.

Then, satisfied, he came to Myrrima's side. She pulled her riding pants up so that the facilitator could place the brand just above her knee, where it would seldom be seen beneath her clothes

The white-hot forcible seared her skin, even as the facilitator drove the blood metal into her flesh.

But even as it burned, Myrrima found herself in ecstasy. The sense of vitality that suddenly flooded into her, the invigoration, were overwhelming.

Myrrima had never taken an endowment of stamina before, had not quite imagined how satisfying it would be. She suddenly found herself covered in sweat. The sweetness of the whole experience overwhelmed her. As she struggled to reckon with her euphoria, she glanced down at the pup in her arms.

It lay there looking haggard.

Moments before, the pup's eyes had been bright with excitement. Now they appeared dull. If she'd seen the pup with a litter, she'd have thought it sickly, a runt. She would have suggested that someone drown it, release it from its misery.

'I'll take that one to the kennels, now that you're done,' the facilitator said.

'No,' Myrrima said, knowing that she sounded foolish. 'I'm not done with it. Let me pet it for a minute.'

The pup would be giving her so much, she wanted to give it something in return, not just abandon it to another's care.

'Don't worry,' the facilitator assured her. 'The children at the kennels are good with the dogs. They'll give it more than a few scraps of meat. They'll love it as if it were their own, and the pup will hardly miss the stamina you've taken today.'

Myrrima's mind felt numb. With her stamina, she would be able to practice longer with her bow, become a better warrior, faster. By taking this guilt upon her, she hoped to help her people.

'I'll hold it,' she said, and put a hand under the pup's white chin and held it for a moment, stroking it.

'That pup at your feet, the one that barked at me, it's ready, too,' the facilitator said. 'Will you take the endowment now?'

She glanced down at the pup in question. It wagged its tail and gazed up at her hopefully. This was the pup with the strong nose. 'Yes, I'll do it now.'

When Myrrima took the endowment of scent, the world changed.

One moment, she sat in the chair with the pups, and then it was as if a veil dropped away.

The aroma of burning hair that had filled the room suddenly became more pungent, overwhelming, as it mingled with the scents of candle wax and dust and plaster and the pennyroyal flowers that had lain for a week upon the floor of the tower. She nuzzled a pup, could even smell its warmth.

The whole world seemed new.

With one pup's stamina to increase her energy reserves, Myrrima felt completely invigorated and awake. With another pup's endowment to heighten her sense of smell, the world seemed . . . remade, when she walked down from the keep.

The odor of horses blowing from the stables was overwhelming, and the smell of fresh-cooked beef in the bailey outside the Duke's Keep made her mouth water.

Yet it was people that thrilled her. She left her pups with the facilitator and walked down into the bailey, where the cooking fires had been guttering only half an hour before. Gaborn had made sure that the fires were doused before he spoke openly of fighting Raj Ahten.

Now Myrrima walked in darkness among the warriors, many of whom sat cross-legged on the ground to eat or lay on the ground on blankets.

Each warrior held such a fascinating combination of scents: the oiled metal armor, the greasy scent of wool, the mixture of soils and horses and food stains and spices and soaps and blood and the men's own natural body oils and urine.

Every scent came to her a hundred times more powerfully than she'd ever smelled it before. Many scents were completely new and alien, scents that were far too subtle for the human nose to recognize: the smell of grasses that had brushed against men's feet, or of their ivory buttons and the dyes in their cloth or on their leather fastenings. She found that dark hair smelled different from light, and that upon a man's skin she could often smell the food he had eaten earlier in the day. Thousands of new and subtle scents lay ready to be tasted. The men in the bailey somehow seemed more tantalizing than before.

I am a wolf lord now, she thought. I walk among men, and no one sees the change in me. But I was blind, and now I see. I was blind, just as all those around me are blind.

With little effort, she would learn to smell those around her, so that she could hunt a man by scent, or recognize someone in the dark. The knowledge gave her a wild and heady sense of power, made her feel a little less vulnerable at the thought of going to war.

Alone, in the dark, Myrrima climbed a tower up onto the wall-walk above the Duke's Keep and stared out over the plains.

Desperately, she wanted to share this wondrous feeling with someone, and her thoughts turned to Borenson, riding on his errand far to the south.

She feared for him, so far away. Down in the bailey, some warriors who either had high stamina, and thus did not need sleep, or who were too excited to sleep, began to sing war songs, promising to slay their foes and give the Earth a taste of blood.

The night was chilly. Myrrima wished for Borenson's arms around her. She placed her right hand above her womb and stood sniffing the night air, waiting for moonrise.

32

CROWS GATHER

Roland trudged up the circular stairs of a dank guard tower where the fog was so thick that it seemed to have snuffed out every second torch. Roland imagined that he'd be hours on the walls of Carris, searching for towers fifty-one and fifty-two in such fog.

He'd taken over an hour to find the armory, only to discover that with the thousands of men who'd come before him, there was no shirt of mail left that would fit a man his size, not even an aged cuirass of boiled leather. All he got for his pains was a small horseman's shield filed to a sharp point on one side and a silly leather cap.

The walls of Carris rose twelve stories above the plain. The castle was an old keep, enormous. In ancient times, a duke from this realm had become betrothed to a princess of Muttaya, but when the woman had tried to cross a particularly treacherous portion of the Dove's Pass, the mule that carried her had lost its footing, so that she plunged to her death.

The King of Muttaya was an elderly ruler, and of course did what his custom dictated was right. He waited a year, the proper grieving time, and then sent a replacement, one of the princess's many younger sisters.

But over the intervening year the Duke had taken a fancy to a dark-eyed lady from Seward. He married her before the replacement bride ever crossed the mountains. When the Muttayin Princess did arrive, the Duke sent her home.

Some of the Duke's counselors claimed afterward that he

had never known that a replacement bride was coming, and that he erred only because he did not know Muttayin customs. But most historians in the House of Understanding were quite certain that the Duke feigned ignorance in order to placate his new bride.

The rejection of his daughter infuriated the King of Muttaya. He'd hoped to unite the two realms and had paid a vast fortune as a dowry. Feeling cheated, he went to the kaifs of his land and demanded to know what to do.

The kaifs said that, according to ancient law, any man found guilty of theft had one of two options: he could either restore what he had taken three times over, or lose his right hand.

So the King of Muttaya sent three kaifs and his dark-skinned daughter back over the mountains and gave the Duke three options. He offered to let the Duke take the princess as a second wife and then disavow the lady of Seward so that he could rightfully elevate the Muttayin Princess to the status of first wife. In the King's mind, this would have rectified the whole situation, and seemed the only plausible solution.

Or the Duke could either return an amount equal to triple the dowry, which would be an apology, or send back to Muttaya his own right hand, thus admitting that he was a thief.

The whole dilemma thus presented to the Duke was quite serious. No lord of Rofehavan would dare marry two women, or turn out a wife who was now heavy with child. Nor did the Duke have the money to pay triple the dowry. But it so happened that on that very afternoon, one of the Duke's young guardsmen lost his right hand in a dueling accident.

To placate the kaifs, the Duke called his torturer to his quarters and faked an act of mayhem. He wrapped a bloody bandage around his right arm as if the hand had been removed, then he placed his own signet ring on the finger of the guard's severed hand and gave it to the kaifs.

The deed astonished and saddened the kaifs, for they thought that surely he would marry the fair young Princess, or at least pay triple the dowry. Instead, they returned to

Muttaya with nothing but a severed hand as an admission of the Duke's theft.

For two years the ruse worked. The King of Muttaya seemed to be appeased.

Until a trader from Muttaya spotted the Duke at the Courts of Tide, somehow having regrown his severed hand.

The resulting war was called the Dark Lady War, named for the dark-skinned lady of Muttaya and the dark-eyed lady of Seward.

The war raged for three hundred years, sometimes skipping a generation without much fighting, only to burst into flame anew.

A dozen times the kings of Muttaya overtook western Mystarria, and often managed to settle there. But eventually the commoners would overthrow them, or the kings of Rofehavan would unite against them.

So it was that castle after castle was built in western Mystarria, and time and again they were torn down. Sometimes the Muttayin built them, sometimes the Mystarrians built them – until the land justly earned the name The Ruins.

Then Lord Carris came along. Over a period of forty years he managed to hold the realm against the Muttayin while he gathered enough stone to build his great walled city, which the Muttayin were never able to conquer.

Lord Carris died peacefully in his sleep at the ripe old age of a hundred and four – a feat that had no precedent in the previous three hundred years.

That had been nearly two thousand years ago, and Carris still stood, the single greatest fortress in Western Mystarria and the lynchpin that held the west together.

The walled city covered an island in Lake Donnestgree, so that most of the walls could not be breached except by boat. Since Muttaya was landlocked, the Muttayan were poor hands with boats. But even boats could not avail much when the castle walls themselves rose a hundred feet on the side, straight up from the water.

The stone walls had been covered with plaster and lime, so a man attempting an escalade could not find a toehold.

From atop the walls, commoners could shoot arrows down through the kill holes or lob stones onto any boat. It therefore did not take force soldiers with great endowments to man most of Carris's walls. Instead, those who sought to assail Carris had one of three options. They could try to infiltrate the castle and overthrow it from within, they could set a siege, or they could opt for a frontal assault, trying to win through the three barbicans into the fortress proper.

The castle had fallen only four times in history. Many castles in Rofehavan had thicker and higher walls or more artillery engines, but few castles were more strategically situated.

Roland climbed the stairs eight stories through a dank guard tower until he reached the top. There a steward with a key unlocked the heavy iron door that led upstairs to the top of the wall.

Roland had expected the fog to be so thick that he'd spend hours looking for his post. But as he neared the top of the wall, he found that the fog receded and he actually saw the last rays of the evening sun before it dropped over the western hills.

When he reached the crenellated wall he elbowed his way forward through the throng of warriors who sat ten deep along the wall-walks. Huge stones and stacks of arrows were piled up everywhere along the walls. Commoners lay asleep in the lee of the crenellations with nothing more than thin blankets pulled over them.

Roland trudged along the wall, past tower after tower, until he reached the baker's tower. The yeasty scent of bread rose from it. The tower was so warm that men thronged to sleep atop it in the cold evening.

Roland could not tiptoe through the press, so he just walked across the men's bodies, ignoring the shouts and curses that followed him.

Past the tower, peasants were hoisting up good food – lamb roast and bread loaves and fresh-pressed cider – and dispensing them to the troops. As the men ate, Roland had to avoid knocking over their mugs and stepping on plates.

Roland continued to thread a precarious path through the crowd, grabbing a loaf of bread and slicing it open, then throwing his lamb atop it so that the bread acted as a plate. A chill wind blew here atop the wall, and gulls hovered on the wind above, eyeing his food hungrily. He wished that he'd not given his thick bearskin robe to the green woman.

He wondered where she was now, wondered if Averan would fare well tonight.

He found his post on the south wall, and there spotted Baron Poll easily enough. Since Carris sat on a lake, and this particular wall faced the waters, no hoardings had been erected between these towers to protect the castle from bombardment. The fat Baron had climbed atop a merlon and sat with his legs dangling over, looking like some glum gargoyle.

Roland would never have dared hang from the wall like that. His fear of heights was such that it made his heart race just to watch a friend sit in that precarious position.

Wisps of fog reached right up to Baron Poll's feet.

Everywhere out around him the crows and pigeons were flapping about in the upper fog.

When Roland approached, the Baron glimpsed him from the corner of his eye, and his demeanor brightened. He smiled joyfully. 'Ah, Roland, my friend, you made it alive after all! I thought Raj Ahten's men would be using your skull for a drinking cup by now.'

'Not likely,' Roland said with a grin. 'They nearly had me, till they saw that my brain was the size of a hazelnut. I guess they figured my skull couldn't hold enough to make a decent mug. They ran off and left me alone in the woods while they hunted for you.'

'Then where have you been all day?' the Baron asked in astonishment.

'Wandering down in the fog,' Roland answered.

The Baron glanced down at the mist curling just under his toes. He spat over the castle wall. 'Aye, a man can't find himself to pee in this fog. I made my way to the castle well enough, but it helps that I'd lived here half of my life, and so knew the way.'

Roland stood beside the Baron, looked out at the birds.

'So, we're way up here with the birds. Looks as if they don't dare find a place to roost.'

'Crows,' Baron Poll said with a wise look. He'd been right. The crows knew where to hunt for food, and they knew that a battle was coming.

Baron Poll glanced over his shoulder, up to a tower in the central keep, higher than any other except the Duke's Keep – the graak's tower. Dozens of vultures roosted there.

Roland looked out over the mist, wondering how a fog that was so low to the ground could have been so thick. He set his small shield down on a merlon, as if it were some huge curved platter, then placed his mug and his loaf with meat on it, and began to dine. He felt guilty eating such a fine meal when Averan had complained of hunger this morning. Likely the girl would go hungry again tonight. Roland's own stomach had been cramping as he walked through the fog, but suddenly he remembered that he'd picked some walnuts for Averan and then forgotten them while evading Raj Ahten's troops. He reached into his pocket and took those with his meal.

He stared across the darkening landscape. He could still see three bluish clouds out there on the downs, but they had moved closer to Carris, and now were but five and a half miles away.

'What news have we?' Roland asked the Baron.

'Little news, much conjecture,' Baron Poll answered. 'The fogs out there have been drifting around all day, never quite stopping. They're like guards marching atop a wall, except that sometimes they come right up to the edge of our own fog, and then they back away. I think that the troops keep moving just in case Lord Paldane should decide to strike.'

'If they've come up close by, isn't it possible that those mists hide nothing but flameweavers, and all of Raj Ahten's troops are a hundred yards from the castle?'

'It's possible,' the Baron answered. 'I heard dogs yapping in the mist not an hour ago. I suspect that it's Raj Ahten's war dogs down there. If you hear anyone scaling the castle wall – grunting, panting – it would be wise to drop a rock on him. But I'm thinking the walls are so slick, not even Raj Ahten's Invincibles could chance an escalade.'

Roland grunted and merely ate for a while, tearing off chunks of lamb and gravy from his loaf. He saved his cider for last.

'Is it true about the Blue Tower?' Roland asked.

The Baron nodded darkly. 'It's true. Not one in ten of the knights on these walls is worth a damned now.'

'And you?'

'Me? My Dedicates are safely hidden,' the Baron said. 'I can still eat rocks for breakfast and crap sand for a week after.'

That was somewhat reassuring, Roland thought. Though the Baron didn't have an endowment of metabolism, and thus could not match an Invincible's speed in battle, he had the brawn and grace of a warrior. It was better to have half a warrior next to him than none at all.

'So, what are we protecting?' Roland looked down at the mist. He couldn't imagine why he'd need to sit atop this wall. No man could have climbed up its plaster surface. Tree frogs might do it, but not men.

'Nothing much,' the Baron said. 'The boat docks are on the other side of the castle, up north, and Raj Ahten's men could try to break in that way. But there's nothing for us here.'

Roland sat beside the Baron for a long time, neither of them speaking. A chill wind had begun to blow from the east. As it did, the magical fog around the castle blew with it, attenuating to the west, so that it stretched along the folds of lowlands like fingers searching for something in the fields.

The same wind began to blow the blue fog away from the armies of the Invincibles, and some men along the walls chattered excitedly as they saw the first signs of Raj Ahten's troops.

A pair of frowth giants, each twenty feet tall at the shoulder, paced along the front of the mist. They bore huge brass shields.

At a distance of miles, Roland could not see them well, of course. Even a giant at that distance seemed only a stick figure, and while others shouted that they could see war dogs and Invincibles against a line of trees, Roland could not see anything smaller than the giants.

They looked nothing like a man, any more than a cat or a cow could be compared to a man. Their fur was a tawny gold, shaggy along the arms. Their enormous muzzles were longer than a horse's, with sharp teeth in long rows, while their small round ears lay flat against their heads. Dark ring mail hid their stubby tails, while they wore shields in rows along their belts. Each giant carried a huge iron-bound stave as a weapon.

To Roland, they looked like some sort of giant rat or ferrin, armed and armored.

In the last light of day, the giants turned their muzzles and stared toward Castle Carris longingly. The mouth of one of them gaped open. A bit later, Roland heard the roar carry across the distance. Roland imagined that the giants were hungry, longing for human flesh.

He finished eating, then strapped his shield over his back, letting it protect him from the bite of the chill wind. Within an hour, he felt miserably cold.

As darkness fell, he suddenly saw lights begin to glow redly through the patch of fog directly to the west. A fire burned there, a big fire.

'That's the village of Gower's Ambush, or maybe Settekim,' the Baron said uneasily. Roland wondered why Raj Ahten's troops had set the village afire, but the answer seemed obvious to everyone else. The flameweavers sacrificed it to the Power that they served. Roland did not much care. He only wished that he could be a little closer to the flames, so that they might warm his hands.

As the darkness deepened, villages off to the north and south also began to go up in flames, and off to the west dry fields burned bright.

It looked as if the flameweavers would raze the whole valley.

A blue spy balloon, shaped like a giant graak, lifted into

the air on the eastern shore of Lake Donnestgree at about ten at night. It came hovering over the castle, its shape dark against the stars. The far-seers in the balloon rode the skies at least a thousand yards above the castle, so that no man could shoot them down, no matter how powerful his bow. The wind pushed them along quickly, so that the balloon landed far to the west.

Up and down the ranks, worried men kept saying, 'They're planning something big. Keep your eyes open!'

Word had it from the north that Raj Ahten had let his flameweavers destroy the whole of Castle Longmot. They'd summoned fell creatures that sent a wave of flame washing over the castle, slaying thousands of men.

Such a plan wouldn't work at Carris, others ventured. Carris was protected by water, while Longmot had only had earth runes carved into it.

Still, the knowledge settled uneasily into Roland's stomach, along with the lamb and loaf.

Who knew what the flameweavers might do? Perhaps they were burning the countryside in an effort to build up some spell powerful enough so that no water wizard's ward could repel it.

Yet for hours he kept watch in the bitter cold, and nothing more happened. The fires burned across the fields and hills outside of Carris. The spy balloon flew over twice more during the night.

On the castle walls, men sat above the fog and told tall tales or sang, so that in some ways the long night's watch took on an almost festive atmosphere.

By the third time the balloon hovered over, at three in the morning, Roland was hunched down behind Baron Poll, shivering violently, wishing for a blanket because, with flameweavers about, the Duke had forbidden any fires on the wall, lest the sorcerers turn the fire against its makers.

The Baron just stared up at the damned balloon. 'Pshaw,' he said to Roland. 'You might as well get some sleep. I'll wake you if anything happens.'

Trembling from cold, Roland lay with his back to the stone and closed his eyes. It was cold, terribly cold, and he would have slept soundly except for the cold.

He managed to doze in brief snatches, sometimes disturbed by nothing more than the wind or someone bumping against him as they stumbled past in the dark. Once, he woke to hear some nearby fellow with a lute plucking an endless bawdy ballad such as a jester might fancy.

He listened to it only distantly, half asleep. The song spoke of a running feud between two men in the King's Guard, and the various embarrassing and dangerous tricks they played on one another.

Roland was not really listening as the tune spoke of a young squire who made a tryst to meet a girl at a pond after dark, only to have his nemesis manage to get the young squire assigned to other duties. Afterward, the nemesis went to the pond himself, under cover of darkness. Roland came fully awake when he recognized a name . . .

> 'Then comes the squire, to catch Sir Poll:
> and it ain't a bass he's kissin' in the fishin' hole.
> For Poll's got the squire's lass,
> and he's making quite a splash,
> with his naked little ass – Uh-oh!
> Diddly-oh!
> Ain't it funny how the story grows?'

Though Roland came fully awake, he suddenly realized that he'd missed most of the song, for in the next verse, Squire Borenson leapt into the pond and chased Sir Poll 'Without any luck, whilst quacking like an angry duck.'

The good squire cornered and stabbed the 'foul' Sir Poll, 'And his fondest wish was to gut him like a fish.'

But the trollop in the pond managed to 'nurse Sir Poll back to life, and become his nagging wife.' Each stanza of the ballad ended with the chorus, 'Uh-oh! Diddly-oh! Ain't it funny how the story grows?'

Roland glanced up to see Baron Poll's reaction. The old fellow took it stoically. There was nothing he could do, after all. Bards were historians, and songs about living lords could only be sung openly by the King's consent. Thus, both Roland's son and Baron Poll had displeased their King enough so that as part of their punishment, their deeds were left open to the 'scorn of bards.'

Roland silently wished he'd been awake during the whole song. When Baron Poll had said that Roland would likely hear his story at the mouths of minstrels, Roland hadn't taken him seriously. Normally, only the most craven enemies of the King were so ridiculed.

But then another thought struck Roland. 'Ain't it funny how the story grows . . .' Now Roland had come into the story, and maybe someday the bards might sing a verse about him.

Roland finally felt so cold that he made his way back to the baker's tower, where the heat of the ovens and the smell of baking bread tantalizingly wafted up from below. But far too many men lay there for him to comfortably squeeze in.

He returned to Baron Poll, who said, 'Can't find a warm place to sleep?'

Roland shook his head, too weary to answer.

'Here's how you do it,' the Baron said. He escorted Roland back to the baker's tower, and Baron Poll growled, 'Up, you slackers! Back to your posts, you lazy dogs, or to a man I'll throw you from the tower into the drink!'

He aimed a few timid kicks, and in no time at all, dozens of men were scurrying from the warm tower. Baron Poll then bowed to Roland and gestured in a servile manner, like some chamberlain eager to ingratiate a visiting lord. 'Your bed, sirrah.'

Roland grinned. Baron Poll was a trickster.

Roland lay down next to the warmth of a chimney, his teeth still chattering, and found it almost too hot. Baron Poll went back to his post. Soon, men began sneaking back to sleep next to Roland.

He lay hoping that sometime before dawn he'd get warm enough to sleep.

But half an hour later, men began to shout when a city to the south was put to the torch. Roland looked up, saw the Baron and other warriors gazing off, the firelight reflecting from their eyes. But he was too tired to watch the flameweaver's show, and he reasoned that if a huge wave of fire did come sweeping toward the castle, the safest place he could be was down there, hidden behind the stone.

Moments later, he heard a deep rumbling sound that filled the whole sky for sixty seconds. The walls of Carris trembled beneath him, and he could feel the tower sway. People screamed in terror, for Raj Ahten had destroyed Longmot, Tal Rimmon, and other castles by the power of his Voice, and everyone imagined that it was happening to Carris now.

Yet as the rumbling subsided and Carris still held, Roland felt intense relief that lasted for only a few seconds. For immediately the rumbling was followed by the shouts of men on the nearby walls: 'Trevorsworthy Castle is down!' 'Raj Ahten has come!'

Roland climbed up, and gazed to the south where everyone pointed. There a city burned, flames leaping high into the sky.

Trevorsworthy Castle, four miles to the south, was not nearly as large as Carris, was not even manned, yet Roland had not been able to miss seeing it earlier in the day. It stood on a hill and had risen like a beacon from the fog. Now the hillside roared in an inferno, great clouds of smoke roiling up into the night, while flames licked at them.

In that light, Roland could see what remained of the castle: a heap of stone and a couple of jagged towers and sections of wall. Dust rose from the castle, and even as he watched, a tower leaned over like a drunkard and crumbled in ruin.

Carris had not been the focus of the attack. Trevorsworthy had. Roland ran back to his post.

'Well,' grumbled Baron Poll, 'at least he's given us fair warning.'

'What do you mean?' Roland asked.

'I mean that Raj Ahten's men have been forced to race at least eighteen hundred miles in the past two weeks, and he knows he can't run them any farther.' Baron Poll spat over the castle wall. 'So he wants a nice cozy place to lay up for a few months, and Carris is the best that Mystarria has to offer.'

'So he wants to take the castle?' Roland asked.

'Of course! If he wanted these castle walls down, they'd be down. Mark my words, he'll be offering us terms of surrender within the hour.'

'Will Paldane accept?' Roland asked. 'He said we'd be down to knife-work by dawn.'

'If he doesn't surrender,' Baron Poll said, 'then just listen for that sound Raj Ahten makes. When you hear it, take a running leap and throw yourself off the castle walls as far into the water as you're able. If the fall doesn't kill you, and a rock doesn't land on you, and if you don't drown, you just might make it.'

Roland was stunned.

He waited for a long hour, until the sky in the east began to lighten in the cold of dawn.

Roland never saw Raj Ahten draw near the castle, though he saw the work of his flameweavers.

A brilliant glow arose beneath the fog, as if a great fire raged on the ground, but that glow moved forward steadily from the south at the pace of a walking man. Accompanying that glow, Roland could hear the creaking of harnesses, the occasional slap of a shield against a breastplate, a man's cough or the yap of a dog.

Raj Ahten's army moved toward Carris almost sullenly, and the troops at Carris accepted them with similar reserve. Duke Paldane and his counselors labored up the stairs above the castle gate, a ragtag band. As they reached the top of the gate, so that Paldane himself could see out over the fog, he shouted, 'Archers, make ready! Artillery, take aim!'

Yet Raj Ahten's progress was undeterred. When the great light reached the causeway west of Carris and suddenly stopped, Roland waited expectantly for Paldane's artillerymen to open fire, or for Paldane to shout some command.

Instead, the glow beneath the fog intensified, as if the sun itself blazed there for several long moments, until at last pure rays of light began to pierce the opal mists. Roland lifted his arm to shield his eyes. The light burned the magical fog back for a hundred yards in every direction.

There at the end of the causeway sat Raj Ahten on a gray Imperial charger, while two flameweavers blazed beside him, pillars of living fire, naked but for the flames that wreathed them.

Raj Ahten wore a simple footman's helm and a shirt of black scale mail under a golden silk surcoat. He looked tired, grim.

Roland found that his heart was racing, and his breath came fast. Raj Ahten was the most handsome man he'd ever seen, more glorious than any he'd ever imagined, and completely unanticipated. Roland had expected a man who would be monstrous in form, cruel and deadly.

Yet Raj Ahten seemed to embody everything that Roland had ever hoped for in a lord. He appeared bold and imperious, powerful yet capable of great kindness.

He had only to open his mouth, and he could bring down the walls of Carris, as he had so many other castles in the past week.

If he is going to kill me, Roland thought, I wish he would do it now and get it over with.

No one shot from the castle walls.

An army rode at Raj Ahten's back. Roland could only see the front ranks protruding from the line of fog. Two dozen frowth giants stood like living walls, their faces grim and troubled. Huge black mastiffs at their feet bristled behind red-lacquered leather masks. Raj Ahten's Invincibles formed ranks behind, men with dark armor and round brass shields that reflected the light of the flameweavers as if they were hundreds of glowing yellow eyes.

For a moment, no one spoke. In a stern tone, Paldane called, 'If it is battle you want, then come against us! But if you hope to find refuge in Carris, you hope in vain. We will not surrender at any cost.'

33

EARTH DREAMS

As Gaborn reached the top step of the landing to his room, he stumbled in the darkness and fell to the floor.

He'd never stumbled and fallen in his life, not that he could remember. Born as a prince among Runelords, he had been endowed as a child with grace from a dancer. It aided his flexibility and sense of balance. Always in the past he'd landed on his feet no matter how far he'd fallen. He'd been granted endowments of brawn to give him greater strength, endowments of stamina to let him work tirelessly into the night, an endowment of sight to let his keen eyes pierce the darkness, an endowment of wit so that he knew every uneven step in every castle he'd ever walked.

Wearily, he climbed up and made for the bedroom Groverman had provided. At the top of the stairs, he said goodnight to his Days.

A boy lay curled on the floor in front of his door. Gaborn wondered if the lad served as a page for Groverman, though he couldn't imagine why the boy would be sleeping at his door. Gaborn carefully stepped over the lad.

To his surprise, in the room he found Iome asleep. She lay abed with five pups snuggling against her. One of the pups looked up at him and barked querulously.

A single candle burned in the room beside a bowl of wash-water. The washbowl had been sweetened with rose petals. Clean riding clothes were draped over a chair. The room smelled pleasantly of roast beef, and a silver platter bearing food sat on a table, as if the feast an hour past had not been enough. A small fire burned in the hearth.

Gaborn looked at it all, realized that Jureem must have been here. No chamberlain had ever served Gaborn quite so well. The fat servant was always underfoot, yet seldom in sight.

Gaborn had hardly had time to speak to Iome tonight. Though she'd said he looked decrepit, she herself had looked overworn. He was glad that she slept. She'd need her rest. In two hours he'd ride for Fleeds.

He did not bother to remove his dirty ring mail and clothes, just lay down beside Iome.

She rolled toward him, laid a hand over his neck, and came awake. 'My love,' she said. 'Is it time to ride?'

'Not yet. Get some rest,' Gaborn said. 'We've got two hours to rest.'

Instead, Iome came fully awake. She climbed up on one elbow, studied his face. She looked pale, worn. He closed his eyes.

'I heard about the Blue Tower,' Iome said. 'You can't get all the sleep you need in two hours. You must take some endowments.'

She spoke only hesitantly. She knew how he resisted taking endowments for himself.

Gaborn shook his head. 'I am an Oath-Bound Lord,' he groaned. 'Did I not swear an oath to you?'

It was not a purely rhetorical question. He'd lost two endowments of wit today, and with that loss, he'd forgotten much. Memories had been stolen, lessons forgotten. He recalled being on the tower above Castle Sylvarresta and watching Raj Ahten's forces take formation on the hills south of the city. But his memory of taking the ancient vow of the Oath-Bound Lords seemed muzzy, incomplete. If he'd spoken the vow, he could not recall it.

Gaborn had feared to speak to Iome tonight. He dared not admit that he could not recall the minute that he'd asked Iome to marry him, or remember his own mother's face, or bring to mind a thousand other facts that he thought he should know.

'You did,' she said. 'And I've heard your arguments against taking a man's endowments. But there has to be some point . . . some point at which you will accept another man's endowment. I'd give you the use of my pups, if I could, but they won't bond to you in time. Your people need you to be strong now.'

Gaborn stared hard at her.

'My love, you must take endowments,' Iome said. 'You cannot completely forsake them.'

Gaborn had been taught as a youth that a lord who had great stamina could use that stamina to serve his people tirelessly. A lord with great brawn could fight for his people. To take endowments was a noble thing, if done properly.

Yet the thought of taking them himself seemed wrong.

It seemed wrong in part because it put those who took the endowments in great jeopardy. Many a man who gave brawn would have his heart stop afterward, too weak to beat anymore. A man who gave wit might forget how to walk or eat. A man who gave stamina could easily be ravaged by illness, though it was perfectly safe to give the 'lesser' endowments that did not endanger the giver, those of metabolism, or sight, or smell, or hearing, or touch.

It seemed wrong in part also because he knew that he put those who offered endowments at risk from outside attack. He'd seen the bloody rooms where Borenson had slaughtered Sylvarresta's Dedicates.

Gaborn felt lost. He recalled the drawings he'd discovered in the Emir of Tuulistan's book, the secret teachings from the Room of Dreams in the House of Understanding.

A man owned certain things: his body, his family, his good name. Though these things were not named in the Emir's book, a man certainly owned his own brawn, his own wit.

To take a man's attributes and never return them so long as both of you remained alive seemed to Gaborn an inescapable violation of another man's domain.

It was evil, thoroughly evil.

Though Gaborn dared not say it, in a sense he felt lighter, happier, right now than he had in years.

For the first time since he was old enough to understand what it cost for another man to grant him endowments, Gaborn felt free, totally free of guilt.

For the first time in his life, he was only himself. True, his Dedicates had died today, and he felt deeply saddened to know that they had died for him, died so that they might lend him their attributes.

But though he felt weak and frail and tired, he was also no longer encumbered by guilt.

'I had hoped to forsake endowments,' Gaborn said. 'I am the Earth King, and that should be enough to sustain any man.'

'It might be enough if you were alone in the world, but is it enough for us?' Iome asked. 'When you go into battle, you will not risk yourself alone. You risk the future of us all.'

'I know,' Gaborn said.

'Your forcibles, your people, offer you power,' Iome said again. 'Power to do good. Power to do evil. If you will not take it, Raj Ahten will.'

'I don't want it,' Gaborn said.

'You must take it,' Iome said. 'Guilt is the price of leadership.'

Gaborn knew that she was right. He could not risk going into battle without endowments.

'Tomorrow, before I leave,' Iome said, 'I will take endowments from my pups. I have been giving it great thought, and I will not stop with them alone. The future is rushing toward us, and we must rush to meet it. I will take enough endowments of metabolism to make myself battle-ready.'

The thought pained Gaborn. Battle-ready? If she were to protect herself from Raj Ahten's Invincibles, she'd need five endowments at least. With so many, she'd grow old and die in ten or twelve years. To take so many endowments was like taking a slow poison.

'Iome!' Gaborn said, unable to express his dismay.

'Don't make me leave you behind,' Iome said. 'Come with me! Grow old with me!'

Of course, that was the answer. She did not want to leave him, did not want to grow old alone. For those who took endowments of metabolism, it became difficult to speak to people who lived in common time. The sense of isolation from the rest of humanity carried a great toll.

Yet he wondered at Iome. He knew that she did not want to take endowments any more than he did. He suspected that she sought to lure him into doing this, or perhaps force him.

'Don't do this on my account,' Gaborn said. 'If you want me to take endowments, I will. I know that I must. But *you* don't have to do this. I will do it alone.'

Iome reached out, squeezed his hand, shut her eyes as if to sleep.

Outside the door, the clubfooted boy stirred in his dreams like a restless pup, kicking the door with a soft *whump*.

'Who is the child outside our door?' Gaborn asked.

'Just a boy,' Iome said. 'He walked a hundred miles to see you. I wanted you to Choose him, but when you passed him in the hall tonight, he was afraid to address you. So I asked him to wait for you here. I thought he might help out here at Groverman's kennels.'

'All right,' Gaborn said.

'All right? Aren't you going to look into his heart before you Choose him?'

'Sounds like a good kid,' Gaborn said, too weary to get up and Choose the boy, or to discuss the matter further.

'We saved the people at Castle Sylvarresta today,' Iome said. 'Every one of them, except for Sir Donnor.'

'Good,' Gaborn said. 'Jureem told me all about it.'

'It was hard . . .' Iome agreed, drifting off to sleep.

Preparing for sleep, Gaborn used his earth senses to reach out and feel how his people were doing.

Sir Borenson had reached the Hest Mountains and seemed to be encamped – or at least stationary for the moment – and like Gaborn, dared not ride until moonrise. But Gaborn could feel danger rising about Borenson, had felt it for hours. The knight was riding toward trouble.

Beyond that, Gaborn had to wonder about the men with him. He'd felt that they were in tremendous danger all day long. Some of that cloud had lifted when Myrrima slew the Darkling Glory.

But death still stalked his warriors – every single man among them.

It was true that the Earth had bidden Gaborn go south into war. It was true that the Earth was allowing him to go into battle. But it was also true that the Earth had warned him to tell his messengers to flee Carris.

Attack and flee? Gaborn felt befuddled by the conflicting inspirations.

He had begun to wonder, did the Earth allow him to attack only because he so craved it? Or did the Earth perhaps want something of him that he could not name? It was possible these men were to sacrifice themselves in some cause he did not understand. Was he taking his men to their deaths?

Perhaps not all of them would die. Certainly some would be killed at Carris, maybe even most of them.

Yet the Earth allowed it. Take them to battle, it said. Many will die.

It seemed a violation of his vows, for Gaborn had sworn to protect those he had Chosen.

Indeed, Gaborn had let young Agunter Orwynne retreat north because he so feared for that boy in particular, though he dared not tell anyone.

How can I save them all? Gaborn wondered.

Outside his door, Gaborn heard the *ching* of ring mail and the thud of iron boots on the carpet as a knight came up the stairs. Gaborn used his earth senses, determined that the man posed no threat to him.

Since Gaborn's room was at the top of the keep, he knew the fellow had come to see him. Gaborn waited for the knight to knock at his door. Instead, he heard the fellow stand outside the door for a while, then sit down and sigh wearily as he put his back against the plaster wall.

The man dared not disturb him.

Wearily, Gaborn got up, then took the burning candle, opened the door. He glanced at the clubfooted boy, saw into the lad's heart. A good kid, as Iome had promised. The boy had nothing to offer in the wars to come. He was perhaps worthless, unable to fight or save himself, unsalvageable. Yet Gaborn felt too emotionally drained to restrain the impulse to reject him.

Gaborn Chose him.

The fellow who sat on the floor across the hall wore the colors of Sylvarresta, the black tunic with a silver boar, and his uniform indicated that he was a captain. The man had dark hair and haunted eyes, a face that was unshaven, filled with pain and terror.

Gaborn had never seen him before, at least not that he could remember, which suggested that perhaps the captain served here under Duke Groverman.

'Your Highness,' the fellow said, climbing to his feet and saluting.

Gaborn spoke softly so that he wouldn't wake Iome. 'Do you have a message?'

'No, I . . .' the fellow said. He dropped to one knee and seemed to struggle, as if unsure whether he should draw his sword and offer it.

Gaborn looked into the captain's heart using his Earth Sight. The captain had a wife and children that he loved. The men who had served under him were like brothers to him. 'I Choose you,' Gaborn said. 'I Choose you for the Earth.'

'No!' the fellow wailed, and when he looked up, tears misted his dark eyes.

'Yes,' Gaborn said, too tired to argue. Many a man who was worthy of the Choosing seemed to feel unworthy.

'Don't you know me?' the fellow demanded.

Gaborn shook his head.

'My name is Tempest, Cedrick Tempest,' he said. 'I was

captain of the guard at Longmot, before it fell. I was there when your father died. I was there when everyone died.'

Gaborn knew the name. But he'd lost an endowment of wit, and if he'd ever seen Cedrick Tempest's face, it was erased from memory.

'I see,' Gaborn said. 'Go get some sleep. You look as if you need it more than I do.'

'I . . .' Cedrick Tempest gaped at the floor in dismay and shook his head in wonder. 'I did not come to ask for the Choosing. I am unworthy. I came to *confess*, milord.'

'Confess, then,' Gaborn said, 'if you feel you need it.'

'I am not worthy to be a guardsman! I have betrayed my people.'

'How?'

'When Longmot fell, Raj Ahten gathered the survivors, and offered . . . he offered life to any man who would betray you.'

'I see no treachery in your heart,' Gaborn said. 'What deed did he require?'

'He was seeking forcibles. He'd brought many forcibles to Longmot, and he wanted to know where they had gone, and when. He offered life to any man who would tell him.'

'And what did you say?' Gaborn asked.

'I told him the truth: that your father had sent them south with his messengers.'

Gaborn licked his lips, barely restraining a painful laugh. 'South? Did you mention the Blue Tower?'

'No,' Tempest said. 'I told him the truth, that the men had gone south, but I knew not where.'

But of course Raj Ahten would have believed that the forcibles had gone to the Blue Tower. Where else would a King of Mystarria send his forcibles? If Gaborn were putting the forcibles to good use, the Blue Tower was the only fortress in all of Mystarria that might have housed forty thousand new Dedicates.

Why didn't I see it? Gaborn wondered. Raj Ahten did not destroy the Blue Tower to bring down Mystarria; he did it to humble me!

Gaborn laughed painfully, imagining how Raj Ahten must have feared him, never knowing that the forcibles lay hidden in a tomb in Heredon.

Cedrick Tempest looked up, anger burning in his eyes. He did not like having a man laugh at him.

'You did not betray me,' Gaborn said. 'If my father sent anything south, it was not forcibles. My father counted on someone like you to tell where the forcibles had gone, so that Raj Ahten might race off on some fruitless quest. By speaking as you did, you served my father well.'

'Milord?' Tempest asked, shame burning in his face.

Gaborn realized that he should have known. His father had been a far better strategist than Gaborn would ever be. Since he'd become the Earth King, Gaborn had relied upon his newfound powers to protect him.

Yet his father had always taught him to use his brain, to plot and scheme and look ahead. Gaborn had not been doing that, or he would have thought to reinforce the Blue Tower a hundredfold, to set a trap for Raj Ahten.

'Tell me,' Gaborn asked, 'were you the only man who offered to trade his life for a bit of useless knowledge?'

'No, milord,' Tempest said, looking down. 'Others offered, too.'

Gaborn dared not tell Tempest the truth. That because of the lie he'd spread in King Orden's behalf, tens of thousands of men had died, and perhaps hundreds of thousands more would die in the war to come. Such knowledge was too heavy for anyone to bear.

'So if you had not borne the news to Raj Ahten, some other man would have?'

'Yes,' Tempest said.

'Have you considered,' Gaborn asked, 'how poorly you would have served your King, if you'd let yourself die?'

'Death would have been easier than this guilt I bear,' Tempest said. His eyes searched the floor.

'Undoubtedly,' Gaborn said. 'So those who chose death made the easy choice, did they not?'

Tempest looked up uncertainly. 'Milord, my wife used my warhorse to bear my children and a wagon here to Groverman. I have my horse and my armor still. I am an uncommonly good lancer. Though I no longer hold any endowments, I beg to ride south with you.'

'You would not survive longer than your first charge,' Gaborn said.

'Be *that* as it may,' Tempest growled.

'As penance for your deed,' Gaborn said, 'I will not accept your death. I want your life in service. I have hundreds of men riding now into war, and many of them will not return. I need warriors. I beg you to stay here at Groverman with your wife and children, and protect them. Furthermore, I bid you to begin training warriors. I need a thousand young lancers.'

'A thousand?' Tempest asked.

'More, if you can get them,' Gaborn said. He was making an outrageous demand. Normally, a knight might choose two or three squires to train to knighthood during his entire lifetime. 'I will notify Groverman of what I require,' Gaborn said with a heavy heart. 'There will be dogs to serve as Dedicates and forcibles for every young lad or lady who joins under your command. You say you are a fine lancer, so you can teach the lance and the care of horses. Other men can teach the warhammer and the bow and how to care for armor.

'Choose only the smartest and strongest that you can find,' Gaborn said, 'for you have only until spring. The warriors' training must be completed by spring. The reavers will come upon us this spring.'

Gaborn wasn't sure why he believed that. Evidence said that the reavers were already rising from their lairs, but it was common knowledge that reavers could not well abide the cold. They made their lairs deep in the hot parts of the Underworld, and when they did make forays to the earth's surface at all, they tended to do so in the summer. They retreated underground with the snow. He hoped the reavers would not travel far in the cold.

'Six months?' Tempest asked. He did not say it was impossible, though his tone spoke for him.

Gaborn nodded. 'I hope for so much time.'

'I will begin tonight, milord,' Tempest said. He rose to his feet, saluted, turned, and marched down the stairs.

Gaborn stood holding his candle. He looked back at Iome through the open door. The bed had not seemed comfortable; it was too soft or too hard or something. He doubted he would be able to sleep, and instead found himself wanting to walk in the Duke's garden.

The smell of the herbs there would be a better balm than sleep, he thought.

Gaborn bore the candle downstairs to light his way out the back door of the keep and into the Duke's herb garden.

In the starlight, he could hardly see. In one corner of the garden sat a white statue of a lord on a charger, spear raised to the sky. Willows hung down to brush the soldier's head, and a small pool reflected starlight at the charger's feet. Gaborn blew out the candle.

He smelled lavender and savory, anise and basil, in the garden. It was nothing so marvelous and large as Binnesman's garden at Castle Sylvarresta had been, before Raj Ahten's flameweavers burned it, yet still Gaborn felt refreshed by its presence. Just being here lightened his heart.

He pulled off his boots, letting his feet touch the cold night soil. The feel of it was like a balm, soothing his nerves, restoring him.

He realized that he needed more. He pulled off his armor and had half removed his robes before he realized what he was doing.

He looked about guiltily, as if afraid that someone might see him naked. To his astonishment, at that moment the wizard Binnesman stepped out from behind a screen of yellow roses.

'I wondered how long it would take,' Binnesman said.

'What do you mean?' Gaborn asked.

'You are a servant of the Earth now,' Binnesman said. 'You need its touch, as much as you need breath.'

'I . . . wasn't going to lie down,' Gaborn said.

'Why not?' Binnesman said, as if mocking the falsehood. 'Does the soil displease you?'

Gaborn was unable to answer. He felt somehow embarrassed, though he knew that the wizard was right. His skin craved the touch of the earth. That is why he had not been able to sleep. Slumber would not suffice. His weary ache required something more.

'It should please you,' Binnesman said. 'May the Earth hide you. May the Earth heal you. May the Earth make you its own.' The wizard struck the ground with his staff, and the grass at Gaborn's feet parted with a ripping sound. Rich dark soil lay exposed.

Gaborn reached down, tasted it.

'Good soil,' the wizard said, 'strong in the Earth Powers. That's why this castle was built here. When old Heredon Sylvarresta first came to this land, he looked for the good soil and built his castles atop such places. An hour asleep here will rest you more fully than many hours in bed.'

'Truly?' Gaborn asked.

'Truly,' Binnesman said. 'You serve the Earth now, and if you serve it well, it will serve you well in return.'

Gaborn resisted the urge to lie down. Instead, he looked up at Binnesman, studied the wizard in the dark. In the starlight, Binnesman's face glowed lightly, and starlight limned his graying hair.

The color in the wizard's face was off. Still too green, so that he no longer looked quite human.

'I have something to confess,' Gaborn said.

'I will help you if I can,' Binnesman said.

'I . . . I lied to my men tonight. I told them that the Earth commanded me to strike at Raj Ahten . . . but that's not exactly right.'

'It isn't?' Binnesman asked in a dubious tone.

'The Earth warns me that many will die if they do not flee,' Gaborn said. 'Yet it allows me to strike. I . . . I'm not sure what the Earth wants.'

Binnesman hunched close to the ground, held his staff loosely. 'Perhaps . . .' Binnesman said, 'you are deceived.'

'Deceived?'

'You say the Earth wants you to strike at Raj Ahten? But are you sure it isn't *you* who wants to strike Raj Ahten?'

'Of course I want to strike him,' Gaborn said.

'So you hold the banner of truce with one hand, and the battle-axe with the other. Do you offer death or peace? And how can Raj Ahten trust you, if even you have not made up your mind?'

'So you think I should offer him peace? But what of the Earth's command to strike?'

'I think,' Binnesman said firmly, 'that you must look beyond illusions. Raj Ahten is not your ultimate enemy. You were sent to save mankind, not to fight it. You must see *that*, before you understand the Earth's will.

'The reavers too are an illusion. You fight Powers unseen. Whether you strike at Raj Ahten, or the reavers, or someone else, you must realize that they are only substitutes for your true enemy.'

Gaborn shook his head. 'I don't understand.'

'I suspect it will become clearer when you reach Carris,' Binnesman tried to reassure him. 'The Earth knows its enemies, and you have the gift of Earth Sight. You will know the Earth's enemies, too, when you see them.'

Gaborn merely hung his head, too weary to puzzle it out.

Binnesman looked at him with concern, touched Gaborn's shoulder. 'Gaborn, I must tell you something now. I don't want to offend you, but it has been much on my mind.'

'What is it?'

'You have determined to go to war,' Binnesman said. 'You will ride to battle, am I right?'

'Yes. I believe so.'

'Then I must wonder: do you understand your role as an Earth King?'

'I believe so. I am to Choose the seeds of mankind, to save them through the dark times to come.'

'That is right,' Binnesman said. 'But don't you understand that no matter how much you want to fight, it is not your place to do so? You would be offended if the stablemaster decided to serve your dinner, wouldn't you? Nor would you allow your chief steward to sit in judgment for the King. It is not the Earth King's duty to engage in conflict. If I understand correctly, it is your duty to *avoid* conflict.'

Gaborn knew that. He knew, yet could not quite live with it. 'Erden Geboren fought battles two thousand years ago. He fought and won them decisively!'

'He did,' Binnesman said. 'But he did so only when his back was to the wall and he could run no farther. He did not lightly put his people at risk.'

'Are you saying that I must not ride to battle?' Gaborn asked, still incredulous.

'You are the Earth King, and you must Choose the seeds of mankind,' Binnesman said. 'I am the Earth's Healer, and I must do what I can to help it recover after the coming scourge. There is another who will be the Earth's warrior. You cannot claim that title.'

'Another?' Gaborn asked. 'Who?'

'I speak of the wylde.'

'The wylde?' Gaborn asked, uncertain. Binnesman had given part of his life to raise a wylde, a creature made of Earth to be its champion. But the thing had leapt high into the air at its inception. Though Gaborn's men had scoured all of Heredon, the wylde had not been seen since.

'Yes, the wylde,' Binnesman said. 'I formed the green knight to fight in the Earth's behalf, and it will fight, once I complete its creation. A wylde lives only to fight, and it is a far more powerful foe than you will ever be.'

'Are you sure it is still alive?' Gaborn asked.

'Yes,' Binnesman said. 'I have studied the tomes thoroughly in the past week. It is alive and aware, I think. It is most likely just lost, wandering in the wilderness. So long as there is enough healing power left in the Earth, the wylde cannot easily be destroyed.'

'You say you have not completed it, but the wylde did take form, didn't it?' Gaborn asked. He had seen the thing take shape in the darkness, at the ruins of the Seven Standing Stones. But the soil and stones and bones that Binnesman had laid out to create the wylde had flowed together so quickly, Gaborn had not seen much before it departed.

'It has form,' Binnesman said. 'But still the creature is not finished. I created the wylde, but I must still *unbind* it.'

'What do you mean?'

Binnesman considered for a moment. 'Think of it as a child, a dangerous child. The wylde is newly formed, but it is still ignorant, and thus needs a parent. It needs my care. I must teach it right from wrong, as I would any child, and I must teach it to fight.

'When it has learned enough, then I will unbind it, grant it its free agency, so that it will be released to fight as it sees best. Only then will it become fully effective, capable of defending the Earth.'

'It has no free agency?' Gaborn asked. 'Is it like a marionette then, waiting for you to move it? If that's so, then it could be lying in the bushes somewhere. We might never find it!'

'No,' Binnesman said. 'It can move. But until I unbind it, it must obey my commands – or the commands of those who invoke its true name. After the unbinding, no man will be able to control it.'

'It will still follow your orders, won't it?' Gaborn asked. 'Eldehar created a warhorse and rode it into battle.'

'He could not have ridden it once it was unbound.' Binnesman shook his head. 'No . . . there are no words to describe the unbinding. The wylde is itself, independent. It can exist only so long as it feeds upon the blood of its enemies. It must fight with or without me. It cannot be constrained. It must be allowed to remain *wild* in ways that you cannot understand, as feral and untameable as the most vicious pack of wolves.

'The wylde is not a beast, so much as it is a concept formed by the Earth, a concept for which we have no words.'

Binnesman sat for a moment, clutched his staff with both hands. He looked up at the starlight. As if he had not sufficiently stressed an earlier point, Binnesman said, 'You must not seek out battles. That is not your domain. I wonder . . . are you striking out in anger?'

Gaborn fixed Binnesman with a calm expression of certainty. 'There is no anger in the Earth's desire,' he tried to explain. 'I do not wish to strike in anger. Instead, I feel the Earth's call as a plea for help. Strike, it begs me. Strike before it is too late!'

'All right,' Binnesman said in a placating tone. 'I believe you. I believe that the Earth begs you to strike. So I will ask you only one thing: to be mindful of your target.'

'I am the Earth's King,' Gaborn promised. 'I will do as it wishes.'

'Good,' Binnesman said. 'That is all I can hope for. You must rest now, milord.'

Gaborn was tired, terribly tired. He pulled off his tunic, lay down naked on the soil.

It seemed surprisingly overwarm to the touch, as if it still held the heat of the day.

Binnesman waved his staff, and soil washed over Gaborn, a comforting blanket.

Beneath the soil, Gaborn lay with eyes closed and felt the tension ease from his muscles.

At first, he felt afraid, for he did not know how he would breathe, but after a long minute of holding his breath, he realized that he did not need to breathe. Even his lungs rested, and he lay with warm humus sifting into his ears, pressing upon his chest and face, filling the tiny spaces between his fingers.

In moments he was fast asleep, and for a time he dreamt that he was a hare on the road outside Castle Sylvarresta, running from some unknown danger to reach the safety of its hole. The hare bolted through some blackberry vines and raced into a nice safe warren, down into the darkness where the scent of young hares came strong.

There, in the very back of the warren, it found its young kits, four small hares that were just a day old.

The hare's breasts were heavy with milk. It lay on its side, panting from its exertions, and let the kits nuzzle, pressing hard against its breasts to release the milk.

As the hare lay there, panting, it heard the wizard Binnesman speaking up above the warren. It leaned its long ears back, heard the conversation distinctly as horses pounded the hardpan of the road overhead. 'The Earth is speaking to us. It is speaking to you and to me.'

'What does it say?' Gaborn heard himself ask.

'I don't know, yet,' Binnesman answered, 'but this is the way it usually speaks to me: in the worried stirrings of rabbits and mice, in the shifting flight of a cloud of birds, in the cries of geese. Now it whispers to the Earth King, too. You are growing, Gaborn. Growing in power.'

Then the horses were gone, and the hare rested peacefully in its warren. The hare closed its eyes while the kits drank, letting its long ears lie flat against its back, and worried about a flea on its forepaw that it wanted to bite.

Silly men, the hare thought, not to hear the voice of the Earth.

In his dream, Gaborn slithered across the forest floor, as if he were a snake. He felt the sleek scales on his belly letting him slide as easily as if the soil were ice.

He flicked a long forked tongue into the air, tasting it. He smelled fur and warmth ahead: a hare in the leaves. He lay very still for a moment, the autumn sun shining bright upon him, as he tasted the sun's last warm embrace of the season.

Nothing moved ahead. He smelled hare, but saw nothing.

He nuzzled among the oak leaves, until he saw a hole, a burrow, dark and inviting. He flicked his tongue, smelled the young kits in their burrow.

It was daytime, and the hares within would be sleeping. Ever so quietly, he slithered down into the depths.

Above him, he heard the heavy tread of horses, and the wizard Binnesman saying, 'The Earth is speaking to us. It is speaking to you and to me.'

Gaborn asked, 'What does it say?'

'I don't know – yet,' Binnesman said. 'But this is the way it usually speaks to me: in the worried stirrings of rabbits and mice, in the shifting flight of a cloud of birds, in the cries of geese. Now it whispers to the Earth King, too. You are growing, Gaborn. Growing in power.'

'Yet I can't hear the Earth,' Gaborn said, 'and I so *want* to hear its voice.'

'Perhaps if your ears were longer,' the wizard replied in the dream. 'Or maybe if you put them to the ground.'

'Yes, yes, of course, that's what I'll do,' Gaborn said enthusiastically.

Gaborn lay in the mouth of the burrow and found himself listening, straining to hear with all of his might. He flicked his long forked tongue, smelled young hares ahead.

In his dream, Gaborn walked through a new-plowed field. The soil had been turned recently, and the clods had been all broken with a mattock and raked. The loam was deep, the soil good.

His muscles ached from long hours of work, yet he could smell the spring rains coming, and he hurried through the field with a sharp planting stick. Using the stick, he poked a small hole in the soil, dropped in a heavy seed, and then covered the hole with his foot.

Thus he worked, sweat pouring down his face.

He toiled mindlessly, thinking of nothing, until he heard a voice nearby.

'Greetings!'

Gaborn turned and looked off to the side of the field. A stone fence stood there with young flowering pea vines and morning glory trailing up it. On the other side of the fence stood the Earth.

The Earth had taken the form of Gaborn's father, had

become a man in shape. But Gaborn's father looked to be a creature of soil: sand and clay and twigs and leaves where flesh should have been.

'Greetings,' Gaborn said. 'I'd hoped to see you again.'

'I am always here,' the Earth said. 'Look down at your feet, and I should be somewhere nearby.'

Gaborn kept working, continued dropping heavy seeds from the pocket of his greatcoat as he walked along.

'So,' the Earth said, 'you cannot decide whether to be the hunter or the hunted today, the hare or the snake.'

'Am I not both?' Gaborn asked.

'You are, indeed,' the Earth said. 'Life and death. Nemesis and deliverer.'

Gaborn looked around, feeling uneasy. The Earth had appeared to him before in Binnesman's garden. But at the time, Binnesman had been there, and the wizard had translated. The very Earth had spoken in the movement of stones, the hissing of leaves, the venting of gases from deep underground.

And the Earth had appeared to him like this, as a creature of dirt and stones. But it had come in the form of his enemy, Raj Ahten.

Now the Earth appeared to him in the form of a friend, his father, and spoke to him as easily as one man speaks to another, as if he were a neighbor talking across a fence.

Wait, I must be dreaming, Gaborn thought.

The Earth around him rumbled as if in the throes of a quake, and the leaves of nearby great oaks hissed in the wind.

He understood the sounds made by the movement of stone, by the hiss of leaves. 'What is the difference between wakefulness and dream?' the Earth asked. 'I do not understand. You listen now, and you hear.'

He looked at the pebbly image of his father, and understood. The Earth was indeed speaking to him, and not with the voice of mice.

'What message do you have for me?' Gaborn asked, for he felt that he desperately needed the Earth's help. He was so confused about so many things: should he take his people and flee Raj Ahten; should he attack; how could he best serve the Earth; should he take endowments from men.

'I brought no message,' Earth said. 'You summoned me, and I came.'

Gaborn could not quite believe that. Certainly there must be some important thing that the Earth could tell him. 'I . . . you gave me all of this power, and I don't know how to use it.'

'I do not understand,' the Earth said, confused. 'I gave you no power.'

'You gave me the Earth Sight, and the power to Choose.'

Earth considered. 'No, those are my powers, not yours. I never *gave* them to you.'

Gaborn felt befuddled. 'But I'm using them.'

'Those are *my* powers,' the Earth said again. 'As you serve me, I serve you in return. You have no power unless I allow you to use mine.'

Gaborn stared at the pebbly image of his father, a distinguished-looking man of forty with a broad jaw and broad shoulders.

Gaborn narrowed his eyes. Now he saw it. 'Yes,' he said. 'I see. You gave me no power. You have only *lent* it to me.'

Earth seemed to consider the word 'lend' for a long time, as if unsure whether that word was appropriate. It nodded at last. 'Serve me, and I will serve you.'

Then Gaborn realized that even the word 'lend' was not right. The Earth wanted his service, and when Gaborn served the Earth, the Earth repaid him immediately by granting Gaborn the power to serve it.

'You are sowing the seeds of mankind,' the Earth said. 'Time and again, you have asked how to sow them all. I do not understand this.'

'I want to save them all,' Gaborn said.

'You see the wheat fields,' the Earth said softly. 'A hundred seeds fall to the ground, but does each one grow? Are none to be left to fill the bellies of cattle and mice? Are none to rot in the sun?

'Do you want the world to be filled with wheat alone?'

'No,' Gaborn said heavily.

'Then you must accept. Life and death, death and life. They are the same. Many shall die, few may live. The Harvest of Souls is upon you. We do not have the power to save all the seeds of mankind. You shall have only the power to Choose a few.'

'I know,' Gaborn said. 'But the more I can save—'

'Withdraw from me, and I must withdraw from you,' the Earth whispered.

'I didn't mean that!' Gaborn said. 'That's not what I'm trying to do!'

'The seeds you hold in your hand,' Earth asked, 'do you wish to plant living seeds, or dead ones?'

Gaborn stared at the pebbly image of Earth, and wondered. He had not looked at the seeds, had not really been aware of their heft or shape in his hand.

Now he held seeds in his palm, and lifted them experimentally.

He could feel them moving, stirring at his touch. Dozens of seeds. Yet some did not move. He opened his hand wide, glanced down.

He held embryos in his hand, dozens of them, small and pink or brown, like the half-formed shapes of young mice. Yet he could distinguish features. Some of them waved tiny arms and legs, and he recognized them: that pink one in the center of his palm with the red down would be Borenson. The beautiful dead brown one beside it was Raj Ahten.

He held them, poked the Earth with his planting stick, and tried to decide which embryo to drop into the deep, rich humus.

When he looked up again, hoping for the Earth's advice, the sun had suddenly fallen. The time for planting had passed, and Gaborn could no longer see.

Gaborn groped and struggled up out of his shallow grave. He sat for a moment in the starlight, heart hammering. He looked about wildly for Binnesman, but the wizard was nowhere in the garden.

He felt as if the Earth had warned him against failure, but failure at what?

The Earth had lent him the power to Choose. Gaborn had accepted it gratefully, and had been doing his best. But was he Choosing too widely? Was he not Choosing well?

In Binnesman's garden, a week ago, Gaborn had accepted the task of Choosing. Because he loved his people, the Earth had given him the task of Choosing which 'seeds of mankind' to save.

But now Gaborn had been fretting, wondering how he might save all of his people in the war to come.

The Earth seemed cold and hard to Gaborn, dispassionate to the point of being cruel. Choose, the Earth said. It does not matter to me. Life and death are one.

Choose a few to save, and then save them. That was his task. Nothing more, nothing less.

It sounded simple.

But seemed impossible.

How was he to Choose?

Did the Earth expect him to let babes die merely because they could not defend themselves? Or the frail or elderly? Should he let a good man die because an evil man might make a better warrior?

How was Gaborn to Choose well?

I've lied to my people, Gaborn realized. I told so many of them that they were Chosen, that I would protect them during the dark times to come, and in my heart I really do want to save them.

But I don't have that power.

The knowledge filled him with dread and cold certainty.

He couldn't save them all, couldn't protect them all. He imagined that in a melee, he would have to choose: let one man die so that three others might live.

But how could he make such a decision in good conscience? What would be his logic?

Could he let Iome die under any circumstances? If saving her cost the lives of a thousand men, would it be worth it?

Even if he spent lives that way, would she thank him for it afterward? Or would she damn him?

What had Binnesman said yesterday morning? That Erden Geboren had 'died not of battle wounds, but of a broken heart.'

Gaborn could imagine such a thing. The Earth had selected him to be the Earth King because Gaborn was a man of conscience. But how could Gaborn hope to live with his conscience if he did what the Earth asked?

He sat thinking about what had happened today. He had Chosen to save King Orwynne, but that fat old knight had defied Gaborn, had ridden into the cloud of swirling night in a vain attempt to defeat the Darkling Glory.

Meanwhile, Iome and Jureem had nearly lost their lives because they stayed at Castle Sylvarresta trying to save those who would not flee, as Gaborn had commanded them.

I can Choose them, Gaborn realized, but that does not mean that they will Choose me. I can try to save them, but that does not mean they will save themselves.

Let that be the first criterion for the Choosing, he decided. I will save those who listen to my voice and thereby seek to save themselves, and I must forget the rest.

Gaborn gaped about in the starlight, until he saw his armor and tunic lying in a heap nearby, atop a bed of lavender.

He got up, dusted himself off, and dressed. By the time he reached his room, Iome was dressing for her late-night ride.

Despite his ominous dreams, Gaborn felt more completely rested than ever before in his life.

BOOK 8

DAY 1 IN THE MONTH OF LEAVES
A DAY OF DESOLATION

34

ANDERS

Years of worry had gnawed at King Anders. Those years had left the flesh hanging slack on Anders's tall, spare frame.

Yet as he lay abed, his eyes staring past the canopy above him, he felt no fear. A deep calm coursed through him, like a refreshing drink of water from a mountain stream. The world was about to change.

Anders stepped out of bed, threw off his robes, and stood naked for a moment. His rooms were in the highest tower of his keep, and the balcony door and windows were all wide open. A cool, titillating breeze breathed through the room, stirring the thin summer curtains.

Anders's wife reached out, pawed at his pillow, as if she sought to find him in her dreams. He brushed back the dark hair from her right temple and whispered, 'Sleep.'

Immediately her whole body slackened, and she dropped into a heavy slumber.

A strong gust of wind lashed at the curtains, entered the room and began to circle. Though the wind was invisible, its movements were palpable.

Anders spread his arms wide in welcome, felt the wind encompassing him, brushing under his arms, delicious to the senses.

He let the wind move him, lead him out to the balcony of his keep.

There, gargoyles splotched crimson, yellow, and metallic green with lichens hunched on the merlons and stared down to the courtyard two hundred feet below.

King Anders leapt lightly to the nearest merlon, teetered upon it a moment, then caught his balance.

He stared out at the night sky until – sure enough – he saw three shooting stars streak overhead in rapid succession.

He took it as a sign. He was not sure of its meaning, but he felt comforted by it, just as he felt comforted by the wind gushing around the tower.

Here, so high above the city, the wind was stronger than anywhere below. It moved forcefully, pleasingly, stirring the hair of his body, tightening his nipples. It seethed across the distant plains below, buffeted him and teased him.

The city just outside the castle gates was silent at this time of night. The streets down in the merchant quarter were empty tonight.

Aroused, King Anders began to circle the tower, leaping lightly from merlon to merlon. Some dark corner of his brain knew that he must look mad. If any of his guardsmen were to spot him, or some inhabitant of his realm up late of night, they would have been astonished to see him leaping in the darkness upon the merlons of his tower, braving death with every step.

He did not care.

Sensation had its own logic. He liked risking death at every step. For years he had been consumed by worry, but in the past few months, he'd begun to overcome all fear.

Now he leapt swiftly, running ever faster. For a king with endowments of brawn and grace and metabolism, it was not a particularly dangerous feat.

Yet as he ran, he felt the danger. For often his feet scraped the lichens from the bare stone, so that his footing felt slippery and unsure, or the power in his legs brought him teetering on the edge.

Ah, to plunge! he thought in those moments. Ah, to be surrounded by air!

The urge was strong in him, so strong that King Anders could deny it no longer.

He raced to a merlon, stepped on the hunched back of a

gargoyle, and threw himself with all his might from his tower.

He plummeted, his legs still pumping, arms spread wide like an eagle's wings, his eyes half-closed in ecstasy.

And then he recognized his peril.

What of it? he thought. What of death? Even if he died, this taste of Air, this liveliest of breaths, was worth the price.

He looked to the west as he fell. The wind there stirred the fields, heaved toward him.

It rushed over the hills at a hundred miles per hour, perhaps two hundred, and then screamed above the city roofs.

King Anders closed his eyes, prepared to meet doom. His stomach rose into his chest as he fell.

Five feet from the ground, the wind caught him. It swirled around his torso, lifted him. It fondled his hair and his skin.

Anders opened his eyes, grinning fiercely.

He stared into a whirlwind. A veritable tornado was taking shape before him. Yet its base did not shift and writhe. Nor did it roar in its fury, but instead breathed as quietly as a sleeping babe.

Silently it whirled, drawing dust up from the city streets. Near its crest, Anders could see stars through the maelstrom as if they were eyes. The monstrous wind held Anders in its hands, lifted him high overhead.

Over the past months, Anders had dreamed of this possibility, had yearned for it. He'd hoped for it only distantly.

Anders cried aloud, 'Well met!,' and he laughed with sheer pleasure.

35

THE FOOD THAT SATISFIES

Averan clawed her way up from her shallow grave. Night lay thick on the village. Her stomach ached for want of food, but something more pernicious assailed her.

As a child of three, when the King decided to make her a skyrider, she'd been granted an endowment of brawn, one of stamina, and one of wit.

She'd always felt strong and tireless, and been able to remember things well. Now, she felt weak in both body and mind. Her thoughts seemed clouded.

I'm a commoner, she realized. Someone killed my Dedicates today.

It must have been horrible. Averan had flown over the Blue Tower on her way to the Courts of Tide many times. The enormous castle sitting out there in the ocean had always seemed so vast, so strong. She couldn't imagine anyone overthrowing it.

But she knew in her heart that someone had taken the Blue Tower, and in the darkness she felt forlorn and desolate, more than ever in her whole life, more even than when she'd had to leave Brand and everyone else at Keep Haberd.

I'm just a girl now, she thought. I'm a commoner, like everyone else. I'll never ride a graak again.

At the age of nine, her life had just ended.

Without her endowments, she imagined that she had no future.

She wanted to lie in the dirt and cry, but remembered

something Brand used to say. 'Riding a graak isn't easy. If you fall off, the first thing to do is to make sure that no bones are broken. Even if they are, you might have to get up and climb back on to fly to safety. If you can't do that, you'll never be a skyrider.'

Averan had fallen from her graak on landing a dozen times. She'd always gotten up.

Now, though she felt more desolate than ever, she merely bit her lip and looked around.

The dark, deserted village seemed much changed. The walnut trees lining the road hunched like sinister old men, and Averan worried about what might be hiding in their shadows. The cozy cottages, with their thatch roofs and hide windows now seemed as stark as tombs in the starlight.

The girl rose, and the air carried the scent of cool dampness. A strong wind lashed the ground. She pulled on her clothes.

The green woman climbed from her shallow grave and searched the sky longingly, squinting at the wind. 'Blood?' she begged.

'I don't know *where* you can get any blood,' Averan said. 'You can't have mine. Here, let's find something to eat.'

Averan gave the green woman her bearskin coat so that she wouldn't be naked.

Then Averan began looking through the garden for something to eat. As she got down on her knees, she told herself, Don't worry if you've lost your endowments. Just count yourself lucky. After all, you're not the one who died.

The garden soil was loose and well tended. Though the folks who had planted the garden had dug up the vegetables and carted them off, they'd done so hastily.

Earlier, Averan had seen a few small carrots and turnips still in the ground; the grape vine that climbed the stone fence still held a few grapes. She felt sure that so long as she stayed in the village, she'd be able to forage for enough food to keep her going for a day or so. She imagined that she'd find a few apples, pears, and plums on the ground by the trees.

Averan got on her knees, looking in the starlight for sign of the carrot leaves. As she crawled through the soil, she felt for the carrots rather than looked for them, since she knew the touch of their feathery leaves. She brushed the top of one carrot, but somehow knew without grasping its base that it was too small to eat. It would be stunted, thin and bitter.

Yet a moment later, she felt the urge to grasp in the soil at a spot where no carrot top protruded. When she did, she found a nice big carrot, hidden there in the dirt. Someone had tried to pull it from the ground and had only managed to rip off the top leaves. With a bit of wiggling, she pulled out a carrot as long as her forearm.

She held it, wondering how she'd known it was there.

For her part, the green woman gaped fearfully up at the sky. Each time the wind buffeted her, the green woman gasped in surprise and whipped about, as if afraid that some invisible hand had touched her.

Averan showed her prize to the green lady. 'Carrot,' she said. 'Carrot. Tastes pretty good, like blood, but it doesn't run away when you try to catch it.'

She held it for the green woman to see in the thin starlight, then took a big bite. The carrot was still dirty, but to Averan the dirt tasted as sweet as the carrot. She offered the green woman a bite.

The green woman bit off the end, then knelt on her haunches, chewing thoughtfully like a pup that has just discovered its first shoe.

Averan swallowed her prize quickly, and wanted more. She closed her eyes, crawled ahead in the garden half a second, trying to sense another carrot.

In moments, she found another with its top torn off, just as big as the first. She pulled it. The green woman inched over, looked at Averan's carrot. In near total darkness, she pulled another that had been hidden from Averan's view.

Of course she can find them it, too, Averan realized. We are creatures of the Earth now, and the Earth knows where its treasures are hid. 'All the fruits of the forest and of the field' are ours.

Something odd was happening. Though she'd lost her endowments, she'd gained something else.

I'm not a commoner, she decided. Not with green blood flowing through my veins.

Averan added some parsnips to her hoard, then walked under the trees at the side of the house, where she quickly 'found' figs that had fallen in tall grass where others couldn't see them. She soon added to her repast some mushrooms and hazelnuts.

When she had enough food, she led the green lady in the darkness to a large building at the center of town, some kind of guildhall or storehouse. Perhaps in the winter it served as a marketplace sheltered from the wind and rain. Or it may have been a songhouse built with a high roof so that the singer's voices would echo and fill the room. Now the building was empty, its huge doors thrown wide.

The green woman padded quietly behind Averan until they reached the open door. The doors were large enough so that a pair of hay wagons could easily drive through them into the building.

Averan peeked in. She could see nothing. But immediately she heard the desperate shrieks and whistles of ferrin. In moments, twenty of the hairy little man-shaped creatures raced from the building, seeking escape, afraid that Averan might try to kill them.

One ferrin ran over Averan's foot and tripped, rolled head over tail, spilling some crumbs that it carried in a scrap of cloth. Averan could have booted it across the street, but though she'd never liked ferrin, she'd never wished one dead, either.

'If the ferrin like it here, then this place should be safe,' Averan assured the green woman.

'If the ferrin like it here, then this place should be safe,' the green woman repeated.

Averan crept into the huge building. In its rafters high above, pigeons cooed querulously.

'I'll bet the ferrin were after those birds,' Averan said. In the pale light slanting in from the door, she spotted a pile of feathers on the floor. 'Looks like they got one.'

The green woman prowled over to the pile of feathers, sniffed at it. 'Blood, no?'

'I wouldn't eat it,' Averan agreed. 'Blood, no.'

The green woman looked mournful. She squatted on the floor and began munching a parsnip.

Averan sat next to her and gazed all about. Averan really had no idea what to do with her life, or where to go. She knew only that she wanted to get north.

She closed her eyes, imagined the big maps in the graak's aerie back home.

She felt the Earth King now, blazing like a green gem. But when she felt for him, her voice caught in her throat. 'The Earth King is coming south!' she said. 'He's come a long way already!'

Averan tried to eat some mushrooms. Even though they were fresh and nutty-tasting, they didn't satisfy. Her stomach craved something else. Aside from a crust of bread that Baron Goutgut had spared her last night, she hadn't eaten in two days. The mushrooms seemed somehow dry and without substance.

Averan nibbled at a fig, but didn't much care for it, either. She wanted better food. She craved a steak, sweet and juicy.

Averan reached into the little purse at her side and got out her wooden comb, began combing the garden soil from her hair. The green woman watched her with unabashed curiosity. When Averan finished her own hair, she took the comb to the green woman.

'Comb,' Averan said, showing her the item. 'I'm going to comb your hair.'

'My hair,' the green woman said. Averan grinned. The green woman had more than repeated, she'd showed that she understood the difference between 'mine' and 'yours.'

'You are a smart one,' Averan said. 'Beast master Brand used to have a crow that could talk, but it only repeated foolishness, and it died anyway. I don't care what Baron Roly-Poly says, you're smarter than a crow.'

'I are a smart one,' the green woman agreed.

Averan began trying to comb the green woman's hair, but the green woman kept moving her head around, trying to look up at the comb.

'Keep still,' Averan said, holding the green woman's head for a moment.

She tried to distract the creature. 'I think we should name you something, don't you? My name is Averan. And Roland's name is Roland, and Baron Poll is Baron Poll, even if I like to call him nastier things. Everyone has names. Would you like a name?'

'What . . . name?' the green woman asked. Averan stopped combing, wondered if the green woman really understood the question. It seemed impossible that she could understand.

'I don't know what to name you,' Averan said. 'You have green skin, so I suppose I could call you Greenie.' It was the first thing she thought of.

When Averan was little, she used to play with a five-year-old girl named Autumn Brown who lived down in Keep Haberd. Autumn had a white cat named Whitey and a red hound named Red. And Autumn's hair was brown, so the last name Brown fit her well enough. But Averan thought it was really stupid to name everything after its color.

'How do you like the name Olive, or Emerald? I know a woman named Emerald. If you squint, you can sort of see that she has greenish skin. But you're a much prettier green than she is.'

The green woman listened to each name, and tried them on her tongue, but did not seem impressed.

'How about Spinach?' Averan joked.

'Spinach?' the green woman said thoughtfully.

'It's a plant, a kind of lettuce.' Averan finished combing the snarls from the green woman's hair. The green woman hadn't yelped or complained even once. 'There, I'm all done. Don't worry, we'll come up with a name that fits you true.'

The green woman grabbed Averan's hand. 'True name?' the green woman asked in a strange tone, as if she had just remembered something. 'True name?'

Averan paused. Magical creatures had true names, names that must never be spoken in public, lest an enemy learn it.

'Yes, true name,' Averan said. 'My true name is Averan. Your true name is . . . ?'

The green woman looked up, but in the shadows, Averan could not really make out her features. The green woman chanted in a commanding tone, 'Arise now from the dust, my champion! Clothe yourself in flesh. I call you by your true name: Foul Deliverer, Fair Destroyer.'

Averan stepped back. The green woman's tone, her whole demeanor, had changed so completely as she spoke that she seemed to be another person. Averan knew the green woman was repeating something she had heard, repeating it exactly. If Averan had doubted that the green woman was magical – if she'd thought even for an instant that she was but an oddly colored woman from some distant realm beyond the Caroll Sea – that doubt was now erased.

Averan didn't want to look afraid, so she stepped close again and stroked the green woman's hair. She didn't particularly like the sound of the green woman's name: Foul Deliverer, Fair Destroyer.

If the green woman was indeed a 'Foul Deliverer,' a 'Fair Destroyer,' whom was she meant to deliver, and what would she destroy?

'That's a nice true name,' Averan assured the green woman. 'But I think we should come up with something shorter. I'll call you Spring from now on. Spring.' Averan touched the green woman as she spoke the name.

A strong gust of wind slammed the huge building, and one vast door swung on its squeaky hinges. Averan hadn't known the building had a chimney, but suddenly she heard the wind moan up its stone throat.

The green woman leapt to her feet and shouted wordlessly in rage or terror.

'It's only the wind,' Averan said. 'It won't hurt you. I think a storm is coming.'

'Wind?' the green woman asked. 'Wind?' She backed to the far side of the room. Averan followed, found the green woman huddled in a corner.

'Good girl,' Averan said calmly. 'This is a good place. The wind won't find us here.'

Averan put her arms around the green woman. The powerful creature felt as if her muscles were made of iron, yet she shook from terror.

Averan had nowhere to go and nothing to do. She held the green woman and sang a lullaby. Averan's mother used to sing lullabies when Averan was young, so Averan now sang:

'The wind blows wild tonight,
sweet and wild tonight.
It shakes the trees,
but don't let it shake your knees.
It's only the wind, my child, good night.'

The green woman didn't go to sleep. Averan felt more hungry than tired herself, so she talked to the green woman long into the night, telling her stories and the names for things, trying to teach the green woman to speak, while keeping her calm and distracted.

Near dawn, the green woman slapped her hand over Averan's mouth, as if warning her to shut up.

Every muscle in the green woman's body tensed, and she climbed to one knee and sniffed the air. 'Blood, yes,' she whispered longingly.

Averan's heart began thumping.

Raj Ahten's men are outside, Averan thought. The green woman smells Invincibles.

Averan looked all around the building. It was huge and empty. It offered nowhere to hide, only shelter from the wind.

But the building's support posts were made of thick oak, and heavy beams crisscrossed the posts every few feet. The beams formed a sort of ladder that led up to the rafters where the pigeons roosted.

If a ferrin can climb those beams in the dark, Averan thought, I can, too.

She went to the wall, put her hands on the nearest beam, which was chest high, and climbed on top of it, then continued up to the next and the next.

She was surprised at how hard it was to climb, without her endowment of brawn. It was dangerous work. Mud-dauber wasps had built nests on some of the beams, and cobwebs were everywhere. The rough-hewn beams had big splinters in them.

Averan worried that she might get stung by a wasp, or bitten by a spider, or cut her hand.

Worse yet, she could lose her grip and fall.

In less than a minute she scurried thirty feet up the wall to the juncture of the rafters.

Here, no starlight made its way into the building at all. She felt secure in such total darkness, though she had to find the rafters and climb onto them by feel alone.

'Spring,' Averan whispered, 'come up here.'

The green woman remained crouched on the floor, like a cat ready to spring. If she understood Averan's plea, she did not show it. She looked instead as if she would hunt, and this frightened Averan.

How strong could the green woman possibly be? Averan wondered. The green woman had fallen thousands of feet from the sky without getting killed or badly hurt – but she did bleed.

If she met one of Raj Ahten's Invincibles, would she stand a chance against him? What if she met a whole bunch of them?

The green woman might be as strong as an Invincible, but she was not a trained warrior with endowments of metabolism.

Against a faster opponent, she'd be killed in seconds.

'Please, Spring!' Averan whispered. 'Come and hide.'

But Spring remained wary. 'Blood, yes,' she growled fiercely. The green woman's hunger made Averan's mouth water.

She'd wanted the taste of blood yesterday morning, when she'd looked at the assassin's corpse on the hillside. Now, though carrots and parsnips partly filled Averan's belly, Averan thought longingly of the assassin, and hoped that the green woman would kill someone.

No, I don't hope that, Averan told herself. I don't want blood.

'Spring, get up here right now!' Averan whispered.

But immediately Averan heard a sound that made her blood chill. Outside the building a hissing erupted, a dry buzz deeper in tone than that of a rattlesnake, a sound she'd heard only once before – the sound a reaver makes as air rattles through the chitinous flaps under its abdomen. At Keep Haberd, Averan had flown low over the reavers. She had heard tens of thousands of them making that rattling all at once.

Now she heard only one, exhaling slowly, just outside the door.

It must have followed me from Keep Haberd! Averan thought wildly. Then, more reasonably, she reminded herself that it couldn't possibly be true. I rode most of the way on old Leatherneck, she told herself. Even reavers couldn't have trailed me. No, this has to be some sort of scout.

Averan had heard that reavers often sent out scouts. She also knew that reavers preferred to hunt on warm, sultry nights, when the weather most closely mimicked the conditions of their lairs in the Underworld. Tonight it was moist and cool, not reaver weather at all.

She'd also heard that reavers hunted by sound, scent, and motion. If she stayed here in the rafters and did not speak or move, she might be safe.

She yearned to yell a warning to the green woman below, but dared not so much as whisper.

Outside the building, the reaver hissed. The green woman raised her head and shouted in delight; then she leapt up and raced to meet it.

The reaver charged to the huge open doors.

It stood some twenty feet at the shoulder, so that even

though Averan hid in the rafters above it, she could have leapt on its back without getting hurt.

Its huge leathery head was as big as the bed of a large wagon, and rows and rows of crystalline teeth filled its mouth. Reavers had no eyes or ears or nose, but along the back of its head, feelers fanned out like snakes. Runes of power were tattooed onto its head, on its forehead and in columns near its leathery upper lips. The runes shone silver in the darkness, glowing with their own ghostlight.

The reaver's four long legs were dark and thin and gleamed like bone. Its huge forearms had three-toed hands with great claws, each claw curved like an assassin's khivar and just as long.

The reaver bore a weapon in its foreclaws, an enormous blade with a hilt of crystal, as if carved from reaver bone. The sword's thick blade was slightly curved and three times the length of a man.

The reaver hissed and swung the blade overhead in a great arc, as if to bring it crashing down upon the green woman, but the blade bit deep into a rafter beam just a few yards from Averan, then stuck, hanging over the green woman's head.

The green woman shouted in glee and raced toward the reaver.

Involuntarily, Averan shouted, 'Spring, stop!'

But the green woman did not stop. She merely drew a rune in the air, a couple of quick movements of the hand, and then raced forward.

When she slapped the reaver's jaw, the effect was astonishing: there was a clap like thunder, and shards of crystalline bone exploded through the reaver's flesh.

Averan gasped. Nothing should do that, she told herself. No warhammer or maul – even if it were wielded by a warrior with twenty endowments of brawn – could have dealt a reaver such a fearsome blow.

But Averan had seen it clearly in the starlight.

The reaver hissed in pain and tried to lurch backward, but could hardly move.

The green woman leapt at it, and slapped the reaver's face again, to the same effect. The sound of the blow echoed from the rafters.

This time the reaver shuddered and dropped lifeless to the ground.

The green woman climbed atop it, stuck a slender arm deep into the reaver's leathery head, and pulled out a handful of its brains.

Ichor streamed from the reaver's wounds.

It was said that a reaver had no scent of its own, but only tried to mimic the scents of those things around it.

Yet as Averan stood clinging to the rafters in terror, she realized that the green woman *had* smelled the reaver.

In the closed room, the stench of the reaver's ichor was overwhelming, and now Averan could smell it, rich and sweet. She had not eaten much for days. Even the food she'd tried had not satisfied her, and she'd thought she craved a nice and juicy steak.

Now her mouth watered as if she were a starving thing who had seldom seen a crust of bread.

She knew what she needed, what she craved.

Averan scrambled down the support beams of the huge shed, too excited to sit still. She wanted to wet herself in terror, for the scent of reaver blood was so alluring that she knew she could not resist, not now, not ever again.

Reavers. She needed to eat reavers. But unlike the green woman, Averan had no way to kill her own.

She raced to the corpse.

'Foul Deliverer, Fair Destroyer,' the green woman had called herself. Now Averan knew what she had been created to destroy.

And dimly Averan understood a bit more of her own destiny. The green woman's blood now flowed through Averan's veins, and somehow they had become one in nature.

Averan could not resist the impulse to climb atop the reaver, thrust in her own hands and eat greedily from the sweet meat that rested warm and juicy inside the reaver's crystalline skull.

'Mmm . . . mmm,' the green woman crooned as she fed. 'Blood, yes.'

'Blood, yes,' Averan agreed as she shoved meat into her mouth.

She knew some lore about reavers. Averan knew that when a reaver died, its kinsmen consumed it. As they did, they took upon themselves the reaver's lore of magic, and its strength, so that the oldest reavers, those that had fed most on their younger kin, became the greatest: the most powerful sorcerers, the most valiant warriors.

Finally Averan had found a food that satisfied, that sent the blood quickening through her veins. Even as Averan sated herself with the sweet meat of her first reaver, she felt herself responding to it.

This shouldn't happen, Averan told herself. People don't get strong from eating reavers. People don't get anything but sick from eating reavers. I'm not a reaver.

Yet she glutted herself and thanked the earth powers for this gift.

36

TARGETS IN THE DARK

As the watchman blew the horns calling for Gaborn's troops to prepare to mount up, Myrrima felt restless. She felt eager to ride to Carris. The midnight ride would be stimulating, and she was glad she would have to carry only two pups with her now, rather than four.

So she saddled her mount, then began doing the same to Iome's. Her pups played in the stable as she worked, running about, sniffing at each horse's stall, chasing one another's tails.

She had just bridled and blanketed Iome's mount when Jureem entered the stables. 'Do not bother,' he said in his thick Taifan accent. 'Her Majesty pleases not to ride tonight, but instead will wait for tomorrow.'

'Dawn?' Myrrima asked. That would waste six hours.

'Later,' Jureem answered. 'At dawn she plans to eat, then take endowments from her pups. She will not want to carry dogs with her into battle, and her horse is fast enough so that it can overtake the main body of the army.'

Myrrima and Iome had claimed their pups at the same time. If Iome was right, Myrrima might also take endowments from her last two pups by dawn. It *would* be better to take those endowments before traveling. Iome couldn't very well ride into Fleeds with four pups in her saddlebags, lest everyone in Rofehavan mark her as a Wolf Lord.

Myrrima hated the idea of waiting. It had very nearly cost her life to wait for Iome yesterday.

Yet she couldn't very well leave without Iome. The Queen

needed a woman to escort her, and Iome thought of Myrrima as her Maid of Honor, thought Myrrima hoped to be more than that.

'Very well,' Myrrima said, vowing that she would not waste the night. At least she could take her bow and practice some more.

She untied the bow from its sheath, grabbed her pups under one arm, and headed toward the stable door, just as Gaborn entered.

She smelled him before she saw him, and what she smelled was death most foul, a stench that made her want to howl in fear and to vomit.

It seemed to stretch from one wall to the other, a vast specter of death that groped toward her. Her vision went black, and her senses reeled.

Myrrima dropped her bow and puppies. She cried out in shock, 'Back! Get back!'

The pups yelped in terror and ran into an empty stall, where they began to bark and howl mournfully.

Myrrima cowered on the floor, crouched in a fetal position, and wrapped her hands over her head. Every muscle of her body seemed to spasm in pain.

'Back, my master!' she cried. 'Please, go back!'

Yet Gaborn stood in the doorway not forty paces off, wearing an expression of alarm. 'What?' he asked. 'What have I done? Are you ill?'

'Please!' Myrrima cried, looking about for some means of escape. But this stable was no ordinary stable. Force horses were kept here, and they needed protection. The only entrance was the front door, and guards who held the portcullis secured that. 'Stay back! You bring the scent of death with you.'

Gaborn stared hard at her for a long moment, then smiled. 'You're a wolf lord now?'

Myrrima nodded mutely, heart pounding, unable to speak.

Gaborn reached into his pocket, pulled out a single dark green spade-shaped leaf. 'It's dogbane you smell, nothing more. I found it growing down the street.'

The smell came fifty times stronger now that he held the horror in his hand, and the terror that it inspired in Myrrima was like a hot branding iron burning into her guts. She cried out and turned her face against a wall, shaking.

'Please, milord,' she begged. 'Please . . .' She could see the leaf, and she knew that Gaborn's powers as Earth King caused him to magnify its normal properties. She knew that the single leaf was the source of this horrible dread that assailed her.

Yet now that she'd taken an endowment of scent from a dog, knowledge meant nothing. The unspeakable terror that the scent inspired to a dog's nose could not be rationalized away.

Gaborn backed off, retraced his steps. As soon as he had left the stable, Myrrima grabbed the squirming pups, bolted out the door.

She saw Gaborn at the far side of the street, where he was setting the horrible leaf on the ground.

'I hoped it would help drive off Raj Ahten and his assassins,' he said. 'I'm sorry it did not occur to me to consider how it might affect you or Duke Groverman.'

'I fear it will protect you from *me* now – and from your wife.'

Gaborn nodded. 'Thank you for the warning. I will throw this robe away and wash the scent from my skin with parsley water, so that when next we meet, you will not find my presence so unbearable.'

'You do me honor, Your Highness,' Myrrima said, finally remembering her manners.

'Everything comes with a price,' Gaborn said. 'May your endowments serve you well.'

Myrrima took her bow and left the King's presence, recovering enough so that after twenty minutes, she no longer trembled. She went out to a green behind the Duke's Great Hall and there found the archery field.

She set her pups down, and let them gambol on the grass.

A steep dirt embankment rose high to the north, and a couple of straw men had been set up before the embankment.

Myrrima measured off eighty paces, studied the straw men.
She had only three blunted practice arrows. The rest were
sharp instruments of war.

Absently, Myrrima strung her bow. She had purchased the
bow only two days before. She loved the feel of its oiled wood,
the strength of it. It was no weak thing made of elm or ash
or laburnum. Instead, it was a war bow made of yew, which
Sir Hoswell had assured Myrrima had the right proportion of
red heartwood in the belly of the bow to white sap wood at
its spine. The bow was six inches taller than herself, and
pulling it was hard.

Only two days ago, Hoswell had warned her to properly
care for her bow so that the wood would not warp from expos-
ure to dampness, or become weakened from idly staying
strung for too long.

He'd told her how to work lacquer deep into the grain,
rubbing it in circular motions clockwise, then counterclock-
wise. He'd taught her the proper way to apply beeswax onto
the catgut strings.

As she strung it, Myrrima felt the string, to make sure it
had dried during the day. She feared for her bow, for it had
fallen into the water.

On each bow, a bit of hollow cow's horn was glued with
a mixture of birch pitch and charcoal dust over the nock
where the bowstrings met the bow's wings. The horn kept
moisture from entering the wood if the wing idly touched wet
soil, but Sir Hoswell had warned Myrrima that the horn should
be dried by fire once or twice a year, then soaked in linseed
oil, so that the horn itself would keep out moisture. As a
matter of precaution, he had warned that she should never
let the end of the bow rest on the ground. Myrrima felt each
of the horns, to make sure that they were also dry.

When the bow was strung, Myrrima took out a practice
arrow, felt its smooth shaft.

All of the lords of Rofehavan used a common method for
honing a straight arrow, but Hoswell warned her against using
any arrow made within the past few weeks. The arrowsmiths

of Heredon had been working day and night, straightening green wood that was likely to warp. Such arrows might not fly straight and would more likely bend on impact with armor than to penetrate it.

Hoswell had taught her the styles of bodkins, the long arrowheads used for war, and warned her to employ only those that had a blue sheen to them, for they were made of the hardest steel and could puncture an Indhopalese helm. He warned her to sharpen each individual arrow in her quiver before battle, and to apply pitch to its tip, so that it would better hold to and pierce armor.

Myrrima nocked a blunted practice arrow, drew it full to the ear, and steadied her breath before she released it. She watched where the arrow fell – high and to the right – then tried a second shot, adjusting her stance in an effort to aim more true.

The second shot also went high and to the right, but not so high.

Myrrima bit her lip, sighed in exasperation. She felt inadequate to the task. She'd shot much better yesterday. A small part of her almost wished that she had Erin Connal here to instruct her.

Releasing her third arrow, she hit the straw man's shoulder.

Once she launched her arrows, she could not see where they landed. She managed to find them in the embankment by scent, along with an extra arrow someone else had lost. Without her endowment of scent, she'd never have found the arrows in the dark. The starlight was not strong enough to illuminate the white feathers.

When she returned to her place, she heard the horn call the troops to mount. She heard creaking armor, the muffled shouts of men ordering their anxious force horses to steady. The fields were awash with starlight, a satin glow. The half-moon struggled over the hills to the east.

She wished she could leave with Gaborn and the other warriors.

A voice from the darkness greeted her.

'Very good. You are taking time to practice.' She looked over her shoulder.

Sir Hoswell walked toward her from the shadows of the Duke's Great Hall.

Myrrima suddenly realized that she was alone with him, here in the darkness, where no one could see.

'What are you doing here?' she demanded. Myrrima reached into her quiver, pulled out an arrow, a good straight shaft with a heavy bodkin, for piercing armor. She quickly nocked the arrow and drew it full, ready to shoot Hoswell down, if need be.

Sir Hoswell stopped, studied her frankly, almost daring her to shoot.

'We are going to war tomorrow, and I am an archer – first and foremost,' Hoswell said easily. 'I came to practice. I didn't know you were here. I am not following you.'

'Why don't I believe you?' Myrrima asked.

'Because, quite frankly, I have not earned your trust,' Hoswell said. 'Nor your respect, nor your friendship. I fear I never shall.'

Myrrima searched her feelings. Yesterday when she'd been in danger, Gaborn had warned her by using his powers. Now she felt no fear, no warning.

But she didn't trust him. Myrrima's heart was hammering, and she watched Hoswell carefully. The man had endowments of metabolism, and could have covered the eighty yards in seconds, but not before she loosed an arrow. Even in the starlight, she could see that his face was still swollen from where Erin Connal had hit him.

'Get out of here,' Myrrima said, drawing back her arrow, taking steady aim.

Sir Hoswell raised his bow and quiver high, regarded her coolly. He smiled as if in appreciation. 'It's hard to shoot a man, isn't it?' he said. 'You have nice control. You're holding your breath, keeping a steady hand. You'd make a fine assassin.'

Myrrima didn't say anything. She didn't want his compliments.

'I'll give you to the count of three,' she warned.

'When shooting at night,' Hoswell taunted, 'the tired eye does not judge distance well. Lower your aim a bit, Myrrima, or you'll never hit me.'

'One!' Myrrima said, dropping her aim a tad.

'There,' Hoswell said. 'That should skewer me nicely. Now, practice shooting quickly. If you cannot take fifteen shots a minute in a pitched battle, you will be of little use.'

'Two!' Myrrima said coldly.

Hoswell caught her eye half a moment, his weapons still in the air. Myrrima's fingers felt sweaty, and she decided to loose the arrow just as Hoswell turned his back and began to amble away.

'We are on the same side, Lady Borenson,' Hoswell said with his back to her. He had not taken a pace yet, and Myrrima wasn't sure whether to drill a hole through him or not. 'Tomorrow night we may be in battle together.'

Myrrima did not answer. He glanced over his shoulder toward her.

'Three!' Myrrima said.

Hesitantly, Sir Hoswell began to stalk away. She kept her eyes trained on him. He walked twenty paces then stopped, spoke loudly over his shoulder. 'You were right, Lady Borenson. I did follow you here tonight. I came because honor demands it – or perhaps dishonor. I came to offer my apology. I did a vile thing, and I am sorry for it.'

'Keep your apology. You're afraid I'll tell my husband,' Myrrima said. 'Or the King.'

Sir Hoswell turned toward her, raised his weapons. 'Tell them if you wish,' he said. 'They might well kill me for what I've done, as easily as you may kill me now. My life is in your hands.'

The very notion of forgiving him came hard. She didn't know if she had the stomach for it. She'd as soon forgive Raj Ahten himself.

'How can I trust you?' Myrrima said.

Sir Hoswell shrugged slightly, still holding his weapons out so that she could see. 'What happened two days ago – I've never done anything like that before,' Hoswell said. 'It was foolish, impulsive – the act of a lout. I thought you comely, and I hoped that you would want me as I wanted you. I was terribly wrong.

'But I can make it up to you,' Hoswell said with certainty. 'My life is yours. Tomorrow, when you ride into battle, I will stand beside you. I swear that so long as I live, you will live. I will be your protector.'

Myrrima searched her feelings. Yesterday when she'd been in danger, Gaborn had warned her using his earth power. Now she heard no warning voice. Only her own natural fear of the man tore at her. She suspected that Hoswell's offer was sincere. She did not want his apology, nor his service, and in the end, perhaps only one thought kept him alive. If Gaborn can forgive Raj Ahten, she reasoned, can I not forgive this man?

Sir Hoswell walked away.

Myrrima stood for a long while, until her heart quit hammering.

By the time the dawn sun came into the sky, Myrrima had practiced for hours.

37

AFTER THE FEAST

The reaver's leathery head was slippery with gore by the time that Averan finished gorging upon its brain. Sated, she lay back upon its skull, her stomach heavy, and sat for a long while feeling muzzy.

Dawn was but a few hours away. She could hardly keep her eyes open.

Flashes of dreams assailed her, terrifying visions of the Underworld, overwhelmingly vivid.

She dreamt of long lines of reavers, marching up from the Underworld, desperately seeking something. A powerful mage drove them where they would not go, a horrid beast called the One True Master.

But the visions showed nothing as she'd ever seen it. For the dreams were revealed not in sight, but in powerful odors and in a sense of quivering movement and the shimmering aura of energy fields that surrounded all living things. The dreams were cold, ghostly, showing energy as waves of blue light, like the evening sky reflecting from snow. Everything in them was preternaturally clear. And the reavers sang songs, eloquent arias emitted in scents too subtle for a human to detect.

For a long while, Averan lay torpid, trying to remember what she searched for in her dream. Then it came:

The Blood of the Faithful.

Averan's eyes snapped open, and she lay for a moment trying to stifle a scream. For deep in her gut, she knew that

she'd not experienced any common dream. These were memories, memories from the reaver she'd eaten.

The reavers were coming. They were coming and would
march right through this town.

Full of reaver's brain, still muzzy, Averan began to recognize her own precarious situation.

'We've got to get out of here,' Averan told the green woman
as she crawled from atop the reaver's head. 'A fell mage is
coming. We might already be too late.'

Averan crawled off the dead reaver, and prepared to begin
her race north.

Desperately, she tried to conjure the images she'd seen in
her dreams. The reavers could not 'see' far with their sense
of energy fields – a quarter of a mile was their limit. Things
close by could be discerned with great detail, while objects a
hundred yards out were often fuzzy and indistinct.

So long as Averan stayed ahead of the scouts, she would
be safe. But the reavers had a supreme sense of smell.

And the green woman had killed a blade-bearer, one that
would soon be followed by countless thousands. The reavers
would get Averan's scent, and would hunt her down.

Averan had to escape – quickly. A force horse would be
best. It could run fast and far.

But Averan didn't have a horse.

The Earth King could protect us, Averan thought.

She closed her eyes, consulted the map in her heart. The
emerald flame was coming, had traveled nearly two hundred
miles. But the Earth King was still far away, in southern
Heredon.

At the rate he traveled, he wouldn't make it here until
tonight or tomorrow. Averan didn't have anywhere near so
much time.

A reaver was over twice as tall as a horse. She'd seen how
fast the reavers ran.

She looked at the reaver, lifeless in the darkness.

Down near its bunghole it secreted its scents, leaving a trail
for others to follow. The monster had been terrified before it

died, to feel the green woman's hand crushing its skull. She could smell it dimly now, the reaver's last emitted garlicky scent.

An hour ago, she'd never have noticed the scent. Now, it seemed to whisper volumes.

Averan raced around to the monster's bunghole, and came up close to it. Her human nose was not nearly as sensitive as a reaver's philia, but she smelled the reaver's last secretion, and the odor hit her not as a flavor, but as if it shouted words: 'Death is here! Beware! Beware!'

The green woman came beside Averan, sniffed. She drew back and shouted wordlessly, flailing her arms. For, like Averan, now that she had fed upon a reaver's brain, the green woman reacted to the reaver's scent as if she herself were a reaver – with abject terror.

Clouds were racing above. In the starlight, Averan looked until she found a long stick that might work as a staff, then she shoved one end into the reaver's bunghole, until the scent of the monster's dying warning lay thick upon her stave.

'Come on, Spring,' Averan called to the green woman. 'Let's go.'

But the green woman could smell death on Averan's staff, and merely backed away. Spring looked about for someplace to escape, held her hands in front of her face. In moments Averan feared that the green woman would bolt.

Averan suspected that if Spring did run away, the reavers would track her down and kill her. Spring had managed to slay a single reaver, but she might not fare so well against dozens of them. Certainly she'd never kill a fell mage.

'Spring!' Averan shouted. But the green woman would have none of it. She turned to run, flailing her arms wildly as she sprinted through the village street toward some cottages that huddled like frowth giants, throwing dark shadows everywhere.

Averan tried to get her attention the only way she knew how. 'Foul Deliverer, Fair Destroyer, follow me!'

The effect was astonishing. It looked almost as if Spring

had an invisible string attached to her back. When Averan spoke, the green woman abruptly jerked to a halt, turned and stared at Averan in dismay. She began walking back.

'That's right,' Averan said. 'I'm your master now. Follow me, and be quiet. We don't want to attract any more reavers.'

Spring's face fell, but she turned and followed Averan obediently.

Averan sprinted along the road north. The night was cold, and the wind blew wild in the lane between the walnut trees. Brown leaves skittered in her path, and clouds raced overhead, carrying the smell of rain.

Averan thought she might be able to run for only a few minutes. Ever since the Blue Tower had fallen, she'd felt weak.

But to her surprise, the warm meat of the reaver that she'd eaten suffused her with unexpected energy. She felt stronger – although not strong enough to crush a man's skull with a single blow, or anything fancy like that. It wasn't the same as getting an endowment of brawn. But she did feel more . . . energetic, more invigorated.

The meat of the reaver seemed to work as a strangely powerful tonic for her body.

Averan raced tirelessly for nearly an hour, running faster than any child her age should, with the green woman loping beside her.

Every two hundred yards or so, Averan would turn and swipe her staff across the ground, and she would imagine with delight how the shout of 'Death! Beware! Beware!' would frighten the blade-bearers on her trail.

Without their proteds, they'll have no choice in how they react, she thought. They'll be forced to close ranks, take defensive formations, and crawl ahead at a snail's pace.

Averan stopped dead in her tracks. How do I know that? she wondered. She couldn't recall anything specific from her dreams, her borrowed memories, that let her know how the reavers would react, how the blade-bearers would be forced to react. But she knew.

Yet many questions continued to puzzle her. Who was the

One True Master? What did it want? She knew that it wanted the Blood of the Faithful, and that it was human blood, but what would it do with it?

An image flashed in her mind: an enormous reaver, the One True Master, crouched upon a bed of the crystalline bones of those she had vanquished, resplendent among the holy fires, instructing her inferiors how to create the runes that would usurp and dismay the Earth.

Averan knew that the reavers were heading for Carris. The Blood of the Faithful was near there.

Poor Roland, she thought. I hope he gets out of there quickly.

Her best hope of reaching the Earth King would be to go into the mountains. Maybe then the reavers wouldn't follow her. When she reached a crossroads, she turned east, taking a mule trail along a canal.

Since the reavers couldn't 'see' more than a quarter of a mile in any direction, she could evade them by keeping far enough ahead of them.

She also knew that when she walked across the ground, she left an energy trail that reavers perceived as a ghostly glow. But half an hour after she crossed a field, the glow would dissipate. And the reaver's depth perception was too poor to let them easily detect her footprints.

Which meant that they'd have to hunt her by scent alone.

When Averan was small, beast master Brand used to tell her stories about how he'd helped the Duke outsmart foxes on the foxhunt.

Duke Habered had been the kind of man who would pay a huntsman to trap a wild fox, then pour turpentine on its back to make sure that his hounds never lost the fox's scent.

So for a fox to survive it had to be crafty.

Whenever the dogs got close, the fox would race ahead and run in circles and curlicues, letting its scent get so twisted that the dogs behind wound up barking at their own tails.

Then the fox would find some low hill and lie behind a

bush, watching the dogs, just to make sure that none ever came close.

The reavers were much like hounds, and Averan had to outfox them. So as she ran along the canal, she sprinted here and there for nearly two hours, often circling.

She was still on the flatlands east of Carris, but the towns had thinned out. She knew this place from maps, and had even flown over it on her graak.

Farther west were a few hills and valleys, then the Hest Mountains. She hoped to make it there, for she doubted that the reavers would follow her into the Hests, where it was so cold.

When she judged that she had neared the end of the canal, she took a brief trip through some woods, racing about in circles, doubling back over her own steps, climbing in trees so that her scent would be lost overhead. She painted every tree with the words 'Beware!'

A cold drizzle began to fall. Averan doubled back to the canal and jumped in, swam for the far shore.

The green woman followed Averan faithfully, if somewhat clumsily, through all of this. But as soon as Spring leapt into the canal, it became obvious that Averan's plan had gone astray.

The green woman didn't know how to swim. She thrashed about, kicking and squealing and bobbing under. She looked about desperately, swatting the surface of the water.

Averan tried to swim back to save her, but without her endowment of brawn, Averan swam slowly, sluggishly. When she finally did reach Spring, the green woman climbed atop Averan, pushing her under.

She fought to get to the surface, but Spring was too strong. Averan realized that it was no use, that Spring would merely hold her. So Averan dove desperately, until she touched the muddy canal bottom, then pushed up and away.

She broke the surface. The green woman went under, thrashing.

Averan caught her breath. The green woman quit splashing; she had gone down for the last time.

Averan's heart pounded. 'Spring!' she called. 'Spring!'

But the surface of the canal remained calm.

For several heartbeats, Averan wondered what to do. Then Spring floated to the top.

Averan swam to her, grabbed the woman's bearskin cloak from behind, and pulled the unconscious form to the far bank. She dragged Spring's head from the water, turned her over.

The green woman coughed and gagged and cried like a child. When she quit throwing up muddy canal water, Averan helped her up the bank. She looked around in the darkness.

Averan had lost her staff in the struggle to save Spring. Even though the water was sluggish, Averan judged that the current had carried them both a quarter of a mile downstream. She'd wanted the staff to help scare off the reavers, but doubted that she'd be able to find it in the dark.

Averan staggered to her feet. By now, she imagined that she was still eight miles west of Carris, and another six miles south. She wanted to turn north, but felt afraid. She could see fires burning on the hills south of Carris.

The wind blew wild, and the clouds had thickened so that Averan could hardly see. Rain pelted her in heavy droplets. There was no way she could get her staff.

Maybe if I'm lucky, we'll get lightning, Averan hoped. Everyone knew that reavers were afraid of lightning, though no one knew why. But Averan had feasted on a reaver's brain and learned its secrets. Now she understood better: lightning did not frighten reavers so much as it blinded them and caused them pain. To be near lightning was like staring into the sun.

I'm the only person in the world who knows this, Averan realized. Somehow, she had done something no one else ever had: she'd eaten a reaver's brain and gained its memories, just as if she were a reaver herself.

Unfortunately, though rain fell, there was no sign of a thunderstorm.

Wearily, after hours of running, Averan limped west, jogging for an hour while the green woman began to lag behind. An hour before dawn, she heard an odd noise in the distance toward Carris, a strange groaning that shook the earth. A bit later, birds in the meadows began to chirp as they wakened. She thought it odd that the birds would make such joyous noise on such a dismal day.

Near dawn she found a wooded hill on the north side of the road, and decided to play the part of the fox.

So she hunkered down in some scrub oak and tall ferns, in the lee of a huge pine. She waited for sunrise. From her perch, she imagined that she'd be able to see the giant reavers coming for miles, if the monsters didn't lose her trail.

Spring lay beside Averan, in her bearskin cloak. Averan pulled Spring's cloak open enough so that she could crawl under 'it. The cloak was still damp, but Averan lay warm against the green woman's breast.

38

A COLD WIND AT CARRIS

The wind at Carris had shifted an hour before dawn, driving from the northeast and becoming bitterly cold. With the fog beneath and lowering clouds rushing in overhead, it became darker rather than lighter as morning approached.

The greatest source of light came from Raj Ahten's flameweavers, clothed in living flame, who had driven back the fog at the end of the causeway. Raj Ahten stood between those pillars of light, gazing up at the men on the walls. Frowth giants, war dogs, and Invincibles glowered at his back.

'If it is battle you want, then come against us!' Duke Paldane called valiantly. 'But if you hope to find refuge in Carris, you hope in vain. We will not surrender at any cost!'

All around Roland, men raised their weapons, began beating sword and hammer against shield in brutal applause.

Raj Ahten gauged and dismissed Paldane all in a glance. Instead, he looked up at the men along the castle walls, and as he did so his gaze strayed to Roland. Roland tried to hold his eyes, but could not. The challenge there, the look of supreme confidence, cut Roland to the quick, and for the first time in his life he realized what a weak, pitiable thing he truly was. One by one, the men on the walls quit banging weapon to shield.

'Brave sentiments,' Raj Ahten said to Paldane. Distantly, from the far edges of the predawn fog below, Roland began to hear distant battle horns, the high horns of Indhopal blowing wildly. With it came a faraway beating of drums, a thunderous boom, boom, boom. A giant at Raj Ahten's back glanced to the south, while warhorses minced their feet nervously.

'They're blowing full retreat,' Baron Poll said in wonder at Roland's side. Somewhere out in that fog, perhaps five miles off, Raj Ahten's troops were in flight. Had the Knights Equitable come? Or warriors from the Courts of Tide?

In rash hope, someone on the wall shouted, 'The Earth King is coming! That's put the fear into them!'

A trio of dark creatures rippled up from the fog, whipped past Roland's ear. At first he thought they were bats. But they were too small, and the things writhed in the air like pain given form. He recognized them as gree, creatures of the Underworld seldom seen aboveground.

'Begone!' Paldane shouted at Raj Ahten. 'You'll find no shelter here! Archers!'

Raj Ahten raised his hand toward the archers, commanding them without words to belay the order. While other mounts shifted about in fear, his gray Imperial warhorse stood calmly.

'It is not the Earth King who comes from the south,' Raj Ahten said loudly enough for every man on the wall to hear. Indeed, the words seemed to slide into Roland's subconscious, piercing him like a knife blade, so that they aroused a subtle fear. 'Nor is it salvation for you in the form of reinforcements. Duke Paldane knows what hails from the south; his messengers passed through our lines. Reavers are boiling from the Underworld by the tens of thousands. They'll be here within the hour.'

Roland's heart hammered and his mouth felt as dry as dust. Reavers, he thought in mounting horror. In sixteen hundred years, men and reavers had not fought a major surface battle. From time to time Roland heard stories of men who lived on the borders of the Alcair who were slaughtered by reavers or dragged to their lairs to be eaten later.

But reavers had never in living memory attacked a castle at full strength – not until they hit Keep Haberd.

Roland would have rather fought Raj Ahten twice over than

face a reaver horde. After all, a lucky blow might bring a force warrior down, but a reaver stood taller than an elephant. No damned little commoner with a half-sword was likely to even pierce its skin.

Still the fog hid everything in the fields around Carris. Distantly Roland began to hear a hissing roar, like the pounding of surf against sand. Minutely, the walls of the castle trembled.

Raj Ahten said, 'You don't have the force soldiers to defend this rock against reavers. But I do.

'Kneel to me now!' Raj Ahten called. 'Kneel to your lord and master. Open your gates! Kneel to me, and I shall protect you!'

Without thought, without willing himself to, Roland found himself dropping to one knee. The command was so persuasive that he could do nothing else. Indeed, he had no desire to do anything else.

Men began to shout and cheer. Many drew weapons and shook them in the air, offering themselves into his service.

Roland's heart pounded. Duke Paldane stood atop the battlements defiantly, his hand clutching the pommel of his sword, a small man, contemptible in his impotence. It looked as if he alone would stand against Raj Ahten, while everyone else embraced him.

Can't the fool see that Raj Ahten is right? Roland wondered. Without the Wolf Lord, we're all dead.

Roland found a cheer ripping from his own throat.

Then the drawbridge came down with a rattling of chains.

Amid the cheers, Raj Ahten strode victoriously into Carris. He began shouting orders. 'Secure the causeway. Banish this fog so that we can see what we're up against.'

His flameweavers turned and began to draw fiery runes in the air at the end of the causeway.

The thick fog collapsed around the flameweavers for a moment, floated back in, so that in seconds the frowth giants that marched into Carris strode waist-deep through the mist, while men on warhorses had their heads barely bobbing above it.

Miles back, Roland could hear men shouting, the sound of horses neighing in fear as Raj Ahten's troops raced for Carris. Warhorns blared retreat.

With it, another distant sound floated over the fields, the buzzing whir that reavers made as air hissed from their abdomens, mingled with the crashing of their thick carapaces against stones as they thundered across the earth.

Reavers were coming, and Raj Ahten's troops raced through the mist to beat them, swelling the castle. The troops came in long lines, mounted knights begrimed and weary, riding their proud chargers. Row upon row of spearmen. Cheers thundered above the clamor of hooves and the clang of armor.

Roland looked over the battlements. Though the flame-weavers had begun to banish the fog, it was not something that could be accomplished in a moment. In the early morning, with the wet earth all around it, the fog had grown to the point that it smothered the ground for miles in every direction.

For long minutes Roland waited, his guts tight with terror. A cold heavy rain began to batter Roland's brow, soak his thin tunic. Men nearby huddled beneath their capes and hunkered under their shields as if the raindrops were a hail of deadly arrows. But the small target that Roland had been given just covered his head. It barely kept the rain off his neck.

More gree whipped overhead as if hurled by slings, a flock of hundreds. With the magical fog beneath and the natural clouds above, Roland's perch seemed strange and exotic. In the dim mist, gulls and crows and doves all began to flap about the battlements, disturbed by the commotion, lost between clouds above and fog below.

As the thrill of the moment began to fade, as the power of Raj Ahten's Voice seemed to dim, Roland found himself shaking.

He suddenly realized, like one waking from a dream, that he was forsworn, that he had let Raj Ahten take the city without a fight.

'What does this mean?' Roland asked Baron Poll. 'What

if the Earth King comes? Will we be forced to fight him?'

'I guess,' Baron Poll said. He spat off the edge of the castle, into the fog. The Baron's calm demeanor showed that he had already reached this realization, and that it did not disturb him.

Roland grumbled to Baron Poll, trying to sound confident, 'I'll not do that. I'll not fight the Earth King!'

'You'll do as you're ordered,' Baron Poll said. 'You'll be Raj Ahten's man when he puts you under oath.'

That was the way of it. If Raj Ahten secured the castle, he'd give the soldiers here the choice: swear fealty to me, or die.

'I'm Orden's man. I'll not forswear myself!' Roland said. 'I'll not bear sword against my own King.'

'But it will be your oath or your life!' Baron Poll said pragmatically. 'Believe me, a smart man will swear fealty quickly – and take his oath back just as quick.'

'I never claimed to be a smart man,' Roland answered. It was true. He couldn't read, couldn't do numbers. He'd never had an answer for the arguments of his shrewish wife. He'd hardly been able to find his way through the fog here to Carris.

But he'd always been loyal.

'Listen,' the Baron said fiercely. 'Take your oath for Raj Ahten. But once the Earth King comes, no one says you have to fight *fiercely*. If his troops come against the wall, you can just growl and wag your half-sword in a hostile manner, demanding that they all go bugger themselves. You don't have to draw blood!'

'Raj Ahten can go bugger himself,' Roland said, gripping his sword.

But when Raj Ahten's warriors began to come up on the walls, Roland dared not draw steel.

Instead he hunkered against the battlements and wished anew that he had not given the green woman his bearskin cloak. The cold now seemed more biting than it had been the night before. It pierced all the way to his heart, left him feeling numb and dazed.

After nearly half an hour, Raj Ahten's troops were still not

all in, but his flameweavers had drawn mystic fiery runes in
the air at the end of the causeway in a great circle. Symbols
hung in the fog like tapestries upon a wall until the
flameweavers pushed them. Then the fiery runes dissolved.
The fog began to back away at about the pace that a man
could run, opening a little window to the land.

All during that half hour, the sound of reavers approaching
became louder, the dull roar of heavy carapaces dragged across
the ground rising like an approaching thunderstorm.

Under the cover of fog, reavers converged around Carris
from everywhere – from the north and south and west.

Warhorns blared in the fog, two miles out. Horses began
to scream in panic, and Roland could hear horses charge first
to the south, then to the west, then reel madly back north.

Men on the walls began to shout, 'They're lost! There's men
lost out there!' 'Cut off.'

Roland empathized with them. He knew how maddening
that fog could be, how easily one might get lost in it.

The flameweavers had just begun to dispel the mist, and
Roland waited breathlessly on the battlements as it began to
peel backward, exposing the green folds of earth, the whitewashed cottages with their thatch roofs and abundant gardens,
the haycocks and apple orchards and pastures and serene little
canals all about Carris. A single mallard duck beside a bricked
well looked up at the sky and flapped its wings in delight at
being able to greet the light again.

It was such a stunningly beautiful landscape that Roland
found it all the more macabre to be standing here on the
battlements in the misting rain, straining to hear sounds of
engagement.

On the castle walls, men began to blow warhorns, signaling
to the armies of Indhopal lost out in that damnable fog, trying
to steer them to safety.

The troops responded by wheeling their horses and racing
toward the castle. Every moment or two, Roland could hear
a horse trip and fall in that impenetrable mist, armor clashing
as some knight met the ground.

And then the first troops appeared at the edge of the fog, about half a mile from Carris.

These were not fierce force warriors. They were archers with hornbows, wearing white burnooses with a little leather armor; or artillerymen with wide bronze helms and nothing more than a long knife to protect themselves; or young squires who were more used to polishing armor than wearing it.

In short, this was the rearguard, the dregs of Raj Ahten's army, all common support troops out of Indhopal come to hold Carris if it was taken. Most of them marched on foot.

Only their leaders rode horses, and once those leaders spotted the castle, they wheeled their mounts and charged for safety in blind panic, leaving the footmen to whatever fate they could manage.

The commoners of Indhopal began shouting, fled through the villages and fields toward Castle Carris. Everywhere around them rose the thunderous roar of reavers rushing through the fog.

The smell of dust and blood began to saturate the air, along with cries of terror, and though Roland had still not seen a reaver, he knew that out in the fog men were fighting for their lives.

All along the castle walls, warhorns blared. Soldiers shouted encouragement. The troops of Indhopal sprinted toward Carris, perhaps twenty thousand strong.

Then the reavers came.

One monster raced from that damnable fog, trailing mist as if it were afire. Roland stared in horror at his first reaver.

It looked like no creature that had ever taken form in the Overworld. It was a blade-bearer in rank, a warrior without the glittering fiery runes that distinguished a mage.

The reaver ran on four legs, reserving its massive front paws to carry its weapon. In shape, the monster might best have been described as formed like an immense crab. The reaver's thick outer carapace looked to be the gray of granite from above, but had muddy highlights beneath the legs.

Its head was enormous, the size of a wagon, something of

a shovel-shaped thing, with rows of waving feelers – called 'philia' – along the back of its skull and down its jaws. Its teeth shone like quartz crystals, and the monster had no eyes or ears, no nostrils.

Aside from its breathing, it made no noise, no hissing roar. It merely ran among the fleeing warriors, racing past them at three times the speed a commoner could run. It sped past warriors like a sheepdog trying to head off a flock, as if it would not bother to kill a man, but sought only to beat their retreat.

But it wisely stopped well short of the castle. When it reached a point near the front ranks of the warriors, it wheeled and went to work.

It held in its paws a glory hammer, a pole made of black reaver steel with six hundred pounds of metal at its head. According to tradition it was called a 'glory hammer' because 'it makes a glorious mess of a man when it hits him.'

The first swing of its glory hammer swept low over the ground without touching it, like a farmer with a scythe cutting through straw. The stroke knocked five men into oblivion, and Roland saw bodies tossed a hundred feet. One poor fellow's head whipped through the air and landed in Lake Donnestgree with a splash a hundred yards from the battle.

Some men drew weapons and tried to fight past the reaver. Others sought to surge past it. Others turned and fled madly or sought refuge in cottages or under bushes.

The monster's glory hammer rose and fell so swiftly, with such astonishing grace and surety, Roland could hardly comprehend it. For such a large beast, the reaver moved with incredible grace. In ten seconds fifty men lay dead, yet the monster's work had just begun.

Roland's mind blanked in horror, and he found himself gasping for breath, heart hammering so loudly that he feared men would think him a coward. He turned to see how others reacted. A lad next to him had gone pale in terror, but stood stiff, his jaw clenched stoically. Roland thought the boy was holding up quite well, until he saw pee streaming down the fellow's right leg.

From the barbicans came the *whonk, whonk* of artillerymen loosing ballista bolts. Shaped like giant arrows, the huge bolts were made of thirty pounds of steel. The first two shots fell short of their mark, tearing into the ranks of fleeing warriors. The sound of cranking gears followed as artillerymen struggled to reload.

Their marksman shouted, 'Hold your shot until the reaver comes in range.'

By then a hundred men had died, and on the walls people began to shout, 'Look! Look!'

At the edge of the fog, reavers charged forward, trailing mist. Not by the dozens or hundreds, but by the thousands.

They bore giant blades, glory hammers, and knight gigs – long poles with enormous hooks on the end.

In their midst were mages, glittering creatures so covered with fiery runes that they looked as if they were clothed in flames. They bore crystalline staves that glowed with their own inner light.

The thunder of carapaces bouncing over the ground made the castle walls tremble. The terrified cries of common soldiers became a roaring in Roland's ears. His legs felt so weak, they probably could not hold him up much longer.

Roland felt urine stream down his own leg.

'By the Powers!' Baron Poll bellowed.

Men began to leap from the castle walls out into the lake rather than face the reavers.

Some nearby fool with a voice like a town crier's shouted, 'Please remain calm! Please remain calm! Please remain *vigilantly* optimistic, and I'm fairly certain we'll all come out of this . . . intact.'

Roland wondered if the fellow was trying to reassure him, or if he only sought to face death like the legendary knights of old – in a spirit of good humor.

If ever there was a time in Roland's life to panic, it was now.

Baron Poll glanced back, his face lit by dawn's first light. The fat knight tried to make a jest, speaking loudly to be heard over the clash of arms and death cries in the background. 'Take a deep breath, lad. It may be your last.'

39

A SEPARATE WORLD

When the clubfooted boy fetched Myrrima from the archery range an hour after sunrise, she expected the lad to tell her that it was time to mount up.

Instead, he told her simply that Iome wanted her at the Dedicates' Keep.

She hurried to meet Her Highness. The morning sun came bright here at Castle Groverman. It was rising in a perfect blue sky, spreading the day before it. Fish eagles wheeled in the distance.

From the courtyard of the keep, Myrrima could see out on the plain for twenty miles: the Wind River winding like a silver thread through the heather, the ranches and cottages at every little hillock by the river's side, the herds of cattle and horses dotting the heather.

Outside the keep proper, doves and pigeons pecked by the hitching posts on the green. Myrrima went to the wall that surrounded the Dedicates' Keep. Its brown sandstone walls could not match the height of the keep at Castle Sylvarresta. Though the keep was large, with a huge open courtyard, it was not designed to hold more than a couple of hundred Dedicates.

As Myrrima approached the keep, she felt surprised to hear something odd: music.

Inside the Dedicates' Keep – even at this early hour – she could hear a song played on pipes, drums, tambour, and lute, accompanied by singing. The Dedicates, those not too weakened from granting endowments, were making merry.

Just inside the portcullis, she found a knot of curious folk standing there in a crowd, looking off onto the green.

As Myrrima passed them, one old woman whispered, 'That's her, the one who slew the Darkling Glory.' Myrrima felt her face turning red. 'They're calling her "Heredon's Glory,"' the old woman continued.

'She's been out all night practicing with that bow,' a young lad said. 'I hear she can knock the eye out of a diving hawk at two hundred paces. Now she's off to kill Raj Ahten himself!'

Myrrima ducked her head, tried to ignore the rumors. 'Knock the eye out of a diving hawk, indeed!' she wanted to protest. 'I'm lucky if I don't get all tangled up trying to string my own bow.'

Myrrima entered the green and felt astonished to see every Dedicate in the keep out on the grass. Tables were filled with drink, and the cooks had made savory pies and tarts by the score. Those Dedicates who had given brawn, grace, or metabolism – and thus could not easily move – lay shaded beneath a huge oak in the courtyard while all other Dedicates celebrated.

Blind men and women danced close together, careful not to step on one another's toes, while the deaf and mute romped to a merry jig. Witless fools capered madly.

Myrrima stood a moment just inside the gates gazing into the courtyard, baffled.

One old blind fellow sat cross-legged on the ground nearby, eating tarts and drinking from a jug of wine. He had weathered features and stringy hair.

'Why are they dancing?' Myrrima asked. 'Hostenfest ended two days ago.'

The blind man smiled up at her, proffering his bottle of wine. 'Tradition!' he said. 'Today we revel, for our lords go to war!'

'Tradition?' Myrrima asked. 'Dedicates always do this when their lords go to war?'

'Ayuh.' The fellow nodded. 'Have a drink.'

'No, thank you.' Myrrima was perplexed. She'd never heard

of this tradition. On the other hand, in all of her life, Heredon had never gone to war.

She looked up at the keep, with its sandstone chambers to house the Dedicates, its broad walls and the watchtowers above.

Once a man entered this place, he forsook the wider world – until either the lord or Dedicate passed away. Myrrima had seldom considered before how this place became its own separate world, untouched by outside affairs.

Amazed, she saw that some Dedicates were now dancing. 'Will this go on all day?' she asked.

'Ayuh,' the blind fellow said. 'Until the battle.'

She wondered. 'Ah, I see . . . Today, if your lord dies, your sight will be restored. What better reason to celebrate?'

The blind fellow gripped his wine bottle fiercely, as if it were a cudgel, and snarled, 'What a rude creature you are! We celebrate because today *we*' – he thumped his chest for emphasis – 'are going to war. Today, my lord Groverman will use my eyes, but I would gladly fight at his side if I could.'

He sloshed wine onto the ground. 'And by this libation, I implore the Earth: may Groverman come home victorious, to fight another day! Long live Duke Groverman!'

The fellow raised his wine bottle in the air and took a long swig, toasting the Duke's health.

Myrrima had spoken thoughtlessly. She understood that she had insulted the fellow, but she'd meant no harm.

Near one wall, in the shadows apart from the revelers, Myrrima saw Iome encircled by three dozen peasants, men and women of various ages and backgrounds. They held hands and circled slowly as Iome spoke. In the background, two minstrels played a soft march on flutes and drums. It was an ancient tune.

Myrrima recognized immediately what was happening. When a warrior sought endowments, he went to the facilitator, who kept a list of all those who had ever offered to act as Dedicates. The facilitator would then gather candidates, and because it was imperative that the Dedicates offer themselves freely and completely, the warrior often would need to speak. He'd tell the candidates of the need that drove him, promise to serve well if granted endowments, and offer support to the Dedicates and their families.

Thus Myrrima was not surprised to hear Iome speaking intently: 'I ask not for myself alone. The Earth has spoken to my husband, and warned that the end of the Age of Man is upon us. Thus if we fight, we fight not for ourselves, but for all of mankind!'

One man in the circle called out, 'Your Highness, forgive me, but you're not trained for war. Might my endowment not serve another lord better?'

'You're right,' Iome countered. 'I have some good training with the saber, and if I had an endowment of brawn, I could bear a warhammer as well as any man. But I don't pretend that I'll fight with great training and skill. To fight with great speed is as deadly as to fight with great skill. So I'll want metabolism instead.' There was a gasp of surprise from the potential Dedicates.

'Why? Why would you want to die young like that?' one older woman in the group asked as she plodded along slowly in the circle.

Myrrima pitied Iome. Myrrima had never engaged in a ceremony like this. She doubted that she could do it. She knew she didn't have a way with words. She'd never be able to talk a stranger into giving her the use of his or her most precious attribute.

'I carry the King's son within me,' Iome explained. 'Yesterday when the Darkling Glory came to Castle Sylvarresta, it sought the child's life, not mine. If I carry him to term, the Prince will not be born until midsummer. But if I take enough metabolism now, I can deliver in six weeks.'

Good girl, Myrrima thought. All of the potential Dedicates could see what she wanted. Iome would become a warrior, give her life to buy a life for her son. Iome's love for her child might sway these people.

The old woman stared at her intently and broke from the

circle, taking a step inward and bowing on one knee. 'My metabolism is yours, and your child's.' But the others continued circling, asking questions.

Someone tapped Myrrima on the back. She turned and looked up into the face of one of the largest men she'd ever encountered. He threw a shadow that could darken a small crowd, and he looked as if he'd more likely be seen carrying a horse about than to have it carry him. He was a woodsman by the smell of the pine on him. He wore a leather vest with no shirt underneath, so that she could see his muscular chest. He looked to be in his mid-thirties. He grinned down at her, his bearded face filled with awe. 'Are you the one?'

'Which one?' Myrrima asked.

'What killed the Darkling Glory?'

Myrrima nodded dumbly, unsure how to speak to someone whose face revealed such awe.

'I sawer it,' the fellow said. 'Flew right overhead, it did. Blackened the sky for miles. Never thought anyone could kill it.'

'I shot it,' Myrrima said. She realized that she was clutching her bow defensively, holding it close to her breast. 'You'd have done the same if you were there.'

'Hah! Not bloody likely.' The big man grinned. 'I'd have turned tail and still be running.'

Myrrima accepted his compliment. He was right after all. Most men would have run.

The fellow nodded, as if too shy to speak. She could tell that he was none too bright. 'You'll need a new bow,' he said.

She glanced at her bow, wondering if she'd damaged it. 'What do you mean?'

'You'll need a steel bow,' the fellow said, ''cause I could crack that one in two, no problem.'

Then she understood. Her reputation – however undeserved – preceded her. This monster meant to give her an endowment of brawn. Many a knight would have gladly paid fifty gold eagles for such an endowment, ten years of a workman's wages. By the Powers, he was big!

'I see,' Myrrima murmured in wonder. She dared not say that she thought his admiration undeserved, for if she had the brawn of a man like this, she suspected that she could become the kind of hero he believed her to be.

Several other peasants standing at this big fellow's back rushed forward. And Myrrima had a second realization. The knot of people waiting at the gates had all been waiting for her. They'd come to offer endowments.

Unlike Iome, 'Heredon's Glory' did not have to talk them into giving her their finest attributes.

40

TALES OF MADNESS

Daylight found Gaborn deep in the lowlands of Fleeds. The northlands had been hilly, filled with shepherds' cottages and narrow roads bordered by stone fences. Huge rocks crowned with twisted pines had stood along the road like ancient sentinels. The starlight fell over the countryside as heavy and palpable as if it were silver coins.

Gaborn had not dared ride hard in the darkness, no matter how great the danger he felt arising at Carris, and so the vast majority of his troops kept pace through the night. Though he had begun to receive endowments, a fall from his horse could break his neck as easily as it could any other man's.

Yet even as he rode, he felt himself swelling, growing in power. He'd taken less than an hour to receive endowments at Castle Groverman. He'd taken one each of brawn, metabolism, grace, and stamina. Then he'd fled, leaving Groverman's facilitator to find others willing to vector endowments through his new Dedicates.

He'd warned the facilitator that he'd need forty endowments by nightfall, and the facilitator had promised to have it done.

So as he rode that night, he grew more refreshed with each passing hour. He grew stronger, faster.

Though the deed repulsed him, he could not deny that the taste of evil was sweet, and unwittingly on one occasion he even found himself wondering, If Raj Ahten sought to use forcibles to become the Sum of All Men, could I not do the same?

Yet he cast the thought away quickly, for it was not worthy of a king.

He rode now with the wizard Binnesman at his side, along with five hundred lords out of Orwynne and Heredon. Gaborn had provided a fast force horse so that his Days could accompany the party.

At dawn Gaborn gazed down from a hill trail that looked over the rolling plains. A cold sun dawdled on the horizon, and a hazy mist hovered over the fields of Fleeds.

In preparation for a race over the plains, he stopped to water and feed the horses by a placid finger lake where wild oats and purple vetch and golden melilot grew thick. The icy water was marvelously clear; fat trout swam lazily among the humped stones beneath its surface.

Yellow larks sang in the willows beside the road; at his approach they flew up like sparks from a smith's grindstone.

'Feed and water here for fifteen minutes,' Gaborn called out. 'If we race, we can reach Tor Doohan within the hour. From there we'll strike south quickly, in hopes of reaching Carris by mid-afternoon.'

Gaborn was raising the time scale. The sense of impending doom at Carris was becoming overwhelming, and the Earth bade him to strike.

'Mid-afternoon?' Sir Langley asked. 'Is there some great hurry?'

Carris was so far away that no messenger could have brought him any news that was less than a day stale. But Gaborn surprised them with some. 'Yes,' Gaborn admitted. 'I believe that Raj Ahten is at the walls of Carris. Five minutes ago, my messengers were in mortal danger . . . The feeling passed for a moment. Yet now once again I feel a staggering sense of danger rising around my Chosen messengers there.'

The lords began talking to one another loudly, discussing strategies. Raj Ahten was notorious for taking castles quickly. Few believed that Carris would hold out through the day. If it did, then chasing him off might be an easy matter.

But no one believed that they'd find him crouched before the walls of Carris.

The consensus was that if Gaborn laid siege to the castle, he would likely be successful in the short term. But how long could he sustain such a siege? With Raj Ahten's armies spilling across the borders, the Wolf Lord would not have to wait more than a week for reinforcements. Which meant that Gaborn would either have to attack Raj Ahten in his stronghold quickly, or stave off armies that came to give him aid.

Either way, Gaborn might well be setting the stage for a battle of epic proportions.

It all sounded so simple. Lords from all across Rofehavan would gather to his banner. Already he had Beldinook and Fleeds, the Knights Equitable, Heredon, and Mystarria. With so many troops, taking Raj Ahten should not be hard. In fact, Gaborn almost hoped that Raj Ahten did take Carris, for it would leave him trapped, like a rat, there on the peninsula.

Yet Gaborn still felt deeply troubled. He felt death stalking every single man and woman in his retinue. There would be a battle royal at Carris, and it would not wait for a week. He feared that Raj Ahten was setting some sort of trap.

He worried that even with Lowicker's aid, and the aid of Fleeds, he would not gather enough troops to do battle.

Gaborn went to the edge of the lake, hoping to be alone with his thoughts. Little yellow posies sprouted between the rocks at the shore's edge. He plucked one, stood holding it. As a child he'd always thought posies to be such treasures, though now he saw how common they really were.

Like people. Men and women and children everywhere. Gaborn still treasured every one of them, though the Earth warned that he could save only a few.

His Days went to the water's edge, drew back the hood of his riding robe to expose his close-cropped hair. His skeletal features looked haggard, marred by worry. He knelt and cupped his hands to draw forth a drink.

'What is happening at Carris?' Gaborn asked.

The scholar dropped his handful of water, startled. He did

not turn to Gaborn to answer. 'All in good time, Your Highness.'

'You cannot simply *record* the deaths of men,' Gaborn said. 'No matter how hard you try to conceal it, you feel for them. Yesterday, when the Blue Tower fell, I saw the horror in your face.'

'I am Time's Witness,' the Days said. 'I do not get involved.'

'Death stalks every man and woman in our party. There are hundreds of thousands of people at Carris, and I believe that death stalks them also. Will you merely witness it?'

'There may well be nothing I can do to stop it,' the Days answered. He turned to look at Gaborn. The morning sun showed a tear glistening in his eye.

What is he saying? Gaborn wondered. That he will not stop it, or cannot?

Cannot, Gaborn decided. But if that was true, what trap had Raj Ahten set that was so diabolical that it could not be thwarted? Gaborn needed to know more.

'You asked me last night if I would ever Choose a Days,' Gaborn said. 'My answer is yes, I will. But only if the Days will give himself in service to his fellow men.'

'You seek to buy my allegiance?' the Days asked.

'I seek to save the world.'

'It may be that you seek in vain,' the Days said.

'How comfortable it must be, to simply remain a voyeur,' Gaborn chided, 'to pretend that indifference is a virtue, and that our fates are all sealed by time.'

'You hope to anger me into breaking my vows?' the Days said. 'That is a deed that I would have thought beneath you. My opinion of you is lowered. It will be noted in the book of your life.'

Gaborn shook his head. 'Beg, ridicule, badger, blackmail. If I ask hard things of you, I do not ask for myself alone. I warn you: I will not Choose you. I am riding into battle with you at my side, and I will not Choose you. You will most likely die today if you do not name the threat at Carris.'

The Days trembled, tried to keep a firm jaw as he turned

away. But his trembling demeanor told Gaborn much. There was a danger at Carris, a threat so enormous that the Days really believed he would die today.

Yet he chose oblivion rather than to break his vow of non-interference in the affairs of mankind.

As Gaborn stood waiting beside the lake, Erin Connal came to him. She'd warned him last night that she wanted to speak to him alone, and now she sat down beside him and said, 'Your Highness, I have news of a plot against you.'

She then gave him the bare bones of King Anders's plot to subvert Gaborn's claims to his throne.

Gaborn felt overwhelmed. He could hardly imagine why Anders would do it. For another lord to fight him was . . . so wasteful.

He'd imagined that people would have rejoiced to hear that the Earth had chosen a new king. Instead, it seemed to Gaborn that the land sprouted enemies like . . . like the banks of this cold lake sprouted posies.

Gaborn spoke to Erin for a few minutes, then she fetched Prince Celinor so that he could get closer to the heart of the matter.

Gaborn sat him down and questioned him. 'Erin has warned me that your father plots against me. How serious is his plot, do you think? Would he go to war, or send assassins against me?'

Celinor answered frankly, as if he'd been worrying about the possibility himself. 'I . . . don't know. My father has never sought war against or tried to assassinate a fellow lord of Rofehavan. He never spoke to me about the possibility. However . . . my father has not been himself lately. Not for the past month, at least. I think he is going mad.'

'Why would you think him mad?' Gaborn asked.

Celinor looked all about, in order to make certain that no one else was close enough to hear.

'About three weeks ago, while all the castle was asleep, he crept to my room with nothing but a candle in his hand.

'He was naked, and wore nothing at all but a beatific smile

such as I'd never seen on his face. His voice was soft and dreamy, and he woke me and announced that he had seen a sign in the heavens, and knew of a surety that he was to be the next Earth King.'

'What sign had he seen?' Erin asked.

'He claimed that he saw three stars falling from the heavens, all at once, bright and flaming. Then these stars, he says, as they neared the horizon, suddenly veered from their course and wheeled about, circling the castle, creating a flaming crown that encompassed all of South Crowthen.'

Gaborn wondered at such a story. Meteors did not figure at all in any legend dealing with the earth powers. 'He thought this an Earth sign?'

'He did,' Celinor said. 'But I took it merely for a sign that he'd had some waking dream, and told him so. As proof I went to speak to the far-seer upon the castle walls, and to the guardsmen there, so that I could convince my father of his error.'

'What did they say?' Gaborn asked.

'The guardsmen in the Dedicates' Keep had seen nothing, for they'd been making their rounds down below inside the keep. Four men were found to be missing. The far-seer upon the watchman's tower was dead.'

'Dead?' Erin asked. 'How?'

'He'd fallen from the tower. Whether he was pushed or had slipped or merely decided to jump, I don't know.'

'The missing men?'

'My father refused to say where they've gone. He hints that they are on some mission. He said merely that "They had duties elsewhere."'

'You think your father murdered his own far-seer, and sent the others away?' Gaborn asked.

'Perhaps,' Celinor said. 'I had men check the borders of South Crowthen, looking for the four men. After a week, we found a peasant who says that he did indeed see one of the missing knights racing south. He said he hailed the man, but the knight rode as if in a dream . . . without seeing him, without speaking.

'On a hunch, I looked harder, and found that indeed all four knights had left the kingdom – one riding north, another south, a third east, and the last to the west. Each man rode away without speaking a word.'

'This reeks of sorcery,' Gaborn said. He did not like it. This had nothing to do with the earth powers. It hinted at something dark and dangerous.

'So I thought,' Celinor said. 'We had an herb woman in the hills nearby, a lady called the Nut Woman, for she was always collecting nuts. She was a witch who lived in the woods and cared for the squirrels. I went to her cave to seek her counsel, to learn if this was the Earth's doing . . . but though I've heard that she'd lived in that cave for a hundred years, she had suddenly gone.

'And this is the odd part: every squirrel in those woods disappeared with her.'

Erin licked her lips nervously. This Nut Woman obviously served the Earth. She was an Earth Warden, like Binnesman, but with a different charge. 'Have you asked the wizard Binnesman about this?' Gaborn asked.

Celinor shook his head. 'I have had little evidence for my concerns. After this one night, my father has not spoken of his delusion again, though it seems to me that his delusion guides every deed.'

'How's that?' Erin asked.

'He very calmly and systematically contacted his lords and began strengthening his defenses, doubling and quadrupling his guard. This did not seem a bad thing, for three days before Hostenfest, he managed to slaughter a group of Raj Ahten's assassins.

'Indeed, my father's demeanor, his reasoned response to his belief, almost convinced me that his fantasy was a good thing, that if he was deluded, this might be a helpful delusion. And I confess that even I began to wonder if perhaps the sign was true.

'Then, something else happened, last week. My father flew into an indescribable rage upon learning that another claimed to be the Earth King. He screamed and threw things about. He ripped tapestries with his bare hands and toppled his own throne. He beat the servant who'd brought the news. When he finally calmed after several hours, he claimed that he should have seen it, that he should have known that pretenders would claim his throne. It was then that he began to plot how he might discredit Gaborn's title. Indeed, his stories seemed so convincing that even I wondered if Gaborn might be a fraud. Yet my father has suddenly become . . . unstable. He will be talking about one thing, and suddenly change the subject or shout some unrelated command. He . . . moves oddly.'

'The man sounds daft – and dangerous,' Gaborn said. 'Why haven't you told others? Why did you wait until now?'

Celinor folded his hands and stared hard at Gaborn. 'When I was a child of ten, my grandfather went mad, suffering from grand delusions and hallucinations. For his own safety, my parents locked him in a cell beneath our keep.

'As a child, I used to listen to him mutter and laugh long into the night, in his cell down below my bedroom.

'At the time, my father told me that it was a curse in our family. He sought to keep his own father comfortable as he lived out his last days. We vectored metabolism to him through four servants, so that he would grow old and die quickly, while we spread the news abroad that my grandfather had passed away.

'My father made me vow that if he should ever show the same symptoms, that I would treat him no better and no worse.

'I have always been loyal. If my father is mad, I would hope that he merits our compassion.'

'As do I,' Gaborn said. Yet he had to worry. It sounded as if a madman haunted the borders of Heredon. He'd hoped to find an ally in Anders, as he had in Kings Orwynne and Lowicker.

At that, Gaborn called for his men to mount up, and he raced for Tor Doohan with renewed vigor. With the clear morning light and dry roads, they made good time. As they raced, the troops began to spread thin, those on the fastest horses taking the lead while others fell miles behind.

An hour later, Gaborn, the wizard Binnesman, and a few lords thundered over Atherphilly Trail into Tor Doohan. The 'palace' at Tor Doohan had stood far longer than anyone knew. It was no palace at all, by modern terms. It was instead only an enormous crimson tent pitched within a circle of crude white stones.

The stones atop Tor Doohan were roughly hewn from the earth. Some were planted in the hillside as pillars so that they rose up like jagged teeth, eighty feet tall and forty feet wide. Atop the standing stones, others had been placed crosswise between each pillar, and these stones too were each over eighty feet long and weighed hundreds of thousands of tons.

Who had placed the stones together, or when, or why, no one rightly knew. Ancient tales called it the 'Place of the White Mare,' for it was said that a race of giants had built the stones as a corral to hold the Star Mare, before she escaped and became a constellation.

Of course, only giants could have placed the stones in the circle, yet even for hill giants like those still living in Inkarra, it would have been a monumental task.

But as for the stones' purpose? Certainly they did not hold a giant horse. To the horse clans, any such stack of stones would have seemed like a corral.

Gaborn suspected that the stones marked the tomb of some ancient hill giant king, though no one had ever dug for his bones.

The horse clans of Fleeds had gathered for annual games and war counsels atop Tor Doohan for nearly three thousand years, until it had become the permanent camp of the High Queen.

The nomadic horsesisters of Fleeds had long sneered at folk who settled in one place. Thus the Queen's palace at Tor Doohan was an enormous tent that had remained erected within the stones now for thirty generations. While the tent stood on the hill, villages had grown up along the Roan River to the west, and eighteen fortresses now dotted the valley. Yet the palace pavilion remained the symbolic heart of Fleeds.

Gaborn felt thankful when they rounded the hills on the Atherphilly Trail and at last saw the Red Queen's great pavilion of scarlet silk pitched inside the ring of stones. Two enormous bronze statues of mares, their hooves pawing the air, rose above the palace entrance.

On the grounds outside the circle, hundreds of clan lords had pitched their own tents in the shadow of the palace, preparing for war. Yet they were remarkably few in number, and Gaborn was concerned. He'd hoped that Queen Herin the Red would offer some troops to ride at his side. But too many men and women had died in the battle against Raj Ahten, and many more had already gone south to retake the fortress at Castle Fells.

Fleeds was a poor land, and it looked as if Herin the Red would have few troops left to offer him. She was a proud woman, and Gaborn could see that she had no one at all to spare.

Still, hundreds of young warriors wildly raced their horses around the palace, for legend said that any warrior who raced his mount seven times around the great stone circle while blowing his or her warhorn would have good luck in battle.

As Gaborn and a few dozen lords rode up to the palace, he listened to those who had never seen it make appreciative sounds of surprise.

The racing young riders now drew in their reins, and stared back in equal wonder to see the Earth King.

Many young women – lancers and archers – urged their mounts to rear up and paw the air as a sign that they were willing to give themselves and their mounts into Gaborn's service. Yet he dared Choose none until he spoke with Queen Herin the Red.

Gaborn, Binnesman, Gaborn's Days, and the various lords rode under the statues of the war mares and dismounted; servants rushed forward to take their weary horses down to the royal stables.

Few things made Gaborn feel quite so humble as to walk beneath the great statues and standing stones of the palace. A cool morning wind blew across the hills, beating against the tent, so that its red silk outer walls billowed and rolled. The sentries posted outside the pavilion pulled back the flaps.

The lords went into the antechamber of the pavilion, into a room that had a ceiling eighty feet high, while a servant went to announce the party to Queen Herin the Red. The sun shining through the top layers of silk cast a scarlet glow, so that even the golden urns along the walls were bathed in a ruddy hue.

Many lords stood gaping about at the vast tapestries on either wall to the left and right. Both tapestries showed the emblem of Fleeds: a great roan mare pawing the air, while flames issued from its nostrils. The tapestries showed the mare upon a green field, and on that field, one could see every blade of grass, every dandelion, every posy, every ant.

Outside, the young knights resumed their race around the palace, blowing their warhorns.

'Well,' Sir Langley joked, 'I don't know how we'll ever hold a council here with all of this racket.'

His ignorance of course was excusable. The Queen's Sanctum at the heart of the palace was virtually soundproof.

The palace was enormous. Its roof consisted of three layers of cloth, one above another, but each nearly five hundred feet across. The interior was divided into rooms by great curtains and tapestries that formed the walls.

Furthermore, wooden ramparts fashioned of logs had been built beneath the great awnings of the tent, forming floors and stairs, further dividing the pavilion into three separate levels. The framework of these logs allowed tapestries to be hung as walls. Thus, the Red Queen's palace was less secure than a palace of stone, yet far more serviceable than a simple pavillion.

Queen Herin soon entered the antechamber. The Queen had red hair and pale skin, eyes as dark blue as bachelor's buttons. She was tall, strong. She smiled, but her smile did not hold any joy at this meeting.

She knows that I must beg for troops, Gaborn thought, and she knows that she can spare me none.

Queen Herin wore scale mail, with a silver buckler at her waist that displayed the symbol of Fleeds in red enamel. In her hand she bore the royal scepter of Fleeds, a rod of gold made like a horseman's crop, with a red horsetail at one end.

'Your Highness,' Queen Herin greeted Gaborn, and did the unthinkable. She dropped to both knees before him and bowed her head.

Then she offered her scepter.

Among the horsesisters of Fleeds, no high queen had ever bowed to a man.

Gaborn had hoped to beg Queen Herin for the use of a few knights and some food for his men and horses.

Instead she offered Gaborn her realm.

41

THE SMELL OF A RISING STORM

In the late morning, Iome spurred her charger onward toward Fleeds, riding hard, with Myrrima and Sir Hoswell at her back. Having no charger that could match her pace, Iome's Days was left behind.

Iome had taken endowments at Castle Groverman – more than she'd expected, but in the end not so many as Myrrima did. She had two endowments of brawn to her credit now, one of grace, one of wit, one of sight, and four of metabolism. With that, she also bore endowments from dogs: one of hearing, two of stamina, two of smell. She felt like a wolf lord indeed, powerful, tireless, and deadly. It was a heady pleasure, one that filled her with a renewed sense of responsibility.

Yet Myrrima had bested her. The villagers had heard how Myrrima had slain the Darkling Glory, and they heaped endowments upon her. So many that Iome had felt obligated to give Myrrima more forcibles from her private horde. Sixteen men and women went under the forcibles for Myrrima, so that between those endowments and the ones from her dogs, she now had nearly as many endowments as did any captain in Heredon's guard.

Myrrima had always been large, beautiful. Now her endowments lent her an air of fierceness. So the three Runelords now rode without any other guard but their own strong arms. Yet as they rode, Iome noted that Sir Hoswell remained a respectful distance behind the women, and Myrrima avoided his presence. She did not welcome his company.

Wind rippled over the grass in steady waves, gusted at
Iome's back, pushing her south. Though the sky was blue,
the wind smelled of a rising storm. The heather had sprouted
tiny purple flowers after last week's rain, leaving the distant
fields awash in their odd gray-blue hue. Iome ran her mare,
for the morning felt cool and her mount seemed eager to
outrace the wind. Though it raced at forty miles per hour,
Iome felt as if it were hardly testing its pace.

In the past when riding a force horse, Iome had never been
able to follow the movement of its hooves with her eyes. Now,
with so much metabolism to her credit, she could follow her
horse's movements easily.

The rest of the world seemed to have slowed dramatically.
A crow beating its wings against the wind seemed to hang
painfully in the air. The sounds of thudding steel-shod hooves
on the road were too deep, more like a frowth giant pounding
on a huge drum.

Even more disturbing, Iome's thoughts seemed to race.
Before, without her endowments of metabolism, riding all day
would have seemed a short journey. But now her journey of
one day would seem like five.

She'd seldom had so much time to merely sit and think.
And after the long day's ride, she would have to live through
the night. With all of her metabolism, thirteen hours of darkness would seem like sixty-five. In the dead of winter, force
soldiers with high metabolism often became irascible and
despondent, for the nights could seem interminable to them.
Iome steeled herself to face the coming winter.

She raced past a few solitary oaks whose leaves had mostly
blown away, the bones of trees, clothed only in ivy twined
high in their branches.

Ahead lay a shallow, muddy creek winding across the
prairie, and there where the road dipped, a fellow sat on a
narrow log bridge watering his horse in the spare shade of an
oak.

Even half a mile away, Iome recognized his tunic. He wore
a courier's colors, the blue of Mystarria with the green man

emblem embroidered on the right side of his chest. In addition he bore a saber on his hip and wore a steel helm with a long visor. A common courier. The fellow was small, with long silver hair, as if it had gone gray prematurely.

Iome raised her hand in signal for Myrrima and Sir Hoswell to slow. There was something odd about this one. Myrrima had met several of Gaborn's messengers before, and she could not quite name her concern.

The messenger saw them, climbed up from his spot on the bridge, dusted off his tunic. The fellow mounted his horse, rode out of the shadow of the oak, letting his horse plod along. He studied them intently, as if he feared they might be outlaws.

Iome reined in her mount as the fellow approached.

He was a strange one, Iome decided. He was grinning, but not shyly or fearfully. Instead she decided that he had an impish grin, mischief in his eyes.

She urged her own mount forward, until she felt close enough to hail him. 'Where are you going, sirrah?'

The courier stopped his mount. 'I bear a message for the King,' the fellow answered.

'From whom?' Iome asked.

'Funny,' the messenger smirked. 'The King did not have tits, last that I saw.' It was his crude way of rebuking her for asking too much about the King's business, yet Myrrima had never heard such comments from even the roughest Mystarrian.

'But the Queen did – last I saw,' Iome said, trying to keep the rage from her voice.

The messenger's smirk disappeared, yet his deep brown eyes glittered as if he laughed at some private joke. 'You're the Queen?'

Iome nodded. His tone suggested that she somehow disappointed him, did not live up to his expectations. Iome had taken several endowments, but none of glamour or of Voice. She did not look like a queen. She was trying to decide whether to have the man beaten, or merely dismissed from service.

'A thousand apologies, Your Highness,' the messenger said. 'I did not recognize you. We have not met before.'

Though he mouthed an apology, there was none in his tone – only mockery.

'Let me see the message,' Iome demanded.

'My apologies,' the fellow said. 'It is only for the King's eyes.'

Iome found her pulse racing. She was angry, yet suspicious.

This man spoke quickly. She knew that he too had more than one endowment of metabolism. That was not common for a courier. She smelled him, but could not detect anything amiss. He smelled of horse and the road, of linen and cotton and perhaps some liniment that he'd used to service a wound on his horse's leg.

'I will carry the message,' Iome said. 'You're going the wrong way, and doubtless your mount is fatigued. You'll never catch the King.'

In consternation, the messenger glanced behind along the road he'd been traveling.

Surely if he'd come from Tor Doohan, he'd have spotted Gaborn on the road. Which meant that he'd not ridden the most direct route last night, but had traveled along some side road.

'Where can I find him?' the courier asked, looking back.

'Give *me* the message,' Iome demanded.

The fellow caught her tone, turned and studied her with one eyebrow cocked. Sir Hoswell caught her tone, too. She heard him slide his horseman's hammer from the sheath at his saddle.

Still the courier did not hand her the message pouch. 'I demand it,' Iome said.

'I . . . I only meant to spare you the trouble, Your Highness,' the messenger said. He reached to his pouch, pulled out a blue-lacquered leather scroll case, and handed it to Iome. 'For the King's eyes only,' he warned.

Iome reached for the thing, and the Earth King's warning rang clear in her mind. 'Beware!'

She hesitated for a moment, studied the messenger. He did not lunge at her or draw steel.

Yet she knew for certain that he presented some danger. From a distance she examined the pouch's exterior. She'd heard of southern assassins who placed poison needles on implements. Perhaps something like that might be at work.

But she could see nothing ominous on the exterior of the case. The pouch was sealed with wax, but no signet ring marked who might have sealed it.

The messenger leaned forward, stared hard into her eyes. A taut smile turned his lips upward as he offered the case.

He's daring me to take it, Iome thought.

She reached out and snatched – not for the case, but for the fellow's wrist. His eyes went wide.

He shouted and spurred his mount so hard that flecks of blood flew from the horse's flanks.

He was a small man, hardly taller than Iome, and without quite as many endowments as she had. He struggled to urge his horse past her, and Iome clamped down hard on his wrist.

As she did, her own forearm brushed the surface of the message pouch. The sensation she felt on doing so was almost impossible to describe – she felt movement over the surface of the pouch, as if thousands of invisible spiders skittered across its surface, bumping into her arm.

In horror she squeezed the courier's wrist and twisted, hoping to force him to drop the case.

To her surprise, the fellow's bones snapped. She had taken endowments of brawn hardly more than an hour ago, and so had not learned her own strength.

The message case went flying to the ground.

The fellow's mount surged forward, but Myrrima had already reacted. She charged to Iome's defense. Sir Borenson's massive warhorse slammed into the messenger's smaller mount.

The courier's horse floundered backward and stumbled.

Torn from his horse, the courier rolled to the ground. Myrrima fought to remain in her saddle, ended up clinging to her horse's neck.

Iome wheeled her charger, fearing that the courier would leap on Myrrima. Though Gaborn had warned her to beware, she saw that they were three against one, and she felt confident.

'Hoof!' Iome commanded her mount. The warhorse reared and pranced forward, pawing and kicking.

The courier leapt up, wild-eyed. He laughed maniacally. Sir Hoswell shouted and spurred his horse forward, wielding his horseman's hammer.

Seeing that he was outnumbered, the courier suddenly leapt into the air – and flew!

He did not flap his arms as if they were wings. Nor did he make any other odd motion. He merely cackled and spread his arms wide, as if he were a flying squirrel, and let the wind take him.

A sudden burst of air whirled around him, battering his blue cloak, lifting him unexpectedly. He soared over Iome's head. His leap carried him a hundred feet in the air and two hundred yards downwind.

He came to rest like a crow in the huge oak tree above the stream where Iome had first seen him. The upper branches bobbed and swayed under his weight.

'By the Powers!' Sir Hoswell swore, racing to the base of the tree. He reached around behind his back, pulled his steel horsebow, and such was his uncommon strength that he actually strung it while in the saddle. He prepared to send a shaft up to hit the fellow.

The courier settled between three branches and chortled like a madman as Iome and Myrrima approached. Iome advanced toward him warily, wondering why this fellow had changed his demeanor so dramatically – from the grinning assassin to the chortling maniac.

'He's a Sky Lord!' Myrrima cried in wonder.

'Nay,' Sir Hoswell growled angrily, 'a Sky Lord would have flown away from here. He's just a damned Inkarran wizard!'

Now that Hoswell said it, the fellow did look somewhat Inkarran. He had the silver hair, which was a rare enough trait here in the north. But his skin wasn't quite pallid enough, and his eyes were a dark brown rather than silver or gray. Not Inkarran, Iome thought, only a half-breed.

Hoswell sent a shaft into the tree, blurring upward from his steel bow, but the assassin merely dodged aside, or perhaps a sudden gust of wind moved the arrow.

'Greetings,' Iome called to the fellow, raising a hand to warn Hoswell not to shoot again. The courier continued to cackle.

Iome studied him. She could feel it, now that she tried. She had always been sensitive to the Powers, and now she could feel the Power that drove him. The fellow was not a cold, calculating assassin. He was passionate, chaotic, and utterly fearless – one who had given himself to the wind. Iome had recognized this *wrongness* in him almost immediately, even when she'd first seen him from a distance.

The courier continued to snicker. Iome tried to smile in return, catching his mood, feeling the power that drove him. She knew little of Air magics. Air was an unpredictable master, wild and variable. In order to harness it, one had to learn its moods, and mirror them.

Certainly the gibbering, cackling creature before her could not have acted the assassin like this. No, I see what he is doing, Iome thought. He adopts this mood to curry favor with the Air. But the wind is an unstable master, as likely to give a man ten times the power he needs as to let him down.

She thought of the Darkling Glory, of the elemental of Air that had escaped it. Could it have sent the assassin? she wondered. Could it have initiated this subtle attack?

Sir Hoswell glowered at the courier. 'Who sent you?'

'Who? Who?' the fellow shouted. He gaily flapped his arms as if he were an owl. His broken wrist left one hand flopping. He looked at it and winced, gazed accusingly at Iome. 'That hurt.'

'Why don't you come down?' Iome said.

'Down?' the fellow shouted. 'Down to the ground? Down to the *ground*?' he cried in alarm. 'Nay! Goose down. Eiderdown. Spider down!'

The fellow's eyes suddenly lit up as if he had an idea. 'Thistledown!' he screamed. 'Thistledown. Pissle down. Why don't *you* turn to thistledown and fly up? You could, you know! You could if you would. You would if you could. In your dreams!'

Iome's heart pounded. She'd dreamt of thistledown last week, of turning to thistledown and flying over Castle Sylvarresta, drifting up into the air away from her problems.

The courier opened his eyes wide, stretched out his good hand and beckoned to her. 'Come to me, O cumbrous Queen of the Sky, you need no feathery wing to fly!'

He's serious, Iome realized. He wants me to join him.

A powerful blast of wind slammed into Iome's back, halfway ripping her from her saddle. Iome grabbed the pommel and clung to it. She remembered Gaborn's warning, and wondered now at her own stupidity.

If she let go, the wind would tear her from the saddle, and she feared where it might carry her. She screamed for help.

Hoswell let a shaft fly. The arrow lodged in the tree near the assassin's head, breaking his concentration. The wind around Iome died.

The assassin spun and snarled like some vicious dog, angered at the unexpected attack.

'No?' he cried. 'No? No! She won't go! She won't grow. Not like the son within her grows!' He snarled as the Darkling Glory had. 'Give me the King's son. I smell a son in your womb. Give it or I'll take it!'

The assassin grasped the arrow, wrung it from deep in the oak where the bodkin was buried, and hurled the bolt back at Hoswell. The arrow flew with astonishing speed, blurring as it whipped toward Hoswell, soaring left and right as no arrow should.

It struck Hoswell on the shoulder, merely to bounce off his armor and go blurring toward the grass.

'Beware!' Gaborn's voice warned Iome.

Iome ducked just as the arrow soared upward and whipped around. It drove past her head, blurring as it picked up speed.

Then it sailed off into the distance, lost to sight. Without her endowments of metabolism, she'd have been skewered.

'Damn him!' Hoswell shouted. 'I'll go into the tree after him if I must.'

'Wait!' Iome warned.

She stared up at the assassin. He looked down at her, gibbering in laughter.

She felt the Power that moved him. She'd never met a wizard of the Air.

She felt confusion around him, indecision, a great buffeting wall. The man had no mind of his own, no will of his own. He moved as the wind moved him. He gave himself to it even further now, hoping that it would preserve him.

She felt his instability. The Air was taking him.

He was no longer human in this state, could hardly think sequentially. He was a gibbering lunatic blown by the wind. A wretched creature bereft of will. The horror of it settled into her as she realized that he wanted her to join him, to become like him.

Her dream of turning to thistledown. She remembered now that she'd dreamt it during a storm, with the wind blowing all around.

No, the wizard didn't want her to become like him. The wind did. The Powers of the Air.

Throw yourself into the sky. Let me take you away.

'So, good fellow,' Iome asked in an effort to divert his attention, 'do you think you can teach me to fly?'

'Fly? Sky fly? Fly. Walk like a fly? Talk like a fly. Talk to the sky? Why? Why? Does she ask why?' the assassin began to gibber. He raked his good hand nervously over the bark of the oak, and Iome was amazed at his strength, for he absentmindedly began to rip huge shreds of bark away.

Iome calmly walked her mount over to Sir Hoswell. He'd nocked another arrow but was unsure whether to shoot. His last shaft had come within an inch of skewering the Queen.

Iome licked her lips and kissed the arrow's point, shaft,

and fletching, wetting it in the same way that Myrrima's arrow had been wetted when she slew the Darkling Glory.

'Shoot him now,' Iome whispered.

The assassin shrieked, searched about for some means of escape. His sudden terror let her know that she had guessed right. Hoswell brought up his steel bow.

The fellow leapt into the air, and the wind shrieked around him, howling as if the wind itself were in fear. It beat his robes, so that they flapped around him like wings.

Hoswell loosed the shaft. The arrow became a dark blur and caught the assassin in the shoulder.

The assassin spun half a dozen times in the air.

Then the strange winds that held him suddenly dissipated, and his body hurtled downward as if he'd fallen from a limb. He landed with a dull thud.

But a groaning sound escaped his throat and moved off through the sky, whirling overhead, circling the great oak.

In horror Iome gazed upward.

The wizard's body might be lying at their feet, but something of him was left still: a swirling expanse of air that circled overhead and moaned of its own accord.

Hoswell dropped from his mount and rolled the corpse over. Hardly any blood flowed from the fellow. The arrow in his shoulder provided a minor flesh wound that should not have killed him.

Yet the Inkarran lay unmoving, unbreathing, his eyes staring fixedly.

We did not kill him, Iome realized. Not the way that Myrrima slew the Darkling Glory. This wizard had chosen to leave his body.

Hoswell wrapped one hand around the throat of the corpse and squeezed, then grabbed a handful of dirt, gouged it from the soil, and began shoving it in the dead man's mouth and nose. He glanced about fearfully as he worked.

'I've heard it said that if you disembody a Sky Lord, you should put him in the ground quickly,' Hoswell said to Myrrima and Iome. 'That way he can't take his body back.

It's best to sew his mouth and nostrils closed, too, but a little dirt shoved up there should hold it for a while.'

Iome knew little of such things. She was not a soldier of the line, had never imagined that she'd find herself battling magical creatures. Yet she had to wonder. She'd not done these things to the corpse of the Darkling Glory. Could it come back?

A strong gust of wind roared from the sky with a sound like a cry, slammed into Hoswell's back and drove him to the ground. The wizard's body suddenly bucked and heaved about as if in its death throes.

Hoswell threw a handful of soil in the air, and the magical wind whirled away in retreat. As if in frustration, it roared up into the heights of the tree and shot through the desiccated leaves, sending them raining down all around.

'Wait!' Iome said, horrified at the gruesome pains that Hoswell was going through to kill the man.

Hoswell looked up at her curiously.

'I want to know what he's after. Why did he attack us?'

'You'll not get any sane answers by questioning one of the wind-driven,' Hoswell said.

'Search the body,' Iome ordered.

Hoswell went through the fellow's purse, but found nothing.

Hoswell pulled off the man's right boot. His foot and calf were covered in blue tattoos, in the style of the Inkarrans, but the image there was not of the world tree, as was common, but instead bore the symbol of the winds among his family names. Iome knew a little of Inkarran glyphs, could barely read what was written there.

Hoswell scratched his jaw, studying the fellow's tattoos. 'He's an Inkarran, all right. His name is Pilwyn. Zandaros is his patriarchal line, but the bitch who sired him is named Yassaravine,' Hoswell said meaningfully. He looked up into Iome's eyes.

'Yassaravine coly Zandaros?' Iome asked. 'The Storm King's sister?' The Storm King was perhaps the most powerful lord in all of Inkarra. Legend said that his line descended from the

Sky Lords, but that his forefather had fallen from their grace.

Hoswell was telling her that this wind wizard she had at her mercy was a powerful lord in his own right.

The Inkarrans did not fight wars. Their leaders settled disputes by battling among themselves. But Inkarran methods of battle were often subtle and perverse. Seldom did two lords actually bear weapons against one another. More often, a victim might be poisoned or humiliated, or driven to madness or suicide.

As Iome considered this man's actions, she gaped in wonder.

He'd probably taken great delight in dressing as a messenger of Mystarria. He'd have enjoyed the irony of riding as a courier of the land he sought to destroy.

Iome understood that creeping sensation she'd felt when she'd touched the message case. Magical runes were written on it, written with wind. Iome had no doubt that if Gaborn had touched that message case, the 'message' written there would have destroyed him.

More than that, this fellow had either sent Iome dreams to trouble her mind, or he'd peered into her dreams.

'Is this what I think it is?' she asked Hoswell

'Aye, I fear so,' Hoswell said. 'For the first time in history, the Inkarrans have come to war against Rofehavan, milady, and they're going to teach us a whole new way to do battle.'

In frustration, Iome clenched her fists and gazed up into the sky. She didn't want to kill another lord, especially not a foreign lord with family members who would seek retaliation. Why would the Inkarrans want war? She wondered if she could reason with him.

The wind was moaning around the upper branches of the tree. She called to it now. 'Pilwyn coly Zandaros, speak to me.'

The mass of whirling air quit thrashing through the branches, stood quivering above the tree, as if listening to her.

'We have not attacked your people,' Iome shouted. 'Nor do we seek battle with Inkarra. We hope to be allied with you in the dark times to come.'

The wind did not answer. She did not know if the Inkarran

lord could speak to her in his present form. Perhaps it was too complex a task, Iome reasoned.

'Sir Hoswell, take the dirt from his mouth and nose.'

'Milady?' Hoswell asked.

'Do it,' she said.

Hoswell did as she commanded, but the corpse did not move. It merely lay smiling mysteriously up into the tree. Iome noted that its eyes had not glazed.

Iome rode her horse back up the road a couple of hundred yards, until she reached the leather scroll case. She dared not touch it. Instead she threw dust on it by the handfuls. For a moment two runes written there in wind whirled about, then at last dissipated, drowned in dust.

Only when they were gone did Iome open the case and read the message that fell out, scripted on yellow parchment.

Ah, to taste the lively air –
no more!

The scroll had carried a curse, then. One that would have strangled her husband, had he dared to touch the scroll case.

She ripped the paper in half and trampled the message case, then rode back to the tree. 'We'll take his horse as a palfrey,' she told the others. 'I don't want him following us. But leave him with money and food, so that he can make his way home as best he can.'

'You'll leave him alive?' Hoswell asked. He did not hide the incredulity in his voice. She was taking a dangerous risk.

'The Storm King may want to wage war against us, but we desire peace,' Iome said. 'Let Pilwyn coly Zandaros bear that message back to his uncle.'

With that, they gathered the Inkarran's horse and left his body beneath the tree. The fellow still had not moved, had not drawn a breath. Hoswell left the arrow in his shoulder.

The three of them had not ridden more than two hundred yards when an arrow whizzed past Iome's head.

Iome looked back. The Inkarran stood with his white hair

blowing in the wind. He'd pulled the arrow from his shoulder, sent it over her head.

'Honor dictates that I repay your kindness, Your Highness,' he shouted at her. 'I give you your life, for mine.'

Iome nodded curtly, as ladies of the court were taught to do, and said, 'Let there be peace between us.'

But the Inkarran shook his head. 'Though the Earth King may shake his fists and cry out against it, the wind blows him war.

'There is no hope for him, or for the vast hordes of mankind. The earth powers weaken. But my offer to you stands, milady. The Storm King will offer you a haven—' He pointed off to a distant cloud, a great cumulonimbus on the horizon.

Iome turned and rode south.

42

A LORD OF THE UNDERWORLD

The walls around Carris shuddered as the reaver horde raced from the mists.

Out in the fields before the city gates, the common troops of Indhopal ran for their lives, even as the castle guards began to crank up the drawbridge. Many of those troops sprinted up the causeway to where the drawbridge had stood open, then threw themselves into the water and swam for safety, relying upon those at the barbicans to pull them from the lake. The water became thick with splashing sounds, pleas for help, and the cries of the drowning.

Others were too slow to escape, and reavers herded them or hunted them mercilessly. To Roland's amazement, many of the men, when confronted by a reaver that blocked their way, merely fled in terror back out onto the plains, into greater danger, or lay down and huddled, afraid to even move. Thousands of men were thus stranded, cut off from Carris.

Roland clung to the castle wall. The crows and gulls all began to wing away from their roosts in the city, so that only gree filled the air, writhing like tormented things.

Nine reaver mages raced toward the castle, heads held high, staves thrust forward, as if drawn by the scent of its men. Soldiers on the walls shouted in terror.

Raj Ahten's flameweavers ran to the wall-walk above the city gates. Soldiers backed away from the flameweavers; they burst into flame and were clothed only in living fire. One flameweaver raised a hand, drew light from the sky so that for a moment he stood in gloom as sunlight whirled and funneled down into his palm.

He traced a shape in the air: a fiery rune took form before him, a magnificent green shield of living fire that glowed like the sun. The flameweaver shoved it forward. The rune floated down to the end of the causeway and hung in the air two hundred yards from the castle gates. In rapid succession, two more flameweavers did the same, and then the first flameweaver created a fourth rune.

The temperature around Carris plummeted by ten degrees as flameweavers drew heat from the sky. The cold drizzle that had been falling turned to sleet.

But within thirty seconds a wall of four fiery shields blockaded the causeway, cutting off the retreat of men, or the reavers' hopes for attack.

All the while, behind the mages, the main army of reavers marched northward, as if they cared for Carris not at all.

A wild hope began to rise in Roland's chest.

We are nothing to them, he realized. Whatever the reavers intend, Carris is nothing to them.

But out on the plain, the reaver mages formed ranks, a group of nine, so that they charged over the battlefield like geese in formation, with the largest mage at their head.

No, Roland suddenly understood. We are not nothing to them. They merely think so little of us, that they only feel the need to dispatch these nine.

The leader of the nine was a huge thing, over twenty feet tall at the shoulder, with fiery runes tattooed across its entire face and along its forearms. It held its head up fearlessly and approached the causeway, its staff high. As it charged, the dull azure glow within its staff began to blush to crimson, and the rod itself began to trail black smoke.

The artillerymen cut loose with a volley of ballista bolts, the *whonk, whonk, whonk* sounds punctuated with shouts of 'Reload!' and the cranking of gears.

At such close range, one of the artillerymen should have

pierced a reaver. But mysteriously, every bolt seemed to veer wide of its mark.

Magic! Roland realized. We can't shoot them. There's no stopping them.

The great reaver mage reached the end of the causeway and halted momentarily before the green shields of flame. It moved its head this way and that, as if studying them. Then it reached out experimentally with its staff and touched the whirling green wheel of living fire.

It will dispel them, Roland imagined. The shields will collapse harmlessly.

The shields exploded with the sound of an avalanche, tearing at the castle's foundations. Roland fell backward on his butt. Bolts of green flame slashed skyward. Hot air surged over Roland in a violent concussion, and he felt as if he were leaning over a blacksmith's forge, even though the flames were over two hundred yards off. Men nearer the inferno cried out in pain and dropped for cover.

Flames blasted Carris. The heat was so intense that the water wards on the castle wall took effect.

A steam cloud geysered upward, surging into the air, forming a vast curtain that obscured Roland's view. Water condensed on his brow, filled his eyes, and he wiped it away with his sleeve.

Roland looked up for one heart-stopping moment and saw the most beautiful rainbow above him.

He climbed up. The clouds of steam rose, darkening everything, and for several minutes he saw nothing.

Though the walls of Carris were bound and strengthened with Earth runes, the explosion had punished the walls, caused stones to shift. Great slabs of white plaster fell from both the inner and outer castle walls, stripping away the bone-white exterior to leave the stone naked to the cold sleet.

Then the men upon the walls nearest the reavers began to shout and cheer and whistle.

Roland spotted the mage at last, lying two hundred yards back from the mouth of the causeway, black as a cinder and uglier than any nightmare he'd ever had.

It lay dead, unmoving. Green smoke issued from its wounds, where the fiery lances had pierced it. Behind it, other flame-blackened mages were canted sideways, feebly pawing the ground with broken limbs.

Four of the reaver mages near the rear wheeled and scurried from the castle, limping or dragging broken limbs.

Roland whistled and gaped at the dead behemoth. He found himself breathing hard in relief. We've beat them, he thought. We've beat their attack. Men clapped and cheered.

Out on the plains, a few thousand footmen had become trapped. Only three dozen reavers bothered to herd them. The reavers stalked among them, slaughtering them wholesale, but hundreds of men made it to the causeway, threw themselves into the water.

For a long moment, Roland gazed across the countryside. The fog was still receding steadily; a mile from the castle, reavers marched northward in great lines.

The rattling sound of their carapaces smashing against stone could be heard everywhere, like roaring surf. On nearby hills Roland spotted reavers by the thousands.

There are many kinds of creatures that men call reavers, Roland knew, but men rarely saw different varieties. Mostly when men painted images of reavers, they showed the most common breed: the hordes of dreaded blade-bearers and the fearsome mages that led those hordes.

But other species existed. Now for the first time, Roland saw some of those among the blade-bearers: the many-legged worms that men called 'glue mums,' each some eighty feet long, and the smaller urine-colored spidery creatures that men called 'howlers' because of the queer howls that they emitted from time to time.

Though these beasts did not look like the more common reavers, they somehow fit within reaver society. Whether they were intelligent species that the reavers had subverted or whether they were dumb animals trained to slave away in the reavers' behalf, no man knew.

Then, from out of the fog, the reaver horde's leader came.

She was the stuff of legend, a reaver lord unlike any to have been seen aboveground for thousands of years.

'A fell mage!' men shouted in dread as she issued from the fog. A hundred reaver mages bore her on a vast palanquin over their heads. Though a reaver stood taller than an elephant, she dwarfed her companions. Thirty feet at the shoulder, and a full length longer than a normal reaver, her entire body was clothed in runes that glimmered like a garment of light. She did not ride upon the palanquin alone, but sat among a pile of glowing crystals so brilliant that at first Roland thought them to be a bed of glimmering diamonds.

But no, he realized, they were merely reaver bones, eaten free of flesh and licked clean by tongues of fire. These were her vanquished foes.

In her paws she held an enormous staff that glowed a sickly citrine hue.

She is beautiful, Roland thought.

Any reaver so terrified him that he did not know how to feel about this one. He looked to see others' reactions, for he suspected that the warriors here would know enough lore to gauge the threat better than he could. The face of Baron Poll, who had joked at the sight of lesser mages, now looked chiseled and bloodless in terror. Raj Ahten himself gaped at her, eyes wide and nostrils flaring.

A moment before, Roland had breathed a sigh of relief. Now hair rose on the back of his head, while goose pimples formed on his arms.

Here was a veritable Lord of the Underworld.

The reaver mages that had tasted the sorcerous fires of Carris raced toward the palanquin.

'Uh-oh,' Baron Poll grumbled dangerously. 'If there's one thing I don't like, it's a tattletale.'

Perhaps the fell mage won't care, Roland hoped desperately. Perhaps she has more urgent work to the north.

The four mages reached the palanquin, and to Roland's surprise they dropped their shovel-shaped heads into the ground and did obeisance, almost exactly as if they were knights presenting themselves before their lord; their leader raised her tail in the air as if she were a stinkbug. The mages bearing the palanquin stopped.

The fell mage swiveled her broad head toward Carris, then did something that Roland had never heard of before. She rose up on her back legs, the way that a marmot might do at the front of her burrow, so that her forepaws and middle legs dangled uselessly.

She shimmered in the gray morning. The philia along the top of her head stood up and waved like the spicules on a sea anemone as it grasps for food in a tidal pool.

'She can't see us from there, can she?' Roland asked, hoping that at such a distance, he might be overlooked.

'She's smelling us,' Baron Poll said. 'Smelling all eight hundred thousand of us.'

The fell mage took her great staff in both hands, then leapt from her palanquin and came loping toward Carris. At her back, her whole army, thousands upon thousands of reavers, followed in a dark tide.

Down above the castle gates, the flameweavers had just vanquished the mages. Now they desperately began pulling fire from the sky, setting down more of their infernal wards before Carris. As they worked, the air grew colder, and the flameweavers leached heat even from the stone walls, until frost rimed them. The falling slush turned to drifting snow.

Rapidly the flameweavers set nine more wards, and in the process exhausted themselves. The fire curling over their skins died, so that soon all three men stood naked in the cold. All of their hair had burned cleanly away long ago. Snow hissed to steam when it touched their hot skin. Roland could see that the flameweavers did not believe that their wards would hinder a fell mage.

As the reavers raced forward, many of them stopped to pick up the ruined corpses of Raj Ahten's foot soldiers in their teeth. These they bore gingerly in their maws, as if to make an offering of them on the causeway, the way that cats might leave dead mice on a doorstep for their master. Some of the men in the reavers' mouths were only wounded, so that they cried out in pain or pleaded for help in Indhopalese.

The cries wrung Roland's heart, but there could be no rescuing those lost souls.

The fell mage closed upon the castle, but at four hundred yards, she halted. A hundred lesser mages, scarlet sorceresses, spread out and flanked her on either side. Tens of thousands of reavers now gathered at her back, a grim horde that covered the fields; nearly every reaver held a man between its crystalline teeth.

The reavers were still far back from the fiery green wards of the flameweavers.

The fell mage raised her citrine staff and played it over the walls of Carris, as if to unleash some dire spell. Men shrieked and dropped for cover.

Now she'll show us what she can do! Roland thought.

43

ON HUMAN FRAILTIES

Gaborn took little rest at Tor Doohan. He felt the need to hurry south, to fight the Earth's battle. The facilitator at Castle Groverman must have been working all night, for by early morning Gaborn had the full complement of fifty endowments that he'd asked for. He felt his muscles straining beneath his armor, and his blood pounded in his veins, pounded for battle.

So he let the horses feed and rest for only three hours that morning, until he could restrain himself no more.

Before noon he rode south. Only a few hundred men and women rode with him: a hundred lords of Orwynne and Heredon, another hundred and fifty from Fleeds. But they were a stout war party in many ways, the best to be had from three kingdoms, and hope swelled in Gaborn's chest. For soon he would unite with King Lowicker's vast army, and as he approached Carris he hoped to band together with Knights Equitable and lords from Mystarria.

He imagined that he might well have half a million men under his command when he reached Carris, and their attack would be spearheaded by some of the most powerful Runelords in the world.

Time and again he thrilled to realize that old King Lowicker of Beldinook would ride beside him. He'd not expected Lowicker to bestir himself.

Some called Lowicker a 'frail' man, though the description was overly nice.

His frailty was more mental than physical. Over the past

couple of years, his reasoning skills had begun to diminish. Some hinted that he'd grown quite senile. Only the fact that Lowicker had taken endowments of wit from three different men – and thus could store memories in their minds – allowed him to obscure the severity of his ailment.

Yet Lowicker had always been one of King Orden's staunchest allies. Not three weeks ago, Lowicker had organized a grand reception in his father's honor as Gaborn journeyed north.

Lowicker had praised Gaborn roundly, hinting that the Prince would make a fine match for his own daughter – a plump girl who had not one single distinguishing virtue but also seemed to lack any vice.

Gaborn recalled a night of drinking mulled wine beside the hearth while Lowicker and his father told hunting stories, since years before, Lowicker had often accompanied Orden north on the autumn hunt.

But three years past, Lowicker had taken a fall and broken his hip, and now the old man rarely rode a horse at all, and then only in considerable pain. He'd never hunt again, and Gaborn's father had lamented the fact.

As Gaborn headed south, he knew that Iome would be angry with him. He had hastened his departure from Tor Doohan in part because of the rising sense of danger that assailed him to the south, the sense that he needed to attack swiftly. But even more than that, he hurried because he hoped to discourage Iome from following.

He knew that she'd confronted some danger on the borders of Heredon once this morning. And as he rode he began to suspect more and more that men in his care were going to die today. He didn't want Iome to be among the casualties.

Kriskaven Wall spanned a hundred and fourteen miles of the border between Fleeds and Beldinook. The bastion of black stone stood twenty feet tall, and was twenty feet wide at the base. Beyond that, a trench had been dug in ages past all along the north face of the wall, so that now a shallow river flowed there at all times of the year except in high summer.

Two horses could run abreast atop the wall, but the lords of Beldinook had not felt the need to keep Kriskaven Wall properly manned in the past two hundred years.

When Gaborn rode near the wall early that afternoon, toward Feyman's Gate, he felt somewhat gladdened to see Beldinook's warriors thick along the battlements, to see horses galloping atop the wall, to hear welcoming warhorns blowing from it. He estimated that a thousand warriors held this gate alone.

The wall would be a formidable barrier to Raj Ahten's troops, if any sought to ride through here again.

But as Gaborn in company with a hundred knights drew close to the wall, he felt a familiar prickling sensation, as if a shroud dropped over them all.

The Earth whispered of danger.

Gaborn called a halt two hundred yards from the open gate, while he studied the sentries ahead. The men wore Beldinook's uniforms, tall silver caps with square tops, and heavy breastplates. Their shields bore the dun-colored field with the white swan. They carried Beldinook's characteristic wide bows. They flew Beldinook's banners. Atop the wall, a captain waved Gaborn ahead.

But something was not right. Feyman's Gate opened wide and inviting, as it had for hundreds of years. The gate itself stood forty feet across, and the top of the wall spanned over it, brimming with archery slots and kill holes by the score.

Silently Gaborn warned the Chosen in his retinue of an impending ambush. The air around him suddenly filled with the clank of metal on metal as lords lowered their visors and unstrapped shields from the backs of their mounts. The chargers knew the sounds of war. Though Gaborn's own mount stopped, it capered to the side, eager to charge.

Prince Celinor rode beside Erin Connal, two horses down from Gaborn. The Prince looked about nervously, wondering what was happening.

'Who opposes us?' Gaborn shouted across the distance. The

ride had been long and dusty, and the dust choked his throat. Though Gaborn felt battle ready, he had not taken a single endowment of Voice. Now the wind blew northwest into Gaborn's face, hurling his own words back at him, so that he felt unsure if the men on the wall even heard him.

The men of Beldinook watched Gaborn's forces uneasily. Many reached for arrows and stepped behind the battlements on the wall.

'Who dares oppose the Earth King?' Queen Herin shouted, and her Voice cut across the distance far better than Gaborn's ever could.

Suddenly the thunder of hooves rose from the far side of the wall. A row of horsemen wheeled from both the left and the right, and the knights converged before the open gate, blocking Gaborn's passage. Through the gate, Gaborn could only see the front ranks, but estimated that more than a thousand knights rode together.

At their head rode old King Lowicker himself. Lowicker was white-haired, with a narrow face and pale blue eyes that were going gray with age. His long hair was all in braids and slung over his shoulder. He wore no armor, as if to say that he held so little regard for Gaborn as a warrior that he needed none.

He frowned as he sat in his saddle, pained at his old injuries.

'Go back, Gaborn Val Orden,' King Lowicker shouted. 'Go back to Heredon while you may! You are not welcome on my soil. Beldinook is closed to you.'

'Your messenger told another tale two days ago,' Gaborn shouted. 'For what reason have you become inhospitable? You and I have long been friends. We can be friends still.' Gaborn tried to sound calm, to keep his demeanor friendly, but inside his blood ran hot. He felt confused and betrayed. Lowicker had falsely pledged support and urged him to ride here quickly, to fight at his side. Yet Lowicker himself had plotted to cut Gaborn down like a dog. Though Gaborn struggled to remain calm, in his heart he knew that Lowicker would be a friend no more.

'*Your father* and I were friends!' Lowicker raged. 'But I am no pawn to a regicide.' He stabbed a finger toward Gaborn as if he'd caught a young scoundrel. 'You appropriated your father's crown as soon as you were able, but found it too small! Now you call yourself the Earth King. Tell me, Earth King, are these hundred men the only ones silly enough to follow you to your doom?'

'Others follow me,' Gaborn said.

But Lowicker studied Gaborn severely and shook his head, as if he pitied those who rode at his side. 'When you began to practice in the Room of Faces, young man, I was dubious. I thought that if you did not want to learn to be a king, at the very least you would learn to act the part.

'But now I see you strutting and preening like a great monarch, and I am not impressed. Ride along north, young imposter, while you still can.'

Gaborn felt a rising sense of danger. Lowicker was not voicing idle threats. Erin and Celinor had warned Gaborn that King Anders had hoped to sway Lowicker and others with his lies, and apparently Anders had managed to do it quite well.

Lowicker had planned to ambush him, and even now was seconds from ordering a charge. Yet Gaborn hoped that he could persuade Lowicker to see the truth.

'You accuse me of regicide, yet plot my assassination?' Gaborn said, hoping to reveal to Lowicker his own error. 'I fear you are but Anders's pawn. How Raj Ahten would laugh to see this!'

'It is not regicide to execute a criminal,' Lowicker insisted, 'even if that criminal is a man I have always loved as if he were my own son. I wish that I could believe you are the Earth King.' Yet his tone was cold, and Gaborn wondered at Lowicker's sincerity.

'I *am* the Earth King,' Gaborn warned. He stared hard into Lowicker, using the Earth Sight.

He saw a man who loved his position, who loved wealth and acclaim more than he loved the truth. He saw a man who had always felt jealous of King Orden's greater affluence, jealous enough so that he'd always greeted Orden with great pomp – but had schemed to grab a piece of Mystarria for his own.

Here was a man who had married a woman he detested so that he could gain greater position.

Gaborn remembered years ago how his own father had mourned the death of Lowicker's good wife. But Gaborn looked into the aging King's mind and saw how Lowicker had feigned love so well that when the Queen took a fall from a horse and died during a hunting accident with no witness other than Lowicker, no one questioned the manner of her death.

He saw a man who thought himself wise, and secretly congratulated himself often for how he'd accomplished his wife's demise.

This was a man who was frustrated because Gaborn had not married his own homely daughter, for he'd hoped that Gaborn would love wealth as much as he did, and Lowicker had long calculated how to arrange both Gaborn's marriage and death at an early age.

As Gaborn searched King Lowicker's soul, the soul of a man he'd always thought a friend, he found only a shriveled husk. Where Gaborn had once believed that he'd seen decency and honor, now he saw only a fair mask that hid a monstrous avarice.

Lowicker was not acting as Anders's pawn. At the very least he was Anders's conspirator.

Gaborn felt ill in his stomach.

'So then,' Lowicker said, grinning falsely. 'If you are the Earth King, show me a sign so that I might believe, and thus become your servant.'

'I shall,' Gaborn shouted. 'This is the sign: all men who refuse to serve me shall perish in the dark times to come.'

'An easy thing to claim, a hard thing to prove,' Lowicker chortled. 'And as all men shall perish whether they serve you or not, I see no advantage in scraping my arthritic knees to you.'

'If you will not accept that sign,' Gaborn said, 'then let me offer another: I have looked into your heart, and found it wanting. I know your secrets. You call me a regicide, but on a hunt eight years ago, you broke your wife's neck with the butt of your spear. In your heart, you felt no more regret than if you had taken down a pig.'

King Lowicker's smile faltered momentarily, as if he considered for the first time whether Gaborn might really be the Earth King.

'No one will believe your lies,' Lowicker said. 'You are a nothing, Gaborn Val Orden – not a king, nor even a fair mimic. You are not even a has-been. You are a never-shall-be. Your nation is at the mercy of the merciless. Archers!'

Upon the wall, hundreds of men raised their bows. Gaborn stood two hundred yards from Kriskaven Wall. Any arrows shot from such a distance would find it hard to pierce his armor, but few of the mounts in his retinue had barding. A rain of arrows would be devastating, and at this moment, Lowicker craved blood.

Yet the vile old King hesitated.

'Wait!' Gaborn called, raising his left hand. 'I give you one more fair warning! I am the Earth King, and as I serve the Earth, so it serves me.

'I have been called to Choose the seeds of mankind, and those who raise their hands against me do so at their own peril! I bid all of you, let me pass!'

On the wall, Lowicker's men began to laugh him to scorn, and Gaborn stared at them, amazed at how one man's evil could subvert so many.

'Go back!' Lowicker said. Gaborn perceived suddenly that something restrained Lowicker, kept him from releasing his hail of arrows even now.

Since Lowicker had carefully pared away his own conscience with the precision of a skilled surgeon, Gaborn imagined that only one thing could stay his hand: fear.

Gaborn glanced from side to side. Binnesman rode beside Gaborn, along with Sir Langley and many other lords from

Orwynne, as did Queen Herin the Red and Erin Connal of Fleeds, and Prince Celinor of South Crowthen.

Shooting at this company would have repercussions that Lowicker did not want to deal with – perhaps most of all because Lowicker feared how King Anders would react to the murder of his own son.

Indeed, Lowicker's eyes flickered across Celinor for half a second, giving the lad an evil look, as if begging him to depart.

Gaborn almost laughed inside. With sudden clarity he saw that the Earth would serve him well right now.

Gaborn hopped down from his horse.

Before making a cut in stone, masons would draw upon it a rune of Earth-breaking, and thus weaken the stone so that it conformed better to their will. Only a week ago, Binnesman had destroyed the old stone bridge across Harm's Gorge in a similar manner.

Gaborn knew that he could wield such power now. Using the Earth Sight, he gazed not at Lowicker, but at Kriskaven Wall itself. The wall was a great expanse of stone, held together by mortar and gravity.

Yet as he studied it, he saw flaws within the stone. A splintering crack here where a root had pried the stone, a weakness there. It was not so much a wall that he beheld, as a network of small fissures.

The wall was so weak that with a little pressure here, and some there, and over there, it would come down.

'If it is a sign you seek, so be it!' he shouted to Lowicker. 'I will give you a sign that you cannot deny.'

Now Gaborn glanced at the wizard Binnesman. The wizard, astride his horse, whispered, 'Milord, what are you doing?'

'I reject King Lowicker and any man who stands with him,' Gaborn replied. 'Lend me your staff.'

The wizard handed Gaborn his staff, saying, 'Are you sure this is wise?'

'No, but it is just.' He looked up. Lowicker still sat his horse, smirking across the distance, confident. But to Gaborn's satisfaction, Lowicker's Days nervously began backing his own horse away.

Gaborn took the staff and carefully traced a rune of Earth-breaking on the dusty road. The rune looked to Gaborn like a mantis with two heads and three claws, all trapped within a circle.

'Is this how it's drawn?' Gaborn asked the wizard, to be certain he had done it right.

'The earth powers are not used to kill,' the wizard warned.

'The Earth permits death,' Gaborn said, 'even our deaths. I will spare all those I can.'

Yet he wondered if he dared spare Lowicker. Gaborn needed to protect his people, and the Earth had not forbidden him from taking the lives of his enemies. Killing an enemy as vicious as Lowicker was no worse than killing a reaver.

Gaborn raised the wizard's staff overhead and shouted a command: 'By the Earth I serve, I command this wall: be thou broken stones and dust!'

With his mind he reached out to a hundred pressure points on the wall, and then he smote the rune of Earth-breaking with the staff, and felt the impact at his feet as the ground began to roll and buck. The earth rumbled as if it would split apart, and suddenly all the smirking bowmen on the wall began to shout in terror.

The command that Gaborn uttered came not from a weak-willed mason who served the Earth only enough to get something in return. It was the command of the Earth King, and so carried more force than that of any other.

King Lowicker's horse reared, tossing the old man from his saddle. The knights in his retinue broke rank, turned, and began to flee. The men atop the wall raced for the stairs or tried leaping to safety.

The breastwork of Kriskaven Wall had stood for a thousand years. Now with a booming of thunder and a screaming protest of stone, the Earth King's power wracked it. The wall shuddered and twisted for half a mile in each direction, writhing like a snake.

Yet Gaborn could not lightly kill those who defied him.

He felt the wall ready to buckle and shatter according to his will, but for a moment longer he sought to hold it together until the men atop could leap to safety.

Then, even he could no longer hold it, and the wall snarled like an enraged animal, and exploded. Stones shot high in the air, then dropped like hail, pinging on Gaborn's helm. Dust rose into the air in acrid clouds, and was captured by the wind and blown to the north.

Archers who had leapt for safety raced from the base of the wall, trying to cover their hands with their heads.

When the dust settled, a mile of Kriskaven Wall had crumbled. Even in ruins, it was an impressive pile of rubbish. Where Feyman's Gate had stood wide, now there was but a tangle of broken stone from the fallen arch.

A few men had leapt from the wall and injured a leg or arm. Another dozen knights had been unseated from their horses.

As far as Gaborn could discern, he had not slain a single man.

Now, beyond the low pile of rubble, Lowicker's knights fled, hundreds of men racing from destruction.

Erin, Celinor, and a dozen other knights raced to the fallen Lowicker. Their mounts circled the old King, cutting him off from any escape.

Gaborn rode forward with his company over the pile of gravel and cracked stone that had once been the arch to Feyman's Gate, up to where his former friend lay on the ground. King Lowicker's face was contorted with pain, and his right leg askew. It looked as if his hip had broken yet again.

'Damn you!' Lowicker shouted. 'I hope you and Raj Ahten kill each other!'

'A likely scenario,' Gaborn said. He gazed down at Lowicker, full of concern. He did not want to kill the man, to kill any man. Yet Lowicker was such a great evil, such a powerful king, Gaborn knew not what else to do.

Gaborn still dared hope that he could lead Lowicker's troops to war.

'I've given you a sign,' Gaborn said. 'Will you swear fealty to me? Will you repent of your crimes?'

Lowicker merely laughed in derision. 'Of course, milord. Allow me to live, and I swear by the Powers, I'll clean your bedpans every morn!'

'Would you rather die, then?' Gaborn asked. 'Would death be preferable to a life of service?'

'If I am to live, let me live to be served,' Lowicker roared.

Gaborn had expected no better. He shook his head sadly. He looked back at his knights. To slay a king even in the heat of battle was a hard deed, for it might easily bring retribution from another lord. Few in Gaborn's company would dare risk it. But to execute a king in cold blood was more perilous still, for it would incite Lowicker's allies to rage.

Though it was a deed best done by a man of equal rank to Lowicker, Gaborn was loath to do it. He turned to the lords accompanying him and asked, 'Will any of you put him down?'

'I will,' High Queen Herin the Red said in a hard tone. 'I always admired Lowicker's wife. I will avenge her now.'

When Celinor heard Queen Herin's threat, he said, 'You should make the cut, milady. But it would please me if you would do the honor of using my sword.'

She leapt from her gelding, took Celinor's sword.

King Lowicker shouted, 'No, please!,' and feebly tried to crawl away as Queen Herin advanced.

Though Lowicker lay wounded, he was not defenseless. He was a Runelord still, with endowments of brawn and metabolism to his credit.

As Queen Herin drew near, he blurred into motion. From somewhere in his robes Lowicker produced a knife, hurled it expertly.

Queen Herin sought to parry with her sword, but the knife blade took her full in the chest.

Her mail blunted the impact, and the heavy quilting of her underjerkin held the point.

Lowicker's eyes went wide as Queen Herin rushed in with the sword.

In Fleeds the penalty for regicide was the removal of the criminal's hands and feet. Thereafter he would be left to languish. Lowicker did not die quickly from his wounds. He had so many endowments of stamina that he could not die quickly.

According to those who followed, Lowicker lived on in torment until sunset, when the cold leached the heat from his body, so that he died like a snake.

44

THE STALEMATE

The fell mage merely stood before the walls of Carris, her sickly citrine rod throbbing with light, the gleaming runes tattooed into her carapace glowing dimly. She played it over the walls, and Roland imagined that at any second she would cast a horrid spell and the barbicans would melt into slag or crumble to ruin.

Instead, she merely pointed her staff toward the castle gate, and for a long time, nothing happened.

Roland was a good swimmer. Given the chance, he would throw off his clothes and dive from the castle wall. He could probably swim south a mile or more, then cut for the shore. From there he might be able to escape.

Then, at last, he saw her plan.

She cast no spell.

Instead, from the ranks of ten thousand reavers, a single reaver strode forward. It was diminutive compared to its companions. Small, wretched, and covered with old scars.

It marched toward the castle alone, toward the nine fiery green shields that the flameweavers had set as wards.

Everyone in the castle saw the reaver's plan at once. The captain of the artillery shouted for his men to fire at the wretched creature, and fire they did.

But as before, the ballista bolts careened away from their target, and the miserable little reaver trundled forward to the mouth of the causeway, into the midst of the green glowing shields.

Roland did not see what happened. He dropped for cover before the small reaver triggered the flame wards. He merely felt the castle walls buck, the roiling heat blast overhead. Light and dust swirled up into the air.

And then the castle's protective wards were gone.

The flameweavers that guarded Carris had spent their power in vain. When Roland got up, he glanced down toward them. Two of the flameweavers, naked now even of flames, began slinking down the steps, as if seeking retreat, while the third merely stood studying his ruined wards in defiance.

With the wards gone, the fell mage turned and began to stride north, as if she were no longer concerned herself with the castle.

But a cohort of a thousand blade-bearers remained in place, forming a long wall before the castle, just a few yards out of artillery range.

Their intent was clear. There would be no escape from Carris.

The fell mage led her horde north, and Roland was glad to see her go. But she did not travel far.

Just north of the castle was a small rise called Bone Hill, where lords had fought for centuries as they sought to take Carris.

The fell mage stopped at the foot of the hill and dropped her head close to the ground, like a hound eagerly catching a scent. Slowly she began to tread in a circle around the base of the hill, while minions stayed back a hundred yards.

When she had circled it completely, the fell mage dropped her head and trotted round it again, more quickly – so that her shovel-shaped head scooped out a perfect circle. Then she galloped around a third time, widening the furrow.

As she did, all of the other reavers began to hiss.

Moments later the wind brought a scent – from beneath the snow and ash – unlike anything Roland had ever smelled before. It was sweeter than the nectar of a rose, more fragile and exotic.

Of anything he'd witnessed that day, the scent alone seemed

the most wondrous. He breathed deeply, sought to fill his lungs with the heady perfume.

'What's that smell?' a farmer asked Baron Poll in a whisper.

'Something the reavers are making,' Baron Poll said.

'But . . . I've always heard that reavers don't have a scent, that they can't be tracked even by dogs.'

Baron Poll shook his head in wonder. 'Sirrah, the smartest man in the world could fit everything he thinks he knows about reavers into a ten-page book, and once you read it you might as well throw it straight in the jacks.

'Some say that reavers don't have a smell, and others say that they mimic the scent of their background, and I've heard some say that they can manufacture any scent at will. But . . . it's been two thousand years since we've fought a surface war with reavers. Most of what men once knew is lost. All that's left are exaggerations and half-truths.'

When the fell mage had paraded the hill six more times, she climbed to its crown.

Reavers pulled crystalline skulls from the mage's palanquin and used them to decorate the crown of the hill, so that eyeless reaver skulls stared from it in every direction.

Then the fell mage raised her staff overhead. Lesser mages formed a circle at the base of the hill. Each carried a dead or dying man in its jaws, and now the mages grasped the carcasses and wrung each man as if he were a rag. Blood and guts and bodily fluids squirted into the trench. Then the corpses were thrown over the top.

When the reaver mages had wrung their victims dry, a new scent began to arise – a ghastly odor that seemed a mixture of smoke and putrefaction.

Then the howlers and blade-bearers left Bone Hill and began to spread over the countryside. They began dismantling every artifact of human manufacture, tearing down fortresses and cottages, uprooting trees and orchards, crashing through stone fences that had stood for hundreds or thousands of years.

They demolished everything, spared nothing, and worked with terrifying speed and efficiency.

The glue mums began eating every plant in sight, masticating whole trees and the thatch from cottages, then spitting it out in the form of sticky saliva. Howlers grabbed the masticated pulp and pulled it into ropes, as if it were taffy that quickly hardened. The howlers dragged the lines to the base of Bone Hill and twined it about, forming a rigid cocoon around the hill, a screen behind which the reaver mages continued to work. They began excavating the hill, forming strange and sinuous patterns in the ground.

At the base of the hill, bladebearers dug burrows for fortifications.

Within an hour, all of the low-lying wizard fog had at last dissipated, and Roland could see into the distance for several miles. When he did, his heart fell.

To the south was an unending line of reavers, all marching from the mountains down to Carris. These twenty thousand or so that held Carris had only been the vanguard of a vast army.

Roland had dared hope that the reavers would head north. Now it seemed they had found what they were looking for: a new home.

Raj Ahten stood on the ramparts of the gate tower and watched the hills to the south. Every quarter mile or so, he could see reavers by the threes and nines, forming a long line that reached from Carris down to the Brace Mountains and beyond. It was a maddening sight.

The wall of blade-bearers outside the castle gates would block any attempt to sally forth and attack.

Raj Ahten's flameweavers and counselors stood beside him, while his Days stood at his back. As he watched the fields below, Lord Paldane the Huntsman climbed up the tower.

'My lord,' Paldane said softly, solicitously, 'may I please have a word with you?'

Raj Ahten studied him curiously. The man's demeanor bespoke utter humility. But Duke Paldane was a brilliant man, a duplicitous man, and a famed strategist. In Raj Ahten's opinion, in a drawn-out war Paldane would have been Raj Ahten's most fearsome opponent. Now, he had come like a dog with its tail between its legs.

'Yes?' Raj Ahten asked.

'I have been considering a plan to abandon the castle,' Paldane said humbly. 'There is a gated aqueduct on the north wall.'

'I know,' Raj Ahten said. 'Seven hundred and fourteen years ago, during the Siege of Pears, Duke Bellonsby pretended to abandon the city by boating men through it night and day. But when Kaifba Hariminah's men entered the city at last, and drank themselves silly in celebration, Bellonsby's men came up from the King's cellars and slaughtered them.'

Raj Ahten let Paldane know that he'd anticipated him. 'You of course have a large number of boats.'

'Yes,' Paldane said. 'I've nearly eight hundred skiffs at hand. We can begin evacuating women and children to the east shore of the lake now, at ten thousand people per flotilla. I estimate that we can make one journey every two hours.

'More than a hundred thousand people per day. If by some miracle the reavers did not attack for five or six days, the whole castle could be emptied.'

Raj Ahten stared hard at Paldane, considering. Women and children. Saving them would of course be the first priority of these soft northerners.

He almost laughed. These people were his ancient enemies.

Besides, had the northerners ever considered the welfare of Raj Ahten's own women and children? In the past five years, northern assassins had struck down most of his family – his father and sister, wives and sons. The war between Raj Ahten and the lords of Rofehavan had been bloody and personal. By invading the north, Raj Ahten had escalated it to the level of being bloody and impersonal.

Raj Ahten could easily evacuate his own Invincibles in a single flotilla, abandoning the people of Carris to fend for themselves. Or he might begin moving all his warriors from the castle now, and be gone by day's end.

'What makes you think that it will be safe on the east shore?' he asked Paldane. 'Isn't it likely that the reavers have set guards around the lake?'

Lake Donnestgree was large, forty miles from north to south, nearly three and a half miles from east shore to west.

'Perhaps,' Paldane said cautiously. 'But my far-seers in the tower cannot make out any guards there.' Raj Ahten could almost see the doubts whirling in Paldane's head, the worries and fears.

Raj Ahten nodded toward the line of reavers marching from the mountains to the south. 'It may be that the reavers are still waiting for reinforcements,' he said, 'or that they've secreted troops behind the hills. I would not underestimate the fell mage. It would be foolish to send women and children into greater danger.'

He knew that villages were scattered to the east of Lake Donnestgree, even some minor fortresses that his people could defend. But the shore was so rocky, the land so mountainous, that only a few sheep farmers and woodsmen inhabited it. Raj Ahten turned to his old counselor, Feykaald. 'Get twenty skiffs and fill them with mixed troops from our company and from Paldane's. Have them check the east shore of the lake for signs of reavers, and then march inland for several miles to make sure that the shore is secure. When they finish, have them hold a fortress and bring me word.'

Feykaald studied Raj Ahten with heavy-lidded eyes, hiding his smile. He understood Raj Ahten's game. Scouting the shore and securing a beachhead was worthwhile, for Raj Ahten would need it if he did evacuate his men. 'It shall be done, O Light of the Universe.'

Immediately Feykaald shouted to some of the captains, began assembling his shore party.

'My lord,' Paldane said, 'we also have plenty of wood here for hoardings, beams from homes and corrals in the city. We could put men to work on the east wall of the castle, lashing together rafts. With enough rafts, we could evacuate perhaps a hundred thousand more people with a few moment's notice.'

Raj Ahten studied Paldane briefly. Paldane was a thin man with a hatchet face, dark hair that had almost completely gone white. His dark-blue eyes showed superior cunning. 'Not yet,' Raj Ahten objected. 'If we begin lashing together rafts prematurely, it will turn men's minds toward flight, rather than on how to better defend themselves. Defending Carris is our first priority.'

'My lord,' Paldane said, 'considering the number of reinforcements the reavers have coming from the south, I suspect that flight is our best – if not the only – alternative.'

Raj Ahten smiled a practiced smile that included more than just a simple movement of the lips. He tightened the muscles around his eyes. 'You are dismissed.'

After the fog dissipated, news spread along the castle wall that Raj Ahten was sending shore parties to the east, so that the castle could be evacuated.

The news buoyed Roland's spirits. It was then that he took his first real view of the city of Carris itself. There were homes below him, and an almond tree that grew against the wall so high that if he dared he could have leapt into its topmost branches without injury. He was right behind some lord's garden, and the city stretched to the north all around.

Down in the inner bailey to the west he could see thousands of townsfolk, and the horses that Raj Ahten's knights had ridden tied in lines along the street.

Against the west wall of the outer bailey hunkered some forty frowth giants, each twenty feet tall. The tawny yellow fur beneath their ring mail looked darker than normal, for it was wet and matted by rain. The giants gazed about with their huge silver eyes, looking doleful and ill-used. The giants needed fresh meat often, and Roland did not like the way they eyed the peasant children of Carris, who peered at the monsters from doorways and windows and from beneath the eaves of inns.

Every bit as fearsome as the giants were Raj Ahten's war dogs, mastiffs that wore armor: masks and harnesses of red-lacquered leather, and collars around the neck with huge curved spikes in them. These were force dogs, bred to war and granted endowments of brawn, stamina, and metabolism from other dogs in their packs.

Yet as fearsome as these beasts were, Roland knew that Raj Ahten's warriors were more fearsome still. Each Invincible had at least twenty endowments to his credit. In battle, the Invincibles were unmatched by any other soldier in the world.

Beyond these forces, the walls of Carris were bolstered with over three hundred thousand common soldiers out of Mystarria, Indhopal, and Fleeds. Indeed, men crowded the wall-walks and were stuffed in every tower like meat in sausage skins. The baileys and streets of the city were replete with spearmen.

A force so large would have seemed enough to repel any attack. Yet Roland realized that if the reavers attacked, all the men in the castle would not be enough.

As he watched the small flotilla of twenty boats row east, he earnestly hoped that they would return soon, that the evacuation would begin. He considered his own best route into the water if the need arose.

Reavers blackened the land and continued marching from the south all morning. The number around Carris was impossible to count, but surely tens of thousands raced over the countryside, toiling feverishly.

No man alive had ever seen a reaver work, had ever seen their cunning or efficiency or astonishing speed.

The wind blew fiercely, and a thin rain began pouring two hours after dawn. A watery sheen covered the reavers' leathery hides. The rain and clouds above offered the people of Carris some hope, for all men knew that if lightning began to flash, the reavers would likely depart.

Howlers grubbed about everywhere, throwing up defenses in the muck. Burrowing holes. They excavated trenches to the south and west, flooding them with waters from Lake Donnestgree, forming a series of four oddly winding moats.

The sounds that arose from the fields west of Carris were

odd, alien: the rumbling and rasping of reavers, the apparently unprovoked and inexplicable bawls of the howlers, the smacking sounds that glue mums made as they worked. Beneath it all was a tittering, like the squeaking of bones, that emanated from gree flying among the horde. The sounds made Roland feel as if he'd been transported to another world.

To the north, reaver mages and glue mums worked at Bone Hill, molding ridges of rock to form an arcane design in bas-relief, a design that was strange and sinuous and somehow evil. As they worked, the mages sprayed certain knobs and protrusions on their sculpture with fluids from their bung-holes, creating a nauseating stench of decay like something from rotting corpses.

Meanwhile, a mile to the south of Carris, the reavers began to form an odd tower – black and twisted, like a narwhale's horn, yet tilted at an odd angle, as if pointing toward Bone Hill.

Beside the tower on the shore of the lake they built several huge domes made of stone bound with glue-mum resin. Some conjectured that these were egg-laying chambers or some sort of hothouses.

But the reavers did not attack Carris.

They dismantled hamlets that had grown over the centuries. They plundered fortresses and converted the stones to their own purpose. They tore up roads and gardens.

But the reavers did not attack. So long as the blade-bearers blocked the only road in and out of Carris, no man could hope to flee that way or sally forth to attack. But then so long as the reavers did not storm the castle gates Roland felt . . . mollified by the arrangement.

As the day wore on, he was able to forget the creeping sense of menace and horror of the morning, the cries of Raj Ahten's foot soldiers as they were carried to their deaths. He dared hope. For long hours as the day wore on, the men on the walls held remarkably silent. By noon they began talking animatedly, easily.

The shore party had been gone for hours, and would surely return soon. Who could blame the men if they did not hurry back to Carris?

But minute by minute, hour after hour, men scanned the waters, and saw no boats return from the east.

45

FRAIL KING LOWICKER

Until a week ago, Myrrima had never been more than ten miles from home, and as she rode through Fleeds, she felt as if everything she'd known were slipping away.

Myrrima had left behind her family, her country. The land was changing subtly as she rode south. First she passed through the plains of southern Heredon, into the canyon lands of northern Fleeds, and now she was moving farther south. Here, the plains were richer and more fertile than back home, a bit more wet. She did not recognize some of the trees at the roadside, and even the people were different. The sheep men of Fleeds were often shorter and darker than people at home, the horse clans taller and more fair. Cottages were no longer made of mud and wattle, but of stone. Even the air smelled different, she thought, though it was hard to tell, given that she had an endowment of scent from a dog.

Most of all, Myrrima had left herself behind. She had the strength of three men in her arms now, the grace of four, the stamina of her dogs, the speed of five.

She'd never been so cognizant of her own power.

Yet she felt an unsettling sameness to her. In her heart she still loved in the same way, still felt her own inadequacies. Even with her new endowments, Myrrima felt impotent. Though she was a wolf lord, she felt all too common still.

She did not know whether Borenson would welcome her on his quest south, but by nightfall she hoped to reach Carris and present herself to him. She hoped he'd think she'd earned the right to accompany him to Inkarra, though she could not pretend to have his skills in battle.

But her encounter with Lord Pilwyn had left her shaken, uncertain. What kind of enemies would she find in Inkarra? How could she hope to fight them? Endowments would not be enough to fight wizards like the Storm Lord and his kin.

At Tor Doohan, Myrrima found everything in disarray. Gaborn's knights were strung out for miles. Some were just reaching Tor Doohan, while a passerby told them that Gaborn himself had ridden south an hour ago.

A knight rode out of the shadows of the great white stones that circled the crimson pavilion and addressed Iome. 'Your Highness, His Majesty King Orden bade me inform you that he has had to ride on to Carris in great haste. He left this letter in my care.'

Iome read the letter, sniffed the paper to make sure that Gaborn's scent was upon it, then wadded it angrily and stuffed it in her pocket.

'Bad news?' Sir Hoswell asked. 'Can I do anything to help?'

Iome glanced at him distractedly.

'No,' she answered. 'My lord is in great haste to reach Carris. He bids us hurry. We won't be able to rest the horses long if we are to catch him before nightfall.'

'Is it wise even to try, milady?' Sir Hoswell inquired. 'You've ridden over four hundred miles since dawn yesterday. Even your fine mount cannot easily bear such punishment!'

It was true. Sir Borenson's force horse had been plump when Myrrima set off for the south, but in the past two days it had lost seventy or eighty pounds of fat.

The lords of Rofehavan fed their force horses special diets when traveling in haste, using a mixture called 'miln.' Miln consisted of rolled oats and barley coated with dried molasses, often with alfalfa or melilot thrown into the mix. For a horse, miln was a heady pleasure, and a force horse fed well on it could run for hours, while a horse fed on grass alone was said to have 'legs of straw,' for they would not hold the mount long.

But even miln would not allow a force horse to race endlessly. Myrrima's mount had three endowments of metabolism. With so many endowments, a few hours of rest would seem like a day to the beast, allowing it to recuperate.

'Gaborn is racing his horse,' Iome objected to Hoswell.

Hoswell shook his head. 'It's not my place to counsel the Earth King,' Hoswell said, 'but Gaborn knows the danger he's riding into. Half of the mounts he's driving to Carris will die at this pace.'

'We'll take two hours' rest,' Iome said to Hoswell. 'We can feed the horses here, and carry extra miln to keep them along the way until we reach Beldinook.'

Hoswell looked at his own mount. It was in far worse shape than Iome's mount or Myrrima's. The beast had been skinnier than these in the first place, and so had been hard-pressed to keep pace with the stouter mounts. Myrrima knew full well that when Hoswell objected to the pace of the ride, he objected mostly for the sake of his own beast.

If the horse lived to reach Carris, it would most likely be in poor condition for battle. Nor would it carry a man far in case of a forced retreat.

'So be it,' he said heavily. He leapt from the mount and led his horse to the stables, intending to give it as much rest as he could. With it he took the palfrey from the Inkarran assassin.

Myrrima watched Hoswell go.

'Why do you give him such a black look?' Iome asked. 'Is there something between you?'

'Nothing,' Myrrima said. Hoswell was Lord of the Royal Society of Archers, a master bowier who had spent years in the south, studying the making of hornbows. He was a man of sound reputation, in the good graces of the King. Myrrima did not want to have to confess that she detested the man.

Myrrima sat astride Borenson's big warhorse and fought the urge to continue south now. Iome must have noted her mood.

'Gaborn begged me to stay here in his note,' Iome confessed weakly. 'He does not think the road ahead will be safe. He says that he fears that "Doom lies upon Carris," and even now the Earth bids him to strike and flee with equal fervor. He's confused. I thought I should warn you.'

'He's probably right,' Myrrima agreed. Iome sounded as if she felt unsure what to do. 'Milady,' Myrrima said. 'If you wish to stay here, I understand . . . But I'm not riding to war at Carris. I hope to accompany my husband to Inkarra. I *must* take the road south.'

'You sound driven,' Iome said warily. 'I fear that you will never forgive me.'

'Forgive you, milady?' Myrrima asked, surprised by the Queen's tone.

'I'm the one who sentenced your husband to perform his Act Penitent,' Iome said. 'Had I known that I was driving you south, too, I'd not have done it. Perhaps I should lay aside the quest . . . It's a hard thing I've done.'

'No,' Myrrima said. 'It was a generous thing. You've given him a way to earn forgiveness, and in Mystarria I've heard that there is a maxim: "Forgiveness should never be given – it must be earned." I fear that in my husband's case, he cannot even forgive himself until he has earned it.'

'Then I hope he can earn it, with you at his side,' Iome said. 'You have a warrior's spirit. I'm surprised that no one noticed it sooner.'

Myrrima shook her head, glad to change the subject. She'd always been strong of will, but she'd never seen herself as a warrior – not until a little over a week ago.

'It's said that when the Earth King Erden Geboren was crowned, he Chose his warriors. I know full well that Gaborn Chose me in the market of Bannisferre on that first day we met. Even though neither he nor I knew that he was the Earth King. He thought me brash and said he wanted me in his court, but he was really Choosing me.

'But do you know what I was thinking when he Chose me?'

'What?' Iome asked.

Myrrima hesitated, for she'd not told this to anyone, had not even recalled the thought until now. 'I was thinking, even when I saw him standing there at the tinker's booth, all dressed like some fop of a merchant prince, that I would fight for that man. I would die for him.

'I'd never thought that about a man before. The notion gave me the courage to take his hand, though he was a total stranger.'

Iome was bemused. 'Gaborn told me how you met, how you took his hand there in the market. He saw it as only an attempt at seduction, a poor woman looking for a good marriage.'

That was true, but now Myrrima recognized that there was also something more. Myrrima tried to express the odd notion that was growing in her. 'Maybe Gaborn did not Choose me, so much as we Chose each other. Last week, you mentioned that one could not be so near his creative powers without wanting a child. I . . . there's more to him than that. Ever since we've met, I look at the earth, and time and again I'm stunned by its beauty – by the yellow of a daisy, or the blue shadows cast by rounded stones, or the rich smell of moss. He makes me feel more awake and alive than ever before. But there's something else: he makes me want to fight.'

'You're a frightening woman, Myrrima.'

'I told you that I'd understand if you wanted to stay here. I know that it will be dangerous in Carris. But I want to go,' Myrrima said, hoping Iome would understand.

'Neither you nor I have enough training to go into battle – yet,' Iome warned. 'It wouldn't be wise.'

'I know,' Myrrima said. 'But that doesn't stop the craving.'

Iome bit her lip, spoke thoughtfully. 'I think . . . that your intentions are good. As a Runelord, you should act upon them. With your stamina you can work ceaselessly; with your brawn, you can strike mighty blows. Our people deserve our best efforts.

'But it frightens me, Myrrima. You have been given so much so quickly. I would not want to see you get killed.'

Myrrima's mount bent low. The ground here below Tor Doohan was beaten, hardly a blade of grass left, but Myrrima's mount snatched at a few blades of clover close to the ground.

'We'll ride fast,' Iome promised. 'Maybe we can reach Carris before sun-down.'

'You're too kind, milady,' Myrrima said, climbing down from her mount. She stood a moment, stretching her legs.

Two hours later, as they were having a meal at an inn, a courier brought word from the south: Lowicker of Beldinook had sought to ambush the Earth King, and had been defeated at Beldinook's border.

Iome reeled from this ill news.

Lowicker had promised to ally himself with Gaborn, had promised to send knights to ride at his side. Lowicker had promised to lead his own troops against Raj Ahten, and to provide supplies for Gaborn and his knights.

What would happen now that Gaborn had slain the King of Beldinook? One by one, Gaborn's allies were fading away. It was nearly two in the afternoon. King Orwynne had died about this time yesterday while fighting the Darkling Glory. Now Lowicker had turned traitor and been slain.

With Lowicker dead, his daughter would either have to go to war with Gaborn or offer terms of surrender. Gaborn was in such a hurry that he would want neither.

Whether Lowicker's daughter offered battle or reconciliation, Gaborn would merely have to ride through her lands.

It might be dangerous to continue on to Beldinook. Gaborn's knights would be spread thin between here and Carris. Gaborn and a few hundred men were racing toward Carris, probably never more than a dozen in a group.

With his ranks spread thin, Gaborn's men would be in no position to fight. Indeed, they offered fine targets for Beldinook's wrath.

No, Iome suspected that Lowicker's daughter would not surrender, but instead would press the attack. She might be on the hunt for anyone caught in her lands.

Gaborn had hoped that Lowicker would spend hundreds of thousands of troops in his defense. Now it looked as if Gaborn might have to fight through them.

Iome sighed, looked from Myrrima to Hoswell, and said in a firm tone, 'We'll need extra food for ourselves and our mounts.'

Myrrima was not prepared for what she saw when she reached Kriskaven Wall. The courier in Fleeds had said that Gaborn had defeated Lowicker's ambush. He had not mentioned that the Earth King had cursed and blasted the wall.

Nor did Myrrima realize that Lowicker would still be alive. The three riders reached the wall and found Lowicker pinned to the ground a hundred yards on the other side, with a dozen of Gaborn's knights in attendance.

A spear had been thrust through his belly, pinning his torso to the ground, and a banner affixed to the spear named Lowicker as a regicide. Lowicker's arms and legs had been hewn off and dragged away, so that only the stump of a man, all still dressed in kingly apparel, lay in the hot sun.

But Lowicker had so many endowments of stamina that he had not yet died. Only a king or one of Raj Ahten's Invincibles, a man with many endowments of stamina, could have survived such mutilation. Blood had pooled about him, and flies swirled around in a swarm. But with so many endowments of stamina, the horrid wounds had begun to heal swiftly.

Myrrima felt astonished to see him lying in agony, still clinging to life. She doubted he could last long, knew for a fact that he must yearn to die.

Such was the penalty prescribed for those who had committed regicide. As they rode near the site, Myrrima gasped involuntarily, for she recalled that Sir Borenson was also a kingslayer, and by rights, Iome could have demanded this penalty from him.

The scent of blood in the air was cloying, now that Myrrima had an endowment of scent from a dog. It smelled surprisingly enticing.

As they reached the spot, King Lowicker turned his head and watched Iome, sweat dripping from his brow. He took one look at Iome, and King Lowicker began to laugh. 'So,

Spawn of Sylvarresta, have you come to gloat?' Lowicker asked. He spoke painfully.

Iome shook her head. 'Give him a drink, at the very least,' she commanded one of the knights in attendance.

The Baron shook his head. 'It would only prolong his suffering, Your Highness. Besides, a creature like this – he'd give none to you.'

She fixed the husk of King Lowicker with a gentle look. 'Would you like water?'

'Ah, she feels sentiment for the damned,' Lowicker snarled. 'Do not pity me. I want it less than your water.'

Myrrima could not believe that Lowicker could be so cold, so hard, even now when he faced death. Yet she'd seen that look of contempt on other faces. At Castle Sylvarresta, when the city guard had caught thieves looting as the Darkling Glory came, she'd seen such expressions on the faces of hardened criminals, men who had hidden from the Earth King lest he look into their hearts and know them for what they were.

Now she saw Lowicker's dilemma. While many kings might search Gaborn out, hope to ally themselves with him and thus save themselves and their people, other kings would be like this – like Lowicker of Beldinook and Anders of South Crowthen – men so corrupt that they felt no choice but to strike out at Gaborn.

Lowicker knew himself to be corrupt beyond all hope.

'I pity you anyway,' Iome told him.

Lowicker cackled insanely. Tears began to cut streams down his dirt-crusted face. Obviously his pain coupled with the hot sun was affecting his mind.

What an evil man, Myrrima thought. He deserves no pity, yet Iome offers it. He deserves no water, yet Iome would give it.

'Your Highness,' Sir Hoswell asked after a long moment, 'shall I do him?' He dared not use such an indelicate word as 'kill.'

Myrrima thought that Iome would consent, would give

in and kill the man now, release him from his pain.

'No,' Iome said, suddenly furious. 'That's what he hopes for.' She spurred her horse past Lowicker, and Myrrima felt a thrill of relief.

46

A HERO BY NECESSITY

In the west tower of Duke Paldane's Keep, Raj Ahten stared from the windows and studied the workings of the reavers.

For now, he was biding his time. His shore party had not yet returned from the east side of the lake, and so he still did not know for certain whether they could flee the castle by water. The fact that they were so long overdue suggested to Raj Ahten that the shore party had been slaughtered to a man.

In the back of his mind, he knew that Gaborn's troops would be heading to the aid of Carris. Perhaps even the Earth King himself would come do battle with the reavers, and he imagined the satisfaction watching that fight might bring.

Raj Ahten was here with Paldane, the men who had served as Wits to King Orden, and Raj Ahten's counselor Feykaald. His three flameweavers stood at his back before a roaring blaze in the hearth, peering into the smoke and the writhing flames. They were drawing the heat into them, trying to regenerate their powers, but they were so drained, Raj Ahten doubted they'd be able to fight for the rest of the day. He dared not engage the reavers until the flameweavers could stand beside him.

After dawn Raj Ahten had quickly set up formations for defending the castle gates. Yet the reavers merely ignored them, continued to build.

'What are they up to?' Raj Ahten wondered aloud. 'Why don't they attack?'

'It may be that they fear to try a frontal assault,' Duke Paldane ventured. 'But they dig well, and might tunnel into the castle, like monstrous sappers.'

The reavers had obviously come here for a purpose.

But for the moment the reavers did not seem interested in taking the castle. Perhaps they were not fully aware of the danger that his men presented. It even seemed remotely plausible to Raj Ahten that the reavers had forgotten that the castle was here; they were after all strange creatures that danced to a pipe that no man could hear.

He glanced toward Bone Hill. The fell mage worked there near its crown, glittering from the fiery runes tattooed in her carapace. Once, her massive head swiveled toward the castle, but then she resumed her work.

Perhaps the fell mage felt secure with her minions guarding the plains. The land was now pocked with openings to subterranean caverns, laced with moats, decorated with that stinking rune that covered the hill. He studied Bone Hill, secure behind its barrier of hardened mucilage, partially wrapped inside its cocoon.

The glue mums had quit towering the walls higher. Raj Ahten suspected that the fell mage's curious defenses might be complete.

Was it merely a coincidence that they came to this place, now, where Raj Ahten planned to face the Earth King? Raj Ahten wondered. Could it be that they prepared this battleground for the Earth King?

It seemed more probable that their plans had nothing to do with any of them. The reavers seemed content to ignore Raj Ahten and his armies, as if he were beneath their notice.

Raj Ahten shook his head in dismay. For the past hour he had been assaulted by strange and distressing emotions for reasons that he could not quite understand.

I should not be dismayed, he reasoned. I am the most powerful Runelord to grace the earth in millennia. My facilitators in Indhopal have drawn brawn and stamina from thousands of subjects, have taken grace and wit from thousands more. A sword driven through my heart cannot slay me. I should not feel apprehensive.

Yet he did. In recent months, he had begun to believe that he was invincible, that he was on the verge of becoming a creature of legend, the Sum of All Men – a Runelord so charismatic that he would no longer need forcibles to draw attributes from his Dedicates. He hoped to become a Power, a force of nature, like the Earth or Fire or Water.

Daylan Hammer had accomplished it in days of old, if legend spoke true.

Raj Ahten had stood on the brink of attaining that distinction; until ten days ago it seemed that nothing could hinder him. Then old King Mendellas Orden had stolen his forcibles.

Surely if the reavers knew that a man like me confronts them, Raj Ahten thought, they would fear me.

Raj Ahten glanced toward the foul rune that the reavers were shaping at Bone Hill. The stink of it had become appalling, and now the odor hung above the hill in a spiral of brown haze.

Death emanated from that place. Raj Ahten felt the pain and rot and decrepitude. To even look at it made the eyeballs twitch, want to turn away. Dim lights flickered beneath the roiling smoke, like the phantom ghost lights that formed when gas bubbles rose from a swamp. It seemed to Raj Ahten that the whole rune was precariously close to bursting into flame.

I feel dismay. Somehow, that rune is the key.

The reavers focused too much attention on it. Their mages swarmed the hill, patiently digging great trenches so that the odd rune took shape in bas-relief, then decorated it with their stench.

Raj Ahten had endowments of scent from thousands of men. He breathed deeply. It was not a single odor. He could detect myriad undertones and flavors. It was a complex medley: a bouquet of rot, of moldering flesh, mixed smoke and death and human sweat, a rich symphony teeming with competing smells. He felt as if he were almost on the verge of revelation, of recognizing the entirety of it.

Certainly the reavers had come to Carris for the sole purpose of shaping that rune.

Reavers scurried about on the rune's walls, and one of them slipped, causing a slide. To Raj Ahten's delight, part of the rune collapsed. Reaver mages raced to build it back up, hold it together, and spray the protuberances with new scents.

The rune was tantalizingly close. A child with a hammer could knock it down.

On a sudden impulse, Raj Ahten slammed a mailed fist through the window of the Duke's Keep, stood for a moment and inhaled the subtle texture of odors coming from the rune.

Raj Ahten closed his eyes in concentration. As he inhaled deeply, he became aware that some scents did not translate simply as smells. Instead they assaulted the emotions. Yes, dismay was the scent that he smelled.

He'd never considered the possibility that a scent might arouse an emotion.

The sour sweat of someone who toiled near death. Raj Ahten tasted the scent, and felt with it that man's despair.

Smoke, and agony. The salty taste of human tears. The greasy scent of charred flesh, and with it another smoky odor: fields of crops rotting under a blight.

Decay. A corpse bloated like a melon to the point of bursting.

Despair and terror assailed him. The coppery scent of blood, a woman's broken water, and decay – a mother giving birth to a stillborn child. Fatigue.

The sour taste of old skin. Loneliness so deep it was an ache in the bones.

After a long moment, Raj Ahten smiled and almost laughed in pain. He recognized that complex scent now: it was a symphony of human suffering, the tally of all mankind's misery.

'It's an incantation,' Raj Ahten realized. He startled himself by speaking aloud.

'What?' Duke Paldane said, staring hard at him.

'The rune,' Raj Ahten said. 'It's an incantation written in scent – an incantation to call a curse upon mankind.'

He suddenly yearned to dash the rune and its makers into oblivion, to drown the thing in water and wash it clean.

Yet he doubted he could accomplish that feat. The reavers were too wise to give him access to his objective, too powerful to be defeated so long as they comprised such vast numbers. A cocoon blockaded much of his path to the rune, although a trail had been left for the workers.

Raj Ahten had to try.

'The reavers may build,' Raj Ahten said, 'but we do not have to let them build in peace. I may not be able to take that hill, but I can surely spoil their party.'

47

WAITING FOR SAFFIRA

High in the Hest Mountains, Borenson's mount clambered down a narrow trail through a flurry of snow. He was leading Saffira and her guards down from the precipitous high passes.

He gazed over a small valley and saw a herd of elephants floundering in the drifts. Most of them had died already, and they lay like elephant-shaped boulders covered in ice. But a couple of big old bulls looked up toward Saffira's entourage and feebly raised their trunks, trumpeting.

These were domestic elephants, with tusks sawed off and capped with copper. But they looked so starved that they would probably never succeed in climbing out of this valley. Their mahouts had abandoned them.

Apparently, the Wolf Lord had tried to bring war elephants over the Hests late in the season – and he had failed. Three times in the night, Borenson's party had passed Raj Ahten's armies of commoners as they tried to make it over the mountains. These were archers and footmen, washwomen and carters by the hundreds of thousands. Not in his wildest dreams had Borenson imagined that Raj Ahten would try to bring such troops over the mountains so late in the autumn. Up so high in the Hests, the narrow trails offered little forage: a few rough grasses and low bushes to eat, snow to quench one's thirst. There was no fuel to burn, and so men burned ox dung in their small fires.

A journey that Borenson made in an hour on a force horse might take these men and women a day. The journey he made in a single night would take weeks of hard work for a commoner. Many of the horses Borenson saw in the last army were in terrible shape. They were beasts whose hides hung limp over skeletal frames. The commoners riding them would likely get stranded in the snow and die up here before midwinter, just as these elephants would die.

Raj Ahten had taken a deadly gamble, with both the lives of his people and his animals.

But he doesn't care, Borenson told himself. The lives he gambles with are not his own.

The mountain air was thin. A biting chill blew through it, piercing his cloak. Borenson wrapped it around himself and waited for Saffira to catch up. He hoped that when she saw the beautiful elephants, she might see her lord's folly. Evidence of it was everywhere. Rumor said that Raj Ahten had taken more than a thousand endowments of wit. With so much wit, he would recall in vivid detail every waking moment of his life. Yet endowments of wit only let a man store memories, not reason more clearly.

So he has a thousand endowments of wit, Borenson thought, and he's still dumber than my ass.

Last night, when Saffira had said that Raj Ahten was the greatest man in the world, and would surely save mankind from the reavers, Borenson had believed her. But now he was not looking at her, and the seductive power of her Voice did not sound as reasonable when he replayed it in memory.

No, Raj Ahten was not all-wise. Only a fool would have sent so many commoners into these mountains.

A fool or a reckless and desperate man, a voice whispered in the back of Borenson's mind.

Perhaps Raj Ahten had been a Runelord too long. Maybe he'd forgotten what a frail thing a commoner could be. A man with a couple of endowments of brawn and metabolism could rush through a battle line and cut down commoners as if they were scarecrows.

They died so damned easily. Last night had brought a thin snow, and it had kept falling all morning. If it held, Raj Ahten's troops would get bogged down. Their animals would die in a fortnight, and without fuel for fires, the people would freeze in a matter of days.

What had made Raj Ahten hope that the fair weather would hold? Certainly he'd studied Rofehavan, knew what a risk he took.

Raj Ahten is a fool, Borenson thought, and Saffira does not see it.

He knew that Indhopal was an enormous realm, comprised of many kingdoms. And though Borenson had ridden through parts of Deyazz and Muttaya, he'd not been farther south, had not numbered the teeming hordes of Kartish or old Indhopal. It was said that before Raj Ahten conquered all of his neighbors, the old kingdom of Indhopal, with its lush jungles and vast fields, had fed more than a hundred and eighty million people. Certainly Raj Ahten commanded two or three times that number now. Yet even Raj Ahten could not afford to throw away half a million of his best-trained footmen and archers.

No, Raj Ahten was a fool. Or he might be a madman, deluded by his own fair face, the power of his Voice.

The horror of it now was that Saffira in her naïveté could not see Raj Ahten's excesses, his vices.

Saffira was a tool in Raj Ahten's hand, and if she could not twist him to her will, then he most certainly would twist her to his.

Borenson waited several long minutes for Saffira. When she arrived, Borenson moved to her windward side, so that his body might shield her better from the stinging wind.

'Ah, look at my lord's elephants,' Saffira said as she stopped, giving her horse a breather. The poor beast put its head down and bit into the snow, began chewing it for refreshment. 'We must do something to save them.'

Borenson looked helplessly at the starving elephants. In the morning light, Saffira's beauty had become a terrible and breathtaking thing to behold. All through the night, the facilitators at Obran must have been working to transfer the concubines' glamour and Voice into Saffira's vectors. Saffira had garnered thousands of endowments. When Borenson glanced at her face for only a moment, her beauty smote him like a furnace, and he felt unworthy to be so near her.

A couple of vultures flapped up from an elephant's carcass.

'What would you suggest, O Star of Indhopal?' Borenson begged. When she did not answer, he looked to Pashtuk and the guards. He could see no way to save the elephants, short of spending the day hauling in hay and food for them from Mystarria.

If Saffira asked him to cart feed for the elephants, he knew that he would obey, but he feared the consequences if he delayed his quest. He needed to deliver Saffira to Raj Ahten, to convince him to turn aside from pursuing this self-destructive war.

'I . . . I don't know what we can do for them,' Saffira said.

'They have grazed this valley to stubble, O Greatest of Stars,' Pashtuk said. 'Perhaps if we drove them down to a lower valley where there is more grass, the elephants would regain enough strength so that they might live.'

'That's a fine plan!' Saffira said in delight.

Borenson glanced at Pashtuk, hoping to convey in his scowl how displeased he was with the idea. But he saw Pashtuk's face, and knew that the big man felt as much in thrall to Saffira as did Borenson himself. Pashtuk only hoped to please her.

'O Bright Lady,' Borenson said, 'your lord tried to bring the elephants across the mountains too late in the season. We cannot save them.'

'It is not my lord's fault if the weather does not cooperate,' Saffira said. 'The weather should be warmer this time of year. It often stays warm, does it not?'

'It does,' Borenson admitted, and Saffira's Voice was so seductive, he could not help but wonder. Surely she was right. The weather often remained warm this late in the year.

'Still,' Borenson said, 'he brought them too late.'

'Do not seek fault with my lord,' Saffira said. 'Blame is easy

to give, and hard to take. My lord does only what is necessary to stop the depredations of the Knights Equitable. If
anyone is to blame, it is your kind.'

Her words were a hot whip that slashed his back. Borenson
cringed, unable to frame an argument, unable to say anything.
He tried to recall his thoughts a moment earlier, but Saffira
had ordered him not to seek fault with Raj Ahten, and so
persuasive was her command that his mind slid away from
any ill thoughts.

So Borenson and Pashtuk left Saffira with her guards and
made their way down to the starving elephants. The herd had
contained fifty beasts, but only five remained alive. The narrow
valley had no water flowing through it, and Borenson
suspected that the other elephants had died of thirst as much
as from hunger.

Borenson and Pashtuk slowed their pace through the
morning and spent most of a long day herding the elephants
eight or ten miles down the mountains to safety. Two miles
of travel took them down to the tree line.

After that, Pashtuk drove the elephants down a side trail to
a narrow valley. Here the light snow turned to a cold drizzle.
The valley had good water and enough grass so that the
elephants might forage for a couple of days before they moved
down to the lowlands, but Borenson had no real hope for them.

The grass here was merely straw that would not give the
elephants energy. Without men to push them on, the elephants
most likely would be too weak to leave this place.

Still, he'd done all that he could.

Saffira's entourage rode down out of the mountains.
Borenson now took the lead. Duke Paldane's soldiers would
be guarding this road; though a large party might pass un-
molested, Saffira and her entourage would be easy targets.

Borenson didn't know where the ambush might come, but
he didn't doubt that he would be challenged.

So he rode at the van of the group, a hundred yards ahead
of the others. All the while, he watched for sign of an ambush.
But with the loss of endowments, his eyes were not as sharp

as before; his ears seemed dull of hearing. Without his stamina, he seemed to tire more easily than ever before.

Still, having endowments wasn't everything. Knowing what to look for was as important as having sharp eyes. So he watched the dark folds of valleys where the pines were thick, and he studied outcroppings of rock that might hide a horse, and he worried each time he came to a new fold in the ground and had to look over a rise.

He hoped only that Gaborn would use his powers to warn him if any danger should present itself.

By mid-afternoon, the rain poured. Borenson was desperate to pick up his pace, but Saffira commanded otherwise.

As they rode down a forested slope, they came upon an old wayfarer's cottage at the edge of a glade. Its thatch roof was sagging and full of holes, but by now Borenson was thoroughly soaked, and any roof looked as inviting to him as it did to Saffira. Besides, overhanging limbs from pine trees offered some added shelter for the cottage.

'Sir Borenson, help Mahket build a fire while Pashtuk and Ha'Pim prepare dinner,' Saffira said. 'All of this travel has left me famished.'

'O Great Star,' Borenson said. 'We are — We must hurry.'

Saffira fixed a reproachful gaze on him, and Borenson raised a hand to shield his eyes.

He went to work building the fire and did not object, for he told himself that a short rest would give their mounts time to forage, chewing viciously at the grass outside as force horses will. Besides, the cold rain had left them all thoroughly chilled. They needed rest.

For the moment, he felt too weary to argue further.

Borenson entered the cottage, found a dry corner where the roof still kept out the rain. Fortunately, the corner was near the fireplace. Dry pine needles and cones littered the cottage floor, and Borenson and Mahket set these in the fireplace. Soon they had managed to get a small blaze going.

As he worked, Borenson remained constantly aware of Saffira so near him. Since he knew there would be no dry wood outside, he went to the far end of the cottage and pulled some dry thatch out of the roof. He used the thatch for fuel while Pashtuk and Ha'Pim fetched water to boil rice and warm the lamb cooked in coconut milk that they'd brought from the Palace of the Concubines.

After dinner, Saffira ordered the men to stand guard while she took an afternoon nap, for she said that it would not do for her to 'appear before the Great Light with baggy eyes from lack of rest.'

So Borenson let Saffira lie in the warm dry corner while he took a guard post nearby.

He could not rest. The day was wasting, and as he turned away from Saffira he soon found that he merely seethed.

He dared not voice his frustrations to Saffira. He feared her rebuke, but he was dismayed by the delays she caused. It was almost as if she did not want to see Raj Ahten, he decided.

Saffira slept, breathing deeply and softly under a brightly embroidered quilt on the floor, the picture of perfect repose.

Borenson wondered if he would have to kill her. With so many endowments of glamour and Voice, she would be dangerous – as dangerous in her own way as Raj Ahten.

He stared into her glorious face, saw the beauty and innocence there, and knew that to kill her, to take her life, would be as impossible as cutting out the heart of his own child.

Borenson left Saffira to Ha'Pim and Mahket. He went outside to Pashtuk, who stood atop a nearby rock beneath the shelter of a low-hanging pine limb.

They'd come out of the higher mountains. Dark pines stood straight along the road below, forming an impenetrable barrier to his gaze. In an hour, they would reach the warmer lowlands, where oak and elm thrived.

Borenson looked down the trail.

'How are your pearls feeling?' Borenson asked Pashtuk. He'd noted how the warrior sat uneasily in his horse, using his thighs to hold himself off the saddle.

Borenson could not stop worrying about what it would cost him to have looked upon Saffira's face.

'I fail to understand,' Pashtuk said, 'how body parts that I no longer have can cause me so much pain.'

'That bad, eh?' Borenson said.

'When we near Carris,' Pashtuk said, 'Raj Ahten will certainly demand his ounce of flesh from you.'

'*Ounce* of flesh?' Borenson jested. 'I'm more of a man than that.'

Pashtuk did not smile. 'I suggest that you turn your horse and escape,' he said. 'Neither Ha'Pim's nor Mahket's horse can catch yours. I might be able to give a good chase . . . but I will not catch you.'

'Why not?' Borenson asked.

Pashtuk shook his head. 'My lord's decree was made to keep men from idly seeking out Obran, and to make sure that palace servants did not dally with the concubines. I do not believe it was meant for men like you, men of honor who would not betray a trust.'

Borenson felt truly grateful. 'Thank you,' he said. 'But what kind of escort would I be if I ran off before I saw my charge to safety?'

In his heart, he suddenly knew he could not run, could never leave Saffira's side. He had to stay beside her now, and he wondered if he would be able to leave even when his journey was done, when it was time to ride for Inkarra. Part of him yearned to stay at her side because to leave would be painful. But he also knew that at the very least, he had to be there to plunge a knife in her back if she decided to betray the Earth King.

Pashtuk shook his head. 'I only warn you for your own sake. I would understand if you ran. And if the chance presents itself, I beg you to do so.'

Borenson gazed off down the road. He wanted Pashtuk to believe that he considered this option, that he had no ulterior motive for remaining close to Saffira. 'Perhaps you're right. It looks as if you may not need me. We should have run into a Mystarrian patrol by now – at least within the past twenty miles – but none seem to be about.'

He did not need to say more. With the Blue Tower destroyed, few men would be capable of acting as scouts for Mystarria, and most of those would be hiding in Carris.

'This is pointless,' Borenson breathed at last. 'You don't need me to protect you. Why is Saffira traveling so slowly? What is she afraid of?'

Pashtuk bit his lip and whispered, 'She is more cunning than you give her credit for. There is a danger in displeasing our lord. It is said in Indhopal, "No one ever displeases our king twice."

'When she delivers her message and sues for peace, she will have only one chance. She must do her best. Be patient. You gave her a thousand forcibles. How soon do you imagine that her facilitators can drain them?'

'I don't know,' Borenson said. 'How many facilitators does she have?' He'd imagined that Saffira would have a dozen facilitators at her call.

'Two,' Pashtuk said. 'A master and an apprentice.'

Borenson licked his lips. Only two. They would each be hard-pressed to drain a forcible every five minutes. The two might be able take twenty-four endowments in an hour, two hundred and forty in a ten-hour day, perhaps four hundred if they drove themselves for eighteen hours.

Saffira's beauty had been growing night and morning. She grew fairer and more radiant by the minute.

Her facilitators had to be working overtime, exhausting themselves. Yet they could not possibly take a thousand endowments in less than two days.

Saffira had been traveling now for only about twenty hours. Borenson calculated that if they rode hard, they could reach Carris in another four hours – or less.

But Saffira needed to wait.

'She can't hold us here another day!' Borenson said. 'By now, Raj Ahten has certainly besieged Carris. Tomorrow, the Earth King will fall upon him.'

'And if Carris falls, is that such a great matter?' Pashtuk asked. 'You seek to divert a single battle. Saffira hopes to end all war.'

'But . . . another day!'

Pashtuk shook his head. 'She will not wait another day. Yesterday while you slept, I spoke to the chamberlain of the Palace of the Concubines. The palace holds fewer than five hundred women and guards, plus a few servants. Saffira's facilitators swore that by sunset tonight, they would drain every person of endowments who is worth a forcible. If their calculations are correct, by then Saffira will have vectored to her over twelve hundred endowments of voice and twenty-four hundred endowments of glamour.

'After that, in the Palace of the Concubines, the only creatures that the facilitators will have left to take endowments from will be the camels.' Pashtuk laughed at his own jest.

Borenson smiled. Certainly Raj Ahten himself did not have half so many endowments of glamour. In all history, Borenson had never heard of a queen who had taken more than a tenth of what Saffira hoped to garner.

She had one chance to persuade Raj Ahten. One chance.

Borenson quietly squatted next to Pashtuk and let Saffira get her rest.

In late afternoon, Saffira wakened, and after several long minutes she said in a voice far sweeter than any song, 'I have good tidings. The facilitators have stopped adding endowments to me. Their work is finished, for good or ill.'

With that news Borenson and Pashtuk saddled up the five force horses.

The roads were muddy, and they would have to ride slower than Borenson wanted. He hoped to make Carris before sunset.

For twenty miles they rode hard and fast, until at last they found the Mystarrian patrol that Borenson had feared.

A dozen knights wearing the green-man emblem lay by the roadside, torn asunder. The body of a horse dangled in the branches of a tree forty feet overhead. Most of the men were hacked into several pieces: a torso trailing guts lying over here, half a leg over there. Some body parts were clearly just

missing. The ground around the corpses was scored and trampled by heavy feet, but the knights had not managed to slay
a single foe. Seldom had Borenson seen such a slaughter. And
it had happened not more than an hour ago. The dead men's
guts still vented steam.

'It looks as if one of your Mystarrian patrols has run into
my lord's men,' Saffira said innocently. She covered her fair
nose with a silk cloth, to clear the air from the smell of blood
and bile. Her voice was calm and she did not tremble, as if
the sight of dead warriors hacked to pieces could not daunt
her.

Borenson wondered what kind of sights she could have
seen at her tender age, to be so hardened.

Perhaps it does not concern her, he thought, because these
warriors are her enemy.

Pashtuk merely shook his head, as if weary of Saffira's
naïveté. 'They did not meet *our* patrol, O Great Star. No human
would tear apart another man so savagely. Reavers did this.'

'Oh,' Saffira said without emotion, as if the thought of
reavers stalking the woods around them did not alarm her in
the least. Her guards let their mounts edge closer.

Pashtuk glanced at Borenson, and his dark eyes spoke
volumes. 'With reavers on the road, we are in trouble.'

48

THE REAVERS SEND A MESSAGE

Roland stood on the castle walls and cheered as Raj Ahten emerged from the Duke's Keep and began shouting orders to his men, instructing them to prepare for a charge.

Proud Invincibles raced down the ramparts to their horses, squires began carrying barding and lances from the armory. It would take a good hour for the men to effect a charge, and Roland could do nothing but wait.

Over on Bone Hill, the reaver mages were hard at work; the fell mage near its crown was a blur of glittering motion. As they labored, a roiling brown haze began to swirl off the rune.

The odor of death and decay rising from Bone Hill left Roland feeling sick. His stomach churned, and his muscles ached, while his eyes burned so badly that he hardly dared look toward the hill any longer.

As Raj Ahten's men armored their horses, Roland noticed subtle changes out on the plain. The huge glue mums had been chewing grass and trees, continuously excreting a thick, sticky resin that howlers used to fuse stone together – stone that formed walls and barricades.

They'd been working on the south shore of the lake, creating several large domes. Men had conjectured that these domes might be nesting sites, but now the reavers flipped the domes over and pushed them toward the water, and Roland recognized that the domes were really ships, enormous vessels without oars or sails, shaped like the halves of walnut shells.

The howlers now began toiling desperately, building up the sides of the ships stone by stone.

A cold terror struck at the pit of Roland's stomach. Until now the reavers had seemed content to ignore the men of Carris.

But now it was evident that, like Raj Ahten in the court-yards below, they were preparing to attack.

To the west, reavers continued to burrow. The barren earth had become pocked and cratered with openings that were strangely taller to the north than to the south.

As afternoon wore toward evening, Roland grew steadily more ill. The air around Carris felt oppressive, with its scent of decay. His head ached, despair settled into his stomach, and a deep-seated fatigue made him feel so worn that he could hardly stand. Some of the men around him tried to hide the fact that they had begun weeping.

In an effort to keep their humor up, some stout warriors began to hurl insults at the reavers, while others laughed and assigned names to the new landmarks that the reavers created.

The huge stone tower to the south rose higher and higher, resembling a twisted narwhale horn or a giant thorn. By mid-afternoon it was over eight hundred feet tall, and still the reavers kept on building. The fell mage twice went to check the progress atop the tower, and men noted that it looked something like a male reaver's genitals, so they called it the 'Love Tower.'

To the east of the tower, along the shore of Lake Donnestgree, glue mums and howlers continued to work on their ships in the Stone Shipyards.

The pile of discarded wood from homes and trees and fences was called Mount Woody. The men delighted in calling the multitude of burrows to its northwest 'Lord Paldane's Slum.'

Yet of all the foul things created that day, the evil rune on Bone Hill was the most appalling. No mere howlers executed the masonry work. Roland half glimpsed them behind the walls of their cocoon. While howlers carted off dirt from the trenches and dragged deadwood to the glue mums, mages with runes tatooed along the ridges of their heads above their philia built the wall of the horrific rune.

So the great rune grew – an obscene badge that slowly began to emanate smoke and power. The lines of it beneath the brown haze were marvelously sinuous, like garter snakes all mating in a ball, or like a plate of hummingbird tongues. Like reaver magic itself, the rune was twisted and vile.

If Roland tried to look at it, his eyes literally throbbed. The knotty cords that controlled the movement of the eyes would all convulse, so that he could not focus. Yet if he turned away, the burning sensation against his skin felt so intense that at times he sniffed the air, fearing that he would smell his own flesh cooking.

But the dismay that the fell mage's rune caused the men was not the only manifestation of its power. For as the rune neared completion, it began to wreak a monstrous change around Bone Hill: the few shrubs and grasses at the foot of the hill began to steam and die.

The grass turned gray and wilted. On the inside wall beneath him, Roland could see the branches of the almond tree slowly begin to writhe. The leaves blistered and fell.

By the time Raj Ahten's troops had barded their horses and donned their own armor, Roland looked out beyond the walls. North, south, and west of the castle grass and trees steamed as they died, miles away.

The men of Carris renamed Bone Hill the 'Throne of Desolation.' As for Castle Carris itself, some men grimly whispered that it might best be called the 'Butcher's Playpen.' Roland imagined that the city held enough people to feed the reavers for a couple of months or more. It was hard to tell, with so many reavers still marching north. Certainly, every man in Carris felt destined to grace a reaver's dinner table.

For a time, Roland searched hopefully off to the east, where the weak sun shone on the choppy waves. Still no sign of boats returning. Roland clutched his half-sword, practiced drawing it.

The reavers built. But they did not attack.

'Maybe they're not going to attack,' Roland ventured hopefully. 'Maybe they're after something else . . .'

'It's Bone Hill that draws them,' a man behind Roland said.

He was a wretchedly skinny farmer with the wiry hair of a goat for a beard. He'd introduced himself earlier in the morning as Meron Blythefellow, and he guarded the wall with nothing more than a pickaxe.

'Why do you say that?' Roland asked.

'All the dead men up there,' the farmer said. 'More knights have led charges and died on that hill than anywhere else in all Rofehavan. There's been maybe a hundred battles fought, and all that blood on the ground poisons the soil, making it ripe for dark enchantments. The blood is so thick that the Duke has even tried to mine it, looking for blood metal. That's why the reavers are here, I think – to build that rune on ground rich in human blood.'

As Blythefellow voiced this thought, Baron Poll frowned. 'I don't think that's it at all. Maybe they're just sending us a message.'

'A message?' Roland asked, incredulous. It was obvious that the reavers were poisoning the people of Carris, sickening them with their twisted magics. 'Reavers can't talk.'

'Not usually,' the Baron argued, 'at least not so that we can understand. But they talk nonetheless.'

'So what are the reavers saying?' Roland asked.

Baron Poll waved his arms across the landscape. As far as the eye could see, the land around Carris was scarred and barren. Cities, farmhouses, fences, and fortresses alike had all fallen and been carted away. Trees steamed on hills five miles distant.

'Can't you read it?' Baron Poll said. 'It's not as hard to decipher as high script: "The land that was once yours is ours. Your homes are our homes. Your food – well, you are our food. We *supplant* you."'

Down in the bailey, Raj Ahten's troops had mounted. The knights sat astride their chargers, war lances held upright, pointed like glistening needles at the sky.

'Open the gates!' Raj Ahten shouted at their head. Chains creaked as the drawbridge lowered.

49

HUE AND CRY

Averan didn't know that she'd fallen asleep until she felt Spring lurch up, ripping the warm cloak from her grasp. The green woman shivered with excitement, sniffing the air.

All night long, Averan had suffered from strange dreams, unreal visions of the Underworld.

The day was cool. The sun lay behind thick clouds. A thin drizzle rained down. Averan had been dreaming that one of the graaks had brought a rotten goat to the aerie, as they sometimes did, and Brand was making her drag it away.

She cleared her eyes. While she'd slept, the ferns above her had all died. They hung wet and sullen, like limp gray rags. Indeed, every bit of moss at her fingertips, every tender vine, every tree overhead, all had wilted as if blasted by the worst hoarfrost ever seen. The scent of decay lay heavy in the air.

Worse than that, whatever had cursed the ground seemed also to affect her. Averan felt nauseous, and her muscles were weak. A dry film coated her mouth.

If I stay here, I'll die, she thought.

In mounting curiosity and horror, Averan glanced up at the sky. Sunrise had come and gone hours ago. Soon the sun would set.

She'd run most of the night. In her exhaustion, Averan had slept the entire day. In that time, a horrible change had been wrought upon the land.

Now the green woman lifted her nose so that her olive hair

fell back on her shoulders, and she said softly, 'Blood, yes. Sun, no.'

Averan leapt to her feet in the evening drizzle, glanced down the long hill. A mile away, a group of huge reavers raced on her side of the canal, following her scent.

The air issuing from their thoraxes made a dull rattle, and they scurried about in a defensive formation called 'nines.' A scarlet sorceress led them, bearing a staff that glowed cruelly with obscene runes.

A reaver mage, Averan realized dully, fighting panic. In dull wonder, Averan realized that the scout she had eaten had known this monster and the blade-bearers at her back. These were no common troops. These were some of the fell mage's most elite guards.

Averan's shouts of 'Beware' must have frightened the reavers, causing them to send some of their most deadly warriors.

Desperately, Averan sprinted through the wilted ferns surrounding the hill, sliding on their slimy surface, hardly daring to make an occasional loop, knowing she could never outrun the monsters, knowing that in moments she would be within their field of vision.

The green woman loped beside her, curious, glancing back like a dog eager to hunt squirrels, unsure whether to fight or flee.

Overhead, the leaves of every tree had fallen. There was no foliage, nothing she could hide behind. With nowhere to go and nothing to lose, Averan did what instinct bade her. She raised a hue and cry: 'Help! Help! Murder!'

Even as she screamed, she thought, If I yelled 'Reavers!' no one would be dumb enough to come to my rescue.

50

RIDE OF THE MICE

'Open the gates!' Raj Ahten shouted from the bailey. Five hundred force soldiers gathered behind the castle gates, the knights and horses gleaming in armor, painted lances prickling toward the sky.

The only monument left to mankind within sight was Carris itself, still tall, its white plaster walls still proud in the fading afternoon light. Rain had fallen on and off all day long, misting everything. Now a bit of sunlight beamed from a break in the clouds.

The walls of Carris gleamed preternaturally, contrasting with the dark wet mud outside.

The drawbridge dropped, and everywhere within the walls, men began to cheer wildly. Raj Ahten led the foray himself, bearing a long white lance of ash, riding his great gray Imperial force horse.

He swept over the causeway at an astonishing speed, and in seconds thundered over the plains toward the Throne of Desolation. Blade-bearers waiting well back from the causeway charged to meet him.

He swept past the first few of the great monsters as if they were but islands in a stream. His troops flowed behind. Each horse had endowments of brawn and grace and metabolism, and thus even in armor could race over the downs like a gale.

Raj Ahten's face shone like the sun. Even at this distance, he drew the eye like no other man could, as if he bore beauty with him.

Now the knights took formation, five columns charging north toward the Throne of Desolation. Reavers rushed to block them, their carapaces gleaming darkly from the afternoon rain.

From such a distance, Raj Ahten and his men looked to Roland like a great herd of mice, charging out to make war upon overfed cats.

Their horses were marvelous and speedy, their lances gleamed in the sunlight like needles. The men shouted war cries that were lost on the wind.

And the reavers towered above them, sickly gray and bloated.

Lances struck home. Some knights sought to strike the reaver's brain by aiming at the soft spot in its skull, or by driving a lance through the roof of its mouth. A reaver so struck died almost instantly.

But others opted to try to drive a lance into the reaver's belly, a maiming wound.

Thus the Invincibles charged and began to strike, but almost as often as a lance went home, it exploded harmlessly against a reaver's hard carapace. The unfortunate warriors who failed to strike a deadly blow were often borne backward off their horses, left weaponless to scurry for refuge while hoping that their fellows would slay their foes.

Roland watched one horse slip on the slick mud and crash into a reaver as if it were a stone wall, so that both horse and rider were broken instantly. Elsewhere a blade-bearer swung a great blade and sliced the legs from beneath a charging force horse.

Half a dozen reavers went down in seconds, along with several men. As each column of knights met resistance, its men would veer away from the foe, so that the columns quickly became irregular snaking streams.

And once a lancer met his target, his lance would be destroyed. Either it would become hopelessly impaled in the reaver, or it would shatter. In either case the lancer was forced to turn his horse and retreat.

Raj Ahten and a few knights bore down on the Throne of Desolation, his mount racing through the brown clouds that continuously swirled out from it, between wide columns of hardened mucilage that formed the cocoon.

He's charging like a fly into the spider's web, Roland feared.

The few dozen enormous blade-bearers rose up to meet him. Atop the throne, glue mums like ugly grubs reared in wonder at the threat, while mages took defensive positions behind the walls of the rune itself. Howlers fled for cover. The fell mage whirled to look at him from her eyeless head, then dismissed the threat and went back to work.

As the Invincibles charged, at the edge of the cocoon reavers reared up on their back legs, great talons gleaming as they clutched their enormous blades or glory hammers.

Then the forces clashed. A dozen reavers were thrust through by the fury of the charge. Lances shattered. Blades whipped through the air faster than the eye could see; Invincibles and their horses were slashed asunder.

In that single charge at the lip of the cocoon, Raj Ahten lost a full dozen men. Those who met the reavers forfeited their lances. Raj Ahten himself brought a reaver down, plunging his lance into its mouth.

But even as it fell, its tonnage blocked the path to Bone Hill. Raj Ahten turned his mount and raced back for the castle, a few knights at his heel.

From the warrens at Lord Paldane's Slums, reavers issued from their burrows in fury, scuttling from the shadows, while others raced from the western shore of the lake. Along the roads to the south, reavers still marched in an unending line.

Raj Ahten saw the threat, wheeled toward the castle. His men retreated for their lives.

Reavers from the west lumbered up to block the causeway – and Raj Ahten's escape.

On the castle walls, men began to shout, encouraging Raj Ahten's troops to better speed, cheering for men who had been their enemies a few hours before.

But Roland merely stood with his mouth agape.

Is that the best we can do against them? he wondered. Shall we halt their work for three seconds and then flee, like a child pelting a knight with rotten figs?

To do so was folly.

No more than sixty or seventy dead reavers littered the plain; Raj Ahten was forced to retreat, and now he would be chastised by the fell mage and her minions.

As if she had been waiting for this moment all along, the fell mage struck.

The huge mage perched atop Bone Hill raised her great staff to the sky, and an odd hissing roar issued from it. Even now, she wore her fiery runes like a coat of light.

There was a noise like a peal of thunder, and a blast of wind surged from her, sweeping across the hill as if an invisible stone had dropped into a pool, sending out a ring. Roland would not have been able to see it at all if not for the gree that writhed through the air. When the wind struck them, it sent them swirling like leaves.

Down on the plains below, the wind smashed into warhorses. It looked as if they had merely been hit by a blast of air, but the mounts suddenly lost their footing and crashed over the stony land, armor clanging. Warriors cried out as they fell to their deaths. Some got up and feebly began to crawl about, while reavers raced in and finished them.

Raj Ahten and his men neared the causeway, a ragged company of three hundred men and chargers. The knights' mounts staggered about blindly, as if stricken, while a wall of blade-bearers charged to meet them.

Then the wind hit Roland with a vengeance. He felt the icy kiss as if it were fear itself, an unmanly fear that sent his heart racing and made him wish to hide. The smell of the air was like burning hair, but a hundred times more intense. A roaring sound raged in his ears, far louder than a thundering waterfall. His eyes burned painfully and, in that moment, everything went completely black.

Suddenly stricken blind, with a roaring like the sea blocking all sound, Roland cried out and clutched the battlements on the castle walls. A disorienting dizziness assailed him, so that he grasped the wall but could not tell which way was up or down.

All about him, men began to scream in terror. 'Help! I'm blind! Help!'

But there would be no help. Such was the power of the fell mage's curse that Roland merely lay in terror, gasping great breaths, struggling to stay alive.

No wonder the reavers do not fear us! Roland thought.

His eyes burned as if a hot drink had scalded them, and the knotty cords within throbbed in pain. He gasped and wiped copious tears from his face. He felt utterly unmanned.

For a long minute he lay thus, until the hammering in his ears began to subside, and through his tears he could see the sun riding dim as the moon through the gray sky. He made it to his knees, peered through his blindness, blinking rapidly. Black clouds seemed to obscure all sight. All along the wall walks, men around him huddled, wiping their faces, squinting to pierce the darkness.

In moments he realized that reavers must have reached the causeway, coming within artillery range. The marksmen called for the artillery to shoot, and from the castle walls men cut loose with ballistas. Loud *whonk* sounds filled the air as ropes thudded against the steel wings of the ballistas, then giant metal bolts whooshed through air, landing with loud whacks as the bolts pierced reavers' carapaces.

Roland blinked into the gloom over the wall, until he could see reavers, gray shapes writhing in the dark. Raj Ahten's cavalry looked as if it would be overwhelmed.

But Raj Ahten was no common lord, and his men were no common warriors. They'd recovered enough from the fell mage's blast so that they could fight.

They charged manfully into the fray. Lances pierced reaver flesh. Horses screamed when blade-bearers slashed through them. Glory hammers rang against armor.

Dozens more reavers died in the onslaught as Raj Ahten tried to win his way back to Carris. Men with great endowments of brawn and metabolism leapt from dying mounts, charged into battle, long-handled horseman's warhammers rising and falling, chopping into the thick skin of reavers.

At the ballistas on the castle wall, artillerymen shouted and struggled to rewind the winches that drew back the ropes on the enormous bows, while boys lifted the heavy bolts and slid them into their grooved channels.

Raj Ahten himself, the most powerful human lord, screamed a war cry that shook the castle, dislodging plaster from the outer walls. As the pain in his eyes eased, Roland could make out reavers falling back, briefly stunned by the sound, but then they attacked more fiercely, as if enraged.

Roland heard men shout in dismay; down at the Stone Shipyards, five dozen ships cobbled together from rock and glue-mum resin had been launched into the water.

They bore no sails, sported no oars. Instead, reavers thrust long steel war blades into the water, using weapons to row.

Roland blinked and fought back tears. The strange craft with their high prows looked like black halves of walnuts floating in a pond. Except that these ships raced toward him with reavers by the hundreds.

Terror seized him. He'd hoped that he would not have to face the enemy. He was on the south wall, after all, and everyone knew that reavers could not swim, but sank like stone.

Besides, he reasoned, the plaster walls of Carris were far too smooth for man or reaver to get a toe-hold, and though the plaster had been damaged, no one could hope to scale the walls.

He clutched his little half-sword, which had seemed adequate protection from highwaymen just two days ago, and wondered what use it would be in the battle to come.

It was folly for him to be here, folly for a commoner to fight a reaver.

Out on the causeway, Raj Ahten shouted again, hoping to stun the reavers. Roland glanced his way, saw that the reavers not only ignored his cry, but scurried toward him all the faster, as if recognizing that he was a threat.

'Get ready!' Baron Poll shouted. 'Get ready!' Howlers began emitting their weird cries in an unearthly chorus.

Everywhere around Roland, men rushed to and fro, hoisting shields, grabbing battle-axes. Some men bellowed for Roland to move, and they came and perched a heavy stone on the merlon next to him, went back for another.

'Damn!' Roland found himself shouting excitedly for lack of anything else to say. 'Damn!'

'Look,' some fellow behind him cried. 'They're at the gates!'

Roland glanced west. Blade-bearers rushed behind Raj Ahten's retreat. They raced in before the gatekeepers could raise the drawbridges, and thus burst past the first two barbicans. Roland could not see if reavers made it into the castle proper, for the gate tower hid his view.

Again the fell mage atop Bone Hill raised her great staff to the sky, and the hissing roar issued from it. All along the castle walls, men cried out, for none wanted to be stricken by the fell mage's curse again.

'Close your eyes! Cover your ears! Don't breathe the fumes!' men shouted.

Roland glanced back, toward the gates, watched men fall as the reaver's curse struck them down.

He crouched down by the wall, clutched his ears and squinted his eyes tightly, held his breath as the second curse washed over him.

It struck like thunder, and the cords in his eyes twitched despite his care. He dropped to the ground, kept his eyes closed for several long seconds, dared not unstop his ears.

To his relief, his efforts helped him somewhat. He felt no disorienting dizziness.

Roland opened his eyes, and though they burned painfully and his sight was somewhat dim, he was not completely blind. He found himself face to face with a lad who was so frightened that the boy seemed leached of blood. The boy's teeth chattered, and Roland knew that he was too afraid to fight, that the boy would lie here and die in exactly this position.

And as he huddled by the wall, Roland also knew that the

fell mage was uttering her curse in an effort to keep him from defending Carris.

Roland had always been a man that life happened to. He'd steered the course of his life by a plan that his parents had set out for him, responded to every prodding from his wife with a snarl of his own. He'd ridden north to find a son he'd never known, not because he felt much for the lad, but simply because he knew that it was the right thing to do.

Now he gritted his teeth, filled with regret for all that he'd never done, for all that he'd never be able to do. He'd promised to be a father to Averan, wanted to be a father to his son. Now he doubted that he would ever get that chance.

Either I can lie here and die like this dumb lad, or I can get up and fight! he thought.

He heard a thud as one of the odd stone ships below collided against the castle wall. He could wait no longer.

'Come on,' he growled to the frightened lad. 'Let's get up and die like men!' Roland rose, grabbing the boy and giving him a hand. He leaned between two merlons, tried to peer through foul vapors that made him weep uncontrollably.

A hundred feet below, a reaver ship nuzzled the walls of Carris. One monster thrust its huge claws into the wall of the castle, piercing the thick layer of white plaster that lay over the stone.

A crow went cawing just over Roland's head as the reaver leapt from the ship. To Roland's astonishment, the reaver thrust its great blade between its teeth, like a dog fetching a stick, and climbed upward, raking the walls with its enormous fore-claws.

We are all commoners on this wall, Roland thought. No man here could stand against a reaver, even if it was unarmed.

Behind Roland, someone shouted, 'Get some pole-arms up here!' Shoving the monsters from the walls with pole-arms sounded like a good plan, but there would be no time to fetch such weapons. Most of the halberds and falchions would be in use down below, by the castle gates.

Roland plunged his half-sword into its scabbard and

grabbed for the huge stone nearby. He was a strong man, and large. But the stone he grabbed weighed upward of four hundred pounds.

With all his might, he strained to lift the damned boulder and drop it over the battlements.

It landed with a thud, hitting the reaver solidly on its eyeless head, some sixty feet below. The reaver halted for a second, stunned, and clung to the wall, as if it feared another rock.

But to Roland's distress, the huge boulder was not enough to dislodge the beast from the castle. Instead it hooked the bonespurs at the juncture of each elbow into the stone and continued scrabbling more carefully. The bone spurs dug into the plaster, finding holds that no human could see.

In three seconds the monster reached the top of the wall and reared, ready to leap over.

The reaver perched on the merlons, its enormous talons raised in the air. It grabbed its great blade and swiped down at the young fellow nearby.

The blade crushed the pasty-faced boy against the stone floor in a spray of blood. Roland drew his small half-sword and shouted a battle cry.

Gathering his courage, he rushed forward. The monster was balanced precariously atop the wall, holding itself to the merlons with clawed toes. Roland could see the joints that held the toes together, knew where to cut so that his blade would separate a toe from the foot.

With all his might, he thrust his blade deep into the joint of the reaver's toe, heard it hiss in pain.

The half-sword buried itself to the hilt, and Roland struggled to wrench it free again. At his side, Meron Blythefellow leapt forward with his pickaxe and hit another joint.

'Watch out!' Baron Poll shouted. Roland looked up to see an enormous clawed talon swipe toward him.

The talon caught Roland's shoulder, ripped into his flesh, and carried him into the air. For half a second he was thirty feet in the air above the tower, looking into the maw of the reaver, row upon row of crystalline teeth.

He was aware that men below were using this moment of distraction to attack the beast. One huge fellow went racing underneath, threw himself against the monster in a shield rush.

Then the reaver fell, and Roland fell with it. He landed upon some defenders below and stared in horror at blood spurting from his right shoulder. The fiery pain was excruciating.

Men cheered as the reaver tumbled from the wall, went splashing into the water. 'Surgeon! Surgeon!' Roland cried.

But none came forward. Roland grasped his arm, tried to hold the gaping wound closed, to keep his lifeblood from flowing out. He shook uncontrollably.

In a daze, he crawled backward against the stone of the wall-walk, tried to clear out of the path of other castle defenders.

He stared hard for a moment at the merlon where Baron Poll had sat for the past day, but the Baron was gone. Other men rushed to defend the wall. Roland looked all around, still fighting the tears and the black fog that threatened his eyesight.

Suddenly in his mind's eye, he recalled the fellow making the shield rush, knocking the reaver into the lake. No commoner could have performed such a feat – only a man with endowments of brawn.

And he knew where Baron Poll had gone.

Roland's heart seemed to pound in his throat; he pulled himself up. To the east and west, reavers gained the top of the wall. Commoners struggled to repel the monsters.

But here the attack had stopped for now. Roland gazed over the wall into the lake below. The water was choppy, for the reavers were still trying to land. But the ship beneath his post was sinking. The bulk of a falling reaver, weighing more than a dozen tons, had been too much for the stone ship. The prow had shattered, and the reavers sank with their vessel.

Sank the way Baron Poll had, in his armor.

Roland shouted to Meron Blythefellow, 'Baron Poll! Where is he?'

'Dead!' Blythefellow shouted in reply. 'He's dead!'

Roland floundered to his knees in a faint. Cold sleet pelted his neck. Gree wriggled overhead painfully.

The skies went black though the fell mage all dressed in light had not yet uttered another curse.

51

STRANGERS ON THE ROAD

'Flee!' Gaborn's voice rang through Borenson's mind. For half a second he drew rein on his horse and peered down the road west toward Carris, squinting to pierce the gloom. He raised a warning hand for Pashtuk, Saffira, and her bodyguards.

Borenson was in the lead. Pashtuk rode up next to him.

'What is it? An ambush?' Pashtuk squinted ahead, trying to pierce the darkness thrown by the shadows of the mixed oaks and pines along the hillside to their left. For the past few minutes, Borenson had been exceedingly ill at ease. Five miles back, they'd crossed some sort of invisible line.

The plants there had been steaming and wilting, blasted by some strange spell. Grass hissed as if it were full of snakes. Branches drooped in the trees. Vines in the ground had been writhing as if in pain, and all of this was accompanied by an odd stench of premature decay.

The farther they rode, the more decrepit the land became. Nothing was left alive. Low brown fumes clung to the ground.

The vegetation here had been blasted with a curse more dire than anything he'd ever seen. It left him feeling anxious, anticipating trouble.

'I . . . don't know if it's an ambush,' Borenson answered. 'The Earth King warns of danger ahead. Perhaps we should turn aside and go cross-country.'

Suddenly, down the road at the corner of the bend, a girl ran beneath the barren limbs of a hoary oak. Distantly her voice could be heard as she raised a hue and cry. 'Help! Help! Murder!'

She turned the corner, saw Borenson, and relief transformed her face. She was a small girl, with long red hair the same color as Borenson's, wearing the dirty blue tunic of a skyrider.

Borenson had been galloping hard for the past hour, hoping to make Carris by sunset. He'd feared reavers along the road, and he'd hoped that if he rode fast enough, he could outrun them. But now they'd slowed the horses to let them cool.

'Help!' the child cried, and a woman came loping behind her. The two raced under blasted trees, over limp grass, as if running from out of some nightmare of desolation. The fading rays of the afternoon sun showed full on their faces.

The woman seemed to have fallen into a vat of green dye. She wore a black bearskin robe that flapped open as she ran, revealing the fact that she wore nothing else beneath that single garment. She had small breasts and a slim figure, and the green dye seemed indeed to cover every part of her body. Yet something about her gave Borenson pause, made him feel unaccountably distracted. It was not the fact that she was beautiful and half-naked. Rather that, even at two hundred yards, she looked familiar.

His heart hammered. Binnesman's wylde! Though he'd never seen the creature, every lord in Heredon had been told to look for it. Borenson wondered how it came to be here.

Pashtuk tensed, and Borenson reached behind his saddle for his horseman's warhammer.

'Flee!' the Earth King warned again.

'Damn it, I hear you,' Borenson shouted back at Gaborn, knowing full well that Gaborn could not hear.

'Is this an ambush?' Pashtuk asked. In Indhopal, women or children were sometimes used as decoys to lure warriors to their deaths, though no decent lord of Rofehavan had ever done this.

'Let's go!' one of Saffira's guards, Ha'Pim, ordered. He grabbed the reins to Saffira's mount, turning her horse, prepared to gallop south across the open fields.

At that moment, a reaver raced round the bend, huge and monstrous, bearing an enormous glory hammer.

'I'll get the girl, you take the woman!' Borenson shouted to Pashtuk.

Borenson slammed his heels into horseflesh, raised his weapon high. He held no illusions. He had no endowments left, no brawn or grace or metabolism, and he wasn't likely to ever get close enough to the reaver to even take a swing. Still, the reaver wouldn't know that. He hoped that the beast, upon sensing two warriors racing toward it, might at least pause long enough so that Borenson could grab the child and make a clean escape.

He shouted a war cry and Pashtuk's mount raced beside him.

'Wait! Leave them!' Ha'Pim shouted at Borenson's back. 'We are here to guard our Lady.'

Pashtuk did not resist. The Invincible drew reins for half a second, and Borenson glanced back to see him racing to his Queen.

Borenson did not know if Pashtuk acted well or ill. He'd heard abject terror in Ha'Pim's voice.

Borenson ducked low, raised his warhammer. His mount had two endowments of brawn, and could easily carry him, the wylde, and the child. But it would be a clumsy ride, and he doubted he'd have time to save them both. Indeed, the wylde was running in the rear, running too slowly, glancing back from moment to moment as if eager to turn and embrace the monster.

Borenson raced for the child, slowed his mount just enough to reach down and grab for her, try to yank her up.

But he no longer had endowments of brawn, and Borenson misjudged the effort it would take. The child leapt up, as if to help him pull her onto the horse.

Borenson had meant to swing her onto the saddle in front of him. Instead, he caught her arm off balance. He tore a muscle in his shoulder, and for half a second the burning pain was so great that he feared he might cripple himself.

Yet he managed to swing the child onto the horse behind him, then race toward the green woman.

But as he glanced toward the wylde, three more reavers raced round the bend. Borenson could not reach her in time. The reaver raised its glory hammer, sprinted toward her, its great crystalline teeth flashing like quartz in the sunlight.

Borenson tried to wheel his mount, leaving the wylde to die.

The girl riding behind Borenson shouted, 'Foul Deliverer, Fair Destroyer: blood, yes!'

The green woman stopped in her tracks, spun to face the reaver, and leapt at the beast as she aimed a punch at its giant maw.

Her deed seemed to catch the reaver by surprise. It had been racing for her at full speed. Now it swung its glory hammer.

The blow fell long and wide. It pounded the road with a loud *thwack*, like the sound of a tree crashing in the woods.

What happened next, Borenson could not quite believe.

The reaver's head was as large as a wain. Its maw could have swallowed Borenson and his horse whole. Had the monster landed on him, its fifteen tons of bulk would have ground him into the dirt like a miller's wheel pulverizing barley.

Yet the green woman twisted her hand as she punched, some weird sort of little dance that baffled the eye, as if she were a mage drawing a rune in the air.

And when her blow landed, it was as if she wielded a glory hammer herself.

Crystalline teeth shattered and flew out like droplets of water, catching the sun. The huge gray reaver's flesh ripped from its face, exposing the skeleton just beneath. Foul blue blood as dark as ink sprayed everywhere.

The reaver collided with the green woman's blow as if it had hit a stone wall. Its entire body lifted into the air six or eight feet, and its four huge legs convulsed in exactly the same way that a spider's will when it tries to protect its belly.

When it landed with a thud, the thing was dead.

Borenson wheeled toward the green woman, but he need

not have bothered. Pashtuk acted the part of a man even though Saffira had taken his pearls, and now he galloped toward the green woman at full speed.

But the green woman was not satisfied to have killed the monster. Though three of its fellows raced toward her, she leapt atop the dead reaver's head, slammed her fist into its skull, and brought out a piece of brain, black with blood, to shove into her mouth.

Borenson gaped in surprise and reined in his horse. Pashtuk reached the green woman, grabbed her from behind.

Borenson spun his mount and raced north toward Saffira and her guards. He glanced over his back to make sure that Pashtuk got clear before the other reavers arrived.

Pashtuk did not take time for niceties. He grabbed the wylde around the waist as if she were a bag of oats. She did not struggle as she feasted on a handful of reaver's brain.

'This way,' Pashtuk shouted, wheeling southeast as he passed Borenson. Borenson glanced back. More blade-bearers thundered round the hill. A reaver mage charged in their midst, but the monsters would never catch force horses such as these. A reaver's top speed was forty miles per hour, and then only in short bursts.

'You saved me!' the girl at Borenson's back shouted in glee. 'I knew you'd come for me!' She hugged him hard.

Borenson had never seen the child before, felt surprised by her tone.

'Well, you seem to know more than I,' Borenson said sarcastically. He had no patience for fakirs who pretended to prescience, even if they were only children.

They raced in silence for a few minutes, and Pashtuk managed to plant the wylde in the saddle in front of him. Behind Borenson, the girl kept leaning forward, trying to see Saffira, as if unable to stop staring.

Finally the child asked, 'Where's Baron Gobble Gut? Didn't he come with you?'

'Who?' Borenson asked.

'Baron Poll,' the child said.

'Hah! I hope not,' Borenson said. 'If I ever see him again, I'll spill his guts all over the road!'

The child pulled on Borenson's cloak, tried to peer up into his face. 'Are you mad at him?'

'No, I merely hate the man as I hate evil itself,' Borenson said.

The girl gazed up at him questioningly, but remained silent.

The sky above filled with a snarling sound that reverberated like a distant hiss. It sounded as if all the heavens drew in a breath at once. Far away, the red of firelight glowed from columns of rising smoke.

'Quickly!' Pashtuk shouted, racing ahead over the dead landscape as fast as his mount would carry him. 'My lord battles at Carris!'

52

IN THE THICK OF BATTLE

Less than an hour from the time Raj Ahten had emerged from the castle gates, Carris stood on the brink of ruin.

In the first moments of battle, reavers drove Raj Ahten's knights back along the causeway, then exploded against the west wall of Castle Carris before men could raise the drawbridges.

They beat the stone arches above the gates with glory hammers, pounding into dust the runes of earth-binding engraved there.

With the walls of Carris thus weakened, the reavers began to batter through the walls as easily as if they were made of twigs.

In less than five minutes they demolished the gate towers and opened a chasm into the bailey.

Raj Ahten could only respond by throwing men into the breach, hoping to drive the reavers back. A wall of corpses – both human and reaver – piled up at the breach some eighty feet, until the reavers were able to leap from their dead onto the castle walls.

Many reavers scuttled over the piled corpses, came sliding down on the dead, their enormous carapaces rumbling as they slid through slick gore. They hurled themselves into battle in such a fashion that the flesh and bones of any man who dared stand before them were ground into mangled ruin.

Might alone could not stop the reavers.

In minutes they butchered a thousand Invincibles before the breach.

Meanwhile, reavers raced up on the south wall of Carris from their stone ships. They decorated that wall with blood and gore. At least twenty thousand commoners died before Raj Ahten's Invincibles managed to slay the intruders.

In desperation, Raj Ahten brought his exhausted flameweavers into the fray and lit several inns and towers afire so that the burning buildings might lend the sorcerers energy to do battle.

For ten minutes his flameweavers had stood on towers to the north and south of the gates, hurling fireballs as best they could into the ranks of reavers that lumbered down the causeway. The flameweavers drove the reavers back, but only for a few moments.

The reavers soon rushed forward over the causeway bearing enormous slabs of dark shale in their great paws, as if they were shields, then set them on each side of the causeway, forming a ragged wall that baffled the flames.

Then some reavers scuttled forward under cover while other lobbed huge boulders against the castle walls in a crude artillery barrage. One tower collapsed so that a flameweaver plunged to his death in the lake.

Fifteen minutes into the battle, Raj Ahten could see that he would lose Carris, for he fought not just the blade-bearers alone, but also the fell mage that drove them.

Six times she cast spells against the men who defended Carris. Her curses were commands, simple in nature, astonishing in effect.

'Be thou deaf and blind,' had been her first refrain. Three times a black wind had issued from her. But after three sweeps, she commanded, 'Cower in fear.'

Six curses, at odd intervals. Raj Ahten was horrified by their effect. Even now, some brave men huddled in mindless terror a full ten minutes after the last curse had blown from the east.

Raj Ahten felt mystified by the spells. No chronicle ever told of reaver mages that uttered such curses.

Now, as Raj Ahten fought in the midst of battle, out on

Bone Hill the reavers' fell mage raised her citrine staff to the
sky and hissed, uttering a seventh curse. Her hiss was a violent
sound that seemed to crawl away in all directions as it echoed
along the cloud ceiling between earth and sky. Men on the
castle walls cringed or cried in terror.

Raj Ahten listened, but knew that the curse that issued
from her could not be understood until he smelled the dark
wind that roiled away from her. He could almost count the
number of milliseconds it would take for the command to
reach him, down here in the castle's bailey.

He led a charge into the reavers' front rank, blurring in his
speed, bearing a battle-axe in each hand. With six endowments of metabolism to his credit, he could work fast, but
needed to make every heartbeat count.

A reaver slid down toward Raj Ahten on the backs of the
dead, glory hammer high overhead. It came with a rumbling
roar, for its carapace ground over the dead with a sound like
a huge log rolling down a hill.

As it slid to a halt, a frowth giant behind Raj Ahten roared
and slammed its huge staff at the reaver's maw, thrusting
upward, forcing the reaver to stop and fall back a pace.

The reaver had little time to choose its mode of attack. It
raised its hammer overhead. Raj Ahten hesitated an eighth of
a second while the frowth held the reaver back, then he lunged
to strike. His first blow was a vicious uppercut that took the
reaver behind the spur of its raised left arm. Raj Ahten's axe
bit deep into the flesh, pried between the monster's joints,
weakening the limb without severing it.

More importantly, the ganglia there in the elbow sent a
numbing jolt that left the reaver hissing in fury, briefly stunned.

In that infinitesimal portion of a second, Raj Ahten's work
began. He had to find a second target. If the monster roared,
it would open its mouth wide enough so that he might leap
in between its deadly teeth, strike up through the soft palate
into the reaver's brain.

On the other hand, if the reaver backed away in panic,
he'd get a blow between the thoracic plates at its soft under-

belly, where he might disembowel the beast.

The monster did neither. The reaver lowered its head and struck blindly through its pain. It swung the glory hammer down viciously, lurching, trying to win past Raj Ahten.

Raj Ahten ducked aside as fifteen tons of monster surged overhead. Even with thousands of endowments of brawn, he could not afford to take a hit from a reaver, for though his endowments of brawn strengthened his muscle, they did nothing to strengthen bones. Even the most casual blow from a reaver would shatter his bones like kindling.

The reaver slammed down its glory hammer, cutting a vicious arc, putting all the power of its good right foreclaws into the blow. The frowth giant shoved harder on its great staff, trying to press the reaver back, and the frowth turned its head and blinked.

In that moment, Raj Ahten glanced up at his giant. The thing was spattered with the red blood of men and the inky blue-black blood of reavers, fouling its fur. It had taken a hit from a reaver's blade earlier, so that a rent showed in its chain mail, and the frowth's own blood added to the mix, matted and fly-covered in its golden fur.

Perhaps blood loss had weakened the frowth, for though the giants were normally tireless, this one saw the blow coming and did little to avoid it, merely shoving meekly with its staff and blinking its great silver eyes as it turned aside.

The glory hammer swiped down, smashing into the frowth's snout, shattering bones and teeth. Blood and gore rained upon Raj Ahten.

Enraged, Raj Ahten struck down with his battle-axe, taking off the two front toes of the reaver's left foreleg. As the reaver's head spun to snap at him, Raj Ahten leapt past its jaws into its mouth, rolled once over its raspy tongue, and aimed a savage blow up into the monster's soft palate.

His axe blade met flesh, scored deeply as it ran between two plates of bone, slicing a cut as long as a man's arm deep into the cleft above the jaw. As the blade cleared, Raj Ahten pulled it back up and in. The long spike on the reverse side of his axe scored deep into the monster's brain.

Raj Ahten was already diving from the reaver's mouth before the blood and brains began gushing from the wound. The monster would die, but so would Raj Ahten's giant.

The frowth reeled back from the battle, staggered into some warriors behind, and fell upon half a dozen men, crushing them.

Raj Ahten glanced about to see if his men needed help. Most of his men fought in teams – four or five men to a reaver. Dressed as they were in yellow surcoats, they looked to Raj Ahten like wasps trying to bring down larger prey with their multitude of stingers.

Now, on Bone Hill, the fell mage's snarling curse ended, and her dark command rolled toward the city. Raj Ahten wondered briefly if the fell mage merely toyed with him.

If she can force us to cower in fear, or strike us blind, why does she not kill us outright? It could not be harder to make a wind that would poison men than to utter these commands.

Raj Ahten could only wonder. It had been sixteen centuries since her kind last attacked. He imagined that she was enamored of her new spells, sought to learn which was most effective.

The fell mage's dark wind struck. Atop the walls, men cried out and covered their noses, and Raj Ahten could not immediately see any effect.

It was not until the scent hit him that he understood. His mouth went dry, and – as one – every pore in his skin began to exude sweat. Tears streamed from his eyes. He fought an overwhelming urge to urinate, and around him he saw weaker men lose control of their bladders.

He felt her command, even as he fought it: 'Be thou dry as dust.'

A hundred yards behind Raj Ahten, Feykaald stood behind the battle lines on the steps of an inn and croaked, 'O Great One, a word!'

Raj Ahten called to his Invincibles to close ranks and raced out of the battle, across the green, to the steps of the inn.

He glanced back. Reavers had crawled atop the mound of their dead, and now one prepared to slide into battle. Raj Ahten glanced at the walls, estimated that three quarters of his Invincibles had already died in this slaughter. He had fewer than four hundred left.

Atop the walls, reavers were battling men. Raj Ahten pulled out a file and began to sharpen his axe blade. He needed no oil for his file. Reaver's blood worked well enough.

'Speak,' Raj Ahten said to Feykaald.

The old counselor worked his mouth, as if fighting back a choking dust. A sheen of sweat dripped from him as he spoke furtively in Raj Ahten's ear. 'Boat arrived. East shore . . . secure. Our men found reavers, but slew them.'

Raj Ahten wiped the sweat from his brow. It was pouring from him, making a sop of his tunic, slicking his hands. Rivulets threaded down his cheeks and into his beard. He drew the file over his axe blade, top to bottom, half a dozen times. As he worked, he studied his crumbling defenses on the walls.

His vassals fought in vain.

The rent in the wall was growing quickly. Half of his artillery outposts were gone. Reavers fought atop the wall. One flameweaver was dead, the others were dwindling from exhaustion despite the fact that Carris was in flames.

His tawny-furred giants fought savagely, but only thirty had survived the retreat from Longmot. They were dying fast. Even as he watched, a blow from a reaver's blade split the skull of one giant, caught another in the back above his stubby tail.

And as the reavers battered the walls of Carris, they widened the breach, so that Raj Ahten's forces were now spread too thin to effectively block the reavers' efforts. Few of Paldane's lords had enough endowments left to fight a reaver. They struggled beside Raj Ahten's men, but their feeble efforts availed little.

Carris would fall despite all that he could do. It was not a matter of hours – it was a matter of moments.

Commoners cried out as the black wind wrung tears and sweat from them. Some fainted.

Ten minutes of this might leave a man dead, Raj Ahten feared. In only one way had his luck held. A light wind was blowing from the east, across the lake, and it seemed to Raj Ahten to ameliorate the effects of the fell mage's spells.

Raj Ahten finished sharpening his axe. A reaver came barreling down, sliding over the slope of carnage. A frowth giant nearby bellowed as the reaver's greatsword struck through its neck. The giant lurched sideways and collapsed on a pair of Invincibles, and the reaver leapt into battle, the first swing of its blade striking through four men.

Raj Ahten made his grim choice. His men were dying. He had fewer than four hundred Invincibles left with which to fight, and fighting at all was vain.

This battle would be lost, but he dared not lose the remnants of his army with it.

There would be other battles, other days.

It was not cowardice that drove him to the decision, but the cold certainty that he did what – in the long term – was best. He'd not sacrifice his men to save the lives of his enemies.

'Prepare the flotilla,' Raj Ahten told Feykaald. 'My flameweavers and Invincibles will take the first boats, my archers next. Spread the word.'

Raj Ahten sprinted back into the fray.

53

THE EARTH'S PAIN

How can I save them all? Gaborn wondered for what seemed the hundredth time that afternoon as he rode for Carris. He galloped fast now. A cool drizzle fell from leaden skies. Few lords rode horses that were able to keep pace: the wizard Binnesman, Queen Herin the Red, her daughter, Sir Langley, and two dozen others.

He felt the fist of doom closing upon the messengers he'd sent to Carris. The Earth warned Gaborn of danger not just for himself, but for everyone who rode to Carris.

The force horses had thundered across the green fields of Beldinook. Gaborn made excellent time – he'd traveled nearly three hundred miles in six hours. But not everyone was able to follow at Gaborn's pace. He'd ridden into Beldinook with hundreds of lords at his back. Now, many of them had dropped from the race. His troops were strung out for hundreds miles behind. The few who remained close rode horses that were spent. Some mounts were dead on their feet, but Gaborn dared not slow. His own Days had fallen behind hours ago, and Gaborn wondered if the man's horse had wearied, or if he feared to travel where Gaborn was heading.

The overwhelming aura of death that surrounded so many of Gaborn's people was suffocating. Gaborn had ridden over the battlefield at Longmot a week ago, seen thousands of good men that Raj Ahten had killed. He'd smelled the charred corpses, the blood and bile. He'd found his own father dead, cold as the snow he'd clutched in his empty hands.

Yet he'd not *felt* those deaths waiting to happen. He'd not been aware of the final moments of those men in the way he now felt the final moments of those around him.

How can I save them all? he wondered.

He felt Borenson riding into danger now, and Gaborn spoke a warning for Borenson's ears. 'Flee!'

As he rode fifteen miles north of Carris, the wizard Binnesman raced beside him and shouted, 'A moment's rest, milord. It won't do us any good to reach Carris on mounts that cannot fight.'

Gaborn could hardly hear the man over the thundering of horses' hooves.

'Milord!' Langley shouted, adding his plea to Binnesman's. 'Five minutes, please!'

Ahead, a pond beckoned to the right of the road. Fish were rising, snapping at mosquitoes. Cattle had come here to drink often, had churned the bank to mud near the road.

Gaborn reined in his horse, let it go to the water.

A pair of mallards began quacking and flew up from some cattails, circled Gaborn and the pond, then winged to the east. In no time at all, mosquitoes were gathering around Gaborn, and he slapped them away from his face.

Sir Langley let his horse drink not twenty paces off, on the far side of Binnesman. Langley grinned at Gaborn. 'By the Powers,' he said. 'If I'd known that I'd have to contend with so many mosquitoes, I'd have worn plate!'

Gaborn was in no mood for jests. He looked back as a few lords straggled to a stop, made a quick count.

Gaborn had no army at his back. Just twenty knights. Worthy lords out of Orwynne, Fleeds, and Heredon. Gaborn's Days was nowhere to be seen.

He did not have an army – just a few people brave enough and foolish enough to follow him to their deaths.

Gaborn felt certain that Castle Carris and its inhabitants could not stand another hour.

Gone were the troops he'd hoped to gain from King Lowicker. The men behind him would be of no use. He'd hoped to find one of his own armies, or perhaps the Knights Equitable that High Marshal Skalbairn had promised.

It does not matter, Gaborn told himself. I do not know what Raj Ahten is up to, but I will ride to him and demand surrender or give him his death.

Binnesman's mount stood and drank, taking draughts of water in great gasps. Gaborn got out his feed bag and held up a last double handful of miln for his horse to eat. The warhorse whickered gratefully at Gaborn. It chewed the sweet oats, malt, and molasses quickly. Its eyes looked dull and tired.

Gaborn wiped his sticky hands on his tunic afterward, and Binnesman must have seen Gaborn's worried expression, for he asked softly, 'What troubles you, milord?'

Night was falling, the last full rays of sunlight streamed through some broken clouds. The wind off the pond blew cold in Gaborn's face.

He spoke softly, not wanting to be heard by the lords who were still converging on the watering hole. 'We're riding into great danger. I have been wondering: how can I set a value on the lives of others? How can I Choose one man above another?'

'Choosing isn't hard,' Binnesman said. 'It's *not* Choosing that pains you.'

'But how can I set a value on the lives of others?'

'Time and again you've shown me that you hold life precious,' Binnesman answered. 'You value most people even more than they value themselves.'

'No,' Gaborn said. 'My people love life.'

'Perhaps,' Binnesman said. 'But just as you try to shield your weaker subjects with your own life, any man in this company' – he nodded to those lords who were closing in behind – 'would give his life for another.'

He was right. Gaborn would gladly give his life in service to others. He'd die nobly for them in battle, live nobly for them in times of peace.

'What is really bothering you?' Binnesman asked.

Hoping that no one else would hear, Gaborn whispered,

'The Earth came to me in a dream, and has threatened to chastise me. It has warned that I must Choose the *seeds* of humanity, and nothing more.'

Binnesman focused completely on Gaborn now, frowning in apparent horror. The Earth Warden drew close. 'Beware, milord. If the Earth chose to speak to you in a dream, it is only because you are too preoccupied to listen when you are awake. Now, tell me exactly, what did the Earth warn you against?'

'Against . . . Choosing too widely,' Gaborn said. 'The Earth appeared in the form of my dead father, and warned me that I must learn to accept death.'

Gaborn dared not admit that he had not yet come to terms with his father's death. The Earth asked something that was impossible for him.

The Earth had warned Gaborn that he needed to narrow his scope, to Choose only the best seeds of humanity to save through the dark season to come.

But who were the best?

Those he loved the most? Not always.

Those who contributed most to the world? Was one man's art of more value than a baker's skill at baking bread, or a humble peasant woman's love for her children?

Should he Choose those who could fight best in his behalf, and thus best defend his people?

How could Gaborn set a value on life? He'd seen into the hearts of his people, and now it seemed that the gift of Earth Sight was as much a burden as a boon.

He'd seen into the hearts of others, and knew that old men loved life more fiercely than youths who should have treasured their days.

He saw into the hearts of others and seldom found men to be as virtuous as he hoped. The best soldiers, the men he most wanted as warriors, often did not value life. Too many of them were brutal creatures who loved blood and domination. Far too seldom did a virtuous man wield a sword.

Far too often Gaborn looked into the hearts of men and,

as with King Lowicker, found the sight unbearable.

How then could he turn away from a simple person who deserved life, but had little to offer: babes and clubfooted boys and grandmothers tottering on the edge of doom.

Binnesman said solemnly, in a whisper that no one else nearby would hear, 'You are in grave danger, milord. Those who serve the Earth must do so with perfect complicity. If you do not serve the Earth, it will withdraw your powers.'

Binnesman studied Gaborn for a long moment, frowning. 'Perhaps I am at fault,' he said. 'When you gained the power of Choosing, I told you to be generous. I should have warned you that a great danger also lies in being too generous. You may have to give up some that you have Chosen . . . Is that what you feel?'

Gaborn closed his eyes, gritted his teeth. At this moment, he could not accept death.

'Milord!' Sir Langley shouted, and he pointed toward the crest of a rounded hill a couple of hundred yards to the south.

Up there, a brown vapor stole over the fields, creeping over the hill like a grass fire, moving at about the pace that a man could walk. But no smoke rose from that fire, no flames burned within it.

Instead, grasses and low shrubs hissed and wilted in gray ruin. The creeping line of brown smoke hit a great oak, and part of the bark on it shattered and split. Its leaves turned a sickly hue and began to drop. Even the mistletoe hanging in its limbs hissed and writhed. The bachelor's buttons at the oak's base went from vivid blue to dullest gray in seconds.

Then the fog of destruction blew downhill.

Binnesman frowned, stroked his short beard.

Gaborn stared at the lurking mist in growing horror. 'What is that?' he ventured.

'I . . . don't know,' Binnesman said. 'It may be a blasting spell of some kind, but I've never heard of one so powerful.'

'Is it dangerous to people?' Gaborn asked. 'Will it kill the horses?'

Binnesman mounted his horse and rode toward the hill.

Gaborn hurried to the wizard's side, loathing the touch of that desecrating fog.

When Gaborn reached the brown haze, he smelled death and putrefaction. He immediately felt corruption around him. Even with his endowments, breathing that mist weakened every muscle. His head reeled, and Gaborn sat in his saddle, sickened to the core of his soul. He could only imagine how the mist would affect commoners.

'Ah!' he cried as he drew near Binnesman.

He looked at the wizard to see its effect on him, and Binnesman suddenly seemed older than before, the creases in his face etched more deeply, his skin grayer. He bent over in his saddle, like a frail and devastated man.

Behind Gaborn, his men left off caring for their mounts and rode up behind the King. Gaborn watched their reaction to the mist. To his surprise, they did not seem as devastated by the mist as he and Binnesman were.

'Forgive me for doubting you, my King,' Binnesman said hoarsely before the others could arrive. 'You were right to insist on riding to Carris. Your powers of perception are growing, and have surpassed even mine. We must strike down whatever is causing this defilement.'

Gaborn crested the hill and stared south in apprehension. In the distance, whole forests lay denuded. Skeletal branches raked the sky. Steam curled in thin wisps from gray mounds of grass.

The Earth was in torment. Gaborn could feel it in every muscle and bone.

Three warriors sat ahorse half a mile in the distance, gazing back at Gaborn. One wore the horned helm of Toom, another carried the long rectangular shield of Beldinook. The third wore full plate in the elaborately decorative style of warriors from Ashoven.

Such disparate styles of armor would only be worn by Knights Equitable. The three peered at Gaborn a moment, and the warrior from Toom raised his right hand in a sign of peace, as he urged his horse toward the hill.

A huge man with an enormous axe strapped across his back and a deadly gleam in his eyes, he raced to Gaborn's side. Horror showed in his countenance. He studied the twenty men at Gaborn's back. 'Is this all, Your Highness? Is this all the army you bring?'

'A few others follow, but they will not be here in time to save Carris,' Gaborn said frankly.

'That I can see,' the warrior said.

'King Lowicker betrayed my trust,' Gaborn explained. 'None will come from Beldinook, only Queen Herin and a few others from Fleeds, Orwynne, and Heredon. We did not ride soon enough, I'm sorry to say.'

'Can you stop this devastation?' the man asked, motioning toward the tide of dead foliage, the putrid haze that covered the land.

'We must try,' Binnesman answered.

The big warrior grunted. 'I was sent to wait back here, in hopes of reinforcements. High Marshal Skalbairn awaits your command. Our troops are moving south, not eight miles down the road, but even the Righteous Horde is no match for so many reavers.'

'Reavers?' Sir Langley asked in astonishment, and the twenty lords who had followed Gaborn abruptly laid propriety aside as they began shouting. 'How many? Where? When did they attack?'

Astonished, Gaborn sat in his saddle, unable to speak. Even with all his powers – his recognition that his Chosen were in danger, his often precise knowledge of how to save them – he still could not tell whether his Chosen fought against bandits or lords or reavers – or were simply in jeopardy of falling off a stool.

He'd expected to find Raj Ahten storming Carris.

The three Knights Equitable all began to answer at once. 'Our far-seers reported the castle taken by Raj Ahten before dawn, but reavers rode in on his heels. There are some twenty thousand blade-bearers, we estimate, plus many reavers of other kinds. Raj Ahten led a charge against them not an hour ago, and lost some men. The reavers are at the castle walls, but Raj Ahten is making them pay dearly for their conquest.'

Gaborn studied Sir Langley. The young lord was full of power. Langley wore scale mail and a helm, yet in some ways seemed not to wear armor at all. He'd been receiving endowments for two days as the facilitators of Orwynne sought to raise him to become Raj Ahten's equal. The man wore his armor now as lightly as a farmer would don his tunic, and the profound strength and power in him seemed to overflow, as if it could not be held within a metal skin.

Now Sir Langley proposed that they should attack. 'We can charge into their flanks, take the reavers by surprise.' He was eager to fight – overeager.

'Charging a horde of reavers should not be considered lightly,' Binnesman argued. 'We don't have nearly enough troops for such a feat.'

'We have the Righteous Horde,' the big knight of Toom said, 'and four thousand decent spearmen who defected out of Beldinook.'

Gaborn weighed what the men had to say.

'Consider well,' Binnesman cautioned Gaborn.

Gaborn glanced at the wizard. Binnesman had an odd green metallic tint to his face and eyes. His service to the Earth had drained him of his humanity decades ago. As an Earth Warden, he was in some ways Gaborn's senior. He'd given himself in service, and fulfilled his duties honorably, for hundreds of years. Gaborn had vowed to serve the Earth only a week ago. Gaborn respected Binnesman's counsel, but he did not want to follow it now.

'The wizard may be right, Your Highness,' High Queen Herin the Red said. 'Against so many reavers, I would think we are too few.'

'I never took you for a coward,' Langley growled at her. 'Did not the Earth command him to strike?'

The Earth has also been warning me to flee, Gaborn thought.

'Think on this,' a lord from Orwynne said. 'Of course

Paldane and his people are in Carris . . . but so is Raj Ahten. Perhaps the reavers will do us a favor and kill the bastard. If the people of Carris die, too, it may not be an easy trade to stomach, but it might not be a bad trade.'

'You forget yourself,' Gaborn warned the knight. 'I can't let hundreds of thousands of good people die just to be rid of one man.'

Though Gaborn spoke of riding to Raj Ahten's defense, he was weary of trying to decipher the message of his dream from last night.

'Be forwarned that if we go forward, every man among us will stand at death's door today,' Gaborn warned them. 'Who will ride with me?'

As one, the lords around him cheered. Only Binnesman watched Gaborn skeptically and remained silent.

'So be it,' Gaborn shouted. Putting his heels to horseflesh, he raced off for Carris. Every bone in his body ached with the Earth's pain.

Twenty lords followed him.

For now, that seemed enough.

54

FOUL BARGAINS

Gaborn reached a low valley three miles north of Carris, and came upon the rearmost contingent of High Marshal Skalbairn's troops trudging across the ruins of a blasted land, through the reeking low mist that infused men with a profound feeling of illness.

Farthest away from him, Skalbairn led a couple of thousand knights at the van, followed by eight thousand spearmen marching in formation. Thousands of archers trailed near their rear.

Last of all came the camp followers: carters with huge wains full of armor and arrows and food; artillerymen who skulked behind knowing that they would be of little use in the coming battle; squires, cooks, washwomen, whores, and boys seeking adventure who had no business marching to war.

How can I save them all? Gaborn wondered.

Scouts at the rearguard blew battle horns, and the people turned to look back at the Earth King and his 'reinforcements.'

If the sight dismayed them, they did not show it. The men in back suddenly raised their fists and their weapons and shouted in triumph.

Mankind had waited two thousand years for an Earth King. Now an Earth King had come to these few at last.

On the horizon, the cloud ceiling above Carris was red with flame.

The sound of a distant hissing roar rumbled over the ruined earth. The Knights Equitable continued cheering, but now the camp followers began to cry out. 'Choose me, milord! Choose me!'

They turned toward him and some began to run forward to plead for the Choosing. Gaborn realized that if he did not act soon, he might be crushed in the press.

Gaborn raced his charger to a roadside farmhouse. Near the house, a sod barn for storing tubers lay next to the ground with its low roof of thatch rising like a small hill. Gaborn rode up to the barn and leapt from his horse, then sprinted to the rooftop and stood holding an iron weathervane shaped like a racing dog.

He gazed out over Skalbairn's Righteous Horde. He knew it would be no match for the reavers. Not if these men fought with nothing more than their own strong arms to defend themselves. Yet Gaborn needed this army desperately if he was to strike a blow.

Gaborn raised his left arm to the square and begged to the Earth Powers he sought to serve. 'Forgive me for what I must do.'

He gazed over the army and shouted in a voice loud enough so that all could hear. 'I Choose you. I Choose you all, in the name of the Earth. May the Earth hide you. May the Earth heal you. May the Earth make you its own.'

Gaborn did not know if it would work. In the past he'd always sought to look into the hearts of men – to judge them fairly to see if they were worthy before offering his gift.

He'd never sought to gather so many at once.

He only hoped it would work. The Earth itself had told him in Binnesman's garden that he was free to Choose whom he would, but Gaborn did not know if he was free to Choose men he thought unfit.

Far away, at the very van of the cavalry near the hilltop, rode High Marshal Skalbairn.

He sat ahorse, in his full black plate mail, and turned toward Gaborn. He lifted his visor and tapped the side of his helm beneath his right ear, as if begging Gaborn to repeat what he'd said.

Gaborn had not used the Earth Sight to gaze into the hearts of every man and woman in the horde. He'd looked into the heart of only one – Marshal Skalbairn – and had sworn never to Choose him.

Now he repented of that vow, but not for the sake of Skalbairn. He hoped only that if Skalbairn fought valiantly, his deeds might save the lives of a few hundred or a thousand common folk who were more worthy of life than was Skalbairn.

As the lines of power formed between Gaborn and thousands of new subjects, Gaborn silently whispered words that only the High Marshal could hear.

'That is right,' Gaborn said, shame making the blood rise hot to his face. 'I Choose you, though you have slept with your own mother and fathered your own crippled, idiot sister. You have committed abomination and have loved the deed as you love your own child. Though I abhor what you have done, I Choose even you.'

I am free to do this, Gaborn told himself. I am free to Choose. He felt in his own heart, wishing that he could know the Earth's will in this matter.

If the Earth objected, Gaborn was not aware. He did not feel his power drain from him or notice some other sign of the Earth's reprisal. All he felt was death's heavy hand waiting to smite every man, woman, and child in the valley before him. And with it he felt the Earth's command, still vague and as yet undefined: 'Strike! Strike now!'

Gaborn spoke to the heart of every man and woman in his army, relaying his message.

High Marshal Skalbairn nodded, signifying that he had heard Gaborn. Then he turned and blew his greathorn, sending his warriors to charge into battle.

Gaborn's eyes look haunted, Erin Connal thought as she rode for Carris. Erin had often seen that same expression, that same heavy weight on her mother's brow. Everyone thinks Gaborn is invincible because he is the Earth King, she realized. They don't know how many nights he sits awake, worrying for them.

Erin guessed from his expression of horror that little good would come from this battle. She resolved to stay at his side, to protect him to the last. I could use my body to shield his, she thought, if I have to. I might be able to trade my life for his.

Erin glanced from Gaborn to her left, to the wizard Binnesman at his far side. Binnesman rode a great gray Imperial warhorse that he'd stolen from Raj Ahten more than a week ago. The beast had so many endowments of wit and brawn that it hardly looked like a creature of flesh and blood. Fierce intelligence shone in its eyes, intelligence equal to a man's in measure but not in kind. No, his mount looked not at all like an animal. It looked like a force of nature, or like a creature of granite.

Though the brown mists that smelled so much of rot made Erin feel weak, she still wanted to kill something. Not one something, she told herself. Many somethings. Raj Ahten, her father's assassin, for one. She wanted to slay reavers, enough reavers to wash away her cold anger.

The sky overhead was leaden, the sun fading like a cinder over the hills. Her mount breathed deeply, its nostrils flaring, its breath coming out cold. It wanted to run, knew it was time to fight.

Yet she had to keep the pace slow to accommodate the footmen of the Righteous Horde. She had not yet seen a reaver.

The smell of horseflesh came strong all around her, and the knights trotted along wordlessly, the *ching* of ring mail singing in the wild autumn air, the sound of the occasional lance or shield clacking against armor, the thud of hooves, the snorting and neighing of horses.

Erin bore no lance, for she'd not wanted to carry one all the way from Fleeds to Mystarria only to have it break on her first pass with some knight.

Now, with all the reavers ahead, she wished she were better armed. A reaver's crystalline bone was hard as rock, and many a weapon would shatter on impact with one of the monsters. But it would be hard to kill a reaver with anything smaller than a heavy lance.

She wheeled her mount, headed back toward the carters' wagons, looking for a wain with a long bed. 'Lance?' she cried.

Ahead, a boy in a long-bedded wagon got up from his seat and jumped into a wagonbed to get a lance while the drover at his side continued to drive.

Erin grabbed the heavy lance.

Prince Celinor raced close to her on a mount borrowed from her mother's stables.

The young man was ashen-faced, his jaw set. 'Lance?' he called to the boy, getting a weapon of his own.

He glanced Erin's way, patted a sheathed Crowthen war axe with its six-foot-long handle and huge single spike. It was a clumsy weapon for fighting men, but it had never been designed for men. The great prong was ideal for cracking a reaver's carapace.

'Don't worry,' Celinor said. 'I'll protect you.'

His sentiment astonished her.

You'll protect me? she wanted to mock. He was not Chosen, after all. Of the entire horde racing toward Carris, she realized, he alone had not been Chosen. Gaborn had raised his hand, Chosen every last blacksmith's helper and whore in the company. But Gaborn's back had been to Prince Celinor at the time.

No, if anyone would be needing protection it was Celinor.

It will be up to me to watch out for him, Erin thought. Her loyalties were divided. She gritted her teeth and nodded toward Gaborn. 'Stay by him!' she begged.

Celinor smiled wryly, adopted the tone of a patron dickering with a street vendor. 'So, I have been wondering, Horsesister Connal, what deed today would convince you that I'm worthy of a night in your bed?'

Erin merely laughed.

'I'm serious,' he said.

'I'd not be worrying about it, if I were you. How could your head be so woolly as to think of such things now?'

'War and women: I find them both exciting. Is it valor you want? I'll be fearless. Is it strength and cunning you seek in a man? I'll give it a try. What if I saved your life today? Would that earn me a night in your bed?'

'I'm not some serf from Kartish. I'd not be your slave just because you save my life.'

'Not even for a night?'

Erin studied his eyes. Celinor smiled at her as if he jested, but behind that smile she saw concern, as if she looked into the eyes of a child.

He did not jest. He wanted her desperately, and he feared her rejection. He was not a bad man, she knew. He was handsome, and strong enough. He had fine composition. If she'd been looking for a man to sire a child on her, she'd have considered him.

So she dared not reject him out of hand. But although she found his looks and build captivating, it impressed her more that he understood the political consequences of what he asked, yet asked it anyway. He was not seeking a mere night of diversion; he wanted to court her as best he knew how. She was not some tender flower of a girl, after all, she was a horsewoman of Fleeds.

'All right,' Erin said. 'Prove yourself in battle today – save my life – and maybe I'll have you for a night.'

'Agreed,' Celinor said. 'But that brings to mind another question. What does it take to prove myself worthy as a husband? If perhaps, let us say, I saved you three times?'

Erin laughed aloud, for she thought *that* unlikely. 'Save me three times, and you will be having three nights in my bed,' she teased. But then she spoke softly, provocatively. 'But if you want to be my husband, you must prove yourself not on the battlefield . . . but in my bed.'

Erin turned her gelding and drove on into the gloom. Her face burned with embarrassment. She watched the leaden skies fade as the sun rode down in the west. It was not a beautiful sunset, not a roaring sky of flame or gold – just a dimming of the day into night.

She glanced back at Celinor, who hurried to keep up.

Their horses crested a small hill. Across a valley stood a tall wall with an arched gate beneath it. 'The Barren's Wall,' someone said.

Beyond the wall, she glimpsed Carris, two miles distant. Its white towers stood tall and proud, but a great black rent marred its western façade. Boats were issuing from a floodgate in the south wall, bobbing on the waves as people fled for their lives.

On the castle walls, men cheered and cheered to see Gaborn's army. Warhorns blared, calling for help.

To the south of Carris, atop a dark leaning tower that twisted up like black flames, she could see reavers working feverishly.

Reavers were visible everywhere now. Tens of thousands of them swarmed on the plains and at the gates of Castle Carris. More marched northward in a line down from the mountains, each reaver taller than an elephant, but looking nothing like any creature to roam the surface of the earth.

Seeing them, she felt loathing.

On a hill north of Carris was a strange thing – a cocoon of fibers that looked like silk from this distance, wrapping the whole hill. At the hill's peak, a fell mage glimmered, clouds of brown fog whirling away from her. As Erin watched, the mage raised her staff and hissed, a roaring noise that filled the valley. A wave of dark wind issued from her in all directions.

In response, a thousand Knights Equitable suddenly raised voices in song. Many warriors spurred their mounts forward, toward the gate in the Barren's Wall.

Her horse began running. Erin had not willed it, had not pounded her mount's flank with her heel, but the horse suddenly surged forward beneath her, eager to race with the other knights.

The knights erupted into song, and Prince Celinor sang clearly at her side.

'We are born to blood and war,
Like our fathers were, a thousand years before.
Sound the horn. Strike the blow!
Down to grief or glory go!'

Erin began racing, and the bloodlust was so strong in her, she cared not whether she raced for her life or to her death. She couched her lance and spurred her horse, screaming in defiance.

55

THE HUNTSMAN STRIKES

Raj Ahten had endowments from thousands of men, could recall in detail nearly every moment of his life. It had been six months since he had glanced at a diagram of Carris, but he knew precisely where to find Paldane's boats.

The courtyard around him was glutted with reavers and Invincibles, locked in a grim struggle. The city burned, and his men were drenched in sweat even as the fell mage uttered another curse. The news of boats that could take them to safety had spread among Raj Ahten's men. Here and there, Raj Ahten saw teams of men dive out of battle, giving ground before the reavers, while the men of Mystarria were left to fill the breaches as best they could.

But he doubted that many of his men would be able to find the boathouse, hidden as it was down in the business district.

Raj Ahten gutted his last blade-bearer, and wheeled back out of the fray.

'Follow me!' he shouted to his men, leading the way to the boats.

As he fled south, toward a narrow street clogged with oxcarts and barrels of tar and nails that commoners had set up as pitiful barricades against the reavers, cries of dismay arose from the people of Carris.

He glanced up to see the cause. Commoners up there – men of Rofehavan that he would leave to their fates – watched him retreat, and their faces were ashen, twisted in grimaces of fear. The mage's spells had so wrung the sweat from them that many had fallen to the wall-walks.

Throwing away the lives of himself and his few remaining Invincibles would not save them.

He hurried away.

Land in Carris had always been at a premium, and that was apparent in the city streets, which were as narrow as the alleys in most northern castles. The buildings canted nearly together.

The fell mage's black wind struck once more, and Raj Ahten stopped a moment and knelt, holding his breath, squinting his eyes, trying his best not to absorb the scent of her curse.

When he breathed again, the mage's command wrung sweat from him more fiercely. He hurried to escape this benighted place.

He had not retreated half the distance to the boats when he turned a corner down a steep hill toward the merchants' quarter and met Duke Paldane the Huntsman, ambling toward him through the narrow alley, with half a dozen of old King Orden's Wits marching at his back.

Paldane raised a hand, signaling Raj Ahten to stop, then wiped the copious sweat from his forehead with his sleeve.

The triumphant grin on Paldane's lips gave Raj Ahten pause. Raj Ahten halted warily.

'Good news!' Paldane greeted him. 'You'll be happy to hear that the first flotilla is off! The first load of women and children are being rowed to safety.'

'What?' Raj Ahten asked. He imagined that it must be a ruse. Paldane could never have loaded the boats so quickly.

'Indeed,' Paldane said. 'I took the liberty of assembling the refugees this morning. The boats have been laden since noon. When my far-seer brought word that he saw a boat returning on the horizon, our first load of women and children shoved off.'

To emphasize his victory, Paldane said, '*Every* boat is gone. Every one.'

Raj Ahten thought to run to the north wall to verify

Paldane's word, but Paldane's tone of triumph was pure and honest. Clearly, Paldane had launched the boats. From the wall, Raj Ahten would only see a thousand skiffs bobbing on the whitecaps of Lake Donnestgree.

Paldane knew precisely what he had done. He had stranded Raj Ahten's men here in the castle. Raj Ahten decided to wipe that superior grin from his face.

With a mailed fist, Raj Ahten swung swiftly for the bridge of Paldane's nose. The blow landed with a crunching sound, and the bone in Paldane's skull shattered with a satisfying *schunk*. Flecks of blood spattered all over Raj Ahten's face, even as the Huntsman of Mystarria dropped like so much meat.

How dare the little man? Raj Ahten thought, as he wiped the flecks of blood from his face.

The King's Wits who had been following Paldane all drew back in a little knot, terrified. They awaited his punishment, and he held it back, knowing that a feast always tastes better on an empty belly.

Raj Ahten considered his options. His Invincibles did not need boats. As a last resort, they could abandon their weapons and armor and swim across the lake.

In that moment, there was an odd, unexpected sound. The wails of pain and despair on the castle walls erupted into cheers and the wild blowing of warhorns.

Raj Ahten glanced up to see the cause of the excitement. People on the walls were waving and pointing to the north, leaping in celebration. 'The Earth King is coming! The Earth King!' men began to shout.

Raj Ahten smiled grimly at Paldane's corpse. With a sudden certainty, he realized, he might yet pull off a strategic victory here.

'So,' Raj Ahten said, addressing King Orden's Wits, doddering old men who trembled before him. 'Your King comes at last – comes to throw himself against the reavers and die. He should offer quite a spectacle. I would not miss this.'

56

THE ONE RUNE

Sweat glazed Gaborn's forehead, drenched the leather jerkin beneath his chain mail. As he drew near Carris, the sensation of illness that had assailed him ever since he'd begun to cross the blasted lands grew more potent. He clung to the reins of his mount, and without his endowments of stamina, he knew that he would have succumbed in his saddle.

He stared ahead, almost blinded by perspiration, as his mount raced the warriors beside him. Only dimly did he hear the Knights Equitable raise their war songs.

In a daze, Gaborn rode to battle, crossing under the stone gate in the Barren's Wall. He felt only vaguely aware of his situation as he drew within a mile and a half of Carris and watched the towers burn. Gree flew about his army, wriggling darkly.

Ten thousand threads bound him to the men and women under his charge. He felt death stalking them all. The weight of the invisible shroud overwhelmed him.

He gazed downhill at the castle, across the blasted earth. He'd never imagined such a scene of ruin, the land so dead and torn, with hordes of reavers scuttling about.

'Where to, milord?' Sir Langley shouted near Gaborn's side. 'Where to strike?'

Dazed and ill, Gaborn peered about, tried to collect his thoughts. His father had been a master strategist, and in his youth Gaborn had learned much from him. He needed to quickly develop a plan.

A few reavers a quarter of a mile away sensed the presence of his knights and cautiously began to scuttle forward. At this distance, as they ran by lunging forward in short bursts, they reminded him of kelp crabs creeping along the shore of some desolate beach.

Gaborn surveyed the reavers' defenses. Directly to the south, the enormous menacing tower leaned like a black flame toward the castle. At the castle gates the reavers had opened a huge rent in the western wall, and now clambered into the city over hills formed by the carcasses of men and reavers. Aided by the light of burning towers, he could clearly see Paldane's men fighting valiantly to defend the walls, but reavers had breached into the city so far that there was no hope of repelling them.

To the north of Carris squatted a strange little hill on an easy slope, entirely encircled by a cocoon of whitish threads. Bone Hill. He knew the place from his studies of ancient battles.

At its crown a fell mage labored, while lesser mages slaved beneath her. Around her, roiling dirty clouds emanated in spirals from the hill. Ghost-lights flickered beneath the rust-colored haze.

Gaborn's breath quickened. Bone Hill immediately repulsed him and drew him.

It repulsed him because the hill was engraved with a rune that itself was loathsome to his sight, was the source of illness and pain. To look at its warty knobs and sinuous lines burned his eyes and made the muscles in them twitch and try to turn away. The rune atop the hill was like a vast heart, pumping poisoned blood to every finger and toe in a human body.

Yet the hill drew him, it was his target. 'Strike!' Earth silently begged. 'Strike before it is too late!'

Gaborn appraised the rune using his Earth Sight, as if he stared into the heart of a man. What he saw filled him with terror.

Ancient lore said that all runes were but parts broken from one great master rune, the rune that controlled the universe.

Gaborn saw now a vast portion of the master rune.

The Earth held sway over growth and life and healing and protection. But in that rune he saw laid bare the end of all earth powers:

Where there is growth, let there be stagnation.
Where there is life, let there be desolation.
Where there is healing, let there be corruption.
Where men hide, let them be revealed.

Gaborn knew the name of that rune, knew it in his bones: the Seal of Desolation.

The rune was incomplete, like a sword newly forged and not yet tempered, but it tortured the land for miles in every direction.

In wonder Gaborn studied his target. The hair rose on the nape of his neck. He'd ridden hundreds of miles hoping to fight Raj Ahten. He'd promised his warriors that he would lead them to battle.

Now he knew that he had been called not to fight reavers or men or any living thing. He needed to destroy this construct, this weapon. And it was a task that no army could hope to accomplish.

Only a wizard with vast earth powers might destroy that hill. Only Gaborn could do it.

He had to draw a rune of Earth-breaking.

A sense of doom assailed him. Gaborn's powers were limited. He had to get close, so that he could focus his spell. Yet the stench that exuded from Bone Hill became more overwhelming the nearer he approached.

Gaborn addressed High Marshal Skalbairn. 'I'm going to attack Bone Hill, and I need diversions. Take a thousand men and head down into the valley, then ride hard toward the Black Tower, skirting the reavers' army at a hundred yards. Make sure that you're close enough for them to sense you. If they do not take up the chase immediately, kill a few of them. But don't engage their main force! Don't waste men. I want

you only to draw them off! And if I should be killed, you'll
need men to bring down the fell mage. Is that clear? She
cannot leave this battlefield alive!'

'As it pleases milord,' Skalbairn said, clearly affronted to be
used as a mere diversion for someone else's attack. He immediately whirled his mount and shouted orders, drawing the
dregs of his cavalry into service.

'And me?' Langley asked. Gaborn needed to send Langley
into far greater danger than he had Skalbairn. Langley's great
strength would be needed if he were called upon to fight.

'Take another five hundred knights along the shore toward
Carris proper. Charge their flanks by the causeway, then
retreat. As with Skalbairn, your task is not to slay reavers, but
to open their ranks. And if I die . . .'

'I understand, milord,' Sir Langley said, no happier to be
a diversion than Skalbairn. Yet it would be a difficult task.
The reavers were thick near the causeway, with little room for
retreat.

Langley raised his hand, summoned his men.

'What of us?' Queen Herin asked.

'You'll ride with me,' Gaborn answered, 'to face the fell
mage.' He was not overly gratified by the cruel smile of
approval that she offered.

'I will give it the deathblow myself, if it please you,' she
said.

Gaborn only shook his head. 'We'll need to fight our way
close to the hill, so that I can destroy it. Nothing more. The
rune that she's drawing must be destroyed. Afterward, we can
regroup and consider how to deal with the mage.'

The High Queen nodded. 'So be it.' She turned to the
knights behind her, called out orders calmly.

'What of the spearmen and foot soldiers?' Erin Connal
asked. 'Could we use them to some advantage?'

Gaborn shook his head. Sending foot soldiers against
reavers would accomplish almost nothing. 'Order them to stay
behind the Barren's Wall. They can hold it against any reaver
that climbs over.'

With that, Skalbairn rode off, charging to the right. A ragged line of a thousand knights raced downhill toward the plains, charged the western slope of Bone Hill.

As they rode, they began to sing. The pounding of hooves and the ring of metal kept time with their deep voices.

Against Gaborn's orders, Skalbairn drove his troops right against half a dozen reavers. With a crash of lances against carapaces his knights left the monsters impaled, then veered away at slow speed, forcing the horses to lope.

The effect of his diversion was astonishing. The plains were pocked with odd burrows – lopsided craters with dark maws. To Gaborn it had seemed that the plain was almost black with reavers, but now hundreds more boiled up from underground, giving pursuit. In moments, perhaps two thousand reavers were chasing Skalbairn's men south.

At Gaborn's back, men began to cheer and raise their weapons. 'Well done!' Queen Herin and others whispered, obviously pleased.

Gaborn sensed little danger to Skalbairn's men. Indeed, they were not in great peril, yet they accomplished much.

Gaborn nodded toward Sir Langley, sent his lancers charging left.

Langley too advanced on Bone Hill at slow speed, this time from the north. But Gaborn felt a pall over the man. Langley was in far greater danger than Skalbairn.

As Langley neared Bone Hill the reaver mage raised her staff to the sky and hissed. Her voice echoed from low-lying clouds like thunder.

A dark wind roiled from her, and Langley's men shouted in fear, turned their mounts and galloped east toward the lake, fleeing the dark wind of her spell, the burnished metal of their helms and armor limned red from the burning citadels of Carris. Hundreds and hundreds of reavers gave pursuit.

The black wind caught the men near the lakeshore, and suddenly the air filled with cries. Knights began to topple from saddles, stricken. Gaborn could not tell why.

Whatever effect the fell mage's spell had upon them, Gaborn

was too far away to feel it himself. Langley's men fought to stay ahorse as reavers closed in.

'Get up,' Gaborn sent to the men. 'Fight now or die!'

After a heart-stopping moment, Langley himself roused in his saddle, shouted and spurred a charge south. Dozens of men followed, though most of his force remained inactive. Their horses milled about or fled from advancing reavers.

Thirty of his men lanced through the charging reavers, losing less than a dozen knights in the clash. The survivors wheeled their mounts and fled north along the lakeshore, with seven or eight hundred reavers giving chase.

The repercussions of Gaborn's feints shuddered through the reaver horde. Reavers near the causeway backed off, fearing an attack on their flank, giving the defenders of Carris some relief. Others continued to race south after Skalbairn.

To Gaborn's relief, the north slope of Bone Hill was momentarily left with few defenders. He saw only some hundred reavers above their burrows, but a hundred reavers were not to be trifled with – especially not when a fell mage stood at their backs.

He had only seconds to strike.

57

IN THE SHADOWED VALE

'Prepare the charge!' Gaborn cried. 'Staggered pinwheel formation! Single line! Ho!' He raised his hand in the air, whirled it, letting the men know that they should pinwheel from left to right.

The staggered pinwheel, or the knight's circus, as it was sometimes called, had proven an effective formation against reavers in ancient times.

Rather than charge forward in a line, as they would against human opponents, the knights rode in a giant pinwheel that gravitated forward as it circled. Deadly lances bristled along the pinwheel's edge, so that fresh men and mounts were constantly racing at an angle to the enemy's line.

Getting the proper angle and attack speed was vital when lancing a reaver. The trick of using a lance to kill a reaver, Gaborn had learned from those who had tried, was to strike the reaver solidly and skewer the damned thing without killing yourself in the process.

Above all, speed was essential. A force horse with many endowments charged at forty to eighty miles per hour. At such a speed, a knight had to take care not to slam into a reaver haphazardly, for in doing so he would break his bones.

Nor could a knight make a pass at a reaver in the same way as he did a man. The reaver was too massive. Besides, even if a knight did make a pass at the front lines of a reaver horde, he would lose his lance in the process, only to find himself behind enemy lines. Consequently, he had to race parallel to the reavers' lines, only daring to touch briefly before he pulled back.

As Heredon Sylvarresta had shown so many centuries ago, the art of lancing a reaver required the lancer to lean toward the beast in such a way that he did not slam into the monster after his charge. While leaning thus, his best hope was to thrust the lance into the reaver's head, into the 'sweet triangle,' an area the size of a man's palm where three bony plates met. A second such area could be found in the reaver's upper palate, if the monster opened its mouth.

And if a lance entered at the right angle, then the knight could send it home to the reaver's brain with a gentle and powerful shove.

Thus, in the staggered pinwheel, lancers rode fast enough so that reavers could not adjust to the knights' breakneck pace. At the same time it allowed the knights the chance to engage the reavers in a viable formation, one that would let a knight escape the clutches of a reaver if he missed his target or let a man who was unhorsed escape while the knight behind pressed the attack.

Gaborn spurred his mount. It leapt downhill, thundered ahead.

As Gaborn neared that odious hill, he glanced to each side and found that he rode alone. Such was the speed of his mount that no others could match pace with him.

'Beware,' the Earth whispered, and its voice took him by surprise. Gaborn was so used to warning others, he felt unprepared to take warning himself.

He glanced back. Behind him, the hill was dark with lords and knights. They came singing; firelight from Carris reflected in their shields.

Erin Connal screamed a war cry. Celinor Anders glowered near her side, with High Queen Connal not far behind. The wizard Binnesman's face was rigid with terror. Gaborn's cavalry charged ahead, streaming out from the Barren's Wall.

Ahead, Bone Hill rose, wrapped in its cocoon. Tendrils of white were strung from it like threads from a spider's web.

Dirt and rock gouged from its slopes made it look a horrid ruin, scarred and maimed.

Warned by the front ranks, blade-bearing reavers suddenly issued from the crevasses in the ground on that hill, climbed atop the cocoon as if it were a fortress wall. Behind the blade-bearers, mages continued their foul work.

The rust-colored mist grew heavy in the vale beneath Bone Hill, lying in thick folds. It seared Gaborn's eyes and made them water. He blinked away tears, saw ghostlights flicker back under the cocoon.

Gaborn grimaced as he tried to draw a breath. Fatigue and illness slammed into him like a fist. His stomach wrenched; his gorge rose. Every muscle in his body strained as sweat coursed down his forehead.

Gaborn galloped past a blade-bearer that spun, swinging its glory hammer too late. He ducked beneath its blow, knowing that he'd be dead by now if he'd not taken endowments at Castle Groverman.

Gaborn heard the crack as a lance exploded into the monster's unprotected side, piercing the beast.

Queen Herin the Red had scored her first kill.

Though his charger carried him toward the foul rune, all Gaborn's effort could barely keep him ahorse. He slowed his mount a third of a mile from Bone Hill, close to the ranks of the reavers, and gripped the pommel of his saddle.

Reavers raced down the slopes of the cocoon to do battle.

Gaborn dared charge no closer. Here in the vale, the sour-smelling mists lay over the ground like a suffocating quilt, and no commoner could have abided the stench. His muscles flamed, aching as if every fiber would rip asunder. Sweat poured from him like a drenching rain. Gaborn reeled, fell hard on the earth.

The very soil beneath him burned; it was almost as hot as a skillet. He writhed upon it, could not breathe.

Silently he wished that he'd taken more endowments of stamina.

He glanced up through the rust-colored mist. His knights

were forming their pinwheel, racing ahead of him in a line to cut off reavers that thundered into battle, their thick carapaces crashing against the stony ground.

Several knights caught up to him, circling him protectively. He glimpsed Erin Connal and Prince Celinor, their faces frozen in dismay to see the Earth King fallen.

Gaborn lay sweating on the ground, gasping in the cruel haze, afraid that he might suffocate, for he could hardly draw a breath for the pain that assailed him.

Desolation lay all around him, a smoke that choked the soul.

Atop Bone Hill, the fell mage raised her citrine staff to the sky and hissed so loudly that the sound echoed from the clouds. With a boom like thunder, black smoke roiled off her.

Gaborn tried to climb to his knees as the mage's curse swept downhill.

Erin Connal rode behind Gaborn, choosing to guard him rather than help form the staggered pinwheel. Almost instantly she was glad that she had.

A reaver sped through the lines as a knight broke his lance against its side, then lumbered through the rust-colored mist toward Gaborn, an enormous behemoth swinging its head from side to side.

Erin shook the streaming sweat from her forehead, shouted a battle cry, and charged the beast. She raised her lance overhead and to the side, preparing for the thrust. She squinted against the haze, for it pained the eye, then leaned out from her saddle.

She thrust home her lance, just as the reaver spun its head back toward Gaborn. The tip penetrated the monster's sweet triangle at a slant.

She felt the lance tip drive shallowly into the reaver's crystalline skull. She suspected that she had the wrong angle, that the lance would merely catch in bone and shatter, but she hurled it anyway, hoping to shove the tip home with brute force.

The lance snagged on bone and snapped at the point. Suddenly Erin was caught still thrusting the damned thing without any resistance. Off balance, she pitched from her horse and sprawled to the ground, just beneath the reaver.

It reared above, raised its greatsword protectively to fend off a charging knight.

'Flee!' Gaborn's voice spoke in Erin's mind as she tried to gain her feet.

As if I couldn't guess, she thought, knowing she was too late. The reaver hunched its massive head and lunged, its crystalline teeth gleaming like quartz.

A dark blur sped past her. Celinor's lance pierced the monster's sweet triangle and heaved into its brain as if it had been shot from a ballista.

In amazement, Erin realized he'd thrown the damned thing like a javelin!

The reaver collapsed at Erin's feet.

Celinor galloped near, as if he'd planned to block the dying reaver from further attack with his own body. Then he whirled and drew his Crowthen battle-axe.

Erin ran for her own horse.

'One!' Celinor shouted, then pointed toward the Earth King. Gaborn had fallen from his mount.

Gaborn lay in the dust. Several knights leapt from their mounts to fight at his side, prepared to die if necessary. Celinor Anders rode near and stood guard over him, screaming and waving his battle-axe as if daring any reaver to come close.

As Gaborn struggled to get up, the thought streaked through his consciousness: I should Choose him.

Reavers surged down from Bone Hill like living monoliths, and the thought was driven off as Gaborn sent warnings to hundreds of warriors. In moments Erin Connal and others reached Celinor's side.

The black wind struck, and it carried with it an unnameable stench – a smell similar to burnt cabbage, but that affected Gaborn profoundly. He felt suddenly as if his muscles had turned to jelly, and he experienced the most profound fatigue he'd ever imagined.

He dropped to the ground, as weak as if he'd just given an endowment of brawn. Everywhere around him, dozens of others did the same, even Queen Herin the Red.

A hundred yards back, Binnesman had stopped his mount. He struggled to sit up, slumped as if in pain. 'Jureem!' he warned. 'Get Gaborn away from here! Get the Earth King away! We're too close.'

Jureem rode hard among the knights, leapt from his horse. The fat servant held a silk scarf over his nose to keep from breathing the stench. He grabbed Gaborn's elbow and shouted, 'Get up, milord! Let us flee!'

With muscles flaccid and mind swimming in pain, Gaborn struggled to fend off his own man, tried to push Jureem back. 'Not yet. I can't go! Help me!' he cried. 'Help!'

Gaborn had to destroy the rune. It was still nearly half a mile off. He had destroyed Kriskaven Wall half a mile out. It was near the limit of his power – yet the cloying mists in the vale were so devastating that he dared not ride closer.

He fought to draw with his finger in the hot dirt, to trace a rune of Earth-breaking.

Jureem tried to grab his elbow, to pull him toward his horse. Jureem shouted to Celinor, 'Hold our master's mount! Help me get him in the saddle.'

'No!' Gaborn pleaded. 'Leave me! Binnesman, help!'

He glanced back. As he did, Binnesman collapsed under the influence of the fell mage's spell, lay draped over his own horse. The mount must have sensed that its rider had fallen, and now spurted north, bearing its master out of battle.

To Gaborn's astonishment some knights around him were less affected by the reaver mage's spells. Some lancers still charged. Some men withstood the weakness. Perhaps I need more stamina? he wondered. Yet Queen Herin had fallen, and she had as much stamina as any other.

'Jureem,' Gaborn gasped as he struggled to trace his symbol precisely on the ground. He felt as if he were trying to write on fire itself. His finger was so weak, he could hardly stir the dust.

Jureem stopped struggling to pull him away. The servant gazed at Gaborn wide-eyed and distressed, as if being unable to help caused him physical pain.

Gaborn finished drawing his rune, studied for a moment to make certain that he'd made every curlicue properly, then he looked fiercely at the hill where the Seal of Desolation desecrated the Earth. The fell mage continued to labor atop it. Strange lights flashed behind the cocoon in shades of palest turquoise. Reavers were boiling up from the south side of the hill.

He gazed at the hill, and used the Earth Sight to look beneath it. There, far below the ground, he could sense a weakness – a place where tons and tons of stone grated together in a fault.

It would take only the merest breath to push it all toward ruin, to split the ground beneath the rune.

Gaborn focused on the object of his spell and shouted, 'Be thou riven!'

He slammed the ground with his fist, and envisioned the soil beneath him heaving, splintering that foul rune and shattering its every wall.

The earth responded.

The ground heaved beneath him, and the knights who surround him all gaped, trying to stand as the earth shuddered.

Horses whinnied and floundered. Reavers stumbled. The earth roared like an animal.

The ground rolled in all directions. Knights shouted, and reavers atop their foul cocoon scuttled back in dismay, clinging to their webs.

Gaborn had not imagined what devastating power he would unleash. Knights toppled from their chargers, crying in terror.

But as Gaborn gazed at the Seal of Desolation, his hopes went dry. The ground beneath it trembled, the soil around bucked, but the Seal of Desolation held as if it were a bit of flotsam riding the waves of the sea.

Only powerful runes of binding could have held it. He studied the construct again with his Earth Sight as he had Kriskaven Wall, searching for weaknesses.

Indeed it was bound. Every knob and protuberance was encased in runes of binding – perversions that did not call upon the Powers so much as twist them against themselves. Gaborn was astonished to find that the reavers had so twisted their powers that they could use the Earth against him.

Even as Gaborn focused on the foul rune, men all around began shouting, 'Look! Look there!'

Gaborn gazed toward Carris.

Reavers crawled over the plain before the fortress. They'd burrowed pits everywhere, but the earthquake had tossed rocks and reavers into the air, throwing monsters from their hidden lairs, or just burying them.

Disoriented, some reavers raced about on broken legs.

Above these monsters, Gaborn saw a tower fall, heard thousands of people cry out.

Sheer horror coursed through him as he saw that his tremor had not struck completely without effect. The walls of Carris, a mere half mile to the southeast, swayed like a willow frond. The white plaster on the walls fell off in sheets, and merlons went splashing into the lake.

The tremor could not destroy the bound rune, but it tore asunder more common structures. Towers toppled. Walls began to crumble. Dust rose in the city as inns and homes collapsed.

Even as Gaborn watched, something unexpected happened. The ground beneath him began to roll once again as a new, more powerful tremor made the castle walls shift and sway. The people of Carris cried in terror.

Gaborn's horse staggered to keep its footing. And in Carris dust and fire rose as more buildings began to collapse.

An aftershock.

He did not need his Earth Sight to warn him that he had unleashed a monster. He could feel the power building. This fault ran deeper, farther, than he'd expected. Just as a shout will trigger an avalanche, so had his small tremor triggered catastrophe.

Gaborn stared at the hapless inhabitants of Carris clinging to its walls. Two minutes ago I sat here congratulating myself, he thought. But by my actions I might have doomed the people I hope to save.

Guilt swept through him. Guilt for what he had done, and for what he knew he now must do.

Gaborn raised his left arm and looked to the castle, to men by the scores who now were crying out in despair.

He shouted to the people of Carris, though at such a distance few men would have had enough endowments of hearing to discern his voice. 'I Choose you. I Choose you for the Earth!'

Surely the Earth will allow it, Gaborn reasoned. I was given the gift of Choosing in order to save mankind, and those at Carris need saving.

He had never sought to Choose a man he could not see. Now he tested the utmost limits of his powers. He stared at the castle walls and hoped that with this one Choosing he could protect all those within.

If Choosing Skalbairn would let Gaborn save a thousand, he hoped that Choosing Raj Ahten would let him save hundreds of thousands.

He gaped at the broken walls of the city and whispered, 'Even you, Raj Ahten. I Choose you!'

He felt the threads of his consciousness lengthen, grasp men who fought in Carris, along with women and babes and elderly who only huddled in its dark corners, fearing for their lives.

He reached out even to Raj Ahten.

Gaborn held the Wolf Lord in his mind and whispered, 'I Choose you,' as tenderly as if Raj Ahten were his brother. 'Help me save our people.'

He felt the tendrils of communication connect, felt overwhelmed by Raj Ahten's danger. Death lay thick upon the Wolf Lord, heavy and nauseating. Gaborn had never felt a man lingering so near it. Even now he wondered if his own powers would be sufficient to save him.

'Flee!' Gaborn whispered to Carris.

Out on the plains, Sir Langley and Marshal Skalbairn saw how the earthquake struck the reavers, leaving them dazed and wounded. Being farther from the fell mage, these knights were not so profoundly affected by her curses.

Skalbairn wheeled into the reavers, led a charge, hoping to draw more of them from Gaborn. A thousand mounted knights raced across that plain, lances bristling.

58

THE UNWORTHY

Raj Ahten was not surprised to learn that the boy Gaborn sought to rescue Carris even from the reavers. It was an ill-considered move, as foolish as it was daring and chivalrous – an act of self-sacrifice from a weak-minded idealist.

He sprinted up the steps of a tower, looked to the north.

On the plains, Knights Equitable pinwheeled at the base of Bone Hill. Elsewhere, some thousand knights charged across the downs to the south, drawing away the reavers' forces, as did another contingent to the north.

Raj Ahten almost wanted to congratulate Gaborn. He'd done a fine job of spreading the reavers thin and baffling their lines.

He watched Gaborn's knights struggle toward Bone Hill, saw the world shiver around them, tearing stumps from the ground, hurling dirt and stones in the air, burying some reavers, tossing others from their burrows, and raising a sound a hundred times louder than the rolling of thunder.

For some reason that he could not understand, Raj Ahten had never been able to see Gaborn. A spell lay on the lad, one that hid him from Raj Ahten's view. But the Wolf Lord knew that he was out there.

He felt the quake strike Carris, set the walls to weaving like a drunkard, while those around him cried out.

Only the Earth King could have loosed such a monstrosity. In the space of a heartbeat, Raj Ahten saw the danger. It would level the city.

Almost as soon as the quake struck, Raj Ahten heard

Gaborn's voice ring through his mind as he performed the Choosing.

So, Earth King, Raj Ahten wondered, you bless me and curse me in the same breath?

Gaborn's troops began to advance on Bone Hill and the fell mage. He rode with two thousand knights at his back, as if hoping that such a desperately small force might, by good fortune, strike a lucky blow.

A black wind rolled over Carris, bringing the fell mage's latest curse.

Raj Ahten tasted the scent, felt fatigue sap his strength like never before, and translated it thus: 'Be thou weary unto death.'

Yes, it was a powerful spell. If it were uttered against commoners at close range, Raj Ahten did not doubt that men would collapse with hearts too weak to beat, lungs too exhausted to draw another breath.

On the castle walls around him, many commoners dropped, too stricken to stand.

But Raj Ahten was no commoner.

As Gaborn's knights in their pinwheel slowly gravitated south, blade-bearers began to amass against Gaborn. Perhaps dismayed by the earthquake, they had turned and charged round both sides of Bone Hill. Indeed, the reavers close to Carris itself were wheeling to meet this new threat.

Gaborn would never repel the attack, Raj Ahten could see. The reavers' lines were too thick. In the battle for Carris, Raj Ahten imagined that no more than five hundred reavers had died so far. Twenty thousand reavers were still left to charge north. In moments they would crush Gaborn's troops, rend him to pieces.

'Flee! Flee Carris,' Gaborn's command rang through Raj Ahten's mind. 'Flee for your lives.'

Even as the Earth King spoke, Raj Ahten recognized the folly in listening. The walls of Carris would come down, true, and many men would die. But they'd die regardless of whether they charged the reavers.

'The clever bastard,' Raj Ahten hissed. He saw the lad's ploy now: Gaborn merely sought to use Raj Ahten and his men as pawns, as a distraction, to draw the reavers from himself.

Raj Ahten was far too cunning to fall for such a ruse.

Raj Ahten's Invincibles had already withdrawn from the battle. 'Stand fast!' Raj Ahten shouted to his men. To Paldane's men, he called, 'Hold the breach!'

The Earth King will die here, Raj Ahten told himself, and I . . . I will idly watch.

Yet as Raj Ahten glanced down at the breach, he realized that Paldane's men suddenly fought as fiercely as reavers themselves. At first he imagined that desperation lent them strength. But it was obvious that an unseen power guided them. These were commoners and warriors of unfortunate proportion. He watched one commoner bait a reaver, stand for it to take a whack with its sword, then leap aside instantly. In the brief opening, two better men lunged forward with axes and took off the reaver's arm. As the monster screamed, one quick fellow jumped into its mouth and thrust a longsword through its palate, into its brain. Before the beast ever fell, Paldane's men rushed forward to take on the next comer.

His men lunged quickly to take advantage of exposed targets, avoided reaver's blows. They choreographed thrusts and parries, so that the battle suddenly became something more than a frenzied free-for-all.

Now it seemed a macabre and deadly dance.

To Raj Ahten's wonder, Paldane's men began fighting so effectively that the reavers at the gates hesitated, withdrew in confusion, unwilling to withstand the slaughter.

Paldane's men closed ranks. Along the walls, men leapt down atop the mound of carcasses and raced forward, forced reavers back to the causeway.

Everywhere in the castle, commoners staggered down the wall-walks, heading for the bailey, trying to obey Gaborn's command to flee the castle. Others threw themselves over the walls into the lake.

Carris was enormous, with nearly four hundred thousand troops on the walls and as many commoners within the city proper. Now these people spilled out into every narrow street, fleeing the quakes.

'Hold!' Raj Ahten shouted to them. 'Stand fast, I say!' His Voice was so powerful and seductive that his words slipped like a dagger into the subconscious minds of Paldane's men, and soon most of them began to hold their positions.

I will not be ill-used, Raj Ahten told himself.

He smiled grimly and shouted across the distance, with a voice so powerful that even Gaborn could not fail to hear. 'We are enemies still, son of Orden!'

Roland thought he heard dogs barking and snarling. He found himself in a tree carved of stone, perched high above the ground.

In a daze, he struggled to raise his head, saw huge reavers racing through the branches above, teeth flashing. An overwhelming fatigue smote him. He fell back. The tree shuddered below, and he heard its great bole snap under so much weight.

'The walls will come down! The walls are coming down!' someone shouted distantly. Raj Ahten's voice rolled through the woods, 'To me! To me!'

Men screamed and died, and nearby Roland heard a woman shouting for help. He glanced down from his perch of stone and saw Baron Poll's familiar face, leering up at him.

'Help,' Roland called weakly.

The Baron laughed. 'Help? You want the help of a dead man? What would you give me?'

'Please . . .' Roland said.

'Not until you call me "sirrah,"' Baron Poll said smugly.

'Please, *sirrah*,' Roland begged.

'Now if only your son would say that word,' Baron Poll laughed. He turned his horse and rode away through a misty field.

Distantly he heard men screaming, heard the rattling breath of reavers. He felt in great pain, almost past caring.

Light flashed overhead, flames dancing in a burning tower. Roland opened his eyes, lay for a long time looking at his arm. It was wrapped in a bloody bandage. Men lay dead all around; gore splattered the merlons above him. The white plaster walls of Carris were turning crimson.

Gloom filled the sky. Feathery flakes of snow fell like ashes. No, he realized, they were ashes. Roland closed his eyes, for it pained him to look. It was nearly dark. Roland judged that he'd been unconscious for an hour or more.

He heard a baby crying, lolled his head to the side. Down in the courtyard just below, a young woman in a gray-blue robe had come out of the back of the manor, and she clucked softly as she tried to shush her fretting child.

Painfully, Roland gathered his strength and rolled to his stomach. Blood began to leak from his bandaged arm. He climbed to his knees and held his arm for a long moment, stanching his wound, trying to make sense of what he saw.

No one was left alive on the south wall with him. Bodies by the thousands lay strewn along it, nearly all human, though a few reavers lay in the mix. Ashes and soot fell from the cold air.

The castle walls were swaying, stones grinding against stone. 'I Choose you. I Choose you for the Earth,' a voice whispered in Roland's mind. 'Flee!'

Roland heard the call distantly, through the tattered remnants of a nightmare of pain. He struggled to comprehend it.

He glanced around. Everyone's killed, he thought. But no, he decided, the wall had been abandoned. The walls were bucking, plaster and stones falling from them.

He looked into the castle. The front gates were down, along with both gate towers. Reavers had broken into the castle. The men of Carris struggled for their lives down in the bailey, clambered up a mound of dead reavers in an effort to retake the causeway. A few frowth giants fought ferociously at their backs.

The plain before Carris was black with bodies – gray reavers by the dull thousands. At the foot of Bone Hill, a human host fought. Hundreds of knights whirled their mounts in a slow-moving pinwheel, lances bristling.

Lances shattered as men met reavers. Horses stumbled with their knights. Blades and glory hammers rose and fell in deadly arcs.

In the midst of the pinwheel, a flag blew in the stiff wind: the green man of Mystarria, King Orden's standard.

At the center of a tiny knot, Roland saw the Earth King himself, Gaborn Val Orden, staggering toward the fell mage at Bone Hill. Guards circled him in a knot, and Roland's heart swelled to imagine that his son would be among them. Ah, if only Averan were here to see this!

It's true, Roland realized. The voice I heard in the dream . . . the Earth King has Chosen me.

Why? Roland wondered. Why me? Surely I am not worthy. I am a murderer. A worthless commoner. I am no warrior.

Roland was not given to fantasies. Even if he had been a fantasist, he'd not have imagined the Earth King Choosing him.

Suddenly he found tears streaming down his cheeks, and Roland wondered how he might best repay the gift. 'Thank you,' he whispered, unsure whether the Earth King could hear him.

In that moment a gray wind swept over the castle walls, sending gree swirling like ashes in a flume, bearing the odor of the reaver's curse.

Roland felt weak from his wounds, had hardly made it to his knees. Now the curse wracked him with a lethargy that sapped all his will.

He succumbed atop the wall-walk, felt it swaying. He could not muster the energy to cry for help, to draw a breath, or even to blink.

59

UNEXPECTED RELATIONS

Four miles from Castle Carris, Averan clung to Roland's back as she rode, afraid that she might fall. One of the men from Indhopal had wrestled the green woman into his saddle, though she struggled against him, trying to climb down.

They'd outpaced the reavers that chased them, left the monsters far behind.

But something was wrong. Averan could not understand why Roland was here with the beautiful woman from Indhopal and her bodyguards. Nor could she understand why Roland was dressed in clothes that were different from those he'd worn yesterday, or why he rode such a grand horse.

With some embarrassment, she realized that this wasn't Roland at all. It was more than the clothes or the horse – this man *smelled* wrong. His clothes smelled of desert sage and greasewood and sand, not the green grass of Mystarria.

'Who are you?' she asked. 'I thought you were someone else, my friend Roland.'

The big man glanced back at her. She saw that this truly wasn't Roland. This fellow had the same red hair, the same laughing blue eyes. But some of his hair had begun to turn gray.

'You know someone named Roland?' the fellow asked. 'From the Blue Tower?'

'Yes,' she whispered. 'He gave me a ride on his horse. He was riding with Baron Poll to Carris. He wanted to go north to see the Earth King, and his son – you. He was going to see you. Wasn't he?'

The big man nodded. 'Roland is my father's name. You can call me Borenson.' He didn't look happy to learn that his father was coming to see him.

'You don't like your father?' Averan asked.

'My mother detested him,' Borenson answered, 'and since I look like him, in time she grew to detest me.'

'I like Roland,' Averan offered. 'He's going to petition Paldane so that I can be his daughter.'

'The man is a lackluster,' Borenson said. 'He'll be no more of a father to you than he was to me.'

The cold way that Borenson spoke of his father unnerved Averan, and she was angry that he dismissed everything she said. It was true that she was only nine years old, and that she had lost her endowments, but she wasn't a stupid child. She'd just told Borenson that she was going to be his sister, and she expected some kind of acknowledgment from him. But Borenson seemed intent on dismissing her.

They charged up a long narrow hill, over dry rye stalks, bent and broken and as gray as ash.

At the top of the hill, an ancient granite sun dome lay in ruins. The perfect orb-shaped crematorium had rolled from its pedestal and cracked. Now it rested on the hill like a broken egg.

Averan could see the lay of the land to the north and south. They were far enough from any cover that no reaver could ambush them.

But as they crowned the hill and wheeled around the ruined dome, they gazed down on Carris, and Averan gasped in dismay.

Below in the distance, fire burned the white towers of Carris, reflected in the waters of Lake Donnestgree.

The barbicans lay in ruins and the western wall of the castle was shattered. The smooth plaster everywhere was stripped.

Reavers blackened a land shrouded in dirty mist. One Indhopalese guard stared hard at the burning castle. 'Our Lord Raj Ahten defends that fortress,' he said grimly, 'along with many men of Mystarria. The Earth King fights in the fields.'

'Perhaps we are not needed,' a eunuch said. 'It seems that our lord has already called a truce.' Averan thought him cowardly, the way his voice trembled.

The fields below were a wasteland. It looked as if Carris might never be fit for human habitation again – not even if men tried to rebuild their homes, replant their crops.

Averan watched the Earth King ride through the thick haze toward the foot of Bone Hill. Her eye was drawn to him. She recognized him instantly, but felt surprised. Gaborn looked like an ordinary man, not the emerald flame she'd seen in her mind when she closed her eyes.

Averan glanced over at the green woman. She sat in the saddle in front of Pashtuk and watched the Earth King, but she watched him with her eyes closed. She smiled wistfully.

The green woman sees it, too, Averan realized. She sees his power. Averan closed her eyes and watched Gaborn. He looked like an emerald flame that glided and bounced with every jostle of his mount.

One Indhopalese guard suggested, 'If we go down to that hill, we can skirt north along the aqueduct to reach the Earth King,'

'I don't like it,' Borenson groused. 'The burrows at the end of the canal won't have gophers in them.' He pointed north. 'We should take the trail up around the Barren's Wall – come in from behind.'

'That's too far!' the Indhopalese fellow argued.

Averan watched Gaborn fight his way to Bone Hill. He had so many endowments of metabolism, that to her the deed seemed swift, almost a race as he crouched and cast a spell that made the whole earth tremble. She saw the walls of Carris begin to tremble, and Gaborn stare off toward it with mouth agape. He raised his left hand and cast a second spell.

'There,' Borenson said. 'He's Choosing. He's Choosing the whole city!'

If Gaborn spoke, Averan could not hear his words. They were lost in the hissing sound of thousands of reavers, in the trembling of aftershocks. But she marveled at the notion that

Gaborn would Choose this whole city, even his enemies.

The men atop the walls of Carris cheered and fled the falling city, while reavers raced to attack the Earth King. Reavers thundered over a barricade at Bone Hill. They scurried up from burrows.

The Earth King urged his cavalry forward, doggedly trying to fight.

'What does he hope to accomplish?' one eunuch asked.

'He's trying to save Carris,' Borenson said with some certainty. 'He hopes to draw off its attackers.'

But even from here, Averan could see that Gaborn could not make it. There were too many reavers, attacking too swiftly. Gaborn would be cut off, surrounded.

Across the valley, the Voice of Raj Ahten roared, magnified by his many endowments. 'We are enemies still, son of Orden!'

Raj Ahten stood atop the city wall, waving his battle-axe in defiance, even as slabs of plaster cascaded around him.

And atop Bone Hill, the fell mage raised a pale yellow staff to the sky and hissed. Thunder sounded and rolled down over the hill to Carris.

The beautiful woman from Indhopal said softly, 'So, it is true. My husband rejects the Earth King, his cousin by marriage, and will leave him to the reavers.'

Her tone was one of solemn revulsion, as if she'd never imagined that Raj Ahten could be so heartless.

'I am afraid so, O Great Star, my Saffira,' Borenson said gently, trying to ease the blow.

Another aftershock made the ground rumble, the horses dance to keep their feet.

Saffira shouted and spurred her mount downhill. It ran with speed and grace and purpose as only a force horse could, racing due west toward Carris as if to reach the city, though ten thousand reavers blocked her way.

Borenson shouted, and Averan clutched his back tightly as their mount shot forward.

Saffira rode east, and at first Averan thought she rode

blindly. But she changed course, veered south, and Averan saw where she headed.

The reavers had broken into several fronts. One front directed its attack against Carris, while a second raced for the Earth King. A third chased after the cavalry that had struck south.

As the reavers split, they left an empty field in the midst of their forces. Into this field Saffira charged.

'Wait!' the eunuchs shouted. 'Hold up!'

But it did no good. Saffira galloped for Carris, until she came within half a mile of its walls, and the reavers down the slope ahead were so thick that she could ride no farther.

Sensing her at their backs, blade-bearers nearby all began to wheel. The rasping at their thoraxes became louder.

For a moment Saffira charged alone to a small hillock, in the last light of day. She wore a riding robe of fine red cotton, embroidered with exquisite gold threads to form curlicues like the tendrils of vines that wrapped about her arms and breasts. On her head, she wore a thin red veil beneath a silver crown.

Now she unbuckled a narrow golden belt, tossed it on the ground, and pulled off her robe. She withdrew her veil, so that for one moment she sat proud atop a gray Imperial charger, wearing only a sheer dress of lavender silk that accentuated the exquisite dark hues of her skin.

At the edge of the horizon, the sun was falling, and a few small rays slanted from the broken clouds.

Many other hillocks were scattered through the wasteland, but now Averan saw that Saffira had chosen this one because she'd seen the wan light upon it and knew it was the best place to display herself.

To Averan, Saffira seemed to be perfection given form. The graceful lines of her neck and shoulders would have kept a proper minstrel writing lines for a lifetime, yet even Behoran Goldentongue himself could not have composed a tune and words that would have captured her grace, or the light in her eyes, or the courage in her stance.

It seemed to Averan that even then Saffira knew she would

die. She'd ridden too close to the reavers. The nearest of them wheeled not a hundred yards down the slope, taking a defensive stance. Reavers are easily surprised, and often hesitate when trying to determine the nature of a threat, but it would only take a moment for the monster to recognize that Saffira stood alone.

But one moment was all Saffira wanted. In that moment, she began to sing.

60

BONE HILL

How do I save them all? Gaborn wondered.

He'd connected to hundreds of thousands of people in Castle Carris, and he felt overwhelmed by the sense of danger around them. A third aftershock began to make the ground swell and buck.

At the castle gates, thousands of men were fighting for their lives. Gaborn concentrated on them, for their situation was gravest. Yet in Castle Carris, Raj Ahten refused Gaborn, smugly chose to hinder his troops from advancing. Surely, his Invincibles could hack a path over the causeway.

Fatigue wracked him as he doggedly advanced toward Bone Hill, a deep-seated lethargy that worried the bone. The closer he drew, the more paralyzing it became.

I have Chosen too indiscriminately, he realized. He led a ragtag band of warriors. Desperately, his men forged on. Unhorsed and without their long deadly lances, they were not as effective as mounted knights, yet they advanced manfully, as if moved by his will alone.

Gaborn climbed down from the saddle and tried to lead them a few paces closer, but the effect of the fell mage's spell was so powerful he could hardly hold the reins of his own mount.

To the south, High Marshal Skalbairn sought to make an ill-fated charge. Gaborn sent the message 'Turn back! Save yourselves if you can!'

He focused on the job at hand, hoping that the warriors

who guarded him now would be able to fend off the impending attack.

Two hundred yards ahead was the great cocoon, with the fell mage atop the hill. Reavers were racing round both sides of Bone Hill. They'd be here in seconds.

When he could go no farther from weariness, Gaborn numbly dropped in the dust and began to draw a second rune of Earth-breaking.

Desperately he searched the rune itself, looking for weaknesses, flaws in its binding.

A wave of reavers rushed toward his battle lines, fifty yards ahead on each side. Near his foot lay a strand of cocoon, a line that ran two hundred yards.

Gaborn glanced up at Bone Hill, trying to see the object of his spell. Reavers blocked the way, climbed the cocoon in droves. A reaver's head was larger than a wagon bed and its paws were longer than a man's body. As monsters surged closer, surrounding him, he could not see over them.

Yet his men held their line, prepared to fight with the strength of desperation.

Gaborn knelt in the fetid mist and struggled to form a rune.

A reaver charged the Earth King, not even slowing as it barreled over two men ahead, crushing them with its bulk. Erin Connal cried out in dismay, lunged to meet it.

'You take it low, I'll take it high!' Celinor shouted at her back.

She ran at the beast. It raised its glory hammer overhead. Erin shouted and struck her own warhammer into the monster's elbow, biting deep into the joint just beneath its protective bone spur.

The jolt should have frozen the reaver in pain for a moment, or perhaps enraged it.

Instead the reaver struck with its glory hammer – eight hundred pounds of steel at the end of a twenty-foot pole. She heard no warning from the Earth King.

The pole slammed into her shoulder, throwing her to the

ground, pinning her for a moment. The reaver raised a massive paw in a fist, ready to pound her into the dust.

Celinor leapt over Erin, lunged in and struck the beast between its thoracic plates. His blow was not powerful enough. No guts gushed from the monster.

The reaver hissed in fear and lurched back a pace, trying to escape.

Celinor leapt in and delivered a second blow. The reaver's guts spilled down in a gruesome rain, and the monster leapt away, slamming into another of its kind.

The Prince of South Crowthen spun, dodged out of battle, and grabbed Erin's hand, helping her up. 'Two!' he warned.

Erin felt her face redden with chagrin.

Gaborn finished drawing his rune of Earth-breaking, raised his fist and looked up.

All around him, reavers thundered forward in a terrifying wall of flesh, pounding into the ranks of his men, overwhelming them.

To his left a reaver smashed a fellow with a glory hammer. The body somersaulted in the air twice, arced toward him.

Celinor raised his shield, threw himself before Gaborn, but the force of both bodies slammed into Gaborn, smacking him to the ground.

Everything went black.

61

IN THE FADING LIGHT

Saffira sang in the voice of her homeland, in Tuulistanese, and because she had thousands of endowments of Voice, her aria rang louder than any sung by a commoner.

So beautiful was her song that Raj Ahten looked up from a wall of Castle Carris where he had been watching Gaborn's debacle of a charge.

Time seemed to freeze.

So loud was her song that even on the causeway, many reavers drew back, philia waving in the air, as if trying to decipher whether her voice presented some new threat that they must confront.

For a moment, the tumult of battle dimmed, as men listened to Saffira's golden voice.

Certainly, most of the men of Rofehavan could not have understood Saffira's words. Tuulistan was a small nation in Indhopal, insignificant. One could walk across its borders in a fortnight. Yet the pleading tone of the young woman's voice struck Raj Ahten to the soul, made him yearn to . . . do anything, anything to placate his bride.

She sat in the saddle on some ruined mound, and all beneath her the land was black with reavers. In the last light of day, her lavender dress seemed but a veil that lightly covered her perfect beauty.

She shone like the first and brightest star in the nighttime sky, and all around him, Raj Ahten heard the rush of in-drawn breath as thousands men gasped in astonishment.

Immediately Raj Ahten saw what Gaborn had done. He saw the glamour of all his concubines, of the loveliest women from every nation he conquered, all bound into one. He heard the sweetness of every melodious voice in his harem.

Saffira sang a common lullaby.

She'd sung it to her firstborn son, Shandi, when she'd first held him, five years ago – before a Knight Equitable slaughtered the child in an effort to rid the world of Raj Ahten's progeny.

The tune was not profound, neither was its message. Yet it moved Raj Ahten to the core of his soul.

'There is no you. There is no me.
Love makes us one. There is only we.'

Of all the men who heard that song, only Raj Ahten understood its message. 'I understand your hatred and anger,' she said. 'I understand, and I feel it, too. I have not forgotten our son. But now you must lay your anger aside.'

Saffira then called in her imperfect Rofehavanish. 'My Lord Raj Ahten, I beg you to put aside this war. The Earth King asks me to bear this message: "The enemy of my cousin is *my* enemy." Men of Mystarria, men of Indhopal – unite!'

She beckoned to Raj Ahten, and in the silence, the reavers near her suddenly responded, surging uphill, as if at her summoning.

Saffira's eunuch guards – the finest of Raj Ahten's Invincibles – rushed to her side and followed her downhill as she raced now to the north, toward Gaborn's forces half a mile distant.

She had far too many reavers ahead of her. The great monsters stood back to back around the Earth King's pitiable army, forming a solid wall. Even with all the speed of her mount, Raj Ahten knew that she would not be able to break those lines.

Certainly she understood that. Yet she rode into danger, into the heart of the maelstrom.

She would force his hand. If you will not come to save

him, then at least come to save me, her actions said.

With a shout of horror and dismay, the men of Carris responded to Saffira's plea.

For several moments now, Paldane's men and the frowth giants had been shoving the reavers back, had managed to scrabble over the pile of dead reavers to the causeway in Lake Donnestgree, then shove them back a hundred yards toward the mainland. The causeway itself was littered with dead reavers.

Now the people of Carris all heaved forward as one. With a great roar they charged for the mainland. The fell mage's spells of fatigue seemed to be forgotten temporarily.

All along the walls and all through the city streets, men picked up whatever arms they could carry and hastened to join Saffira and the Earth King.

Raj Ahten watched in amazement.

This was a mistake, he knew. Hundreds of thousands of men, women, and children in Carris would race to attack; the vast majority of them were only commoners.

The reavers would have them for dinner.

Yet they charged.

He could not say what drove them. Whether it was a belief in their Earth King or the desire to heed Saffira's call. Perhaps it was neither. Perhaps they fought only because there was nothing left for them to do.

He himself raced down the tower steps, shoving aside slower men so that he could join the battle. His heart hammered and pulse quickened. Invincibles surged from alleys to back him.

62

CHASMS

On the road to Carris, time and again Borenson had wondered about Saffira. Would she have the courage to stand up to Raj Ahten? Did she truly want peace? Would she betray Gaborn and his people?

Yet now, with danger all around, this woman – hardly more than a child really – rose to Gaborn's defense.

Saffira finished her song. For a breathless moment Borenson sat enthralled, unable to think, unable to do anything but mourn the fact that her song had ended.

Cheers arose from the city, thunderous cheers like the voice of a distant sea, assuring that the people of Rofehavan would heed her call.

Saffira's courage had been sufficient. In that moment, Borenson loved her as fully and innocently as he could love a woman. His heart pounded, and he wanted nothing more than to stand in her shadow, to breathe her sweet perfume, to gaze at her ebony hair.

She sat tall in her saddle, breathing hard. The light in her eyes was a marvel, and as she sat listening to the cheers from Carris, she bowed her head in silent exultation.

'Come, my friends,' Saffira called, 'before it is too late.' She spurred her mount north, galloping downhill toward Gaborn, but not making a direct charge.

She was angling west, away from the main force of the reavers.

Smart girl, Borenson thought. She's pretending to charge,

hoping to divert the reavers' forces from Gaborn, even as she races west past Bone Hill. From there she would angle back around from the north, come at Gaborn from behind.

Ha'Pim and Mahket struggled to catch up, to ride at her side. Ahead lay Bone Hill, the fibrous cocoon around it gleaming dully like icicles in the evening, the fell mage at its crown gleaming from the opalescent runes tattooed into her carapace.

The great reaver stood with her citrine staff raised to the sky; the philia on her broad head rose and waggled as she sought to catch a scent.

Suddenly her enormous head swiveled toward Saffira, as if she'd taken notice. She pointed her staff toward Saffira's entourage.

She thinks we're attacking! Borenson realized almost too late. He did not know if anyone else saw her response. 'Veer left!' he cried.

The fell mage hissed and light pulsed in her crystalline staff. The air around it exploded as a dark-green cloud issued from its tip.

Saffira charged sharply left as the green haze pulsed out and slammed into the ground on her previous trajectory. The cloud carried an odor of rot so foul, so abominable, that Borenson did not merely smell it, he could feel his body struggle to respond, as if his skin would slough away and flesh decompose as he watched.

Saffira covered her face with a golden silk scarf, weaved a course perilously close to the nearest reaver. The ground trembled.

Pashtuk and the green woman were unceremoniously dumped from their mount.

Pashtuk grabbed the wylde and quickly tried to remount. The wylde struggled lightly in his grasp, as if eager to battle the reavers.

Saffira looked back, saw his predicament, and stopped her own horse, waiting for him.

'Watch out!' the child behind Borenson cried out. A blade-bearer rushed Saffira's back. Her guards shouted, warning her.

Saffira lowered her head, wheeled and spurred her charger, as if hoping to draw the beast away from Pashtuk.

Almost casually the reaver swung its great talons, talons that gleamed wickedly on a forepaw that was as long as a horse.

The reaver smacked Saffira's mare, breaking the horse's neck and slapping it backward. Saffira tumbled over the top of her horse, bounced against one great claw, and vaulted into the dark recesses behind the reaver.

Three other reavers raced toward the spot.

Ha'Pim shouted in dismay and drew rein, leaping to dismount. A blade-bearer smacked him with a glory hammer as he landed. Blood and gore spattered Borenson's face.

Mahket rode full of furor into the reavers, swinging a great battle-axe. He leapt into the mouth of the reaver that had struck Saffira, delivered a tremendous blow through its upper palate, and danced back out, swinging at another monster's leg. His body was a blur of motion.

Pashtuk quit trying to mount his horse – simply hurled himself toward the closest charging reaver. He leapt up several feet in the air, struck down with his battle-axe at the base of the monster's neck.

Borenson reined in his horse. There was a slim chance that Saffira would live. The blow she'd taken might only have broken a few bones.

Yet if she lived, she was now behind three reavers – or under them.

If they did not kill her outright, she'd be crushed.

'Get us out of here!' the child behind Borenson cried, clutching Borenson's waist. The odor of rot that the fell mage had exuded was filling the area, gagging him.

He gritted his teeth in frustration. He was Saffira's guard. She owned him more completely than he could ever imagine himself being owned again.

Yet he was also bound to Gaborn. He knew where his duty lay. Borenson had the wizard Binnesman's wylde at hand. She was a potent weapon. Borenson needed to deliver her to Binnesman.

Weakly, Borenson heard Saffira cry out in Tuulistanese, 'Ahretva! Ahret!'

Though he could not understand her plea, he now knew that she lived. The power of her Voice was more compelling than cold logic. The woman who had so courageously charged into the midst of the reavers to deliver her message now held his heart too firmly for him to resist.

So, Borenson thought dully, this is where I will make my battlefield. This is where I make my stand. It is not a battlefield I would have chosen.

With no endowments to aid him and with no apology to the child who rode behind, Borenson leapt from his mount and charged into battle.

Averan sat on her horse for half a second in dismay. Borenson and Saffira's bodyguards had abandoned their mounts – all to defend Saffira.

The green woman remained in her saddle. A reaver's blade arced overhead as two monsters raced toward her.

Averan shouted, 'Foul Deliverer, Fair Destroyer: blood, yes! Kill!'

The green woman leapt from her horse onto the nearest reaver so swiftly that Averan almost did not see it. Spring slammed a fist into the reaver's brain, shattering its skull, as if she'd finally figured out that this was the quickest way to get some of the goo that she liked.

Ahead of Averan, the two Indhopalese guards lopped the forearms off a reaver. The creature reared, tried to back away, while with terrifying slowness and clumsiness – or at least compared to warriors with endowments – Sir Borenson rushed up under its belly and started trying to chop between its thoracic plates. The guards turned to a reaver at their backs, trying to hack a path to Saffira.

To Averan's left and behind her, reavers all raced to converge. 'Help!' Averan screamed. 'Help!'

But no one came to her side. She didn't have Saffira's allure. She was only a little girl.

She dropped from her horse. A reaver swung a glory hammer behind her, bludgeoning Borenson's fine mount into a spray of blood and guts.

Averan scampered, hunched over and tried to make herself small. Desperately she sought someplace to hide.

Ahead, the green woman had just slaughtered a reaver. It lay gasping mechanically, mouth open, its raspy tongue nearly two feet wide hanging from its mouth. Averan wanted to roll under the monster, to hide in the crook of its legs, but the beast had fallen to the ground.

Its mouth, she realized. I could hide in there.

She leapt into the monster's cavernous mouth. Its palate formed a hollow nearly as tall as a man, but the sides were covered in slime. The warty flesh of its gums was nearly black, and the reaver's teeth around her, row upon row of them, were all as clear as crystal knives. She clung to two of the longest teeth, hanging on, lest she fall down.

The reaver's breath smelled fetid, added to the horrid stench of decay that the fell mage had created. Averan almost imagined that the beast was rotting apart in her hands. Her own hands itched, and dark blotches were forming on them.

The reaver's mouth convulsed mechanically, and the tongue she stood on shifted. Then the reaver's maw slowly began to close.

Averan's stomach clenched in terror. She pushed on its gums with all of her might, struggled to keep the mouth open. She feared that even though the reaver was dead, it might swallow her still. She'd seen how dying animals sometimes moved by reflex. 'Help!' she screamed. 'Help!'

'I'm coming!' Borenson shouted. He'd sliced cleanly between the reaver's thoracic plates and now backed away as the reaver came crashing down, its forepaws landing almost atop him.

He's coming for me, Averan thought.

But now as the eunuchs continued to fight a blade-bearer to Borenson's left, he lunged beyond them, into a dark gorge formed of reaver corpses. Borenson raced to Saffira.

But I thought you were going to help *me*! Averan wanted to shout.

The evening sky was going dark. The land was covered in a cloying, sickly mist, and in the deep shadows, reavers rose up black and monolithic. As a new attacker scaled the bodies of the dead, the light above Averan was nearly cut off.

Averan cringed in terror, struggled to push the reaver's mouth open again. As she did, she squinted, and in her mind's eye she could see the emerald flame burning brightly.

It's so close now, she thought. I could almost touch it. She'd been drawn to it for days. Now, she thought she understood why.

Safety. I would be safe with the Earth King, she told herself – safe as his Chosen. A wild hope thrilled through her.

'Foul Deliverer, Fair Destroyer,' Averan cried on sudden impulse, 'go get the Earth King! He'll help us.'

Then the reaver's mouth closed, despite all that she could do.

Averan screamed.

63

THE BRIGHTEST STAR IN INDHOPAL

Raj Ahten raced down from the stone walls of Carris, struggling to be the first to reach Saffira. He shoved aside some
slower men on the stairs, then leapt from them onto the back
of a dead frowth giant, catching his foot in the beast's chain
mail. He pulled his foot free.

Once released, he leapt from the back of one dead reaver
to another, using the dead beasts as if they were ghastly stepping stones. Thus he reached the fallen castle gates well before
most of his people did. Only a few of Paldane's men were
ahead of him out on the causeway.

For half a heartbeat, he stood on a reaver's corpse above
the causeway and felt the tremors of an earthquake. It shook
the very foundations of Carris, with a roar far louder than the
surf. As it hit the shore, it caused a mighty wave to ripple
out.

Paldane's finest men fought ahead down the causeway,
embroiled in a melee.

He could imagine how they would fare.

He raced now, leaping along the backs and bellies of dead
reavers.

As the quake rocked a reaver beneath him, Raj Ahten
vaulted into the air, then landed in the fray atop a living
reaver's head. He slammed his warhammer deep into its sweet
triangle, killing it instantly.

A hundred thousand human voices cried out as one as the
earthquake surged beneath the castle. Raj Ahten glanced back

just as the west wall of Carris sheered away in thunderous ruin, spilling outward.

He dared not hesitate. He climbed the reaver's sloping head, raced toward Saffira.

He did not watch the fall of Carris, but he heard it, smelled the acrid scent of stone dust in the air. The people wailed as Carris collapsed. Towers toppled. Shops disintegrated.

With six endowments of metabolism, Raj Ahten fought swiftly and furiously, daring attacks he'd never have tried if not for Saffira. He leapt on reaver heads and sought to crush them with his hammers. He raced past one monster, pausing to shatter its leg so that men behind would have an easier time with it. For long moments, his existence became an obscene dream of death and maiming, while Paldane's men and his Invincibles fought at his side.

Behind him, he could hear hundreds and thousands of commoners charging toward Saffira, racing to do battle in the midst of the reavers. To do so was suicide, Raj Ahten thought. But in his heart he knew that to do less was also suicide.

In the midst of the city, several towers flamed. As they crumbled, they spewed burning wood and cinders up into the evening sky.

As Paldane's men slaughtered a reaver, Raj Ahten climbed atop it to get his bearings. Behind him in the castle people fled for their lives: warriors and merchants, women with babes in arms, lords and paupers.

Raj Ahten marveled at how many had survived the quake, for if he'd not seen it, he'd have thought that not more than a few hundred would escape the fall of Carris.

For what seemed a long hour, Raj Ahten fought on, though it could not have been more than ten minutes of commoner's time. Paldane's lords and Raj Ahten's Invincibles fought at his back, while the commoners of Carris streamed into the battle lines.

Their effect astonished Raj Ahten: many reavers began a careful retreat, balking at the challenge. Confronted by a dozen men, most reavers backed away.

Until now, none of his tactics had impressed the reavers. But so many people – a mass of people attacking as one – gave the reavers pause. It was easy to guess why: the reavers could not distinguish a commoner from a Runelord. All men smelled the same. To a reaver, any man who dared attack presented a potentially devastating challenge.

We are wasps to them, Raj Ahten realized, but they can't tell whether we have stingers.

Pockets of resistance grew around his Invincibles and among Paldane's most powerful lords. But though many reavers balked, they did not flee.

Blade-bearers waded into the commoners and commenced a truly horrific slaughter, cutting down men and women by the thousands and tens of thousands.

The people of Carris threw themselves against the reaver lines, commoners wielding pickaxes and hammers. They gave themselves for their Earth King in ways that they'd never have given themselves for Raj Ahten.

The commoners' efforts were almost futile, except that they provided some diversion for those warriors who had the grace and brawn and metabolism needed for the melee.

So their struggle was not completely in vain. But Raj Ahten would never forget the spectacle that presented itself before the gates of Carris: human blood by the barrels, the splintered bones, mangled flesh, the expressions of horror in dead women's eyes.

He battled on, fighting an endless host toward an unseen goal. Twice he took wounds that would have killed another man, and wasted precious seconds waiting for his great stamina to perform its miraculous healing.

Ironically, it was the voice of a child that led him to Saffira.

Behind him, lords fought on thirty or forty different fronts. Added to this chaos was the sound of Gaborn's knights somewhere to the north of Bone Hill – men yelling and dying.

Even with his endowments of hearing, Raj Ahten could barely discern among the hissing and rattling of reavers a girl wailing over and over again, 'Help! Help!'

He heard the child and raced through the battle lines to reach the girl. With six endowments of metabolism, he burst past several reavers before they could even react.

Dead and wounded reavers lay everywhere ahead, forming a grizzly maze. The smell of putrescence, the fell mage's last spell, was overwhelming. He leapt between the limbs of two tangled reavers, squirmed through a narrow chasm.

In moments he reached a clearing. A dozen reavers lay dead in an irregular circle, forming a ghastly little chasm between the reaver corpses.

When he leapt down into the clearing, a dead horse and knight littered the ground at his feet. Raj Ahten could hear men skirmishing with a reaver around a little bend.

The girl herself was trapped in the mouth of a dead reaver. Raj Ahten left her shrieking in terror.

But the wound on the reaver she hid in intrigued him. Someone had bashed the reaver's skull. Aside from a frowth giant wielding an enormous maul, Raj Ahten could not imagine any weapon that would so decimate reaver bone.

He raced round the bend to find Pashtuk, bleeding from a bad leg, still fighting like a berserker while Mahket joined the fray beside him.

A reaver was trying to wedge its way between two dead comrades in an effort to charge the men. Raj Ahten could not see Saffira, but with so many endowments of scent, he found her easily. The delicate scent of her jasmine perfume drew him to the spot, in a little chasm off to his right.

She lay crushed beneath the paw of a fallen reaver. King Orden's man, Sir Borenson, lay with her, his arms wrapped around Saffira, seeking to protect her. Borenson struggled to breathe with the weight of the reaver's paw so heavy upon him.

A huge gash crossed Saffira's forehead. Blood flowed from it freely.

Raj Ahten grasped the reaver's paw by one long talon. The paw weighed seven or eight hundred pounds. He dragged it from atop Saffira, pushed the red-haired knight away.

Behind Raj Ahten, all around Carris, thousands of people battled. But the dead reavers formed a solid wall that would hedge commoners out. Those who sought Saffira would likely bypass this place.

Saffira's eyes stared fixedly upward. She breathed erratically. He knew that she would die soon.

'I'm here, my love,' Raj Ahten said. 'I'm here.'

Saffira grasped his hand. She had but three endowments of brawn, and so her touch seemed feather-light to him.

Saffira smiled. 'I knew you would come.'

'The Earth King made you do this?' Raj Ahten asked. His voice was hot with wrath.

'No one forced me,' Saffira said. 'I wanted to see you.'

'But he bade you come?'

Saffira smiled secretively. 'I heard . . . I heard of an Earth King in the north. I sent a messenger . . .'

It was a lie, of course. None of the palace guards were to speak openly of the wars and conflicts. None would have dared.

'Promise you will not fight him! Promise you will not kill him!' she begged.

Saffira began to cough. Flecks of blood spattered out as she did. Raj Ahten held silent.

He wiped blood from her chin and held her close. The sounds of battle seemed distant, as if monsters roared in a faraway wilderness.

He was not quite aware of when Saffira died. But in the coming darkness, he glanced down and saw that she had gone still. With her death, the endowments of glamour she had borne returned to her Dedicates.

Saffira faded like a rose petal wilting away in a blacksmith's forge, so that soon the young woman in his arms seemed only a pale shadow of herself.

The greatest beauty of all time was no more.

Gaborn's consciousness swam in a place where there was no present, no pain, and no understanding.

It was a place with violet skies of a remembered sunset, a field of wild flowers he might have roamed in childhood.

The scent of summer grass was profound, rich, buttery, full of roots and soil and leaves drying in the sun. Copious daisies spread their golden petals. They smelled bitter compared to the grass, but only served to intensify the earthy atmosphere.

Gaborn lay in a daze. Distantly, he thought he heard Iome calling, but his muscles had gone slack, would not respond.

Iome. He wanted her desperately, craved her touch, her kiss. *She should be with me,* he thought. *She should be at my side.*

She should see this perfect sky, touch this perfect ground. Gaborn had not seen anything so lovely since he'd visited Binnesman's garden.

'Milord?' someone called. 'Milord, are you all right?'

Gaborn tried to respond, could think of nothing.

'Get him on his horse, he's injured! Get him out of here!' someone shouted. Gaborn recognized the voice now. Celinor. Celinor Anders was shouting, worried about Gaborn.

'All right.' Gaborn tried to comfort him. *I'm all right.* He tried to raise his head, fell back – and recognized something amazing. His fatigue, the sense of illness and the pain he'd felt for hours, had almost totally departed.

Instead he felt as if he stood in a fresh spring wind, totally invigorated. As he lay still, the sensation grew more potent.

Earth power. He felt earth power, as he'd felt it in Binnesman's garden, or at the Seven Standing Stones of the Dunnwood. It was growing stronger. Stronger. He could almost turn his face toward it, as a flower turns its leaves toward the sun.

Iome is coming, he reasoned deliriously. *That is it.*

The sensation grew suddenly intense, until he could feel it warm against his cheek, like a sunbeam caressing him.

His eyes came open.

In the semidarkness stood a woman who wore only a bearskin coat. Not Iome.

Yet he recognized her instantly. Her face was beautiful, innocent, immaculate. Her small breasts sagged forward beneath her coat. Her skin was a delicate green. Gaborn could feel the power blazing inside her. She reached down and grabbed his throat gently. With her touch, all weariness and pain fled.

He knew her at once: Binnesman's wylde.

The wizard had raised her from the dust of the Earth a little more than a week ago, raised her in the night, giving her a form taken from his own mind. Binnesman had said that he'd hoped to form a great warrior, like the green knight who had aided Gaborn's forefathers. But upon creation, the wylde had leapt high into the air and disappeared.

Now Gaborn's eyes flew wide as the wylde lifted him with one hand, pulling him to his feet. 'Go get the Earth King!' she blurted.

Dimly, Gaborn realized that the green woman wanted him, wanted him to follow her somewhere. Or perhaps the Earth itself had sent her.

Gaborn looked around him. He lay on the battlefield about a hundred yards back from his previous position. Prince Celinor, Erin Connal, and several other knights had all backed away from the green woman, staring at her in shock.

Gaborn's knights had abandoned their mounts and now skirmished furiously with reavers in a ragged front. The reavers were pushing his men back. Everywhere he looked, a sea of reavers crawled atop one another in an effort to break the line, hunting men as dogs might hunt hares. His people fought valiantly, but in vain. Even as his glance swept across the battlefield, he saw a dozen men hurled into oblivion as blade-bearers swung their enormous swords.

On Bone Hill, surrounded by minions, in her protective cocoon the fell mage raised her citrine staff to the sky, prepared to utter another curse. The air was already filled with an unspeakably foul scent. But ghostlights flickered at the base of the rune, suddenly blazing like never before.

'Get the Earth King,' the wylde said, pulling Gaborn toward the battle line.

He understood. Someone had sent the creature to him. But

Gaborn had been present at her creation, knew the wylde's true name.

Now Gaborn grabbed her wrist and summoned the wylde for his own purposes. 'Foul Deliverer, Fair Destroyer: stand with me.'

The green woman stood panting, as if she'd forgotten her previous errand.

'Strike now,' the Earth warned.

Gaborn knelt. Taking the wylde's finger, Gaborn concentrated as he began to trace a rune of Earth-breaking in the grime.

Yet as he studied the foul hill before him, he could see no flaws, no way to break that thing.

Curiously, an image came to mind. Not a rune of Earth-breaking, but a rune nonetheless. A strange coiled shape within a circle, and single dot above.

He drew the rune, and then he gathered the wylde's hand into a fist.

He looked up. Staring at the fell mage atop her monstrous creation, Gaborn imagined annihilation. He imagined the soil blasting upward in total ruin, the hill and the rune ceasing to exist – scattered so far on the winds that they utterly perished, never to be rebuilt again.

He did not know if he could do it. Can earth destroy earth? he wondered.

Gaborn shouted, 'Be thou dust!'

For two long seconds Gaborn held his fist clenched, waiting for the earth to respond.

Far below him the ground began to tremble, slowly at first, a distant rumble that grew steadily more powerful, as if a quake were building, far huger than any he'd felt before. He could feel the might there, struggling for release. Soon the ground pulsated as if shaken by a mighty fist.

The fell sorceress raised her staff in the air, the runes in her flesh glittering like a garment of sunlight, and her citrine crystal flashed with inner fire.

She issued a hissing roar that resounded from the heavens,

that bounced from the walls of Castle Carris and rebounded from the near hills. An impenetrable black cloud began to form at her feet, joining with the corrosive mists that swirled out from the Seal of Desolation – a curse that Gaborn imagined his men would not survive.

Still Gaborn let the earth power build, a measureless force surging toward him. He held the image of destruction in his mind, letting it grow and expand until he could hold it no more.

Gaborn opened his fist, releasing his power.

64

THE SHATTERED EARTH

Iome Sylvarresta was still forty-two miles from Carris. She had stopped with Myrrima and Sir Hoswell to eat some bread and drink a draught of wine while the horses took a rest. The wind was blowing softly through the leaves of the live oak above her, whispering through the grass as it surged downhill.

She felt the earth trembling long before she heard the end. The ground ripped and snarled beneath her feet, and she looked south in wonder and horror.

From Iome's vantage, she saw only a vast dust cloud that thundered into the evening air, rumbling as it hurtled upward mile after mile.

Though the sun had fallen moments before, the dust cloud rose so high that the evening light slanted off its top, while lightning forked around it.

'By the Powers!' Myrrima said, leaping to her feet, spilling wine from her wineskin.

Iome grabbed Myrrima's arm, for though she had endowments of brawn, she suddenly felt weak with fear. She knew that her husband was in Carris, and that no one could survive such a blast.

Many long seconds later, the sound of the explosion came. Even at such a distance it shook the earth, making it rumble beneath her feet, then the echo sounded from the distant mountains. She was not quite sure if there had been a single explosion or more than one.

In later days, she would always imagine that there had been

two explosions: one when Gaborn cast his spell, and a second explosion a moment later when the world worm surged upward, creating a vast hole where the Seal of Desolation had been.

But witnesses closer to the blast said, 'Nay, there was but one explosion as the world worm burst from the ground at the Earth King's summons.'

The Earth snarled as the world worm ascended. Erin Connal fought at Gaborn's side when it came, and that is how she would always describe the sound: 'the Earth snarled.'

Dust exploded upward from the Seal of Desolation and the world worm reared so high that for a moment a full half of its body shot skyward hundreds of yards in the air, blotting out the last rays of sunlight. It spewed dust in its wake.

The ground snarled at the blast site, and some walls of Carris that had not yet fallen now tumbled into Lake Donnestgree.

Erin hardly remembered anything for a long time after that. She stood gaping up at the vast worm, a hundred and eighty yards in diameter, her heart nearly frozen within her breast, awed by its complex musculature, the magma streaming from the crevasses in its skin, the spectacle of its scythelike teeth. The air was suddenly awash with the odors of sulfur and the metallic tang of dust.

She could only have seen it for a moment, yet time seemed to stand still.

When she came to her senses again, she became dully aware that men and women had begun to cheer. The world worm was receding into its vast crater, where Bone Hill had once stood. Dust was falling everywhere.

Lightning bolts ringed the sky as dust shot through the cloud ceiling.

The reavers began to flee.

It seemed too much to hope for – a full rout. But with the destruction of Bone Hill and the fell mage who led them, the reavers saw no reason to remain.

They began fading into the night, racing back to their dark tunnels, until the time when they would return in greater force.

'Flee,' a distant voice called. Sir Borenson struggled to obey. 'Run now, while you may.'

The earth rolled and bucked beneath him, throwing him two feet in the air. A vast rumble sounded, far louder than the snarl of any thunder. Lightning crashed overhead, while dust and pebbles rained down.

The earth is broken! Borenson thought dully.

Borenson's legs kicked almost of their own volition, and he reached out for Saffira. He'd found her bleeding and half dead here on the battlefield. Pashtuk and Mahket fought ferociously to protect her, and when the reavers came in full force, Borenson had no recourse but to throw himself atop her, try to shield her with his own body, even as a dying reaver collapsed upon them, crushing the air from his lungs.

He would not leave her now.

He coughed, struggled to breathe, though dust clogged his nostrils.

'Flee now!' Gaborn's voice warned once again.

It did not come more clearly, but Borenson realized whose voice he heard, and he struggled to obey. The air was filled with the stench of rot.

Borenson reached for Saffira, searched nearby. 'O Bright Star, we must go!' he mumbled, struggling up. He tried to focus his eyes, but everything had gone black. Night was swiftly falling, and with dust filling the air here in the shadows of the reaver corpses, he could see almost nothing. He looked up. A vast cloud of dust hung overhead, though some light still silvered the north and south horizons. He crawled to his knees. Lightning flashed overhead.

'Where would you take her, little man of the north?' Raj Ahten asked, his voice soft and melodious but seething with subdued rage.

Borenson blinked, trying to focus, to see Raj Ahten in the

flicker of lightning, to hear his voice above the pealing thunder.

He could see them now in the deep evening gloom. Raj Ahten's saffron-colored surcoat gleamed in the darkness. Saffira lay gently in Raj Ahten's arms, as still as the waters of a pond on a windless morning, her pale teeth and eyes hardly visible. She did not move. The glamour had dissipated from her.

For one eternal moment, Borenson knelt. All the air left his lungs. All the willpower seemed to drain from his heart, and he wondered that he could even remain on his hands and knees.

She was gone forever, and he feared that because she was gone, his mind would break.

Not all beauty is gone – he tried to console himself – only the greatest. Life is not empty. It only seems that way.

Yet he felt as if a great void suddenly yawned open inside him, and he could not breathe the dusty air, and he did not care that he could not breathe.

He'd known Saffira only for a day, and if it had been but a short time, it had been . . . He found no words for it.

Every breath he'd breathed had been for her. Every thought in his mind had revolved around her. In that day, he had been completely devoted, had become her creature. His devotion might have been short in duration, but it was intense.

To go on living now would be . . . fruitless.

'Run,' Gaborn called to Borenson.

He was safely encircled by dead reavers, as if in a narrow canyon. Beyond them, on the shadowed battlefield, Borenson could hear sounds of war amid men shouting and cheering in the distance. Some reavers still fought, but none fought nearby. The battle had turned.

Borenson gazed warily at Raj Ahten. The Earth King had warned Borenson to flee, but now Borenson realized that he was not meant to flee from reavers.

'Answer me, man of the north,' Raj Ahten said calmly. 'Where would you take my wife?'

'To safety,' Borenson managed to croak. He licked his dry mouth; grime came thick on his tongue.

'Yet you brought her here, didn't you? You brought her to her death, at your master's insistence. The most exquisite and finest woman in the world. You brought her here.'

It was not an empty accusation. Blood rose hot to Borenson's cheeks. Even if Raj Ahten had not been struggling to convey Borenson's guilt through the power of his Voice, Borenson would have felt ashamed, damned beyond all hope.

'I did not know that reavers would be here at Carris,' Borenson apologized more to himself than to Raj Ahten. 'She didn't fear them. We wanted her to stay back, but she would not listen . . .'

Raj Ahten growled low in his throat, as if mere words could not express his rage.

He hates me, Borenson knew. The lies I told pried him loose from Castle Sylvarresta, and I slaughtered his Dedicates there when he left. My deceptions caused him to retreat from Heredon at Gaborn's ruse. I delivered his wife to her death.

'You were a worthy adversary,' Raj Ahten whispered.

Borenson tried to lurch to his feet, to run, but he was no match for Raj Ahten with his endowments of metabolism.

Raj Ahten had taken brawn from more than two thousand men. Borenson could not fight him or escape his grasp any more than a newborn could withstand the wrath of its father.

The Wolf Lord of Indhopal caught Borenson's ankle, jerked swiftly and brought Sir Borenson down hard upon his back.

'I found you cradling her like a lover,' Raj Ahten whispered fiercely. 'Were you her lover?'

'No!' Borenson shouted.

'Do you deny that you loved her!'

'No!'

'It is forbidden fruit to look upon my concubines. There is a fee that one must pay!' Raj Ahten said. 'Have you paid your toll?'

Borenson did not need to answer. The Wolf Lord swiftly pulled him near, ran his hands up Borenson's leg beneath his coat of ring mail and his tunic, to explore his private region.

Sir Borenson howled in outrage and grasped for his dagger, but Raj Ahten was swifter still.

He pinched hard with fingers as strong as a blacksmith's tongs, and he pulled.

The incredible burning pain that assaulted Borenson caused him to black out for a moment, to drop his dagger.

When Raj Ahten brought his hand away, Sir Borenson was much less of a man.

Raj Ahten shoved Borenson hard into the ground, wrenching his back and scraping his face.

Sir Borenson writhed in pain and horror, barely able to retain consciousness. Raj Ahten climbed to his feet.

'Thus,' Raj Ahten said, flicking a gobbet of flesh on the ground beside Borenson's ear, 'I dismiss you.'

Averan cried for help and tried to pry open the dead reaver's mouth. Lightning pounded, and now a gree whipped past her head, wriggling in the air, having also decided that the dead reaver's mouth was a fine dark place to hide. The cloying scent of decay filled the air, and it was so powerful that her hands and face were blistering wherever the air touched them.

'Help me, please,' she cried, trying to be heard above the thunder. Only the dimmest rays of evening light filtered through the dust clouds.

But her heart leapt. Through the flickering lightning she saw Raj Ahten suddenly enter a clearing between the dead reavers, not twenty feet away. He'd gone back there a minute before, to where Saffira and Borenson were, and he had exchanged some harsh words with Borenson.

Borenson's cries filled her with fear.

Raj Ahten shouted now in some language of Indhopal. Averan did not know what he said, but obviously he was calling orders to his men. He held his face up, so that dirty rain streamed over his helm, down his cheeks. Lightning flickered, and Averan could see him clearly. With so many endowments of glamour, he was the most handsome man that Averan had ever seen. He carried himself so proudly, with such grace, that it made her heart flutter.

'Please!' she cried, trying to pry open the reaver's mouth.

Raj Ahten glanced at her distractedly, as if he wanted nothing to do with a child.

But to her relief, he strode to her.

Averan had imagined that it would take several common men with pry bars to open the reaver's jaw, but Raj Ahten sheathed his warhammer on his back, then pulled the reaver's mouth wide with his fists. He gave Averan his hand, let her step out daintily, as if she were a lady of the court.

He had blood all over his gauntlets.

In seconds, half a dozen Invincibles leapt into the clearing between the dead reavers. Raj Ahten jabbered at them, talking so fast she was hard-pressed to follow.

Averan understood only one word: 'Orden.'

Then Raj Ahten and his men all raced north. They ran so swiftly that it seemed almost as if they merely vanished. For one moment they stood still in the shadows, then she heard the *ching* of ring mail and the Invincibles fled in a blur.

In the sudden silence, Averan stood. Dust and mud fell from the sky. Thunder boomed. Lightning split the sky.

Reavers fear lightning, Averan recalled. It blinds them and fills them with pain. They're all going to run away. At least that's what I'd do, if I were a reaver.

Nearby, she heard gagging; someone was in pain.

The sound came from where she had last seen Sir Borenson.

Averan crept toward the sound, huddling close to the body of a reaver, until she could see past its head. There in the shadows lay Saffira and Sir Borenson.

But only Borenson was alive. He was curled on his side like a baby. He'd vomited, and tears were streaming from his eyes. Saffira's glamour was gone from her, so that now she seemed to be only a pretty girl.

Averan feared that Borenson would die from his wounds, and there was nothing she could do to stop it. 'What's wrong?' Averan asked timidly. 'Are you hurt?'

Borenson gritted his teeth, wiped tears from his face. He didn't speak for a long minute, until finally in a strange voice, all filled with pain and fierceness, he said, 'You're going to grow up to be a beautiful woman – and there's no way that someone like me would ever be able to do anything about it.'

65

THE EARTH BETRAYED

'Flee!' the Earth warned Gaborn.

He was sitting on the ground, looking skyward in astonishment. He'd never imagined that he had the power to
summon animals to his aid.

The world worm had hardly risen from the ground. Dust
and stones and pebbles gushed skyward above it. The vast
beast towered there, twisting and writhing half a mile in the
air.

The force of the blast had propelled Gaborn backward. The
green woman sprawled beside him.

Lightning flashed amid the dust, creating a crown around
the great cloud, a crown of light that for a moment seemed
to Gaborn to be his own. All around him, the reavers were
turning, fleeing from the battle in terror.

'Go!' the Earth insisted.

Death was coming – Gaborn's own death. He'd never felt
the overwhelming presence of the shroud so completely.

Darkness hovered above him, an immense black cloud of
dust and falling debris that hid any remnant of daylight.

In that unnatural darkness, split time and again by lightning, Gaborn lurched to his feet and raced for his horse,
calling for his troops to retreat.

Of course, he realized. He'd felt it all along. Strike and flee,
strike and flee. That is what the Earth had wanted of him at
Carris.

'Come!' he shouted to the green woman, offering his hand.

She leapt twenty feet to land at his side, and Gaborn reached down, pulled her onto his horse.

'This way!' Gaborn shouted to his men. He began racing for his life.

He felt inside him.

In seconds, the entire course of the battle had shifted. Tens of thousands of people had fled Carris, and hundreds of thousands more had not yet even exited the city gates, but were still rushing out as fast as possible.

Much had changed for the better.

The reavers fled. Lightning strobed the sky, and reavers abandoned the field. Everywhere the threat to his people suddenly diminished.

Galloping past two living reavers, Gaborn careened north filled with a sense of dull wonder and terror – wonder at his victory here, terror at the rising sense of personal danger that assailed him.

The Earth no longer bade him to strike. Now the Earth bade him flee with all haste. He raced past reaver and man alike. He was no longer needed at Carris.

Thus he rode through the dust cloud thrown by the world worm, half blinded, until he found his way north to the gates of the Barren's Wall.

The wall was a twisted ruin. Though Gaborn had focused all his attention to the south during the battle, the quakes had struck here, too. Much of the wall had fallen. The parts left standing leaned at precarious angles.

Miraculously, the arch above the Barren's Wall held, and as he rode toward it, Gaborn glanced back toward Carris.

Several castle towers had collapsed, and others were still burning. Clouds of dust filled the valley. Dead men and reavers littered the plain. Every bit of soil was churned and ruined. Every plant had been blasted and destroyed. The great Black Tower had collapsed in the distance, and a fire raged there. The world worm was slithering back down into the hole where the Seal of Desolation had been. Lightning bolts played overhead, striking through clouds of dust. A sickly brown mist still wreathed the field, carrying a marvelous stench of rot and illness.

No scene of destruction that Gaborn had ever imagined could begin to rival what he now beheld.

A few hundred yards across the battlefield, the wizard Binnesman spotted him. The old man had apparently retreated from the front line; now he galloped toward Gaborn, shouting.

Gaborn felt such a desperate need to escape that he dared not wait for Binnesman.

With only Jureem, Erin, and Celinor still at his back, he wheeled and raced on beneath the Barren's Wall.

'Milord,' Pashtuk called. 'There he is!' Raj Ahten had swiftly gathered a dozen Invincibles and ordered them to help find the Earth King.

Raj Ahten peered through clouds of dust, while thunder pounded overhead. The rising dirt had mingled with the clouds; now a muddy sleet fell. Raj Ahten stood atop a hill formed by two dead reavers and peered through the grit to where Pashtuk pointed.

Raj Ahten had never seen Gaborn's face. Some protective spell made it so that every time Raj Ahten tried to look at the lad, he saw a stone, or a tree, or nothing at all.

Now he studied the horse that Pashtuk pointed toward. As for the Earth King, Raj Ahten spotted his mount – an unassuming roan – but he could discern nothing of Gaborn himself, only a dark-skinned woman sitting oddly atop it, and a piece of oak brush that appeared to be caught before her on the saddle. He rode north with several knights at his side. The wizard Binnesman raced to catch up with him.

'Where do you think he is going?' Mahket asked.

It seemed odd for the Earth King to retreat so swiftly when the victory here seemed secured. Lightning flashed overhead, and everywhere the reavers scattered, leaderless and without purpose.

'I don't care where he is going,' Raj Ahten answered simply. 'I'm going to kill him.'

'But . . . O Great Light,' Pashtuk said. 'He is your kinsman . . . He seeks a truce.'

Raj Ahten glanced at Pashtuk and recognized the face of an enemy.

Raj Ahten had no words that could adequately express his rage. Gaborn had evaded his assassins since youth, had repelled him from Longmot with a humiliating ruse, had stolen his forcibles. Gaborn had brought Saffira to her death, turned her against him. Now Gaborn turned Raj Ahten's most loyal followers against him.

He wanted revenge.

'The reavers are fleeing,' Raj Ahten said as if speaking to a slow-witted child. 'The danger is past, and the truce may now safely be put aside.'

'A battle may be won, but not the war,' Pashtuk replied.

'What makes you think the reavers will return?' Raj Ahten offered in a reasonable tone. 'We can't know that they will return.'

'O Great One,' Pashtuk said, 'forgive me. I do not mean to offend, but he is the Earth King. He has Chosen you.'

'I too came north to save mankind,' Raj Ahten reminded Pashtuk. 'I too can destroy reavers.'

Raj Ahten heard Gaborn's warning in his mind: 'Beware!'

Pashtuk raised his warhammer and lunged forward to swing, but the man could not have had more than three or four endowments of metabolism.

Raj Ahten dodged Pashtuk's blow and struck him in the temple with his mailed fist. The blow shattered Pashtuk's skull and drove bone into his brain.

'Beware!' Gaborn's voice warned again.

Raj Ahten spun. Two Invincibles at his back had drawn weapons, intent on murder. He briefly engaged them, and two others who joined the fray.

But Raj Ahten was no fool. Though his Invincibles might seem awesome to the common man, he had always known that some would turn against him.

He dispatched the four men swiftly, taking only a few light

wounds. With his thousands of endowments of stamina, the wounds healed over before the last man fell.

He stood a moment, panting, watching eight other Invincibles who surrounded him. Lightning flickered, thunder pounded. None of the eight dared try to withstand him, yet he wondered dully if he should kill them anyway.

Gaborn's voice rang in Raj Ahten's mind. 'Men lie dead at your feet, men whom I have Chosen. Your own death hovers nearby. One last time I offer you protection and hope . . .'

'I did not Choose you!' Raj Ahten screamed. The force of his Voice was so great that the words rose up louder than the thunder.

As Gaborn galloped from Carris, rivulets of sweat poured down his face. A thousand tiny battles raged around him at once. Sir Langley and Skalbairn slaughtered the reavers mercilessly, attacking to good effect. Though many reavers fled Carris, not all were discouraged.

Yet Gaborn was aware that one intense battle raged nearby. Raj Ahten stood among his Invincibles. Gaborn had thought them all in danger, perhaps from some reaver mage.

But in warning Raj Ahten of danger, Gaborn had unwittingly aided in the slaughter of other men.

Appalled and hurt, Gaborn made one final attempt to make peace with the man. But Raj Ahten's rebuff rose above the sounds of battle and thunder: 'I did not Choose you!'

Gaborn could not bear his guilt. He couldn't allow Raj Ahten, one of his Chosen, to continue killing men and women around him. Desperate, Gaborn could see no alternative but to strike back.

Even as he sought to fight, Gaborn feared that he committed sacrilege. The Earth had given him the power to Choose and protect mankind. To use his powers for any other purpose might well incur the Earth's punishment.

But in destroying Raj Ahten, Gaborn reasoned, I protect thousands of others.

Gaborn could almost see the setting: Raj Ahten was ringed

in by his Invincibles. They'd seen him murder their brethren, and even now steeled themselves for a fight.

Doubtless, these were powerful men. Otherwise the Earth would not be sending Gaborn such intense intimations of Raj Ahten's peril.

This time, Gaborn did not warn Raj Ahten of the rising danger that began to crest all around him. Gaborn fought the urge to warn Raj Ahten, fought it with all his will. It pained him to do so.

Gaborn called on the warriors near Raj Ahten. 'Strike now!'

Raj Ahten heard no warning. The Invincibles around him lunged as one, moved by some inaudible command.

His old friend Chesuit, one of his greatest and most trusted servants, whirled and sought to put the spike of a warhammer through Raj Ahten's helm.

Raj Ahten dodged, narrowly escaping death. He buried his own warhammer in Chesuit's shoulder, and then drew a long dagger for fighting at close quarters.

Gaborn felt danger flash around the Invincibles he'd commanded to slay Raj Ahten.

But he felt it only dimly, as if the earth power within him were a candle that had just been snuffed out, and now all that lit the room was a single ember glowing at the candle's wick.

He was granted light still – enough light to know that it still burned, but nothing more.

In abject horror Gaborn raced to a hilltop, and looked back. He knew where Raj Ahten stood. Even now Gaborn fought the urge to warn him that he was in danger.

The struggle that took place happened too fast for Gaborn to see much at this distance, through the rusty haze and dirty rain. Lightning flickered overhead, and in its glare, Gaborn witnessed a swirling mass of bodies.

He felt the Invincibles' danger, perceived each blow as it fell. Bones were broken, muscles savagely torn. Blood flowed and men cried out in agony and horror as they met their own deaths.

He knew intimately when each Invincible fell and died.

With their deaths, something within Gaborn tore. He had said it plainly to Molly Drinkham: when his Chosen died, he felt as if somehow he had been uprooted, as if part of him died with them.

Now he felt it ardently, seemed more profoundly torn than ever before. For as each Invincible succumbed, he sensed keenly the loss of his own earth powers.

So swiftly their deaths came – each like the tolling of a death bell atop a city tower.

But that tolling did not proclaim the death of a few Invincibles. It heralded the death of the hope of mankind.

'Once there were toth upon the land,' the Earth had warned Gaborn in Binnesman's garden. 'Once there were duskins . . . At the end of this dark time, mankind too may become only a memory.'

Is this how my people are to die? Gaborn wondered. Betrayed by me?

He'd tested his powers imprudently, like a well-endowed archer who pulls the strings of a bow long enough to see if the bow or the string will break first.

The Earth had given him dominion, granted him a circle of power.

Save whom you will, it had declared, and now Gaborn found himself trying to kill one that he had Chosen.

He'd violated the Earth's will.

Now his powers were stripped away, and Gaborn gaped in wide-eyed horror, awaiting the moment when they would extinguish completely.

Lightning flashed above Carris, and by its light Gaborn saw when the Invincibles' struggles ceased: a single man rolled from that gruesome fray.

Gaborn spurred his mount, galloping north as fast as he could. He shouted to those nearby, 'Raj Ahten is coming! Run!'

66

APOLOGIES DUE

Invincibles lunged at Raj Ahten from eight directions. Some struck low, some high. Some swung at his face while others tried to slip in from behind. They came with warhammers, daggers, fists, and feet.

Even his superior speed and decades of training would not allow him to leave such a row unscathed.

A warhammer caught Raj Ahten cleanly in the right knee, ripping ligaments and shattering bone. A dagger slipped through his scale mail and pierced a lung, while a half-sword sliced his neck, severing his carotid artery. A mailed fist dented his helm and probably fractured his skull. Other wounds were not so dire.

Raj Ahten managed to survive. Thousands of Dedicates in Kartish channeled stamina to him. Raj Ahten clung tenaciously to life as he fought.

In moments, he cut the eight down, and Raj Ahten slid from the back of a dead reaver, struggling to heal.

The wound to his neck closed quickly, the flesh knitting, though blood had sprayed everywhere. His head ached, and when he pulled his helm away, the dent in it drew flesh off with it.

The knee wound caused him the most agony. The hammer had chipped deep into bone, breaking the patella and twisting it sideways, so that the wound healed quickly but improperly.

When he tried to stand on the leg, it ached so much he

wondered if the head of the warhammer had broken off inside.

So Raj Ahten found himself in great pain as he ran north.

With so many endowments of metabolism, grace, and brawn, he should have been able to run fifty or sixty miles per hour. Under normal circumstances he could keep up that pace all day. Perhaps in the short term, Gaborn's mount could outrace him. But Raj Ahten could run forever. In time he could catch the lad.

So he ran through gloom over the blasted lands. He sprinted hard past the Barren's Wall, north along the highway through the villages of Casteer and Wegnt and Breakheart, until he left the sounds of battle far behind.

Sweat poured from him. He had fought for a long while. Though the melee had lasted for only the last two and a half hours in common time, with six endowments of metabolism it seemed to him that he had fought for fifteen. Since noon, he'd had little to drink, nothing to eat. The fell mage's ghastly spells had left him weak and dazed, and now he'd been sorely wounded.

It was folly to chase Gaborn under such conditions. He was no force horse fed on rich miln and fattened by a week of idleness.

He'd been on short rations now for weeks, marching first north to Heredon, fighting his campaign there, only to have to flee south.

In the past month, he'd grown lean. Then he'd been forced to battle all day long. Though his wounds healed quickly, even that took energy.

So as he ran, a tremendous thirst plagued him. He'd sweated out far too much of his life's water.

It had rained on and off all day. Ten miles north of Carris he dropped beside the road and slurped from a puddle.

The grass around lay wilted, as if it had baked in the hot sun. He marveled at how the fell mage had so cursed this land, and he wondered if it was safe to drink from such a pool. The water tasted odd . . . of copper, he decided. Or maybe blood.

He rested for a few minutes. Got up and raced on. After five more miles, he still had not seen Gaborn. But amid the acrid haze he could taste the scent of horses, and of those who rode with Gaborn.

He kept running. He had made a mistake in wearing his mail, he decided. It was too heavy; it wore him down. Or maybe it was the painful wound to his knee.

He wondered if he'd lost stamina, somehow, if maybe some of his Dedicates had died.

Or perhaps the Earth King or his wizard has cast a spell on me, Raj Ahten thought. He found it oddly difficult to keep running.

Or maybe it is this land. The land itself was cursed, why not the people in it?

He raced until he smelled a change ahead. All along the route from Carris, the grass and trees had been dead, smelling of rot and decay.

But now he detected the cool scent of lush grasses, ripened in summer fields, and of mint; the taste of autumn leaves and of mushrooms growing wild in the woods; the honeyed aroma of vetch and other wild flowers that one did not notice until they were gone.

Twenty-eight miles north of Carris, he reached a barrier. In a single pace it seemed as if a line of demarcation had been drawn. To the south, every blade of grass was blasted and dead.

But on the far side of the line, the hills were rich and vibrant. Trees thrived. Bats fluttered in the night. A burrow owl called out.

On the other side of the line, Gaborn sat on his mount, though Raj Ahten still could not see his face. Instead, it looked very much as if a gourd balanced precariously on his saddle. Two lords rode at his side: a princeling wearing the livery of South Crowthen, and a young woman of Fleeds. And behind them were gathered perhaps sixty other knights of Heredon and Orwynne. It looked as if Gaborn had happened on a party of his own knights, a party that had seen the devastation and

feared to cross over the boundary into the blasted lands. Men
and women in that group brandished bows and axes. He
recognized his cousin Iome among the lords.

Binnesman the wizard sat atop Raj Ahten's own great gray
Imperial warhorse. He held his staff high in his right hand.
Fireflies swarmed round it in a cloud, lighting his face. In his
left hand, he brandished a few leaves.

At his side stood his wylde, a woman in a bearskin robe
with skin as green as the flesh of an avocado.

Raj Ahten halted. He'd seen her from behind earlier, had
seen Gaborn flee with her. He had not recognized what she
was then. Had he known that the wylde was here, he might
not have dared follow.

Raj Ahten tried to feign unconcern as he drew close.

A strange and disconcerting numbness began to steal over
him, over his face and hands, anywhere that his flesh was
exposed. It became difficult to draw a breath. Everything felt
cold.

He did not know what spell so dismayed him, what herb
the wizard used, until Binnesman warned, 'Stay back. You
cannot resist the monkshood. Your heart will stop if you
advance much farther.'

Raj Ahten knew the herb now. He had brushed against it
as a child and felt it numb his skin, but it had not been in
the hands of an Earth Warden then, had not been magnified
by his powers.

'Far enough,' Binnesman said. 'So, Raj Ahten, why do you
follow the Earth King? Have you come to do obeisance at last?'

Raj Ahten halted, gasping for breath, his whole body numb
and tingling. Even with all his endowments, he could not
fight an Earth Warden – especially one guarded by a wylde
and sixty lords. The wylde now raised her nose in the air,
sniffed. 'Blood – yes!' she cried in delight. She smiled, fangs
gleaming.

Raj Ahten had never before looked into the face of someone
who intended to eat him, yet he did not doubt the meaning
behind her beatific expression.

'Not yet,' Binnesman whispered to the wylde, 'but if he advances, then he is yours to play with.'

Raj Ahten swallowed hard.

'You have my forcibles,' Raj Ahten said to Gaborn, as if to dismiss the wizard. 'I want them back – nothing more.'

'I want my people back,' Gaborn said. 'I want the Dedicates you killed at the Blue Tower. I want my father and mother, my little sisters and my brother.' To Raj Ahten, it seemed a singularly odd moment, to hear that gourd speak. Raj Ahten studied the Earth King's voice warily.

'It's too late for them,' Raj Ahten said. 'Just as it is too late for my wife Saffira.'

'If it's vengeance you're after,' Gaborn said, 'take it from the reavers. If any man here has been injured, I have the greater claim, and if it was vengeance I wanted, I could take it even now.'

Raj Ahten smiled. 'Is this why you stopped, Gaborn Val Orden – to make petty threats?' he asked. 'Do you need the comfort of wizards and knights at your back just to snivel at me?' Raj Ahten stood panting, determined to hide how much the monkshood affected him. He wished he could see a face, to learn what the lad might be thinking.

'No, I did not come to make threats. I hoped to warn you that you are in grave danger. I felt such danger myself, yesterday, just before you destroyed the Blue Tower. It was a cloying, indefinable rot. I tell you that Mystarria is not the only land where reavers are massing. I fear that *your* Dedicates will be next.'

He sounded sincere, though the lad had no cause to wish Raj Ahten well. 'So, you want me to flee home?' Raj Ahten said. 'To chase phantoms while you strengthen your borders?'

'No,' Gaborn answered. 'I want you to go home and save yourself. If you do, I will use all the powers at my command to aid you.'

'Not half an hour ago, you tried to kill me,' Raj Ahten pointed out. 'What has brought about so great a change of heart?'

'I Chose you,' Gaborn said. 'I did not want to use my powers against you, but you forced me to it. I ask you one more time: join with me.'

So the boy seeks an ally, Raj Ahten realized. He fears that he cannot stop the reavers on his own.

Raj Ahten wondered if Gaborn still might be persuaded to return the forcibles.

'Look around you, Raj Ahten,' the wizard Binnesman cut in. 'Look at the land behind you, the death and ruin! You faced the fell mage. Is that the world you want? Or would you come with us, to this land, to a land that is fair and green, hail and living?'

'You offer me land?' Raj Ahten said, genuinely disappointed. 'That is gracious: to offer land that I could so easily take, land that you are incompetent to hold.'

'The Earth bids me warn you,' Gaborn said. 'A pall lies over you. I cannot protect a man who does not want my protection. If you stay in any of the kingdoms of Rofehavan, I cannot save you.'

'You cannot put me out,' Raj Ahten said. He glanced back toward Carris, toward his own troops.

In that moment, something changed in Gaborn. He began to laugh. Not a mere nervous chuckle, but a laugh of such deep and profound relief, a laugh from so deep in the gut, that Raj Ahten wondered at the source. He wished he could see the boy.

'You know,' Gaborn said in a cordial tone. 'Once, I might have feared you and your Invincibles. But I have just realized how I could defeat you, Raj Ahten. All I need do is *Choose* your people – man by man, woman by woman, child by child – and make them my own!'

Beside Gaborn, the wizard Binnesman smiled and also burst into laughter as he realized Raj Ahten's predicament.

Raj Ahten cringed inwardly as he saw the truth. He himself no longer had an army at Carris. He doubted that he could bring any men against Gaborn at all.

'Go back to Carris if you dare,' Gaborn suggested coldly.

'You defeated twelve Invincibles, but I have hundreds of thousands of followers there: your men. Will you fight them all?'

'Give me my forcibles,' Raj Ahten demanded clamly, hoping that through the persuasive power of his Voice, he still might reach some settlement.

But Gaborn Val Orden shouted, 'No bargaining, you foul cur! I offer you your breath, nothing more! Begone, I order you one last time – or I'll take even that!'

Raj Ahten's face flushed with rage, and his heart began to pound in his chest.

He shouted and charged.

A dozen knights loosed arrows. He whipped his hands around, tried to knock them aside, but one lodged in his injured knee. He fought the bone-chilling numbness that sapped energy from his heart.

And then the green woman rushed to meet him. She took him by his coat of mail and lifted him, her nails digging so powerfully that bits of scale mail scattered from his coat like scales from a trout.

He tried to grapple with her, aiming a punch at her throat with his mailed gauntlet.

The force of his blow shattered his right arm, though it also knocked the green woman backward a pace. She seemed surprised to be affected at all – surprised, but not injured.

She screamed and drew a small rune in the air, her right hand twisting in an intricate little dance that baffled the eye.

Then she slugged him in the chest. His ribs shattered, ripping into his lungs and heart. Raj Ahten flew backward head over feet a dozen yards, lay gasping for a moment, staring up at the evening sky.

He had not noticed until now that the clouds had begun to scatter, that brilliant white stars pierced the heavens. With his thousands of endowments of sight, he could see more stars than a common man could, infinitely more stars – swirling masses of light, dazzling orbs – all very pretty.

He lay choking on his own blood, heart beating erratically.

Every fiber of his chest seemed to burn, as if each individual muscle were demolished. Sweat broke upon his brow.

They've killed me, he thought. They've killed me.

Blood pounded in his ears, and the green woman rushed to him, grabbed his throat, and prepared to yank out his windpipe.

'Hold!' the wizard Binnesman shouted.

The green woman merely held him. Her dark-green tongue darted out, slowly played over her upper lip. In her eyes, he could see an endless longing. 'Blood?' she pleaded.

Binnesman rode his mount up close to Raj Ahten, and several knights surrounded him, bows drawn. Fortunately, the wizard had dropped his leaf of monkshood. The wizard asked Gaborn in mock sincerity, 'What say you, milord? Shall we do him now?'

Raj Ahten was healing. The shattered bones in his chest were knitting askew; his right arm throbbed from fingertip to shoulder. He began healing, and in a few minutes he felt sure that he'd be able to fight. He needed to stall them.

Yet he healed slowly. More slowly than he'd have thought possible. Even with thousands of endowments of stamina, he could not heal.

He lay at their mercy while they ringed him like hounds.

Myrrima looked over at Gaborn, studied the Earth King. She could see the righteous anger flaring in his eye, could see how livid he was. His muscles were taut, hard. She'd been astonished that he'd asked the Wolf Lord's forgiveness, sought an alliance even now.

But that was past. Gaborn fumed, and she thought that Gaborn would kill him himself, though she yearned for the honor.

Myrrima had not lied a few hours past, when she'd told Iome that the presence of the Earth King made her want to fight something. Gaborn was someone whom she would willingly die for.

No man on the face of the earth deserved an execution

more than did Raj Ahten. She felt fortunate to have met Gaborn here, this fine evening, so that she would be present to see the demise of the Wolf Lord.

Yet with pain and regret and a tone of finality, Gaborn answered Binnesman. 'No. Leave him.'

'Milord!' Prince Celinor shouted in outrage, as did Erin Connal and a dozen other lords, though Celinor's voice rose above the rest. 'If you will not kill him, give me the honor!'

'Or me!' other men shouted.

Iome tried to remain calm. 'My love, you make a mistake here,' she told Gaborn through clenched teeth. 'Let them have him.'

Rage burned in Myrrima's veins. She'd seen Gaborn's father alive at Longmot five hours before the castle fell, and he'd refused her entry to the fortress, knowing that in doing so he probably saved her life. She'd seen him cold dead, along with thousands of other warriors, later that night.

She recalled Hobie Hollowell and Wyeth Able and a dozen other boys from Bannisferre who had died in that battle, while closer to home the farmers all around her house had been decapitated by Raj Ahten's scouts as his army sought to slip unnoticed through the Dunnwood. Even her neighbor, ninety-three-year-old Annie Coyle who couldn't have hobbled to town to save her life, had been butchered.

Gaborn's own wife had been robbed of her glamour, had watched her mother die at Raj Ahten's hand. She'd been present when her own father was assassinated because of Raj Ahten's deeds, and her armies had been decimated.

Yet Gaborn had the audacity to forbear.

And as Myrrima gazed around at the hard faces of the knights in that company, she knew that not a man among them had lived a life untouched by Raj Ahten's evil. All of them had lost their kings and queens to his assassins, seen friends or brothers or parents die at his hand.

To think that Raj Ahten should live another minute seemed unbearable. The blood sang in her veins, demanding vengeance.

'As you love me,' Gaborn said to his lords, 'as you love your very lives, I beg each of you to spare him. The Earth bids me to let him live.'

In outrage Myrrima studied Gaborn's eyes. Every muscle in her was tense. She reached into her quiver and drew another arrow, nocked it. The first shaft she'd fired was still lodged in Rah Ahten's knee, though she'd hoped to hit the bastard in the chest.

'This is unconscionable!' Sir Hoswell shouted. 'To let him live is—'

Other men roared agreement.

But Gaborn merely raised his hand, asking for silence.

Gaborn said solemnly, 'I Chose Raj Ahten in desperation, and sought afterward to use my powers to slay him. For my sin, the Earth has withdrawn. My powers have diminished, and it may be that I cannot make amends.

'I only know that for the sake of the world, I must lay my wrath aside. No man here wants to see him dead more than do I . . .'

Gaborn trembled with impotent rage. He groaned in despair. He put the spurs to his charger and fled south toward Carris as if he no longer trusted himself to remain and let Raj Ahten live.

He raced half a mile ahead, and stopped at the brow of the hill, on the blasted earth, looking back. 'Come!' Gaborn cried. 'Get away from there!'

Aspen leaves whispered behind Myrrima in the evening wind; the grass rustled. She gritted her teeth and waited.

Binnesman climbed down from his own mount, touched the green woman's shoulder. 'Come,' he whispered into her ear. 'Leave him for now.'

The wylde backed away, though no one else did. The knights held steady on their horses in the gloom, weapons bristling. Myrrima could hear the hard breath of their anger, smell their sweat.

Raj Ahten sat up, pulled the arrow from his knee. The wylde had torn his surcoat and so decimated his kingly scale mail that the coat now looked a ragged mess, ripped and shredded in the front.

The Wolf Lord of Indhopal stared at the lords, regal and imperious even now. He wheezed as he breathed, as if something inside him were torn. 'Were I the Earth King,' he said softly, 'I would not be such a pathetic little man.'

'Of course not, my cousin,' Iome said, 'for you so need to show yourself to be every man's superior, you would of necessity be both much larger, and far more pathetic than he.'

Iome turned from the odious Raj Ahten and spoke to the lords. 'Come. Let us go.' She turned and followed Gaborn. Other lords began to file off after her, slowly at first, but then faster, for they feared to be alone with Raj Ahten.

Myrrima stayed, determined to be the last to leave, to show no fear. Sir Hoswell stayed at her back, while Binnesman kept his wylde at his side.

When the others had all fled, Myrrima held Raj Ahten with her glare. Still seated on the ground, he stared up at her as if amused.

'I'll thank you for the return of my arrow,' Myrrima said, nodding toward the shaft in Raj Ahten's hand. She wanted him to know that it was her shaft that had scored on him, for all the good it had done.

Raj Ahten climbed to his feet, presented the arrow and answered in a seductive tone. 'Anything for a beautiful woman.'

She took the arrow and surreptitiously sniffed at him, to catch his scent, so that if she ever needed to track him, she'd be able to do so.

Raj Ahten said, 'I have but three words for you, young woman: Wolf . . . Lord . . . Bitch.'

Raj Ahten turned southwest, headed off through the blasted lands.

Myrrima left the blood on her shaft and dropped it back into her quiver. She turned her horse and followed her King, though leaving Raj Ahten alive was the hardest thing she'd ever done.

She did not suspect how much she'd come to regret it.

67

IN THE BLASTED LANDS

Averan stayed with Borenson after the battle. Some healers from Carris came and looked at him, learned the nature of his wounds, and then left him in search of others who were closer to death.

She could only vaguely guess what was wrong with the big knight. Though the healers said he would not die of his wound, one woman offered nightshade anyway.

Borenson only growled angrily and lay on the ground, still curled up like a babe.

Averan found herself a cloak from a dead man to keep her warm. She looked for the green woman, but Spring had apparently run off during the battle – or gotten herself killed. Averan didn't know which, and she found herself worrying, constantly listening for the sound of feet squishing through the mud.

By an hour after nightfall she realized she was hungry, so she took Borenson's knife for protection and began wandering through the maze of dead reavers toward Carris, searching for the right piece of meat.

Up in Carris, buildings were still afire, and she managed to pick her way among the dead reavers by this faint light.

The causeway was well guarded by thousands of men: warriors of Carris, Invincibles, and footmen from Indhopal. They'd cleared most of the reavers' corpses from the causeway, shoving them into the lake. The men seemed terrified that the reavers might return under the cover of darkness. They sat beside campfires and swapped tales, sometimes laughing apprehensively. Theirs was still an uneasy peace, but Averan could never have imagined that they would have formed a truce at all.

But she heard little laughter in the camp. Instead, the men spread nasty rumors that the Earth King had died, or had forsaken them all. Others related nervously how they had discovered in the midst of battle that their leader had fallen silent.

Averan tried to conjure up a vision of the Earth King, but when she closed her eyes, she could not see him.

He was dead, she decided.

At the head of the causeway, the warriors had just dragged up part of a huge reaver mage all wet and blackened. Flaming runes still burned all around its head, and its mouth had been propped open with a fence post so that one could see how wide its jaws were.

'What's this?' Averan asked the men camped nearby.

'The fell mage, or what's left of her,' one man replied. 'We fished it from the lake. Be careful now, she's still twitching, and she might bite you!' The men all laughed at their stupid joke. Even a little girl of nine could see that the corpse of the fell mage wasn't twitching.

She was by far the largest reaver killed today, ancient and venerable in her way.

Averan stared at the mage in amazement. She climbed into the mage's mouth, and outside the men hooted and cheered. 'There's a brave one,' one of them said.

Averan walked to the far back of the reaver's mouth, until she found the soft spot in the mage's upper palate. She plunged her knife up into it and sliced quickly, afraid that someone would stop her.

She was hungry, and this was the only food that would satisfy.

When the blood gushed out, she reached her arm up as high as she could and grasped some of the reaver's brains. The fell mage was so huge that her brain was still hot and steamy.

For a long time Averan gorged, then she lay down in a

groggy stupor on the reaver's palate as strange dreams assailed her, carrying her through unimagined realms.

From the fell mage, Averan began to learn much about the One True Master's magic. What Averan learned terrified her to the core of her soul.

She desperately wanted to tell someone, especially the Earth King. But when she closed her eyes and tried to visualize him, she still could not see him.

'Hey, little girl, what are you doing in there?' some fellow asked. Averan looked up. She still had some bloody meat in her hand, and she wiped it on the reaver's tongue.

A man stood outside the reaver's mouth, bearing a torch. He was not a knight, just some common fellow. 'Here now, you can't eat that. Let me get you some real food!'

The look of wide-eyed horror in the man's eyes let her know that she should not touch him. He thought she was mad, and if she got close enough, he'd try to put her in a cage.

Averan grabbed her knife in both hands and held it up for him to see. 'Back!' she shouted.

'Here now,' the fellow answered, backing away cautiously. 'I won't hurt you. I only want to help.'

Averan got up and darted past, dodged away from him and raced down the causeway between the campfires.

When she reached the end of the causeway, she turned for a moment and shouted to the frightened warriors camping there. 'The reavers won't return – not here, not tonight! Don't you see, they *won* this battle! They've destroyed all of the blood metal in the ground, they have no reason to come back here.'

Everyone looked at her as if she were crazed. 'I mean it!' she said. 'The One True Master is preparing the Seals of Desolation. If you don't stop him, no place will be safe!'

But of course everyone just stared at her as if she were mad. No one would listen to a crazy girl. She turned and fled.

'Milady,' Myrrima begged Iome. 'I would like to go on into Carris. There will be other wounded to attend.' She realized belatedly that she used the words 'other wounded' because she saw the wounds so deeply in Gaborn.

'Of course,' Iome said, releasing her from service. The sixty warriors had gathered in a circle not far from where they'd fought Raj Ahten.

Gaborn looked up in the starlight. 'Your husband is about a third of a mile northwest of the castle,' he said. 'He is alive, but has not moved in a long time. I regret that I cannot come with you. I need . . . I need to speak to the Earth, and the soil here is dead and powerless.' He glanced toward the north, as if he would ride that way.

Gaborn did not say more. His tone warned her that Borenson would be wounded, that she needed to steel herself for what she might find. She could not imagine her husband, one of the most powerful warriors in Mystarria, lying wounded, near death. She imagined that all his bones were shattered, or that his neck was broken.

'Please go with her,' Iome begged the lords. 'There will be many wounded. We must do what we can.'

'I will accompany you north,' Erin Connal said to Iome. 'I've business in my own lands to attend.'

Myrrima and the rest of them turned and rode south, leaving Gaborn, Iome, Binnesman, the wylde, Jureem, Erin, and Celinor alone. The lords rode in silence for several minutes, until they were far out of earshot, and at last one lord of Orwynne asked, 'What do we do now?'

In order to fill the uncomfortable silence that followed, Myrrima said, 'We'll do what we have to. We fight on.'

'But what of the "dark times to come" that Gaborn spoke of? He said he Chose us to save us through the dark times to come.'

'The times grow darker still,' Sir Hoswell answered.

'If we stay close to the Earth King, he can still warn us of danger,' one man said. His voice was full of fear.

Myrrima tried to imagine her future, to see herself at Gaborn's side, a wolf lord with a few hundred other men and women, hiding in the woods, struggling to survive the incursions of the reavers.

But as she rode through the blasted lands, the smell of decay rising from the dust all around her, she realized that there would be no woods to hide in.

Rocks, then. We will hide under rocks, she consoled herself. We will do as we must, Myrrima told herself silently.

She gritted her teeth, drew reins on her mount, and since she was in the lead, the lords behind all did the same, looking at her expectantly.

'I'm a wolf lord now,' she said, examining the man's faces. Their expressions were dulled by grief. 'There is no one who will save us. But Raj Ahten's forcibles lie hidden in the king's tombs in Heredon, and perhaps with them we can save ourselves.'

The men looked up at her, uncertain. One proud knight of Fleeds said, 'What are you saying? Do you want to be our lord? Is that not presumptuous?'

Myrrima held up her bow for all to see. 'I'd not ask to be your leader. No one should ask such favor. I forswear *all* kings,' Myrrima said, 'until the Earth King comes again.

'But I tell you this: I swear fealty to you all. I swear fealty to mankind – heart, might, mind, and soul! Wherever one stands in need, you will find me fighting beside him, using whatever weapons I may find: the endowments of dogs, my own teeth and nails if I must. I swear fealty to you all, for mankind, and for the Earth!'

The lords looked up at her bow in dull wonder, while the blood sang in Myrrima's veins. She was makind herself a Knight Equitable, sworn to protect mankind. The men she rode with were powerful Runelords, noblemen with a long history of service to Heredon, Fleeds, and Orwynne. She did not expect them to follow suit, but was astonished and grat-ified when one by one, each man brandished his own weapon and raised it to the sky, shouting, 'For mankind, and for the Earth!'

Thus the Brotherhood of the Wolf was forged on that dark day.